THE SECRETS OF TIME

A Portal Fantasy (Chosen Origins, Books 1-3)

AMY PROEBSTEL

BETHANY HALL

Cavaliers Publishing

BookBub: https://geni.us/BBFollow

Goodreads: www.goodreads.com/aproebstel

Facebook: https://geni.us/FB-LOA

Twitter: https://geni.us/Amy-T

Instagram: www.instagram.com/amyproebstel

BookBub: https://geni.us/BBFollow

Goodreads: www.goodreads.com/aproebstel

Facebook: https://geni.us/FB-LOA

Twitter: https://geni.us/Amy-T

Instagram: www.instagram.com/amyproebstel

BOOKS IN THIS SERIES

Chosen Origins Trilogy
Book One: The Keeper of Secrets
Book Two: The Secrets of Magic
Book Three: The Magic of Time

The Chosen Series
Book One: The Time of Shadows
Book Two: The Shadows of Destiny
Book Three: The Destiny of Hunters
Book Four: The Hunters of Souls
Book Five: The Souls of Children
Book Six: The Children of Fire
Book Seven: The Fire of War
Book Eight: The War of Realms
Book Nine: The Realms of Rising
Book Ten: The Rising of Dragons

I dedicate this book to all of the wonderful people in my life who encouraged me to keep writing. To my brilliant husband, Richard, thank you for knowing when I needed quiet time to get my writing done, for being my biggest cheerleader, and for all of the encouragement to keep going. To my sister, Ginger, for reading the almost endless re-writes, edits, and revisions over the years. To Ann, my favorite mother-in-law, for always being so eager to read and edit the latest versions. I also extend a huge thank you to Bridget for your friendship, coaching, and encouragement.

To the readers of this series, I greatly appreciate all of your kind words, suggestions, and support along the way. None of this would be possible without your enthusiasm for the world of Tuala.

THE KEEPER OF SECRETS

BOOK ONE OF THE CHOSEN ORIGINS

CHAPTER 1

Amanda isn't ready to die tonight. But one false move could prove her last.

Nine weeks ago, Amanda did not have skulking around in the darkness with a stranger in mind when she set out on her first adult adventure. The two parallels between then and now were the silence of the evening and the racing of her heart. Only now, it practically beat out of her chest from fear instead of anticipation.

The realization came too late of her mom's wisdom to worry about the sailing trip she embarked on with her newly minted fiancé. What she wouldn't do to get her mom's outdated advice, be pulled into one of her warm hugs, and know her unconditional love. It went beyond imagination that she may never set eyes on her mom again.

Amanda would never have predicted that danger could come from something as impossible and mysterious as the Bermuda Triangle. Not with Neal. All her worries then revolved around spending time alone with Neal. If only things could have been that simple. She would give anything to have her boring, predictable life back. How could she have been so naïve about life only nine weeks ago?

Eager to prove her independence, she completely disregarded everything her parents painstakingly taught her. She struck out on her own, bold and empowered. Yet, neither of those emotions held her captive now. Far from it. How could she with a sadist hunting her down?

Another stolen glance at Bryon caused a lancing pain through her heart. He didn't know how much he resembled Neal. Yet, here he guided her through the empty marketplace, facing unknown dangers for her, simply because Barla asked for his help.

Who did that? Why would he want to put his whole life on the line for her? Would she do the same for a stranger? In all honesty, probably not, which made her sound terrible for thinking that way. But nobody ever depended on her or needed her help. She wouldn't know how. A crippling fear coursed through her that she might fail someone when it mattered the most.

Once again, pushing the encroaching fabric of her hooded disguise from her eyes, she appraised her surroundings. Barla, the mother figure she'd found here in Tuala, admonished her to pay attention to her surroundings. Yet, the fabric kept obscuring her vision and making even that simple task onerous.

Nothing in this world seemed easy. Even escaping the City of Cresdon needed to be accomplished in the dark of night while the town slept. Yet darkness held secrets of its own, ones she didn't want to discover. Shying away at every noise, she conjured up shades of Petre creeping out of every crack and crevice to retake her captive. Even knowing Bryon would protect her, fear kept a firm grip on her imagination.

Bryon's massive presence should have given her reassurance, but Neal's equally impressive build didn't keep her safe. Why would this stranger be any more effective? Granted, he did have several inches of height and a good fifty pounds of muscle more than Neal. Also, he knew the dangers of his homeworld better than either Amanda or Neal possibly could. And Bryon had magic.

Just knowing about this strange ability left Amanda in awe. What kind of world had she fallen into? The outlandish idea of an alternate universe left her head spinning, but adding magic seemed a bit much. Maybe she landed on a movie set where someone went to a lot of trouble to punk her.

But Barla insisted on the reality of this whole Tualan world. So real, even God lived here, only they called Him Jehoban. The two weeks she spent with Barla may have given her more knowledge about this world, but it didn't prepare her for how to fend for herself.

Now, she wished she'd taken kickboxing instead of the dumb aerobics class in high school. The closest they got to fighting skills were air punches to increase their heart rate. Even then, seeing herself in the mirror, she looked foolish and uncoordinated. Hardly intimidating.

At least with kickboxing, she could have looked convincing in her ability to fight off someone. Who was she kidding? Given her current streak of luck, she'd probably only manage to pull a muscle and miss her target at the same time. Then she'd be injured and even more defenseless.

Every step they took away from the safety of where Barla lived seemed like a failure. When she escaped imprisonment from Petre, she imagined swimming to shore and miraculously finding Neal. He'd have figured out how to get home, and they would be back on Earth before the evening fell. But that fantasy fizzled immediately.

Neal vanished as effectively as the helicopter David Copperfield made disappear in front of a live audience. Only this wasn't a fancy trick of smoke and mirrors; this was her reality. A reality that scared the crap out of her. How would she manage without the support of her fiancé or family? How could she survive on her own?

A touch on her shoulder almost made her cry out. She only barely managed to stifle the scream threatening to erupt even now. Poor Bryon. He merely wanted to get her attention. She'd let her mind wander too far, and that kind of inattentiveness could not be tolerated. Not here. Not now.

Bryon turned abruptly from the broad street. Peeking dubiously around his muscle-bound torso, only darker shadows loomed in the narrow alley. Did Bryon honestly think this was the best plan?

Of course, he hadn't watched all the scary movies Amanda had. In fact, she doubted movies existed here at all. Those experiences taught her that darkness held untold danger. The fact that complete blackness stood only inches from her feet didn't inspire much hope for surviving this leg of the journey.

Yet, Bryon led the way, and he didn't seem fazed by the lack of light. Maybe his magic helped him. Although, even with Barla's extensive tutoring, Amanda couldn't recall any mention of such an ability.

Sweat dripped between her shoulder blades as she pressed in closer to Bryon. The hair on her arms stood straight as goosebumps prickled her skin. Her breathing came in halting gasps as her heart galloped faster than her speeding imagination.

Amanda stumbled over every uneven cobble in the alley; her eyes darted from side to side, her ears strained to catch any sounds other than their own. How much farther did they have to go? Peril could come with every uncertain step.

A hand snaked out faster than she could register and pulled her against a sweaty, muscular chest. Rank wafts of liquor mixed with an unwashed body assailed Amanda. She struggled against his groping hands, waves of fear clouding her judgment.

Her overactive imagination easily put together the worst possible scenario. This could not be happening to her right now.

Fear and reality merged. Petre somehow found them, and she would endure torture at his hands yet again.

A breeze flashed past her face, followed immediately by a sickening thud. In only a fraction of a second, the man's body went limp and dropped like a stone into a still pond. Only the ripples of her fear remained as evidence of the trauma. Amanda didn't even know what happened, but Bryon's voice broke through her befuddlement.

"Stay quiet. Let's keep going."

This time, Bryon slung his arm across Amanda's shoulders. She leaned into his body, eager for the shelter he provided. How could she seek solace in someone's arms other than Neal's? Was it a betrayal?

But as her body began to shake uncontrollably from the shock of the close encounter, she let go of her self-condemnation. Amanda didn't follow Barla's instructions to pay attention as Bryon led her out of the alley and down several more streets. Eventually, a shuddering sigh coursed through her. Only then did Bryon withdraw his arm. Instantly, she missed his warmth and security.

"What just happened?" Amanda asked, appalled at the quiver making her voice small and weak.

"I'd say he was drunk and didn't know what he was doing. He didn't put up much of a fight, and he went down easily enough; I doubt he knew I was there. He'll have quite the headache tomorrow, though." Bryon chuckled as he shook his hand out.

Instantly, Amanda recalled the man's stench as if it still lingered on her clothing. Suppressing a shudder of disgust, she asked, "Are you okay?" Without asking, Amanda took his hand in both hers and intently searched for any damage in the poor lighting.

He gently pulled away from her grasp and said offhandedly, "These hands have seen far worse; I daresay it'll be just fine.

Thanks for the concern." He smiled to take the sting out of his words. "Are you okay?"

"I'm fine. He just startled me, plus I'm pretty sure my imagination provided even more danger than that man posed. Besides, I think you're right about him being drunk. He reeked like he fell into a distillation barrel."

He stopped walking and turned to face her. "I'm really sorry I put you in danger. It was dumb of me to take a shortcut when we know Petre's looking for you. Will you forgive me?"

With such a sorrowful expression in his eyes, Amanda could not possibly refuse. "There's no need to apologize." Guilt danced through her mind. Why would he need to apologize? He was the one taking risks for her. Besides, she didn't know how to respond to such a sincere apology. She doubted her sister's sullen, grumbled apology only spoken because of their mother's glare could possibly count.

"We don't have much further to go until we get to the next stage of our journey," Bryon said, his tone light and untroubled.

Because he didn't give more detail, Amanda assumed he didn't want anyone to overhear their plans. She politely nodded. Why did they need to go to all the trouble and risk of walking when they could have simply teleported?

Surely, these people knew the best way to get her to a safe place, but it started to chafe a bit. Nobody explained anything to her, and her powerlessness to offer suggestions of her own grated even more.

CHAPTER 2

The storefronts gave way to large residential lots, allowing the fresh air to swirl around them freely. They came to a property with an enormous barn set off to the side. Enclosed entirely by a split-rail fence, they entered the yard at the open gate.

The country setting in front of her could have been transplanted directly from Earth. Almost, could she imagine herself back home right now, only Bryon stood beside her instead of Neal. Her heart clenched painfully in his absence.

Was she doing the right thing by leaving the Port of Cresdon? Neal could easily be somewhere in the city searching for her as well. She could not let her mind dwell on the idea of him lying somewhere hurt or even dead.

Maybe she should take a chance and approach an Elder for help. He might assist her in getting home. If Barla had been right with her assessment of the Elders, then they'd be eager to get her off of their world.

She didn't have any remarkable insights into Earth's technology. They wouldn't have any reason to keep her. Just like a grandparent hands back their cranky grandchildren to their mother to take care of them, she felt just as useless here. Heck, she'd even throw a tantrum if it helped expedite her return.

Bryon tugged on the fabric covering her arm, jolting her from her reverie. Just as they stepped onto the property, the porch lights beamed brightly along the pathway. "It looks as though someone's expecting us," Amanda said nervously.

"Oh, we're expected," Bryon assured her, "but anyone passing through the gates would activate these lights."

"Oh," Amanda replied stupidly. *I'm going to have to be more careful than this.* Already, her ignorance of details in Tuala began to show. Who knew? Maybe everyone had lights like this.

Bryon took her hand and led her away from the lit path toward the barn. More than a little confused, Amanda followed along, occasionally tripping and wondering how Bryon could walk so sure-footed. It seemed like she always had someone to help her out when she tripped and fell in life. Why should today be any different?

"Just a few steps more," he whispered back to her as he reached forward, opened a door, and pulled her into the darker interior. Once the door closed behind them, he spoke a little louder, "Wait right here. I'll be right back."

Amanda nodded then realized he could not see the gesture in the darkness, so she said, "Okay." As soon as he stepped away from her, she began shaking again. Crossing her arms over her torso, she hoped she could hold herself together long enough for him to return. To keep herself from babbling nervously, she strained to listen to Bryon's movements.

Hearing his retreating footsteps, she listened intently to the sounds of metal clinking, the soft rustling of hay on the floor, and the opening and closing of another door. Surprised by the feel of warm breath on her cheek, she hastily stepped back.

"It's okay," Bryon assured her, suddenly standing next to her.

"Put your hand out and greet Maga; she's a four anon old horse. She's very gentle and won't bite."

With the identity of the hulking shadow revealed, she reluctantly held up her hand. Instantly, her mind retreated to the few encounters she'd had with horses, none of them very good. How had they gone from walking to this new nightmare? Did Bryon really think she should actually ride this horse? Why couldn't they just teleport out of here and be done with this stressful evening?

A velvety nose came down to touch her palm, and warm air wafted up to her wrist. "It doesn't smell like horses in here," she commented, mainly to keep herself from flinching at the whiskers tickling her hand, which she strained to hold flat to prevent the horse from biting off her fingers with her huge teeth.

"They don't usually have horses. This barn is mostly just for storage anymore. I brought the horses here before coming to town to get you. They've only been here for a couple of hours. They're all saddled and ready. Do you need help getting mounted?"

Alarmed at the idea of him wanting to assist her, Amanda hastily replied, "Oh, no; I've ridden before. I think I'd like a moment to get acquainted with her before I get on, though."

"Good idea," Bryon replied.

Amanda ran her hand across the horse's broad shoulder until she found the edge of the saddle. Her fingers clenched the leather as a long-forgotten memory overtook her vision. Her sister, Deanna, sat on a horse who stood just as calm as Maga here. Then, for some unknown reason, the stallion had gone wild, bucking and snorting his way across the pasture with Deanna clinging with all her might to remain seated. But, her young strength could not contend with the stallion's wild gyrations, and she'd been thrown over the horse's head to land in a still heap in the dirt.

But Maga was not that horse. And she was not Deanna. Still, the disturbing image would not leave her head as she felt her breath coming faster at the idea of actually mounting Maga.

Maybe she should tell Bryon she'd changed her mind about leaving. She didn't have to go through with this.

"Are you ready?" Bryon asked, his words slightly clipped as if he were eager to get going.

Even as she shook her head to say no, her mouth spoke, "Yes. Just mounting now." Bryon had already risked himself for her; she could hardly repay his bravery with her cowardice. Besides, she'd ridden horses since Deanna's accident, but the fear remained. She forcefully stamped down her overactive imagination and lifted her foot to the stirrup.

She hoped the darkness would cover any clumsiness in her mounting. While she had not lied about knowing how to ride, she did not mention the number of years since her last attempt. When Maga did not even flinch as she flung her leg over the saddle, Amanda breathed a sigh of relief. She could do this. She had to do this.

Bryon led his horse forward. "I'll get the door. You can ride out; the door's high enough."

A narrow shaft of light pierced the enclosure, bright now in contrast to the absolute darkness inside the barn. The horse already knew to follow Bryon's horse, rendering Amanda's heel tap on the horse's side unnecessary.

Amanda nervously waited while Bryon closed the barn door and mounted. Maga's ears twitched backward as if warning Amanda to calm her nerves. She knew horses could feel their rider's emotions, and she needed to relax before her sister's nightmare became her own.

Riding single-file through the property's gate, Amanda brought Maga beside Bryon's horse as they traveled the winding road out of town. "Shouldn't we have told the people at the house that we took the horses?"

"No, nobody's home anyway." He glanced at her, then clarified, "Captain Ahn and Barla own the place, but Ceren and his family live here. For discretion's sake, they told me to leave the horses here and come get you on foot."

"That makes sense. Where are we headed?"

"Barla didn't tell you?" Bryon asked in amazement.

"No, she said the walls could hear."

"You must be in more danger than I imagined if she wouldn't even talk in her own home," he mused quietly. "We're going to ride until sunrise; by then, we should be in Matza. These horses belong to a friend of mine who lives there. We'll sleep the day in his house; then, at nightfall, we'll take my telepod to my house in Kirma."

"How long will it take us to get to Kirma?" she asked excitedly. Her mind raced ahead in anticipation of her first telepod ride.

Bryon looked at her for a few seconds as though trying to understand her question. His silence triggered Amanda's heart to stutter in alarm. She realized again she had said something wrong. "I'm sorry. That didn't come out right. I wondered if we're going straight to where I'll be staying, or do you have other errands to run first?"

The silence stretched out even longer before Bryon slowly nodded and replied, "You'll be staying at my house. And yes, we'll go straight there, so you can meet my wife and family, get unpacked, and then rest. I'm sure you'll need it by then."

She hadn't realized Bryon had a family. Her chest constricted with pain at how much she missed her own. Unable to stop herself, she asked, "Are you sure I won't be an imposition to your family?"

"Absolutely not! My wife's thrilled to have another woman in the house. I'm sure you'll love her."

They rode silently for a few minutes before Bryon quietly but swiftly said, "It seems as though there's more to your story than you're telling me."

Amanda's gaze cut over to him sharply, appraising his expression. *Should I tell him?*

Not for the first time, wishing she could share her story. But, without absolute certainty she could trust him, she had to defer to Barla's warning to keep her origins secret.

Barla trusts Bryon with my safety, but would he not want me in his house if he knew I was an old soul? She had to give him an answer, so she said, "There is, but Barla has asked me not to talk about it just yet. I hope you'll understand."

"Do you think there might come a point where you'll tell me everything?" he asked hopefully.

"I honestly don't know. Can we play it by ear?"

"Fair enough."

Amanda's curiosity was piqued, so she asked, "What made you think I had something more to tell?"

He shrugged offhandedly and replied, "Oh, it's just little things here and there which you do or say differently."

"Am I terribly obvious?"

"No," he replied, "My wife tells me I always read too much into things, but more than once, it's come in handy!"

"Will you do me a favor and let me know when I make a mistake?" she asked him quickly before she lost her nerve. If Bryon could see through her so easily, how could she possibly handle integrating with another community? Just the idea of being kept hidden made her have second thoughts about leaving with Bryon.

"Sure. Do you want me to cough or stumble or something?"

"Whatever fits the situation."

"That sounds fun," he replied.

To fill the strained silence, Amanda asked, "Tell me about your family." Maybe she could gather her thoughts while Bryon spoke about himself. As long as she kept him talking, then she wouldn't have an opportunity to say something alarming.

"What would you like to know?"

"How long have you been married?"

"Six anons, last mesan in fact," he replied promptly. "One thing

I learned; never forget your anniversary; it might just be the last thing you do!" He chuckled.

"I hear a story behind that laugh!" Amanda replied and then added, "I'll have to ask your wife what happened. By the way, what's your wife's name?"

"Alena," he spoke with pride.

"You also said you had a family at home. Do you have kids then, too?"

"Yes, we have our oldest son, Justan, who's three anons old; then there's his betrothed, Andera, who's almost three anons; and lastly, we have our youngest son, Kyelon, who just turned two anons."

"Betrothed," Amanda sputtered, staring at Bryon with her mouth hanging open. She'd read about the arranged marriages, but she didn't think they meant them to be for babies. It almost felt as though she'd fallen back in time when she entered Tuala. How could they possibly think that was a good idea?

"There you go again," Bryon smiled and then coughed to cover his amusement at her expression.

"But you said your three anon old son is betrothed!"

"Yes, it is the Tualan custom. Where did you say you were from?"

His question brought her back to Tualan reality. She shook her head to clear her mind. "Sorry, I don't know why, but it just took me by surprise. I thought only the Elders' families had betrothals anymore." Her cover story came a bit late as her mind reeled. Every time she began to relax, the drastic differences of Tuala smacked her in the face.

Bryon nodded, but he noticed she had not answered his question. Turning his attention back to the road in front of them, he considered who this woman might be who would be living with his family. If he did not trust Barla as he did, then he might have considered placing her with someone else. However, he promised Barla he would look out for her and would honor his word.

Amanda let Bryon's statements sink into her mind as she contemplated what other distinct customs she might not know about Tuala. Apparently, Barla had forgotten to mention betrothals happened to children, which seemed a pretty important detail to Amanda. She decided to ask Bryon more questions about his life and firmly told herself to accept anything he said as 'normal' even if it seemed bizarre to herself.

"How did Andera come into the picture?"

Bryon kept his head facing forward but allowed his eyes to glance curiously at the woman riding beside him. "We made arrangements for her to come live with us when she was three mesans old, as is the custom. Our two families have been business partners for generations. When both wives discovered their pregnancies at the same time, we agreed that if Alena had a boy and Zeka had a girl, then they would be betrothed."

"I see," Amanda said as she assimilated the information. "So, if Andera is Justan's betrothed, what do you call her in your family... your daughter?"

"You're doing it again, but I'll answer because you obviously need to know. A betrothed girl is considered a first-daughter. So we can introduce her as our first daughter or as our son's betrothed; either is acceptable."

Wow, I am not doing a good job of hiding my curiosity. He already suspects something, so what's the harm. Then she asked, "How come your younger son doesn't have a betrothed?"

"They don't usually get one unless something happens to the older son or if circumstances called for it, which is pretty rare."

"What would've happened if your son had been a girl? Would you have given her away to be betrothed to someone else?" She tried to wrap her thoughts around the idea of not raising your children.

"We might if a reputable family approached us, and we could make the proper arrangements within the allotted time frame."

"What's the allotted time frame?" It seemed insane to discuss child marriage as if nothing seemed morally wrong. Yet, her curiosity kept her asking.

"Usually within three to six mesans after they're born."

"What would happen to Andera if something happened to Justan? Would you keep her or send her home?"

"If she were younger than seven, we would have the option to send her home. Older than seven, we would give her the option of either becoming our adopted daughter and staying with us or going back to her birth parents."

"What if they grew up hating each other?"

"That doesn't happen. It's the reason they're raised together, so they'll have the same parenting style, same morals, and same beliefs."

"What if one of them found someone else they wanted to marry? Could they break it off themselves? If they did, what would happen to them?"

"It's been known to happen, luckily, not very often. The parents usually feel obligated to care for the girl for the rest of her life. If she refuses their help, she can go on and find someone else to marry, or she can return to live with her birth parents. It's considered one of the greatest insults to the family of the girl, and it can have serious social consequences for her and her family."

"Don't you feel a little bit sorry for the two kids not having a say in their choice of spouse?" She shuddered to think of her parents picking someone for her to marry. If that had happened, then she would never have gotten to know Neal. Then she never would have ended up in Tuala, she realized with a sinking sensation. Maybe they had things right here in Tuala, after all.

"Not at all; it's considered a blessed union and gives them an even higher status in the community. What parent wouldn't want to give their child a leg up in life?"

"Why is it considered blessed?" She almost dreaded the answer. If she had to choose between discussing child marriage or traveling on horseback, she didn't know which actually seemed worse. Together, it seemed almost too much to bear.

"Because it has to be approved and been blessed by the Elders before it can occur."

Amanda desperately wished for a blessing from the Elders. Maybe they were her only hope for finding Neal. Barla's fear of discovery may have tainted her opinion of Jehoban's representatives. The Elders might not be as bad as Barla made them out to be.

In that instant, Amanda decided to give everyone a week to locate Neal. If she didn't hear any progress in that timeframe, she would ask to speak to an Elder. She longed to have Neal hold her again and tell her everything would be okay.

CHAPTER 3

Only the dull thuds of the horses' hooves striking the dirt road sounded as they passed through the country-side. With the houses left far behind, they rode past fallow fields and small tree groves. Looking up at the clear, bright stars and half-crescent moon, Amanda wondered if Neal could see the same heavenly bodies. If only she could find him, then maybe they could discover a way back home.

Her imagination must have been in overdrive. She could have sworn she spotted the silhouette of a massive dragon in the sky. Of course, if dragons existed here, she was certain Barla would have said something about it. Rather than make herself sound even more alien to Bryon, she kept her mouth shut but cherished the idea that she'd seen something miraculous.

Expecting more questions from Amanda, Bryon finally looked over at her when the silence stretched longer. The moonlight showed her deep in thought, making him wonder more about her story. Where was she from that she would not know about betrothals and the Elders? Even stranger yet, she had known about the crystal ceremony for newborns. Once again, he wished he had

had more opportunity to discuss this matter with Barla before he had to return home.

The longer she thought about missing Neal, the more depression settled over her. She had to remain strong until Captain Ahn could execute a proper search of the ocean where she had last seen him. She couldn't dwell on the possibility that he might not have survived the passage between worlds. She needed a distraction. Just as her throat began to constrict with emotion, she managed to squeak out, "What kind of work do you do?"

Startled out of his reverie, Bryon slowly responded as he processed her question. "I work with the shipping warehouses in Kirma. I make arrangements for the storage and transportation of various goods needed throughout the region."

Good! Something boring to distract her morbid thoughts. *Keep him talking*, she coached herself. "How long have you been doing it?"

"For the past eight anons. I wasn't as lucky as some others when it came to the lottery. Since I didn't go to post-study, I had to draw from the short list.

"Alena was luckier. She gets to stay on retirement for another declan. I guess it worked out okay. She can stay home while the kids grow up, and I can build my reputation before I'm too old to care about it."

Smiling at his own joke, he looked over at Amanda when she remained silent. She actually looked confused, and he wondered what she knew of the retirement pool. Taking pity on her, he asked, "Do you want me to tell you how the retirement pool works?"

"I'd love to hear you tell it."

Bryon's fingers drummed against the saddle's pommel as he tried to think of an easy way to explain something so commonplace. "Okay, let's see. When you finish your education, you begin retirement. During retirement, you're encouraged to pursue hobbies and build skills in your chosen field. After retirement, you go to work. The length of a retirement depends on two factors; how much education you obtain and which lottery pool you are assigned."

"When you say retirement, are you saying you get paid to *not* work?" Amanda asked in disbelief.

"Yes. Exactly."

"Who pays for it?"

"The Elders do, of course!" He laughed out loud at the incredulous expression on Amanda's face.

"Why would they do that?" she asked, still not believing what she was hearing.

"It's simple, really," he began, "older teenagers aren't ready to settle down to a job and do it well. This way, they can have their adventures, get married, start families, and, most importantly, grow up, before having to enter the working world."

Amanda nodded as she thought through all of the pros and cons. "It sounds pretty interesting."

"Have you really never heard of this?" Bryon asked, not fully believing the possibility.

Trying to decide if she should lie, his look of sincerity convinced her to tell the truth, and she replied quietly, "Yes."

Bryon whistled. "Wow! Are you sure you can't tell me where you're from?"

"Sorry, not yet." Feeling uncomfortable, she kept her gaze locked between her horse's ears at the road. How could she possibly tell him the truth? She had a hard enough time believing in Tuala, and she had lived through the strangeness of crossing over from Earth. She wouldn't want Bryon to think her crazy and decide to withdraw his help.

"I'm sure when the time's right, it'll be a fascinating story. I look forward to it."

You don't even know how right you are. A restless breeze whipped her hair across her face, mirroring exactly her own feelings. The rustling of the leaves grew louder as they rode through another small patch of trees.

As her thoughts raced out of control again, Amanda asked, "What does your wife do to keep busy if she's still retired?"

"Well," Bryon answered, "I wouldn't exactly say Alena *is* retired, even though she receives retirement pay from the Elders. She's a healer, and she works out of our house."

"Is a healer the same as a wise-woman?"

"All wise-women are healers, but not all healers become wise-women."

"How do they become a wise-woman?" *Would the medical procedures performed here compare to those of Earth?* She greatly admired anyone who went into medicine ever since the doctors worked tirelessly to save her sister, Deanna, from an almost fatal bout of pneumonia.

"They start as Alena has, and if they receive enough recommendations to the Elders, then they go and study with the Elders. If the Elders certify them, then they are supplied with ceremonial crystals and receive a ring showing their status as a wise-woman."

"Is Alena a wise-woman?"

"Not yet, but she has been asked to study with Elder Debbon. She hasn't given her reply yet."

"Doesn't she want to go?"

"Yes, she does, but she doesn't want to leave the children alone."

Amanda pondered the dilemma. Alena should not miss such a fantastic opportunity. Then an inspired thought occurred to her. "Do you think she would go if I agreed to take care of the children for her?" Even as the offer left her lips, she wished she could take it back. She didn't plan to stay in Tuala longer than a week. Surely, the wise-woman training would take more time than that.

Bryon smiled at the idea and then replied, "You'd have your work cut out for you. The kids are a handful. Alena still has a couple of weeks to give her answer. Maybe you could talk to her about it after she gets to know you a little better. I'd be grateful if you could give her this opportunity."

"It'd certainly make me feel better about staying with your family. After all, I don't have any money to help out with my expenses." In for a penny, in for a pound, Amanda decided. After all, Alena didn't know Amanda. So, of course, she'd turn down her offer.

Leaving the shelter of the trees led them straight into a fierce, cold wind. Immediately, Amanda grabbed the hood resting over her back to cover her head from the gust of frigid air. Hopefully, they were getting close to where they would stop for the day. Unfortunately, the saddle had only been comfortable for the first couple of hours. If the ride lasted much longer, she would be lucky to retain the ability to stand.

As if reading her thoughts, Bryon yelled over the wind, "We don't have too much farther to go. Let's push the horses faster before this storm really blows in."

"Sounds good to me," she yelled back as she applied her heels to the horse's sides. All too willing to go faster, Maga promptly quickened her walking stride to a smooth trot.

The change in gait instantly reminded Amanda of her sister's rough ride, but Maga appeared stable and not ready to fling her off. One hand remained clenched on the pommel while the other gripped the reins until her fingernails bit into her palm.

Amanda glanced up at the once-clear sky to see dark clouds rapidly obscuring the twinkling stars. Within minutes, the bright moon and its comforting light were gone. Did the dragon bring this storm, or was she flying away from it?

The fierce wind threatened to tear the hood back from her head. She had to let go of the pommel to clutch the fabric close to her neck.

The scenery blurred past them at their faster pace. Occasionally, raindrops hit their faces as they raced along. The fitful gusts of wind caused brush to roll across the road ahead of them, making the horses startle and break their stride.

Amanda barely managed to contain her scream the first time Maga lifted her front hooves to soar effortlessly over the rolling weeds. This once-easy ride became more frightening by the second, but Amanda reminded herself to remain hopeful with Bryon's remark of it ending soon.

Seeing lights ahead on the sides of the road, Amanda hoped it was their destination. Her initial peace with riding expired long before, and the faster pace continued to drive her bones further into the already uncomfortable saddle.

A searing pain struck the back of Amanda's right hand. She let out a piercing scream of pain and fear. Maga panicked at the sound and reared up on her hind legs. Not expecting the sudden tilt, Amanda slid right off the back of the saddle. As she fell, Amanda twisted around and put out her hands to break her fall. All too soon, she felt the impact of the ground, coupled with another intense jolt of pain as she felt her wrist snap on impact.

Rolling to her left side, she cradled her broken wrist with her other hand, a groan of agony erupting from her lips. She could not decide if the wrist or the initial hand injury hurt worse. Leaning forward, she strained to see the back of her hand in the driving rain and darkness and came face to face with the biggest beetle she had ever seen. Screaming again, she brushed madly, trying to dislodge the insect from her flesh.

Bryon appeared at her side. Reaching forward, he plucked the beetle from her hand by pinching it just behind the head. Then, he dropped the insect on the road with an exclamation of disgust and crunched it under his boot heel with a satisfying twist. "Hold still. I'll be right back," he said as he ran to his horse.

In a few seconds, he returned carrying something compact.

Without moving her hand, he brought a small pouch forward to squeeze some ointment into the hole left by the beetle.

"What was that…that thing?" she stammered as shock started to set in.

"It's called a beetlesnatch, but this isn't the right season for them or even the right region. The wind must've brought it in."

"What did it do to my hand?" She shuddered to think of why her hand hurt so badly.

"They're flesh-eating beetles. Nasty bugs, really. Once they tear the flesh from you, they inject their saliva into your muscle to break it down. The ointment should stop the saliva from destroying more of your muscle tissue. I'm afraid you'll still have a scar where it tore your skin off, though. Now, how is your arm?" He reached forward to examine her.

The beetlesnatch wound sounded too much like that of a brown recluse spider. A shiver of disgust coursed through her as her mind dredged up her fear of spiders. Amanda shifted to prevent him from jarring her again. "My arm's fine, but I'm sure I broke my wrist."

"Let me help you up," he said as he bent down behind her to hook his arms under her armpits.

Amanda rose clumsily to her feet but immediately felt light-headed. Starting to sway alarmingly, Bryon rushed to sling his arm around her waist to steady her. This time, she didn't feel at all bad about leaning against him for support. If he hadn't been there, she would have fallen flat on her face in the mud.

"Do you think you can walk to the horses, or should I carry you?"

Mortified at the idea of him trying to carry her, she hastily shook her head and managed to say, "I think I can manage, just don't leave my side." *Was this wound fatal? Will I die in a strange dimension and never know what happened to Neal? How come nothing ever works out as I plan?*

Bryon leaned her against his horse while he rummaged in his saddlebags. Using one of his shirts, he fashioned a sling by tying the sleeves around her neck so the shirt's body could snugly cradle her arm.

Looking over his handiwork with satisfaction, he asked, "How's that?"

Trying to remain calm, Amanda lied, "Fine. How much further do we have to go? I saw some lights before I fell. Is it our destination?"

"Yes, it is. We were only five minutes from stopping. Can you manage to ride your horse, or should we walk?"

The idea of getting back up on Maga horrified her. The horse appeared calm now. She couldn't really blame the horse for shying at her obnoxious outburst. "How long will it take to walk?"

"About fifteen minutes."

"Let's ride." She really wanted this nightmare to end. *Could things get any worse?* No sooner had she answered when the rain started to come down in earnest. Amanda almost chuckled as the elements mocked her.

Much to her embarrassment, Bryon practically needed to lift her in the saddle. Yet, she knew she could not have managed it on her own. Moreover, because of her lightheadedness, she could not bother with the horse's reins. She clutched the pommel with her left hand, determined to remain seated this time.

Seeing her pained expression, as well as her fierce determination to stay in the saddle, Bryon reached up and took the reins. "I'll lead your horse," he unnecessarily announced as he walked her horse over to his own.

The rain continued unrelentingly in its unseasonal downpour, which soaked them through to the skin. Amanda kept her head low as she moaned in pain and clutched the pommel harder to hold as still as possible against the horse's wretchedly unsteady gait. She almost exclaimed her relief when they finally came to a halt.

Bryon lifted her down from the saddle and put his arm around her waist, leading her down a lit pathway to a small cottage. Amanda's head swooned to the point where she wished Bryon would have just carried her the short distance. When they got to the front door, Bryon knocked three times swiftly and waited. Within a few seconds, the door opened, and a little old lady ushered them into the living room.

"The lady has broken her wrist falling off of a horse just moments ago after being bitten by a beetlesnatch," Bryon said to the old woman.

"I'll get my medicine kit," she replied and shuffled out of the room.

Bryon settled Amanda in front of the lowly lit fire on the broad, stone hearth. Cradling her arm, she tried to will the throbbing ache traveling up her limb to stop. Rocking back and forth, she hoped to distract herself from the pain while they waited for the woman's return.

With shuffling steps back into the overly warm room, the elderly lady carried an oversized wooden crate. Setting it down at Amanda's feet, she opened it to display the vast array of medicine bottles and cloth bandages. Sorting through the contents, rattling the glass, and occasionally pulling one out and reading the label, shaking her head and putting it back, she repeated this until she found the correct vial.

A pungent odor wafted from the container as soon as she opened it. Digging into her apron pocket, she produced a large spoon onto which she poured a generous amount of the foul-smelling liquid. Bringing it to Amanda's lips, she said, "This'll taste bitter, but the pain will stop."

Amanda fleetingly debated the sterility of the spoon, but with the pain flashing through her, she impatiently leaned forward and swallowed the contents in one quick gulp. Her eyes instantly watered from the intense bitterness, but she remained hopeful that the disgusting dose would promptly take effect. Of course, the most effective medicine always tasted the worst, right?

"Help me get her out of this filthy, wet coat," the woman ordered Bryon. Then, while the two of them worked together to remove her soaked and soiled cloak, she untied the sling and supported Amanda's wrist.

Amanda tried assisting with the removal, but all of her limbs felt heavy and not her own. With her thoughts wandering aimlessly, she heard the woman tell Bryon her wrist was broken more severely than she could handle. *What would happen now?* But she could not get her mind to care about it anymore as she drifted off to sleep.

"The beetlesnatch venom has also gone too far for my experience. I need to contact an Elder," the wise-woman's tone clearly expressed her urgent concern.

"Do whatever you need, just do it quickly!"

Bryon watched the wise-woman close her eyes and silently mouth a petition for help. Suppressing a momentary concern about involving an Elder given his suspicion of Amanda being an *old soul,* Bryon knew she would rather stay alive.

CHAPTER 4

Elder Debbon hardly ever received urgent mental petitions for help; they usually came through the patil. Even more unusual, since he respected Copa's competence as a healer. Her case must truly have extraordinary circumstances. After translating himself directly into Copa's consultation room, Elder Debbon kneeled beside the sick woman on the cot.

Gathering elemy to create healing energy for the woman's seemingly simple injuries, he realized the amount of energy required would not work at all. At once, he knew this person did not belong in Tuala, which both intrigued and excited him. Glancing sidelong at the wise-woman, he wondered if she felt the difference as well.

He needed time alone with her. Now. Effortlessly gathering massive amounts of elemy to surround himself and this woman, he used his gift to translocate both himself and the unknown girl to his Elder Isle Residence. Alone in an upper bedroom, he leaned heavily on the power of the ley lines flowing under the Residence to finish the healing which Copa barely began.

As an Elder, his responsibilities included locating any

foreigners and questioning their reasons for being in Tuala. Yet her potent but latent power surprised him more than he cared to admit.

Foregoing the usual questioning techniques, Elder Debbon took advantage of Copa's sedative. Gently resting his hands on the girl's temples, he delved into her unconscious mind. Amazement and anger warred inside him at the story he encountered. Her thoughts quickly became his own as her story unfolded…

NEALAND SETTLED his arm more comfortably under Amanda's head as they cuddled closely on the bed. She could not believe she was lying naked next to him; this had definitely not been in the plan.

"What are you thinking about right now?" Nealand's soft inquiry broke the peaceful silence which settled over the nestled pair. His fingers, suddenly restless, ran along the length of her long, brown hair. He loved the feel of the silky strands as they fell across his chest.

"I was just wondering…," she sighed and looked earnestly into Nealand's beautiful brown eyes, "what we're going to do now?"

"I can think of lots of ways to answer your question," his lowered voice devilishly answered while he moved down to nuzzle his smiling lips against her neck.

"You're terrible!" She pushed herself away from him with mock indignation, trying to restrain an undignified giggle. "I was talking about our future!"

"You don't think that's what I had in mind?" He leaned up and reached for her again.

"I'm sure *your* future only involves the next ten minutes."

"Ouch!" He groaned as his muscular frame fell back against the bed, pretending to stab himself through the heart. "I was thinking more along the lines of the next half hour, at least!"

"You wish!" She settled back next to him. Tracing the contours of his incredibly muscled abdomen and chest, she considered her next words. "Seriously, Neal, what're we going to do when we have to go back home?"

"Get married, of course!" He wrapped his arms around her petite frame and held her snugly again.

"No. Before that! After spending weeks with you alone on this yacht, I can't bear thinking about going back to my parents' house and being away from you. Doesn't it bother you, too?"

"Sure, but what else can we do? My mom would kill me if we didn't allow her to plan an embarrassingly huge wedding along with your mother. It's going to take months, you know."

"Ugh! Why don't we just elope and tell them about it later? I'm not a prize horse to dress up and show off, you know!"

"You're my prize. We'll be so dazzlingly gorgeous that people will talk about our wedding for at least a week." He flashed her another devilish grin, loving to egg her on.

"Months of planning just so people can talk about us for a whole week, huh? I don't think so!" She sat up and leaned over him with a hand on each side of his head. She used the advantage of her naked torso to invite him to agree with whatever she wanted from him. "C'mon! Let's elope before going back."

His resolve weakened as his eyes looked over her body longingly while his hands reached up automatically, unable to resist the silken fall of her hair. "Do you want to stop off somewhere in Mexico? I'm not even sure if that's considered a legal marriage in Florida if we did."

"Oh, I don't know, and I don't care! I just want you with me every night for the rest of my life." Amanda groaned as she realized she failed in her attempt at seductive persuasion. Growling, she flopped onto her hip at Nealand's side.

"We'll figure something out to make everyone happy," he assured her as his hand caressed the soft skin on her shoulder and traveled along her spine to try to get her back in the mood. His hand braced her hip as the bed swayed violently under them. His forehead creased, and his head whipped sideways to allow him to look out the porthole window.

"What?" Amanda asked as she felt his body tense.

"I just realized how much the yacht is rocking. There must be a storm blowing in. I checked the weather warnings earlier today, and they didn't say anything about any small craft advisories."

"Do we need to do anything to get the yacht ready if it gets worse?" Amanda asked. *Was this the reason Mom didn't want me to go?*

"Nothing right now," he answered, wanting to reassure her but continuing to look troubled.

Amanda flinched as a flash of light erupted in the sky outside the window right next to them, and she automatically counted in her head *one, two, three, fo*—bang. She was pleased to remember learning about counting the seconds between the flash of lightning and the sound of thunder to calculate the storm brewing less than a mile away.

Nealand shook his head, deciding he could do nothing about the storm. He cleared his expression and resumed his prior exploration of Amanda's naked body. The waves crashed against the yacht from unpredictable angles, making them both clumsy and awkward. As the rough waters made even cuddling difficult, the romantic mood dissipated with the same speed as the oncoming storm.

"Ahh!" Amanda squealed in alarm as a boom of thunder immediately followed another flash of lightning. "That was right next to us!"

"I'm going to check the radar in the wheelhouse," Nealand announced as he threw his legs over the mattress. Taking one step away from the bed, he hastily grabbed a pair of previously discarded sweatpants from the floor and struggled to put them on with the unpredictably pitching floor.

Another wave aggressively rocked the yacht, making him fall sideways onto the bed. Amanda squealed as he fell against her legs.

"Sorry," Nealand said over his shoulder as he continued to dress. Pausing in the doorway, he turned to Amanda and said, "Stay put, I'll be right back. I love you." Nealand smiled flirtatiously before racing down the corridor to the stairs and out of Amanda's sight.

The yacht rocked brutally again, and Amanda made up her mind. "Stay put, he says! What am I? A dog? He may be big and muscular, but I can help too!" She ripped back the covers and threw her legs over the edge of the bed.

With her legs splayed wide for some semblance of steadiness, she leaned over to grab a discarded shirt from the corner of the bed just as another rogue wave hit the port side of the yacht. Amanda stumbled, toppled over backward, and hit her head on the bedside table. The last thing she remembered was a flash of lightning piercing her closed eyes and a thunderous roar splitting her eardrums…

Elder Debbon had never even considered an electrical storm becoming a conduit into Tuala. He would have to ponder the possibilities which this phenomenon could produce. Returning to Amanda, he noticed some time had elapsed, and the setting had changed drastically as her unconscious stream of thought continued…

She could not keep two thoughts straight in her head. For some reason, staying awake seemed equally problematic. Her thoughts shifted with confusing, disturbing, and almost otherworldly images. She tried to focus when she drifted into another dream...

I sure hope this map is accurate, she mumbled to herself as she navigated the open-air hallways through the school.

Finally arriving at the orientation room, she sat at the front row desk. During the orientation, she learned the location of the cafeteria, called The Commons, and which lunch shift was going to be hers. The rest of the orientation spiel passed in a blur until the woman announced the dance team tryouts. Excitedly, she wrote down the tryout information on the front of her new PeeChee.

Starting to stir from her dream, she blinked slowly to clear her eyes and looked around warily at her unfamiliar surroundings. Taking in the strange room, she was startled when she spotted the pudgy man leaning casually beside the bed. A frown pulled her full lips down as she barely managed to croak, "Where am I?"

"You're on my water craft. You're safe, don't worry," the man replied softly.

She saw his lips moving, but she couldn't make out anything he said. *Did something impair my hearing as well?* Trying to create some moisture in her mouth, she swallowed with difficulty. "Who are you?"

"I'm Petre. Do you think you could manage to swallow some broth? It might soothe your dry throat." Petre moved over to her purposefully, one hand balancing the broth as he used the other to steady her as he brought the cup to her lips.

She struggled to sit up and brace herself against his spongy arm. Her nod was rewarded by feeling the warm liquid in the cup being pressed to her lips. The heavenly moisture soothed her parched throat as she swallowed.

The broth drew away too soon, and Petre held it out of her reach. A faint whine of protest came unbidden, mortifying her as tears sprang to her eyes. She stared into his bright blue eyes. *Who is this stranger, and how did I come to lie unconscious in bed?*

Petre gently pulled the cup farther away from her as he said, "Easy now, too much liquid will make you sick." He set the cup on the counter just out of her reach. Her eyes remained fastened on the mug as if it contained her lifeline. He chuckled and said, "Relax, you can have more in a minute."

She sighed and wilted onto the sleeping platform. Her head dropped back on the cabin wall, and she gasped as pain instantly engulfed her. "What happened to my head?" She reached up to assess the damage.

"You must have fallen; I found you on the floor." But all she heard was another mumbled response.

"I don't remember what happened." She drew up her knees and wrapped her arms around them protectively. Realizing she was naked, her eyes darted around her before widening in panic. "What happened to my clothes? Why don't I remember anything? I don't even remember my name. What's my name?"

She clutched his arm but then realized she did not know him either. Suspicion made her eye him warily. He could be a kidnapper. A rapist! He could be the one who hit her on the head!

She spoke quietly, trying to force the words out without her voice breaking. "I don't remember you. I don't remember how I got on this boat. Who the hell are you?" Fear and frustration overcame her, and tears rushed down her cheeks.

"My name's Petre. Remember?"

Even through her tears, Amanda noted the odd way he pronounced his name, as though it was short for something else. "Peter?" she asked, careful to pronounce it like she thought it should be spelled.

"Close enough, honey. Now, now; don't cry." He tried to soothe her by rubbing her arm. *What is a boat? It must be an* old soul *word.*

She mistook his comforting gesture as an aggressive move, and she reflexively jerked out of his grip.

"I'll tell you everything just after you finish your broth," he said, but she could not understand him. He turned to the counter and thought about what to put in her drink to make her sleep. Epeny *should do it*. He focused his thoughts on her cup.

The *epeny* now floated in her broth. Swirling the liquid gently, he brought the cup back to her lips. With a calculated look of satisfaction mixed with anticipation, he stared into her brown eyes as she gulped the fluid down eagerly.

CHAPTER 5

With the broth gone, her mind clouded again, and she felt the man tucking the covers around her. She curled up on her side and swiftly drifted into another dream. She'd take anything to divorce herself from her throbbing headache and fear of the unknown.

She and her best friend, Sherry, stood behind the noisy crowd of girls, watching the hopeful candidates as they read the final selection list for the dance team's newest members. She did not have much hope of making the cut since the team seldom picked freshmen.

Sherry impatiently shoved her way through the crowd to look for her friend's name on this list. Intently watching Sherry's face as she scanned the list, she tried not to let hope bloom and saw Sherry's expression grow sad.

Tears welled up in her eyes, and she lowered her head to allow her long hair to cover her face. Hoping nobody would see her tears, she turned away from the crowd and swiftly walked toward the parking lot where her mother waited for her.

Sherry caught up with her and put her arm over her shoulders. "I'm sorry, Amos," Sherry whispered, using a silly nickname for her best friend's first name. "I was just so sad because you and I aren't going to be spending much time together this summer." Sherry turned her toward herself to make sure she had her attention before she shouted, "YOU MADE THE TEAM!!!"

The tears of sorrow rapidly changed to those of joy. "What?! What?! Seriously?" She shoved Sherry's arm. "How could you let me think I hadn't made it? You know what this means to me."

"Hey, I said I was sorry, and I meant it both ways."

"Mmm-hmm," she hummed, then grabbed Sherry's arm and said, "Let's go back and see when the first practice starts. Oh, and who else is on the team with me!"

SEEING Petre MacVeen in her memories raised immediate concerns. Without another thought or even a moment to allow himself to calm down, Elder Debbon used his power to locate Petre and immediately transport him into the room adjacent to where Amanda now rested comfortably. He angrily shot up from the chair at her bedside and strode across the room. Just as he closed the door to Amanda's room, loud complaints issued from where Petre now found himself.

Elder Debbon calmed his expression to neutrality and opened the door. Petre aggressively faced him. Not willing to hear any accusations of impropriety from Petre, he sliced his hand in front of his body and Petre's voice immediately silenced.

He shut the door solidly behind himself and strode confidently into the room. He pointed to the chair. "Sit, Petre. You have some serious questions to answer. Unfortunately, I don't have time for your cooperation; you will submit to my questions by compulsion."

His anger amplified the amount of elemental energy he accessed. Using his considerable talent to compel compliance, Petre meekly sat in the indicated chair. He stepped behind Petre and placed his fingers on Petre's temples. "Show me how you found the water craft and the girl," he ordered as his thoughts delved into Petre's mind and retrieved the answers he sought…

PETRE DREW briny air in through his nose and blew an impatient breath out his mouth over the calm, sun-sparkled ripples of water under his water craft. His hands clenched hard on the railing as he surveyed the water. His day was not going well.

This halted sail through the Gulf of Thulen after his fruitless, not to mention illegal, business venture in the City of Thulen did nothing to improve his mood. All he needed now was to rip a hole in the bottom of his vessel on some stray coral reef to make his day truly special. His eyes squinted against the newfound sun. The dark storm clouds just passed behind him, and he could see for several gania in every direction. It seemed his was the only water craft out that day.

Suddenly, a bright flash of lightning ripped through the sky, and the once calm waters boiled with unexpected rage. Automatically bracing his legs against the sudden sway of his ship, he blinked in amazement, unable to believe what he saw. Scrubbing his hands roughly over his eyes to clear his vision, he still did not trust his sight.

Where seconds before the sea had been his only companion, he now saw another water craft directly in front of him. If he did not act immediately, his water craft would tear through the middle of the other listing ship. He closed his eyes, and with all his mental strength, he concentrated on making his vessel stop. He felt the scanty forward breeze dwindle and the waters still. When he dared to open his eyes, he saw mere hand spans remained between the two water crafts.

Now I know a ship wasn't there just a second ago. He shook his head in confusion and mumbled out loud, "What just happened?"

Immediately intrigued over this unexpected bounty, Petre grabbed a thick mooring rope. With practiced ease, he tossed it over the railing to lash the two water crafts together before he jumped aboard the yellow and white ship.

Funny colors. He curled his upper lip in vague distaste. *Why would someone want their ship to be so bright?*

From the sleek shape and the odd type of wood used in its construction, Petre knew he discovered something of great value to the Elders. He could feel the familiar rush of adrenaline coursing through him as he calculated what the Elders would pay for such a find.

Petre walked around the slanting deck, not recognizing any of the equipment. His heart rate accelerated, and his mouth fell open as he unconsciously licked his lips.

This has to be a ship from one of the old souls.

If this lucky streak remained on his side and he happened to discover an *old soul* survivor, the Elders would make sure to set him up for life. Excitedly, he called out, "Hello! Is anybody aboard? Does anyone need help?"

Pausing, he slowly turned his head from side to side as he listened intently and nearly fell over when he actually heard a faint groan from the depths of the ship.

Petre found the stairs leading below, and he called out again, "Is anybody down there?" Clutching the rail and barely breathing, he tried to pinpoint the location of the faint sound. A victorious smile burst forth at the sound of another groan, and he rushed to investigate before the ship took on any more water.

Once below deck, he noted some of the doors were already flung open. He hastily searched each room with the hope some people were still alive. Another sound, louder this time, issued from the last door in the corridor.

Practically leaping forward in his eagerness, he grabbed the latch and shoved himself against the door. Another faint noise sounded. A rapid scan of the room revealed more strangely polished wood throughout the sleeping space. The noise came from behind the sleeping platform. Several steps into the room brought him around to the far side of the bed, but what he found was not what he expected.

He looked down on the petite body of a completely naked and utterly still woman. Her eyes were closed, and her skin appeared unnaturally white. Excitement coursed through him as he moved closer to kneel beside her to put his trembling hand on her cold arm. With a rough shake, he asked, "Lady, are you all right?"

She groaned again as her head lolled to the side. Petre spotted a pool of blood forming beneath her long dark hair. Petre guessed she probably fell and split her head open. If he did not get something on the wound soon, she could bleed to death.

Then he'd lose his prize.

If she died, he would never get any money from the Elders. Without another thought, he grabbed a sheet from the sleeping platform and used his teeth to rip it into long bandaging strips.

Petre roughly propped up the woman against the sleeping platform. Ignoring her moans, he felt through her hair until he found the bump and a nasty three-inch gash. Disregarding sanitation or comfort, he jammed a wad of fabric over the wound and used another strip to tie it in place. With the injury covered, he struggled to lift her small, limp body off the floor to place her on the sleeping platform.

As much as it thrilled him to see her nakedness, she needed clothes. If she didn't get warmer, she'd go into shock.

Petre rummaged through the strange box-like things next to the sleeping platform and found what appeared to be women's clothing. He pulled out an armload of items and dumped them on the sheet next to the woman.

With everything bundled inside the sheet, he cradled her in his arms. Staggering under her weight, Petre retraced his steps to the upper deck, awkwardly hopped across to his craft, and dropped her on his own sleeping platform.

Tearing himself away from her luscious nakedness, he could not resist scavenging for more items from which he could profit. He jumped across to the other craft, descended the same stairs, then down yet another flight to look for any more survivors and also to see if he could find out why the ship leaned so precariously. He didn't want his prize to sink into the ocean before he had a chance to sell it.

While wading through knee-deep water, he didn't find any other people, but he did discover the pump below not running, which allowed the water to seep in swiftly. He located the reset button on the machine and pushed it. The pump hummed to life, and the water level stopped rising. Nodding in satisfaction, he hurriedly ascended the stairs to continue rummaging around.

When Petre finished his cursory inspection, he noticed the unusual vessel rested squarely in the ocean as she should. A smile slowly spread across his thin lips as he mentally tabulated the money he would receive for selling this strange beauty and the woman to the Elders.

Maybe it was going to be a good day after all…

Elder Debbon struggled to control his anger at seeing the vessel which Petre had found. Revulsion slithered through him at Petre's thoughts regarding Amanda but hoped Petre would contain his sick curiosity concerning the girl. He took a moment to compose his mind before he continued to delve into Petre's recollections of the past…

First thing first.

He hopped back to his craft and unfastened the rope line from the bow rail. He felt the deck under his feet shift slightly and adjusted his stance to compensate as he mentally maneuvered his craft so he could attach the tow line to his craft's rear anchor bolt. Once securely fastened, he concentrated on moving his vessel around the *old soul* ship and changed his course to the nearest Elder's islet. During this shift, he noticed the writing on the side of the *old soul's* craft which read, *The Golden Jesisca.*

Petre knew he would have a few days before he reached the Elder's islet. It should give him enough time to question his new guest, that is if she survived. Satisfied with the set of his course, he returned to his cabin, not sure what he should expect. A quick visual assessment assured him the woman had not stirred from where he left her.

He never entertained a woman on his water craft. As if drawn by a magnet, he found himself standing next to her prone form. Before he could stop himself, he removed the blanket from her pale, still form and stretched himself out beside her.

His sweaty hand trembled as he drew his palm over the side of her shapely, smooth, white thigh. She did not even stir. Illicit thoughts swirled through his mind as he wondered what it would be like to take her. His hand wandered further to stroke the silky skin of her stomach. She was so soft.

Why shouldn't I? She might die anyway, and nobody would ever know if I did...

CHAPTER 6

Rage over Petre's actions poured through Elder Debbon. He hoped Petre would at least have some decency, but it appeared too much to expect concerning this depraved man. Just seeing the activities of this man made him feel soiled. Skipping ahead in Petre's memories, Elder Debbon continued to review what had happened…

He wrapped the woman in warm blankets and then routed around his cabin for some dry clothes to wear. The clothes he found were tattered but serviceable, and most importantly, dry.

Ravenous hunger ruled his thoughts. With practiced ease, he concentrated on the empty counter beside him. Instantly, he created a thick slab of hot, juicy foxl steak smothered in béarnaise sauce, creamed corn, a baked gourd with soured cream and green onion, and a cup of java for himself. He picked up the platter, ready to eat and his eyes rested on the woman.

She should probably have something to eat as well. Another cup filled with hot foxl broth laced with epeny appeared on the table almost as an afterthought. Pushing the cup of broth aside to cool, Petre sat at his table and dug into his feast.

He was just mopping up his platter with the skin of the gourd when the woman's moans became louder than Petre's smacking lips. Setting aside the almost clean platter, he moved over to the sleeping platform where the woman's eyes began to flutter but remained closed.

After a brief—mostly one-sided—conversation, Petre gave the woman some of the drugged drink and watched with anticipation until she passed out.

While the young woman slept, Petre sat out on the deck to think about this fantastic new turn of events. His eyes lingered on the sleek, yellow and white vessel that followed lazily behind his shabby, brown craft.

The Elders don't need to know I found the woman. I could just keep her drugged in my cabin until I sell her water craft.

He would have money and a woman. What more could a man want?

Better yet, I could tell her she's my wife, and she'd be mine forever. She looks young, probably eighteen or so. I really like them young; they seem to be more adventurous in the sack. Now, what do I tell her about her name?

A tailwind caught the side of the trailing ship and shifted it enough for him to see *The Golden Jesisca* written on the side.

"Yes! That's perfect! I'll tell her that her name is Jesisca."

With her name decided, Petre stood, took a deep breath of clean ocean air, and brushed his hands down the front of his pant legs. He turned to go back into his cabin when an idea struck him.

He'd have to get all of Jesisca's things from her water craft, or else the Elders might suspect something. Also, Petre wanted to search it again to see if he had missed any valuables to pilfer before turning the vessel over to the Elders. Who knew what types of treasures these *old souls* collected. Until the water craft appeared in the ocean before his craft, he was not sure he believed the stories about the *old souls*.

Now he believed.

Petre first walked to the center of the strange craft and carefully inspected the tall pole with fabric tied down with rope.

I wonder what it does.

While he had a central pole on his craft, he only used it to hoist his identification flag when he came close to landfall.

The upper main cabin contained complicated-looking equipment. Here, he found a familiar land and water map, but all of the names were wrong. He put it in the back waistband of his pants. Next to the map rested a small, flat, round object with a dial in the middle. Because of its size, he pocketed it, even though he had no idea what it did.

The kitchen contained shiny containers and implements. The unusual food left out on the counter gave him a hint as to the actual function of the room. Everything else in the space remained a mystery to him.

Not recognizing anything of value in the kitchen, he proceeded down the stairs to the living quarters. The first two rooms were empty except for the sleeping platforms, which had undisturbed sheets and pillows.

The next room was obviously a bathroom. Many odds and ends in there caught his interest. On the counter were a couple of white squares in satiny wrapping. One was open, so he picked it up and dumped the contents out into his hand. The dry, smooth square seemed rather peculiar. He turned it over and brought it up to inhale its clean scent.

The ship rocked suddenly, and his hip crashed against the counter. As he reached out to balance himself, he dropped the square into the washbasin and bumped the faucet. The water rushed out of the spout directly onto the curious object, which caused foam to form on it. He turned off the water and touched the slimy, smooth surface of the square.

Rubbing together his finger and thumb, he turned on the faucet to rinse the film from his fingers. As soon as he turned off the water, he discovered two perfectly clean fingers where the slime had touched him.

I could find a use for this.

He picked it up and put it back in the wrapper. He rinsed them clean in the basin using the residual slippery stuff to rub all over both hands. He gathered up the three blocks of cleaner and left the bathroom.

Only the room where he had found Jesisca remained for his inspection. He rummaged through all of the box-like containers and pulled out anything which looked like a woman might use. These items he piled onto the sleeping platform.

Since he planned to keep her, he needed to erase all evidence of her existence. He grabbed a towel from the floor and retraced his steps to the bathroom. He soaked the towel, returned to the bedroom, and smeared the blood from the floor behind the oddly raised sleeping platform.

With the floor cleanish, he took the soiled towel to the bathroom, rinsed it out, and wrung it as dry as he could. Returning to the sleeping room, he dropped the damp towel onto the heap of items he planned to take. He gathered up another of the many blankets from the sleeping platform, tied it around his bundle, and hoisted it up over his shoulder.

Convinced he had everything he wanted, he returned to his vessel. Carelessly dumping her pile of clothes in an almost empty cupboard, he let out a satisfied breath when he saw she slept on undisturbed.

As he shuffled through the confined cabin, his gaze roamed greedily over Jesisca's body. He wanted her again. She had consumed enough *epeny* to keep her unconscious throughout the night. His lips drew back wickedly. His hands reached forward of their own accord.

I can do whatever I want to her, and nobody will even complain…

Not only had Petre abducted an injured girl, but he also drugged her and then took advantage of her while she slept. Did this man have no limits to his depravity? Repulsed at the idea of touching Petre but needing to find out how the story continued, Elder Debbon replaced his fingers on the man's skull. He gasped as he witnessed Petre beating the woman until bruises and cuts covered her body.

So disgusted with the multiple violations he had just seen, Elder Debbon almost struck Petre dead right where he sat. Instead, he pulled his hands away from Petre's temples and hastily left the room. Another second spent with Petre, and he would do something he would regret.

Pacing the hall several times helped to cool his thoughts before he returned to Amanda's room. Since he knew what happened to her, he wanted to discover how she managed to get herself away from Petre. Taking a seat in the chair at the head of the bed, he rested his fingers on her temples. Immediately, he picked up her story where they left off before…

The following day, she awoke groggy, disoriented, and frightened. The dream felt so real, and vague impressions lingered of her friend, Sherry. As awareness grew, so did her hunger. She groped with the pillows and covers in her weak attempt to sit up.

Her head ached and throbbed abominably. Reaching up and using her fingertips, she tentatively felt the wadded bandage at the back of her skull. Even the gentle touch caused her to cry out in pain, which she swiftly tried to silence with one hand across her mouth. The makeshift bandage was stiff with her matted and crusty hair mixed with dried blood. She winced, just thinking of the pain it would cause to remove the mess later.

Looking around the room for the first time with almost clear vision, she realized nothing looked familiar. Holding back a sob, she covered her eyes with her hands. Overcome with confused emotions, her hand dropped to her lap, suddenly feeling too heavy with the weight of her situation.

A sound outside the door gave her a familiar stab of fear.

Who is on the boat with me? Will I ever remember?

Sniffing loudly, she hastily wiped her nose with the back of her hand. This new challenge needed her complete focus, not her sniveling.

The door flew back, and a medium-sized man stood framed in the opening. His features remained a mystery as the bright light poured in behind him and cast his face in shadow.

Taking one step into the cabin shifted the light enough for her vaguely to recognize him. Relief spread through her. She released her breath before inhaling deeply through her nostrils.

The man rushed to the side of the sleeping platform and sat. He took her limp fingers between his clammy hands. "How are you feeling today? Any better? Do you remember your name yet?"

He looked both troubled and eager when he asked her about her name. She managed to croak out, "No."

"It's okay, Jesisca; I'll take care of you. I always have," he softly reassured her. He reached for a cup.

Her confused mind latched onto the word *Jesisca;* recognition warred with relief. "Jesisca? Is that my name?"

Nodding, he turned back to her. "Yes, honey, doesn't it sound familiar?"

After only a moment of thought, a flash of memory surrounded the name. Slowly nodding, she sighed. "Tell me everything, please. I'm going crazy with not knowing."

Even as she asked, the room started spinning with black dots, while she felt hot and cold at the same time. Her concentration on his answer evaporated as she felt on the verge of passing out. The longer she sat upright, the more her head throbbed, and the whooshing sound of her blood filled her hearing. She could see his lips moving, but nothing made sense.

"Okay, let's start with the date. Today is Elul 22, 3442. It's the sixth day of the week, and we're heading home to Cresdon. You and I got married on Heshvan 28, 3440. Any of this sounding familiar yet?"

She tried to shake her head to clear her thoughts, but the pain intensified and caused larger black splotches to obscure her vision further. "No," she said and started taking deep breaths to keep from losing consciousness. "Keep going," she prompted and hoped something he said would trigger a memory.

"You and I got married just before the terrible storm hit Reesun, which killed all of your family."

She heard him say something about her family dying, and she gasped; tears of despair and anguish sprang to her eyes, even though she could not remember who they were. She suddenly felt even more alone, thinking she did not have any family to turn to for help.

Petre held her limp hand as though to comfort her. "We had a nice memorial service for them, and we've been working together really hard to try and forget about the loss. I probably shouldn't have mentioned it, but I figured that part of our history would trigger a deeper memory. I guess it didn't work, huh?"

Confused, she closed her eyes and tried to focus only on the things she could piece together. The next thing she knew, he offered her another cup of liquid. Carefully reaching for the cup with both hands, she peered into it. She desperately wanted water, not this warm, brown liquid.

Jesisca instinctively knew it would make her fall back to sleep. But she still needed to find out where she was. She looked up at the man—*her husband*—and mouthed the word *water* to him. A small crease, which may have been a controlled frown, appeared between his eyebrows. He sat on the edge of the sleeping platform again.

"You look beat. Why don't you drink some more foxl broth to help you relax? You need to get your strength back, Jesisca," he said in a petulantly quiet voice. Petre hoped she would drink it all down since he had laced it again with *epeny*, not quite as much this time, though. He wanted to get the dose just right so she could participate when they had sex.

He sounded reasonable. She set her lips to the edge of the cup drank a small sip to ease her parched throat. Just out of the corner of her eye, she spotted a fleeting expression of triumph on Petre's face.

"Now, Jesisca, you'll have to do better if you ever expect to get your health back." Petre nudged the cup again toward her lips. When she hesitated, he frowned and pushed more insistently on the cup.

Jesisca did not have the strength to resist. This uneasy feeling about Petre's expression needed to stay with her. She raised the cup to her lips and drank all of the liquid. Immediately, she felt lighter, and the room spun faster than before. With unexpected euphoria, a smile formed on her lips as she groggily looked up at him.

Petre smiled back, leaned forward, and pressed a kiss to her lips.

Jesisca moaned softly and whispered, "Thank you, Petre."

Jesisca thought she saw Petre stand and unbutton his shirt. She was sure of the wicked and joyous gleam in his eyes as he looked at her intently. The last thing she remembered before she drifted into an uneasy nightmare was hearing Petre chuckle.

She was falling...she reached out to grasp for help...she tried to grab the warm hand being offered to her.

If she could hold on long enough, then she would be safe...the hand slipped away.

She opened her mouth to call for it to come back.

Something filled her mouth.

She choked.

She struggled, but her head was trapped.

Thrashing her head side to side drove the bandage into her fresh wound. She moaned in torment.

Oh, the searing pain between her legs.

Something fell on her.

She screamed for help, but a warm, wet slug crawled into her open mouth.

She struggled to get out from under the tree which fell on her, stabbing her so excruciatingly.

Every time she moved, another part of her body felt burning agony. The bark on the tree tore at the tender flesh of her groin, then her chest.

She couldn't breathe with the slug lodged in her mouth...she couldn't fight it anymore.

Her body went limp as she gave up and let the tree crush her.

Horrible laughter erupted from the victorious tree.

CHAPTER 7

Hours passed quietly since the nightmare ended; Jesisca drifted in and out of consciousness before finally moving into normal sleep. With her traumatized, limp body tightly wrapped in a blanket, she sighed as she entered a friendly, warm dream...

She finished her Thursday dance team practice. As she showered and changed her clothes, she looked down on her figure and noticed how well her body had toned from all the dancing. Pleased, she grabbed her school bag out of the locker, unceremoniously slammed shut the flimsy metal door, and twirled around on her toes all in one motion.

She had a mission regarding the cute guy with the short-spiked, brown hair who usually sat in The Commons. Sherry dared her to sit next to him, find out his name, and as much as she could about him, all without telling him her name.

Feeling up for the challenge, she raced up the stairs leading to The Commons. When she reached the top, she could see him seated at the same table where he always sat, reading a school book. Jesisca stopped to really look at him.

Man, his muscular body looks impressive in his polo shirt and tight jeans.

She pulled her shoulders back before boldly walking across The Commons to his table. "Mind if I sit here?" she asked as she dropped her school bag next to the chair as she pulled it out.

"You know, every morning, I come up from dance team practice and see you sitting here all by yourself. Why is that?"

"I work after school. I don't have time to do my homework at home." *He shrugged and leaned back, his muscles flexing with his every move.* *"So, I come in early to get it done. Any more questions?"*

"Just a couple." She chuckled, liking him even better up close as she looked intently into his brown eyes. "What's your name, and what does your girlfriend think about you working every day?"

"My name's Nealand Taivas, but everyone calls me Neal, and I don't have to worry about upsetting a girlfriend because I don't have one. What's your name?"

Scooping her bag off the floor, she jumped to her feet. "Oh, sorry; I forgot something back in the locker room. I gotta go!" She ran out of The Commons and down the stairs to the gymnasium. Mission accomplished.

She woke up, whispering the name *Neal*. Disappointment fell thick and heavy around her. If only she had stayed in the dream just a little longer, how much more would she have found out about herself?

Again, Petre held her feverish hand in his damp, clean hands. Even with her partially opened eyes, she could see him frowning deeply.

Why is he frowning? Oh, I spoke Neal's name aloud from my dream.

Again, Petre pressed a cup of broth into her weak hands. Jesisca refused to drink anything more until he answered some of her questions. She lowered the cup to her lap and tried to talk, dismayed when only a whispery squeak emerged. She cleared her throat, tried more forcefully the second time, and succeeded in saying, "Where am I?"

Petre cocked his head and replied, "Where do you think you are?"

Irritated, Jesisca answered, "On a boat with you." She could clearly hear the ocean lapping on the vessel's sides and feel it rocking gently on the water. The knowledge didn't give her any specifics, and she wanted answers.

There's the boat word again. Could she be talking about my water craft? Petre then asked, "Do you remember your name, honey?"

Panic rushed through her.

What should I tell him? He called me Jesisca.

But instinctively, she knew it was not her name. It sounded familiar, but then she distinctly recalled her friend—

What was her name—oh yeah, Sherry, that's right.

Sherry had called her Amos. It seemed an odd nickname since her name was supposed to be Jesisca. She had to answer his question. "Jesisca," she replied.

"It's a start," said Petre as he lifted her hands, still holding the cup, to her lips. He tipped it enough to force her to either drink or get drenched. "Don't worry, babe; I'll take care of you like I always do. Don't be afraid."

Jesisca looked directly into his eyes as she gulped. She desperately wanted to believe he told her the truth, but she had too many unanswered questions. She was almost convinced he would care for her until she saw the wicked gleam appear just as her eyes closed into another random dream.

She turned to leave dance practice when her teammate, Jenny, called out to her, "Hey, Amanda, wait for us! We want to talk with you about some formations to use at the homecoming halftime performance." She plunked herself down on a bench and waited for her teammates to change into their school clothes.

When they were ready, the girls left the locker room in a tight group. As usual, they all spoke simultaneously because each one had a different idea of what they should do. So engrossed in conversation, she didn't see Neal sitting at the table as she passed by.

One of the other girls noticed Neal waving to her and started to tease her, "Oh, aren't you cold, just walking by Neal when he's obviously flirting with you."

Looking over her shoulder, she saw Neal sitting at the table, reading as usual. "Whatever!" she drawled back to her. But the seed had been planted. Did Neal try to talk to her, and she missed it?

When she woke again, she felt more alert and aware than the other times. As though it were a life vest and she was drowning, she clung to the details of this last dream. The dance team girl, Jenny, called her Amanda. Sherry called her Amos. Amanda, Amos, Amanda.

Yes, that's it; my name is definitely Amanda. Sherry made up the ridiculous nickname of Amos because she said Amanda was too formal sounding.

She kept her eyes closed and concentrated on taking even breaths while she gathered her thoughts. These dreams were not as random as they seemed; they were pieces of her past!

If they're true, then what's Petre's real story?

She shifted on the bed and winced. Deep, intense soreness encompassed every part of her body, not just the gash on the back of her head.

What happened to me?

Her head still throbbed abominably, but it, too, felt improved.

Before she realized her mistake, she tossed her arms in frustration. Petre's attention immediately snapped to her. She looked into his blue eyes and saw pure lust looking down at her nakedness. He reached down and replaced the covers she had thrown off her torso. Amanda blushed violently and bunched the covers tighter to her neck with tight fists.

"Feeling better, I see," Petre commented as he looked at her

flushed cheeks. "Pretty soon, you'll be back on your feet and helping me out around here."

He smiled what Amanda assumed was supposed to be a comforting smile. She would have believed him had she not remembered the conflicting emotions she saw in his expression before.

Slowly, the pieces of her past fell into the blank spaces of her mind—she hoped. Already, she figured out her real name. Petre obviously wanted to make her think otherwise. She would have to watch her step with him and not share what she learned about herself before figuring out where she was and how to make contact with other, more sane people.

She believed Neal held a major part of her life. If she could just find him, she felt sure everything would be fine. A shiver of apprehension raced through her body. What if Neal were not around anymore? What if he were lost somewhere in her past?

Curling onto her side, she brought her legs closer to her torso and tucked her hands between her thighs. Immediately she gasped in pain as her hands brushed over scrapes and bruises on her inner thighs.

What is going on here?

Panic replaced her apprehension. She didn't want to know the truth about her current situation. She wanted her dream life back.

Petre promptly produced the dreaded cup of broth. "Drink. You're not yet ready to be awake for so long. You'll feel better after your body heals, trust me."

Amanda almost snorted with disbelief when she heard him say, 'trust me.' Yet, she wanted to go back to sleep if only to remember more about herself. At least while she slept, she felt safe. She reached for the cup and drank, then closed her eyes so she would not have to see Petre looming over her. Escaping to her dreams seemed like her best option for the time being.

Amanda sat on her parents' front porch, bored to tears when a gorgeous red Ferrari drove into their driveway. She jumped up, squealed at seeing Neal in the driver's seat, and ran to him as the car rolled to a stop. "So this is why you've been working yourself ragged after school! Your job must have paid really well to get this!"

Neal threw his head back and laughed. "I don't think so. This was a graduation present from my parents. What do you think? You like it?"

She clutched the window sill, leaning down to check out the interior and get closer to Neal at the same time. "Yes! It's totally awesome. Red really suits you. Do I get to take a ride, or is that reserved for someone else?"

Neal reached over and placed his hand on top of hers. "Hop in! I'll take you out to dinner."

Amanda nodded excitedly and said, "Just a sec. Let me get my coat." She ran back into her house, where she found her mom in the kitchen. In a rush, she blurted, "Neal's here! He just got a new car and wants to take me out to dinner. May I go? Please? Please? Please?"

"Fine. Just remember it's Friday, and you need to get home before sundown, okay?"

Amanda immediately nodded and kissed her mom on the cheek. At the last second, she grabbed her coat off the back of the dining room chair before racing out the front door.

Neal held open the passenger door for her. Dropping into the seat of the Ferrari made her feel like a princess. For the whole drive, a grin remained plastered across her face.

The scene shifted. *Amanda could tell she was older, maybe sixteen or so. Neal picked her up for the dance, and he softly whistled when he saw her. "Amanda, you know I really respect you and care for you, right?"*

Amanda nodded.

"I would really love it if you would agree to be my girlfriend and date me exclusively."

A thrill bubbled up inside her. She threw her arms up around his neck. "It's about time you noticed I was a woman and not just your best friend."

Again, the scene shifted. *At eighteen, Amanda found herself at Neal's college graduation party at his parents' house. The guests seemed as excited as the man they celebrated since they all knew the yellow and white yacht which Neal had admired was really his graduation gift. They played along as though they knew nothing.*

As the evening wound down, the guests walked to the pier as if to go home. Neal, walking hand in hand with Amanda on the dock, finally got the chance to ask his parents, "Which one of your friends owns the wonderful yacht?"

Nealand, Sr., and Jessica looked at one other and grinned mischievously. Jessica gestured to the yacht in question and spoke to her husband, "That one? It's lovely, isn't it, honey? I think anyone who owned it would be the envy of all our friends."

"Well, whose is it then?" Neal inquired again.

Amanda turned her face away to keep Neal from seeing the grin she couldn't contain.

His mom gently clasped her son's arm and exclaimed, "It's yours, Neal! You've made us so proud over all these years; you deserve the best that life offers. Happy graduation!"

A cheer rose from the guests as they came over to congratulate Neal on his new beauty and to wish him happy sailing. Some people even asked him to give them a tour of his yacht.

Enthusiastically, Neal boarded the yacht and gallantly helped Amanda aboard. Together, they looked over every detail. Neal repeatedly commented that nothing was less than perfect.

After all the guests but Amanda left, Neal asked his mom, "How did you pick her name?"

"Well," she replied, "your Dad wanted to name her 'The Golden Jessica.' He thought you'd be more careful while you sailed if it had my name on it. However, I thought it could get way too confusing to talk about your yacht and think you were talking about me. So, I took the best

of both worlds and mixed up the letters a little. This way, you'll be reminded of me, but not talking about me. You see?"

"*I do, and I think it's the perfect name. Thanks.*"

Amanda woke, and, as usual, Petre sat by her side, touching her somewhere. Suppressing a shiver of revulsion, she asked, "Can I please have some more broth?"

The soreness remained in her body, but her head seemed better. She believed this last dose would allow her enough memories to cement her true identity and history.

Petre smiled lustfully, brought the cup to her saying, "It's for the best, isn't it?"

Amanda closed her eyes as she rested the cup against her lips. She knew, with every fiber of her being, Petre would continue to touch her while she slept. She drank rapidly and silently prayed this would be the last time she would need the drugged broth. She felt confident she knew almost everything.

Her opened high school graduation presents littered the grass around her. After eating their fill of the outdoor buffet at Amanda's parents' house, the guests settled into small conversation groups. Neal stood and tapped his glass with a knife to capture everyone's attention. Then, he extended his hand down to Amanda and drew her up to stand in front of him. She looked at him almost straight in the eyes as he was only an inch or so taller than herself.

Turning toward Amanda, Neal spoke loud enough for everyone to hear, "Everyone here knows what a beautiful woman you are; that goes without saying. You have so many wonderful qualities it would take me years to express them all. I do, however, have something to ask you." Still holding Amanda's hand, Neal dropped onto his left knee and continued, "Would you do me the honor of becoming my wife?"

As a graduation gift and a celebration of their engagement, Neal invited Amanda to a Caribbean cruise with him on The Golden Jesisca. Amanda worried about what her parents would say about being alone together on the yacht before getting married.

As much as she respected her parents, she didn't ever want to disap-point them with her decisions. At length, she discussed the trip with them, and they told her she was eighteen and could decide what she should do. Moreover, they told her they trusted her to be good, and they were very happy for her.

Amanda's packed bags waited along with her on the front porch. Neal would pick her up in just a few minutes. Her heart hammered inside her chest. If anyone stood close to her, she knew they'd hear it as loudly as she did.

She was about to be alone with Neal. Were her parents right to trust her? She was engaged, after all, and it was almost like being married.

When Neal pulled into the driveway, Amanda hugged her parents, picked up a couple of her duffle bags, and headed toward the car. Neal rushed around the car to help her with the luggage. Smiling, he kissed her on the cheek and took the duffle bags from her hands.

He stowed them into the back of his car and then went up to the house to get the rest of her things. When he got to the door, he shook hands with Chris and then hugged Diane and kissed her cheek.

He felt a particular closeness to Diane as she was a slightly older-looking version of Amanda with a similar personality to his own mother's easy-going temperament. He bent to retrieve the last of the bags. When he stood straight, he told Chris and Diane, "I promise to take excellent care of her."

"We know you will, Neal," Chris said. "Thanks for giving us your itinerary. It's nice to know where your child is, even if it's in the middle of the ocean."

"Don't say it like that, Chris," admonished Diane, "it scares me to think of her out there protected only by a small floating boat."

Neal decided it might be wise if he just turned around and put the bags in the car. After helping Amanda into the passenger seat, he walked around to settle himself behind the steering wheel. Chris and Diane continued discussing their trip. With a glance at Amanda's parents, Neal leaned closer to Amanda and said, "We should probably make our escape before they change their minds about letting you go with me."

Their voices rose. "Oh, Diane, I wouldn't consider a sixty-foot yacht as small. Besides, Neal has been sailing for years, and he knows what to do if anything should happen—which it won't," he hastily added.

Diane frowned.

Chris nudged her arm. "Smile, honey, you don't want your youngest daughter to see you frowning as she's beginning her first big adventure, do you?"

"I guess not," she replied as she forced a smile over her concern and waved goodbye from the porch.

"Good call, Neal. Let's get out of here!"

Both he and Amanda waved and smiled as the car backed out of the driveway.

Days passed by in a flash—it was dark—the boat was pitching fearfully, and the screeching wind made conversation impossible. Neal got out of the bed and told her to stay below. She watched him grab pants and rush to cover his nakedness. He wrenched open the door, paused, looked back at her, and said, "I'll be right back, Amanda. I love you."

Lightning flashed as Neal shut the door behind him. Amanda, not wanting to be left alone, hastily sat up and threw her naked legs over the edge of the bed. Another flash of lightning—the boat rocked violently.

She blinked her eyes open in the dimly lit cabin and blessedly discovered herself alone. Running a mental assessment of her physical condition, she found residual tenderness on her scalp, but not painfully so, and the rest of her body ached dully but was bearable for now. She looked around warily to see what she was up against.

She remembered everything. Newly engaged, she and Neal sailed to celebrate the occasion. Their yacht was named *The Golden Jesisca*, which explained why Jesisca sounded so familiar. Petre must have counted on her remembering enough to believe his lie.

Glancing down at her left hand, the diamond ring shimmered,

and she almost cried with relief. It was all real. Her panic heightened. The storm was real as well, and she didn't know what had happened to Neal.

But first, she needed a plan to escape from Petre. Then, she could find Neal.

CHAPTER 8

lder Debbon made a mental note to find out about her friend, Neal. Did the man end up with another Elder somewhere? It wouldn't do to have these two separated. Thus far, Amanda turned out quite resourceful from her story, and Elder Debbon was intrigued to discover what this remarkable girl did next. So, with fingertips once again touching her temple, he allowed the story to continue…

WHEN SHE WOKE AT LAST, Petre told Amanda she slept for six days. She felt it in the aching of her bones and muscles. Petre offered her eggs, toast, and juice, which she gratefully accepted.

She managed to sit and arrange the blankets to cover her nakedness with more than a bit of pain. After a quick prayer, she ate slowly and savored the flavors in her mouth. It seemed like years since she had last eaten. From the cramps in her stomach, it agreed.

Petre watched her eat. His eyes fixated on the blankets covering her. Finally, he asked, "Are you feeling better today?"

"Yes," she replied, around a bite of eggs.

After finishing the plate of food, she looked around nervously. She cleared her throat and asked quietly, "Where's the bathroom?"

Petre smiled. "It's through this door." He gestured to a wood panel across from her.

It took all her strength simply to gather herself together enough to stand. Feeling weaker than a day-old kitten, she stumbled, and her blanket came loose, exposing one of her breasts. Petre promptly reached forward and pulled up the blanket. His fingers brushed over her breast as he tucked in the fabric to secure it.

Amanda cringed, and her body shifted as far from Petre as she could while still relying on him to keep her upright. Her fingers crushed the fabric in her fists, ensuring such a mistake wouldn't happen again.

Petre seemed not to notice as he casually commented, "We don't want you to catch a chill. Let me help you use the bathroom."

Wishing she could figure out a way to stop him, she had to admit she wouldn't make it to the room without him. They shuffled across the floor and squeezed into the small space. She leaned against the wall and put her hand on his arm. "I think I can manage from here. May I please have some privacy?"

Petre's nostrils flared, and his hands flew to his hips, elbows touching the walls on either side of him. His flinty eyes widened, almost bulging. "I'm more than capable of helping my wife even in the most private matters. It's not like I haven't already seen everything!"

Amanda inhaled sharply. She didn't want to dwell on what Petre meant by that statement. Instead, she squeezed her eyes shut and pinched the bridge of her nose. "It's not that, Petre. This room is so small, and I'm feeling a bit claustrophobic. I just need a little space right now. Please?" She wasn't above begging if it meant he would leave her alone for a few minutes.

He tipped back his head on his neck and sighed. He flatly mumbled, "Fine. But I'll be right outside if you need me." He turned and stepped out, but he left the door ajar.

Amanda felt the trembling of her fingers against the door as she shut it herself. She leaned against the rough wood for support and let the blanket fall to the floor. She used the toilet to relieve herself and winced as she wiped.

Her gaze fell onto her chest. "What? Oh, my goodness!" Black, blue, purple, and yellow bruises covered both of her breasts. Lifting her hands as if to conceal the truth, she discovered both wrists were covered with them as well.

Bile rose in the throat as she continued to look over her body. The insides of her thighs looked worse than anything. Yet, even in her confused state, she knew the fall which injured her head could not inflict this.

She promptly threw up her breakfast into the sink next to her. She continued to dry heave until Petre opened the door and offered her a glass of water, "Sip this," he said, "it will ease your stomach."

His hands touched her bare flesh, causing her to heave even more. She didn't have the strength, let alone space, to bend down to pick up the discarded blanket. She drank the offered beverage and allowed him to lead her back to the bed. Belatedly, she realized the only blanket from the bed remained on the bathroom floor. To conceal her nakedness, she pulled her legs up and crossed her arms over her chest.

"We should get you dressed so you won't be so cold," Petre announced and turned to open another closet. He rummaged through a pile of clothes and pulled out an unlikely pairing of a silky shirt and an old, worn pair of sweatpants. He held them out to her and asked, "Would you like help getting these on?"

"No!" she sharply replied as she snatched the clothes out of his hand. "Thank you, I can manage," she added to take the frostiness from her tone. Since Petre refused to turn away, she dressed as rapidly as she could just to end her embarrassment. Intently aware of his eyes on her, she plunged each leg into the sweatpants.

Looking at him straight in the face, she put her arms into the silky shirt before lifting it over her head. She gasped in shock as her head came through the shirt, and her face was inches from Petre's as he had stepped forward to "help" the shirt down over her breasts.

"This color looks good on you," he said softly as his head started to tip toward her neck.

With nowhere else to go, she sat hard on the lumpy mattress to escape his unwanted advance. She swallowed more bile, forcefully willing herself not to throw up again.

Petre did not seem fazed by her reaction and sat next to her with his arm around her shoulders. His hand stroked her bicep as he asked, "Do you want to try to eat something else?"

"No, I don't think it would stay down." New convulsions racked her body from his unwelcome touch.

"Are you still cold?"

She nodded. "A little." Goosebumps rose on her flesh, yet her stomach blazed like fire.

"Let me get you something." He rummaged for another blanket from the drawer below the sleeping platform and handed it to her. "Do you feel like lying down or drinking some foxl broth?"

The room reeked of vomit, sweat, and unwashed clothing. "No, I think I need some fresh air." Steeling herself against his touch, she required assistance to make it up the stairs and outside. "Could you help me out onto the deck?"

"It would be my pleasure." He manhandled her into a standing position and escorted her out into the bright sunlight on the deck.

With the blanket tightly wrapped around her, she sat on the

deck to look out over the ocean. An odd shimmer surrounded the boat. *What was that?*

Momentarily dismissing the anomaly, she looked beyond it to search for any land on the horizon. If only she could spot some islands, other landmasses, or better yet, another vessel, then she might discover a way to escape.

A couple of times, boats did pass within about thirty feet, but nobody even seemed to acknowledge Petre's boat.

These people aren't very friendly with one another.

A few minutes after the last vessel passed, Petre sat next to her and familiarly put his arm around her waist.

He seems anxious about something.

She glanced at his face and fought her loathing to his touch. She tried to imagine Neal sitting next to her instead of this loathsome man. Her fantasy vanished the instant she heard Petre's voice.

"You and I have always liked how peaceful it is out here." Petre looked out over the ocean. "We can go for mesans without seeing any other water crafts or people."

"What do you mean? Other people sail out here too, don't they?" Amanda felt like she were in an episode of the Twilight Zone. *Did Petre not see the other boats?*

"Oh no, these waters are dangerous, not to mention nowhere near any land. I wouldn't even be here if it weren't for the storm pushing me off course. It'll take us weeks to get back to regularly sailed seas."

Amanda noted his mixture of singular and plural when he spoke of sailing.

He really isn't very bright.

Just then, Amanda saw another boat cruising by them. She opened her mouth to ask Petre about it, but the intense and anxious look he leveled at her changed her mind. "Is there any danger of pirates out here then?"

Petre gave her a puzzled look. "What're pirates?"

Another stab of fear constricted her stomach.

They must call them something else here.

As she explained, his face lit up with understanding.

"A deckhopper!"

Amanda nodded, agreeing to the adequately strange name.

"You don't have to worry about them. I've easily taken care of them before! Here's what I do." He jumped up and grabbed the fish club off the deck. Then, holding it like a baseball player, he made a great swing at a sheet of metal attached to the mast. The club struck the edge of the metal and immediately rebounded straight into Petre's nose. The club clattered to the deck as Petre dropped to his knees and cupped his profusely bleeding nose with both hands.

Amanda burst out laughing at the comedy of the whole scene. She instantly looked contrite at the look of bitter hurt in Petre's watering blue eyes. Grabbing her blanket, she created a makeshift compress for Petre's nose and tilted his head back.

When the bleeding finally subsided, she noted his ineffectual swing narrowly missed breaking his nose. "I'm feeling kind of cold out here. I think I'll go back inside for a while." She beat a hasty retreat before she started laughing in his face again.

Three weeks passed since Amanda started counting the days. Her almost-healed head wound lost quite a bit of hair around the gash when Petre yanked the crusted towel off one rainy afternoon.

Petre constantly found non-existent reasons to touch her. Yet, he never made any sexual advances on her or pressured her at all in that way. Her bruises faded and then disappeared altogether.

Had she jumped to the wrong conclusions about Petre?

Petre told her stories of their adventures together on the ocean. She smiled and nodded, yet knew the lies behind all of his words. From the way he spoke about sailing, it sounded as though he didn't intend to make landfall anytime soon.

Petre constantly inquired about her health. Amanda discovered a direct correlation between her improved health and his increased need to touch her. Because of this, her recovery progress rapidly declined. Luckily, Amanda didn't have to fake her nausea. She threw up every morning and sometimes in the afternoon as well.

"The bump on your head must've messed up your equilibrium. You've always had an iron stomach while we've sailed. You'll get better soon. Don't worry."

Amanda wondered how long she could convincingly stay in 'recovery.' She pondered different plans for escaping from Petre. For sure, she needed herself completely healed before making any attempts.

Amanda puzzled over the odd things which happened since she started helping out around the boat. First, she counted twenty-six vessels that passed them in these *deserted* waters and noted none of them ever seemed to see Petre's ship. Then, as unbelievable as it seemed, she started to suspect the odd shimmer surrounding the boat was some sort of invisibility shield.

Second, Petre always had food ready and available to eat. Yet, strangely enough, she never actually saw him prepare anything, and they never had any dishes to clean. She even had vague impressions from when she was disoriented about the food just magically seeming to appear from nowhere.

Since she spent all her free time on the deck, she never witnessed him creating their meals. Amanda determined she would discover what he did before she made her move to escape.

Third, Petre never appeared to steer the boat. Even when he stood in the control room, he never seemed to pay much attention. Watching him intently, Amanda noticed how his lips constantly moved as if he mumbled something over and over, kind of like he tried to talk around non-existent food.

His annoying habit reminded her immediately of her childhood pet. She secretly nicknamed him gerbil. Every time Amanda thought of the resemblance, it made her smile. More than once, Petre caught her smiling at him.

Does he think my smiles are meant for him? No doubt. He's undeniably conceited enough.

CHAPTER 9

Amanda took up her usual place on the port side bow. One hand trailed over the edge to caress the water if a swell brought it up high enough to touch her. She enjoyed listening to the birds, the wind, and the water as it sloshed against the sideboards. Neal once told her the presence of birds indicated either fishing boats or land nearby. Either scenario worked fine for her.

Her back nestled into the round metal railing, and her hair blew freely in the breeze. She searched the horizon for any signs of land. Whenever Petre came around, she pretended to sleep; but she watched the other ships in the ocean around them as soon as he left.

Most definitely, the ships passed in a predictable pattern. Every third day a large vessel would pass slowly by, first heading toward them, then away. One thing was sure; the boat did not sail after dark, ever!

Petre didn't intend to let her go. His constant references about her being his wife made it quite obvious he expected her to stay with him forever. Amanda also did not appreciate his not-so-subtle references to her neglect of his 'manly needs' during her illness. So far, she successfully thwarted his advances, but she did not know how much longer it would last.

Recognizing her window for remaining sick was swiftly closing, Amanda decided the time arrived to take advantage of the large vessel predicted to pass by the next day. She did not know whether it sailed toward land or away from it. Not that it mattered much since it would turn around within three days to go the other direction anyway. One part of her escape plan was sure; she had to swim. Fortunately, she would swim in the daylight. Just the idea of jumping into the black ocean at night gave her the shivers.

Sorting through her jumble of clothing, she organized them into piles of usefulness in her escape. The first pile of sexy see-through garments mysteriously found their way outside at night.

Best not to have these around to give Petre any more ideas! She tossed them overboard in a giant heap.

The next pile contained practical undergarments, swimsuits, and socks. She neatly folded them and put them in the drawer Petre instructed her to use.

Another mistake. She loaded the drawer. *If I really were his wife, my things would already be in the drawer and not in a messy heap in the cupboard!*

The third pile contained light fabric clothing for warm weather. Finally, the last mound consisted of heavier fabrics for colder weather. As she folded each item, she weighed their usefulness against their bulkiness.

Unable to take much more than what she could wear when jumping overboard, she wished she could find some means to strap more to her body without making it impossible to swim. Drowning was not in her plan of escape!

Her 'escape outfit,' as she termed it in her mind, consisted of a matching set of undergarments, white ankle-length socks, a pink short-sleeved t-shirt, blue cotton shorts, a gray sweatshirt, and a faded pair of blue jeans. It would give her a couple of different choices of clothing until she could find means to get others.

The lack of suitable shoes troubled her the most. With only a pair of blue ballet-type slippers, she knew they would not last very long as walking shoes. But without any other options, they became the final addition to the 'escape outfit.'

As night fell upon the deck, Amanda had not figured out a solid plan to escape the next day. *Now for the hard part*, she thought, *how do I distract Petre so I can get away? It won't do me any good to jump in the water and start swimming if Petre can just fish me out. He'd probably keep me locked in the cabin if I failed the first time. I'm only going to get this one chance!*

She thought briefly of ways to kill him but swiftly dismissed the idea with revulsion. As much as she detested Petre, she could not murder him. She would simply have to knock him out. But how could she manage to incapacitate him for at least an hour? Longer, if possible.

Thinking this hard actually gave her a headache. *I really wish I had some aspirin.* Then the perfect plan popped into her head. Feeling happy for the first time since awakening on Petre's boat, she picked herself up off of the sun-warmed deck and retired to the cabin to eat dinner and prepared to have a terrible night's sleep.

As planned, Amanda slept lightly, frequently waking up and rolling over. During the middle of the night, she firmly removed Petre's hand from her breast then added a few more details to her escape plan. When morning finally arrived, she pretended to sleep with her back to Petre while he shuffled around the cabin in his normal morning routine.

She ticked off the things Petre would do as he did them: stand up and stretch, pull on a pair of pants, slip on his deck loafers, inhale the scent of java when he took his first sip. He should have opened the cabin door to leave, but it did not happen this morning. Something in his routine changed. Amanda rolled over and opened her eyes in the sudden silence. She was startled to see Petre standing over the sleeping platform, watching her wake up.

"Good morning, Jesisca," he said cheerfully. "You didn't sleep well last night. You look terrible."

Amanda sat up and scowled, "Good morning to you, too! You're full of compliments." She swung her legs over the side of the bed and ran her fingers through her disheveled hair.

"Just calling it as I see it!" Petre smiled at her. "Do you want me to get you a cup of java?"

Last night, she had decided not to eat anything he prepared today just in case he took liberties to drug it. Sticking with her plan, she shook her head. "I don't think my stomach is up for it this morning. Excuse me." Amanda suddenly bolted for the washroom. "I'm going to be sick again."

Amanda just made it to the sink when she vomited what little was in her stomach. When she felt the last wave of nausea leave her, she looked at herself in the mirror, really just a polished metal plate. "Petre wasn't kidding when he said I look terrible," she murmured to herself, inspecting the dark circles under her brown eyes and the bird's nest she usually called her hair.

"I look ridiculous," she whispered, a wry grin forming as she picked up the frayed stick to brush her teeth. She soaked it in the running water before scrubbing her teeth vigorously. Then, when her teeth felt smooth against her tongue, she cupped her hands and filled them with cool, refreshing liquid.

She lowered herself to drink deeply, hoping the motion would not upset her already touchy stomach. Finally, after refilling her hands several times, her thirst and hunger pangs subsided. She finished by scrubbing her face with the invigorating water.

Since she hoped to swim in the salty ocean in a few hours, she decided against washing her hair. Instead, she took up the small comb next to the sink and began the tedious task of sectioning off her hair to tease out the tangles. When she managed to tame and smooth her hair, Petre gave up waiting for her in the cabin.

Leaving the washroom, Amanda crossed the cabin to her clothing drawer. Hurriedly, she removed her sleeping sweats and pulled out the items for her escape outfit. After putting on so many layers, she struggled into the jeans and sweatshirt. Next, she sat on the bed to don her socks. Just as she pulled on her shoes, a shadow crossed over her. She promptly looked up and blurted, "Oh, Petre, you startled me!"

"I think you might be overdressed," Petre suggested, gesturing to her ensemble. "It's looking like it's going to be a warm day."

"I'll be fine. I still feel a bit chilled." She tried to hide her anxiousness. "Some fresh air will help with my nausea." She stood and brushed past Petre at the doorway.

Petre turned and followed her out, saying, "I think I'll walk with you."

"As you wish." Crossing her arms self-consciously, she continued walking out the doorway. *I'd rather walk on nails than have to endure your endless prattling of lies and sexual innuendo. Besides, I still have to decide my final plans for leaving; and none of those include hours of walking with you on the deck.*

Unfortunately, Petre's prediction for the weather proved correct. As the day grew warmer, she feared he might suggest she change. Hopefully, Petre wouldn't notice the sweat starting to bead at her hairline. Walking closest to the deck's outside edge, she kept her face turned toward the water's cooling breeze as much as possible.

They made two slow circuits of the craft when a bird, swooping in front of Amanda's face, broke into her private scheming. Startled, she stopped and watched the swallow turn into the breeze and swiftly fly away.

Almost at the exact moment, Petre exclaimed, "Ugh! That bird just crapped on my face!"

She turned around just in time to see Petre step forward and angrily grab a deck rag from a pile of rope on the capped water barrel. In his haste, he grabbed the rope as well. A sound hissed overhead from the cord releasing its hold on the auxiliary pole on the mainmast. The pole, usually used for hanging laundry to dry, landed squarely on the top of Petre's head, sounding almost exactly like striking a ripe watermelon. He dropped like a rock to his knees, and he grabbed his head and moaned.

"Oh my!" Amanda exclaimed, raising her hands to cover her smile. She turned around to prevent him from seeing her laugh. Her shaking shoulders gave her away, though.

"Don't laugh!" Petre barked, still holding his head and dropping to his bottom onto the deck.

Feeling almost sorry for his injury, Amanda faced him, struggling to hold her lips in a straight line. She held out her hands, uncertain of what she could do to help. "I'm sorry, it's just..." Then, at a loss for something nice to say, she blurted, "The whole thing looked so comical. You can admit that, at least?"

Petre's face screwed up as he squinted to see her with the sun behind her back. With his face covered in bird excrement, his lip twitched minutely. "I guess it would be funny if I were in your shoes. But right now, damn, my head hurts! Do you think you could help me stand?"

Amanda took his outstretched hand and hauled him to his unsteady feet. With no other choice, she put her arm around his waist to stabilize him. They walked toward the cabin, and Petre continued to stumble, which made Amanda wonder if he might be acting just a little too weak so he could drape himself all over her.

Back in the cabin, she gladly deposited him onto the bed. She busied herself by looking over his scalp to ascertain any injuries.

Too bad you didn't split your skull open. I could've put a wad of fabric on it and then ripped your hair out by the roots like you did to me! Oh well.

Immediately remorseful for entertaining such thoughts—even if he deserved it—she was not ordinarily sadistic.

It's a good thing today will be my last day with him! He must be rubbing off on me.

Stepping back from him, she announced, "Nothing bleeding! I guess you'll live."

"Now, who has the great bedside manner? You used to like me!"

I doubt it. Then, she said out loud, "You should probably rest. I'm going out on the deck for a while." She turned to leave and heard rustling sounds behind her. Looking over her shoulder, she stared in amazement as Petre actually took her advice.

He smiled and said, "Night, night." He crossed his hands over his stomach and closed his eyes.

Amanda continued out the door without replying. She returned to her spot at the front of the boat and removed her sweatshirt. She folded it and used it as a deck cushion, where she sat and looked out at the water.

It'll be a while before I see any boats—water crafts. She corrected herself as she remembered Petre not knowing about the word "boat." She closed her eyes and enjoyed the warmth of the sun on her face.

CHAPTER 10

After what seemed only moments, she opened her eyes to discover the sun had moved quite far across the sky; she must have slept for a couple of hours. Panicked, she scanned the water for any vessels. The usual ship should become visible on the horizon at any time.

As she searched, something seemed different, but she could not quite place it. Suddenly it dawned on her that the twinkling haze, which usually obscured part of her vision, was barely a ripple of disruption around the boat. It would stand to reason that if Petre created the shimmering around the vessel, it would weaken while he slept.

Petre must really be knocked out to let the shield down so far. Even as she had this thought, the haze strengthened until it looked as it usually did. Forewarned to Petre awakening, Amanda pulled the sweatshirt out from underneath her and put it back on.

Deciding it was time to put her plan in action, she stood, stretched, inhaled deeply, and returned to the cabin. She walked through the doorway just as Petre got out of the bed. "Did you have a good nap?" she asked innocently.

"Yeah, I slept like the dead. I'm starting to wish I was dead with this headache!" His palm pressed against his temple, and he squeezed his eyes shut.

"Maybe we should eat something. I haven't eaten yet today, and I'm starving!" she announced cheerfully.

"Yeah, I'm hungry too. Any suggestions? I can't seem to think straight."

With his hands cradling his head, she could not see his eyes. "Hmm, let's see." She already knew what she wanted but paused for his benefit. Then, snapping her fingers, she said, "How about foxl soup with lots of barley?"

"Sure." He turned around to concentrate on creating it onto the counter. It took longer than usual, but a single bowl of the requested soup appeared on the counter. Petre lifted it and handed it to Jesisca, saying, "Here you go, one soup made to order!"

She took the bowl, keeping a sullen expression plastered to her face. "Aren't you going to have some, too?"

"No. I'm too tired to create another. I'll finish whatever you don't end up eating."

With an overly dramatic sigh, she sat at the table with the warm bowl. "Okay, but you know I don't like to eat alone." She leaned over the soup and inhaled, pretending to savor the aroma. "It smells wonderful." She fought to keep herself from gagging at the rancid odor.

Petre handed her a spoon. She daintily dipped it into the soup. She sipped and rolled her eyes in feigned delight. She hurriedly spooned a bigger bite, then another, pretending to be ravenous. "Could I have some water, please?"

Petre filled a cup from the bathroom with exaggerated slowness and set it on the table next to her. He sat, wearily slid his elbows on the table, and covered his eyes with both hands.

This plan is working better than I thought.

Usually, Petre watched her so closely she would have to work much harder to pull this off. She gulped down the water and then filled the cup with soup. Finally, she shot out of her seat with her cup in hand and announced, "I'm going to be sick!" She raced into the washroom.

Slamming the door behind her, she immediately tossed the cup's contents into the toilet and flushed. She made loud retching noises while leaning over the sink. Then, she ran the water to rinse the cup and dampen her face to complete her performance. Slowly, she opened the door, leaning on it as though it helped her to stand in her weakened state.

Petre rushed to her side and asked, "Are you okay? Can I get you anything?" He helped her to sit again.

"Could I have some of your special foxl broth, please? Just like I had while I was sick with my head injury? I feel so queasy; I should probably try to get some sleep."

"That sounds like a good idea." Petre concentrated on getting the request ready. Petre doubled her usual *epeny* dose, hoping she would get some in her before she vomited again. He handed her the cup. "Here you go. Anything else while I'm still standing?"

Looking sheepishly up, she asked quietly, "Could I please have another cup of water? This one's all gone." She held out to him the empty cup.

Sighing and trying to keep from moving his aching head, he took the cup and returned slowly to the washroom.

Amanda immediately dumped the drugged foxl broth into the soup bowl. She pretended to finish the contents of the cup just as Petre returned with the requested water. Then, clumsily, she put the empty cup down on the table.

"I guess you'll get to eat my soup after all." She pushed the soup over to his side of the table. She stifled a yawn and let her eyelids droop. Finally, she lay on the bed and curled her legs up into the fetal position.

"Waste not, want not." Petre weakly smiled at her and began eating the foxl soup.

"Hear, hear," she mumbled. Then, for added dramatic effect, she sighed and pretended to fall asleep.

She stayed 'asleep' until she heard Petre's spoon clatter to the floor. Then, peeking through her long lashes, she checked on his progress. She could not risk him catching her act should he not really be knocked out.

Even as she watched, his head drooped forward until his forehead touched the table. When his snoring echoed loudly through the small cabin, she knew she could safely get up. A quick check on the contents of the bowl showed only a couple of bites remained.

Briefly, she thought about trying to move him onto the bed but decided against making the effort. Instead, she rushed out the door and searched for any ships. Right on schedule, tacking across the horizon and heading directly for them appeared the vessel she had chosen for her escape.

With an estimated twenty minutes until it would sail close enough, she fretted over her jump into the ocean. Petre's obscuring haze might pose a problem. She needed to swim at least thirty feet from Petre's boat to ensure the haze did not hide her from the rescue ship.

Amanda twitched with anxiety; the wait seemed like an eternity. She checked on Petre no less than fifteen times. He continued to snore without moving. The rescue vessel inched closer with each passing minute.

Time's up!

With one last check on Petre, she walked to the edge of the boat, jumped feet-first into the water, and started swimming.

Amanda could not believe her luck. The passing ship plucked her from the sea as though it were a common occurrence. Then, the crewmen gave her a small yet serviceable room to freshen up and informed her they would be going ashore in just a few minutes! They did not even ask her any questions which would have been awkward to answer.

Rage bubbled up inside her with this news. All this time, she had been close to land but unable to see it because of Petre's ability to make her believe a lie. She could have saved so much time and energy had she known she could simply swim to safety as soon as he had fallen asleep.

Oh well. I can't undo the past, but I can certainly have a say about my future here!

Inside her room, the discovery of its private bathroom pleased her. Immediately, she removed all of her clothing and dumped them into the bathtub. The next few minutes had her shampooing her hair and washing her body free of the salt residue.

Bending, she picked up each item of clothing and rinsed them out in clean water. Twisting as much water out as she could, she placed her clean clothes over the side of the tub.

Amanda stepped out of the tub and dried her body with the plush towel. Using the damp towel, she wrapped up her hair. She laid the dry towel on the floor and arranged her wrung-out clothing on top. She carefully rolled the towel and clothing tightly to wick out as much water as possible.

Although moist and incredibly wrinkled, she had to put all her clothes back on. After a bit of struggle with the damp clothes sticking to each other, she managed to get dressed again. She could not style her hair because it was wet, but she managed to comb it smooth.

Deciding there was nothing else she could improve, she left her room to find the captain. She wanted to find out as much as possible about living accommodations and potential jobs before they made landfall.

Walking down the narrow, dark hallway, she found the captain in the first room in which she looked. This must be what she would call the wheelhouse, except for the absence of any wheel, just the captain sitting in an easy chair, staring intently out the window.

He looked like a typical captain with a lean build dressed all in white. He even wore a unique white hat with a black stripe around it. He had salt and pepper hair trimmed as neatly as his equally brown and gray beard. She paused in the doorway, not wanting to interrupt his concentration.

The captain must have heard the creaking floor because he turned toward her and smiled while beckoning her to enter the room. "So, you must be the swimmer we picked up. My name's Captain Issyn. I see you've gotten cleaned up."

Taking a moment to think fast, she settled into the offered seat. "Yes, thank you. It's nice to meet you. My name's Amanda Covington." Now that she had his attention, she did not know what to ask him without sounding incredibly stupid. "So," she said to fill the lull in the conversation, "Do you have cargo to drop off or pick up at this port?"

"We're going to drop off important cargo for the Telepod Engineering Company. We heard the big shot himself is coming over from Durseni to get it. Luckily for him, it's only a few minutes from the Port O'Plenty. Otherwise, we'd've had to arrange for land portage, which can be plenty of trouble for us.

"We're going to take a long break here at the Port O'Plenty. We'll probably board at the tavern and get some bruskins and some fine women to keep us warm at night!" He laughed and winked at Amanda, "Where're you heading 'lil miss?"

Amanda shrugged. "Where's a good place to look for work?"

Captain Issyn pursed his lips while he considered his answer. "Well, you sure wouldn't fit in at the tavern—you don't seem like that kind of girl to me—so, I'd suggest you go to the diner and see if they might have some ideas for you."

"Where do I find this diner?"

"Well, now, I suppose I could point you in the right direction since it's not too far from the tavern."

"I'd really appreciate that. You've been so wonderful. I don't know how I can repay you since I don't have any money, but I will pay you back once I get some!"

"Well now, I don't believe any payment is needed since you were on our way and haven't been a bit of trouble."

"Still, you didn't have to pull me out of the sea."

"Oh, now there you're wrong again; you see, we got this ethic, you know. We take aboard every person we find because we'd want the same for us, you know, should we find ourselves left without a ship.

"We know there's payback for picking up souls out of the water, but it's paid by the water and not the person saved. So we don't expect anything from you but good wishes for safe sailing in the future, you know?"

Amanda nodded and accepted it as the only answer she would get. Of course, it did make some backward sort of sense.

"Now, my little lady, if you wouldn't mind giving me some peace, I've got to concentrate on getting this ship into that dock without hitting anything, and it takes all my attention. I'll look for you when we're all ready to go ashore. I'll get you steered in the right direction, okay?"

"Oh! I'm sorry to have interrupted you. I didn't realize you were operating the ship right now." In her haste to leave, she almost knocked over her chair. But, she managed to get out the door without too much more fuss and commotion. To her utter embarrassment, she heard him chuckling at her clumsy departure.

She did not have anywhere to go but back to her room. Although, she would have liked to stand on the deck to watch the captain skillfully dock the ship. But she did not dare go out there for all to see. What if someone told Petre where she had gone? So, no, it was better to stay below deck and wait for her escort.

She entered her room and sat on the bunk. Relief washed over her since her captivity was nearing an end, but she was still lost. Unbidden and unwanted, tears welled in her eyes. Unable to stop the flow, her shoulders shook before she wrapped her arms across her middle to hold herself together. She couldn't see where her tears dripped on her already wet sleeves.

What is this strange place? Both Petre and this captain operated their ships without any equipment; this did not make sense.

Her whole life had turned upside down in a few weeks, and now she needed to fit into a society where she did not know the rules or roles of the people. She did not know where she would stay, how she'd make money, how she'd eat, or any other important survival details.

The hopelessness of it all overwhelmed her. When she was with Petre, her only thought was to escape. Now, the plethora of details seemed endless.

The slight chattering of metal touching wood as the ship brushed up against the dock warned Amanda to pull herself together. Tears never fixed anything, and she had a lot to accomplish.

Amanda threw water on her face and just finished folding the towel when someone knocked on the door. She turned, opened the door, and came face to face with a skinny young man.

"The captain's ready to take you ashore, miss. If you're ready, I can show you the way."

Having nothing to take with her, she replied, "Lead on then. I'm as ready as I'll ever be!"

Trekking through to the opposite side of the ship, up a narrow staircase, and into the bright sunshine, they walked the short distance across the littered deck to the simple wooden gang-plank without any side rails. She made the mistake of looking over the edge and stumbled nervously.

The young man caught her arm. He smiled and winked. "Just

look at the wharf on the other side and nothing in between! It gets easier with practice." His assurances instantly made Amanda feel better.

Below, the captain conversed with a stern-looking man on the pier. Amanda stepped forward to talk to the captain when the young man stopped her with a hand on her arm, saying, "The captain will finish with the Harbor Master in a minute. You never want to interrupt this discussion because it affects our pay!"

Amanda nodded. Her lack of cultural knowledge almost caused her to make another social blunder. How much else she did not know and how much trouble it would get her into shortly?

As it turned out, the captain had already completed negotiating the docking fee and moved on to ask about employment opportunities for his passenger. As Amanda watched the interaction, both the Captain and Harbor Master stopped their conversation to appraise Amanda. Seeing their scrutiny, Amanda immediately blushed.

The Captain gestured for her to come forward, and she stepped into their circle. The Harbor Master asked, "Well now, do you have any record-keeping experience?"

She nodded since her tongue felt glued to the roof of her mouth.

"I could use some help logging the shipments from the past couple of mesans if you wouldn't mind helping me out. Of course, I don't know what I'll pay you until I know how efficient you are, but I gave my word to the Captain here that the wage'll be fair. What do you think? Sound like something you would be interested in doing?"

Amanda could hardly believe her luck. Having no idea what a 'mesan' was, she was glad to offer her services if it meant she would have an income. Again, she could only nod and smile.

The Harbor Master looked at the captain and said, "She sure doesn't have much to say, does she! That's okay, though; we have some customers who won't shut up. It might make for a nice change around the office!" Then to Amanda, he asked, "When do you want to start?"

Amanda found her voice and said, "Right now, if you don't mind!"

"You've got a deal, miss. Just go through the door right there and ask Ceren to show you to the filing room."

She moved away from the two men as though in a daze. When she opened the office door, reality struck her straight in the face. Musty and smelling of unwashed sailors, the odor inside the office overwhelmed her.

She walked over to the only person she saw and said, "Excuse me. I'm looking for someone named Ceren. Do you know where I might find him?"

The man looked up from his desk and gave Amanda an appraising look. She could tell he liked what he saw. He paused so long as to make the conversation somewhat uncomfortable and finally answered, "I'm Ceren. How may I help you?"

"The Harbor Master said you could show me where I could get started on logging the past few..." she momentarily paused as she struggled to remember the word the Captain had used, "...mesans' files."

"Sure thing, miss. Right this way." He rose so suddenly he almost overturned his chair.

They must really hate this part of the job to be so eager for my help.

She followed Ceren through the back door, down a short hallway, and into a cramped room full of filing cabinets, piles of papers, and general chaos. Luckily, the foul odors lessened the farther they retreated from the front room. He cleared a spot on the desk by sweeping his hand across the surface, unceremoniously scattering the paperwork in the air to flutter to the floor.

Amanda made a move to catch it until she saw the floor. It wouldn't make any appreciable difference.

Ceren gestured around the room. "Every item listed on each of these papers needs to be logged into this patil."

Amanda did not know what a 'patil' was but saw he gestured toward what looked similar to a computer.

He continued, "Only after all of the items are entered can the papers be filed alphabetically in the filing cabinets. I'd say this doesn't usually look this bad, but that would be a lie. Captain Ahn never did enjoy this part of the job when he got elevated to the Harbor Master position. So, he leaves it all here for some poor sap to handle.

"You should see the scramble of activity for the quarterly audit, which is due to happen within the next couple of weeks. The 'poor sap' is usually me, so I'm really glad the captain brought you in to help. If you have any questions, I'll be back at my desk." He turned to leave.

Panic rushed through Amanda, and her heart pounded furiously at the idea of him leaving her with such a scanty explanation. "Wait! I've never even seen one of these forms before. Can you go through one while I watch? I'm a quick learner."

Ceren groaned. "You've never done this before? I knew it was too good to be true!"

He dropped onto the edge of the table with a look of utter despair. "Miss, I can't teach you everything by just going over one; it's too complicated!"

"Try me!" She squared her shoulders and crossed her arms. She readied herself for this challenge and to prove him wrong.

The patil, Amanda discovered, used a basic spreadsheet-style program which she found easy to learn. After a fifteen-minute patil tutorial and a few specific inquiries during the initial training, Amanda started making a dent in the colossal paper stacks covering the office. The bills of lading mostly contained similar information; only the quantities changed.

"I think I'll leave you to your task! Good luck," Ceren called over his shoulder, and he shut the door behind him.

Alone, she had a moment to reflect upon her situation.

I don't know what's going on! I thought for sure the ship would dock in Mexico, but nobody seems to speak Spanish. And now, I've got a job, working on a computer – which they call a patil – but it's in English as well. I just don't get it!

In her mind, guilt warred with practicality. She wanted to search for Neal, but without any means to survive, she would fail. At least this job would bring her into contact with the port authority or whatever they called him. He seemed like a friendly and reasonable man. At her first opportunity, she would ask for his help.

Turning her attention back to her new job, Amanda sighed as she surveyed the enormity of the task ahead of her. "First thing first," she whispered out loud.

She cleared a space to work. Then, she organized enough stacks together to leave an empty area to sort her finished paperwork.

To break up the monotony, she designated the last hour of each day to file the day's completed paperwork. By the time she ended work and exited the office on her first day, she had discovered everyone else had already left. The doors were locked, and the lights were off.

She meant to ask if she could make up a cot in the corner of the office. She did not have anywhere else to stay.

I guess it'll have to be okay.

She shrugged and walked back to her workspace, and shut the door behind her.

Amanda removed her jeans and laid them on the floor behind the desk. Then she pulled her sweatshirt over her head and rolled it up into a makeshift pillow. Finally, standing behind the desk, facing the door, she leaned back against the wall and slowly sank to the floor in exhaustion.

Even with her neglected stomach growling, her utter exhaustion kept her from dwelling on it for long. Besides, without the means to buy anything made it impossible to contemplate.

I'll need to talk to Captain Ahn about getting an advance to buy some food in the morning.

The gnawing ache in her stomach didn't even compare to the clenching pain in her heart. With the excitement of the day ending, her reality came crashing down on her. Hard.

What if I sleep here while Neal desperately needs my help? Have I already failed him?

A tear slipped between her closed eyelids, and she let the sobs escape her lips without even attempting to remain quiet. Nobody would hear her crying out in pain. Nobody cared whether she lived or died. She didn't have anybody to help her figure out this terrible mess.

Knowing morning would come all too soon, she curled up on her makeshift bed. For the first time in weeks, she fell asleep feeling completely safe but more alone than ever.

CHAPTER 11

Elder Debbon removed his hands from Amanda's temples. While he already knew about the rules in place for swimmers, it shocked him to discover nobody reported any swimmers. He would have expected Captain Ahn to take his job seriously and immediately follow through on this crucial detail. Elders were always notified straightaway of a swimmer to investigate the origin of the person involved. He had to wonder what Captain Ahn hoped to gain by ignoring this particular rule.

He looked down at Amanda's lovely features as she slept peacefully on the bed. Unwittingly, this woman captured the attention of Petre MacVeen, Captain Issyn, Captain Ahn, and himself. What about her caused so many people to act in unordinary ways, if not outright defying the rules set in place by their society?

He needed to ponder these implications further while the woman slept. He left the room to get something to eat from the kitchen downstairs. He encountered people from Earth before and never knew them to be so disruptive to the Tualan way of life. There must be something different about Amanda, but Debbon could not imagine what.

With a foxl sandwich in front of him, Debbon sat and ate without any attention to his food. His mind turned over all of the possibilities which Amanda represented in Tuala.

He went to take another bite and discovered the sandwich was gone. With a growl, he shoved the plate away. He was still no closer to divining Amanda's influence, but he also had not enjoyed eating one of his favorite meals.

Without any further reason for the delay, Debbon left the mess in the kitchen. He trudged up the back stairway to the guest rooms. Momentarily pausing, he mentally collected himself before quietly turning the doorknob and entering the room. Debbon debated whether it pleased or disappointed him to discover Amanda still sleeping. If she had awoken, he would have questioned her to make some sense of why the two respected captains were willing to risk their careers to keep her safe.

Once again, he sat at the head of the bed. Focusing his thoughts on divining the truth of Amanda's journey into Tuala, Elder Debbon gently rested his fingertips on the woman's temples. Then, with his mind connected once again to Amanda's, he urged her to pick up her story where they left off earlier…

DISORIENTED, Amanda awoke in a semi-dark room. She slept deeply until strange and startling noises began near her head; she heard people laughing, animals walking, and rolling carts. After a moment's confusion, she realized the office wall must adjoin the street outside. This noise was the port city's waking routine.

The all-too-familiar sound of her stomach growling competed with the outside noises. She sat up on her makeshift bed. Rubbing the sleep from her eyes, she finger-combed her hair. Deciding against wearing her sweatshirt, she picked it up, neatly refolded it, and placed it on a clear space at the edge of the desk. Not relishing the idea of wearing two outfits again all day, she exchanged the shorts she wore for the jeans on which she just slept.

The movements caused her mind to focus solely on relieving her bodily needs. She needed to find the bathroom. Fast.

She opened the office door and walked into the hallway. Heading in the opposite direction of the front office, she investigated further into the building. On her way in the day before, she knew she had not seen a bathroom. Several doors along the hall proved to be locked. Finally, the last door opened when she tried it; luckily, it turned out to be the bathroom.

After she relieved herself, she washed her hands, splashed water on her face, and rinsed her mouth. She should have stuffed her toothbrush in her waistband before escaping; then, she'd feel more refreshed.

She carefully inspected her reflection in the real mirror above the sink. With a frown, she noted the dark smudges under her honey-tinted brown eyes, thin cheeks, and the sallow skin color against her sun-reddened glossy brown hair.

If only she could get rid of her nausea. But then again, she had not eaten anything in quite some time. "Maybe I'm coming down with the flu or getting close to having my period," she said to her reflection.

I don't really remember when I had my last one. That must be my problem.

Raising a wrist to her forehead, she checked for a fever just in case. "Cool as ever," she said and smiled.

Maybe I just need to eat something to get my color back. How am I going to get any?

Captain Ahn walked through the front door holding a paper sack in his hand. "Come out here," he called to Amanda when he saw her exiting the bathroom, "I've brought something for you."

Amanda rushed to the front office, where he waited for her behind the counter. Hoping to get some idea of exactly where she made landfall, she held out her hand to the Captain and said, "We didn't have a proper introduction yesterday. My name's Amanda Covington."

Taking her hand and pumping it hard, he smiled down at her and replied heartily, "Right you are, Amanda! You can call me Captain Ahn. Take a seat back here with me." He gestured toward a stool next to him.

Amanda didn't even have time to sit before Captain Ahn kept talking. "I don't want to intrude on your privacy, but Captain Issyn spoke to me briefly yesterday about your situation. You don't have to tell me anything, mind, but should you want to, I won't tell a soul. Captain's honor!" He held out the paper sack toward her. "I thought you might like something to eat."

"Thank you!" Tears instantly sprang to her eyes, blurring her vision. She took the bag from his outstretched hand. "I was going to ask you for an advance so I could buy some food! Unfortunately, I don't have any money at all."

"I won't hear anything of it! Captain Issyn told you the rules for picking up swimmers, right?"

Amanda nodded.

"Well, I have rules for pretty women who need help, too."

Suspicion made her pause in the middle of unrolling the top of the paper bag. Inwardly, she groaned, knowing this was too good to be true. Of course, he'd have some conditions for her. People always had some agenda.

'No such thing as a free meal.' Isn't that what Mom always says?

"What rules do you have?"

"First of all," he paused to wink at her, "there will be no more talk of advances for food! This job comes with three meals a day."

"Okay. I like that rule." She smiled, and a glimmer of hope blossomed. Then, continuing to open the paper sack, she hesitated and asked, "What're the other rules?"

"Are you going to eat or just play with the bag? I can talk while you eat." He urged her to remove the food. "I hope you like glawlets; they're a pretty common breakfast, but my wife used her special family recipe to make this one for you."

Amanda reached into the bag, more hesitant than ever.

Glawlet isn't a Spanish word. What else will I learn about this culture?

She brought out a fresh warm roll filled with a poached egg covered in what looked to be a sausage gravy. She held it up and asked, "Is this the glawlet?"

"It sure is. Have you never had one before?"

"No, this'll be my first!" She leaned over and took a big bite. "Mmm!" The savory, rich flavors exploded in her mouth. She swiftly chewed and swallowed. "This's amazing! Tell your wife she could sell this and make a fortune!" She stopped talking to continue eating the perfectly warmed meal.

"I'll certainly pass it along since I've told her the same thing on more than one occasion. Of course, she says that I'm biased!" Captain Ahn smiled so wide his back teeth showed. "There's a second one in there if you want it. I also packed a cup of steena tea." He gestured back toward the bag. "Have you tried that before?"

Amanda swallowed another bite. "Nope, another first."

"I find it really settles my stomach and leaves me feeling refreshed." *Where did this girl come from?*

Amanda sipped the semi-warm tea and discovered its sweet flavor and minty finish. The odd expression on Captain Ahn's face caused Amanda to squirm. Her ignorance of their food must trouble him more than she wanted. "I hope it'll help my stomach; it's been bothering me for weeks now." She finished the first glawlet and unwrapped the second one.

"I want to thank you for helping us out in a tough spot, what with the quarterly audit right around the corner! Ceren tells me you're a quick learner. I never was very good at keeping up with the patil work, as I'm sure Ceren told you.

"But it has to get done. I keep Ceren too busy running errands and working the front desk to bother him with it, either. So, you see, you came at a very advantageous time for us, and we're very thankful."

"I'm glad to be of service," Amanda replied, halfway through the second glawlet.

Captain Ahn's stool creaked as he adjusted himself. With an elbow on the front desk, he continued, "Anyway, back to those rules I mentioned earlier. The second rule is, I pay your previous days' wages first thing the morning after."

"That's not normal, is it?"

"It is now." He pulled some coins out of his front pants pocket and placed them on the table. "I thought there might be some things you'd want to purchase; it'd be selfish of me to make you wait a week to get paid!"

"How much money is this?" She looked over the one gold and four silver coins to see if they had any peso markings on them. She noted the ribbons of leaves curling around the edges of the silver ones while the gold coin only showed a rose on the front.

Pretending it was customary to explain money to an adult, he replied, "It takes ten of these silver shills to equal one of these golden taj. The common terms are just a shill or a taj."

"How many taj would the average person earn in a year?" She couldn't think of a subtle way to ask to determine their value.

Good grief—silver shills and golden tajs? This place is most definitely not Mexico or any other place I've ever heard of!

Getting a funny feeling about Amanda, Captain Ahn replied, "If by *year* you mean *anon*, then the answer would be around 350 taj. There're 252 working days in an anon."

Amanda nodded, soaking in this vital information. "Thank you.

I want to buy a comb and a toothbrush. Maybe even a couple of changes of clothes, too."

"Oh," Captain Ahn exclaimed. "I almost forgot. My wife asked me to give this to you." He pulled a small package out of his coat pocket and handed it to her.

"Thank you," she automatically replied as she received the package. She deftly untied the twine and peeled back the brown tissue paper. "But—how did she know?" Amanda asked as she looked down at a woman's hairbrush, a pair of frayed twig brushes, and a tube of mint paste.

"Well," he said slowly, "I told her about Captain Issyn bringing in a swimmer and about you working for me through the audit. She knew you wouldn't have anything, so she put together this package and your breakfast for me to bring to you. My wife has a soft spot for swimmers since she was one, too!"

"Really!"

"Yep, I picked her up out of the ocean myself, back when I ran my own ship. She's been with me ever since. The best thing to ever happen to me, my Barla's been!"

"Well, I'm glad you two found one another. Please tell her these items are most welcome!"

"You'll get the chance to tell her yourself since she'll be here later this morning." The front door opened, and Ceren walked in carrying an awkward bundle. "Perfect timing, Ceren! Can you take that into the back office for me, please?"

"No problem. Do you want me to set it up while I'm at it?"

"Please, if you don't mind. I'll tend the desk until you finish, then I'll be on my errands until mid-morning," Captain Ahn replied.

Ceren nodded in affirmation. "Morning, Amanda," he added as he walked past her.

"Good morning, Ceren." Finishing the second glawlet, Amanda picked up the steena tea and sipped again before asking Captain

Ahn, "Could I purchase a change of clothes with this amount of money, or should I wait a couple more days?"

"You'd do better to ask Barla about it when she comes in. She loves shopping!" replied the Captain with a smile on his face.

Amanda looked away, biting her bottom lip and curling her fingers into a fist. *The captain did say I could ask him anything. Well, here goes.* "Captain Ahn, this may sound strange to you, but—could you tell me what city this is? I thought it would be Mexico, but these aren't pesos." She indicated the coins on the counter as if that proved everything.

"I'm so sorry, Amanda. I assumed Captain Issyn told you where he was docking! Captain Issyn picked you up in the Gulf of Thulen on his regular route along the coastline of Thulen. You're now in the port city of Cresdon."

"Cresdon," Amanda muttered while trying to recall where she heard the name before. "Thanks for letting me know."

"As for the money," he continued and poked his index finger on the golden taj, "this is standard currency throughout the entire known world. There're different denominations, of course, but I've never heard of pesos."

"You must think I'm so strange." She shook her head in confusion, wishing any of this made sense and worrying that Captain Ahn would turn her out for being deranged.

"Only a little," he confessed, "but then water sickness can have such an effect on people. Give it a few days for your body to return to normal. Ah, Ceren," he called, straightening and leaning to the side to get a clear view of his employee. "Is everything in order now?"

Stepping behind the front counter, Ceren replied, "Yes, sir. I'm ready to man the desk if you like."

Captain Ahn vacated the stool and gestured for Ceren to take the seat. "It's all yours! I'm on my way then." He turned to Amanda and said, "I'll see you again by lunchtime."

Amanda watched Captain Ahn walk around the tall counter and out the front door. She scooped the coins together and slid them off the countertop before slipping them into her pants pocket. Then, she gathered her gifts and hopped off of the stool.

With the steena tea in her other hand, she announced, "I guess I'd better get started on those stacks of paper before you bury me in more from today's shipments!" She walked down the hallway to her office and stopped short of entering the room. "Ceren," she called over her shoulder, "what's this all about?"

Ceren poked his head around the corner of the hallway. "The Captain said you'd be sleeping here. He thought you might be more comfortable on a cot than on the floor."

"Oh. Thank you for setting it up, Ceren." She rushed into the suddenly blurry room as tears filled her eyes. *These people are so kind.*

She went around the desk and sat on the cot, wiping tears from her eyes with the back of her hand before they could spill down her cheeks. Captain Ahn was right; this mattress would make for a better night's sleep. She touched the edge of the sheets, appreciating the luxurious softness—nothing at all like Petre's rough-woven, scratchy linens. Even the blanket was smooth and silky, yet weighty enough to stave off any evening chill.

I sure seem to cry a lot lately. She chuckled at her own foolishness. *I really need to get to work!* She turned on the patil and began the day's task with a full stomach and a happy heart.

After what seemed no time at all, Captain Ahn loudly cleared his throat to catch Amanda's attention. Looking up to investigate, the Captain stood in the doorway with a beautiful woman beside him.

"Amanda, I'd like to introduce you to my wife, Barla. Barla, this is Amanda Covington."

Barla stepped forward with her left hand outstretched while Amanda hastily stood for the introduction. She extended her left hand to accept the handshake. "It's nice to meet you, Amanda," Barla said quietly.

Without letting go, she looked down at Amanda's hand and noticed Amanda's ring. "This's a beautiful gold and diamond ring." She returned her eyes to Amanda's face and smiled while she released her hand.

"Gold and diamond, you say?" Captain Ahn asked with a surprised expression as he looked at his wife. "I think I'll leave you two to get acquainted." He spoke over his shoulder as he hastily retreated down the hall back to the front office.

"What was that all about?" Amanda asked Barla.

"You really don't know?"

"Know what?"

"I see. Now I know why the Captain asked me to come here to meet you. He told me you said some peculiar things which might interest me. I believe he's correct. We'll have many things to discuss."

Dread consumed Amanda's thoughts, and she lifted her hands to her suddenly pale, cold cheeks. This was it—the pivotal moment she wanted to avoid. "Oh no! I knew this was too good to be true. Does he want me to leave?"

CHAPTER 12

"No, no! Don't be silly," Barla admonished. "The Captain believes you're special, and I'm beginning to believe you are as well. Let me ask a few questions before I explain."

Before continuing, she went and quietly shut the office door to assure their privacy. She gestured for them to sit on the cot. Turning to face Amanda, her expression softened. "Have you ever heard of North America?"

"Of course," Amanda replied instantly.

"How about Mexico?"

"Yes!"

"Dollars and pesos?"

"Yes, it's the money they use in the U.S. and Mexico. What of it?" Amanda couldn't understand how any of these questions were relevant. Everyone knew the answers to these fundamental questions.

"Just confirming something because none of those things exist here."

"I know they don't use pesos, Captain Ahn already told me."

"Not just that, Amanda! Think back on all of the answers to the questions I just asked you. North America, Mexico, dollars, and pesos. None of those things exist in this world!"

"What're you talking about? *In this world*—you say it like I'm on a different planet!" Amanda scoffed; a blurt of laughter escaped at the absurdity of Barla's insinuation.

Barla sighed. Her hand reached out like she wanted to touch Amanda's arm, but she let it drop to her lap instead. "No. It's the same planet, just a different dimension. We call this planet Tuala instead of Earth."

"What're you talking about?" Amanda repeated. *This woman is crazy, and they think I act strangely!*

As though she could read her mind, she replied, "I'm not crazy, and neither are you, Amanda. Unfortunately, I can't read minds either to answer your next question. I can read your face, though, and this *is* hard to accept! Amanda, somehow you managed to slip into our world's dimension. We just have to figure out how it happened so we can get you back to Earth."

Amanda sighed, long and soft. Everything started clicking into place, all the odd circumstances, equipment, and abilities. "Oh my. Tuala!" Amanda whispered violently. "I must be crazy because I believe you, Barla! Nothing else made sense until you came to explain."

Barla chuckled. "You took this news a lot better than I did. I came from Earth, too, you know."

"Are you serious? Why're you still here? Does this mean I can't go back?"

"To answer your questions in order: Yes, I'm serious. I fell in love and decided to stay. Yes, you can go back."

"Okay. What do I have to do?"

"Let's start at the beginning, shall we?" Without hesitation this time, Barla put her hand on Amanda's arm. "Tell me everything you remember ever since the last time you knew you were on Earth, and then we'll go from there. Okay?"

Amanda sighed again before she replied. "Okay. The first thing I remember is opening my eyes and seeing Petre MacVeen."

Barla raised her hands to her mouth and gasped. "Petre MacVeen? Are you sure?"

"Very sure, I was on his boat for over a month. We talked a lot," she added lamely.

"Talked?" Barla's skepticism made her tone sound odd. "I'm sorry. The name caught me off guard. But, please, tell me everything. I promise to keep quiet until you finish."

Amanda talked until her voice went hoarse, only stopping when Captain Ahn knocked.

The Captain popped his head around the edge of the door. "I brought you ladies some lunch."

"Please set it on the desk, dear," Barla instructed with a smile on her face. "I think Amanda and I will be talking for the rest of the day if you don't mind. Will you be able to bring us dinner as well?"

"No problem at all." He nodded approvingly to Amanda, winked at Barla, and shut the door on his way out of the room.

"Let's eat while you continue with your story," Barla suggested.

Amanda began where she left off. Barla remained faithful to her word and never interrupted. Amanda finished recounting her story and then nervously waited for Barla's response. Amanda picked at her food, wishing Barla would say something. Anything.

Several minutes passed as Barla remained in silent contemplation. "Thank you," she said quietly. "I believe I hear Ahn in the front office with our dinner. Would you mind if I shared your story with him?"

Amanda immediately wanted to protest, but she owed Captain Ahn more than distrust. With a slight nod of her chin, she replied, "If you think it's for the best."

"I do. He's kept my secret for over twenty-two years—anons, as they call them here. Ahn's extremely trustworthy, and we may need his help to get you back home."

"I don't want to go back before I find out what happened to Neal."

"No, of course, you wouldn't want to go. Ahn may be able to help with that as well. There has to be some record of a found water craft or another swimmer." Her voice trailed off thoughtfully just when Captain Ahn knocked on the door to deliver dinner. Barla smiled at her husband and said to him, "I'm so glad you asked me to come to visit with Amanda. We've had the most interesting talk about her journey."

Ahn hesitated at the door, indecision clearly written on his face. "Would you like me to leave you alone with the dinner?"

"What I'd like, Ahn," Barla replied as she patted a spot on the cot beside her, "is for you to come over and sit here and eat dinner with us. Please shut the door behind you."

Ahn's expression brightened as he entered the room, burdened with a large basket crammed with food.

"Whose kitchen did you raid?" Barla peered into the basket he set on the floor by her feet.

"I stopped by the Trilli Deli on the way back from my errands."

"Lovely!" She clapped her hands like a small child, and her face lit up with expectation. "Amanda, you'll love this food; it's almost like home cooking." Barla spread out hamburgers, salad, an unidentifiable side dish, and several drinks. "Let's eat while I catch up Ahn!" Barla declared as she handed out food and beverages on serving boards also included in the basket.

She turned to Ahn and spoke softly, "She is like me."

Captain Ahn swallowed his bite of hamburger, slowly shifting his gaze from his wife's face to Amanda's. He nodded his head quickly as if confirming something. "I thought so." He looked back to his wife and had another bite of hamburger.

As the Captain's gaze left her face, Amanda breathed a sigh of relief. She did not realize until just now how scared she had been of the Captain's reaction. It only took him seconds to decide, and, amazingly, he didn't seem to care at all.

"We need to search the records for any other swimmers and hopefully their water craft as well," she continued.

"Another swimmer, hmm? Male or female?"

"Male; his name's Nealand. He's my fiancé," Amanda supplied with relief to be able to add to the conversation.

"And the ship; what did it look like? Did it have a name?" Ahn continued his questions.

"Yes, it's a sixty-foot yacht, yellow and white, with the name *The Golden Jesisca* on both of the sides."

"That'd be hard to miss with those colors," the Captain mused. "I'll ask around and see what I can come up with."

"Thank you, honey!" Barla squeezed Ahn's knee in appreciation.

"Did you ask Amanda if she wanted to go to the Elders?" Ahn asked Barla.

"Not yet. Amanda just finished her tale when you arrived." Barla turned to Amanda and quietly considered what to say. Finally, she sighed, and her shoulders dropped. "What would you like to do next?"

"I'd like to finish my assignment for Captain Ahn so he can pass his audit. Maybe by then, you'll have some news about Nealand or the yacht."

The Captain nodded. His gaze swept around the room. "Sounds good. The audit will be in two weeks. At the pace Amanda's been going, I think she'll finish before then." He smiled at Amanda, and she turned her head away with a blush flooding her cheeks.

Barla cleared her throat and added, "I think it's best if Amanda stays here in the workroom and the bathroom. Given what she's been through, I don't think we should tell anyone about her being here. We should also ask Ceren not to mention her to anyone, including his wife.

"As much as I'd love to have the company at home, I don't want any chance of Petre finding out you're here. We know how much the people at the dock love talking about anything new! You're definitely a new story to tell!"

Anger and concern warred for possession of Captain Ahn's expression. Finally, he turned to Barla and asked, "Petre? Are you talking about Petre MacVeen?"

Barla glanced swiftly into his eyes, and she nodded the affirmative.

"Gah!" He stood to pace the confines of the room. "This changes everything, Barla! I can't stand that vile piece of trash. He knows better than to come to any of my docks. After our last argument, I made sure he knew where he stood with me! The moment we finish here, I'm going to let all of my people know Petre is not allowed anywhere near this port!"

Amanda understood Captain Ahn's opinion of Petre. "Should I leave right away? How will I get all of the supplies I need to continue my journey and have clothes to wear?" Her companions merely smiled.

"Don't worry, honey," Barla replied and reached over to pat Amanda's knee and squeeze it for comfort. "We'll take care of everything for you the same as Ahn here took care of everything for me when I arrived unbidden in his life.

"You just concentrate on your work. It's more important than you know! Audits can make or break our annual revenues, so you are doing us a great service. I know how disorderly Ahn's paperwork can get. I used to come down here to help until I found my real calling in this society."

"What was that?" Amanda inquired. *What made this amazing*

woman who came from my same Earth decide she never wanted to return?

"Well, the Captain and I started taking in orphaned children from the fishing community. It's incredible how many men don't come back after storms. The mothers couldn't handle the strain and would give them up, move on, or die trying to do too much.

"I can't stand to see those poor children suffer, and I decided to do something about it. So, first, I took a few in, then a few more. Then, we had so many children running around at one point, and I wondered what I had been thinking. But the children kept coming, and they needed me.

"Ahn here suggested we start training them to learn trades, and it gave me the idea to create a finishing school for them all. So now we have over one hundred children from six to seventeen anons old, currently learning how to read, write, and work at various trades in our community.

"I've been fortunate enough to have wonderful connections within our community. So many businesses hold jobs, especially to train our students. The kids get real-world training and have the experience to take with them when they graduate."

"I don't know how you get it all done. But, it sounds wonderful, tiring too!"

"Very tiring," Barla agreed, "but mostly very rewarding when you see all of the young people graduate with a sense of confidence and make a positive contribution to our society. These children would've been living lives of crime and poverty otherwise. We also have five children living with us who're too young to start school. They certainly keep me on my toes as well." Barla chuckled and smiled lovingly at Captain Ahn.

The Captain returned her smile and nodded his head. "We both love kids and wish we could've had more ourselves, but these other kids kind of took their place. Ceren is one of our first graduates. We got him when he was about twelve. Skinny little shaver, he was. Remember, Barla?" Captain Ahn winked at Barla with a small smile of remembrance for the scrawny youngster.

"How could I ever forget?!" Barla turned to Amanda and continued, "He was just standing on the pier looking out over the ocean as the sun went down. The Captain and I were working late, preparing for another audit, and we almost fell over him as we headed home. He kept his face turned away from us, but I could tell he'd been crying as his shoulders were shuddering uncontrollably. I asked him if he were okay, but he only nodded.

"I suddenly realized there was more to his story than we were going to find out in the dark of the dock, so I asked him to come home with us for supper. He was so eager he almost fell off of the pier into the water. The Captain barely caught him by the scruff of his collar as he tumbled so close to the edge.

"When we got home, we turned on the lights and saw just how filthy the little boy was. We offered him a bath which he refused. I told him he needed to wash his face and hands at least before we ate. He agreed and busied himself in the washroom while the Captain and I looked at each other and decided on the spot we would keep him with us until we found out about his parents.

"Our first meal together taught both of us lessons in how much little boys could eat. We had to raid the pantry twice before he finally sat back with his engorged belly and said he couldn't eat another bite without bursting. The Captain and I both laughed, and poor little Ceren looked like we were going to beat him for making a pig of himself. We assured him we didn't mind, but he was still wary.

"Ceren stood, saying he needed to be on his way. We asked him where he was going to go, and he just shrugged. I suggested he sleep on our couch for the night, and he just shrugged again, but I could see relief in his eyes. I can't tell you how much his sad look tore my heart! We tucked him right in, and he fell asleep before we finished banking the fire for the night.

"There were times I thought he'd run away, but he has been with us ever since. He was kind of our first experiment in the work experience program. We never did find out what happened to his family. The most we could ever get out of him was that they were lost at sea. That anon we had had more than our share of storms, so it was hard to find out who they could've been. He couldn't remember much of anything, but he was ours, and we loved him.

"Anyway, back to you." Barla smiled, her eyes refocusing when she turned to look at Amanda. "When your work here is complete, and we have whatever information we can get about Neal, we still need to decide if you want to take your case to the Elders.

"I'd be remiss if I didn't caution you about them; the Elders are a group of their own. Some of them are good, and some are bad, and it's hard to tell what you'll get when you ask to speak to one of them. They have their own opinion about people like you and me.

"We're called *old souls* by them, and they're always very curious about what we might know. Of course, some Elders will be kind about their questioning, but I've also heard stories about people being kept by them if the Elders feel the person knows enough about Earth to help our society."

"Don't be too harsh about the Elders, Barla," Captain Ahn cautioned. "They also have large ears and many spies. They govern our society, and most of them do a respectable job. So, we can't blame them for wanting to glean new knowledge, now can we?"

"Come now, Ahn," Barla rebuked, "You've heard the stories as much as I have. How would you feel if they'd taken me and not returned me to you? I've never regretted not turning myself over to them."

Barla turned back to Amanda and added, "The Tualan citizens are required to turn over any *old souls* they come across. If we don't, then the punishment can be very severe. So you can also see

the wisdom of asking you to remain hidden in the back offices here until we know more, right?"

Amanda nodded. "Oh, Barla. If that's the case, I should leave so that I won't bring you any trouble." Her throat clenched, preventing her from saying more. After all the help she'd received from these kind people, she didn't want to repay them with problems. As much as it pained her to think about leaving, she would do it for their safety.

"Don't be silly, Amanda. How will you find your fiancé without help? As you said yourself, where would you go? How would you eat? We know how to take care of you and get you back on your feet. Just be careful to do what we ask and don't tell anyone where you came from unless you find you can trust them as you trust us. Sound fair?"

Barla gave her a quick hug and then stood. She straightened out her clothing and looked down on Captain Ahn with love in her eyes. "I've enjoyed our time together, Amanda. But, I must be getting back to the house to put the children to bed. Will you be joining me, Ahn?"

"I think I will," he replied and stood beside her. He peered into the basket and said, "I'll just leave the rest of this here with you, Amanda. There's enough left for breakfast."

Barla gripped Ahn's hand. "I'll make arrangements for Amanda while you try to find her fiancé. I've got two weeks to get something together, and I must say, this is kind of exciting!"

Captain Ahn winked at Amanda over his shoulder as he spoke to Barla while they left the room. "You always did have a reckless streak. That's what I first loved about you." As he shut the door behind them, he called out, "See you in the morning, Amanda. Please sleep in, okay?"

CHAPTER 13

As it turned out, Amanda did end up sleeping in. She reveled in the comfort of the plush mattress, thick blanket, and fluffy pillow. She was exhausted from a full day's work and didn't remember laying her head down or even dreaming. Slowly awareness returned as she woke, stretching luxuriously and feeling her muscles stretch and joints crack.

Hearing the noises of regular business coming from the front office caused her to smile and feel at ease. Reality set in as she sat at the edge of her cot, and nausea struck her instantly and violently. It was all she could do to bolt to the washroom and wretch into the sink.

After rinsing her mouth, she returned to the office to retrieve her new toothbrush and hairbrush. *I must've overeaten yesterday.* Then, with slow, measured steps, she trekked back to the washroom and entered her morning ritual of brushing her teeth and washing her face.

Water dripped from her nose and chin as she looked at her haggard reflection in the mirror. *Ugh! I look disgusting. And my hair's a disaster. I'll feel better if I wash it.*

Back on Earth, she never worried about trivial matters like finding shampoo—it was always there. Nothing came easily on Tuala.

She searched the cabinet under the sink and found what appeared to be shampoo. She took it out, opened it, smelled it, put a little bit onto her fingers, and ran a little water on it to see if it would bubble. *That was easier than I thought!*

Convinced it was at least soap, she dunked her head under the faucet. She worked the soap into her scalp, rinsed with care, then wrung out as much water as she could. The hand towel came in service to wick the residual moisture from her hair. She appreciated her hair's soft and shiny look in the mirror. Finally, the brush Barla gifted her came in handy to work out the tangles.

With her hair done, the rest of her body felt like it needed a thorough washing as well. Without a proper shower or tub, she took off all of her clothes. Using warm water on a washcloth, and hand-bathed the best she could. Then, she shrugged offhandedly about shaving her legs since she didn't have a razor—not that she had anyone to impress in the back office anyway.

Once again dressed, she gathered her bathroom supplies and returned to the office to begin another day of work. As she put her things onto her cot, her gaze spotted the edge of the food basket. She pulled the basket closer, suddenly ravenous, which surprised her since she had just been nauseous.

She rummaged through the containers and discovered some fruit at the bottom of the basket. She took out an apple, said a quick prayer of thanks, and ate it slowly. *Better not push my luck.*

As she chewed, she reviewed the previous day's conversation with Barla. There was something about her that made her feel safe. She could not decide why that might be, but she waffled between three choices.

First, it could be as simple as Barla taking in stray children and making them feel welcome and at home; Amanda definitely felt like a stray. Second, Barla admitted her origins from Earth, so maybe she could feel the connection. Or third, it could just be because Barla reminded her of her own mother, whom she desperately missed and wished she could see again.

With her apple gone, Amanda licked her fingers and brushed her hands off on her jeans. These stacks weren't going to enter themselves. Besides, she neglected her duties the entire day before while speaking with Barla. With the papers already organized, she had no trouble entering invoices into the patil. She plowed through the first two stacks, both towering at least two feet tall.

When she entered the last invoice from the second stack, her stomach growled. She should have taken time to eat or drink, but she lost track of time.

Returning to the food basket, she selected a salad with crumbled cheese and a vinaigrette dressing. She ate another piece of fruit. At first, she thought it was an orange, but the taste and texture ended up surprising her. It started tangy and crunchy, but the longer she chewed it, the softer and sweeter it became. Once she realized her mistake, she decided it was pretty good after all.

It was easy to convince herself that she was back on Earth, but little things like the fruit brought reality crashing back on her. Working distracted her from her problems, but sitting idle let the crushing truth almost overwhelm her. What happened to Neal? Was he still on Earth?

She couldn't let herself think these things. Work. She refocused on her present task.

Originally, she planned to wait until the end of each day to do her filing, but she was tired of sitting, so she grabbed up the first stack, moved the papers over to the filing cabinets, and began to alphabetize them. Each stack took about half an hour to complete.

With the filing finished, she kneeled, grabbed the first stack of papers beside the desk, and set it next to the patil. Then she picked up a second stack and put it on the desk alongside the first. Her day continued in this vein until she plowed through another four full stacks of invoices.

She became so engrossed in filing the last stack it took her several seconds to notice the subtle difference surrounding her. Then, pausing, she turned around to contemplate what had changed. No customer noises filtered back to her office from out front.

How late is it? She poked her head out of her office door to look out the front window. It was fully dark. The office was locked and vacant. *Why didn't Ceren say goodnight? Why didn't Captain Ahn come by to see if I needed anything? What am I thinking? They have lives, too. I'm not their only concern.*

Her jaw popped loudly with her yawn. "I guess I've done enough work for today." She stretched her arms over her head, wincing as the muscles along her back pulled sharply. She went to the bathroom and freshened up.

Back in the office, she picked up the vegetarian sandwich and another apple, the last food items from the basket, and ate them. She didn't have anything left to do except sleep with her meal finished, so she lay down on the cot and covered herself with the blankets.

The work alleviated her guilt about staying there. *Did Barla or Captain Ahn have any luck in locating Neal or the missing yacht?* She chastised herself immediately because it had only been one day, and they probably had other things to work on. Even though she did not have anything pressing to do, it didn't mean they could drop everything just to help her out.

None of these thoughts helped. Instead, she reviewed all the things she remembered since first coming to Tuala. Maybe in her recounting things to Barla, she had overlooked or mistaken something because she didn't know she wasn't on Earth anymore.

She sat up straight, slapping her hand on her thigh at her apparent oversight. Petre must have seen the yacht. There was no other way he would have called her Jesisca unless he had read it on Neal's ship. If they could find Petre, then they would find out what happened to the yacht. Maybe Petre would also know what had happened to Neal.

She should tell Barla and Captain Ahn which vessels she saw sail by them while she was Petre's captive. It also might be crucial to mention the timing of her jumping from Petre's boat to being picked up by the shipping vessel. If they could pinpoint the last known location of Petre's ship, they might have a better idea of where he might have gone after she escaped from him.

No, that won't work because he didn't have the Golden Jesisca *with him then. I would have seen it, too, and I didn't.* She needed to figure out exactly how many days she was with Petre before she could calculate the time she was sick and recovering with drugged sleep. That would have been the time when he would have seen the yacht or possibly done something with it. Figuring out her timeline was going to take a lot more time.

Concentrating so hard on counting the days, she never noticed when she fell asleep. All night she dreamed of the days and nights spent with Petre. Then, after tossing and turning until she tangled herself in the blanket, she was thankful for the arrival of the morning. She woke feeling dirty; all she could think of was getting into the bathroom and cleaning herself.

Gathering her bathroom supplies, she all but ran to begin her morning ritual; unfortunately, this also included retching into the toilet. This time felt more like a reaction to the night's dreams. She made quick work of her routine because she wanted enough time to write up a timeline before starting work.

As she left the bathroom, she glanced down the long hall to discover the complete darkness outside. Also, she didn't hear any noises from outside to indicate anyone was up and moving yet. Even though it was way too early to be up, she didn't want to go back to sleep.

She found a new assignment for her future. Finally, she could take an active role in locating Neal. Having to rely on strangers for everything not only gutted her, but it also made her feel useless.

She found a pencil and some paper in her office and began writing down each day she could remember, starting with the previous day. She only made brief notes to encompass the entire day, just enough to mark the passing of each day. To her surprise, she remembered every day in bizarre detail, almost as if her mind were in hypersensitive mode. Thirty-five days.

Just as she put her pencil down, voices filtered to her from the front office. *What time is it? It must still be early since there's not much traffic noise on the other side of the office wall facing the alley.* Her curiosity grew just as a knock on the office door startled her.

What should I do? Who's at the door? Should I say to come in or just stay quiet? Panic took hold of her just as Captain Ahn's voice spoke through the door. She grabbed the collar of her shirt and twisted. Her heart rate spiked, and she looked around the room, ready to dive into hiding if necessary.

"Amanda, are you awake?"

Sighing with relief, she answered in a rush, "Yes, Captain Ahn. Come on in."

The door opened, and Captain Ahn motioned for Barla to precede him into the room. He closed the door behind him. Barla carried a bag of food that she brought forward and handed to Amanda.

"You look tired, Amanda," Barla spoke quietly. "Is the bed too uncomfortable?"

"Oh no. I had nightmares last night, so I didn't sleep well, and I got up way too early." She shrugged and then pointed down to the paper on the desk and said, "I did create a timeline of my days since coming to Tuala. I thought it might help our investigation in some way. It occurred to me last night that Petre saw Neal's yacht.

He had called me Jesisca, after all. That's not a common name here, is it?"

Barla shook her head and reached for the paper. "I think this might be very helpful, Amanda. You're right. Jesisca isn't a common name on Tuala. And, I agree, Petre probably does know something about your yacht."

She turned to Captain Ahn, "Maybe Petre towed the yacht to the nearest Elder to sell. That sounds like something a man like Petre would do. After all, there could be a lot of money involved. Maybe he even sold Neal to the Elders. What do you think, Ahn?"

"Maybe, Barla," Captain Ahn replied. "Let's sit and talk about this while Amanda eats. She looks a little peaked."

Reaching into the bag, Amanda retrieved a wonderfully warm glawlet. Her mouth salivated just thinking about eating it. Then, smiling at Barla, she said, "You make the most wonderful glawlets. Thank you for this."

While she ate, she discussed her ideas from the previous night with them. They sat in contemplative silence when she finished. Amanda wondered what had happened the previous day as she looked back and forth from the Captain to Barla. Again, she felt the familiar pull to Barla when she looked closely at her. Uncomfortable with the continued silence, Amanda asked, "Is something wrong?"

Barla smiled and patted Amanda's hand, "Nothing that concerns you, dear. We had another fishing vessel capsize yesterday, and all aboard were lost. We spent most of the day telling the next of kin and making arrangements for the children who are now orphans.

"Ceren handles the older boys very well, so he closed shop early yesterday to help us out. We're just a little preoccupied, but we still want to get things moving for you." She held up the list Amanda created. "Do you mind if I take this to read through?"

"Go ahead. I made it to help."

Captain Ahn remained quiet throughout this exchange, and he inspected the room. "You sure are making good progress in here. At this rate, I don't think you'll need the full two weeks."

He smiled and shook his head. Then, he turned to Barla and commented, "You might as well make arrangements for Amanda's move by the end of next week. Otherwise, she'll get bored just looking at these four walls."

"I'm already ahead of you, Ahn."

Amanda looked from Captain Ahn to Barla. *Move? What were they talking about?*

Barla noticed and commented, "Ahn and I agreed you'd be safer farther away from the harbor. Once you complete your work here, I have a friend who'll take you further inland and farther away from Petre MacVeen. Bryon doesn't know anything about Earth, other than the usual childhood fairy tales, so don't mention anything to him about it, okay?"

Amanda nodded. "Sure. I understand. I should probably get to work now if you want me to finish in another seven days."

Her heart fluttered uncomfortably, and her stomach churned at the idea of leaving. She would have to leave the only friends she had made since arriving in Tuala. Besides, going farther inland also meant putting more distance between herself and Neal's last known location.

Captain Ahn turned to Barla and said, "Maybe you should spend a few days with Amanda teaching her about Tualan culture and terminology."

Barla pursed her lips. Her glance shifted from Ahn to Amanda. "I was just thinking the same thing! Amanda, I'll bring you lunch today, and we can start your Tualan lessons, okay?"

"Sure. That sounds great. I'm sure I have a lot to learn."

CHAPTER 14

The morning sped past uneventfully as Amanda finished entering and filing four bills of lading stacks. She just picked up another two stacks from the floor when Barla poked her head through the door and asked, "Are you ready for lunch yet?"

Sighing, Amanda eagerly replied, "More than ready! Come on in, Barla!"

Opening the door the rest of the way, Barla pushed through the entry, laden with books and food. She used her hip to close the door behind her. Amanda jumped from her chair to help.

"Is there this much for me to study?" Amanda inquired. "I hope you don't expect me to learn it all today!"

"No, no, my dear; we have days to get you up to speed!" Barla replied, maybe a bit too cheerfully. "Food, however, will come first."

She continued across the room and set a small basket onto the desk. She reached into the container and removed a loaf of fresh-baked bread, a block of soft, white cheese, a jar of what looked like marinara sauce, a knife, and a couple of plates. She assembled sandwiches and placed them on two separate plates.

They ate in companionable silence. The sandwich made a nice light lunch, satisfying without making Amanda too full.

Barla sorted through the many books. She stacked them up in a particular order. The top book looked like an atlas, piquing Amanda's natural curiosity.

What were the differences between these two worlds? Barla did say the landmasses remained the same, just with different names. Were significant cities located in the same places on both planes of reality? She finished her sandwich and said, "I guess we should get started with my lessons, so my ignorance won't get anyone in trouble."

"This book," Barla nodded and picked up the first book. "Is very special because I have gone through and marked the Earth terms in parenthesis next to what they're known as in Tuala. Please don't let anyone see this, or there'd be a lot of unwanted questions to answer."

She flipped through the text until she found a particular page. Turning the book around, she laid it on the table for Amanda to view. With her finger, she pointed at Cresdon, "This," she said, "is where we are. You'd know it as Cancun, Mexico, right?"

Amanda leaned in closer and nodded; then, she pointed at an area called Pantano on the peninsula of Florida and said, "Neal and I set sail somewhere along here at Boca Raton." She traced their sailing path with her index finger and finally came to Cook Island, noted as Isla Mivua, inside the Bermuda Triangle, and said, "And this, I think, is where we ran into storm trouble. It's not very far from here, is it?"

"It's farther than you think, but, given the time you were with Petre, it makes sense. You'll also note that America and Mexico don't have individual states, just regions divided by the Elders.

"Since you've given me your sailing path, I'll talk to Ahn about possible places to look for Neal and his yacht.

"I think you'll notice the land masses on Tuala appear in the same locations as those on Earth; however, the topography isn't always the same. Geography has never been my strong suit, so this is as far as we'll go with the lesson. I'll leave the book with you to review on your own. Okay?"

Curious to check out other locations, Amanda reluctantly shut the atlas. Setting it to the side of the desk, she said, "Okay, what's next?"

"Well, you need to know Tualan history as it's taught to the children. I brought this children's book to give you the easiest explanation. I'm sure you'll have questions after you've read it. Let's wait until you finish before we go over anything together."

Amanda reached for the text, flipping it to the side to read the title on the spine: *Genero*. "What does this mean?" Amanda asked.

"It's an old term which I think we'd translate as *To Create* or maybe *Creation*," Barla replied. "The book covers the creation of the worlds, Jehoban and his wayward student named Lucinden, and the creation of the Elders which we have today. It's very interesting. I look forward to discussing it with you once you've had a chance to look through it."

"It sounds interesting," Amanda replied as she placed *Genero* on top of the atlas. "What's next?"

"This one's a little in left field, but I thought you'd better know the history of transportation. You won't need to read it cover to cover; just scan through it and read the sections you find interesting." Barla handed it over and indicated that Amanda should add it to the stack since she picked up the next couple of books.

"I think you'll enjoy this book about Tualan food. This one's about Tualan occupations. You should know what people are doing around you."

Barla paused in the act of picking up the last book. Running her fingers lightly over the title of the book, she spoke the name softly, "*Facultas* means *Ability*. This book is significant. It explains the abilities which the Tualan people possess and use daily."

"What makes it so important?"

"It explains how people do the most extraordinary things. They don't think anything of it—things like teleportation, telekinesis, translation, deception, healing, amplification. Basically, if the mind can think of something, it can create it. There aren't any limitations.

"That's the main difference between people from Earth and people from Tuala. This is why the Elders are so interested in the *old souls*. We're genetically the same, but without these abilities. Personally, I think the Elders are trying to figure out how to block Tualans from using their abilities so that the Elders will have absolute power. At least, that's how it seems to me."

"Wow, how interesting! So everyone but us has some kind of ability, huh?" Amanda asked. "I remember seeing an odd shimmer around Petre's boat. Does it have something to do with his ability?"

"I'm sure it did. Do you remember if Petre wore a ring on his left hand?"

Petre's ring was about the first thing she remembered seeing when she woke up on his boat. She answered, "Yes, it had a silver band with an onyx stone in it. Does that signify something?"

"Yes. Let's look it up in the book." Eagerly, Barla flipped to the back of the book and looked in the index for stone colors. She found the page for onyx and turned to it hurriedly. "It says here:

The onyx stone symbolizes deception. If the stone is set in wood, the bearer has minimal control, usually only in the realm of making a person believe a verbal lie. If the stone is set in gold metal, the bearer can control an easy deception, but not for long periods. If it's set in platinum metal, the bearer is considered a master at all aspects of deception, including illusion. Extreme care should be taken around a master, and nothing the ring bearer says should be believed.

"That would explain why all of the boats who passed us never made any indication they could see us. Right?" Amanda asked and then continued when Barla nodded, "But how come I could see through it?"

"As I said, people from Earth aren't as affected by the abilities. You saw a shimmer because he was holding the illusion, but you saw through it because you aren't from Tuala."

"Wow! That's actually pretty cool," Amanda sighed. Looking around the office, she said, "I guess I should probably get back to work."

Gesturing toward the stack of books, she added, "With this fascinating reading material, I may find it harder to concentrate on all of this mundane paperwork."

"I have complete faith that you'll get everything done—including your homework," Barla replied as she gathered up their dishes and leftovers to repack them in the container.

Tucking the basket handle onto her elbow, she stood. "I'll be back with your dinner tonight. At least this way, I can be sure you won't work too late." Barla hesitated for a moment before she leaned forward and gave a quick hug to a surprised Amanda before she turned away and swept out of the room.

Amanda's previous work rhythm eluded her. Each time she finished entering an invoice pile, her eyes wandered back to the stack of books. She constantly fought the urge to open a volume just to see what it might contain.

Shutting her eyes until she turned away, she picked up the stack and moved over to the filing cabinet. On her way back to the patil with a new stack, she found she had to quicken her step as she walked past the desk.

A chuckle escaped, sounding harsh in the quiet room. *Those books are like a drug to which I'm addicted.* She desperately wanted to know everything about the Tualan culture. Barla had probably barely scratched the surface of exciting things to introduce to her. Disgusted with herself, Amanda picked up the stack of books and deposited them on the floor behind the desk to get them out of her sightline.

No wonder Barla stayed here. I might even consider staying for a while longer after I find Neal, if only to learn more about these fantastic people.

A movement caught her attention just as she stood from behind the desk. Several papers fluttered to the floor as she was severely startled when Ceren opened the office door.

"Sorry," Ceren apologized, "I didn't mean to surprise you."

"Don't worry about it. I just wasn't expecting to see anyone right there." To cover her embarrassment, she ineffectually waved her hands before kneeling to retrieve the fallen papers. Once she caught her breath and stood again, she saw Ceren holding yet another stack of documents. "Are those for me to enter?" Immediately, she felt like a fool for asking the obvious.

"Yeah, I'm sorry to add to your workload. It looks like you're making good progress, though. Have you had any trouble with anything?"

"No. Other than some atrocious handwriting, it's been pretty easy."

"Easy?" he asked incredulously, shaking his head in wonder. "This is the most tedious and boring job in all of Tuala. I wonder how you don't fall asleep after the tenth one!"

"I'm grateful for the work, you know," Amanda replied. "I don't have very many labor skills, but I do have to admit it isn't very exciting!" She chuckled along with Ceren, feeling her shoulders relax with his easy companionship.

"Where would you like me to put these?" He looked around the office with more than a little bit of wonder at her progress. "It looks like you've created order out of this chaos, and I don't want to mess it up for you."

"Right there's fine," she said while pointing to the corner of the desk where she had just removed Barla's books.

He deposited the new stack and turned to Amanda, his expression suddenly serious. "I also wanted to apologize for not checking in with you more. I left you abruptly on the first day, and it wasn't fair for you. We've had so much happening these past couple of days. Honestly, things haven't been normal since you showed up!"

Noting her scared expression, Ceren rapidly backtracked. "No, that's not what I meant. It doesn't have anything to do with you. First, we've had more vessels appearing all at once. Then we had a big storm hit in the middle of the Gulf. And then everyone got so busy talking to all the families of the lost seamen. It's just been hectic; that's all I meant to say. Sorry."

Instantly Amanda felt stupid for thinking so much about herself. Of course, life would continue with everyone in Tuala, regardless of where she ended up. Needing to say something to fix things with Ceren, she said, "No, Ceren. I'm the one who should apologize to you! I just don't want to cause trouble for anyone, and I'm overly sensitive about it. Please understand," Amanda pleaded.

"Believe me, I do understand! Captain Ahn and Barla took me in, too, when I was young. Besides, I wasn't nearly as helpful then as you've been now," he chuckled. His smile transformed his features so much that she had to smile back at him.

A noise out front made Ceren turn. He headed for the door and said, "It was good talking with you. I gotta get back to the office. See ya later."

As soon as he left, the room felt lonely. Only then did Amanda know how much she missed just being around people. Of course, having her movements restricted to remain hidden probably made it feel worse. *Nothing like wanting what you can't have.*

She crossed the room and opened the door, where she listened carefully to make sure she could leave without being seen. Hearing the heated conversation from the customers and Ceren's calm response, she hurried in the other direction and closed herself in the washroom.

She filled a glass of water and drank slowly while looking at herself in the mirror. Not for the first time, she noticed how her skin had an odd tone, which only accentuated the dark circles under her eyes. *Maybe some exercise will help.*

Even though the room was barely large enough, she executed a series of jumping jacks. After completing the second set of fifty, she looked at her reflection again in the mirror. While her cheeks had a pink flush to them, the underlying tone was still off. It made her feel foolish and exhausted to believe that a little bit of movement would make any appreciable difference.

Shaking her head, she gave up on the notion of looking any healthier. Besides, maybe her body was simply incompatible with Tuala, although Barla seemed unaffected. Mentally shrugging, she returned to work.

Back in the office, she sat and sighed as she settled Ceren's new pile in front of her. "At least Ceren's handwriting is more legible," she muttered as she picked up the top piece of paper and began entering the information into the patil. The clacking of the keyboard reverberated around the room.

Amanda missed music. She began humming her favorite song, letting the beat dictate the rhythm of her typing. The task seemed less tedious when she created games out of it. Besides, with this stillness surrounding her, it gave her entirely too much time to worry about Neal.

Was he looking for her? Did Petre know what happened to

him? Was she making a mistake staying in the office? She couldn't answer any of these troubling thoughts. Starting another song, she redoubled her efforts, if only to drown out her doubts and fears…

ELDER DEBBON WITHDREW his fingertips from Amanda's temples. Mentally returning to his present time proved challenging. He groaned as the muscles spasmed all along his spine. How long did he spend delving through her memories?

From the amount of stiffness throughout his body, he could only assume hours. Using a bit of elemy, he relieved the worst of the cramping and soreness before he stood.

Whatever he decided to do with Amanda would require careful consideration. She might still pose a threat even though she appeared so innocent.

CHAPTER 15

Elder Debbon took a few hours to review everything from Amanda's recent memories. How many *old souls* resided in Tuala without discovery? While he knew many people feared the people from Earth, he did not share their views.

Furthermore, he wished to discourage the other Elders from cultivating this fear throughout the Districts. As the elected leader of the Elders, he had this right, but he never found the appropriate time to take action with it. More than once, he thought to ask Jehoban why the two worlds were kept separate even though they clearly had access to one another through the Ascension Gates.

He didn't want to detain Amanda much longer. He resumed his place at the head of her bed and once again touched his fingertips to her temples…

Amanda's days developed into a routine where she never worried about getting bored. Waking early, she discussed Tualan trivia while eating breakfast with either Captain Ahn or Barla. She spent her morning hours with data entry and filing, followed by quiet, solitary lunches—usually provided by Ceren—where she ate while studying various subjects from the books.

As the office started clearing out, cleaning became a part of her afternoon schedule and the paperwork. Once the office closed down for the evening, her isolation ended when either Captain Ahn or Barla would keep her company by bringing her something to eat.

Again, they would discuss random customs and ideas about the Tualan culture, which sparked Amanda's interest even more. Consequently, she would then stay up late into the night, reclining on her cot to devour more knowledge about different subjects as they caught her eye.

Sometimes she skimmed through the material, only reading the captions under the pictures. Usually, this would then lead her to research something in another book. Amanda eagerly delved into the diverse topics to round out her accelerated Tualan education.

As Barla suspected, Amanda developed a fascination with the Tualan modes of transportation which most citizens utilized. At first, she thought she had misread the passage. But upon re-reading it, she discovered the vehicles, known as telepods, were truly powered by crystals. These exceptional engineers managed to eliminate the problem of dirty emissions completely.

The color and clarity of the crystal drive determined the speed and reliability of the telepod. Regardless of the crystals installed, the transport used the mind of the person operating the vessel for control and steering. The telepods did not need tires or even paved roads since they levitated.

Yet even those innovations paled in comparison to the most interesting aspect of how they traveled. The telepods employed almost instantaneous teleportation to move between locations. Only the poor people suffered with the slow and tedious travel which Amanda knew and used on Earth.

When speaking with Barla about the telepods, Amanda discovered how diverse they were throughout the world. Barla explained how single people or small groups in home settings mainly utilized such transportation, much like cars on Earth. She also talked about the larger models used for mass transportation similar to airplanes on Earth, although most people didn't use them.

Barla explained the crystal drive technology was only as good as the operator using it. Smaller telepods proved unpredictable in high wind, so most Tualans feared flying over water, where the wind could pose many dangers to the novice operators. As a result, they did not usually bring telepods to the harbor for fear of being blown out over the sea.

"Wait, I thought the telepods teleported! Why would water be an issue?"

"Telepods don't usually teleport to their exact landing location. Therefore, manual flight must occur until they land. If the coordinates bring them in too close to the water, then the winds can cause a lot of disturbance which then makes the telepod difficult to operate manually."

Not all people had telepods, which Amanda thought odd, not just because of financial reasons, but because they did not have the mental capacity to operate them. She chuckled as she told Barla, "I guess it brings home the idea of driving being a privilege and not a right, as they say on Earth."

Amanda's limited interactions with people wouldn't have allowed her to see a telepod. With the only two places she had stayed, the boat and the harbor town office, she wouldn't have had an opportunity to glimpse any of these marvels. Would she ever have the chance to get a ride in one?

It sure would be something to talk about when I get home. When I get home, she repeated to herself, the idea both intoxicated and depressed her at the same time. *Will anyone believe what I've been through when I get back? Will they think I'm crazy or delusional? Will I get to go back? Will I be alone, or will I find Neal?*

Shaking her head to redirect the flow of negative thoughts, she again picked up the transportation book, searching for other aspects she should already know if she were a Tualan. *Barla found happiness here. If I can't go back, I pray I'll find the same kind of contentment.* The thought brought her some comfort, but she still worried about her fate.

Amanda struggled over what to make of the book entitled *Genero* or *Creation.* Barla did say it was a historical document written for children, but the story was so fantastic as to border on a fairy tale. If everything from the book were to be taken at face value, that would mean God, using the name Jehoban, lived on Tuala with the people. More disturbing, however, was the idea of the devil, known in Tuala as Lucinden, also lived among them.

Well-versed in the teachings of Earth's Bible, Amanda's natural curiosity wanted to know what other cultures believed about creation. Right from the beginning, she felt a tug of recognition. This book spoke of the world starting from nothing and Jehoban thinking it into being—and it was.

Another pleasant discovery was the common practice to rest on the last day of each week, which they called Sabtu. She followed the same thing on Earth. Amanda then realized she counted Sabtu as one of her working days. *That's why Captain Ahn told Barla that I had many things to learn. A Tualan would know work wouldn't get done on Sabtu.*

The next day, Barla showed up at the office earlier than usual with dinner and an armload of cloth. "I have something different planned for us this afternoon; consider it as a part of your education of Tuala," she said as she deposited her burdens on the now-empty desk. Barla's usually calm and casual manner seemed slightly off.

"What's going on?" Amanda touched the fabric on the desk. "Did you bring me clothes?"

"I did," she replied. Her gaze remained fixed on assembling

their simple dinner of rich foxl soup with hearty vegetables and dipping bread. "Here," she said as she handed over the bowl, "let's hurry and eat, so you don't miss everything this afternoon, okay?"

Amanda took the bowl, still frowning while trying to understand Barla's strained manners. Was her presence causing a problem after all? Was Barla being too polite by not asking her to leave?

She halted these questions. Not everything was about her. Too often, lately, Amanda fell into that worrisome trap. Besides, Amanda relished the idea of getting outside these four walls.

Dipping her spoon into the bowl, she brought the steaming soup close to her lips. When the smell of the foxl broth reached her nose, Amanda immediately put the spoon down and exclaimed, "I can't eat this. It'll make me go to sleep!" She held out the bowl to her confused host.

Barla frowned and shook her head. She didn't attempt to take the bowl back as she said, "No. You must be mistaken, Amanda. I've heard of people wanting to take a nap because they were full, but not because of the soup itself. What makes you think it's the broth?"

"Every time Petre gave me this broth, I would pass out and have weird dreams." Just saying it out loud brought the reality slamming back into her mind. Her hands shook enough to slosh some soup over the bowl's rim.

"Then he must have drugged it, Amanda," Barla softly replied.

Amanda's gaze shot up to Barla, eyes wide with realization.

Concern evident in her expression, she held Amanda's free hand and said, "Amanda, we told you not to trust anything to do with people who wear the deceptor's rings. Remember, Petre wears a master's ring?"

Amanda's shoulders slumped as the tension eased. Barla would know. She knew she could trust Barla with her life; she already had. Seeing both the concern and reassurance in Barla's face, she lifted the bowl to her mouth and took a sip. "Oh, this is wonderful. It's nothing like the broth Petre made for me. This soup is thicker and richer. I'm sorry to create such a fuss."

"It's no problem," Barla replied instantly, again touching her arm with concern. "You've been through a lot in a short time. Some things will take longer to get over than others. Believe me! I understand completely."

Once she started to eat, Amanda realized how very different it tasted from Petre's version. It didn't take her long to finish the soup; she even wanted to use the bread to sop up the remainder of the delicious liquid from the bottom of the bowl. As soon as she stopped worrying about her food, her curiosity rose about their upcoming outing. What exactly did Barla have planned for them?

"Okay." Barla grabbed the empty bowl from her hands and practically threw it into the dinner basket. "Now we can get to the fun stuff." She reached for the clothes on the desk and held them up for Amanda's inspection. "Well, what do you think?"

Amanda didn't know how to react since the clothes were rather large with an overall shapeless cut. What polite thing could she say?

Barla burst out laughing.

"What?" Amanda asked.

"Oh, the look on your face is precious! These aren't designed to be a fashion statement; they're meant to make you anonymous. Trust me; this isn't how people your age dress here or anywhere else on Tuala, for that matter," she replied through her chuckles.

"I can't tell you how relieved I am to hear that!" Amanda exclaimed. "What exactly are we doing?"

"We're going to give you a social education tonight. I'm taking you out to the market so you can see Tualan's interacting with one another. I also want you to get a better sense of how Tualan's use their money and the types of things available at the market."

"Is it safe? What about Petre?" Looking carefully at Barla, it seemed as though she were anxious about something other than their outing.

"It's okay, Amanda. This outfit will take care of any casual observers," Barla reassured her as she gestured to the bulky garment.

"As long as you're sure. Are we going to be buying anything or just watching?" Amanda inquired, secretly hoping for the former.

"There *are* a couple of things I should get while we're out. Don't worry, you can participate, too, if you want. Now hurry and put this on so we can go."

Amanda tugged the fabric over her head and let it fall shapelessly down the length of her body. The dark red fabric was plush and soft where it touched the bare flesh on her arms and legs.

Lifting the hood at the back of the garment Barla covered Amanda's head until only her nose remained visible. "I think this should do it." Leaning over, Barla plucked the atlas from the cot and shoved it into her basket. Grabbing the basket off of the desk with one hand and Amanda's hand with her other, she very nearly towed Amanda out of the building's back door.

Seeing Barla's covert maneuver with the book combined with their rushed departure, she knew something had happened. "What's going on, Barla?"

Without breaking her stride, Barla glanced sidelong at Amanda. As if she needed to decide what to say, she waited several seconds before responding. Sighing heavily, she answered, "We got a note from a friend saying that someone alerted the Elders to the possibility of an *old soul* being in our office. Lucky for us, we had enough notice to get you out of there while they investigate."

Amanda's eyes widened with worry. This was her worst fear manifesting. "Barla, I can't stay with you any longer. I don't want to bring any trouble. Obviously, my presence is going to be a problem. I can leave right now."

"Definitely not. You don't have any resources or skills to

survive for any length of time outside of our care. Don't worry, Amanda. We've got everything under control. Now, here's the market. It's time you learned how our money works." Barla gave Amanda's hand a gentle squeeze, and her voice remained calm and confident.

Without any other options and recognizing Barla's wise but painfully honest words, she relented for the time being. "What're we buying today?" Amanda breathlessly asked as they nearly ran through the alleyway and out into the street. Amanda looked around curiously. After so long in seclusion, it felt like the first time seeing everything around her.

"I just need to get a few vegetables and medicinal herbs. There're a couple of sick kids at the school, and we're running low on some common remedies," she replied as she continued towing Amanda along the bustling street.

"Don't you think we should slow down, so we don't draw attention to ourselves?"

"Oh, I'm just so excited for you. I remember my first time in the market. I had so much fun, and I want you to enjoy it!" Her pace did slow, however. She drew Amanda's hand into rest in the crook of her arm, and together they continued down the street at a more leisurely pace.

Barla pointed out the street signs and reminded Amanda to pay attention to the direction they headed. "If, for some reason, we get separated in the marketplace, you should know how to return to the office."

They turned down a series of narrow streets, getting increasingly crowded until they reached an open square full of farmers' carts and their wares. Voices raised and lowered depending on the stage of the bargaining. People carried goods and herded children.

Amanda almost felt drunk viewing all of the activity bustling around her. The scene forcefully reminded her of her isolation over the past several weeks. Already, she dreaded returning to the lonely and empty office.

As if sensing her thoughts, Barla leaned sideways and whispered to Amanda, "I've made arrangements for you to spend the next two nights at our house. I know you've been cut off from people, and a change of scenery will do you some good. If nothing else, maybe it will get some color back into your cheeks!"

"That sounds wonderful, but are you sure?" Amanda's emotions warred between eagerness to see their home and worry about bringing them unwanted attention with the Elders.

"Yes. Remember we've had some experience with your particular kind of problem. You'll have a great time. Trust me."

With a grin plastered on her face, Amanda sighed with relief. Now she could relax and enjoy this new experience without dreading the foray's end.

They wandered up one side of the market and circled to the other side to get familiarized with the quality of the different wares before negotiating any purchases. Amanda couldn't help but think she was back home at a farmer's market. Granted, some of the items on display didn't exist on Earth.

Barla quietly quizzed Amanda about various items they saw displayed in between booths to test her knowledge of the more obscure fruits and vegetables. She showed her some of the everyday household items which Amanda may not readily recognize.

Overall, Amanda accurately answered the questions. At least her studying hadn't been in vain. The many differences between Tuala and Earth made this lesson quite educational. Now, she only needed to put her education into practice.

CHAPTER 16

She kept her arm linked with Barla's as they walked through the busy market. Amanda watched the crowds as much as she did the stalls. Nobody seemed to pay them any attention, which caused her fear to subside, but she still couldn't relax. Maybe Barla had the right idea to go out and act normal doing mundane tasks.

The Tualans dressed in various styles and qualities, but the children puzzled her the most. No matter how rich or poor they appeared, without exception, they each wore a pendant with colored stones on expensive-looking chains around their necks. She'd have to ask Barla about it when they finished their shopping.

Together they sidled up to an herb vendor, which they agreed had the freshest and most varied selection. Barla discreetly indicated the different herbs and the most readily known use for each. She gathered a couple of herb bundles to replenish her diminished supplies.

She made a point of bargaining just loud enough for Amanda to listen and learn. Tucking her newest acquisitions into her oversized basket, they ventured to another vendor's stall to finish. Again, Barla negotiated the price while Amanda listened.

With her purchases wrapped and stored away, Barla turned to Amanda and said, "I'd like you to negotiate for this next one. I want to pay less than five shills for a bushel of cucumbers. Are you ready?"

Amanda smiled and nodded with enthusiasm, "Do you want me to pick the booth as well?"

"Sure." She handed Amanda the money purse.

Tapping her bottom lip with her index finger, Amanda glanced from one end of the market to the other, trying to remember where she saw the best-looking produce. They started to walk back the way they came when she remembered the stall closest to the entrance seemed to be the freshest.

Walking with confidence to her selection and without seeming too eager, she asked the merchant, "Excuse me, do you have a bushel of cucumbers available?"

"Yes, ma'am. Just picked this morning, I say, and only seven shills for the bushel," the wizened old man replied with a saucy wink.

"Seven!" Amanda exclaimed while displaying a shocked expression to Barla. "I couldn't possibly afford so much. I'll have to keep looking. Sorry to waste your time."

She made a move to leave the stall at once, but the man displayed more agility than she would have expected when he grabbed her arm to halt her departure.

His bold move triggered her fear. Did he recognize her? To her credit, she remained still and didn't pull away. The man's following words let her exhale and relax.

"No need to rush off, my lady, it's late in the afternoon and all, and I'd rather not return to face the missus with such inventory still in the cart. How about five shills for the bushel?"

Amanda pretended to hesitate and slowly replied, "How about

four shills with four ears of corn added to it as well? I've never seen corn look quite so tasty, and I suddenly have a craving for it, but my purse is small." She winsomely smiled at the man, ignoring the deepening creases along his forehead and between his brows.

His smile quivered, and he wrung his hands as if in pain over making such a small profit. "On the condition, you won't tell anyone else how low I sold it to you, even though my wife will skin me. Fine—you have a deal!" He gestured for her to choose her bushel from the three available behind the cart.

She made her selection before she counted out the four shills. As she had seen Barla do earlier, she shifted enough to prevent the merchant from peering inside her purse.

At the same time, the vendor selected the four largest ears of corn and added them to the top of her bushel.

Amanda smiled at his kindness and handed him the four shills delicately. "Thank you for your generosity. Please tell your wife she's lucky to have you in her life." Hoisting the bushel and resting it against her hip, she nodded cordially to the vendor and walked away from the cart with Barla at her side.

When they walked sufficiently far away, Barla smiled openly at Amanda and said, "You were brilliant! I'll have to remember the added benefit to my next deal. Oh, Ahn will get a kick out of it! He loves corn, too. Well done!" She positively beamed at her pupil's first purchase as she led them back.

At first, Amanda worried that Barla had changed her mind as their travels led toward the office. A few minutes later, she managed to hold back a relieved sigh when they veered off the previous road to take them toward Barla's home.

The streets widened not too far from the office, and the buildings were spaced much further apart. Instead of weathered gray wood, the house colors varied between shades of white or salmon-colored stucco. Immaculately sculpted yards became the norm as the two-story homes set further and further back from the road.

And then she saw it—her first glimpse of a telepod. Even at more than a few hundred yards away, it was unmistakable. With a rapid intake of breath, she stopped dead in her tracks. Raising her hand to point in the direction of the telepod, she asked Barla incredulously, "Is that what I think it is?"

Confused, Barla looked over and then smiled. "Yes. Thank goodness we were alone the first time you saw it, too." She shook her head, and her expression turned serious. "If you want to blend in, then you'll have to pretend it's as normal as it is."

Accepting the kind censure, Amanda instantly put down her hand and kept pace alongside Barla. "How big do you think it was? Was it what I'd typically see?"

"It's hard to tell from this distance, but I think it's safe to say it was a family telepod, not as big as they can be, but not as small, either. And now," she stopped walking and turned to her right, "we are officially home. What do you think?"

Amanda turned and appraised the white, two-story house. The four columns on the front porch and the symmetrical windows around the entry could have been transplanted from a plantation back home. The landscaping was an immaculate showcase—the green grass neatly clipped, and the walkway carefully planted with dainty purple, yellow, and pink flowers she couldn't identify. "It's very grand and perfect. You must adore coming home every night," she exclaimed.

Pleased, Barla smiled. "Just wait until you see the inside," she said, grabbing her elbow and propelling them along the crushed seashell walkway, up the three broad steps of the front porch, and through the massive double-door entry.

"We've called this home since Ahn's election to the Harbor Master position. That's another thing you should know about: housing. All elected offices come with living accommodations— some better than others, depending on the prominence of the occupation. As you can see, people view the Harbor Master's position with the utmost importance. Harbor management directly affects the livelihoods of almost everyone in the coastal towns since it's how we receive almost all imported items."

Amanda complimented the grandeur of the foyer. She loved the way it led into a sweeping staircase to the second floor, and several doorways opened on both sides into various rooms of equal opulence. They walked through a wide hallway alongside the stairs, past a library, a formal dining room—which could easily seat thirty people, and a butler's pantry before they reached a vast and immaculately clean kitchen.

"Just set the cucumbers down on the island, if you will, and I'll put this corn away," Barla said as she placed her picnic basket on the work surface before she took the corn and crossed the room to the cooler. Clapping her hands together, Barla's eyes gleamed in anticipation when she turned. "Do you want to see your bedroom?"

"Yes, please."

Unburdened by the groceries, they retraced their path to the stairs and ascended to the second level. Barla led her down an equally grand hallway past several closed doors. Beautiful artwork hung on the walls, as well as fine furniture adorned the edges of the hallway. Almost at the end, Barla turned to her left and pushed open the door gesturing for Amanda to enter the room first.

The massive bed was the room's focal point—the four posters reaching almost to the ceiling. The carved wooden headboard provided the perfect backdrop for the cushions and pillows piled against it. No detail was left to chance. Even the pattern on the silky green comforter matched the intricate carvings in the bed frame.

Beyond the bed, two tall windows on the far wall had broad, deep cushions. Crossing the room to investigate the view, Amanda paused when her feet landed on the plush carpet covering the glossy, wood plank floor. Leaning forward, she touched the soft fibers and exclaimed, "This feels wonderful! What type of material is this?"

"That's foxl hair. Amazing, huh?"

Amanda frowned while she struggled to recall if the books she studied contained any pictures of a foxl. Coming up blank, she asked, "Does your library downstairs have anything on the animals of Tuala? I should probably know how to identify them as well, don't you think?"

"Probably. We can look for it if you like. A foxl reminds me of a cross between a sheep and a cow."

"I can't even imagine what that would look like," Amanda laughed. "But I can't wait to see it. Is it relatively common?"

"Yeah, almost everyone eats it in at least one meal a day, unless they're vegetarians."

"Do they call them vegetarians here as well?"

"Surprisingly, they do."

Amanda walked over to the window and looked out at the view. The house stood just high enough to see the Gulf of Thulen and a small land jetty protecting the harbor. "The view is spectacular," Amanda said. Her vision blurred, and she hastily reached up to wipe the unwanted moisture away. "I really miss home, Barla!"

Immediately coming forward, Barla tightly circled her arms around Amanda's shoulders. She rubbed her back and murmured, "We'll find a way to get you back. Don't worry. It's okay, it's okay, hun."

"Do you think so?" Amanda sniffed as she tried to control her tears. "You didn't get to go back."

"No. No. You're wrong, Amanda. I chose to stay. I fell in love. Remember? I sometimes miss home. My family probably believes I died in the Gulf of Mexico, and that makes me sad. But other than that, I have everything I've ever dreamed of in my life.

"Come on, no more tears now. Let's try to enjoy your time here, okay?" To distract Amanda from her troubling thoughts,

Barla moved her across the room to another door. "This is your private bathroom. Why don't you take a nice bubble bath? Then, when you're relaxed, put on this robe and come down to the library. We can look for more books for you to continue your research. Does that sound good?"

Amanda nodded and crossed the threshold into the bathroom. She took the offered robe from Barla's hand and set it down on the chair next to the tub. "Barla?"

Barla stopped midstride on her way out of the bedroom and turned around to reply, "Yes?"

"There's something that's been bothering me." Amanda's hands clenched the chairback, wishing she'd kept her mouth shut.

"What is it, dear?"

"I was wondering," Amanda paused to gather her thoughts, "since you have so many students apprentice with businesses, how come none of them are helping Captain Ahn with his paperwork?"

"Oh," Barla exclaimed and hastily raised a hand to cover her smile. "That's my fault, really. Ahn kept telling me he could do the work himself if someone showed him how to do it efficiently. So I finally sat down with him and figured out a system so he could easily stay organized."

"Well, that didn't work out too well," Amanda scoffed, unable to stop herself from rolling her eyes.

"Tell me about it!" Barla concurred. "So when Ahn said he needed someone to come and take care of it, I made other arrangements for the five students old enough to help. I'd hoped to force him to do it himself."

Amanda laughed. "When do you think he was going to get around to it?"

"Ahn and I talked about it the same morning you showed up. When he came home that night, you would've thought he'd just won the lottery! I guess the joke was really on me then because my grand plan backfired. I'm glad about how it all worked out, though. We had plenty of work for you. Anyway, enough about that, it's time for you to get into that tub and start relaxing!"

Lifting her arm playfully, she sniffed her armpit. "Do I smell that bad?"

Barla chuckled and shook her head, but she didn't deny the claim.

Using her most diplomatic tone, Amanda said, "Thanks, a bath sounds like just the thing I need right now."

"Okay. I'll leave you to it then. Everything's going to be fine, all right?" Smiling warmly at Amanda, she quietly closed the door as she left her alone.

Turning the faucets, the tub filled rapidly, speaking to the house's excellent plumbing. Amanda tried and failed to recall the last time she had taken a leisurely bath. Gratefully removing the unflattering cover Barla loaned her, she shrugged out of her shorts and t-shirt. Once folded and neatly stacked on the chair beside the plush robe, she removed her undergarments and added them to the stack.

Balancing her thigh on the edge of the tub, she swirled her hand through the warm water. After a generous dollop of pearly liquid poured from the decorative bottle, Amanda waited for the magic to happen. Fragrant bubbles almost immediately obscured the water altogether.

She turned off the faucets and slowly lowered herself into the blissful pool. Never before had she noticed each part of her body contacting the soothing warmth as she immersed herself into the bath. A low moan escaped her lips. Resting her head against the curved rim of the tub, she closed her eyes and truly relaxed.

Clearing her mind of all of her troubles, she concentrated only on the warmth seeping through her skin and muscles. She continued to take deep, relaxing breaths as she allowed her arms to float. "Wow, this is wonderful," she whispered to no one but herself.

CHAPTER 17

With the water cold around her, she woke from her pleasant dreams. Although loath to move, the coolness decided it for her. Without looking, she reached behind her head. Rather than finding the towel on the rack, she screeched at the sound of a voice.

"Here you go, miss," a little girl said as she deposited a warm towel into her hand.

Water sloshed out of the tub as Amanda rushed to cover herself and turn to face her visitor. "How long have you been sitting there?"

"Sorry if I startled you," she said promptly. "Lady Barla asked me to check on you about an hour ago. When I told her about you sleeping, she asked if I'd sit by you quietly, warming your towel until you awoke, just to make sure you didn't slip under the water."

"Well, I should be thanking you for keeping me safe then, shouldn't I?" Amanda smiled at the cute little girl. She noticed the beautiful blue crystals formed into the shape of a tree hanging from an ornate chain around the child's neck. *Oh, I need to ask Barla about those.* Smiling at the girl, she said, "I like your necklace."

Her little hand rose to cradle the pendant as she looked down at it and said sadly, "It was a gift from my mommy and papa."

"They must love you a lot to give you something so pretty."

The little girl looked sad as she said, "They're dead."

"I'm so sorry. It must make you happy to have it to remind you of them. Hmm?"

"Yes, it does," she whispered.

At a loss of what else to say, Amanda asked the next thing that came to mind, "Would you mind running down to let Lady Barla know I'll be ready to meet her in the library in a few minutes?"

"Okay," she pertly replied as she hopped down from the chair, scampered across the room, and out the door leaving Amanda alone.

Remembering she hadn't finished cleaning, Amanda returned the towel to the rack and dunked her head into the cold water. She picked up the bottle of bath liquid and poured it into her hand to give her hair a good wash. After scrubbing her scalp until it tingled, Amanda again dunked her head into the water to rinse it out.

Amanda tugged the stopper from the tub's drain, stood up, and retrieved the towel. Stepping out of the tub into a giant puddle, Amanda scrambled for another towel to sop up the mess before it ruined the flooring. She wrung out the wet towel into the now-empty tub.

Scanning the room, she couldn't find her clothes. The robe appeared to be her only option. She picked it up and put it on. Looking down, she saw a matching pair of slippers on the floor under the chair, so she slipped her feet into them. *These must be made from foxl hair.* She wriggled her toes against the softness, thankful for Barla's thoughtfulness.

She walked across the bathroom to the vanity and picked up the hairbrush on the counter. She watched her reflection as she ran the brush rhythmically through her long, brown hair. *I still look tired.*

After leaving the bathroom and crossing the bedroom, she hesitated at the hall door. She looked back at the room where she'd spend the night. Would her future hold happiness and security such as she felt in this house, or would it bring sorrow and uncertainty like the little girl knew? *I'll just have to take one day at a time and hope for the best.* She opened the door and strode into the hallway, intent on making the best of the present moment.

Amanda found Barla sitting in one of the plush chairs in front of the library's blazing fireplace. Captain Ahn sat opposite her in a matching chair. Amanda smiled at them both as she entered the homey room.

"Grab that chair, Amanda. Enjoy the warmth of the fire with us," Barla instructed as she pointed to another chair a few feet behind her.

Amanda pulled the chair over and sat facing the fire. Only then did she see the child curled up asleep on the floor with her back to the fire. She was the same child she met in the bathroom. "Who is this?" Amanda asked Barla.

"Her name's Corva; she's one of our foster children," Barla replied as she tenderly looked down at the sleeping girl. "She came to us two anons ago after her parents died in a house fire."

"How awful," Amanda replied. "In the bathroom, I complimented her pretty necklace; she told me her parents gave it to her and that they were dead. She seemed pretty sad about it. I hope I didn't upset her."

"I doubt it. Corva was pretty young when it happened. She knows us as her parents now. I think she'd like to remember her real parents more, but as time passes, her few memories fade," Barla assured her promptly.

"Speaking of those necklaces—they're another aspect of Tualan culture you should know. When a child is born, the parents give them a protective crystal pendant to wear at all times. They're all similar to Corva's in size, but the colors can vary greatly."

"How does it protect them?"

Barla leaned over to whisper directly into Amanda's ear, "Parents can see what their children are doing because of their connection with the crystal. The children never know about it until they become parents themselves."

"Really?" Amanda exclaimed, thinking the crystals held more power than she had imagined. "Can they do anything else?"

"Yes, depending on the color," Barla replied. "The darker the color, the more protection it instills, including keeping them from harming themselves or allowing others to harm them."

"Then how do you know what color to give to them?"

"All children are presented to either an Elder or wise-woman usually within the first day of birth, but no later than their seventh day of life. They look into the child's soul through their eyes and are instructed by Jehoban about what color is required. It's a mystery to everyone else how it's done, but they're always right. I believe they read the child's future; the more dangerous it is, the darker the crystal assignment. I may be completely wrong, but that's how it seems to work out."

"You've never said such a thing to me before." Captain Ahn leaned forward, looking intently at Barla as he spoke for the first time since Amanda entered the room.

"Am I to assume your theory isn't common knowledge?" Amanda inquired.

"Definitely not! It's probably because of where I come from; I look at things closer and question more than people from here.

"Think about it, Ahn," Barla continued with her thought, "What colors are the stones of the kids we foster? They're almost always in dark tones, right? Think about our friends' children; they're all in lighter tones. Do you see what I mean?"

"Like you said, as a native Tualan, I've never actually thought about it. But I'll be looking more closely from now on!" He smiled at Barla and relaxed back into his plush chair to shut his eyes and enjoy the fire's warmth.

"There's something else about the stones: they can change colors," Barla continued. "When Corva first came to live with us, she asked me why her stone had changed to blue. At the time, I asked her what color it used to be, and she told me it was always black."

Captain Ahn opened one eye and said, "You never told me that, either."

She dismissively waved her hand at him. "I didn't think you'd believe me. Anyway, I've witnessed our foster children's stones. Their stones would get lighter or darker as they go through adolescence, depending on their friends or activities. Parents would probably do well to watch the color to see if their children should be kept at home more often to stay out of danger."

"Hmph," grunted Captain Ahn, once again closing his eye. His fingers tapped against the arm of his chair.

"Where do the crystals come from then?" Amanda interrupted hurriedly, hoping to forestall an argument.

"Oh, the Elders and the wise-women keep a stock of them. I'm pretty sure they're supplied to them directly from Jehoban. Once the color is determined, they then provide the pendant to the parent and a phrase they should use when they put it on the child; the words differ slightly from child to child depending on what they see in the child's eyes.

"The parents typically hold a crystal donning ceremony in front of all their family and friends. Once the parents place the crystal pendant around the child's neck and say the proper phrase, the necklace cannot be removed until they turn eighteen. When the ceremony ends, everyone celebrates by congratulating the new parents, complimenting the crystals, and then discretely speculating amongst each other on the reasons for the color assigned."

"How interesting," Amanda commented, not knowing what else to say about it.

They sat in contemplative silence for a few minutes. Barla stared without seeing or blinking. Suddenly she shook her head and loudly exhaled as though she had been holding her breath. "Sorry," she apologized, "I lost myself for a moment thinking about the different stones I've encountered in my twenty-two anons on Tuala. Where were we?"

"We just finished talking about the crystal ceremony," Amanda supplied helpfully.

"Oh, yes," she said brusquely. "I was just thinking about how the children change when they receive their birth crystal. The massive amount of elemental energy, which we all call by its shortened term 'elemy,' which surrounds the crystal, matures them more rapidly. I've noticed their motor skills become enhanced along with their abilities to think, reason, and speak.

"Ahn told me this was important for our children so they'd readily understand the concepts of their world in a much safer and more productive manner. Without the crystals, the children would remain at risk of so many more dangers.

"I found this while you were bathing." She reached beside her chair, picked up a hard-cover book, and handed it to Amanda, saying, "This has pictures of the foxl in it." Moving a tray to the table beside Amanda, she added, "I put together a snack for you since you slept through dinner."

Barla stood slowly and stretched, "It's getting late, you two, and we need to get poor little Corva into bed before she scorches her back. Ahn, would you mind carrying her for me? She's getting so big. I can barely hold her anymore."

"I think you say such things simply to stroke my ego, Barla," Ahn exclaimed as he gently lifted the sleeping girl. "She's as light as a feather," he whispered as he straightened and led the way out of the room.

"Goodnight, Amanda," Captain Ahn and Barla said in unison as they left.

Amanda picked up a sandwich triangle to nibble. Should she stay and read by the fire or go back up to her room? She didn't know the household's weekend routine; sleep in, get up early, wait for a bell to come down. Who knew?

Almost as if on cue, Barla reappeared in the doorway and said, "You can stay in here as long as you like. Leave your dishes here once you finish. Also, feel free to look over the books on the shelves to see if anything else catches your eye."

Seeming unable to help herself, Barla rushed back into the room and hugged Amanda. Seeing the dark circles still under her eyes, Barla took Amanda's chin in her hand and spoke seriously, "I want you to sleep as late as you can tomorrow. You need the rest. Don't worry about breakfast; everyone eats as they get hungry on Sabtu. Nothing formal. Okay?"

Once again, Amanda felt as if she were with her mother. She smiled and replied, "Yes, Barla. I'll probably sleep the entire day on such a wonderful, plush mattress."

Barla's smile mirrored Amanda's as she patted her cheek. "Good girl. I'll see you tomorrow."

Amanda already missed Barla's company but decided to stay by the fire's warmth to give her hair a chance to dry. She finished the sandwich while she looked through the book of animals. More than once, she chuckled at the different names the Tualans had given to the same creatures found on Earth. Ordinary house cats, for example, were called kittilees.

She agreed with Barla's description of the foxl. It had fur about five inches long, straight when dry, curly when wet. The foxl's head was more like a sheep than a cow, but the body size and shape looked more bovine.

The fire's heat seeped into Amanda, causing her to yawn repeatedly. Instead of looking for more reading material, Amanda opted to take the animal book with her as she made her way up to bed.

Once back in her room, she let her robe slide to the floor. She slipped her naked body between the silky sheets and rested her head on the perfect pillow. The luxury of it all made her sigh with pleasure before she became oblivious to everything as she immediately fell into a relaxed and peaceful sleep.

After what felt like only a moment, an odd sensation stirred Amanda's awareness. An intense light shined directly in her eyes, and warmth spread across the side of her face. Because her mind didn't want to make any sense of it, she rolled away from the troubling light.

Wait! This bed wasn't her cot. Her hand swept along the soft, silky sheets covering the plush mattress. Definitely not the cot. Her eyes popped open to verify she wasn't dreaming. Several seconds passed before her sleep-muddled brain remembered this was Captain Ahn and Barla's guest room.

At first, she felt guilty about sleeping so late, but then she recalled Barla's orders to sleep until she felt fully rested. Trying to determine her fatigue level, she decided a bathroom break would be in order.

She reluctantly slid from the warmth of the bed to cross the room. Sunlight filled the bathroom, dazzling her vision with its brightness. She washed and rushed back to the warm bedding.

She snuggled into the covers with her body in the fetal position. With her eyes clenched, she wanted to return to her blissful sleep, but it proved elusive. After several minutes she sat up with her back cushioned by pillows against the headboard. She picked up the book on animals from the night table.

Neal would love to learn about this. Her heart hurt just thinking about what might have happened with him. Was he safe? Was he worried about her? What would they say to one another when they were finally reunited?

CHAPTER 18

Amanda spent quite a bit more time studying the book than she did in the library the night before. The more she found out about Tuala, the better the likelihood she'd pass for a native Tualan, the faster she would be able to find Neal and then find a way to get home. *Get home, get home,* repeated as a regular mantra in her head.

Studying the material provided the needed stimulus to return to sleep. Returning the book to the table, she tugged the covers over her shoulders as she lay on her side, facing away from the sun-drenched windows. In no time at all, she drifted back into pleasant dreams.

When she awoke again, the light changed in the room since the sunlight no longer came directly through the window. "It must be close to noon," Amanda whispered to herself as she pushed back the covers and sat on the edge of the mattress.

Her gaze scanned the room, but she couldn't find her personal items. As she thrust her arms into the plush robe she retrieved from the floor, she luxuriated in its warmth and softness. She didn't miss her clothes, but she should find something more suitable to wear.

With the fuzzy foxl slippers covering her feet, Amanda walked down the stairs and across the foyer, making her way back to the kitchen. In no hurry, she took more time appreciating the pictures adorning the walls. She stopped to admire a family portrait of Captain Ahn, Barla, a young boy who looked so much like Ahn he could only be his son, and a blonde-haired little girl with Barla's features stamped on her round face.

Surprised, Amanda stepped closer to the portrait to pick out all of the little girl's features. She shifted her position from side to side to catch different angles in which to view her. The hair on the back of her neck rose as Amanda realized the little girl reminded her so much of herself at the same age that it was unnerving.

Just then, Barla walked out of the formal sitting room and noticed Amanda's interest in the portrait. She came to stand next to her and said, "These are my two children, Gravin and Rasa. When we had this taken, Gravin was six, and Rasa was just four anons old."

Amanda stiffly nodded as she continued to stare at little Rasa.

"Are you okay?" Barla asked as Amanda failed to respond to her casual conversation.

"I just can't believe this picture."

"What do you mean?"

"This little girl, Rasa, looks just exactly like I did at that same age," Amanda spoke quietly. "She and I could be twins."

"How interesting," Barla commented as she looked closer at the portrait and then at Amanda to compare. "It's too bad you don't have any childhood pictures of yourself to really be able to put them side by side."

"How old are your children now?"

"They're twenty-one and nineteen anons old."

"Do they still live here?"

"No, Gravin's in his last anon of post-study over on Reesun. Do you remember where Reesun's located?" Barla asked, suddenly turning this into an impromptu geography lesson.

Amanda paused, her brow creased, and she bit her bottom lip, then answered with some uncertainty, "Cuba, right?"

"Very good," Barla replied, beaming with delight at her newest student's success.

"What about Rasa? Is she here or still in school as well?"

"No, Rasa's not here, but she's not in school either. Almost three anons after we took this picture, an administrator from Jehoban came to us and asked if Jehoban, Himself, could teach our daughter. With such a great honor, we could hardly refuse," Barla replied.

"You mean you let them take your daughter from you?" Amanda's shock finally broke her intense study of the portrait to stare at Barla in astonishment.

"Oh, no! It's not like that at all. Our whole family was offered the opportunity to go along with her, but Ahn couldn't very well leave his post, and I had all of the orphaned children to look after as well. We talk with her all of the time, and, remember, I can keep track of her through her necklace as well. Rasa's an amazing girl. She begged us to let her go, and she has accomplished so much since she went. We're very proud of her.

"I must admit, I did miss seeing her grow up and mature. I can only imagine what a handful she would've been when she became a teenager," Barla spoke sadly.

"Does this kind of thing happen very often?"

"No, it's infrequent anymore; only one or two children are chosen in a declan to be taught by Jehoban," Barla spoke with pride.

"Where does Jehoban live? Have you ever visited her?"

"Jehoban lives on Acaim, Jamaica as you know it, and visiting isn't allowed. She'll come home to see us when she feels her studying is complete," Barla spoke quickly, as though she were trying to convince herself it might be soon.

"Are you saying you haven't seen her in person since she was six years old? That's been thirteen years!" Amanda exclaimed in amazement.

"What she's doing is much more important than my desire to see her!" Barla admonished. "And, as I said, she'll come home when her education is complete."

Clearly, they had reached the end of this conversation, and Amanda felt uncomfortable enough to want to change the subject. Clearing her throat, she asked, "I was wondering if you knew what happened to my clothes? I hope it isn't considered indecent for me to be running around in nothing but this robe."

"Oh, don't worry about the robe; we're the only ones at home right now. Yesterday I sent my maid to the seamstress with the measurements I took from your clothes to make a new wardrobe. Ahn and I noticed you only had the two outfits to wear. They don't exactly blend in with the Tualan fashions, as you may have seen when we were in the market yesterday," Barla offhandedly replied as she turned and walked toward the kitchen.

Amanda followed Barla's lead and hoped she could get some lunch. They walked into the kitchen, and Barla gestured for Amanda to seat herself on the stool at the island. "What would you like to eat?"

"You don't have to serve me," Amanda hurriedly replied as she jumped up from the stool, fully expecting to make the meal herself.

"Don't be silly, Amanda. You don't know anything about this kitchen, and you're my guest! Now sit down and tell me what sounds good!" Barla pertly replied as she pointed back to the stool and tried to keep a stern expression on her face even though her mouth twitched with restrained mirth.

Amanda raised her hands in surrender as she moved back

around the island. "What kinds of things do you have that I might recognize?"

"Would you like breakfast or lunch?" Barla asked as she mentally reviewed the various items available in the cooler.

She considered for a second and then replied, "Lunch sounds wonderful right now."

"How about a sandwich and chips?"

"Perfect," Amanda replied, then hesitantly asked, "Can you make it without pork? I don't eat it for religious reasons."

"No problem. I don't either," Barla said as she gathered sandwich supplies. "Do you like tomatoes on your sandwich?" She held up a plump, red tomato.

"I love tomatoes. Do they taste as good as they look?"

"Oh, just wait!" Barla replied with a wink. "You won't believe how much better the fruits and vegetables taste on Tuala. Since they're grown aquaponically, they actually have flavor!"

Amanda closed her eyes to remember what she had read about Tualan aquaponics. "That's where they use fish to fertilize the water in which the plants are grown, right?"

"Exactly, Amanda. You've learned a lot in the past few days." Barla smiled smugly.

"Why don't they grow food like this on Earth?"

"I imagine they would if they realized how much healthier it is. Not only is it more nutritious, but it's also guaranteed organic since any traditional chemicals used on the plants would kill the fish."

Barla worked efficiently and quickly. Each time she questioned whether or not Amanda would like something added to the sandwich, she held it up and raised her eyebrows in question; Amanda would nod or shake her head to answer.

In just a few short minutes, Barla had the sandwich prepared and on a plate. She rummaged in a cupboard until she found the bag she wanted and turned around, holding it in front of her as if it were a prize.

"These," she excitedly said, "are my absolute favorite chips. They're a little different than you're probably used to, but they are amazing." She tipped the bag over the edge of the plate and poured out a generous helping of the bright red chips. She picked up the finished dish and placed it in front of Amanda with a flourish.

"Thank you, Barla," Amanda said. She bowed her head to pray. When she finished, she picked up the strange-looking chip before turning it over to look at both sides, smell it, and then take a tentative nibble. Flavors burst through her taste buds, and she instantly craved more. She popped the entire chip into her mouth and smiled as she hummed, "Mmm-hmm."

"They're wonderful, huh?"

Amanda swallowed and replied, "Yes, but what are they? I thought I knew, but then another flavor came at the end, which threw me for a loop."

"They're called tocolas. They're a corn-based chip, colored and flavored with tomato juice, and the flavor at the end is the lime juice and salt." She sat with a smug look as she reached into the still-open bag and started munching on them.

Not wanting to appear rude, Amanda forewent the desire to have another chip to sample the sandwich. Unsure whether the sandwich was seasoned with hunger or just the most amazing ever, she found the flavors intensely appealing.

"I feel like I've never tasted food before!" Amanda commented to Barla as she took another bite.

"As I said, the food on Tuala actually has flavor. Here, let's try an experiment," she turned swiftly and grabbed one of the cucumbers from the bushel Amanda purchased the day before. She held it up and asked, "Do you like cucumbers?"

Amanda could only nod since she had just taken another large bite of sandwich.

Barla smiled and sliced off a couple of sections. She picked up one and handed it across the island for Amanda to sample.

Amanda swallowed her bite of the sandwich at the same time as she took the proffered cucumber. She bit into it and chewed. "Oh my," she said, "I just can't believe how wonderful this tastes! It's amazing! I feel like I keep repeating myself, but there just isn't a strong enough word to describe it."

"Want more? I can cut up the rest for you."

"Gladly!"

No sooner did Amanda accept the cucumbers, there was a pounding on the front door. Immediately, Amanda's eyes grew wide. "Are you expecting someone?"

"No. I'm sure it's nothing. Just stay in here, and I'll get rid of whoever that is." Barla brushed her hands down the front of her tunic, nodding at Amanda as she passed.

Amanda turned in her seat to follow her progress. As much as Barla wanted to reassure her, Amanda didn't feel safe. As quietly as she could, she left her chair and stalked the kitchen, searching for a spot large enough for her to hide.

Barla's voice rose in alarm.

Almost desperate, Amanda flung open the cupboard under the kitchen sink. She crammed herself inside, pulling the door shut behind her and arranging a few larger items in front of her.

"We've been instructed to search the premises, Barla. I'm sure you understand that we have to follow orders. Who was here eating?" A man's voice asked only a few feet from where Amanda held her breath.

"I was having a late lunch," Barla answered, her voice tinged with sarcasm and a little fear.

"The upstairs is clear," another man's voice said. "There was a bedroom with an unmade bed."

The first man asked, "Who was sleeping there, Barla?"

"Oh, honestly. Do you realize how many orphans we have here

every night? Do you expect me to know who slept in which room?"

A third man's voice said, "Give it a rest, Guerin. We've finished our search."

Guerin wasn't finished. "Where are all of your supposed orphans, Barla? Where's your staff?"

"My staff has the day off, and the kids are spending the afternoon with their friends. This was *supposed* to be my quiet day for relaxation. Are you done interrupting my afternoon meal?"

"We haven't checked everything here in the kitchen," Guerin stubbornly replied.

"It's not like I shoved somebody under the kitchen sink," Barla said. "Feel free, knock your socks off. Look in the flour jar if that makes you feel better. But just know that I'll be talking to Captain Ahn about this intrusion—and on Sabtu, no less. Have you no shame?"

At Barla's mention of her hiding spot, Amanda scrunched her eyes shut, and she held her breath. Hugging her knees hard against her chest and willing herself to disappear, she didn't flinch when she heard each cabinet slam shut. *Don't look, don't look. I'm not here; there's nothing here.*

The wood shook, and a breeze brushed against Amanda's face as her cabinet opened and banged shut again. "There's nothing here, Guerin," the third man said.

"Fine. Let's head out and file our report," Guerin said, his voice practically dripping with disappointment. His feet stomped against the floor as he left the kitchen and went down the hallway to the front door.

"I'm really sorry about all of this, Barla," the second man said.

"Yeah," the third man chimed in. "Guerin has it out for the Captain. We tried to get this canceled or postponed until tomorrow, but Guerin insisted we should come today."

"C'mon, Tren. Guerin'll wonder what's taking us so long," the second man said.

"I'll walk you out," Barla said. A few minutes later, Barla returned to the kitchen. "Amanda? Are you in here? It's safe to come out now."

Even with Barla's assurance, Amanda couldn't move. Her body remained frozen with fear. Tears rushed down her cheeks only to absorb into the soft fabric of her robe. She couldn't stay here with Barla and Captain Ahn. Just thinking about leaving brought another wracking sob.

The cabinet door opened, and Amanda flinched. "Hey, Amanda, it's okay." Barla's hand touched Amanda's shoulder. "Have you been here this whole time?"

Amanda didn't move other than to nod her head. "What if they come back? It's not safe for me here. I can't get you guys in trouble any more than I already have. I have to leave, Barla." Her chin trembled, and more tears escaped from her lashes.

"Oh, stuff and nonsense, Amanda. Come out here at once." Her fingers curled around Amanda's arm and began tugging on her to get moving.

With more trouble than she had getting in, Amanda knocked over several items as she exited the cupboard. She kept her arms crossed over her middle, wishing she could be home, safe and away from all of these problems. "That's something my grandma used to say," she managed.

"Mine, too," Barla said, still holding Amanda's arm and leading her back to the seat at the kitchen island. "Relax here for a few minutes, and then you can finish your meal."

Amanda did as she was bid, although food was the last thing on her mind. She stared at the mostly empty plate, her mind replaying the last few minutes of the search.

Barla cleared her throat. "Amanda, where were you hiding when they were searching for you?"

"What do you mean? You saw where I was hiding." Amanda and Barla stared at one another, each trying to understand the other.

"But I saw them look inside there. You weren't there."

"Yes, I was."

Barla tipped her head, and she hummed softly. "It appears you might have a little magic of your own, Amanda. Or Jehoban stepped in to help you. Either way, I'd say you're quite blessed."

Amanda snorted. "Considering I'm hiding out in an alternate dimension, I'd hardly say I'm blessed. Barla, how am I going to get out of here?"

"What do you mean? Here is the safest place you could possibly be. They've already searched here; they won't be back."

"But that Guerin guy—," Amanda started, pointing toward the front door.

"He's a jerk who's held a grudge against Ahn ever since he got elected. Guerin was running against him and is a sore loser. Now, don't waste another minute thinking about him. We can discuss this matter with Ahn when he gets home. Until then, I don't want you to think about leaving."

"But, just by my staying puts Captain Ahn's job at risk."

Barla slapped her hand onto the counter.

Amanda flinched and stared at Barla's hand.

"Listen, Jehoban knows all and sees all. If He wanted you found, then those men would have discovered you. But they didn't. That tells me that Jehoban has other plans for you. Until you can prove otherwise, you'll have to trust me on this."

After cleaning up their lunch mess, they retired to the library to resume Amanda's education on Tualan culture. Barla introduced books by popular authors, others on childhood education, and still more on games.

"I don't expect you to learn about all of these things because I don't think you'll be in Tuala very long, but it's fun to see what's important to Tualans. Don't you think?"

With a hopeful expression, Amanda looked over the edge of the book she held to ask, "Do you really think I'll be going home soon?"

Barla leaned forward and touched Amanda's arm to add strength to her words. "Yes, I do."

Amanda closed her eyes and sighed, letting hope flow through her like a tonic.

"I was wondering," Barla began and then paused.

Amanda opened her eyes and saw Barla struggling with some inner conflict and prompted, "Yes?"

"When you go back to Earth, could you please let my family know I'm okay?"

"Absolutely! It would be the least I could do to repay you, Barla. How could you think I'd refuse?" Amanda admonished gently.

"Well, you do realize it'll be tough to convince my family. This whole realm would be difficult to explain to anyone, but I've been gone so long they may not take it very well if you know what I mean."

"I can handle it," Amanda assured her.

"There's another difficulty as well," Barla began, "something I haven't told you about yet." She didn't continue but seemed to be gathering her thoughts.

"What is it?"

"I've heard—but I don't know if it's true—when Jehoban created the barrier which separates the two realms, He made it so the people from Earth wouldn't remember their time here. Because of it, I couldn't risk going back to Earth since I have my husband and children here. I can't chance not remembering anything about them."

"So," Amanda began slowly, "how will I remember to tell your family about you if I won't remember my time here?"

"I think if I wrote down everything for you in a letter, maybe it would bring it all back. I can't be sure it'll work, but I think it'd be worth a try. Don't you?"

"Sure. Why not?" Amanda agreed.

"You'll have to keep the letter with you at all times because you won't know if you'll have any advance warning when your opportunity arises to go back."

"I can't see where that'd be a problem either," Amanda assured her again. "Do you want to tell me about your family?"

"I'd rather not," Barla replied rapidly. "I get pretty emotional when I think about them. It's been so long since I've seen them, I wouldn't know what to tell you about them anyway," she finished lamely.

"It's okay. The letter will be fine," Amanda said as she picked up the book on poetry from her lap and pretended to be interested in the passages on a random page.

They spent the next few minutes in companionable silence. Amanda scanned through the different books she had pulled from the shelves while Barla stared into the fire and contemplated what to include in the letter to her family. They both jumped when a log shifted in the fireplace and sent sparks flying with a loud crack. The tension left the room as they both laughed.

After a couple more hours of reading, analyzing, and discussing various Tualan customs, Amanda retired to her room to take another bubble bath. Unsure when she'd have another opportunity, she wanted to experience the total relaxation that only the warm water could provide.

Amanda dragged herself from the tub over to the bed with her muscles warm and limp from the hour-long soak. She pulled the covers up under her chin as she relaxed onto her side, facing away from the windows. Her last conscious thought was how cheerfully the birds chirped outside of her window. If only she could be as content and carefree as those birds, able to fly away home.

· · ·

ELDER DEBBON'S hands flew away from Amanda, and he stared with dumbfounded fascination at the sleeping girl. He almost lost his connection when he felt her flowing power at her memory of nearly being apprehended.

Where did she learn to use elemy? Who was she to have Jehoban's protection? And more importantly, who ordered the search?

The room seemed lit with another kind of light when Amanda's eyes fluttered open. What disturbed her sleep enough to bring her to full awareness? Then, more shuffling came from the other end of her room.

Were the guards back to get her? She froze, trying to think herself small. Her heart hammered against her ribs, and she couldn't seem to draw any air into her lungs. She didn't have anywhere to hide this time except under her sheets.

"Oh, this's going to be fun," Barla murmured from across the room.

If that were Barla, then Amanda didn't have to worry. Relief erased her panic as fast as an ocean wave washed away footprints in the sand. Sitting up on the bed, she held the sheets to cover her naked torso and saw Barla arranging various packages on the now-darkened window seats.

"What's going on, Barla?" she asked.

"Oh good, you're awake," she excitedly exclaimed while whirling around to smile at her guest. "Come and see your new clothes." She gestured impatiently for Amanda to leave the bed and inspect her booty.

"Where's my robe?" Amanda asked as she prepared to get out of the bed but couldn't find anything to cover her nakedness.

"Don't bother," Barla replied. "You'd have to take it off to try these on. Don't be shy; I've seen women's bodies before. I have one, too, you know!"

Feeling foolish and self-conscious, she got out of bed and crossed her arms over her chest while she walked over to where Barla pulled garments out of paper boxes. Kneeling on the floor, she soon abandoned her modesty in favor of touching various fabrics to see if they felt as lovely as they looked. Amanda picked up one dress from the selection and held it in front of herself while trying to envision it on her.

Noticing her interest in the dress, Barla directed, "Try it on."

Enthusiastically, Amanda nodded and started to unbutton the front of the dress.

"Oh, just a minute," Barla interrupted as she hastily rummaged through another bag until she pulled out a pair of garments and held them up proudly. "You'll need these first to wear underneath."

Amanda took the undergarments and donned them swiftly, wishing Barla had offered them sooner. With new vigor, she finished unbuttoning the dress, stepped into the skirt, inserted her arms into the long sleeves, and began to button it back up. The fit was perfect; the color and cut were also equally excellent. Amanda twirled and smiled as Barla looked on with happiness.

"It's perfect!" Amanda squealed and rushed forward to hug Barla.

"I knew it would be," Barla replied cheerfully. "Here, try these on as well." She handed Amanda a shirt and a pair of pants. "Pants can be kind of tricky, and I want to make sure they got the fit right."

Amanda stripped off the dress and donned the other outfit.

Again, a perfect fit. She went through the rest of the clothes with equal success. Everything was perfect, including the colors. "After trying all of these wonderful things on, I don't care if I ever see my other two outfits again. I was getting thoroughly sick of them, I must say!"

Barla laughed out loud and said, "We could have a ritual burning of them if it'd make you happy!"

"No, I don't think that'll be necessary, but these new clothes really are appreciated," Amanda replied while suppressing a childish giggle. Then a sobering thought struck her, and she asked, "What am I supposed to do with all of these clothes when I go back to Earth? I won't be able to wear them when I return, and it seems a waste for you to give them to me only to have me leave them behind."

"So practical," Barla clucked her tongue at Amanda and continued, "and here I was having so much fun!" She shook her head, then said, "I thought about that as well. When you're done working down at the dock and you leave with Bryon, I'll let him know if anything should happen to you, your clothes should be given to his wife if they'll fit, or to charity if not. Will that suit your sensibility?"

Amanda instantly stilled, her festive mood shedding off of her like rain on the window. "So you've made the travel arrangements for me?"

"Yes, dear, I have. Bryon's an old friend of mine, and he has business in these parts in the middle of this next week. When he leaves, you'll be going with him. He lives further inland and doesn't have much to do with the people around here, so you'll be safer from Petre and the Elders where Bryon resides."

"Plus, it'll make things safer for Captain Ahn and yourself. What came of the surprise inspection at the office?" Amanda suddenly realized she had never heard anything more about the Elder's *old soul* inquiry.

"Oh, Ceren handled everything perfectly. He explained how we hired an orphan to come in temporarily to get us prepared for the audit. It's pretty common knowledge how Ahn hates the paperwork. It also explained the cot as well as the schoolbooks left in the office." Barla's radiant expression clearly showed her love for Ceren.

Sighing with relief, Amanda's mind raced with her ever-present worry. "But what about finding Neal and *The Golden Jesisca*?" Amanda practically pleaded as she realized how soon she'd leave, and with all of her might, wished she could stay longer with Barla.

"Don't worry, Amanda, we'll continue the search and forward anything we find to Bryon's house. You'll know everything we do almost instantaneously," she reassured Amanda by reaching out and grasping her forearm gently to reinforce her words. "And remember, I'll have the letter for you to deliver to my family, so I'll be just as anxious about getting you back to Earth as you are!" She warmly smiled but then pulled Amanda in for a tight hug.

Amanda's arms automatically reached around Barla to return the embrace. They stood holding one another for reassurance as much as comfort for at least a minute until Barla pulled away.

"Now," Barla said as she rearranged the clothes on the seat. Patting the stack, she said, "I think these outfits will work best for the office, don't you?" As if the tender moments before hadn't happened, Barla was all about business and practicality.

"Do you think it's safe for me to go back there?" Amanda worried, but she also felt obligated to finish her assignment to help repay the captain's generosity.

"Absolutely. It's probably the safest place for you now. Are you okay with that?"

Amanda struggled to collect her emotions but managed to nod. As much as she feared getting arrested, a part of her wanted the opportunity to speak with one of the Elders. They might be her best chance for returning to her world. But, knowing Barla's opinion of the ruling class, she didn't dare voice her thoughts.

Instead, she asked, "On what occasions would I wear these nicer clothes?" Her fingers ran along the delicate stitches of a beautifully crafted tunic.

Barla eagerly answered, "Tualans find a lot of reasons to get together socially: dinners, crystal ceremonies, dances, and the like. You won't have any problem on that account, don't worry."

Amanda couldn't imagine being as social as Barla. Maybe her solitary experiences since coming to Tuala impacted her more than she imagined. Before her time here, she liked large crowds and meeting new people. Likewise, she never had any problem fitting in with a group.

Shrugging, Amanda imagined everything Barla explained and said, "I'll have to trust you on that! I can't thank you enough for this unexpected bounty of clothing. It's almost like getting a birthday present!"

"When's your birthday?" Barla asked curiously.

"It's next month on the twenty-eighth," Amanda replied, then asked, "Why?"

Clapping her hands together gleefully much as a child would do, she exclaimed, "That's perfect! We'll call this an early birthday present!" Barla's pleased smile turned into a laugh as she heard Amanda's stomach growl loudly. "It seems all of this excitement has made you hungry. Do you want to wear one of your new dresses down to dinner?"

"Definitely," Amanda agreed as she picked up the first dress she tried on, excited for an opportunity to wear it in public. *Well, in front of Captain Ahn's family.*

As she entered the room, Captain Ahn complimented Amanda's new outfit. They sat in the kitchen around the island instead of the formal dining room due to the late hour, and only the three ate.

"I'm sorry to delay your dinner for so long."

"Don't be silly," Barla admonished, waving her hand dismissively. "You needed your sleep, and I needed the extra time to have all of your outfits completed by the seamstress."

Barla made it all sound so commonplace, but Amanda knew they made special dispensations for her.

"Where's Corva?" Amanda asked.

Barla smiled and answered, "Oh, she's staying over at the neighbor's house for the night."

"What about the other four kids you said lived here with you? I haven't seen anyone except Corva the entire time I've been here."

"I made arrangements for them to have a campout with some friends of mine. You should've seen their excitement for the adventure, but Corva's just a bit too young to go. Likewise, I gave the household staff the weekend off."

"You sure went to a lot of trouble just so I could spend a couple of nights here," Amanda said quietly and looked down at the counter.

"It wasn't any bother at all. As I said, everyone is having a good time this weekend. Call it a win-win situation all the way around. I've enjoyed spending time with you and talking about Earth. It's been forever since I could speak freely and have someone understand what I was talking about!" Barla turned and patted her husband's hand and said, "No offense, honey."

"None taken, my love. Let's eat, shall we?" Ahn announced with a broad smile.

"I wouldn't want to keep my man from his food!" Barla laughed and began serving the dishes.

Dinner consisted of roasted foxl served with foxl gravy and krumpli, a mashed tuber, much like a potato. It was a simple dinner, but filling and flavorful. They ate mostly in silence until the forks scraped empty plates.

"Barla tells me you're going to be leaving mid-week," Captain

Ahn cut right to the chase. "Do you think the shipping records will be updated before then?"

"I believe so, as long as I can work on it tomorrow as well," she rapidly assured him.

Barla scowled at Ahn then spoke to Amanda, "Don't let him pressure you, Amanda. Just work at your own pace, and whatever doesn't get done, my disorganized husband can enter himself!"

Ahn grunted but smiled at Barla as he said, "Or I might persuade my pushy wife to help out."

"Don't count on it, mister," she replied sarcastically. She turned back to Amanda with her eyebrows drawing down as she said, "I'm serious, Amanda. I don't want you to overexert yourself trying to get it all finished. Just do your best. I can complete anything that still needs to get done. I've had lots of experience at it!" She rolled her eyes back toward her husband and pursed her lips.

Amanda smiled and said, "I don't think that'll be necessary. At the rate I've been going, I should have it done in time. You saw the office yesterday, Barla. Didn't it look like I had it well in hand?"

"Yes, dear, your progress has been nothing short of miraculous. I believe you'll finish, but please promise me you won't burn the midnight oil just to make us proud."

Amanda looked down at her folded hands, abashed because that was precisely what she had planned. She nodded as she looked up at Barla and said, "I promise."

"Well," Ahn spoke into the awkward silence, "since that's settled, we should retire to the library for an after-dinner drink. I'd like to hear what progress you've made in learning about Tuala."

With warm tea in delicate cups, they sat in front of the fire and talked. Captain Ahn's curiosity about Earth led to Amanda describing her family, friends, and hobbies to a captivated audience. The more she spoke of Earth, the more homesick Amanda became. Not having to feign fatigue, Amanda set her empty cup on the coffee table and said, "It's getting late. I think I'll head up to bed now."

"Goodnight, Amanda." Barla gave her a brief hug. Holding her at arm's length, she added, "Don't bother getting up early, either. We won't be getting out of the house until after lunch. Okay?"

Amanda kept her face neutral and answered, "Yes, Barla." Unable to withhold her smile, she grinned over at her hosts, where Barla had resumed her place beside Ahn on the loveseat and said, "Goodnight." She left the room and headed off to spend her last night in the luxurious bed.

Amanda slept later than she intended and had just enough time to take a short bath. She dressed in one of her new work outfits and went downstairs to see if her tardiness had kept the others from eating. She was early, but not by much.

Barla and Ahn, busy preparing lunch, gestured for Amanda to seat herself at the island while they finished the provisions.

Amanda didn't see or hear anyone else in the house on her way through to the kitchen, so she asked, "Where's Corva?"

"We'll pick her up from the neighbor's house on our way back from the office," Barla replied cheerfully. "We think the fewer people who see you, the less likely Petre or the Elders will know where to look for you. Don't you think?"

"Definitely," Amanda agreed and then frowned. "So, what are the chances of Petre coming after me?"

Captain Ahn looked up from watching the skillet he tended and replied, "One hundred percent. He's already been asking questions a couple of gania south of here. I heard from some of my friends that he's looking for a woman named Jesisca."

"Has anyone told him about me?" Amanda's fingers curled up until her fists turned white. She was never going back with him, not alive.

"I highly doubt it. Not many people would tell him the truth in any event. He doesn't have an outstanding reputation around here," Ahn reassured her.

"Well," Barla commented, "I guess it's a good thing the arrangements for Amanda to leave so early worked out the way they did, then, huh?"

"To be sure, Barla," Ahn replied. "I'll hate to see you leave so soon, but I'll sleep better knowing you're safely out of Petre's reach. Now, who's ready to eat?"

They ate grilled cheese sandwiches and more of Barla's tocola chips as they discussed the arrangements for getting Amanda safely back to the office unseen. Barla decided Amanda should wear a couple of her outfits under the shapeless garment Amanda originally wore to the marketplace.

With the concealing hood, she could walk through the streets and into the harbor office without anyone identifying her. Barla told her she'd bring the rest of her things the next day in a duffle bag she could also use for traveling once Bryon arrived.

With all the plans set, Amanda returned to her room one last time. With much sadness, Amanda walked around her room, touching the window casing, one of the four posters on the bed, wandered through the bathroom, letting her fingers trail over the vanity and the items resting on it. She wanted to memorize every detail. With an unknown future alongside a stranger named Bryon, she mentally prepared herself for the next part of her adventure. She was ready.

CHAPTER 20

Amanda donned the shapeless garment and pulled up the hood to cover her hair. Checking her disguise in the bathroom mirror, she smiled at her reflection. Even though she was leaving the house's luxury, she imagined herself taking one step closer to going back home to Earth.

Barla met her at the bottom of the stairs in the foyer. She smiled at Amanda and offered her arm as she stepped toward the front entrance. "Are you ready?"

"As ready as I'll ever be," Amanda said with forced cheer. Knowing Petre lurked somewhere in town looking for her made her stomach clench with nerves. She didn't know how she'd react if she saw him even though she wore a disguise. As if that weren't bad enough, now she knew the Elders would be watching Barla and Ahn's every move.

"Everything will be fine," Barla spoke easily, leaning toward Amanda and squeezing her arm closer to her side. "We'll get you back to your room at the office, and you can stay tucked away until Bryon comes. We'll have the two of you leave town after nightfall, just in case, though."

"That sounds good," Amanda replied as they left the house's safety and walked down the crushed shell walkway. "Where will we go?"

"Oh, I think you should ask Bryon once you're well on your way. Sometimes I think even the walls have ears around here," Barla replied too casually as she turned to the left and led them down the wide street toward the harbor.

Once they reached the office, they walked straight to the back as planned. Luck was on their side; the office was empty of everyone except Ceren, so they didn't have to pretend to be other than they were. As soon as they made it inside her private room, Amanda removed the shapeless garment and held it out for Barla.

Barla shook her head and said, "Keep it. You'll need to wear it again when you leave."

Amanda nodded, folded it neatly, and set it at the end of her cot. She looked around the room and realized just how abysmal it looked compared to the last two nights' luxurious accommodations. However, the setting's familiarity did offer a measure of security.

"I'll have Ahn bring dinner down here tonight," Barla said to fill the silence that entered the room with them.

"Okay," Amanda replied as she slowly sat on the cot.

"I guess I'll leave you to your work then. I'll come by tomorrow morning with the rest of your things," she said as she turned to leave.

"You're right; I do need to get back to work. Thank you for the wonderful weekend, Barla." Amanda smiled and stood to watch one of her only friends close the door, leaving her alone in the office.

She sighed as she looked at the stacks of invoices and bills of lading around the perimeter of the room. When she first arrived, the paperwork filled the room until only trails remained. At least she had made significant headway. With the rhythm already established, she felt confident she'd have everything entered into the patil in time. However, with almost four days left to work, she decided to finish one wall's worth of papers per day. Picking up the first stack, she sat in front of the patil.

Amanda kept up with her work schedule, interrupted only by meals and Barla dropping off her newly made clothes. She started work early and ended late each day, but she'd finish as planned because it was as important to her as finding Neal and going home.

She finished! Sitting on the cot, leaning her back against the wall, Amanda looked around the paperless room and smiled at her accomplishment. Captain Ahn should bring dinner shortly, and she wanted to see his expression as he entered the room.

Unexpectedly, several voices conversed outside the office door. Should she try to hide under the covers of her bed or hope they'd go past the office door? When the door started to open, Amanda looked around rapidly to assess her options; she almost dived under the desk until she recognized Captain Ahn walking into the room first.

His smile reassured Amanda as he entered the small room, followed by another man, and, lastly, Barla came in and closed the door behind her. Immediately, Amanda was struck silent by the similarities between this new man and Neal. While he was significantly taller, his build and coloring were the same. They even had the same short, brown, spiked hair.

Barla stepped forward and addressed the stranger, "Bryon Kesh, I'd like you to meet my friend, Amanda." She gestured toward Amanda, then turned to Amanda and said, "Amanda, this is Bryon." Barla smiled and stepped back.

Bryon swiftly crossed the room at the same time that Amanda came out from behind the desk. They shook hands and said in unison, "Nice to meet you," and then smiled together as well.

Barla stepped forward into the momentary silence and said,

"We brought food for dinner." She held up a large basket and deposited it onto the desk. First, she noticed the clear desktop, but then she comically twirled in a circle before she gasped. "Did you finish?"

Amanda proudly beamed as she answered, "I did!"

"Well done, Amanda," Captain Ahn praised her and smiled while looking around the room. "I knew you could do it."

"I must say, I'm thankful I won't have to come down here to bail you out again this anon," Barla teased Captain Ahn.

"You only do it so you'll have the bonus money to go shopping after the audit is complete, Barla. Don't try to pretend you do it to help me!" Captain Ahn bantered back.

"Let's eat dinner," Barla replied suddenly, as she tipped her head down to hide her grin. Rummaging around the basket, she pulled out four plates and handed them around to each person. She set up a buffet on the empty desktop and gestured for Bryon and Amanda to go first.

After everyone filled their plates, three sat on the cot while Bryon took the desk chair facing them. They made small talk while eating the foxl stew, corn on the cob, krumpli salad, and garlic bread.

"I brought my letter for you, Amanda," Barla said quietly to Amanda as Captain Ahn and Bryon discussed the new shipping fees. Barla reached into the deep pocket of her tunic, and she pressed it into Amanda's hand. "I wrote the events of your time here as you've told me, so you'll be able to explain where you've been. I also wrote the last memories of my family, including their names and the last places where they worked and lived. They may not be there anymore since it's been twenty-two years. For all I know, they may not even be alive anymore, but it's all I have."

"It'll be enough," Amanda assured her as she discreetly took the letter and slid it into the side pocket of her duffle bag under the cot.

"When you change clothes to leave tonight, remember to put the letter in your pocket so you'll always have it on your person, okay?" Barla insisted with an almost desperate plea.

"Don't worry, Barla. I promise you when I get back; your letter will be with me!"

Barla nodded as her eyes misted. She hugged Amanda and whispered, "As much as I want you to find your way home, I'll miss you. I've come to think of you like my other daughter," she confessed.

"I've felt it," Amanda replied and added sincerely. "You've been like a second mother to me, and I love you for it."

"Do you know what makes this so hard for me?" Barla asked suddenly.

"No, what?"

"It's just I'll be saying goodbye to you forever. I'll never know how you spend the rest of your life, if you get married, or if you have children. This'll be our end, and for that, I'm sad."

"This may be goodbye, but I'll still be alive. You know I'm marrying Neal, so there's something you won't have to worry about. I'm sure we'll have children, but how many, I can't say for sure." Of course, she'd have to find Neal, but she kept her thoughts positive. She smiled at Barla and thought about what else to tell her. "I won't be alone either; I'll have my parents and my two older sisters, too."

"Those thoughts do help, but I won't be able to talk to you or see you, either."

"What if you were to give me a crystal, like the children? Would it work across the veil, do you think?"

"I think it would, but it would mean I'd have to tell a wise-woman or an Elder about you, and that won't work at all."

"Well, look on the bright side. With the letter you gave me, I'll be able to help your family know you're alive and happy," Amanda smiled and reached out to touch Barla's arm in comfort.

"True! Thank you, Amanda. Now, do you want to take any of these books with you when you go with Bryon?"

"No, thank you. I think I've read through enough to have them memorized," Amanda responded. "When do you think we'll be leaving?"

"It should be late enough in about half an hour. The streets should be nearly empty as everyone'll be home eating dinner."

"Let me know when I should start getting ready, okay?" Amanda asked. Jitters fluttered in her stomach at the idea of leaving with a stranger and not knowing their destination.

Barla shooed the two men out of the room about fifteen minutes before they planned to leave. She selected the best outfit for Amanda to travel in, along with the shapeless garment over it all. Barla retrieved her letter from the duffle bag and handed it to Amanda to place into her pocket. Barla rechecked the contents of the duffle to ensure everything was in order before she buttoned it closed.

Amanda remembered the items she left in the bathroom, so she went out of the office to retrieve them. On her way back, she overheard Captain Ahn and Bryon talking. While not planning to eavesdrop, she paused to hear what they had to say when she heard her name.

"Petre MacVeen's in town, and he's looking for Amanda. I don't know which direction you're planning to travel, but he was staying just south of town last I heard. Please try to steer clear of him. Amanda has been through enough without having to deal with him again," Captain Ahn spoke quietly.

"Good to know," Bryon replied, then continued, "I'd planned on heading south to visit some friends, but given this new information, I guess I'll have to visit some other time. No problem. We'll head straight out of here tonight and not stop until we are well west of here."

"Good, good," Captain Ahn spoke. "Well then…"

Amanda realized she was now officially eavesdropping, so she shook her head and hurriedly opened the office door and shut it behind her. Her entrance startled Barla, so Amanda said, "Sorry. I just heard them talking in the front office about us heading west tonight. How long do you think it'll take us to get wherever we're going?"

"It shouldn't take you more than two days' travel time," Barla assured her.

"Are we going to walk the whole way?" Amanda realized she didn't know anything about the surrounding towns or terrain.

Barla chuckled and then reassured Amanda by saying, "Certainly not. You'll walk until you get to the edge of town; then, other arrangements have been made. Don't worry. Now, are you all set to go?"

Amanda hastily stowed her bathroom items into the duffle bag and hoisted the strap over her shoulder. She looked around the room and spotted Barla's stack of books on the floor beside the desk. "What about the books?"

"Don't worry. I'll have Ahn carry them home with us after you leave. I'm glad you could use them to learn what you needed, especially the atlas. So, if the books are your last concern, are you ready?"

"Yep, set and ready."

Unable to maintain a cheerful expression, Barla started tearing up. She hugged Amanda tightly and said, "Be safe. Be quick. Get home. I love you, Amanda." She hugged her tighter yet and then released her hurriedly as she brushed the tears away from her cheeks. "Ahn always tells me I'm too sentimental!"

Amanda pulled the hood up over her hair, opened the office door, and led the way to the front office. The men's conversation ceased when the two women appeared from the hallway.

Captain Ahn came forward and held out a bulging pouch toward Amanda.

"What's this?" Amanda asked curiously.

"It's a bonus for finishing early," the Captain replied with a wink.

"Thank you, Captain Ahn. Good luck on your audit; I'm delighted I could help you out," Amanda replied formally. Amanda tried to decide if she should hug the captain or shake his hand when he pulled her into a rough embrace.

To cover her momentary confusion of emotions, she spent the next few seconds adding the bulging pouch to her pack alongside the matching one from her previous days of pay. While she knew Captain Ahn was way too generous for the amount of work she performed, she felt grateful all the same.

"You have a safe journey, you hear?" spoke the Captain, a little too gruffly.

Amanda glanced up, surprised to see tears sparkling in his eyes. Her own emotions matched his at this bittersweet parting. To lighten the mood, she said, "You can't give Barla a hard time about getting too emotional if you're going to be sad to see me leave, too!"

"I'm just sad thinking I'm going to have to start entering in those bills of lading once you leave!" he replied tersely.

Everyone burst out laughing, glad for the excuse. Bryon spoke up, "I hate to break up the party, but we should get going so we can make our rendezvous."

After another round of hugs, they finally managed to leave the office. Once outside on the street, the two parties went their separate ways; one to go home, the other to go to parts unknown.

CHAPTER 21

Elder Debbon sighed at the amount of information he had just assimilated. Feeling confident he knew the rest of Amanda's story consisted of traveling for a couple of days with Bryon, he didn't think he required further delving into her memories. He only had a few inquiries for her while she was awake before he'd be through with his questioning.

It both troubled and saddened him to hear about the people's fear of the Elders. He never wished to make such an impression on the Tualan citizens. Rectifying that new problem would take some deep thought on his part. Fear never made a good motivator, and he wanted to show the people how love always overcame everything.

Unfortunately, Amanda's story uncovered yet another problem, possibly more pressing. Another person from Earth lived in Tuala, one who apparently had lived here for quite some time. Never in his wildest dreams would he have imagined that lineage for Rasa's mother. After all, Jehoban did favor Rasa with a personal education from Him.

Thinking he should probably tell Jehoban what he learned about Rasa, he laughed aloud even to imagine Jehoban Himself didn't know already. With Rasa's impressive skills, he had to admit that he would have kept her close as well.

With a sigh of resignation and wanting to be rid of Petre's presence, he left Amanda's room again and walked the few feet to the room Petre occupied. The compulsion to remain seated in the chair kept Petre from investigating the room, but Elder Debbon's anger allowed Petre's mind to be free even if his voice weren't. He hastily strode behind Petre and gripped his skull harder than necessary as he said, "Let's get to the bottom of this mystery. Tell me everything you know about this girl."

PETRE'S HOPES soared as he neared the Elder's islet. He took the extra precaution of giving Jesisca a larger dose of *epeny* to keep her asleep and quiet. Grunting with the effort, Petre picked her up and moved her limp body below the main deck into the hidden storage area where he usually kept his illegal cargo.

His hands freely traveled over her nakedness while he arranged her body into a more comfortable position. He left the storage area, shut the door behind him, locked it with his brass padlock, and then muttered a confusion illusion over the entire area to discourage anyone from looking at the cargo hold.

Within an hour, Petre docked his water craft at the main harbor of the Elder's islet. People rushed toward the dock to better look at the yellow vessel tied to the back of his water craft. Petre couldn't help his cocky jump onto the pier. *How many others can say they've found something as grand as this?*

Petre puffed out his chest and announced to the growing crowd, "I have important business with the Elder. Who can direct me to him?"

The crowd started to murmur and stir. A middle-aged woman in the group announced, "Gatson has left the Residence to see what's going on!" At the same time, a man yelled, "Make way for Gatson! Make way!"

A well-built, nicely dressed, and equally cocky man, who could only be the man named Gatson, parted the crowd in front of him. He crossed his arms as he looked down on Petre and noted his silver and onyx ring. Raising one eyebrow at Petre's disheveled appearance, he asked in a quiet but authoritative voice, "State your name and your business."

"I'm Petre MacVeen, and as you can see behind me," Petre spoke loudly for the crowd and gestured with a grand sweep of his arm, "I've discovered an artifact which I believe the Elder Debbon would have an interest in acquiring. Please be so good as to escort me to the Honorable Elder."

"I will speak with Elder Debbon," replied Gatson, "and see if he has time to meet with someone like you. He's a very busy man, in case you didn't know. He usually demands an appointment." He turned on his heel and swiftly walked away.

Petre's confidence waned as minutes slowly ticked by without any indication of Gatson's return. The dock's crowd continued to grow, and people pointed to *The Golden Jesisca*. Petre again puffed up his chest, knowing he'd negotiate a substantial bonus for this find.

He returned to his water craft to wait for Gatson. Petre didn't want to look too desperate, so he worked on straightening out some items on the deck while keeping one eye trained on the dock.

After what seemed an eternity, Gatson returned to Petre's water craft and yelled from the dock, "You're in luck! Elder Debbon has decided to allow you to grace his presence. He has allotted you fifteen minutes of his time, beginning now! Feel free to dally at your own discretion."

Grace aside, Petre jumped to the dock and rushed to Gatson's side. Even though Gatson walked at a measured pace, Petre's shorter legs had to take two steps for every one of Gatson's. Petre could barely hide his look of disgust toward the tall guard for making him look like a fool beside him.

They turned to follow a narrow flagstone path lined with tall hedges to the Elder's Residence. Another guard stopped them at the gate for Petre to sign his name in the visitor's ledger. Gatson then led Petre through a side entrance, fully two times taller than any man and made from a single plank of wood at least eight inches thick.

Petre let his hand trail over the intricate flowers carved into the entire face of the door as he hurried after the broad back of Elder Debbon's head bodyguard. By the time they reached the interior double doors of the Elder's reception room, a full five minutes of Petre's allotted fifteen minutes had passed. Gatson reached up and double-tapped the rose-shaped brass knocker on one of the doors.

"Enter," Elder Debbon called.

Gatson pulled one door open and gestured Petre to enter the room without him.

Facing forward with squared shoulders, Petre stepped through the doorway and winced as the door shut painfully on his heel.

Elder Debbon sat at the far end of a long, elegant, dark wood table and gestured for Petre to sit at the end opposite him. Elder Debbon steepled his fingers below his chin as he waited for Petre to settle himself in the uncomfortably-carved wooden chair.

Petre looked at Elder Debbon before hastily glancing around the room to admire the fine sheen on the polished, darkly paneled walls. To his right, two tall, narrow stained-glass windows allowed colored designs to enter the room and sparkle on the opposite wall.

"So," Elder Debbon said suddenly, startling Petre, "I've been told that you've brought something which I may find of interest," he spoke each word clearly as though he spoke to a slow child.

Oblivious of the intended insult and also fearing he would run out of time to make his claim, Petre spoke immediately. "I've found an *old soul* water craft intact and filled with artifacts. As an honorable and revered Elder, I'd like to give you the first opportunity to purchase from me this rare and valuable artifact."

"Quite to the point, I see," mused Elder Debbon.

"I find it's the best way to conduct business."

"Hmm," replied Elder Debbon noncommittally. He let the silence draw out while he stared intently at Petre. He hid a smile as Petre started to fidget in his seat as he timed his following statement for the best effect. "How much were you looking to receive for your rare and valuable artifact?"

"Well," Petre drawled as he hurriedly calculated the sum he'd require to lead a comfortable life. "I believe it's worth at least fifty thousand taj."

Elder Debbon's eyebrows rose. "That much, you think?"

Petre shifted uncomfortably and replied, "That much and more, Honorable Elder Debbon. The *old soul's* water craft is the finest I've ever seen." As soon as the words left his mouth, he realized he should have addressed the Elder as First rather than merely Honorable. He hoped this grave mistake wouldn't impact his profit.

"How many have you seen, Petre MacVeen?" Elder Debbon asked in a tone soft enough to make Petre lean forward to hear him.

Petre blushed mightily and cleared his throat softly. "Well," he gulped, "to be completely honest—"

"I've often found honesty to be the best policy," Elder Debbon interjected.

"This is the first I've seen." Encouraged by Elder Debbon's nod, Petre continued briskly, "I wasn't even sure if the *old souls* existed before this appeared in front of my water craft out of nowhere! You can imagine my surprise when the ocean was empty and dead calm, then bam," he loudly clapped his hands together, "a burst of light so bright I couldn't see for a full minute, and then my water craft is on a collision course with another vessel that wasn't there a moment before."

Petre's jaw clicked shut. He hadn't intended to say so much and silently cursed himself for admitting to doubting the Elders' *old soul* stories told from his childhood.

"Childhood fantasies come to life," Elder Debbon spoke as though reading Petre's mind. Clicking his tongue, he tapped a stack of paperwork on the table in front of him and said, "Petre, I must say I'm saddened that your name had to be shortened. Although, I can't say it surprised me overmuch to see it has come to this."

Petre bristled with insult, "I can't see how those matters factor into this proceeding!"

"Petre, Petre! Don't you see? It has everything to do with it, just like the onyx ring on your finger. You expect me to pay a lifetime's sum for an artifact even you didn't believe in. Your only life's work has been about making people believe in your deceptions!"

"I've paid my dues for those things! I was introduced with my new name, wasn't I? How much more should I be punished for my past?" He silently cursed himself for not turning his ring around. Everyone knew onyx was the stone for deceptors.

Although, he probably would've been called out for trying to hide his talent from this most observant Elder. Petre cursed himself anew for not approaching a different—and less perceptive —Elder with his find.

"Unfortunately, Petre, I don't believe your past is as far behind you as you would lead me to believe. Am I correct in this state-ment?" Elder Debbon cocked his head to the side and waited for Petre to reply.

Petre decided to play ignorant and hope the Elder merely fished for additional reasons to lower the sum for the prize. "I don't know what you're talking about." He shrugged, attempting to lend innocence to his statement.

Not fooled in the slightest, Elder Debbon sighed and opened the folder beneath his hands. "Let's see," he began, his lips pinched into a thin line of disapproval as his eyes scanned the document. "Do you know that this stack of documents reports every offense Petren MacVeen has ever made? What about the illegal shipment seized on Ishal's coast? It appears as though you still have an unre-solved warrant for your arrest and sentencing in the matter."

Elder Debbon cocked an eyebrow at Petre and continued with, "Hmm, then there's the matter of the sexual assault complaint issued by Hashma at the Lookout Tavern thirteen mesans ago. The complaint is quite detailed. Not too subtle on your part, if I do say so myself. Hashma claims she lost income for more than twelve mesans due to the bodily damage you inflicted during your thirty-minute stay with her." He shuffled through a few pieces of plasfilm and pursed his lips.

"That's ridiculous!" Petre shouted. "She can hardly claim twelve mesans disability for a bloody lip and a broken arm!"

"I quite agree with your assessment of that matter," granted Elder Debbon, "however, the resulting pregnancy did end her career prospects until she gave birth."

"Pregnancy!" Petre sputtered, "I was never informed! If the child is mine, I demand to see it. It belongs to me anyway, not with some stinking whore!"

"My report indicates multiple notices were posted for you to reply to the charges." Elder Debbon reviewed his documents for a moment before he continued, "Since you didn't respond, the child was placed with an adoptive family according to the law on unwanted pregnancies. Permanently. You don't have any recourse to the child. Since you've now been informed of Hashma's assault complaint, you must make restitution for her losses."

Petre hadn't expected any of these issues to encroach on his deal. He forgot how extensive and current the Elders' information database could be. None of this seemed to work out as he planned. He asked the first thing which came to mind, "Does your report say whether the child was a boy or a girl? Or a name? Anything?"

Elder Debbon slowly shook his head. "Petre, even if it did, I wouldn't tell you. You've lost all your rights to the child. Forget about it and let the child live the peaceful life you wouldn't be able to give it."

"You're cold and heartless! What if this were your child? Would you be so cavalier about it? I think not!" Petre felt his self-control rapidly dissipating.

"On the contrary, Petre," replied Elder Debbon, "I would never have been with a whore to get her pregnant in the first place. I know where my seed goes. My wife and son are quite content with their lives. Your child with Hashma is better off without either one of you to taint its life with your suffering, miserable lifestyles."

He paused for emphasis and then continued, "Now, back to the matter of the artifact. You've requested fifty thousand taj for delivering it safely to my harbor. Here's my counter-offer: I'll have the arrest warrant, the resulting ten anons jail time, and the fifteen thousand taj restitution removed from your record for the sum of thirty thousand taj. Next, I'll arrange to have Hashma paid seven thousand taj restitution for her losses and her agreement to revoke her complaint against you. You, however, must agree you'll not have any further contact with Hashma or her place of business. This is my offer. Will you agree?"

"Does it mean you'll pay me the remaining thirteen thousand taj?" Petre hopefully inquired.

Elder Debbon lifted another piece of plasfilm and reviewed it for a moment before replying, "You drive a hard bargain, Petre; however, I believe I'll use the remainder to pay the creditors who've issued the 'death or dismemberment' order for you in Cerid."

Petre gulped. He didn't know things went so bad during his last trade route these past fifteen mesans. With his leverage evaporating like smoke into the ether on a windy day, he nodded as he sullenly replied, "You are most kind to help me. I am in your debt."

"Yes, you are, Petre. Since we have agreed on your payment terms, you're dismissed," Elder Debbon closed the folder in front of him and rose from his chair.

Petre scrambled to his feet and blurted out, "What would you like me to do with the water craft?"

"Don't worry, Petre; we've already relocated it to the Old Soul Engineering Facility. Do try to stay out of trouble; I may not be inclined to help you as much in the future. Please shut the door on your way out." Elder Debbon picked up the thick file before him, turned, and left the room through the back door while Petre stood gaping after him.

Petre left the room, disgusted with himself. Here he'd made the find of a lifetime, but instead of looking forward to a wealthy retirement, he got to pay for all his past problems.

Well, not all my problems, but at least the death or dismemberment order will be revoked. As he stomped along the path back to the harbor, he cursed himself for not selling the vessel on the black market instead.

With no reason to stay in the harbor and no money to purchase supplies, Petre released his water craft from the dock and maneuvered his way into the open sea. His black mood lifted as soon as he passed the door leading below deck.

He still possessed a treasure in Jesisca. He smiled as he realized how much excitement he'd receive from his newfound wife. He descended the stairs, anticipating the pleasure of his first payment...

· · ·

WAVES OF DISGUST coursed through Elder Debbon from Petre's following thoughts about hurting Amanda in unspeakable ways. He briskly shuffled through his memories until he reached the part where Amanda wouldn't have known what happened to Petre once she escaped.

CHAPTER 22

Elder Debbon honed in on the next series of events to discover Petre's actions after learning that Amanda managed to escape his imprisonment on the water craft.

INTENSE PAIN ACCOMPANIED by a loud cracking sound effectively woke Petre. Grabbing the side of his head, he blurrily looked around, trying to remember what happened and wondering how he ended up on the floor. He clutched the edge of the table with an unsteady hand before he could leverage his body back into the chair out of which he fell.

Once seated, he noticed the partially eaten bowl of foxl stew on the table. *Why didn't I finish my soup?* All at once, he remembered Jesisca. A rapid sweep of his eyes around the empty cabin confirmed her absence. *She must be out on the deck.*

On unusually shaky legs, he stood and staggered to the door. Catching the door frame to steady himself, he narrowly escaped another fall onto his face. He didn't see her as he looked toward the aft end. Abandoning his grip, he steadied himself against the cabin wall as he walked along the starboard side to view the forward deck. It, too, was empty.

Did she go below deck? Petre went to the hold door and yanked it open. Misjudging the first step, he slipped and fell the eight steep steps, scraping his shins and hands the whole way until he fell onto his rear, which jarred every part of his already aching body.

"Damn it," he yelled as he looked down to survey the damage. Luckily, he didn't have any broken bones, but he'd definitely be sporting a lot of bruises. The new tear in his pants outlined a deep gash on his shin. Blood dripped from the wound, which he attempted to smear off with the heel of his hand. This action led to the discovery of multiple splinters in his palm.

"She better be down here after all this trouble," he mumbled as he struggled to regain his footing. Stomping through the narrow passageway, he peered into each storage area and around the various cargo items still on board. Everything was in place, yet there was no sign of Jesisca.

Now more than a little concerned, he hurried back to the stairs, which he carefully ascended to the main deck. Petre decided she must be in the washroom where she could assist him with his numerous injuries. At least with his anger rising, his steps became surer, and he stomped into the cabin, yelling, "Jesisca, get out here and help me!"

The silence continued in the cabin as he waited for a response. Forgetting his injuries, he grabbed the washroom door handle and threw the door open.

Empty.

The room was empty.

"Jesisca!" He yelled as he turned around and faced the disheveled cabin, "Jesisca, where in hell are you!" Petre went back out and stamped across the entire upper deck. He looked out over the empty ocean surrounding the water craft and realized his invisibility shield was gone. *How'd that happen?*

Understanding dawned on him as he reviewed all of the evidence. He must have accidentally eaten the food he drugged for Jesisca. Once he passed out, she must have panicked and gone out on deck to get help. Without his invisibility shield, she would've seen the land and either jumped or fell overboard.

"I should go ashore to get her back and let her know I'm okay, so she'll stop worrying," he said out loud even though nobody else could hear it. With his plan set, he concentrated on changing the course of his water craft. He returned to the washroom and tweezed the splinters from his hands.

Within half an hour, Petre tied his craft to the southern port dock of Cresdon, which was the closest port to his vessel. This seemed the most likely location where Jesisca would've come ashore. Not knowing how long he'd been passed out, he couldn't gauge how far Jesisca might've gone.

He went first to the Harbor Master's office of South Port. Inside, he spoke to the clerk behind the desk. "Good day, sir," he said as he swaggered up to the counter.

"Good day, MacVeen," the clerk replied coldly.

Petre raised his brow at the formal and decidedly unfriendly reception. He chose to ignore the slight and asked, "Has a woman named Jesisca come in today to report a craft accident?"

Clearly startled by the question, the clerk stammered his reply, "No, why? Did you encounter some difficulty you'd like to report?"

"No, I just ate something which didn't agree with me, and I hit my head. My *wife* must've panicked and jumped overboard. Were any swimmers reported?"

"I didn't know you'd gotten married," the clerk replied sharply.

"It was only a matter of time before I found the right woman," Petre replied easily. "Any swimmers reported?"

"No, none reported," he answered promptly. "You might want to check with the main port."

"Will do. Thanks for your time," Petre said as he turned and left. Walking back to the dock, he spotted a familiar building. *Should I check in with the local wise-woman to ask if she's seen Jesisca?* Wanting to exhaust all possibilities before leaving, he trekked the short distance to the healer's workplace.

As he opened the door, a bell rang, letting the healer know she had a customer. He went into the office and waited. Petre left the office a few minutes later without any better idea of where Jesisca might have gone. *Now what?*

Contemplating his next move, he caught a delectable scent in the wind. As luck would have it, a deli that served his favorite sandwiches was just past the healer's office. He turned up the narrow side street and walked a couple of hundred yards until he came to the brightly painted door which had *Porino's Café* hand-written on the glass.

He walked in and surveyed the room; two out of the ten tables were occupied. *It must be too late for lunch, but not late enough for dinner.* He chose a table and seated himself to wait for the waitress.

A few minutes later, a smiling young woman came up to the table to take his order. "What can I get for you?" she asked while holding a pad and pencil at the ready.

Petre looked up at the question and watched as the smile fell into a frown when she recognized her patron. Although a common reaction he grew used to, it still angered him. "I'll have the fried foxl sandwich with dip, please."

"Right away," she said and turned hastily to leave.

Petre's hand shot out and grabbed her arm to stop her. "Just one moment," he said briskly.

"Let go of my arm, MacVeen," she said through gritted teeth.

"I didn't mean to startle you," he said as he took his hand away, "it's just, I wanted to ask you if you had seen an eighteen anon old woman with shoulder-length brown hair come in here?"

"Why would I tell you?"

"Because she's my *wife*," he shot back angrily. Sighing with annoyance, he tried again by saying calmly, "I believe she's lost, and I am anxious to find her."

"MacVeen, *if* she *is* your wife, then I hope for her sake, she stays lost. She'd be safer on the streets after dark than with you," she retorted sarcastically.

Petre closed his eyes to keep from throttling her and then spoke evenly, "Have you seen Jesisca?"

"I have to put in your order," she replied and stalked away to the safety of the kitchen.

Petre waited at the table, wondering whether or not Jesisca did come to this restaurant. If not, he needed to think of where he'd go next. The last place he wanted to go was to see the Cresdon Harbor Master. Captain Ahn had made it quite clear he was not welcome down at *his* harbor.

A largely built man dressed in a white shirt came out of the kitchen carrying Petre's dinner plate. He set the meal down so hard the dip sloshed out of the bowl and across the table.

"Two things, MacVeen: first, the woman you're looking for hasn't been here; second, if you ever lay a hand on any woman working here again, I'll personally break every bone in your hand. Do you understand?" Even though he spoke with a low tone only Petre could hear, his intent came over loud and clear.

"Thank you for answering my question. Please apologize to the lady for me; I didn't mean to upset her," he calmly said. All the while, he seethed inside because the insipid waitress involved the head cook in this matter. He made a mental note to repay her in the future…

ELDER DEBBON SMILED in recollection of his dealings with Petre. Upon reflection, he believed he handled the situation quite admirably. It also pleased him to see Petre thwarted time and again concerning Amanda.

The twists and turns of Petre's foul mind made the Elder's head hurt. Petre's brain functioned with an odd quality that he couldn't place, yet he'd undoubtedly have to review it at a later time. He sat slowly on the bed behind where Petre sat, unresisting in the chair.

With his eyes closed, he contemplated adequate punishment for Petre's crimes. He felt sorry for everything Amanda endured at this seasoned criminal's hands. Petre's problems all seemed to stem from his sexual appetite; maybe he should do something to keep him from performing in the future.

When he opened his eyes, at last, he glimpsed a dark shadow in the corner directly behind Petre. Once he blinked, the shadow disappeared, and he assumed it was a trick of the light, causing him to think he saw the anomaly. Immediately, he discounted the idea of Lucinden sending a minion into his household as it simply didn't happen to the powerful Elders.

Putting the shadow out of his mind, he smiled at the simple answer to his question. He stood and moved toward Petre when an amazingly vivid vision struck him. His feet felt rooted to the floor as he saw quick flashes of a child in danger being presented to him.

Once his hands touched this child, he knew she belonged with his family. He'd do anything to protect this little girl. Just as abruptly as the vision began, it faded.

In the silence after the stunning revelation, Elder Debbon inexplicably knew both Petre and Amanda were integral parties to this child. Abandoning his plans at punishment or further questioning, the Elder would alter the thoughts of both Amanda and Petre to keep either one of them from remembering their time spent with him. With uncommon desperation, he wanted the child, and he'd do almost anything to make sure his vision came true.

Stepping behind the chair, he placed his hands on Petre for the final time. With speed and precision, Elder Debbon replaced Petre's memories with a pleasant dream involving a woman. He spun the vision powerfully into Petre's warped mind and then removed his hands. In the same instant his fingers broke contact, Debbon translocated Petre back to his water craft while simultaneously removing the silencing compulsion.

Relieved to have Petre away from his Residence, he wiped his palms against his thighs as if to rid himself of Petre's feel while he returned to Amanda's room. She sat on the bed and intently watched him enter the room. Both surprised and pleased, he pulled a chair around to the side of the bed and sat. "I'm glad to see you're awake, Amanda."

Amanda tilted her head as she considered the man sitting across from her. He appeared only slightly older than her father, and he looked like someone she could trust. Yet looks could be deceiving, as she well knew.

He wore a simple white outfit consisting of a long tunic covering equally white pants. For some reason, his soft-soled shoes struck her as impractical for their setting. This particular detail seemed strange even as she attempted to dismiss it entirely.

She could almost believe power emanated from him. While she didn't know this man's identity, she could tell, without any explanation, he wasn't someone to whom she should even attempt to lie. She looked down at her completely healed hand and wrist. How much time did she lose?

Elder Debbon watched Amanda's assessment of himself with amusement. Her pleasant face with her big, brown eyes was easy to read. He wished he could spend more time with her before returning her to the wise-woman's house.

Her expression registered surprise with his opening statement. Tilting her head in question, she asked, "How do you know my name? Who are you?"

With a reassuring smile, he answered, "I know many things. My name is Elder Debbon." He nodded toward her hand and asked, "Does your wrist feel alright?"

She rubbed it unconsciously and simply answered, "Yes."

He nodded, seemingly satisfied to have come to some conclusion without speaking. Abruptly rising, he crossed the few feet to Amanda. Before she could think to resist, he placed his hands on either side of her head. "It's time I got you back to where I found you. You're not going to remember your time with me, Amanda. For that, I'm sorry. I'd love to get to know you better."

Using his ability to manipulate time and space, he returned Amanda to the wise-woman's shack only a fraction of a second after he initially took her. He erased his earlier presence from both the wise-woman's and Bryon's minds with just a thought. Without allowing his body to materialize, he ensured Amanda slept precisely as he found her before he, too, left.

CHAPTER 23

Dr. Stephen Gascon set down his newest patient's file. Amanda Covington's case gave him a thrill he hadn't felt in years. Somehow, he believed he could make a significant difference in the field of Psychiatry if only he could figure out how to get through her obviously disjointed mind.

He would use this case to write his long-held theory on multiple dimensional disorder or MDD for short. Over the years, he experienced many instances in which his patients had delusions of interacting with other dimensions, but Amanda was the most severe of all. She insisted she had lived in this different dimension for almost fourteen months.

"What are your thoughts on Amanda, Jasmine?" Dr. Gascon asked the hypnotherapist sitting across from him at his immense mahogany desk. He had already decided his take on the patient, but he wanted to humor his fellow physician by asking her opinion.

"Her accounts are very specific and consistent. She sounds convincing."

Dr. Gascon frowned at Dr. Medin's response. In his expert opinion, she took too much interest in her patients to maintain proper objectivity. He returned his attention to the paper notes on his desk. He ran the tip of his pen across each line until he came to another incident he felt he could explain with his knowledge of the human psyche.

"Amanda has displayed the classic signs of 'daddy issues' by referring to the Elder stealing her away and acting as her protector. First, the man heals and subjects her to involuntary submission when he reads her thoughts while unconscious. We should find out from her parents about the relationship Amanda had with her father; this might go a long way toward explaining her desire to please him."

"I'd like to try a few sessions with Amanda without any medication." Jasmine looked down into her lap, hoping Dr. Gascon wouldn't see her disapproval for the doctor's methods of keeping his patients heavily medicated. She knew she could treat her patients faster with clear minds during their sessions.

This longstanding argument between the two professionals wouldn't likely find a resolution on this case. She could see the interested gleam in Dr. Gascon's eyes. Suppressing a shudder of distaste, she knew that he envisioned other ideas for Amanda, none of which actually included helping her get better.

"As long as I'm in charge of Cannon Memorial Asylum, you *will* abide by my decisions regarding the patients, Jasmine."

"I always have, Dr. Gascon." She looked up and stared him directly in the eyes. "When would you like me to have my next session with Amanda?"

"Fit her into your schedule this afternoon. Also, I'd like to be present."

"I'll clear my caseload," she said as she stood and turned to leave the room.

"Furthermore, I want to make sure you still include the post-hypnotic suggestion, so she won't remember what we discuss during the treatment."

Jasmine's spine stiffened as she turned her head to look back at the older man sitting behind the desk. He might have been considered handsome, but Jasmine knew the evil poison running through his veins. "I hope you're not implying I don't know what's expected of my job, Dr. Gascon. I've always complied with your wishes on that matter."

"No, my dear Dr. Medin, I know you'll do your job. Occasionally, I like to remind my staff just so there are no discrepancies."

Jasmine shut her mouth on her reply and nodded curtly before escaping the office. Times like these made her wonder why she stayed at the facility. There were so many rules and regulations that she believed were unhealthy, if not downright unethical.

If not for the patients themselves, she would've left long before. She knew her sessions helped her patients to recover faster than those on medication alone. Amanda needed her continued support, and she'd do whatever she could to get her through this challenging time in her life.

Once back in her own office, Jasmine looked over her day's calendar and scheduled seeing Amanda first thing after lunch. With medications dispensed immediately following each meal, she'd have at least half an hour before the full effect of the drugs kicked in. Maybe Amanda would have a few minutes of lucidity at the beginning of their session, where a breakthrough might be possible.

Jasmine messaged Dr. Gascon regarding Amanda's next hypnosis session. Secretly, she hoped he'd have a conflict and either not come to the session or at least be late. She considered having a second doctor in the room during the session, both unprofessional and disruptive. Unfortunately, she could hardly refuse to allow the Program Director to observe.

She opened a drawer, grabbed her lunch, and set it on her worn and scratched desk. Anticipating Amanda's session to go long, she didn't want any interference from her growling stomach. Jasmine opened the paper bag, took out the peanut butter and jelly sandwich, and slowly unwrapped it.

Holding the soggy misshapen bread in her hands, she sighed. How could Dr. Gascon ruin her appetite so easily? After re-wrapping the sandwich, she angrily shoved it into the bag and tossed it back into the still-open drawer. The satisfying bang of the metal drawer sounded precisely like a gunshot, which made her mind think dire thoughts toward Dr. Gascon.

With an hour to go and nothing else to do, Jasmine returned her attention to her computer, pulling up her written notes from Amanda's last session. Something about this case struck her differently. Usually, the patients would have discrepancies in their memories. Amanda remained quite clear on her facts.

Too clear, actually.

Jasmine finally realized what bothered her about this case. Amanda told her story as though she had read it from a book. Amanda described what happened to other people even when she wasn't present. Jasmine thought this might be a point to bring up with Dr. Gascon or at least noted in her own file on Amanda, yet she hesitated to share what could possibly be a vital breakthrough detail.

With sudden inspiration, she typed the word 'Tuala' in the search engine of her computer. She found many entries for random bits of information on the word. Just as she was about to abandon the line of thinking, she saw an online store called TualaShop.

She clicked on it and discovered several interesting items for sale. The online store seemed fascinated with the tree of life symbol that Amanda had mentioned several times. She clicked on the About Us page and simply stared in disbelief as she saw the store owner's name was none other than Riccan Stel. Was it too much of a coincidence?

Before she knew it, her computer alarm chirped a five-minute appointment warning. She hastily shut down the web page and gathered her notepad and pencil before getting up from her desk. She moved across the room to where she could sit across from the patient couch on the other side of her office.

Jasmine liked to have as little commotion as possible in her office when patients arrived. She thought it helped the patient relax if she was already seated and prepared to begin the session when escorted into the room.

CHAPTER 24

"Alright, Amanda, are you going to cooperate today, or will you need restraints?" The orderly crossed his arms and looked down at the young woman sitting on the edge of her bed.

"I don't know why I have to keep taking these pills. They make me feel terrible, and I can't remember anything until after they wear off."

"The doctor ordered you to take them every six hours, so we're going to make sure it happens. Are you going to be difficult?" He unfolded his arms and held out a small paper cup containing three large blue pills.

Amanda reached up, resigned to take the dose. She didn't stand a chance against this brute of an attendant. She had learned the hard way that if she refused to take the medication, they just injected her with something that made her unable to resist and ultimately made her feel even worse.

"Good girl, here's your water." He poured water into a cup from the nightstand and held it out to Amanda.

She took the offered cup and rapidly swallowed the pills.

Amanda imagined she could feel each tablet as they scraped their way down her esophagus and plopped down into her stomach to begin dissolving into her bloodstream. There had to be some way to get out of this place and back home to her parents. The longer she stayed here, the crazier she felt.

"It's time for another session with Dr. Medin." He started to help her up from the bed to make sure she came willingly but realized Amanda planned on remaining cooperative.

At the mention of Dr. Medin, Amanda was unaccountably eager to go. She equated safety to the good doctor's presence. The large attendant stayed glued to her side; they left Room 426 and walked down the long, echoey hall to the treatment rooms. Amanda focused on the floor, distracted by her guard's squeaky shoes on the overly polished linoleum flooring contrasting with the swishing sound of her paper booties.

After rapping sharply on the door, the attendant opened it without waiting for a reply. He remained in the hallway and gestured for Amanda to enter. She passed by him; her gaze still focused on the floor, he closed the door quietly behind her.

Amanda imagined the big man standing just to the side of the door like a sentinel waiting to spring into action should she decide to go crazy on the doctor. The idea was so ludicrous she smiled at her imagination. She walked toward the waiting doctor and sat across from her on the long, brown, leather couch.

"You're in a good mood today, Amanda. Do you have anything you want to talk about before we begin our session?"

"I'd like to get through all of this so I can go home. I miss my family terribly. Do you know when I might be able to leave?"

"I'm sorry, Amanda, but that's up to Dr. Gascon."

Amanda frowned. None of this made sense. "Why exactly am I here, Dr. Medin?"

"You were missing for fourteen months, Amanda. You've experienced some memory loss, and we need to find out where you were. There could've been some people involved in your disappearance, so we need to go over everything you remember to see if we can find those who may have taken you. Are you okay with this?"

"I don't have much choice, do I? Besides, I don't think this hypnosis thing works very well because I don't remember anything from our previous sessions. Although, I like how relaxed I am when we're done." She smiled at Dr. Medin and hoped she didn't offend the doctor with her previous remark. Out of the corner of her eye, motion caught her attention. Dr. Gascon let himself into the room. Her body stiffened. Why is *he* here?

As if reading her mind, Dr. Medin said, "Dr. Gascon has asked to sit in on this session to evaluate your progress. Shall we begin?" She was irritated anew. He obviously made her patient nervous, which wasn't conducive to relaxation. If he had only arrived a few minutes later, then Amanda would've been under hypnosis and wouldn't have known. She hoped the session would still be as productive, with her patient uneasy.

Amanda swung her legs up onto the couch and positioned her body as comfortably as she could. Maybe it was a good thing Dr. Gascon came. If he's satisfied enough, then he'd let her go home. She reluctantly closed her eyes, ordering herself to ignore the man's presence, and said, "I'm ready whenever you are."

Dr. Medin spoke soothingly to Amanda, instructing her to imagine a safe place where she could reside in her mind so she could recall all of her memories without fear of being hurt by any revelations. Amanda relaxed, and warmth spread throughout her limbs as the doctor's voice faded into the distance...

THE COVERS SHIFTED around her body. How long had she slept? No matter how hard she strained, her eyes refused to open. Her right hand felt bulky and odd. She raised her other hand to her eyes and touched a cool cloth.

"Do you want me to take it off of your face?" a woman's voice asked.

"Yes, please," Amanda replied. As the cloth lifted, the cool air rushed in to caress her damp brow. Amanda used the back of her left hand to wipe it off. She opened her eyes but could only see blurry images in a too-bright room.

The woman's face appeared above Amanda, yet she wasn't the same old, healer woman she had just met. This tiny woman had shoulder-length brown hair. Her dark brown eyes, framed by black eyelashes, had very expressive, narrow eyebrows accenting them. Unlike the wise-woman, she had a small nose above well-shaped, full lips. Amanda couldn't place her identity in her fuzzy thoughts and asked, "Who are you?"

"My name's Alena."

Amanda frowned; Alena was Bryon's wife's name. Was it such a common name then? "Where's the other woman?"

"I imagine she's still at her house. Bryon teleported you home just after the first light this morning. I've wrapped your wrist as a precaution to keep down any swelling," she replied offhandedly.

"He teleported me!" She struggled with the covers to sit. How could she have missed the most exciting part of this journey?

Alena looked confused as she asked, "Was he not supposed to?"

"No, that's not it," Amanda said. What could she say to cover her outburst? She lay back down and sighed as she said, "It's just I thought we weren't supposed to travel until after dark. Bryon told me about his plan."

Looking relieved, Alena said, "It was the plan until Bryon thought you broke your wrist. Bryon understands for breaks to heal properly, they need prompt treatment. He didn't actually take any chances since it was still so early when you arrived here."

"Are you sure it was okay? I didn't mess anything up, did I?"

"No, not at all," Alena reassured her as she perched herself on the bed's edge. "The only reason he planned on waiting until dark was because he didn't think you two would make such good time to Jern's house. I should be the one thanking you for injuring yourself so he'd come home sooner!" She smiled at Amanda and asked, "How does your wrist feel? Any discomfort?"

Amanda turned her attention to her wrist for a moment. She frowned. There wasn't any pain. She wiggled what she could of her fingers outside of the wrapping and looked up at Alena wide-eyed with surprise. "It feels perfect! Bryon wasn't kidding when he said you had a gift with your healing!"

"I do enjoy it," she smiled shyly back at Amanda. "But I think Bryon mistook the extent of your injury. I couldn't find anything wrong with it. The bandage is just a precaution to appease Bryon. He was quite upset when he brought you home. He even said you appeared to fade away on the wise-woman's bed. Do you feel like getting up and walking around?"

Amanda nodded and moved her legs over to the side of the bed. Why would Bryon say something so strange to his wife? Alena reached behind to steady her as she leaned forward and pushed herself off of the mattress. Together they walked around the bed and over to the door.

"This'll be your room for as long as you want to stay with us," Alena said. They continued down the hallway, and Alena kept up a running commentary, "And this is the washroom you can use; unfortunately, you'll have to share it with the kids. I hope that's okay?" She scrutinized Amanda's reaction to having to share.

"I'm grateful for any accommodation. Don't worry about it," Amanda hastily replied, grinning and scanning the places in the house she could see. "Where are the kids?"

"I sent them next door so that you could sleep in peace. They'll be back before dinner, so we still have a couple of quiet hours until they return. It'll give us time to get acquainted. Are you hungry?

We could go to the kitchen and get something to tide you over until dinner."

"Sure, I am a bit hungry, but I don't want to put you to any trouble," she answered briskly.

"It's no bother," she assured her as she continued to steer her guest through the house. "These are the kids' rooms," she announced as she pointed out two doors on either side of the hall as they walked past them.

"This is the living room where we spend most of our time. The far room over there is where I take my clients for simple healing. And here's the kitchen," she said as they walked through the living room and straight into a brightly lit room.

A small table occupied one side of the room, and Alena stopped at one of the chairs and pulled it out for Amanda. "Do you feel like eating some fruit salad and iced tea? I'd offer you some iced java, but I wouldn't recommend it in your condition," she said solicitously.

"The iced tea and fruit salad would be wonderful as long as it isn't too much trouble," Amanda replied. Why would Alena think the iced java would be bad for her newly-healed wrist?

"No trouble at all," she said as she opened the cooler and pulled out a pitcher and a bowl. She retrieved a bowl and two glasses from an overhead cabinet and served the two items. She removed a fork from one of the drawers and placed it into the bowl before bringing them to the table. She set the bowl and one of the glasses in front of Amanda and pulled the other one over to her side of the table, where she sat. "It's nice to have a peaceful moment to relax," she said as she poured the cold steena tea into both glasses.

Amanda quickly prayed before she picked up the fork. She stabbed one of the pink melon pieces, expecting watermelon, and was surprised when it had a tangy taste and firm texture. She tried to remember whether or not she had seen this fruit in any of her reading materials but soon abandoned the thought as her hunger took over her curiosity. She sipped the iced tea between bites and was surprised again at how refreshing and cool the beverage tasted.

"This is all so wonderful," Amanda praised in between bites. "Does it take long to prepare?"

"No time at all," Alena replied as she looked curiously at her guest.

"Why did you say iced java would be bad for me right now? I thought my wrist was fine," Amanda asked as she picked up her iced tea for another drink.

"I wasn't referring to your wrist," she replied, "I was talking about your pregnancy."

Amanda sputtered and coughed as the iced tea went down the wrong pipe. "What? What are you talking about?" she managed to ask, between coughs.

"Are you saying you didn't know?" Alena asked, now thoroughly confused.

"Didn't know would be an understatement. It isn't possible since I've never even had sex!" she replied indignantly. "At least I don't think I have," she added quietly. How much of her past had she forgotten if she didn't remember something as important as having sex for the first time?

"Well, I can assure you, you are most definitely pregnant," Alena said calmly.

No way! There had to be some mistake. She couldn't be; her parents would never forgive her. She needed to get this matter clarified right now. Setting her fork down, Amanda rubbed her suddenly aching forehead and asked, "How do you know?"

"Your baby spoke to me while I was examining you. She wanted to make sure you'd be okay."

"What!" Amanda shook her head and stared down at the fruit bowl. Was the food tainted and causing her to experience delusions? This sounded more and more like a prank. "Babies in the womb don't speak!"

"She's very vocal." Alena watched Amanda closely. Her eyes never once wavered but only showed concern.

"Are you sure?" Amanda asked. It made perfect sense—all of those mornings where she threw up. She made up so many excuses —nerves, motion sickness, the head wound, or bad food. Never once did it occur to her that she might be pregnant. The idea of a child growing inside her made her feel nauseous all over again.

Alena nodded with a grin on her face. She had witnessed this same reaction many times in her healing career. She waited patiently for the last response to set in and smiled wider as she saw it happening in Amanda's expression.

"You said it was a girl. Are you sure?" Amanda's lips trembled, and her hand drifted down to cover her flat stomach.

Alena emphatically nodded. "Quite sure. You'd better start thinking of a name for her. I'd say you're due in about six mesans."

Amanda could hardly think; this was all happening so unexpectedly and fast. "Six mesans?" This news changed everything. Now more than ever, she needed to find Neal. They were supposed to raise their children together, and she wanted him to experience the whole pregnancy alongside her. What if she had a craving in the middle of the night? Neal was supposed to be there for support.

Alena nodded and said, "Approximately. Without knowing when your last cycle was, I can't be absolutely certain. Do you recall when you had your last cycle?"

Amanda couldn't remember. She shook her head and said, "I never really kept track of it; I didn't need to since I wasn't sexually active."

"If you want, I can give you an exam to see if I can get a better idea of the timing."

With her mind reeling in shock, she couldn't handle a bodily intrusion. Not wanting to seem rude, she asked, "May I think about it a little longer?"

"No problem; you've got six mesans to think about it!" she laughed at her joke.

"Well, I guess this would explain why I kept throwing up every day. I thought it was many things, but pregnancy never even entered my mind. Wow! A baby!" Amanda shook her head in complete disbelief and wonder. *It has to be Neal's baby if I'm three months along. When did we have sex? What else did I forget?*

The clock was ticking. Six months. That's it. Nothing was going to stop her from locating Neal in that timeframe. Besides, she wasn't about to face her parents alone with this news. There wasn't any way she'd give birth to her baby in Tuala. Hopefully, news of Neal's whereabouts would come much sooner. She needed his reassurance so badly right now.

"Let's take our tea and drink it in the living room," Alena suggested when Amanda finished eating. "Besides," she added, "the chairs are more comfortable in there."

Amanda smiled and stood. Awkwardly she started to gather up her dish and glass when Alena reached over and took the bowl from her grasp.

"I'll get it," she said as she deposited it into the sink with a flourish. She walked back over to the table and picked up her glass, and led the way from the room. Once in the living room, she said as she chose her chair, "Sit anywhere you like. Ah. Much better."

Amanda smiled and selected the one directly across from Alena so they could more easily converse. Without realizing it, she had placed her hand on her belly after she sat. She smiled when she looked down but did not remove her hand. *A daughter!*

"I could hardly believe it when Bryon told me a beetlesnatch bit you!" Alena said, her eyes wide. "Luckily, he'd taken my medicine kit with him; otherwise, you might have lost your hand to its saliva before he got you to the healer."

"Are you serious? I could've lost my whole hand?" Amanda didn't realize the severity of the simple, albeit painful, bite.

Alena nodded gravely over the rim of her glass as she drank. She assessed Amanda's reactions and compared them to Bryon's comments about Amanda being 'different.' He refused to answer Alena's questions about what he meant; he only said *you'll see.* Alena began to understand. Amanda's responses proved intriguing, to be sure, and Alena looked forward to getting to know her.

"Wow, I'm going to have to thank Bryon again for taking such good care of me." She shook her head. *I don't remember reading anything about beetlesnatches in any of Barla's books. Who knew they were so dangerous?*

Changing the subject, Amanda said, "I can't believe I don't remember anything about being brought here. The old woman's medicine must've been pretty strong." Gasping, her fearful gaze darted to Alena at the same time her hand covered her stomach. "Could the medicine have harmed my baby?"

"Luck was on your side again," Alena replied with confidence. "She gave you the same medicine we'd normally give a woman who's in difficult labor and would need to be asleep for us to take the baby swiftly."

"Thank goodness!"Relief washed through Amanda, and she gently rubbed her stomach. It may terrify her to contemplate having a baby, married or not, but she didn't want any harm to come to her.

I'll take better care of myself for you, honey. If something unspeakable happened to Neal, then their daughter would be her only connection to him. Not knowing what else to do, she took another sip of her iced tea.

"So you said you've been having bouts of nausea?"

"Yes, for almost two mesans now," she replied, pleased to have easily remembered to use the Tualan term for months.

"Have you noticed anything else out of the ordinary, any bleeding or spotting?"

Amanda paused to consider the question. "I've just been drained. Exhausted, really. I just thought it was part of my recovery from the head injury."

"What head injury?" Alena asked, leaning forward and frowning.

"The first I remember was waking up on Petre MacVeen's water craft. He told me I'd fallen and hit my head. He'd wrapped it with a cloth, but it was really bloody and hurt like crazy for at least a week."

"Would you mind if I looked at it?" Alena asked with great interest as she stood up and moved over next to Amanda.

"No, feel free," Amanda replied as she lifted her hand to the back of her head. "It was right here," she indicated as she turned her head and touched the welted scar with her index finger.

Alena's cool and gentle fingers parted Amanda's hair before she prodded the edges of the roughly healed wound. "Do you get headaches or shooting pains anywhere?"

"Yes, both."

"You said 'the first I remember.' Did you lose your memory?" she asked as she continued to probe the scar.

"Yes."

"Did it come back?"

"Well, I thought it did until you told me about the pregnancy."

Looking relieved, Alena asked, "This injury could explain why you don't remember the timing of the conception. I wish I could've taken care of this wound when it first happened. How long did it take to get your memory back?"

Amanda mentally reviewed the timeline notes she made for Barla and Captain Ahn. "I'm pretty sure it was about a week, maybe a little less."

"Did it come back all at once or in stages?"

"That's what was weird. It only came back through my dreams."

Alena raised her eyebrows and nodded to encourage her to keep talking.

"Petre kept giving me foxl broth with some sleeping drought in it. Each time I drank it, I dreamed about my past. When I was awake, Petre told me my name was Jesisca and that I was his wife. At first, I believed him because I couldn't remember anything. I never told him when my memory returned." Amanda kept her gaze fixed on the corner of the coffee table as she spoke.

"You did the right thing, Amanda. Petre MacVeen's a dangerous man. How long do you think you were with him?" Alena asked with measured words.

"Right at two mesans," she replied. Knowing where Alena's questions led, she asked, "How do you know Petre?"

"There're very few people in the shipping business who don't know Petre," she replied quickly. "He's a known liar and a cheat who regularly ships illegal items."

"Do you think the drug Petre gave me might have hurt the baby?"

"It's hard to say without knowing what drug he used." She resumed her seat and crossed her legs, but her foot bounced as she considered. "Did it have any smell or taste?"

"I don't think so; he put it in the foxl broth."

Alena pursed her lips. "Hmm. There're only a couple of possibilities. How much broth did you have to drink before you felt any effects?"

"Just a couple of swallows. Then I'd start feeling light-headed. By the end of the small cup, I couldn't even remember setting the cup down."

"Really," she replied with surprise. "If it worked that fast, there's only one possibility: *epeny*. Did you ever hear him say the word?"

"No, sorry."

"That's okay," she reassured her, "*epeny's* a powerful sedative. I personally wouldn't recommend it to a pregnant woman, but since you didn't become addicted to it, I'd venture to say he didn't give you a dosage that'd be detrimental to a young fetus."

"I could've become addicted to it?"

"Yes, but you didn't," she reassured. "If it were the drug Petre gave you, then you were fortunate because it also has anti-inflammatory properties."

"I guess that's one good thing," Amanda mused. "I sure hope my baby's going to be okay."

"Well, if it's any consolation when your baby spoke to me, she sounded very healthy and coherent."

"Really?" Amanda asked in amazement. "I wish I could hear her, too." She sighed. *I have a little life growing inside me!* "Thank you for the reassurance. It does make me feel a lot better knowing you think she sounds healthy."

"So what happened with Petre? You said he told you that you were his wife; it sounds as though he meant to keep you around."

"I thought the same thing, and it scared me," Amanda shuddered. "Just the memory of being alone with Petre in the small cabin makes my skin crawl!"

"So he never knew you got any of your memory back?"

"Not that I know of. I never spoke of it. I feel bad about the *epeny*, though. I figured out the correlation between the drug and dreams. I kept asking for it so I could remember faster," Amanda confessed as she wrung her hands together.

"Amanda, hey, don't worry about it. She sounds fine, and you've probably gotten most of your memory back. Think positively, okay? You've been through enough. It's time you started relaxing."

She gave her a gentle nudge and then changed the subject, "So how did you get away from Petre? Bryon didn't know."

Amanda devilishly grinned, looked over at Alena with a sparkle in her eyes, and said, "I tricked him into drinking the drugged foxl broth."

Alena burst out laughing. "Oh, how perfect! It serves him right. Then what happened?"

Amanda laughed, too, and realized it felt good to smile again as she continued, "Well, he fell asleep almost immediately, and his head hit the table. I jumped overboard just as a shipping vessel passed nearby.

They picked me up and brought me to Captain Ahn. I'm sure Bryon told you about me working for the Captain these past two weeks, getting his paperwork ready for the quarterly audit. And that's the whole story."

Alena nodded affirmation and commented, "Well, that's the short version. Hopefully, you'll feel comfortable enough to share your daily experiences with Petre. I'm sure it was never boring with everything I've ever heard about him."

Amanda nodded and said, "I don't mind talking about it. In fact, there were some pretty funny moments."

Just then, they both turned toward a commotion at the front door; it burst open, and three little children came barreling into the living room, throwing themselves all over Alena. "Momma!" They each cried as they hugged her legs and fought for space on her lap.

Amanda sat back to keep from getting kicked by the rambunctious children. They hadn't even noticed her in their excitement to see their mother. Suddenly there was silence as three faces stared over to where Amanda sat quietly, looking back at them.

"Who's she, Momma," the oldest boy asked with his precious little face turned up to look at his mother. "Is she your patient?"

"As a matter of fact, yes, she was my patient this morning. But she's not like my other patients. She's going to stay here at our house in the guest room down the hall from your bedroom."

"Why, Momma?" Justan asked seriously. "Is she family?"

Alena looked pleadingly over at Amanda, who nodded hastily, then turned back to her son and replied, "Yes, she's family."

"How long's she staying?"

"We're not sure, Justan. It might only be for a few weeks, but it may also be a couple of mesans. She's working on a project, and we don't know how long it might take."

"What kind of project? Can we help?" he asked, excited for a new adventure.

"Sorry, honey, this is something just for the adults, kind of like my work," she replied gently, not wanting to discourage his helpfulness.

Even though Alena spoke kindly to her son Amanda saw his shoulders droop as his spirits diminished with his exclusion from the activity. Amanda thought fast, "If there's anything where you can help me out, I'll let you know, okay?"

A smile lit up Justan's face as he enthusiastically nodded. "Really? You're not just saying it?"

"As long as your mother says it's okay, I'll ask for your help whenever I can include you, all right?" Amanda grinned at his enthusiasm.

Justan immediately turned to face his mother, "Momma, you think I can help, don't you? You think I'm big enough and smart enough, right?"

Alena stroked his unruly dark curls and said gently, "You're my brilliant little boy. When the time comes for you to help, we'll all do it together, okay?"

"Okay," he smiled brightly at his mother and then at Amanda. "What's your name?"

"You can call me Aunt Amanda," she replied hastily. "And you must be Justan."

All the kids giggled, but Justan solemnly nodded.

Alena put her hand on the little girl's head who sat on one of her knees and said, "This is Andera, our first-daughter, and this little scamp," she moved her hand to rescue the other little boy from slipping off of her other knee without breaking her stream of conversation, "is our youngest son, Kyelon."

She sniffed and playfully wrinkled her nose. "And I think it's time you three washed up for dinner; you smell like you rolled in the flowerbeds. Off you go now. Be sure to clean under your fingernails," she cried after them as they raced out of the living room.

CHAPTER 26

Alena turned to Amanda and sighed, "Are you up for this?"

"Sure, bring it on," Amanda laughed. "I bet they keep you on your toes."

"That's an understatement!" Alena replied with a grin. "I better get dinner started. Do you want to keep me company?"

"Sure, I can help if you want," she offered as they both stood and headed toward the kitchen.

"Not tonight," she replied offhandedly, "you can watch and get the layout of the kitchen. I'm sure there'll be plenty of time for you to practice with these three ravenous children."

Amanda seated herself at the little table again and took mental notes of where Alena got different containers. Only then did she realize the difficulty she'd face trying to pass herself off as a Tualan; Alena didn't physically get the ingredients out of the cupboard because she *thought* them out.

At first, Amanda believed she missed seeing her get an item. Still, upon closer inspection, the ingredients would simply appear in the dish without Alena having to get them physically. Thinking more on this idea, Petre had prepared food in the same way. Back then, Amanda convinced herself she had imagined it because of her injury. Now, she knew it was the Tualans' unique talent.

Amanda's mind raced with doubts. *How am I going to pretend to get ingredients out? Maybe, not all Tualans do it. Captain Ahn and Barla didn't. Or do they not because Barla can't, like me? Perhaps I can say my injury makes it too painful to practice the talent. That'll have to work.*

Decided on that course, she once again concentrated on Alena's dinner preparations. In total, it only took about ten minutes to prepare dinner and set the dining room table. It was a simple dinner of seasoned foxl steaks and fried krumpli with a fresh mixed green salad. Everything looked and smelled terrific, and Amanda's stomach growled in anticipation.

"Since dinner's ready, Bryon should be walking through the door," Alena announced as she turned to face that direction.

As if on cue, Bryon came inside, his eyes immediately locking onto his wife's. His grin widened when he spotted Amanda alongside her. "It looks like my timing's as impeccable as ever," he said as he strode over to hug and kiss Alena.

He turned to Amanda and nodded toward her wrapped wrist. "And how are you feeling? You look much better than you did when I left you this morning."

"Alena's done wonders for me," Amanda replied with a grin on her face. She lifted her wrist and wiggled her fingers. "It's all back to normal; the bandages are just a precaution, according to the doctor!"

Bryon looked over at Alena and raised his eyebrows, and received the expression mirrored back. "How wonderful, Amanda. I'll get washed up, and you can tell me all about your day."

"There's our cue, Amanda. Let's use the kitchen sink," Alena offered as she turned back toward the kitchen.

"How did Bryon know it was dinner time?"

"I have no idea," she replied, "but he does it every day. Sometimes I serve dinner a little early or a little late, but it doesn't make any difference; he's always walking in as I set it on the table. It's almost as if he has a food service alarm built into his brain." She chuckled as she finished washing. She moved to the side with the dishtowel in her hands to make room for Amanda.

"Come on, kids, dinner's on the table and Papa's home," Alena yelled over her shoulder.

Amanda heard them giggling and chattering as they ran into the dining room and sat at their seats around the table. She reveled at their joyful noise, imagining she and her sisters must have sounded the same when they were little. Homesickness threatened to overwhelm her, but she firmly stamped it down and plastered on a happy face for her host family.

Alena led the way to the dining room, and they paused in the doorway. Amanda didn't know where she'd sit, but just then, little Justan spoke.

"Can Aunt Amanda sit next to me?" He pumped his legs in excitement, causing his body to bob up and down on the chair.

Alena looked at Amanda to judge whether or not to allow it; Amanda shrugged indifference. "It's very polite of you to offer, Justan. I'll get another chair for Amanda, and I'll put it on your left."

Dinner was delicious but uneventful. The children animatedly told about their adventures over at the next-door neighbor's house. They constructed a telepod in the backyard, and the neighbor's kittilee played a game of hide-and-seek with them.

After everyone finished and the dishes were clean and put away, the group retired to the living room. The children brought out their favorite books for their parents to read to them. Obviously, this was an evening ritual since everyone knew what to expect and where to sit.

Amanda chose a chair off to the side to observe without getting in the way. Full and satisfied, she curled up in the overstuffed chair, and her eyelids became heavy. By the time the kids were tucked in, Amanda announced, "I can't believe how tired I am. If you don't mind, I think I'll retire for the night as well."

"Don't think anything of it, Amanda. Good night," Alena spoke, and Bryon nodded in agreement.

"Thank you for everything," Amanda said as she left the room and made her way down the hall.

"How did your day go, honey?" Alena asked Bryon as Amanda left the room.

"Just the same as ever," he replied offhandedly. Alena practically burst with her desire to talk to him about Amanda. Excitement danced in her eyes as she watched Amanda leave. They'd make small talk until they were sure Amanda slept. "We received a shipment of telepod crystals from Mavuno. There was a problem with the packaging, and some of the crystals were damaged. Of course, nobody wanted to accept responsibility, so we'll have to appeal to Elder Debbon to resolve it.

"How was your day? Did it take long to heal Amanda's wrist?"

"My day was exciting, although there was nothing wrong with Amanda's wrist."

"Wow, are you sure? I saw it twisted at the wrong angle!"

Alena shrugged. "I don't know what to say. Copa must've taken care of it. I did discover something rather amazing, though. Can you guess what it is?" Alena asked with a mischievous glint in her eye. She loved trying to stump her super-observant husband.

"Let's see," he mused, "did it have to do with the injury or something else?"

"I'll answer this one question, but then you're on your own!" she replied smartly. "It didn't have anything to do with the injury."

"Hmm," he tapped his pursed lips as he reviewed what little he knew about Amanda. "Did you discover where she's from?"

Alena clapped her hands together with glee. It happened so seldom, and she felt an inordinate amount of pleasure. "No," she replied thoughtfully, "but hopefully, I will eventually. This doesn't have anything to do with it, but I'd like to talk to you about it after I tell you my discovery. Do you give up?"

"Yes, but only because I know it'll make you happy since I didn't figure it out."

"Amanda's pregnant!"

Bryon sat in stunned silence. "How far along is she?"

Alena swiftly reassured him, "Don't go there, she's at least three mesans along, and she was only with Petre for two. The baby must be Nealan's, but she doesn't remember sleeping with him either."

"Well, how can that be?" Bryon asked in amazement.

"Apparently, when Petre found her, she had injured her head and lost her memory. She said she recovered her memory, but I guess not everything came back. It's something I'd never forget!" She chuckled at her joke.

"So, how did you come to know she was pregnant?"

"You'd never guess this one, either; the baby spoke to me while I was examining Amanda," she said with awe apparent in her tone.

"That's never happened to you before, has it?" he asked as he added yet another oddity to Amanda's story.

"No, not to me, but I've heard stories of other wise-women who've experienced the phenomenon. I never believed it before now."

Bryon sat listening to the noises of the house. Deciding everyone must surely be asleep by now, he spoke what was really on his and his wife's minds, "What do you think about her?"

"I think you're right to say there's something different about her. She had a very odd, almost disappointed reaction when she learned you teleported her while she was unconscious. And then she asked me if a fruit salad took a long time to prepare," she told Bryon as though it were proof positive of Amanda being different.

Bryon shrugged, not convinced with Alena's proofs. "Maybe she comes from a small town without telepods or fruit."

"Yeah, that sounds about right, a small town that has aunts and doctors. What in the world is an aunt or a doctor?"

"I couldn't possibly guess about the aunt without knowing the context in which she used it, but I can hazard a guess that a doctor where she comes from is what we'd call a wise-woman," he spoke with certainty.

He nodded to himself as he recalled the previous night's conversation with her, "Last night, she was very curious about the duties and responsibilities of wise-women. I had the distinct impression that almost everything I told her about them was the first time she'd heard it."

"So what do we do? Pretend everything's normal?"

"Let's just say it'll give us something different to talk about in the evenings!" He put his arms around her and held her close. "You smell good," he said as he nuzzled her neck.

She giggled and tried to move away from his nose, tickling her neck. "Dare I ask what you're thinking right now?"

"I don't think you'd have to if you haven't figured it out already. Are you ready for bed yet?" he asked as he nibbled on her ear.

"Yes, I am," she announced happily, "and I noticed you didn't mention anything about sleep!" She wriggled free of his grasp, took one of his hands in hers, and said, "Let's go to bed."

"Gladly," he replied as he stood and smiled down at her beautiful face.

Afraid of interfering with Bryon and Alena's alone time, Amanda decided to go to bed at the same time as the children. Tired didn't even begin to describe her mental state. Entering the room, she closed the door behind her and leaned against it.

With her eyes closed, she sighed before whispering, "What am I supposed to do?" She pushed away from the door and fell face-first down onto the bed. With the pillow scrunched up under her torso, her mind raced. This baby had to be Neal's. To think otherwise made her want to hurl.

She could envision her mom's expression when she told her the news. It wasn't good. Her parents may have outdated ideas, but they were crystal clear on their marriage requirements before sex. Obviously, that hadn't happened.

"I wish Barla could've told me more about how long it might take to go back home." Immediately, she sat up on the bed, frantically searching the room for her belongings. Amanda promised to have Barla's letter on her at all times. Panicked, she patted down her body but didn't find the letter anywhere.

"Oh, no! Where'd I last see it?" Inhaling slowly to focus her thoughts, she at last remembered. "It's in that awful coat!"

Rummaging through the various clothing items, she finally located the soiled cloak draped across the back of the chair in the corner of the room. She grabbed it up and started rifling through the pockets until her fingers touched the envelope's paper. She pulled it out to check for rain damage; the paper was rippled but dry and okay for the most part.

Sighing with relief, she held it tightly to her chest with both hands. "Now, what'll I do with it?" she whispered out loud to herself as she looked around the room for a safe place to store it while she slept. Moving to the bed, she carefully set the envelope on the bedside table to easily reach it when she got up.

She carefully removed her clothing, found her bedclothes in the duffle bag, and pulled the gown over her head. She lay down on the mattress and sighed when she pulled the covers up to her chin. Amanda considered different ideas on how she'd help out around the house so she wouldn't be a burden to Alena.

As she relaxed in her warm blanket cocoon, her thoughts wandered. *Will I be allowed to leave the house and go to the market? Is Kirma far enough away from Petre to keep me safe? Should I offer to watch the children while Alena learns healing skills from the Elder? Do I want to commit myself to so much time on Tuala? What would happen to Alena's children if I went back to Earth before she completed her training?* She fell asleep during her ruminations.

One day ran into another, and Amanda learned the routine of the household. The children started asking Amanda to read them their bedtime stories. Alena and Bryon just shrugged and enjoyed watching the children find entertainment without them.

Amanda constantly worried about Alena missing the Elder's opportunity to train her. Maybe, this gave her something else to think about other than the fact that no news had come about Neal or her increasing shame over her pregnancy.

Surely, Alena needed to give a response to the teaching invitation. Amanda started to broach the subject with Alena more than once, only to be interrupted by one of the children or even by Bryon.

Bryon had said Alena had two weeks to give her response. Amanda had been in their house for almost that amount of time, and nobody said anything about it. Amanda decided regardless of what interruptions might happen, she was going to talk with Alena. Her opportunity presented itself nicely later the same day.

The children were all finishing their lunch in the kitchen when the doorbell rang. The kids ignored it as usual, and Alena's hands were elbow-deep in dishwater, so Amanda said, "I'll get the door if you don't mind?"

"Go for it," Alena answered appreciatively.

Amanda recognized the petite and friendly next-door neighbor as she opened the door. She smiled in greeting and said, "Hi there, Tana."

"Hi," Tana said, slightly at a loss for what to say. "I was wondering if I could borrow Alena's children for the afternoon. I have a planting project in the backyard, and I know how the little ones love digging in the dirt." She smiled as she talked.

"Come inside. Alena's just finishing the lunch dishes. Let's go ask her," Amanda said as she stepped aside to allow the young woman to enter the house.

Once in the kitchen, Tana repeated her request for assistance. In unison, all three kids chimed in that they wanted to help. Alena held up her hands in surrender and laughed as she said, "It looks as though the children are up for it. They just finished eating, too, so they should have plenty of energy. Are you sure you want all of them?"

"I wouldn't dare split them up!" Tana spoke with sincerity as she smiled adoringly down at the children's upturned faces.

Alena turned and addressed her kids, "Since you're all so eager to help out in Tana's yard, hurry up and go change into your play clothes."

As the children stampeded out of the kitchen toward their rooms, their laughter and bantering echoed down the hall. "You don't have to do this, Tana," Alena protested.

"I know," she replied. "But I want to. They're great entertainment, and they do love to dig in the dirt. I'm afraid they'll come home quite dirty, though."

"I'd expect nothing less!"

Tana ushered the now appropriately dressed children out the front door and toward her house. "I'll have them home for supper," she called back over her shoulder.

Alena stood at the front door and waved as her three kids laughed and skipped alongside Tana. She smiled as she closed the door and said to Amanda. "As much as I love my kids, it's also a relief to have some peace and quiet."

Amanda pounced on the opportunity to talk before anything else could interrupt them. "Alena," she began and waited for Alena's full attention.

"Yes, Amanda? Is something wrong?" Concern washed away Alena's blissful moment at Amanda's suddenly serious tone.

"There's nothing wrong with me, but I'm afraid there will be with you if we don't talk," she replied cryptically.

Alena frowned. "Let's go sit in the living room and talk, okay?"

Not knowing how else to say it, Amanda blurted almost all in one breath, "I don't know how to bring this up subtly, so I'll just say it—Bryon told me you have an opportunity to train with the Elder to be certified as a wise-woman, but you're afraid to leave the children for the time it'd take to get trained.

"I was hoping it wasn't too late for you to accept the offer and let me watch your children for you while you're gone. Please know I'm not trying to be nosy or take over your house, family, or anything. I just know that you're a wonderful doctor, and I think you should get the training and recognition for it as well." Since it was finally all out there, she took a deep breath and sat back, and waited for Alena to reply.

"Well," Alena started and then looked at Amanda with consideration. "Well," she repeated. "I didn't know Bryon told you about it, but you're right; I haven't replied to the summons because of the children."

"The kids like me, and I like being with them," Amanda supplied helpfully.

"I've noticed, Amanda," she replied but then didn't continue.

"So, will you go?" She leaned forward, anticipating Alena's answer and inwardly pleading with her to say yes.

"I don't know how long I'll be gone," Alena spoke, sounding as though she were trying to talk herself out of it.

"If you're half as good as Bryon said about your skills, then surely your training won't take very long. What's typical?"

"I've heard of as short as three weeks up to fourteen mesans," she replied slowly.

"I'm sure you'll be on the shorter end of it. Bryon and I can handle the kids," she assured her again.

"But you're pregnant!"

"I'm not due for another five and a half mesans, so you better hurry up and get going before you lose the opportunity forever," she answered smartly. "Besides, I'd be honored for you to be the wise-woman to present my daughter with her birth crystal."

The idea astonished Alena; she'd only ever focused on the healing end of the training. She'd learn a new skill for the crystal assignments, and she really wanted to know how to do it.

"Well, I don't know," Alena slowly drawled as she pondered the possibilities for school success as well as the problems which could occur with her absence.

Amanda saw Alena teetering on the edge of agreeing, so she prompted, "Please say you'll do it. I'd love the opportunity to repay you and Bryon for all of your hospitality. Once my future is set, I'll be happier knowing I helped to improve your career as well as your household stability. I know how much status is attached to being a trained wise-woman. Your career will skyrocket. Please say yes."

Alena saw the wisdom of Amanda's words, even as she wondered what a 'skyrocket' was, and finally conceded, "Alright, you've worn me down. I'll discuss it with Bryon tonight after the children go to bed; you can stay up, too, and let him know this was your idea."

"Wonderful," Amanda gleefully clapped her hands. "I already talked to Bryon about it on the night I fell off of the horse. He said it was a wonderful solution, but it was up to you."

"He knows all about it, huh?"

"Now, don't go getting all mad at him," Amanda pleaded. "Bryon didn't have anything to do with it. While we traveled here, I asked him how healers became wise-women, and he told me about it. He also told me you were a healer, and when I asked if you wanted to become a wise-woman, he shared your dilemma with me.

"I was the one who came up with the idea of taking care of your house while you did what you needed to do. Bryon seemed glad for my suggestion, but he never even hinted he thought I should do it."

Slightly mollified, Alena smirked, "I don't have to let him off so easily. It'll do him good to sweat it out a little before I tell him I've decided to go."

THINGS SWIFTLY FELL into place after their discussion. Alena sent her acceptance to the Elder and made arrangements for her to leave within two days. Alena sat with the kids and told them about

Amanda taking care of them while she trained with Elder Debbon.

While the children knew something important would happen, they didn't understand why their mother had to leave. They sat on their parents' bedroom floor with Amanda and watched as their mother packed several journey bags. "Why can't Elder Debbon come and stay with us like Aunt Amanda?" Justan asked for the fifth time.

"Because Elder Debbon has lots of students to train, and they all won't fit in this house, Justan," Alena explained patiently to her eldest child. She gave him a quick hug.

"Aren't you too old to be a student, Momma?" Kyelon asked.

"I'm going to a special school where you have to be older to attend, silly boy!" She continued to select items to pack and asked, "Amanda, can you hand me the tunic from the chair back?"

Amanda held out the blue tunic for Alena to pack. "Do you honestly think you'll need this much stuff?" She indicated the four suitcases already packed and lined up by the door.

"I don't know," Alena laughed. "I keep telling myself I won't be gone long, and then I think of something else I might need 'just in case' I'm gone longer."

"I think you should pack for no more than one mesan. You can send home for more if you end up being there longer," Amanda answered.

"I know you're right. I just can't get my head to agree!" She chuckled at her dilemma.

"What time is Bryon coming home to take you?"

"Oh, Bryon's not taking me. I just found out Elder Debbon's sending a telepod to pick me up." She stopped and looked at the clock. "Goodness, I need to hurry; it should be here within half an hour."

As if on cue, Bryon arrived home and rushed into the bedroom. "I'm sorry, honey," he said, "I tried to get home an hour ago, but of course, there was a problem, and only I could take care of it. Do you need me to get anything for you? Do you want me to carry your bags to the front door?"

"Yes, I do need something from you," she said hastily. "I need you to come and give me a hug and a kiss that I won't forget while I'm gone." She held out her arms, inviting Bryon to embrace her.

"Gladly," he said as he walked over to her.

"Come on, kids," Amanda scrambled off the floor and held out her hand to Kyelon. "Let's get some juice so your parents can have a couple of minutes alone!"

She herded the giggling children out the bedroom door and toward the living room. Amanda settled them on the couch and went to get them each a cup of juice to keep them occupied until their parents finished saying goodbye to one another.

Once the kids were busily sipping on their juice, Amanda sat beside them. Her heart raced; both fear and anticipation warred for attention inside her head. As much as she wanted Alena to get this opportunity, guilt popped up. If Neal showed up right now, she'd leave without a second thought, and that made her feel selfish.

But this wasn't her world, and she didn't belong here. Her hand rested across her belly, and she imagined she felt a flutter of movement. This baby couldn't be born here. Somehow, someway, she'd find a way home before the baby's time came.

Several minutes later, Bryon came through the doorway carrying four suitcases and pretending to be staggering under the weight of them all. The children all loudly laughed, just as Bryon intended. He deposited them by the front door and imitated wiping the sweat from his brow. "Whew," he said, acting as if drooping with exhaustion, "It's a good thing she won't be gone very long, or I might break my back carrying all of her necessities!"

"Very funny," Alena said as she walked into the room, easily carrying the last of her baggage; she set it down next to the rest. "They hardly weigh anything at all," she said.

"Well, the last one didn't because you packed everything you owned into the four I carried," Bryon insisted.

Refraining from commenting, Alena turned to her children and said seriously, "Now remember, while I'm away at school, you three are to behave. Amanda and Papa will be in charge, and you're to do as you're told even when Papa isn't around. Understand?"

Three heads solemnly nodded. Kyelon's lower lip trembled. "But you're coming back, right, Momma?" he spoke in a tiny quavering voice.

Alena hurriedly kneeled in front of the three kids and put her arms around them until all of their heads touched in the middle. "Of course, my little angels. I have a special opportunity to learn about healing. You want your momma to be the best wise-woman ever, don't you?"

Again, the three little heads nodded. Justan smiled and puffed out his chest as he said, "You already are the best ever, Momma. Elder Debbon knows how good you are, and he wants to learn from you too!"

Alena laughed as she replied, "I'm afraid it's the other way around, Justan. Elder Debbon's going to be my teacher. Just the same, I won't be gone any longer than necessary to get my certificate, and then I'll be home for good. Amanda's doing us a big favor agreeing to take care of the three of you, but I don't want to take advantage of her goodwill. I love you kids so much; I can hardly stand missing one day of your growing up. Give me a hug I won't forget, okay?"

In turn, the children wrapped their little arms around their mother and hugged her. Alena praised their hugging strength and made little jokes about not being able to breathe. She pulled back and looked at their faces as she said, "Remember the new song I taught you. When you sing the Unity Song, you'll know I'm thinking about you."

Soon enough, the doorbell rang and Alena, and her luggage, was escorted to the waiting telepod. The family and Amanda stood on the front porch and watched as the telepod lifted from the ground and winked out of sight. Amanda's slack-jawed awe of the spectacle was cut short when Kyelon started crying. Duty called. She picked him up and hugged him, saying soothing words to comfort him.

Amanda used the gesture to cover her reaction to seeing her first telepod in action. To hear about their abilities was quite different from actually watching one perform. *Will I ever get the chance to ride in one, preferably when I'm conscious?* She grinned at her own joke.

The family went back into the house and tried to maintain some semblance of normalcy for the children's sake. Amanda prepared dinner; they all cleaned the kitchen afterward; stories were read, the Unity Song was sung—which caused Kyelon to cry again, and then the children were tucked into bed.

After the children were asleep and all was quiet in the house once again, Bryon and Amanda sat in the living room and predicted how long each of them thought Alena would be gone. They both agreed it would only be a short time because neither wanted to think about what would happen if her training took longer than the duration of Amanda's pregnancy.

The days turned into weeks, and the household continued to run in Alena's same orderly fashion. The children ate regular meals, they visited with Tana while Amanda went to the market for fresh groceries, and Bryon went to work in the morning and came home in time for dinner.

Eventually, the children stopped asking every morning when their momma was coming home, and, for some reason, this broke

Amanda's heart. She loved the little children, but they deserved to have their mother home with them just as she had growing up.

My hormones must be working overtime. Even as she thought it, the baby responded by stretching and kicking against her belly, bladder, and spine. *Is this all normal? Who knows! If only I could talk to Alena about it. But no! I sent her away. I'll be fine, I said. Wow, was I ever ignorant?*

Amanda's proficiency in the kitchen improved, which was a good thing since her own appetite increased as enormously as well as her waistline. The most unusual cravings caused her to buy new and exciting foods from the market. Bryon commented more than once about some of the selections Amanda presented for dinner, although Amanda noted, he always ate everything without any trouble.

CHAPTER 28

The clock was ticking down. Alena left four and a half mesans ago. Amanda's busy schedule with the three children kept her from dwelling on the lack of news regarding Neal. *Did he stay on Earth, after all? What am I supposed to do?* Her hopes dwindled, and discouragement set in. From the current state of things, she'd have to figure out how to raise her daughter without Neal. *Everything happens for a reason. Maybe it's for the best since Neal never actually said he wanted any children.*

Every time she caught sight of herself, she frowned with disgust, making her avoid any reflective surface. *Was it normal to be as big as a cow at eight months?* Her once-elegantly long fingers reminded her of sausage links and no longer brought her pride. Most of the time, she hid them in her pockets so nobody would comment on their grotesque puffiness.

Even the baby's constant movement should've brought her some contentment, but because of that activity, she spent more time in the bathroom than she cared to talk about. Did her bladder shrink to the size of a pebble? She hated anyone seeing her so fat and round and occasionally was thankful that Neal wouldn't witness her bloated condition. Such thoughts then poured on more guilt for her cowardice about seeking an Elder's help.

She no longer pined to go home, not now, not with the idea of disappointing her parents, but she couldn't undo the past. Eventually—hopefully—she'd have to face her parents and live with their disapproval. Several times a day, she changed her mind about staying in Tuala or going home. Undoubtedly, her raging pregnancy hormones played a role in her indecision.

Guilt and shame warred inside her as her belly grew, giving evidence to the child she carried. Amanda worried about Alena not returning in time for herself to travel back to Earth before the baby came. More than anything, she wanted her mom's comforting hugs and outdated advice.

Bryon noticed Amanda's quiet withdrawal from her typical self, and he worried about the baby's health for her to be so sad. He tried to think of something they could do to take her mind off her problems, even for a few hours to relax.

The perfect activity came to him one afternoon while at work. The telepod races were coming near their town the following weekend. Given Amanda's keen interest in telepods, he believed she'd enjoy watching the races in person.

Taking matters into his own hands, he arranged for Tana to watch the kids. When he got home for dinner, he asked, "Amanda, would you like to go to the telepod races this next weekend?"

"They have races?"

"Yes, they do," he replied. *How could she not know such a thing?*

"What about Petre?" Bitterness colored her question. She hated having to think about him every time she left the safety of the house. The evil man's influence over her life never seemed to relent.

"I received a report about him being busy in Cerid on race day!"

"What about the children?" Conflicting emotions warred inside her. Between the fear of running into Petre and her shameful appearance, she grasped for any excuse to remain hidden inside, away from gossiping people or their pitying looks.

"We can have Tana watch them. Besides, you need a day off from these monsters!" He smiled at the kids as they each protested their new title.

"You've thought of everything, haven't you? Okay, then. It sounds like fun." Inside she felt a strange bubble of excitement. After all, it'd be nice for a change of scenery. It seemed odd to feel something other than guilt, but she liked it.

CHAPTER 29

At the market, the conversations surrounding Amanda were markedly different than usual. Someone named Riccan was coming to race. Everyone commented on how he put on a good show and how excited they were to watch his performance.

Through careful questioning of multiple people, Amanda learned that his racing pod was unique. He never used elemy enhancements—whatever that meant—to make his telepod go faster, and he almost always won.

When she heard his pod also stood out because of its blazing red color and innovative design, she felt a connection with him. The Golden Jesisca also stood out against the Tualan water crafts. Now Amanda was even more eager to go, and the days seemed to drag slower.

Finally, the day came, and she slept poorly because of her bulky belly and excitement. Amanda didn't know what to expect of the races but knew the diversion would be good for her. Everyone, both young and old, seemed to agree the races were very entertaining and especially worth seeing when Riccan participated.

She finally picked an appropriate outfit to wear, tucked Barla's letter in her pocket, and waddled out to meet Bryon in the living room. Today was the day for her first telepod ride. Amanda's spirits rose just thinking about it. She asked, "Are we all set to go?"

He held out his arm and said, "This way, my lady, your telepod awaits."

She giggled and took his arm, thankful for his assistance with her unsteady footing. Outside he helped her up the ramp into the telepod. Not quite sure what she should do, she looked around the confined area.

Bryon stepped in behind her and placed his hand over a wall panel to shut the door. "You can sit right here," he said as he gently guided her by the elbow to the seat on the right at the front of the cabin. "It'll only be a short ride, but in your condition, it'd be wise to wear the safety belt."

She nodded and pretended to look around while she covertly watched him fasten his so she could see how it worked. Once belted in and ready, she excitedly sat, eagerly anticipating the unknown adventure.

Bryon looked over to her and imagined he could see her glowing with anticipation. He smiled, inwardly pleased about giving her some amount of pleasure in her sad, lonely life. "Let me concentrate on the coordinates, and we'll be there in about three heartbeats," he said as he closed his eyes.

She avidly watched as Bryon toggled a switch that lit up several green lights on the panel in front of them. He used a manual lever that lifted the telepod quickly from the ground, and then darkness instantly engulfed her.

She counted her rapid heartbeats, grateful that Bryon had given her a hint. Did he do that on purpose? Because of her nerves, it wasn't until the tenth beat when light poured through the window, and the scenery wasn't even remotely similar to their home neighborhood.

Bryon set the telepod down in a vast field obviously serving as a landing lot. "We're a bit early," Bryon told her, "I wanted to get here before the crowds so we could get decent seats." Bryon didn't mention this luxury cost a bit more, but he knew it'd be worth it.

Amanda stared out the window at the rows upon rows of brightly colored tents beside each pod trailer. Already, crowds formed around their favorite drivers' tents, where the crews tuned the crystal drives of various styles of racing pods. They exited the telepod and walked into the racing grounds.

"I don't know anything about telepod racing. Would you mind giving me a brief tutorial?" Amanda asked.

Bryon explained to her how there were three different classes of pod racing, and Riccan's racing class was always last because it was the fastest, the most dangerous, and the most popular. They bought two tubes of liquid at a concession stand that conveniently wrapped around their wrists for walking around.

Amanda sipped her drink while they walked from pit to pit as Bryon explained the differences between the racing classes. Some things were quite apparent such as the size of the pod. The smaller pods were generally slower since their crystal drives were sized accordingly.

Some of these racers used expensive technology to enhance power. This started to cause contention and talk about splitting the class to allow similar pods to race against each other.

Officials kept reminding the people in this class that it was supposed to be for fun and entertainment and not competition. The operators scoffed at the last part of their spiel. It was painfully obvious this statement had been spoken around them since they started racing.

Bryon whispered to Amanda, "This's a beginner's class of racing; it lets them get the feel of real racing. The sponsors approach only the best self-funded operators for what they call Top Sportsman racing, which is Riccan's class."

Enthusiastically, Amanda nodded even though she didn't understand most of it.

Bryon continued, "The only difference is Riccan's still self-sponsored, so he doesn't have to conform to what the sponsors want him to do. That's what's made him into what they call the rebel racers class. Everyone loves him for standing alone and still beating the *big dog pods*."

Bryon and Amanda circled through the pit area and came to the mid-class Sportsman section. "Some of these racers have sponsors," Bryon explained, "while others just have a lot of money to burn."

Crowds passed them and assembled in front of a huge black trailer. Bryon pointed to it and stated, "There's Riccan's trailer. He won't bring out his pod until the races begin. The crowds are hoping he'll allow some sneak peeks, but he never does."

Amanda smiled and nodded even though she wasn't sure why they'd be so eager to see it just sitting there when the races would start soon, and they'd see it then. Her feet ached, and pain radiated up her spine, and she hoped they'd find a place to sit soon. She deeply sighed.

Bryon turned away from the trailer to get a good look at Amanda. "Are you okay, Amanda?"

She nodded, but her smile wasn't very convincing.

He took her elbow and guided her through the crowds toward the grandstands. The people's voices and the pods were quite loud by now, and he shouted into her ear. "I'm sorry, Amanda, I didn't think about how badly your feet must feel. The seats are right over here. Where do you want to sit?"

"Probably close to the bottom since I'll most likely have to go to the bathroom at least fifteen times while we're here. Speaking of which, where is the bathroom?"

Bryon changed course midstride, and suddenly the bathrooms were right in front of them. Bryon waited for her to return and then directed her to the stands. They chose second-level seats, but high enough to see the finish line and race time boards.

The race announcers asked the Stock class to start lining up. The crowds converged over to the stands. People crowded in from all sides, surrounding Amanda with noisy but happy spectators, all talking about which racer would do what.

Bryon leaned close to Amanda's ear and explained, "The pods are going to pair up to race. Watch the tree of lights; when it goes green, the pods will go."

Just then, the first two pods revved their crystal drives. The crowds went wild as the sounds roared over the stands. Side-by-side, the pods crept up to the starting line, which activated both sets of lights, and then they raced down the track before Amanda could take it all in.

Her adrenaline-activated heart raced. She got caught up in the cheering when the finish lights showed who won as well as their finish times. She didn't even care if the race times were good; she just knew she was having fun.

In subsequent match-ups, Bryon leaned over to explain the sport's finer points as the elimination rounds continued.

Amanda saw why everyone loved this pastime. She started picking who she thought would win based solely on whether or not she liked the pods' paint jobs. The announcer called the Sportsman class to the staging lanes. A deafening roar erupted around them as the crowds renewed their cheering.

Bryon winked at her and asked, "Do you have to use the restroom?"

Amanda instantly became aware of her body's pressing need. She nodded.

"The few moments before the racing class change is the best time for a bathroom break," he explained when they finally escaped the seating stands' noise.

Because of their bathroom break, they missed the last two

racers of the first class. They also missed the massive crowd at the bathroom. Amanda could barely get to the sink to wash because of the crush of women waiting to get into the facility. Finally fighting her way out the bathroom door, she met Bryon outside.

"Are you hungry?"

She cocked her head to the side and replied, "What a silly question! When am I ever not hungry these days?" They laughed as he directed them toward the food vendors.

They stopped at a snack shack, and both ordered shredded foxl sandwiches. They ate while they meandered back to the grandstand. Since people had taken their previous seats, they found new seats on the track's opposite side.

The crowds filed back to the grandstands just as the Sportsman's class came up to the staging line. These racers also revved their crystal drives, generating a rumbling vibration that traveled throughout Amanda's body.

Initially exhilarated, Amanda frowned. Did one of those racers just disappear for a split second? Confused, she turned to Bryon and raised an eyebrow. "Did I just see the pod disappear?"

"I wondered if you caught it! It's a trick they're allowed to do, but only in the staging process, not during the race," he answered. His grin threatened to split his face as he turned back to watch the track.

The crowds grew louder, and Amanda leaned close to Bryon to say, "I was wondering about that. Why do they race down the track when they could just teleport instead?"

His gaze flicked to hers, his brows furrowing with displeasure. "Where'd the fun be in that?" He turned his attention back to the race in progress.

This class proved to be almost twice as fast as the first class and quite thrilling to watch. Amanda enjoyed the different styles of pods and tones of the crystals as they raced.

However, Amanda noticed that one racer's crystal drive

sounded odd as he blinked in and out in rapid succession at the staging lane. Glancing over at Bryon to see if he noticed, he just turned and smiled without any concern, so she returned her attention to the upcoming event.

The race began, and, midway down the track, the crystal exploded from the rear of the pod. The mid-track spectators ducked from the crystal shards, which managed to infiltrate the active force fields meant to protect the viewers from just such an occurrence.

Amanda continued to watch as the pod dropped to the ground and skidded from side to side, narrowly missing the other pod in its uncontrolled slide along the track. She gasped and clutched Bryon's arm. "Is the driver going to be okay?"

"I don't know," he replied and glanced at Amanda. Concerned the stress might be bad for her, he hastily reassured her by saying, "The drivers are very protected by shields and padding. He's more than likely just shaken up."

Amanda paid attention to the onlookers surrounding her. They speculated on possible injuries or if the racing pod's body was too damaged to be reused. Afraid for the driver, she whispered a prayer for his safe deliverance.

A rescue squad teleported to the accident scene, where they immediately swarmed the pod. They set up additional force fields in the event of further explosions. One rescuer managed to open the pod's side, allowing the driver to step out, dazed but otherwise unharmed.

The temporarily silent crowds erupted in cheers at the driver's appearance. Amanda let out a relieved breath for her answered prayer.

The cleanup crew removed every particle of debris from the track, which delayed subsequent Sportsman races. Meanwhile, the rescue squad entered the grandstands to treat the spectator's injuries. Amanda saw a couple of people receiving medical attention, but nobody left, so Amanda assumed the injuries were relatively minor.

"They'll impound the racing pod to investigate why the scatter shield failed," Bryon explained as the damaged pod drifted past on a transport vehicle in front of their seats. "The crystals aren't supposed to explode onto the track."

The lull in racing gave Amanda time to think. The last time she'd seen an event like this was with Neal. Neal loved watching drag races and even driving to events when they came close to where they lived. He would've enjoyed seeing this event. But he wasn't here.

Eventually, the racing resumed, and the final four pairs of the Sportsman class were directed to activate their crystal drives again. "Top Sportsman racers, please come to the staging lanes," boomed the voice over the loudspeakers. Another cheer went through the crowd, and Amanda heard people begin to chant, "Riccan! Riccan! Riccan!"

People craned their necks to see what order the Top Sportsman racers would race. Speculation was wild whether Riccan would run first or last. He was first.

When he came to the line and revved his crystal drive, his pod blinked in and out of sight at least twenty times with breathtaking speed, causing the crowd to surge to their feet, whistling, clapping, and yelling his name. Pandemonium reigned as nearly every spectator surged toward the track's sideline to watch.

Amanda's attention remained riveted to Riccan's pod; it was the brightest red she ever saw, and the shape seemed oddly familiar. An odd feeling nagged the back of her mind as she watched him stage his pod. Had she seen his telepod before? The idea was impossible since this was her first show. The lights activated, turned green, and then Riccan raced down to victory in a fantastic display of noise and speed. He won this round and would return for the subsequent elimination round.

She and Bryon exchanged goofy grins as she clapped and cheered along with the most seasoned spectators. Bryon gestured for them to go down from the stand, and Amanda raised an eyebrow in question. He winked and gestured again.

Amanda shrugged but led the way off the grandstands. Amanda assumed they were going on another bathroom break, but he steered her in the opposite direction when they got near the building. They arrived in short order at Riccan's tent and trailer.

Riccan's team had already pulled the pod into the stall and removed the shell to check the crystal, supply lines, and connections. Riccan stood confidently, speaking with his crew chief and smiling.

Amanda thought he was amazingly handsome with his beautiful brown eyes, radiant smile, and booming laugh. She appreciated his lean, muscular build and was glad they came over. Bryon and Amanda edged closer to get a better view of the racing pod design on the shell when Riccan glanced over at them and smiled at Amanda. She smiled back and blushed prettily.

They didn't stay long since the crowd was getting too much for Amanda. She was sorry she couldn't have personally met Riccan. *Was I just flirting? I must be moving on with my life. As if he would be interested in a hugely pregnant woman!* She chided herself for even thinking such foolishness.

They revisited the restrooms and finished watching the races. Of course, Riccan was the Top Sportsman champion after five elimination rounds. He gave his victory speech over the intercom. Amanda was strangely pleased about his win and that she got to hear his voice again.

Eventually, the time came to leave, and Amanda was thoroughly exhausted but happy at the same time. They meandered through the hordes of people also trying to get to the landing grounds. When they finally got to Bryon's pod, Amanda gratefully escaped into the quiet, empty space inside the pod.

"Thank you, Bryon, for the wonderful day," she said, smiling with delight as she fastened her safety belt.

"It was my pleasure."

Within moments of relaxing in the comfortable seat, Amanda fell deeply asleep. Deciding against teleporting directly home, Bryon levitated the pod and began the manual process of navigating home instead.

For the duration of the ride home, Bryon glanced over at Amanda. More than a couple of times, he caught her smiling in her sleep. He was pleased to give her this fun day off. His wife would be happy, too, even though she wasn't a racing fan.

What took three seconds to travel in getting there took almost an hour via manual navigation. Bryon didn't mind the change of pace. Amanda needed the rest more than she needed a quick flight home.

Besides, once they got home, she'd again feel obligated to get the children and care for them instead of resting.

Bryon worried about Amanda. Every day without news added more sorrow to Amanda's already emotionally burdened mood. She hardly ever smiled anymore.

He also worried over the idea that Amanda, now two weeks shy of delivering her baby, would need help with the imminent arrival. He better not be called into action. They hadn't received any word from Alena to know when to expect her arrival. Unfortunately, Alena was also the only healer within a reasonable distance from their home.

Amanda no longer slept through the night. How was she going to find a way back to Earth before her baby's birth? Each passing day forced her to realize she'd have her daughter in Tuala. *Alena, please finish your training and get home. I'll only trust you to deliver my baby.*

The children helped around the house as much as they could, given their ages. They cleaned the kitchen after their meals and helped Amanda carry groceries when they went to the market. Justan and Andera took over many household chores such as sweeping, cleaning the floors, and dusting.

Justan shadowed Amanda everywhere because his mother told him to take care of Amanda in her absence. Her huge belly and breathlessness scared him. She told him it was because she was going to have a baby. He finally asked, "Why is your stomach so much bigger than other pregnant ladies at the market?"

"I don't know, Justan. Every woman is different," Amanda said, but one of her swollen hands held onto the side of her stomach, and the other pushed against her back. She grimaced and bit her bottom lip. "She sure likes to wiggle around in there," she said. A smile crossed her lips, but her humor didn't reach her eyes.

Justan wasn't convinced. He wanted his momma to come home and make sure Amanda was okay.

Another week went by, and then it happened. Everyone just settled down in the living room to read stories after dinner when an odd-sounding knock came from the front door. Amanda and Bryon exchanged questioning glances, each wondering if the other were expecting someone. Both shook their heads, and Bryon stood and went to investigate.

He opened the door and immediately stepped outside and started whooping. Suddenly, turning around with a broad grin on his face, he announced, "Look who's here, kids. Your momma's home!" He swiftly grabbed the bags out of Alena's hands, which kept her from opening the door herself. Looking at her with a grin, he asked, "Did you use your foot to knock?"

Alena playfully quirked her eyebrows and said, "I wanted to surprise you!" She barely made it through the door before three ecstatically happy children clambered all over her. She joyously exclaimed, "I'm so happy to be home again! I've missed you all so much." Tears filled her eyes as she kissed each one of her children in turn.

Bryon retrieved the remaining luggage from the telepod and stood behind Alena, waiting for the doorway to clear. When his arms tired, he cleared his throat and said, "Okay, okay! Kids, let your momma inside so I can bring in her suitcases."

The children let go of their mother's neck, but they each kept a hand fastened to her clothing as if expecting her to try to leave again. They pulled her into the living room and made her sit on the couch, so they could climb on her lap and stay close to her. "I missed you, Momma," Kyelon whispered in her ear.

"I missed you too, Kyelon," she whispered back to him and gave him a hug and a kiss on the forehead.

"Momma, I'm glad you're home now," Justan said when Alena finished kissing Kyelon, "Amanda needs your help; her belly's awfully big."

In the crush of the family reunion, Alena hadn't seen or even thought of Amanda. Guilt threatened to override her newfound professional confidence. How could she allow her reunion to take precedence over the welfare of the woman who had cared for her family in her absence? She looked around the living room and didn't see her anywhere. "Where's Amanda?"

"She went into the kitchen," Justan replied; he glanced in that direction and back to his mother, his expression torn between fear and relief.

She didn't want to startle her children with her worry. She scooted to the edge of the couch and moved Andera off her lap onto the cushion beside her. "All right, children, I know you're all thrilled to have me home, but remember why I went away? I earned my wise-woman certification. Now, it's part of my responsibility to take care of pregnant women. I need to check Amanda and make sure she's doing okay."

Bryon picked up Justan out of Alena's lap with one arm and Kyelon with the other. He stood and waited for Alena to stand in front of him. "Kiss your momma, and we'll do storytime in your beds tonight. When your momma finishes looking after Amanda, she'll come and tuck you in. Okay?"

Justan squirmed to be let down and said, "May I pick the story tonight, Papa?"

"You surely may, Justan. Lead the way." Bryon swooped up Andera, causing her and Kyelon to giggle.

Alena's family walked away from her as she inhaled and mentally prepared for seeing Amanda. She could hardly believe she was home again; it felt as though she'd been gone forever. It brought tears to her eyes again as Kyelon and Andera waved at her over their papa's shoulders as they rounded the corner into the hallway.

Duty called. She rushed into the kitchen, where her first sight of Amanda alarmed her. Justan's concern over Amanda's size was warranted. Her stomach was huge, and she looked exhausted as she rested against the kitchen counter in front of the sink. Alena immediately cataloged Amanda's conditions to evaluate her overall health. Her skin color was flushed; she looked weary; her ankles and fingers were terribly swollen.

"Amanda, how're you doing?" Keeping her voice calm and hiding her alarm, she hastily crossed the room and stood in front of her.

"Much better, now that you're here," she replied with a sigh. Her hand rested across the top of her bulging belly. "I was afraid Bryon was going to have to deliver this baby, and, frankly, that scared me!" Her attempt at a joke fell flat as the baby rolled across her belly, causing intense shooting pain along her back. She couldn't withhold the small squeak, and she groped to sit in the kitchen chair.

"What's going on, Amanda?" Alena asked hurriedly.

"She just moved across my kidney and spine," she replied as soon as she caught her breath. "I'm okay. I haven't had any contractions or anything else abnormal. Tell me about your training."

"Okay," Alena said, still concerned. "While I already knew a lot about healing, there was so much more I didn't know, and it was utterly fascinating."

Alena sat down across from Amanda at the kitchen table and started talking. As she spoke of the different healing techniques with the ley lines and crystals she hadn't known about, she also evaluated Amanda's pregnancy with a wise-woman's new awareness.

After speaking for about fifteen minutes, Alena was convinced Amanda had spoken accurately about her own health. "You should go to bed, Amanda."

She shook her head and picked at a spot on the table. "I'm not quite ready yet," Amanda replied. "I think I'll go sit in the living room and relax in front of the fire."

"Okay," Alena replied. "I'm going to go finish tucking in the children. I'll see you in a bit."

"I'm glad you're home," Amanda smiled as she struggled to pull her bulk out of the kitchen chair. "The kids have missed you terribly."

"I've missed them, too. And you know, I'll be relieved to sleep in my own bed tonight, I can tell you!" Alena chuckled as she left the kitchen to go to the children's bedrooms.

The kids were all bright-eyed when Alena entered the boys' bedroom. Andera perched on the end of the bed as Bryon read with Kyelon on his lap and Justan beside him. Alena scooped Andera up and settled her on her own lap as she seated herself on the bed to listen to the story's end.

Andera cuddled into her momma's lap, breathing deeply of the scent she had almost forgotten in her absence. She reached up and touched her momma's cheek and sweetly smiled as Alena lovingly looked down at her. Even though she didn't enjoy this particular book as much as others, Andera was content to stay silent and listen. The family was reunited, and that was enough.

Bryon finished, and Alena read them another before

announcing bedtime. She tucked in the two boys, kissed them on their foreheads, and said, "I'm glad to be back at home with you. I'll see you in the morning." She picked up Andera, walked to the bedroom door, turned out the light, and as she shut the door, she whispered, "Sleep tight." Bryon walked with her as she carried Andera across the hall and repeated the same routine.

Back in the hallway, Bryon pulled Alena into his arms and whispered in her ear, "I'm so glad to have you back." He kissed her soundly on the lips and then pleaded, "Please promise me you'll never leave for so long again."

"I promise!"

"I'm also relieved you're here for Amanda."

"How's she been? Really?" She leaned back in his arms to look up at his face.

"Big," he answered immediately with a grin.

"So I saw," she quipped and raised an eyebrow for his honest answer.

"Pretty good, actually, up until this last week. I don't think she's been sleeping very well, and she's started to swell. I believe she's been pretty depressed because we haven't heard anything from Captain Ahn and Barla about her fiancé or their water craft," he finished.

"Oh! I forgot to tell Amanda what I learned from Kiya today!" She brushed a kiss on Bryon's cheek and pulled out of his arms entirely. She grabbed his hand and hauled him along behind her as she rushed to the living room.

Amanda looked up at their unexpected entrance, noting Alena's excited expression, and asked, "What's going on?"

"I forgot to tell you, I've found *The Golden Jesisca!*"

"What? When?" Amanda leaned forward eagerly. She would have stood for the fantastic news, but her bulk prevented her from any more enthusiasm.

"Just today! It was the most amazing coincidence. The telepod bringing me home had to drop off another student at the Old Soul Engineering Facility where her husband works. While we were waiting for her to unload her luggage from the telepod, I was looking out the window, and I saw your water craft," she replied with her voice rising with her excitement.

"Are you sure it was mine?" Amanda asked, not wanting to get her hopes up, but her heart raced with anticipation.

"Oh, yes; the yellow and white paint is quite unique. And when Kiya returned for her last bag, I asked her if she knew anything about it. Luck was on our side again. She told me her husband was the one assigned to work on it," she answered triumphantly.

"So, did she know anything about Nealand?" Amanda asked with renewed hope.

"I'm sorry, Amanda; Kiya said it was turned in after a storm without any survivors on board," she answered.

"What did she mean by 'no survivors'?" Amanda asked nervously.

"I don't know, Amanda. Kiya had to leave before I could ask her anything more. I'm sorry," she repeated sadly.

CHAPTER 31

I'm on my own, Amanda despaired as she hugged herself and leaned back into the chair in disbelief. *Neal either died, or he never even made it here! I've wasted all these months in Tuala for nothing! If I don't make plans in the next few days, my baby will be born here, and then I'll never get back home!*

Amanda leaned forward and moaned in frustrated agony; this wasn't how she ever envisioned having her first child. She wanted Neal with her; she wanted her mother; she wanted to be surrounded by friends and family.

She wanted to be on Earth!

Angry at her situation's stupidity, she propelled herself up from her chair and said, "Thank you, Alena, it's good to have some closure. I'll be going to bed now."

She waddled as fast as she could from the room to keep her hosts from seeing the tears which threatened to spill from her eyes. Amanda rushed to the safety of her bedroom, where she quietly closed the door behind her and then lay on the bed in the fetal position and cried with uncontrolled sobs.

Alena and Bryon exchanged worried looks as they watched

Amanda try to make a graceful exit from the living room. "I wish I hadn't said anything to her," Alena said into the silence.

"You didn't know how she'd react," Bryon consoled.

"I know, but I should've waited." She thought about Amanda's water craft again and then asked, "Do you suppose it means anything that her water craft is being studied at the Old Soul Engineering Facility?"

"Well, it might explain the questions we've had about her," Bryon conceded.

"Do you believe in the *old souls*?" Alena asked incredulously.

"Of course, don't you?"

"I don't know. I mean, I heard stories about them when I was little, yet I never knew whether or not the tales were true." She thought about it for a second and then asked, "What makes you so sure they exist?"

"Because I've been to Earth myself," he announced unexpectedly with a mischievous smile.

"What!?! You've never said anything about it before. You'd better start explaining!" She turned to look him straight in the face and crossed her arms to hear his story.

Bryon opened his mouth to answer when they were interrupted by an alarming cry.

"Alena, help me!"

Alena reacted first, followed immediately by Bryon. They both sprinted across the living room and down the hall. The children were popping their heads out of the bedroom doors, and Bryon was forced to stop and keep them from interfering with Alena and Amanda.

"Let me know if you need my help," Bryon yelled after Alena and then continued, "I'll tuck the kids back into bed."

Alena, at Amanda's door, nodded confirmation to Bryon and then rushed inside the bedroom. Just as she thought, Amanda was going into labor. She wished she had brought her healing kit in with her but knew it could wait until she had made her initial examination. "Tell me what's happened," Alena asked without preamble.

"I started to get up off of the bed when I felt this horrible pain down low," she indicated a spot at the base of her enormous belly, "and then I felt a gush of fluid come out."

"It's okay, Amanda, your water broke. You're far enough along. We can safely deliver your baby."

"That's what I was thinking, too," Amanda replied with both relief and regret. All plans for returning to Earth were now officially on hold for the foreseeable future. Her sole focus was on bringing her daughter safely into this strange new world.

"Let me help you to take off your pajama pants so I can check if you've started to dilate," Alena said as she put her arm around Amanda's waist to help lift her from the side of the bed. "Carefully now," Alena cautioned as Amanda rose too swiftly.

With Amanda properly disrobed, Alena helped her lie back on the bed to perform her initial evaluation. "Wow. Okay. You're almost fully dilated. Are you feeling any contractions?" She rose hurriedly from the bed.

"My stomach's been getting tight; are those contractions?"

"Most likely. I need to ask Bryon to get my healing kit; I'll be right back."

Alena rushed to the door and yelled for Bryon. She hurriedly told him, "Amanda's almost ready to deliver the baby. Can you please get my healing kit from my luggage? It's in the smallest bag. Please hurry. I've only got a few minutes to prepare."

Bryon gave Alena a double-take at her request's urgency. "I'll be as fast as I can. Are you going to need anything else once I have it?" He tightly clasped his hands and prepared to spring into action.

"I'll need some towels and a basin of warm water with a washcloth," she hurriedly replied, and she turned to go back into the bedroom. "Just bring them right in when they're ready," she called over her shoulder.

Amanda looked uncomfortable as she leaned back against the headboard with just the sheet covering her body. "I think I'm having a contraction," she gasped as she tried to catch her breath.

Alena touched Amanda's stomach and noted the muscles' stiffness at the height of her contraction. She nodded her head and asked, "Is this one harder than the others?"

"Yes."

"How much time has been in between each of them?"

"I don't know. I was distracted and didn't pay attention."

"I'm going to check your progress again," Alena announced as she lifted the sheet. "Oh, we're having a baby right now. Don't push, Amanda! Your baby's head is crowning. I feel her hair."

"Bryon, I need my kit! Now!" she yelled impatiently.

The bedroom door flew open an instant later, and Bryon almost threw the kit into Alena's hands. "Is it time?"

"Yes, I'll need those towels and water immediately. This baby is going to be born in the next few minutes."

Bryon's complexion paled, and he anxiously glanced at Amanda. He turned on his heel and bolted from the room. He stumbled on the doorway's threshold in his haste while he promised himself to have Alena's supplies ready before the baby came.

Alena pushed the sheet above Amanda's stomach to clearly view the baby's progress and Amanda's stomach to track the contractions. She opened her healing kit and withdrew an alcohol sanitizer. She poured a generous amount onto her hand and then rubbed both hands together to eliminate any contaminants.

"Sorry about my cold hands," she said as she massaged around the edges of the baby's head to see if she would need to make more room for it to pass through. Satisfied with the elasticity in Amanda's skin, she monitored her belly to decide when to instruct

Amanda to push. She used this moment to gather some elemy and tie into Amanda's life-line. She used this link to evaluate and control her patient's pain level and the labor's progress.

Before the next contraction, Bryon rushed into the room, carrying all of Alena's supplies. He kept his eyes averted from Amanda's body and concentrated on only looking at her face. He set the supplies on the side table and turned to leave.

"Stay," Alena ordered.

"But…," he began, searching for an excuse to escape.

"I may need your help," she said briskly. "This baby's coming fast. Sit beside Amanda and hold her hand."

Unable to refuse, Bryon reluctantly complied. The power of Amanda's grip made him feel foolish for thinking of his own discomfort. Amanda needed his strength to help her through this ordeal. This was going to be his first birthing experience as well.

"Okay, Amanda, I want you to push gently but consistently," she instructed. She watched as the baby's head progressed until it was halfway present and said, "A little more, now stop pushing." She wiped the baby's face and cleared the airway with the suction device from her kit. "One, maybe two, strong pushes, and we'll have ourselves a baby," she announced happily.

Amanda focused solely on Alena's instructions. She was amazed and not just a little alarmed at the speed of this birth; she had always heard it took hours of hard labor. While she felt a lot of pressure, it surprised her how little pain was involved. She had no way of knowing how much Alena shielded the pain from her.

Alena glanced over at her husband and dictated, "Put a towel across Amanda's chest, Bryon."

Bryon pried his hand away from Amanda's to comply with his wife's instruction. He grabbed a towel from the bedside table and unfurled it over Amanda.

With the baby's head presenting, she wanted to have Amanda feel like she was an active participant in her daughter's birthing.

Without missing a beat, Alena instructed her patient, "Give me your hands, Amanda." She brought Amanda's hands over the baby's head and then guided them to deliver the baby. Alena released Amanda's hands and held the baby's body, and together they lifted the wet and bloody baby onto the waiting towel.

She vigorously rubbed the baby's skin to clean her and stimulate her to cry with the towel. Within moments, the little girl gave a gusty cry of displeasure at the rough handling, and Alena smiled with satisfaction. She left the towel on the baby and told Amanda, "Keep her warm while I help you deliver the afterbirth.

"Bryon, can you please get a set of clamps and a pair of scissors out of my kit to cut the cord," she instructed as she gently tugged on the cord inside Amanda to see if it had come free. The placenta had not yet been released, so Alena clamped and cut the cord with only a few drops of blood released onto the towel.

After a cursory exam of the crying baby, she looked between Amanda's legs and exclaimed, "Oh, my goodness!"

"What's wrong?" Amanda asked worriedly.

CHAPTER 32

"You're having another baby, Amanda! Bryon, please take the baby while Amanda gets ready to push again."

Awkwardly wrapping the bloody baby, Bryon took the little girl. One-handed, Bryon flung another towel across Amanda's chest.

As an experienced father, he washed the baby while the other came into the world. Glad for something to do, he soaked a washcloth in the warm basin water and swabbed the pink little girl. She was perfect with ten perfect fingers and toes.

A few minutes later, Amanda held a second crying daughter against her chest. Alena then discovered the babies were identical twins sharing the same afterbirth. The two babies also explained the reason for Amanda's enormous girth.

Once both babies were washed, wrapped in clean clouts and towels, and resting on either side of Amanda, Alena asked the most obvious question, "What're you going to name them?"

"The first one I'll name Juila," she promptly replied as she turned to the little girl on her left and smiled. She turned to her right to smile even broader and said, "I don't have any idea what I'm going to call this little surprise! Do you have any suggestions?"

"I've always liked the name Jena," Bryon suggested helpfully.

"Juila and Jena," Amanda mused thoughtfully. "They sound beautiful together, similar, but not so close as to be confusing." Satisfied, she nodded. "I think that's the perfect name!"

"Wonderful," Alena said to no one in particular as she clapped her hands together quietly. "Bryon." She turned to address him. "Can you get the bassinets we used for Justan and Andera out of the attic? We need to get Juila and Jena into them so Amanda might get a little sleep before they decide to wake up and eat."

Alena noted Bryon leaving the room and turned to look at Amanda lying in bed with her two daughters. Her first experience as an official wise-woman didn't turn out as she imagined. She could kick herself for not taking the time to give Amanda a proper examination to know she was carrying twins.

Granted, Elder Debbon's invitation seemed impossible to accept. She couldn't figure out how to go until Amanda came along. It wasn't a good excuse. She prided herself in thinking of her patients' welfare over her own. In that aspect, she failed. This will be the last time she made such an egregious mistake in her wise-woman practice.

Alena thanked Jehoban that everything turned out well. She reached forward and shifted the blanket covering Jena's eye; the baby twitched at her touch. She smiled down at the infant and then moved her attention to Amanda.

"Thank you for their safe delivery," Amanda said softly. She snuggled closer to her daughters while attempting to get comfortable. Never before did she feel so tired and excited at the same time. What would her mother say about being a grandmother—twice over now? What will her children's future look like? Will they grow up on Tuala, or will they be able to go back to Earth? Only time would tell.

"What are you thinking?" Alena asked.

"I was thinking about my mom."

Maybe Amanda was tired enough to let something slip about her past. Alena followed Amanda's lead and asked, "Do you want to let her know about the twins?"

"I can't," she replied sadly.

"Why not?"

"Because she doesn't exist here."

"You mean she's passed on?"

"Yes, she's on the other side."

"I'm sorry, Amanda, I'm sure she'd be proud," she finished lamely. "Do you have any other family?"

"Not anymore," Amanda replied and squirmed uncomfortably.

"Are you hurting? Do you need me to check you to make sure everything's okay?" Alena asked. She used her newfound skill to touch Amanda's life-line to check her vitals.

"I'm fine. I'm just sore and feel used. How long do I have to stay in bed?"

"You could get up right now if you felt like it. Gravity will help you to heal and dispose of any residual blood. Do you want to try to go to the bathroom?"

"I think I'll wait until the babies are in their bassinets before attempting anything. It's really nice just having them in my arms right now," she answered with another sigh.

Muffled curses and a crash echoed down the hall as Bryon fell down the attic ladder. He appeared in the bedroom doorway, disheveled yet smiling as he pulled the two bassinets into the room. "It was a war, but I won," he exclaimed triumphantly. Then he asked, "Where would you like these put?"

Alena and Bryon moved a couple of furniture pieces so the two bassinets could rest side-by-side near Amanda's bed. Satisfied with the arrangements, Alena dusted the bassinets and left the room to get clean bedding for the two infants.

Returning swiftly, she made up one bassinet in pink and the other in yellow. After a few minutes of fussing, she gently picked up Jena and settled her in her new yellow bedding, ensuring her blankets were sufficiently snug to keep her warm.

Amanda lifted Juila, settled her into her other arm, and struggled to sit up. Taking the two steps to reach the other bassinet, she gently placed Juila into the small bed and then looked down at her perfect little daughters. She could hardly believe these two babies had come from her.

For the first time, she was able to get a good look at both of them. Try as she might, she couldn't find any resemblance to Neal in either of them. *Oh well. I've heard all babies resemble little old men, and you don't really know who they'll look like until they're older.*

Since the excitement of the birth was over, fatigue seeped through Amanda's muscles and into her very bones. She wished for nothing more than the chance to curl up and sleep for a hundred years, but she had to wait until Alena changed the soiled sheets on the bed.

Once she completed the task, Amanda melted onto her side in the freshly changed bed, facing the bassinets, and pulled the covers up over her shoulder. Alena ushered Bryon out of the room and closed the door leaving her alone with her children for the first time ever. She smiled as she drifted off to sleep.

Within a few hours, the babies started crying. Alena came in to help Amanda change their clouts and then show her how to nurse the girls. While it was possible to nurse them both simultaneously, Alena insisted it was better for the girls to feed separately. Alena supplied a pacifier for the baby temporarily denied sustenance while the other ate her fill.

The three other children loudly spoke on the other side of her bedroom door. She understood how intensely curious they'd be to meet the new arrivals. She smiled, anticipating their reactions to finding two babies when they thought there'd only been one. She asked Alena, "Would it be okay if the kids came in to meet Juila and Jena? I'm sure they're bursting with curiosity."

"I don't mind if you don't. I told them it'd be up to you when they're allowed in. I didn't tell them there were two since I thought you would like to see their reactions."

Amanda smiled and nodded, "I am very interested in what Justan will say. He's been the most attentive with me, and he did voice his concerns more than once about how big I was getting."

Alena nodded, smiling, and said, "It was the first thing he mentioned to me when I got home last night!"

"Was it only last night?" Amanda asked incredulously. "It feels as though a whole lifetime has passed since you came home!"

"Well, two lives have begun since I came home, at least," Alena replied as she walked over to the bedroom door. She poked her head out and said, "All right, children, Amanda said it was okay for you to come and visit as long as you behave."

Justan pushed his way ahead to appear first in the doorway. As anticipated, his reaction to the two bassinets was priceless. "There're two babies?" He looked incredulously at Amanda for confirmation.

"There sure are," Amanda said with a smile. "I've named them Juila and Jena."

Justan sidled up alongside the first bassinet and looked in on the baby, and asked, "Which one is which?"

"The one you're in front of is Jena."

"How will we tell them apart?"

Amanda hadn't thought about it yet and looked to Alena to answer the question.

"We'll keep Juila dressed in pink clothes and Jena in yellow," she replied. "Do you think you can remember to keep track of who's who then?" she asked, sounding as though this wouldn't be an easy task.

"Sure, Juila has an "i" in it like pink, and Jena has an "e" in it like yellow," he replied smugly.

"Well, my smart little boy, it sounds as though you do have it all figured out. Why don't you move closer to Amanda so the other two children can have a chance to look at the new arrivals?"

While the kids were staring at the babies, Alena asked Amanda, "Have you thought about when you'd like to have their crystal ceremony?"

Amanda stared blankly at her, having forgotten entirely about the Tualan custom. Needing to cover her momentary alarm, she scrambled for something to say. "I had hoped Nealand would be here for it, but I guess that isn't going to happen," she began sullenly. She shook her head to clear her negative thoughts, "I guess we can have it as soon as it can get arranged. I don't know very many people, so the guest list would be pretty short."

"Do you want me to perform it, or would you rather have another wise-woman brought in?"

"Alena, I can't believe you'd think I'd even consider allowing someone else to do the honor for my children! Of course, I want you for it! Besides, it was one of our terms of agreement for me to watch your kids while you went off to school, remember?"

"Well, I had to ask. You might've changed your mind since I was gone until the very night you delivered," she said as though ashamed of her poor timing.

"It just proves how wise you are to come home in time to help me," Amanda pointed out and smiled smugly.

"Thank you, Amanda. This ceremony will be my first, and I believe it's extraordinary and important since they're twins."

"When can we do it?"

"Since it'll be small, we can do it this afternoon."

"I think that would be ideal. Do I need to wear anything special?"

"No, I'll take care of everything; you'll just need to bring the babies to me just after they eat their dinner. I should be ready by then."

Amanda could see how excited Alena was to perform this first official ceremony as a wise-woman. Grateful for Barla's detailed explanation of the crystals and their associated ceremony, Amanda was slightly concerned about Alena not reading clearly into the children's futures since their parents were from Earth.

She'd wait and see what transpired. If a problem arose with the reading, she could always pretend to faint from just having had the babies, and it would end the entire scene.

True to her word, Alena transformed her workroom into a bright and cheerful area for the ceremony. She set up two pillows on the floor at the far end of the room for the babies to lie on so she could perform the reading without fear of them falling.

She carefully dressed in a wise-woman's costume, ready to do a formal reading, which consisted of a red tunic, a yellow belt embroidered with scenes of nature, a black pair of pants, and soft-soled shoes. She pulled her hair back into a bun secured tightly to the base of her head to keep it out of the way. She set out two bowls of green liquid, one for each child, along with her new box of crystals.

Alena watched as her entire family, as well as the next-door neighbor, filed into the room and took seats on either side of where she'd perform the ceremony. Since there were so few people, everyone would have an easy time seeing the entire procession. Alena hoped she would remember every step so as not to jeopardize the children's futures and bring shame to her new status.

Once everyone sat, Amanda entered the room with one child in each arm. She walked up the center of the room and delicately placed each sleeping child on a pillow, as indicated by Alena.

Amanda then kneeled on the floor opposite Alena and waited for the ceremony to begin. The short walk was tiring, and Amanda gratefully rested in comfort for the duration of the ceremony.

CHAPTER 33

"Friends, family, and neighbors, we have gathered together for the important task of assigning the protective crystals for these two infants. Amanda, as their mother, do you agree to allow me to look into your children's minds to assign their crystals?" Alena waited for Amanda to reply before continuing.

"Yes, I do," Amanda replied. Immediately she thought this seemed almost like a wedding, which made her smile at her answer. Apparently, it was the correct thing to say because Alena nodded solemnly and continued the ritual.

Alena dipped her finger into the bowl of green liquid beside Juila's head. She marked a green line across Juila's forehead and chanted, "I mark Juila's forehead to be able to divine the thoughts and intents of this soul." She dipped her finger again in the bowl and marked a circle in green on the back of each of her tiny hands, chanting, "I mark each of Juila's hands to be able to divine the actions for which she'll be responsible in her lifetime."

The room was utterly silent as Alena held each of Juila's hands in her own. With her eyes closed, she rocked back and forth with a thin smile on her lips, as she spoke, *"Pencipta langit, silakan panduan dalam pencarian. Membuat bacaan saya benar dan penugasan kristal yang tepat."*

Bryon leaned forward and quietly asked Amanda, "Would you like me to translate?"

Amanda nodded without taking her eyes from the ritual.

Bryon listened carefully to Alena and then translated into Amanda's ear, "Creator of heaven, please guide me in the quest. Make my readings true and the crystal assignment precise."

They waited as Alena continued to rock silently. Amanda worried about what was going on when Alena finally spoke again.

"This child will have many obstacles to face in her youth. She'll grow to be strong and independent. She'll have a strong sense of right from wrong," Alena finished, and she released the baby's hands. She grinned and looked up at Amanda and said, "Juila's the one who spoke to me before she was born. She said she's glad I was performing this ceremony because it makes you happy."

"She's right," Amanda quietly stammered as she remembered her amazement over Alena's ability to hear her unborn child. She fascinatedly watched Alena open the hinged box on the floor. It was beautifully ornate with many gemstones set into an elaborate design of leaves and flowers. The open lid obscured her view of the contents. However, Amanda assumed the box contained the protective crystals.

Alena didn't hesitate as she reached into the open box. She brought forth a one-inch-sized pendant with deep red stones which seemed to shine with a light of their own. She purposefully closed the box as she deftly threaded the pendant onto a delicately ornate chain which she produced from an almost hidden pocket of her tunic. She handed the necklace to Amanda and said, "As you place this crystal of protection on your firstborn daughter, say, *Saya memberikan ini untuk Anda dengan cinta.*"

Amanda solemnly took the necklace. She saw it contained the

shape of a tree, and the crystals were the tree's leaves. She clasped it around her daughter's neck and somehow managed not to stumble over the awkward phrase. Once finished, she looked at Bryon for the translation.

He leaned forward and whispered in her ear, "You said, *I give this to you with love.*"

Pleased with the progress of Juila's ceremony, Alena used a warm, wet cloth and cleaned the green liquid from Juila's forehead and hands. She rinsed the fabric in another bowl of clean water. Alena removed the material, picked up the cup, and handed it to Amanda.

Confused, Amanda automatically reached for the proffered cup and hesitated.

To cover any awkwardness, Alena announced, "I give you this water to drink. By the drinking of the liquid, which contains your daughter's essence, you'll seal the bond between your life and Juila's."

Amanda brought the cup to her lips and tasted the minty flavor. She paused after the first couple of sips and raised her gaze above the rim of the cup to look at Alena. How much was she supposed to drink? Alena's hands twitched to indicate she should finish it, and she did so with haste and then returned the cup.

"With this child, Juila, safe and protected from harm, we'll now turn to her sister."

Alena performed the same ceremony again and dipped her finger into the second bowl of green liquid beside Jena's head. As she marked the line across Jena's forehead, she chanted, "I mark Jena's forehead to be able to divine the thoughts and intents of this soul." She continued by marking the circles on the back of each hand, chanting, "I mark each of Jena's hands to be able to divine the actions for which she'll be responsible in her lifetime."

Again she held each of Jena's hands in her own. With closed eyes, she rocked as she petitioned Jehoban to guide her. Suddenly,

Alena gasped and almost dropped Jena's hands before recovering her composure. Her eyes popped open; she momentarily locked her gaze with Amanda and then purposefully shut her eyes to continue to see into Jena's future.

"This child's life will be an amazing journey. She'll always have those around her who unconditionally love her." Alena finished, and she released the baby's hands.

Unlike with Juila, Alena didn't open the crystal box. She then said, "I don't have the crystal which this child requires. I must ask Jehoban to send it to me." As if this statement explained everything, she turned around, remaining on her knees. With hands clasped and her head bowed low, she spoke quietly, *"Jehoban, ini anak membutuhkan hitam berlian untuk perjalanan berbahaya. Harap kirimkan kepada saya bersama dengan berkat dari hasil positif."*

Bryon saw Amanda turn to him for a translation, but he only shook his head. He translated it to himself as *Jehoban, this child requires a black diamond for her perilous journey. Please send it to me along with a blessing of Godspeed.* Amanda was better off not knowing the severity of the situation. If Jehoban refused the petition, Jena wouldn't be granted a protective crystal, which would essentially be a curse.

Silence permeated the room as everyone continued to wait. The wait seemed an eternity, but in reality, it was only a couple of minutes. Something happened above Alena—a shimmer and a sparkle followed swiftly by a sharp cracking sound like thunder. Alena unclasped her hands and closed her right hand on itself as she turned around with a smile turning up the corners of her mouth. "Jehoban has answered my petition."

She opened her hand to reveal a pendant of black stones nestled in a delicate gold setting already on a beautifully ornate chain. She handed it to Amanda and said, "As you place this crystal of protection on Jena, your second-born daughter, say, *Saya akan kasih Anda di manapun Anda berada.*"

Amanda completed her task. She watched as Alena wiped Jena's forehead and prepared the second cup of liquid for her to drink. She leaned toward Bryon for his translation of her second phrase.

With only a moment's hesitation, Bryon whispered, "You said, *I will love you wherever you are.*" He ignored Amanda's expression of a concerned query.

Seeing she wouldn't get anything more from Bryon, she waited for Alena to offer her the cup. She received it and brought it to her lips. After the first gulp, she tasted a drastic difference; this drink was bitter instead of minty. She forced herself to finish hurriedly and returned the cup to Alena.

Alena spoke to everyone in the room, "With this child, Jena, safe and protected from harm, we can all celebrate."

Amanda glanced at Tana and Bryon to see their reactions to the ceremony; they appeared pleased yet anxious at the same time. With the distinct impression that something serious had happened, Amanda assumed it turned out well in the end.

She gazed down at her now bejeweled daughters, and all worry melted away. She picked up Jena, supporting her onto her left arm, and thanked Alena as she passed Juila onto her other arm; they slept through the entire ceremony.

Tana approached her first. She kissed each baby's forehead and said to Amanda, "They're both beautiful, with equally beautiful crystals to protect them. May happiness bless your lives." She leaned forward and kissed Amanda on her cheek before turning aside to allow Bryon to greet her likewise.

Even Bryon and Alena's children kissed the babies and offered Amanda a blessing, which Amanda found curiously memorable. Alena was last to approach. Amanda did a double-take since Alena had changed her clothes yet accepted her blessing as she had everyone else's.

Amanda sidestepped to prevent Alena from turning away. Quietly, she asked, "Alena, did something go wrong?"

"It could have," she seriously replied before she smiled and continued, "but everything turned out wonderfully. And look," she pointed to the children sleeping peacefully, "they have their protection, and I'll teach you how to use the crystals to watch over them."

Like a dog with a bone, Amanda persisted by asking, "What did you see in Jena's future, which made you look at me?"

"I'm sorry, Amanda. I'm not allowed to share those things which I see, not even with the mothers. What's important for you is knowing we assigned the correct crystal for her life."

Unsatisfied, Amanda knew she wasn't going to get anything more out of Alena. She looked down on the two crystals with admiration and then remembered something Barla said. *The more dangerous the child's life, the darker the crystal assignment.*

Juila's stones were dark red, but Jena's were pure black, which struck a fearful and despairing stab through Amanda's heart. Hugging Jena closer to her, Amanda vowed to herself she'd protect her daughter with her very life if necessary.

Once the ceremony ended and Tana returned home, the children sat with Alena and Bryon on the couch. Amanda returned to the living room after settling the twins in their bassinets in the bedroom. Amanda sat by the fire and waited for storytime to finish and the children put to bed. Questions about the ceremony swam through her head, but she thought it prudent not to have the kids present.

"Okay, children," Bryon said, "Why don't you stand and sing us the Unity Song before going to bed."

Immediately the children left their parents' laps, and the boys added their voices when Andera began the song:

Crystal around the neck,
Follow the next step,
Changes today,
Changes tomorrow,

We all become one.

Both Alena and Bryon smiled as the children ended the song by holding each other's hands in a circle. Alena clapped and said, "How wonderful! You obviously practiced while I was away. Now, who wants me to tuck them in first?"

Several minutes later, Alena returned to the living room. She knew Amanda would have questions. She settled on the couch and cuddled against Bryon's side, expecting a long night ahead.

Without preamble, Amanda asked Alena, "Why didn't you have Jena's crystal in your box?"

Clearly not expecting the question, Alena answered simply, "My crystal supply is only equipped with common crystals. I needed to ask for a rare stone to handle Jena's exceptional situation."

"What exactly is her situation?"

"You know I'm not allowed to say."

"Okay," Amanda drawled. "Why did the two cups of water taste so different from each other? Did you use two different kinds of green liquid?"

That, too, surprised Alena into asking, "What do you mean they tasted different? What did they taste like?"

"Juila's was minty," Amanda started and saw Alena's confirming nod. She then continued, "Jena's was bitter."

"How interesting," Alena began. "I used the same steena tea on both of them. They should've tasted the same; I've never heard of them tasting different."

"You said you'd teach me how to use the crystals. When can I start training? I get the feeling I should learn immediately to be able to help them."

"We can start training tomorrow if you like," Alena sincerely said as she tried to restrain a yawn.

"I'm sorry, Alena, I'm acting selfishly. You must be exhausted from doing both ceremonies without much preparation. We'll begin my training tomorrow. I'll head off to bed before my little girls decide it's time to eat again."

Bryon watched Amanda leave. He hugged his wife tighter to his side and asked, "I don't suppose you can tell me what happened tonight?"

She gave him a disgusted look, poking him sharply in the ribs with her elbow, and said, "Not you too!"

He raised his hands in surrender and pleaded, "I was just asking. I didn't think you could."

"I can tell you this," she paused, "there're some interesting things which are going to develop. Rest assured, one way or another, those children will both be raised with a lot of love."

"Well, you managed to be both cryptic and unhelpful at the same time," Bryon said with a wicked grin. "Are you ready for bed? I know I am."

"Bed sounds like a dream right now," Alena sighed just at the thought of it.

CHAPTER 34

Dr. Gascon kept one eye on Dr. Medin as he read through her latest notes on Amanda. He knew Dr. Medin was looking at the wall of framed articles he had published in The American Journal of Psychiatry, the New England Journal of Medicine, the Journal of Behavioral and Brain Science, and the Archives of General Psychiatry. He was proud of his research and publishing accomplishments and hoped Amanda's case would again bring his work to mainstream attention.

Even with the risks involved in bringing a new disorder to his medical field's attention, he felt an obligation to his life's work to keep pursuing the human mind's intricacies. Amanda's multi-dimensional disorder appeared rather extreme, yet he remained convinced that he would soon have a breakthrough in her case with enough time and medication.

"I'm concerned about Amanda's latest recounting of having delivered two children. She appears to have abandonment issues, which she is trying to come to terms with in her account of Alena coming back home just in time to deliver the children. Also, while she seems to feel she's done her part for society by taking care of

Alena's children, she doesn't seem to have much interaction with other people. What are your thoughts on this?"

"I think taking care of three small children would be exhausting enough. She probably didn't feel she had enough hours in the day to interact with other people."

"Dr. Medin," Dr. Gascon dropped the folder onto his desk and turned his full gaze to the doctor standing across the office from him. He frowned and said, "it sounds as if you believe these things actually happened to Amanda. We know this can't be the case, so how do you explain her desire to have her own children?"

Dr. Medin shrugged and looked over her shoulder to reply, "Well, she was gone for fourteen months, so it's possible she got pregnant."

"Her medical reports from the time when she was found don't have anything to support your hypothesis." He waved his hand as though dismissing the conversation. Picking up the file and leafing through the pages, he glanced over the latest session's details again.

"Aha, here," he looked up and kept his finger pressed on the page. "Amanda has residual guilt regarding the disappearance of Nealand and the Golden Jesisca. She admitted she found the yacht by saying Alena told her its location at the Old Soul Engineering Facility. Obviously, she knows something about Nealand's location. I want you to delve further into that angle to get some closure for the Taivas family. They deserve to know what happened to their son."

Jasmine turned away from Dr. Gascon's trophy wall of articles. She knew he was an excellent research doctor; however, it didn't mean she agreed with his methods for producing the results of his studies.

More than once, she found herself dialing the phone to initiate an investigation on the facility to force him to leave a patient alone. As though Dr. Gascon knew she was close to breaking, he'd always find a way to calm her enough to allow the study to continue.

"I'm meeting with Amanda this afternoon. I'll see what I can find out about Nealand. If that's everything, I must get going. I still have some other notes to dictate before my next session." Jasmine walked toward the door.

"I look forward to reading your notes, Dr. Medin."

Jasmine returned to her office and thought about her next steps with Amanda. She couldn't get around the medication order that Dr. Gascon set up on her chart. But maybe she could figure out a way to meet with her before the administration of her next dose.

Only a few steps into her office, she turned on her heel and marched down the hall to Room 426. She'd be at her most lucid with the medication five hours in her system. Instead of eating lunch, Jasmine decided to have an impromptu session in Amanda's quarters.

She politely knocked on the door and waited for a reply. She knew the attendants didn't offer such courtesy to the patients, so she made a point in being more considerate. A few seconds later, a female voice told her to enter. She slowly opened the door, poked her head into the room, and asked, "Do you mind if we talk before your next session?"

Amanda cocked her head to the side and smiled as she answered, "I'd love to have some company. Come in."

Jasmine hurriedly entered the room when she heard an attendant talking at the nurse's station just around the corner. She didn't need the staff telling Dr. Gascon about her breaking protocol by meeting with a patient in their room—one more point of contention between herself and the good Dr. Gascon.

"We don't have much time before your next scheduled medication round. I wanted to hypnotize you while you're still unmedicated and lucid. Would you mind?"

"I'll try anything if it'll get me out of here sooner." Amanda hastily stowed her book on the bedside table and crossed her hands over her stomach. Already lounging on her bed, she just had to close her eyes to prepare. "I'm ready."

Jasmine smiled at Amanda's eagerness and began immediately…

GOOD ON HER WORD, Alena immediately began teaching Amanda how to use the crystals. Amanda appreciated the complexities of the pendant necklaces while she learned more about their capabilities. If used properly, not only would Amanda both see and hear everything her daughters did, she could deflect harm from them as well.

Alena insisted she learn how to set up simple protection wards to keep the twins from ill intent and neglect. She seemed oddly intent on making sure Jena's wards were thorough and specific. *What did Alena see in Jena's future to make this precaution so urgently necessary?*

By the time the twins were two weeks old, they slept through the night, which allowed the household routine to almost return to normal. When the twins were about a mesan old, Amanda took an hour to go to the market to buy some groceries. Andera assured her she'd be around to help Alena watch the sleeping children.

As it turned out, Andera's maternal instincts proved extremely helpful with the babies. Even though she was young, she took it upon herself to be a second mother to the twins, always staying close by and ensuring Amanda had everything she needed, including an extra pair of hands to hold a baby. Amanda depended on Andera to be by her side whenever the babies ate. Andera would hold and entertain whichever baby wasn't being fed.

Andera was eager for an opportunity to show Alena how well she could care for the babies. Alena smiled at her first-daughter's enthusiasm for the task and said to Amanda, "Take your time at the market; the fresh air will do you some good."

"Thank you," Amanda replied. "I don't think it'll take me very long to get the few things we need."

She left the house with a light heart and an open mind. She was going to ask discreet questions about crossing the veil to get back to Earth. It was a long shot, and she didn't know if this were even possible, yet she was going to keep alert for any opportunity to bring it up.

She almost felt guilty for trying to find a way to leave, yet at the same time, she didn't want to burden Bryon and Alena for so long with the addition of her twins. Besides, it might be easier to take the girls across to Earth while they were still little.

Most importantly, she wanted her mom to share in her experience of raising them. With her maternal instinct operating in full force, she truly began to appreciate how hard her mom must have worked in raising her three children without the protective crystals' assistance.

She strolled to the market, looking around the neighborhood as she went. This neighborhood could easily be transplanted onto Earth and be utterly unremarkable. At the market, she felt the same thing except for the odd varieties of foods available.

She kept her ears open for any opportunity to discover any mention of Earth. Once she thought she heard the term *old soul*, but she didn't know who spoke it when she turned around. Disgustedly sighing and deciding it was a useless endeavor, she purchased her supplies and turned to head home.

Amanda used this quiet time to look in on her daughters from a distance. She concentrated her thoughts through the colors of the crystals and found she could both see and hear everything happening around the twins. Satisfied because they were both still asleep and the household was in order, she stopped at the park to rest for a few minutes while enjoying the sun.

Amanda reflected on her time spent in Tuala. She'd been there for just over nine months. She had arrived at the end of June, known here as Elul, and now it was the end of March, called Sivan. Amanda hadn't noticed the seasonal changes due to the temperate climate.

What must her parents be going through thinking her dead? Pain lanced through her heart, making her catch her breath against the unexpected emotional onslaught. As much as she loved her daughters, she wished she'd never gotten on that yacht with Neal. She'd be safe at home, probably heading off to college. But that wasn't ever going to be her future now. Her daughters needed her —just as much as she needed her mother right now.

She patted the pocket containing Barla's letter; if nothing else, she'd bring closure to Barla's family regarding her disappearance. She was so conscious of this responsibility; she never left her room without Barla's note.

What began as a warm, sunny day suddenly turned cloudy. A chilly breeze and rain sprinkles brought Amanda's attention back to her current reality. She collected her grocery bags and set a brisk pace for the short walk home.

AFTER COMING up empty-handed in his search for Jesisca in Cresdon, Petre gathered supplies to continue his trading business. Entering the cabin reminded him forcibly of his loss. More than once, he looked through her clothes and tried to envision what she'd look like taking them off.

He missed having her warm body beside him in bed at night. He missed having her smile at him across the table while they ate. He missed watching her sit on the bow of the water craft, looking out over the water. Petre finally had to admit he had honest feelings for Jesisca, beyond even simple lust.

At every port, he asked his usual contacts if they might have any information on Jesisca. Every time the answer was the same, nobody saw her. *Had she been discovered and taken by an Elder? That'd explain a lot of things.*

After traveling along the coastline, he found himself back in the Port of Cresdon. There, he won a shipment of telepod crystals that he'd have to deliver personally to Kirma's distribution center. Petre looked forward to the change of scenery, plus it'd give him a chance to ask more people if they'd seen Jesisca.

Petre rented a transport telepod and loaded his cargo. The transport was so ill-kept that he was forced to travel quite some distance inland before teleporting into Kirma effectively. Once there, he made immediate arrangements for the delivery and payment of his telepod crystals with the manager named Bryon.

"I've got a shipment of telepod crystals to be delivered to you," Petre said to Bryon.

"Where did they come from?" Bryon asked suspiciously.

"I received them from Kenen at the Beewa quarry. He specifically asked me to bring them to you," Petre replied assuredly, taking an immediate disliking to Bryon, who seemed pompous and overly confident with his tall, muscular frame and rugged good looks.

"From Kenen, huh?" he questioned and then shrugged. "How many crates did he send?"

"I've twenty-eight of them, each containing four crystals."

"Let's just check a couple of boxes to see what the quality is like, shall we?" Bryon said as he opened the first box to inspect the goods for breakage. What he found was typical of Kenen's products, primarily inferior quality. "I can give you one taj and five shills for each crate," he said with finality.

Indeed, Bryon paid him less than his cargo was worth, but since he won the payload in a card game, it didn't cost him anything except the transport rental, and he needed the money.

With their business concluded, Petre opened his mouth to ask Bryon about Jesisca but was interrupted by another warehouse worker needing Bryon's attention. He scowled at Bryon's back when he left with the other worker. Disgruntled, he turned toward the office to get his payment.

A young, green-eyed beauty with striking auburn hair greeted him. Petre looked down at her nameplate and smiled. He addressed the petite woman with his request, "Hi, Frasnia. Bryon just agreed to pay me forty-two taj for my twenty-eight crates of crystals. I assume you're the right person to issue payment."

Frasnia took an immediate dislike to the disheveled man who stood in front of her. She definitely didn't want him to see where she kept the money box key, so she replied as nicely as she could, "Please take a seat over there, and I'll have your money in a few minutes." She gestured to the seating as far from her as possible and hoped he'd take the hint.

Petre smiled what he thought of as his sexy grin and said, "Are you busy after work?"

Frasnia tried to control her shiver of disgust when she looked up at him and replied, "Yes, my boyfriend and I are going out to dinner. Please take a seat now."

Petre complied with good grace and sat in the indicated chair.

With the man no longer hovering over her desk, she typed a quick query on her patil to ensure the quoted price was valid. Once she received confirmation, she counted the coins into a small cloth sack while seated at her desk.

Petre made sure his fingers touched hers when he accepted the payment she brought to him across the office. He always appreciated a woman's slender figure, and hers was just about perfection. "It's too bad you're not available," he said with a final attempt.

"Have a nice day," Frasnia replied curtly and turned to walk back to her desk. She wanted to have her patil at hand if this disgusting man didn't leave immediately. Thankfully it wasn't necessary as he left the office with a parting grin over his shoulder.

Seeing Petre MacVeen's name on the invoice shocked her, considering Bryon's feelings about the man. She had never met him before, but since she had, she'd be glad when he was once again out of their town.

His pocket bulged with the money sack. Petre's jaunty steps led him to the market where he could pick up supplies only found inland. He took his time wandering through the aisles. He enjoyed how everyone treated him respectfully; the people here didn't know his name or reputation.

He spoke with the vendors casually, trying to glean any information about whether or not the Elders might have found any *old souls* lately. People looked at him oddly and immediately shook their heads. Almost before the discussion began, it ended. Petre gathered his items together to head back to Cresdon before it got too much later.

Making his final purchase of fresh fruit, he heard an oddly familiar voice. At first, he couldn't place it, but then he caught a glimpse of a woman's profile and hair. *That has to be Jesisca.* He couldn't believe his luck. Even though she was heavier than he remembered, it had to be her.

Rushing the vendor to package his items, he shoved money at the old man and hurried to catch up with the woman he could no longer see. Petre pushed rudely through the crowd and hopped up to attempt seeing over their heads. She must have gone in this direction. He'd find her and bring her back with him in his rented telepod. She'd be his again.

CHAPTER 35

Dark clouds gathered on the horizon and rolled toward town. Amanda stared at them, not liking their ominous look at all. *Are we going to have an electrical storm?* She chided herself for delaying longer while she searched the skies for any sign of a dragon. *Why would there be one just because a storm was coming? It's not like there's any correlation between the two. Besides, I was probably mistaken when I thought I saw one before.*

Seconds later, the rain came down in earnest. She quickened her pace to a trot. The first flash of lightning followed immediately by a thunderous boom hit just as Amanda reached the front door. She rushed into the house and shut the door solidly behind her, thankful for the safety from the storm.

Her body shook from the aftermath of her journey. She wasn't as physically fit as she'd once been, and the storm rattled her to the core. Thunder and lightning scared her now. Before her accident with Nealand, she was always fascinated by nature's raw power at its most powerful.

Amanda checked on the twins on her way through the living room to the kitchen to calm her nerves. They both slept peacefully through the thunder and lightning raging directly overhead outside. Alena smiled at her as Amanda deposited the parcels beside her on the kitchen counter. Amanda spoke first, "They didn't have any taro root yet. They said it's still too early in the season for it. They might get their first shipment next week."

"I was afraid of that," Alena replied. "I guess I'll have to use the canned taro root for the foxl pie tonight instead. It's always so much tastier when it's fresh."

Together they prepared dinner. They talked about the twins and the weather. Even though Alena told her this storm wouldn't last, Amanda believed she was mistaken. Having been outside in it, she thought it was going to be a monster of a storm.

However, as this was the first weather system of the season, it was short-lived. After the initial downpour, the clouds swiftly blew through, leaving only a rainy drizzle behind. Amanda was thankful for the storm's brevity. She dreaded more of the major electrical storms she'd heard Bryon and Alena discussing throughout the winter season.

Another mesan passed, and still, the rainy season remained elusive. A palpable tension hung in the air as everyone seemed to anticipate its beginning. And still, nothing happened. Amanda felt even more anxious since Alena adamantly refused to let her venture out to the market again, coming up with one excuse after another for her to stay home.

Bryon told Alena about his encounter with Petre at the warehouse. They worried about Amanda's trip to the market coinciding with the day Bryon bought the crystals from Petre. If Petre happened to have seen her, then maybe he'd hang around. Several weeks went by before Bryon got word from one of his contacts about Petre being back on his regular trading route nowhere near Kirma or Cresdon.

Bryon needed to give Amanda a distraction to help alleviate some of her everyday monotony. "I have the day off. We should go for a hike in Cresdon's foothills." Seeing Amanda's doubtful expression, he rapidly added, "We can take a telepod ride to get there and back, making it a short trip indeed. I think you'll love seeing the spectacular coastal views."

Amanda perked up immediately. "Okay! That sounds perfect!" She went into her room, changed into her working clothes, safely tucked Barla's letter in her pants' pocket, and donned her sturdiest walking shoes. In the kitchen where Alena was just handing Bryon a satchel containing their lunch, she met Bryon, similarly dressed.

"All set?" Bryon asked when Amanda appeared in the doorway.

"I think so. Do I need to bring anything special?"

"Nope. Alena was thoughtful enough to pack us some snacks, and I already have our water bottles in the telepod. I think we're ready. Goodbye, my love," he said as he leaned down and kissed Alena soundly on the lips.

"You'll know if the twins need you," Alena said to Amanda as she hugged her swiftly before Amanda followed Bryon out the door to the waiting telepod.

"Thank you for watching them for me."

"It's my pleasure," she answered and then shooed her out the door. "Go! Have fun!"

Amanda practically skipped to the telepod in her excitement to finally leave the house. *If only I had a camera to capture these spectacular images.* She reached the telepod door, stepped in, and fastened her seat harness with enthusiasm.

Amanda glanced over at Bryon, smiling at her readiness as he activated the control to shut the door. She watched him concentrate on fixing their coordinates in his mind. She remained silent as the telepod rose from the ground. She anticipated the few moments of nothingness before the new surroundings of their destination would soon follow.

Bryon's description didn't hold a candle to the spectacular views before her. The telepod wasn't even settled down on the ground, but Amanda plastered her face against the side window. "Wow," was all she could manage to say to express the vastness of the terrain at sea level.

"Just wait," Bryon said as he gathered their gear and went out the telepod door. "The view from the top of the mountain is even better."

Amanda exited the telepod and glanced behind them at the mountain trail Bryon indicated. *That looks like a rather daunting day hike.*

"Let's hurry," Bryon said as he headed for the trail. "I'd like to get to the lookout point before those clouds settle further down on the mountainside to obscure our view."

Bryon set a grueling pace on the trail that followed alongside a seasonal stream. Amanda soon found herself panting for breath and hoping they'd take a short break so she could enjoy the nature sounds and look for any wildlife around. Shortly after that, Bryon took pity on her; however, they only rested for a few minutes.

When will we ever reach the lookout Bryon promised? No sooner did this thought come to her when they rounded the final corner and came to a broad plateau overlooking the shoreline vista.

"Let's sit on these boulders," Bryon said. He spread out the contents of their lunch. It was a simple fare of shredded foxl sandwiches and mixed fruit salad.

Amanda ate with an appetite she didn't know she still possessed. After satisfying her stomach, she said, "I'm going to rest my eyes for a second." Bryon nodded and turned to enjoy the view to give her some privacy. Uncertain of her crystal skills, she didn't dare tell Bryon that she wanted to check on her daughters. What would she say if it didn't work?

Despite the distance separating them, in just a few seconds, Amanda saw Alena holding both girls and the three other children, entertaining them all. Amanda smiled and returned her focus to her present surroundings.

Bryon grinned at her and asked, "How are Juila and Jena?"

"How'd you know I was checking on them?"

"I've seen the same expression on Alena's face enough times to know when a mother's checking on her children. What were they doing?"

"Alena was holding them while your children were taking turns making funny faces at them," she answered with a smile on her face.

"Alena simply adores babies. I'm afraid she's catching the baby bug again, and I can feel another baby in my future within the next nine mesans or so!" Bryon's attempt at looking pitifully put out failed miserably, and they both ended up laughing.

They sat for a few more minutes in contemplative silence, enjoying the view. The cool breeze reminded her of a childhood trip to Lake Tahoe with her parents. Closing her eyes, she let the memories slide through her thoughts. She missed her parents. She hated thinking they were missing out on their granddaughters.

While she had convinced herself that she wouldn't be welcomed back to her family because of the twins, she knew this wouldn't be true. Her parents would do anything to know their daughter was alive. She knew that so profoundly, it shamed her to have doubted their love for even a second.

In that instant, she decided to take action. If Neal couldn't be located, then she'd find a way to get herself and the twins back without him. As soon as they returned to Kirma, she'd tell Alena and Bryon about her history. Once they knew the truth, then they'd take her and her children to an Elder. Then she could ask for the Elder's help.

It felt terrific finally to decide her future. She'd take charge of her life. Besides, it didn't seem fair to keep living with Bryon and Alena, even if they said they loved having her. She needed to go home.

At this altitude, the cold ocean breeze buffeted their bare flesh.

Goosebumps rippled along Amanda's arms, and she rubbed them to add back some warmth. She looked up, shocked to see the clouds which had seemed so far above were now mere feet above their head. They shifted with the wind, and she smelled rain.

Before she could open her mouth to suggest heading back to the telepod, the clouds parted. Her eyes rounded with disbelief and fear. She remained frozen where she sat on the boulder, unable to move even if she wanted to.

A massive dragon soared gracefully to land only feet in front of their boulders. Her feet landed so softly that none of the dust even shifted. Shafts of sunlight sparkled against the purple scales along her back, and gold scaled neck. She tucked in her wings and leaned forward, her long neck outstretched as her head dropped lower.

She turned slightly to view Amanda, ignoring Bryon entirely even when he scrambled backward behind their boulder. With a huff of warm air wafting over Amanda's whole body, she spoke into Amanda's mind, *"Almost. Hmm. Interesting."*

Amanda's mind refused to work beyond the wonder of this encounter. Was this the same dragon she'd seen in the storm on her perilous journey with Bryon? Instantly knowing this dragon's name, Aaliyah confirmed her unspoken question.

Aaliyah backed up a single, shuffling step and unfurled her wings. With a twist of her body, she leaned forward and dropped off of the mountainside. Seconds later, she soared upward and disappeared back into the clouds.

Amanda and Bryon exchanged incredulous looks. "Did that really just happen?" Amanda stammered.

"Yeah, but nobody'd believe us. I don't think we should tell anyone. Dragons are supposed to be myths."

"Looks like they're just as mythical as the *old souls*," Amanda murmured, never realizing Bryon could hear her.

"Do you realize that the strangest things happen around you?" He said.

She quirked her eyebrow at his remark. She would do without all of it if she could have her simple life back. "What do you think she meant when she said *almost*," Amanda asked.

"What are you saying? I didn't hear her say anything. What did she sound like?" Bryon picked up their picnic bag and stuffed the wrapper he held into it.

"Royal," Amanda answered immediately, not knowing where that came from but feeling the truth of it. Amanda searched the clouds for another glimpse of her.

She should've paid more attention when she stood so close, but it all happened so fast. Amanda wished she could soar with the dragon—ride on her back to Earth. Such fanciful thoughts would get her nowhere.

Bryon saw her upturned face and looked at the clouds himself. "We can talk about this dragon encounter once we're back in the telepod. Right now, it looks like the weather's telling us it's time to start heading back. Going downhill is better and worse at the same time. It's certainly quicker, but it's a lot easier to trip and fall, too!"

Amanda wished he didn't say anything about tripping since she was notorious for that very action. *I'm older now and haven't tripped the entire day, and that has to count for something!* Inwardly smiling, she stood and brushed the grit from her trousers. She searched the skies while Bryon meticulously gathered every last bit of debris before they began their return.

He stowed the items in his small backpack and said, "I think I got everything. You'd better take one last look before the clouds obscure everything, and then we need to get going."

Amanda looked out over the vista. She prepared a photo of it in her head to remember always. This way, she could describe it to her parents when she finally made it back home—although she'd probably leave out the dragon encounter. Bryon was right—nobody would believe it. A few moments later, she followed Bryon back down the steep trail.

As her intuition indicated, it did start to rain; not the soft, happy rain, but hard, cold sheets of rain. It looked like the rainy season began in earnest.

Amanda's drenched hair clung to her scalp and cheeks, and her clothes became saturated and heavy. Her feet slipped and slid on the now muddy track they followed.

Why didn't we leave much earlier to avoid this whole mess? But then I would've missed the dragon. Well, there's that consolation.

At first, Bryon was sure-footed on the trail in front of Amanda, making her feel clumsier still. After five more minutes of rain drenching the soil, he, too, began to slip and slide as they descended the mountain. Each turn in the trail brought them closer to their destination, but they still had a long way to go, and the steepest part was closest to the bottom.

They just reached the steep straight stretch that would lead them to where they had parked the telepod when the ground rumbled deep under their feet. *Was that thunder?* One look at Bryon's face disillusioned her of the idea. What she saw on his face was pure terror, and she didn't know what caused it.

"What happened?" Amanda yelled urgently to Bryon as he started slipping and sliding to get off of the trail.

"I've seen the aftermath but never heard the beginning. If I'm not mistaken, that sound was the start of an avalanche!"

She didn't need any more prompting. She'd rather slide down the remainder of the trail on her rear than get caught in a muddy avalanche. Amanda fell more in the next thirty feet than she had in the past ten years of her life, yet she didn't care.

The trail's end stood about three hundred yards ahead of them. Branches broke behind her; she looked back to see a wall of mud, trees, rocks, and debris a hundred feet away and heading straight for them.

"Run, Bryon!" Terror rose inside her, and she screamed with renewed fear.

Hearing Amanda's fear, he also looked behind them and understood their peril. With a surge of energy, he charged down the trail, heedless of grace. Amanda stayed right on his heels. Without paying close attention, Bryon missed the dip in the track and lost his footing entirely, causing him to fall flat on his face. He skidded to a complete halt.

Amanda immediately began to help him up, repeatedly saying, "Please be okay; please be okay."

Scrambling to his feet, Bryon overcompensated and almost tumbled into the stream beside the trail. Again, Amanda reached for him and pulled him swiftly away from the edge. Unfortunately, where she planted her feet gave way, and she tumbled over the edge of the bank and fell headlong into the creek.

The water was freezing, and she surfaced and gasped for air. Urgently regaining her feet, she only took one soggy step toward the bank when the avalanche caught up to them.

Bryon could only watch as the wall of mud turned away from where he stood to follow the lower course of the creek where Amanda just fell. "Amanda!" he yelled over and over as he searched for her in the swells of mud. He ran again beside the creek, keeping one eye on the trail and the other on the stream for any signs of Amanda. He thought he saw her hand surface about two hundred yards ahead. He didn't have much time before she drowned.

Bryon came to the end of the trail and helplessly watched the muddy waters drain into the boiling surf of the ocean. It seemed highly doubtful that Amanda could've survived through all the debris and boulders mixed in with the mud. If the debris didn't kill her outright, drowning was the next hazard.

As he rounded a pile of boulders strewn on the beach, he witnessed a massive explosion. A mass of boulders fell into the ocean just where he imagined Amanda would've been.

The dragon's shrill cry overhead forced Bryon to look up and away from the accident scene. *What does she know? Can she help?* Even as he watched, she disappeared just like a telepod blinking out of sight, taking away his last hope for a miraculous rescue.

Bryon turned back to the ocean and knew he was looking at a hopeless disaster. No way could Amanda have survived everything that just happened. He raced back to his telepod and hovered over the destruction zone, vainly searching. He continued his search until the sun sank behind the mountain that took her.

Bryon didn't want to face Alena with this news. This outing was his idea. He was responsible for Amanda's tragic death; her children would never know their mother. "What am I going to do?" Bryon despaired out loud to himself in the telepod.

With nothing else left to do, he noted his coordinates in his log and then teleported to the nearest rescue authority in Cresdon. After hours of questioning, signing statements, and pouring over maps, Bryon finally returned to his home in Kirma. Alone.

CHAPTER 36

It was already late, and Alena would know something went wrong. Bryon couldn't avoid the conversation any longer; he fixed the coordinates in his mind for home and teleported instantaneously to his yard.

As expected, Alena stood waiting for him on the front porch. As soon as the telepod touched down, Alena jumped to her feet and ran across to open the telepod door. "What happened?"

"I lost Amanda," Bryon said simply and dejectedly.

"What do you mean you lost her?"

"We were heading down the trail to come home, and then it started to rain," he began and looked into Alena's eyes.

"And?"

"It rained so hard, so fast, then there was a mudslide, and Amanda got swept away in it," he finished briskly.

"Why didn't you rescue her?"

"I tried!"

"I'm sorry, honey, I'm sure you did," she hugged him to her tightly, disregarding the filth covering him, released him, took his arm, and steered him toward the house. "Let's go inside, and you can tell me everything." Alena was confident they'd locate Amanda if she could just hear the whole story.

They sat at the kitchen table, and Bryon recounted everything that happened throughout the eventful day, except for the dragon sighting. He told her about the rescue authorities, saying they'd let them know if they ever found anything. Once he finished the story, the weight of the whole day bore down on him. He brought his hands to cover his face and broke down completely. "What're we going to do?"

"We're going to wait," Alena simply said. Bryon's tale did nothing to reassure her. A horrid feeling settled deep inside her about the whole ordeal. She'd do her best to keep her thoughts from her husband.

"But what about the babies?"

"We'll keep them, of course!"

"But, they're not ours."

"We'll keep looking for Nealan."

"Did Amanda ever talk about her parents?"

"She did," Alena replied, "she told me they were dead."

"So her daughters really don't have anyone but Nealan to claim them," Bryon simply replied. "Oh, Alena, I'm so sorry to bring this burden to our family. You just became a wise-woman, and you should be using your vocation, not starting another family! This's all my fault. It was my idea to go hiking; I should've checked the weather first!"

"Bryon, stop this right now!" Alena scolded her husband. "You had no idea things would turn out this way. You can hardly blame yourself for this bizarre accident. Let's wait for a few days and see if the rescue authorities can find her before we start making other arrangements."

"But I searched and searched," Bryon sobbed and started to rock back and forth in his chair.

Alena recognized the signs of shock and thought up a draught of *epeny* for Bryon to drink. The drug reminded her of Amanda's ordeal with Petre. She held it to his lips and said, "Drink this, Bryon. It'll help." Forcing the drink through his lips, she continued to tip the cup until Bryon was required to swallow.

Once he finished the contents, she set the cup on the table and helped him out of the chair. "Come on, Bryon, let's get you to bed," she said gently to him. She put her arm around his waist and guided him toward their bedroom.

She laid him down on the bed, clothes and all. After removing his shoes, she took the spare blanket out of the closet to cover him. Gently, she kissed him on the forehead and brushed the hair away from his face. She whispered, "I love you."

Only by liberally lacing his drink did he fall fast asleep. Quietly, Alena left the room to check on the twins in Amanda's room. Both slept peacefully, without a care in the world.

Will we be the ones to keep them? She saw their futures and knew she'd be a part of their lives. If Amanda were truly gone, it must be they were meant to keep them. As much as she loved the babies, she fervently hoped Amanda would be found alive.

With tears blurring her vision, Alena searched through Amanda's things for any clue about another family member they could notify. *Should I contact Barla and Captain Ahn and let them know? I'll wait, especially since they only knew her as a swimmer. Neither one of them mentioned any next of kin to Bryon when they asked him to protect Amanda.*

JOSE SLOWLY WALKED along the beach, heading back to his home in Cancun. Once again, he disappointed his girlfriend and made her mad. She told him not to come back until he gave up his drinking. Even though he'd tried so many times to give it up, his friends always had a party going on where it would be readily available, not to mention rude to refuse.

With his head down, he kicked at a rock on the shore, watching as it skipped along the sand and landed in an incoming wave. A flash of fabric beside a boulder and then what looked like a human hand caught his attention. He rushed forward to investigate, glad for something to take his mind off his problems.

He hurried around the outcropping of rock and through the small stream that came down off the highland, spilling into the ocean. At first, he thought the woman was dead because of how unusually dirty and still she looked. He spoke as he got near her, "Señora, ¿estás bien?"

He reached forward and touched her cheek. She was cold, but her skin was soft, and her eyelids fluttered. Relief rushed through him that she was indeed alive. He shook her shoulder and said, "Despertarse. Déjame ayudarte."

The man's voice roused Amanda from her stupor. She felt horrible; every part of her body hurt. The stream's water flowed around her. *Why am I lying in the river?* Try as she might, she couldn't remember how she ended up where she was. Hands pulled on her, and she tried to sit up. Pain coursed through her body, making her cry out and remain flat on the ground.

Jose needed to leave her to bring back help, so he said, "Está bien, la señora. Permanezca donde usted es. Yo le traeré ayuda a usted."

Amanda couldn't understand what he said, but since he nodded to her while he spoke, she nodded back as best she could. She watched with more than a bit of concern as he stood and ran away from her. She closed her eyes and prayed he'd bring back help.

She must've fallen asleep or passed out because the next thing Amanda knew, people swarmed around her. They asked her questions, and she finally recognized the language as Spanish. She didn't know why this idea made her so happy, yet joy rushed through her mind.

The medical crew strapped her to a board and lifted her from the stream. Six men, three on each side of the stretcher, carried her until they reached an emergency vehicle. They lifted her into the back of the sport-utility vehicle. Four of them sat beside her while the other two ran to the front.

Amanda only caught a fleeting glimpse of the first man she saw as they shut the doors. She wished she could've thanked him for bringing help. They drove away from the beach.

Will he come to the hospital to check on me? Is he someone I know?

Everything happened swiftly once she arrived at the hospital. The staff finally brought someone over who spoke English. The man in the white coat held a clipboard and a pen as he faced Amanda and said, "Hi, my name is Dr. Flores. Can you please tell me your name?"

Amanda was relieved to hear his almost perfectly spoken English, "Yes. My name's Amanda Covington."

"Amanda, can you give the name of someone I can contact to let them know you're here?" he kindly asked as his pen scratched over the paper.

Amanda thought about it for a minute. *I don't know why I'm here myself.* She shook her head in frustration and answered, "I don't remember."

"It's okay," he assured briskly, then continued, "Do you know the name of the town or the state you're from?"

Again, Amanda wracked her brain and came up blank. She shook her head.

"It's okay. Can you tell me where you hurt?"

"Everywhere, really," she answered and then reassessed her body. "My left arm hurts bad as well as my shoulder and ribs on the left side. Everywhere else just feels banged up and bruised."

Dr. Flores nodded, set down the clipboard, and moved over to her left side to feel the indicated areas for damage. He nodded and spoke something in Spanish to a waiting staff member.

He turned back to Amanda. "I've ordered a set of x-rays for your whole side and a cat scan of your head since you're having some difficulty with your memory. Nurse Bota will take you right now to get it done and then bring you back. Once I've taken a look at the films, I'll let you know what we'll need to do. Okay?"

"Okay," Amanda replied. "Can you give me something for the pain, or do I need to wait?"

"How bad would you rate the pain on a scale of one to ten?"

"It's at least an eight, bordering on a nine."

"I'll instruct Nurse Bota to give you something to take care of it. Are you allergic to anything?"

"No. At least I don't think so," Amanda replied with less confidence, yet anticipating the idea of the pain subsiding soon. Dr. Flores spoke again to the nurse, presumably ordering her drugs. Dr. Flores walked away to another emergency as Nurse Bota filled a syringe. Amanda watched the nurse inject the contents into the I.V. drip attached to the back of her right hand.

Dizziness clouded the edges of her thoughts as the drug began to take effect. She watched disconcertedly as Nurse Bota moved to the head of the stretcher and steered her toward the x-ray room. The ceiling lights blurred together as her eyes drifted closed.

She never remembered getting the x-rays, the scan, or talking with Dr. Flores afterward. The next thing she recalled was waking up alone in a white, sterile room, flat on her back with the covers pulled up to her chin. Her left arm was heavy, and her chest felt compressed. She blinked her eyes open and discovered her left arm was casted. Upon inspection with her right hand, she found her chest wrapped tightly with bandages.

She remained lying in bed for a few minutes before a nurse noticed she was awake. Before Amanda could ask for someone to speak with, the nurse hurried away. In a few moments, she returned with Dr. Flores and a broad smile on her face.

"Ah, I see you're finally awake, Amanda," he said as he settled a hip onto the side of her bed. "How're you feeling today?"

"I'm still really sore, but a lot better than when I got here a couple of hours ago."

"It's been more than a couple of hours, Amanda. You've been unconscious for forty-six hours," he replied gravely.

"What?"

"With as much trauma as your body sustained, I instructed the staff to monitor you to make sure your vital signs stayed strong and let your body heal itself. How's your pain level right now?"

"It's probably about a four," she replied. She struggled to process the idea of being asleep for almost two whole days; it only felt like a few minutes.

"Good," he replied. "I've got good news for you as well. We've contacted your family in Florida. They should be arriving in the next couple of hours."

"How on earth did you find my family?"

"I contacted the local police department and asked them to search your name to see if anyone reported you missing in the last twenty-four hours. From the extent of your injuries, I thought it'd been at least that long since anyone last saw you."

He enjoyed recounting his story, and she nodded for him to continue.

"Anyway, the police entered your name into the computer; a missing person report did come up along with your photo. The report was filed fourteen months ago. When the police contacted your mother, she fainted. Luckily your father was home, and he took down all of the information on where you are. They booked the next flight out and will be here shortly."

"Wait, did you say I've been missing for *fourteen months*?"

"You don't remember anything?"

"No."

"It's okay. The mind is very resilient. Given enough time, you'll probably get all your memories back," he assured as he patted her hand. "Do you want something to eat while you wait for your parents to arrive?"

"I could probably hold something down."

"Glad to hear it. I'll have some chicken-noodle soup brought in for you," he said as he stood from the side of the bed. "Welcome back to the land of the living."

"Thanks, I think," she mumbled to his retreating back.

A cheery young girl brought in the soup. She set it down on a rolling trolley and pushed the tray close to Amanda. With a curt nod, she left Amanda alone to eat. Amanda dipped the spoon into the broth and brought it to her lips. It tasted like ambrosia; she was ravenously hungry and eagerly ate the entire bowl's contents.

With nothing more to eat, she set the spoon down inside the bowl and pushed the rolling tray away from over the bed. She carefully rested herself back against the pillow and sighed contentedly. She shut her eyes for a moment and fell back into an easy, restful sleep.

CHAPTER 37

Someone held tightly to Amanda's hand when she regained consciousness. After a brief struggle to open her eyes, she blinked several times in quick succession. Shifting her gaze to the side where her mother sat crying. She drew in a hasty breath and said, "Momma!" Even through her excitement, she winced as her ribs pressed painfully against the compression bandages.

Relief spread across Diane's face as she heard her daughter's voice, which she had never thought to hear again. "Yes, my baby, it's your momma." She squeezed Amanda's hand a little to let her know how grateful she was to be talking with her. "Are you feeling okay, honey? Do the doctors need to give you anything?"

"No, Momma, I feel wonderful. Better now because you're here. Did Dad come with you, too?" She looked past her mother to find her father.

Diane nodded and said, "He went to find a bathroom; he'll be right back. Oh, he'll be so excited to see you're finally awake." Her smile positively beamed across her face in anticipation of her husband's reaction.

As if on cue, Chris came quietly into the room, expecting Amanda to be still asleep. He walked up behind his wife and looked over her shoulder to check on Amanda, and his eyes rounded with shocked happiness. "Well, good morning, sunshine!"

"Oh, Dad, I'm so glad to see you!" Amanda gushed as tears started gathering on her lashes.

"Thank goodness! She really is our daughter, isn't she, Diane?" Chris spoke quietly to Diane.

"She sure is. She recognized me immediately and asked for you right afterward," she announced proudly. She stood and took Chris's hand and exchanged her hold on Amanda to Chris. "Stay with her," she said as she walked toward the door. "I'm going to find a doctor to let us know when we can take her home." She opened the door and left immediately.

Chris sat in the chair Diane vacated and smiled at his youngest daughter. *She looks terrible.* Out loud, he said, "You look wonderful. Are you feeling okay?"

"I'm fine, now, Dad. I'm glad Momma's finding out when I can leave. I want to go home so badly it hurts."

"I don't want to put any pressure on you, but Dr. Flores said you couldn't remember anything about the last fourteen months. Has anything come back to you yet?"

Amanda thought about it for a few seconds and then quietly said, "I'm sorry, Dad, no. Dr. Flores said, given time, it might come back to me, though."

"Maybe so, maybe not," Chris reassured her and then continued, "it doesn't really matter. We're just glad to have you back. Your mother was scared to have you go sailing with Neal, yet she tried her best not to ruin your first adventure because of her fears.

"And then, not more than a week after you left, the Coast Guard contacted us when a mayday came from Neal's yacht. Then we got word from the Coast Guard when they found Neal, but not you. Your mother was distraught since her sister was also lost at sea all of those years ago. She kept saying it was happening all over again, and she couldn't bear it."

"I didn't know that's how Aunt Barbara died," Amanda said into the silence.

"Yes, your mother doesn't like to talk about it."

"I'm glad to hear Neal's okay."

"Well, I'm not sure *okay* is exactly accurate," Chris began but then stopped talking.

"Tell me what happened, Dad."

"As best as we could find out, a squall hit where you two were sailing. Neal said the wind rose, and he went up on deck to check the coordinates. While he was up there, the yacht hit something, and Neal called in a mayday.

"He was on his way back to get you when a rogue wave hit the side of the yacht and launched him overboard. He said he was plunged under the water for a few seconds and then broke the surface in time to see a flash of light. Neal said when his eyes adjusted to the dark again, the yacht disappeared. We were sure he meant it sank; however, rescue crews have yet to find it.

"When he found out you were missing, he went berserk. His family hired search parties to cover a vast area of the Gulf of Mexico to search. The crews looked for three weeks before they finally conceded you most likely drowned and were eaten by sharks."

"That's horrible! How's Neal now?"

"He hasn't been the same, but he finally moved on. I have to tell you, Amanda, he searched for you for almost a year until his parents forced him to stop. Once they convinced him to move on, he started dating again. About three months ago, he met a woman named Angie, and they appear to be pretty serious about one another."

"Oh," Amanda replied as she looked down on her left hand and noticed the engagement ring still on her finger extending out from the cast. "I guess that means our engagement is off," she ended lamely.

"We'll see, Amanda. Don't worry about it right now. You need to concentrate on getting yourself healed so we can get you home."

"I'll heal faster if I can go home right now!"

"I'm sure your mother will get it taken care of right away. It's all she talked about the entire flight over here," Chris assured her as he stroked her hand and looked lovingly at her face.

A short time later, her mother came striding confidently back into the room with Dr. Flores in tow. He came forward and looked at Amanda's chart at the foot of her bed. He nodded, looked up at Amanda, and said, "If you feel up to it, I can sign your release papers right now, and you can go home with your parents." He raised his eyebrow, waiting for Amanda to reply.

"I can't think of anything I'd rather do," she replied with a delighted smile on her face.

"I'll have the discharge nurse handle everything right away then," he said and then turned to her parents. "She'll need to have her arm checked when you get back home since it broke pretty badly just below the elbow.

"Make sure she drinks plenty of fluid, especially on the airplane, and put her to bed as soon as you get home. Her body is pretty beaten up, and rest will be the best medicine."

He waited to see if they had any questions, then when nothing was forthcoming, he walked to the door and said, "I'm glad we were able to reunite your family. Take care." He opened the door and walked out.

A short while later, a nurse appeared with two bundles and a folder of paperwork. She set the bundles at the end of the bed beside Amanda's feet and then turned to Chris and Diane while opening the folder. In broken English, she said, "Need here you to sign." She pointed out the various spots for Chris and Diane's signatures.

She smiled at them as she closed the folder, and then she pointed to the two bundles. "Good clothes home for Amanda to wear. These dirty when in she came. You good to leave. Have good day." She nodded at the family and then left the room.

Diane shooed Chris out of the room in her haste to get Amanda dressed and ready to leave. She opened the first bundle and removed an obviously Mexican shirt and a plain pair of pants. A pair of Mexican sandals was at the bottom of the bag, which were a little big for Amanda but better than nothing.

With a little bit of a struggle, Amanda dressed and sat on the bed's edge, ready to leave. She was exhausted, yet she wasn't about to let anyone know just in case they decided she needed to stay longer. She wanted nothing more than to go home and sleep in her own bed.

CHAPTER 38

After an uneventful flight home, Diane put an unresisting Amanda straight to bed. Amanda luxuriated in the feel of the mattress beneath her, and she breathed deeply of the familiar scent of home. She slept immediately and woke up quite a while later.

Amanda gingerly pulled herself out of bed, relieved herself in the bathroom, and then made her way through the house looking for either of her parents. She found them both in the kitchen. Amanda noticed her bag of dirty clothes on the floor by her mother's feet.

Looking up inquiringly at her mother, Amanda raised an eyebrow as she asked, "Find anything in there to tell me where I've been?" Although she tried making a joke about it, she immediately changed her mind when seeing her mother's face. "What is it, Momma?" she asked as she limped across the room and sat at the kitchen table next to her mother.

Diane held a tattered bundle of papers in her hand, and she shook her head, trying to figure out what to say. "I found this in your pants pocket," she said as she waved the papers carefully.

"What does it say?"

"The envelope said, 'Open this when you get home.' I opened it and read it to Chris, but we're having a tough time believing what it says. Why don't you read it and tell me what you think." Diane handed the water-wrinkled papers to Amanda and sat back while she watched Amanda.

At first, Amanda was as baffled by the story unfolding on the page as her mom. She didn't recognize the handwriting, yet images popped up in her head of the events described as she continued to read. By the time she got to the end of the narrative of her time on Tuala with Barla, she remembered her promise to find Barla's family. She excitedly asked her mother, "There was another envelope with this letter, right?"

Diane exchanged concerned looks with Chris and replied, "Yes. I haven't opened it yet. Amanda, can you explain what this is talking about?"

Amanda almost burst with excitement; she remembered Barla and how she taught her about Tuala. "I promised Barla I'd find her family and let them know she's okay," she announced with enthusiasm.

"Did this Barla woman write this letter? Are you trying to say everything written here is true? You expect us to believe you were on Tuala, which is really on Earth, but a different dimension?"

"Yes, that's exactly what happened. Barla told me I wouldn't remember anything once I passed through the veil because Jehoban placed a protective barrier to keep us from interfering with their lives. Where's the other letter, Mom? Barla wouldn't tell me who her family was while I was there, and I'm dying to get started on finding them for her."

Diane hesitantly reached into the tattered envelope and pulled out a smaller sealed envelope that read, 'For finding my family' on it. She scowled as she saw the handwriting, but she handed the envelope over to Amanda.

Amanda's shaking fingers fumbled while she clumsily tore the envelope open. She quickly read the following:

My name on Earth was Barbara Silnack. On January 21, 1945, I was born in Oconto, Wisconsin, to Sydney and Ellen Silnack. The last place I knew of my mother, Ellen, was living in Chico, California. She worked for an egg carton manufacturing plant called Spade Manufacturing. I have a younger brother named Saul Silnack, born on January 19, 1946, who joined the Navy to avoid the draft. I also have a younger sister named Diane Silnack, who was born on October 1, 1947. I don't know if Diane ever married or her occupation since she wasn't out of high school when I disappeared.

I hope this is enough information to get you started on finding my family. Thank you from the bottom of my heart.

P.S. Please tell my family how happy I am and about my son and daughter. My mother will be pleased to know she has at least two grandchildren.

Love,

Barla (Barbara)

AMANDA GASPED as she finished the letter; it all made sense now. She finally understood why she felt Barla was so much like her mother; Barla was her mother's long-lost sister! She remembered Barla's daughter looking so much like herself; they were first cousins. Her hands shook harder as she held out the letter for her mother to read. "I think once you read this, you'll believe."

Diane scowled as she took the proffered letter. She read the first line and gasped. Chris jumped up and started to read it over her shoulder. "Oh, my!" Diane exclaimed over and over as she read it through. "This's Barbara's handwriting! She's alive, Chris! She's alive!" She looked up at Amanda, tears coursing down her cheeks, and said, "Tell me everything about her. What does she look like? Tell me about her husband and her children."

"I can't believe I didn't see it while I was with her. I even told her she felt like a second mother to me, and now I understand why. Her husband is a wonderful man named Ahn, the Harbor Master; that's considered a very high position in their society.

"Together, they have a twenty-one-year-old son named Gravin and a nineteen-year-old daughter named Rasa. I didn't get to meet either of them since they were away at school, but I saw a painting of them when they were children, and Rasa looked exactly like I did at the same age. I even commented on the similarity between us and told Barla it was kind of spooky."

Just then, the phone rang, interrupting their conversation. Chris crossed the kitchen to answer it. He returned rapidly and said, "Neal's on his way over to see Amanda for himself. He doesn't believe she's back!"

"I've got to get myself presentable then," Amanda exclaimed as she stood from the chair and tried to hurry back to her room. After fumbling around in the shower, she finally yelled for her mother to help her wash her hair; it proved too difficult to keep her casted arm out of the water.

Diane toweled her hair dry and then proceeded to brush it straight. Amanda paused while applying her makeup and looked up in the mirror to watch her mother's expression as she applied the brush to her hair. "I'm glad to be back home, Momma," she spoke quietly into the silent room.

"You've brought me back my sister too, you know," Diane remarked as she continued to brush Amanda's hair. "We're all very blessed to have you safely back in our family. Now, let's find you something nice to wear. I think I heard Neal's car in the driveway."

They picked a short-sleeved button-up shirt to make it easier for Amanda to get into it. She rummaged one-handed through her drawer until she found her favorite pair of slacks. Her mother put black dress socks on her feet, and then she slipped on a pair of black flats. With one last look in the mirror, it was time to go out and greet Neal.

For some reason, she was unaccountably nervous to see him. *Is it because he moved on, and we're no longer getting married?* Something she almost remembered rested on the edge of her mind.

She walked into the living room alongside her mother. Neal and her father sat across from each other. Neal stood and stared at her as though she were a ghost.

All at once, Amanda remembered what had been so important back in Tuala. "Oh!" Amanda exclaimed, startling everyone in the room.

"What is it, honey?" Diane came closer to Amanda and held out her arms to hold her up, if necessary. "Are you hurting?"

"No, it's just I remembered I had to tell Neal he's a father!"

"What?" was the chorus of exclamations from everyone in the room.

"Eight and a half months after I arrived in Tuala, I had twin girls. They're yours, Neal!"

"That's impossible. I mean—we didn't—I mean—I don't remember if we ever—," Neal stammered and stuttered as he tried to imagine being anyone's father. "How come nobody told me about any kids? Where are they?"

Full realization dawned on Amanda as she stood facing her family. She spoke with dread as well as resolve, "They're still in Tuala. I've got to go back and get them—."

AMANDA'S STORY so intrigued Jasmine that she forgot to pay attention to the time. The door rattle as the attendant did his medications round, and she hastily ended Amanda's session by saying, "Amanda, you're going to awake at the snap of my fingers feeling rested and refreshed." She snapped her finger just as the door opened.

"Dr. Medin, what are you doing in here?" the attendant asked suspiciously.

Without missing a beat, she replied, "I found myself just down the hall from Amanda's room when I realized it was almost time for her next session. I decided to wait with her until you arrived so we could walk together back to my office. Now, can we please get this taken care of? I do have a schedule to keep."

The man seemed to think the doctor's answer sounded reasonable, so he walked forward and handed the cup to the woman on the bed.

Amanda took the medication readily enough, but she had questions for Dr. Medin. Something was different about this session—she remembered.

❧

THE SECRETS OF MAGIC

BOOK TWO OF THE CHOSEN ORIGINS

CHAPTER 1

Amanda didn't know where to start. Everyone in the room sat in stunned silence at her announcement of the birth of the twins. All at once, the full meaning hit everyone, and they spoke simultaneously, demanding answers.

Finally, unable to hear anyone through the commotion, Amanda raised her hands in surrender, hissing as the sudden motion jarred her broken arm and yelled, "Stop! Give me a second, and I'll tell you everything I remember."

Her parents were the first to stop talking while Nealand continued to sputter and demand answers. Her experiences in Tuala had changed Amanda more than she knew, and she now looked on Nealand in a new light.

What she had once thought of as classical features now just looked ordinary. The eyes she used to love gazing into appeared beady and too close together.

What did I ever see in this man who wouldn't shut up? If he really cared about me, he would've hugged me at first sight. He would've been happy with the announcement of his daughters and then demanded to lead the charge to get them back.

"First, Neal," Amanda began by pointedly staring at Nealand to make him stay quiet while she spoke, "I was rescued by a merchant trader who then held me captive for five weeks before I jumped overboard and escaped.

"I got a job at the Port of Cresdon, where I happened to meet my Aunt Barbara, who goes by the name of Barla there. Aunt Barbara and her husband, Captain Ahn, sent me to a safe house in the City of Kirma. It was in Kirma where I found out I was three months pregnant with your children."

"But I don't remember us ever doing anything," Nealand sputtered.

"Well, explain this—Petre found me naked. Why would I be naked unless we did something?" She awkwardly folded her casted arm with the other arm and waited for him to deny it again.

"Do the math, Nealand. You and I were alone on your yacht from June seventeenth through the twenty-fifth. I gave birth to Juila and Jena on February twenty-second. That's just over thirty-five weeks, Nealand. That's considered full-term for twins, and they weren't even that small when they were born."

"But we didn't have sex," Nealand insisted.

"Whatever, Nealand! You don't have to worry about claiming your own daughters; they aren't even on Earth right now. If I can't figure out a way to get back to Tuala, you won't ever have to set eyes on them." She paused to let that sink into Nealand's brain.

She saw him forming a rebuttal and decided she didn't want to hear it. She preempted his following comment.

"You know what? Everything in our lives has changed. We are too different from one another. I think now that you know I'm alive and well, you can just go back to your new girlfriend and have your own life without me in it anymore! Just leave, Nealand."

All the vitality drained out of Amanda, and she wilted dejectedly into the chair behind her. Her chin came to rest on her chest. Just as her hands dropped into her lap, she saw the sparkle of her diamond engagement ring just beyond the edge of her cast.

The ring's sparkle that used to bring her so much joy only served to remind her of her lost future. Tears welled up, both from jarring her arm yet again and the final shred of hope in reconciling with Neal disintegrating into vapor.

At that moment, she was glad the cascade of her long hair hid her tears from Nealand. She didn't want to deal with Nealand trying to be nice to her on the account that she was alive, and he didn't have to feel guilty about causing her death. He could leave with a clean conscience and forget about her and her children that he obviously didn't want anyway!

Concerned to see his daughter so upset after all of her injuries, Chris stood and gestured for Nealand to stand and said, "Come on, Nealand. Amanda's a little too upset right now. I think it'd be for the best if you left now."

All too eager to leave behind Amanda and her outrageous story, he stood, delivered one last disgusted look toward Amanda, and then followed Chris to the front door. He stopped on the threshold, turned toward Chris, and spoke in a confidential whisper, "I don't know what happened to Amanda, but I can assure you, if she really did have any children, they aren't mine.

"My parents can get you the name of a good psychiatrist to help get her back on her feet. She's obviously very confused. How does she expect us to believe she was on a different planet where she happened to run into her dead aunt? It's all a crazy fantasy, Chris!"

"I seem to recall you being a bit disoriented when you were rescued, Nealand. I, for one, choose to believe my own daughter. Thanks for stopping by. If you do plan on coming over again, please be sure to call first," Chris coldly finished as he shut the door on Nealand's incredulous expression. He quickly returned to the living room to continue hearing his daughter's accounting of her journey.

"Tell us everything you remember," Diane began when her husband was once again seated next to her on the couch facing their now-composed daughter.

"Well, you read the letter Barla—I mean, Aunt Barbara—wrote. That was the outline of my adventures. But there were some fantastic things that Aunt Barbara took for granted since she'd been there for so long. The first weird thing I noticed was that Petre didn't have to steer his boat with any controls. He did it with his mind!

"I found out later that not everyone there can do it, but the ones that can't are definitely the minority." She paused to let this new information sink in and watched her father's expression since he was the technology buff of the family.

"That's pretty amazing!" He said after a moment. "What else was different?"

"Well, let's see," she said as she paused to think. She tapped the tip of her index finger on her pursed lips as she tried to organize the overload of thoughts flashing through her mind.

"The food was terrific. Most people there can prepare it using their minds as well. Aunt Barbara obviously couldn't do it because she's not from there, but nearly everyone else does it that way. As long as they have the food in their possession, they can create a dish by thinking of the ingredients and assembling them. Within an instant, the meal can be prepared and cooked!

"Aunt Barbara had me try lots of different things, and she told me it tasted so much better because they use aquaponics to grow their food. She said that in aquaponics, they raise fish in a vast tank and use the fish water to circulate through troughs to provide nutrients for their floating produce. The plant roots purify the water, which is returned to the fish tank to continue the cycle.

"They eat meat from an animal called a foxl for almost every meal of the day. Aunt Barbara showed me a picture of it, and it looked like a cross between a cow and a sheep. The meat was delicious, too.

"They have horses just like here. I got to ride on one, which I fell off of when a beetlesnatch bit me. I broke my wrist badly when I landed. I found out later that Bryon saved my hand by counteracting the beetlesnatch venom as swiftly as he did."

Diane gasped at the thought of her daughter's injuries and almost permanent maiming.

"Relax, Mom, everything turned out okay. It was actually because of my injuries that I found out I was pregnant. You see, Bryon took me to be healed by a wise-woman before he teleported me to his house, where his wife looked over the after-care of my injuries. Oh, that's another thing; the healers use the ley lines and crystals to assist with their talents to treat their patients.

"Alena, Bryon's wife, is a very talented healer who took care of my delivery. She went away to become a wise-woman while I took care of her three children. A wise-woman is the equivalent to a doctor here, except their healing works faster on Tuala than here on Earth." Amanda held up her casted arm and said, "Alena could've had these breaks healed in a matter of hours instead of the weeks it will take here on Earth."

"Wait," Diane interrupted, "Alena knew you were pregnant but still left you to take care of her kids while she became a doctor?"

"Wise-woman," Amanda automatically corrected her mom, then continued, "Yes, but it was my idea. I had to repay them somehow for taking me in and keeping me safe. Besides, Alena came home the same night I delivered the twins, so she didn't miss anything important."

"Her timing was a bit too close, don't you think?" Diane insisted. "I shudder at the thought of how close you came to delivering your twins all by yourself."

"I was glad to have her there. As big as I was getting, I was afraid Bryon would have to deliver the baby without Alena's help at all! None of us knew I would have twins until the second baby came. At that point, it was obvious why I was so fat." Amanda chuckled.

"Good grief, Amanda, are you saying that not only did you not have any prenatal care, but you also delivered those babies at Bryon and Alena's house?" Diane gasped.

"Yes, it's perfectly normal there. There's no such thing as prenatal care because their food is so nutrient-dense that their bodies get sufficient vitamins and minerals for their babies without supplements like here. They don't even have hospitals as far as I discovered."

"What else do you remember that your Aunt Barbara didn't write about?" Chris prompted to keep his daughter talking.

CHAPTER 2

"Let's see. The day after my girls were born, Alena performed their crystal ceremony. Oh, Mom, you'll like this; the children wear the crystals until they're eighteen, and the parents can watch and hear what their children are doing through the crystals.

"The best part is, the children never know about it because it's a closely guarded secret among the parents. Can you imagine if you'd been able to watch my two sisters and me as we were getting into trouble? That might've saved you a few sleepless nights!"

The three laughed together as they all considered this technology's possibilities for the parents on Earth. Chris was the first one to ask the next question, "Do you think you could look in on Juila and Jena right now?"

"I don't know," Amanda said seriously. She sat back and closed her eyes, concentrating on the lessons she learned from Alena on the technique of using the crystals. She didn't have much practice with this art before being swept away in the mudslide and brought back to Earth.

Amanda strained her thoughts, trying to piece together the

connection she felt so effortlessly on Tuala. Minutes went by, and sweat beaded on Amanda's forehead before she admitted defeat. "Nothing," she said with disappointment quite evident in her voice.

"Hey, Amanda, don't get discouraged. Maybe you're too weak right now. Let's try it again in a couple of days, okay? You had said the healers used ley lines to help facilitate healing. Maybe we could find some here to help you communicate with your daughters!" Her dad excitedly said as he started thinking about gathering that information to help his daughter. Then to take her mind off of the communication failure, he prompted, "What else do you remember?"

"The children are changed when they receive their birth crystal. The massive amount of elemental energy, shortened to 'elemy,' which surrounds the crystal around their neck, matures them more rapidly. It enhances their motor skills and their abilities to think, reason, and speak.

"I had noticed that the children, while being relatively young, were very articulate and coordinated. While I haven't had that much experience with kids, I was more than aware kids shouldn't be that helpful at three and four years old.

"It was extraordinary but also encouraging to see. You never knew what would come out of their mouth since they are so much more aware of their surroundings than we're used to here at home. It's almost like they are little geniuses, but they still need nap time!"

Chris noticed that Diane was interested in this new line of conversation, but he still had questions about the technical aspects of these Tualans. To steer the conversation back to his interests, he said, "You mentioned something about being teleported. Is the meaning of that the same there as it is here?"

"Oh, Dad, you'd be astounded by that technology. It's amazing! Families can own their own small telepod, and they use giant telepods instead of airplanes as well. As I understood it, they're crystal drive powered and controlled, again, by the operator's mind power.

"One moment you're sitting in the telepod at one location, then three heartbeats later, in utter emptiness, you appear out of thin air at your destination. It wouldn't matter if it were ten feet or ten miles; it'd take the same amount of elemy and time to get there.

"They even have telepod races like the drag races we have here. Bryon took me to a show when one came close to town. They don't use the teleporting in the races, just the raw power of the crystal drive to race to the finish line. It was exhilarating," she finished with a massive smile as she remembered the event's rush as well as the famous racer named Riccan. She definitely wouldn't mind meeting him again!

"What did the telepods look like?" Chris asked interestedly.

"They reminded me of a UFO," she replied as she thought back on her first impression of them. "They were almost all silver in color with windows all around the front. They had a side door that you walked through to get to the pair of seats at the front.

"I was only ever in a two-seater model, but Barla said they had family versions. I can only guess those would have more seats, as well as the larger airline versions."

"Hmm, I wonder," Chris mused as he suddenly jumped up from his seat and left the room.

Amanda and Diane looked at each other, startled when Chris left abruptly. "Don't ask me," Diane said with raised hands. While they waited for his return, Amanda drank water from the cup on the coffee table in front of her. She carefully set the cup down and gingerly sat back in her chair.

She closed her eyes and tried to gather as many memories as she could muster to share with her parents. Amanda was relieved her parents were taking all of this information so well as it could have gone the other way just as easily.

A few minutes later, Chris returned to the room carrying a giant encyclopedia. He was flipping through the pages and muttering to himself. He settled down next to Amanda on the loveseat as he still feverishly turned the pages until getting to the one he remembered seeing.

"Aha," he exclaimed, startling both women in the room. "Take a look at this picture and let me know if it reminds you of the tele-pods," he said as he passed the book onto Amanda's lap.

Amanda looked down, and her eyes got wide as she looked at an exact replica of Bryon's telepod. "That's it," she exclaimed, "that's the telepod!"

Diane rushed over to take a look as well. She noted that the article next to the picture read: 'July 7, 1947; RAAF Captures Flying Saucer on Ranch in Roswell Region.' "What are you think-ing, Chris?" Diane asked with growing excitement.

"I'm thinking we might need to take a trip to Roswell, New Mexico," Chris stated with certainty as a huge grin spread across his face.

"Dad, I don't understand." Amanda looked from her mother to her father, waiting for one of them to explain.

"Back in 1947, a UFO was found on a ranch outside of Roswell. Of course, the media had a heyday claiming that a UFO had been found as well as a couple of aliens. Then the military jumped in, and suddenly, the story was changed from a UFO crash to debris from an experimental high-altitude surveillance balloon belonging to a classified program called 'Mogul.'

"Nobody believed the military statements, and people started comparing their stories. Eventually, they opened a museum in Roswell to honor the crash. I think," he paused to make sure Amanda was paying attention, "maybe the key to getting back to Tuala will be in or near Roswell."

Amanda gasped at the concept but was eager to see if the idea had any merit. Anything that would get her girls back was worth the try. "That's brilliant, Dad! When can we go?"

"I'll call a travel agent and make the arrangements," he answered. He turned to his wife and asked, "Do you want to come, too?"

"Chris, how can you even ask that? Of course, I'm coming!" She scoffed while scowling at her husband.

"Just making sure," he replied innocently. He took the book back from Amanda's lap and stared at it more closely. "Wow," he said and looked up again at his daughter, "You really flew in one of these?"

"Several times, actually," she replied with a massive grin. "Dad, it was amazing and scary all at the same time. I wish you could try it, too."

"Me, too, honey. Me, too," Chris said wistfully. They hugged each other in their excitement.

CHAPTER 3

The new information Petre received from his contact in Kirma thrilled him. Ever since he sold his shipment of crystals and thought he saw Jesisca in the marketplace, he couldn't concentrate on much of anything.

With his pockets full of the taj he received from Bryon, Kirma's distribution manager, for those crystals, he could spend some leisurely time in contemplation of how to get the information he needed without letting anyone know his motives.

In the three weeks since he left Kirma, he still wasn't any closer to finding out if the woman he saw was Jesisca. His obsession with getting her back took over every aspect of his life, including his dreams. As fate would have it, the solution to his dilemma presented itself in the Port of Cresdon tavern.

Petre sat at the bar contemplating his next steps to get Jesisca back when he noticed a good-looking man entering the building in his late twenties. The man sat next to Petre and talked about his rotten luck with Captain Issyn.

"I've had some dealings with Captain Issyn. He's a hard man to work with, that's for sure."

"Yeah, he's okay. It's just that business is slow, and I had the least seniority, so I was the first one let go."

"That's rough," Petre drawled, "What's your name?"

"Ninan."

"It's nice to meet you, Ninan," Petre replied as he took a sip from his bruskin. "Let me buy you another drink."

He looked at the man, noting he hadn't been on the sea so long as to age him prematurely. He had short, sun-bleached hair, hazel eyes, and a couple of days' beard growth. But he might want to do Petre a favor. With the idea growing in his mind regarding the unemployed seaman, Petre asked, "Do you have any experience operating a telepod?"

"Sure thing," was his quick reply.

"So, are you looking for a job right now, or do you have something else lined up?"

"I might be persuaded to look into something else," Ninan replied and then hastily added, "if the money was right."

"Of course, of course." Petre shifted gears and asked, "Are you married?"

"Oh, no," Ninan replied with a low chuckle, "I never could convince a woman to stay with me while I was at sea eight mesans out of the anon." He picked up the second bruskin that Petre bought him and drank deeply, savoring the full-bodied flavor of the amber liquid.

"Speaking of women," Petre began, glad for the easy opening to his subject, "I'm looking for my wife."

"How'd you lose her?" Ninan asked with interest.

"She fell overboard while we were sailing, but I don't believe she drowned. You see, the problem I have is that the people around here don't like me much, and nobody will tell me if they've seen her. I need someone to be my eyes and ears for me," Petre reasonably spoke as he folded his hands on the bar to wait for Ninan's reaction.

Ninan's glance happened to look at Petre's hands where he spotted Petre's silver ring set with an onyx stone. He instantly looked away and contemplated leaving the tavern and the master deceptor behind, but the idea of making some easy money kept him in his seat. "What would I have to do?" He was naturally wary.

"Nothing too difficult," he replied quickly, not missing Ninan's discovery of his ring. "I need someone to get a job in Kirma and watch for any signs of my wife."

"Why would I need to be able to operate a telepod?" Ninan inquired.

"I just thought you might be able to get a job at the distribution center there in Kirma," he replied.

"How much are you going to pay?"

Petre thought about it for a minute and replied, "I'll pay ten taj for any information that'll lead me to get my wife back."

Ninan gulped at the offered price. It was more than he had imagined. He would've thought about it more if the price were lower, but this amount was impossible to refuse. He was about to accept when his eyes rested once again on Petre's master deceptor ring. He'd need to get some assurance first. "How can I be sure you'll pay me?"

"Well, I could pay you five shills a week until you find out what I need to know, and then I'll pay you the remainder. Does that sound fair?" Petre said with a pleasant smile on his face.

"Sure," Ninan replied and then said, "When do you want me to start?"

"Let's go over to that booth, and I'll tell you all about my wife." Petre stood and gestured toward the booth furthest away from the bartender's nosy ears.

Ninan picked up another mug of bruskin, for which Petre had nodded to the bartender, and followed Petre to the specified booth. He sat and sipped his third bruskin while Petre told his tale of losing his wife.

"Nine and a half mesans ago, Jesisca injured her head when she fell on our water craft. She lost her memory and didn't even remember her name for a while.

"We were just on the verge of getting back to normal when I ate something bad, and it made me pass out. I think Jesisca must've panicked and jumped overboard to get help for me, but she's not a good swimmer, you see.

"Anyway, when I came to, she was missing, and I've been searching for her ever since. About three weeks ago, I thought I saw her in Kirma, but I lost her in the crowded marketplace."

Petre paused in his storytelling to reach into the breast pocket of his jacket. He pulled out a folded sheet of paper and spread it open on the table between them. "I had this picture of her drawn from my description so the person I hired would know what she looked like."

"Why don't you just go back to the marketplace and show the vendors this picture?" Ninan asked and then felt like kicking himself for giving Petre an option that wouldn't include getting himself paid.

"As I said, the people there don't like me much and are most uncooperative. I need someone they don't know to do the asking for me, but you'll have to be very discreet, or they won't trust you either," Petre cautioned.

"I can be discreet," Ninan assured him as he picked up the drawing and admired the young woman's delicate features.

"Now, you can't just start asking around for her. You'll need to look for her at the market or maybe in the surrounding neighborhoods since I saw her walking with her groceries," Petre instructed as Ninan continued to admire the drawing of Jesisca. With Ninan's lack of attention, Petre drummed his fingers against the wooden table and asked, "Do you understand?"

"Sure, sure," Ninan replied offhandedly. He could easily see himself getting along just fine with Jesisca. He may not even need to get the ten taj from Petre if he had a good job and the beautiful Jesisca with whom to spend his time.

"Okay, I'll do it," he said suddenly and then added, "but I'll need one taj up front to give me transportation, room, and board until I can get a job at the shipping warehouse."

"That's fair," Petre replied and fished a taj from his pants pocket. He passed it across the table's surface with his index finger and said, "I'll expect weekly updates from you. When I receive an update, I'll forward the five shills to whatever address you give me."

"Perfect. I'll leave tonight then," he said with a broad smile.

"One more thing," Petre said as he stood from the bench, "If you try to cheat me, I'll know. Trust me; you don't want to know what I can do to you. Do I make myself clear?"

Ninan's smile lost some of its eagerness, but he held up his hands and replied, "You won't need to worry. I've got you covered."

"Good, good. Here's an address where you can send your first update next week." Petre pulled a small card from the back pocket of his pants and a pen from his breast pocket and hastily wrote down the address of the brothel where he'd be staying for the next week.

"Remember, the sooner you find my wife, the sooner you'll have your remaining nine taj."

"No problem, I'll start tomorrow," he said with renewed confidence.

CHAPTER 4

Good to his word, Ninan found a transport telepod to take him to Kirma later that same night. After asking the telepod operator for eating and sleeping suggestions, he arranged to stay in a boarding house in Kirma for the next two weeks.

Ninan figured that would either give him enough time to find a job and a more permanent place to live or find Jesisca. Then, he could return to Cresdon and collect his finder's fee.

Early the following day, Ninan left the boarding house to locate both the market and the distribution warehouse. He'd get the lay of the land under his belt before he started looking for Jesisca. This time would also help him decide if he really wanted to help Petre find this woman. Maybe there was a good reason she didn't go back to him.

Maybe she decided to leave him, but he forced her to stay. As much as he wanted the other nine taj, Ninan respected women. He didn't trust Petre's story to be entirely accurate based on the evidence of Petre being a master deceptor.

Ninan strolled along the business district where the boarding house was located. He continued through a deserted park given the early hour. Before long, he found himself outside of the shipping warehouse where Petre told him he'd be able to get a job.

The place looked neat and orderly, not at all a terrible place to work. As the day was Sabtu, the area was deserted, so he could look around pretty extensively, which suited his needs perfectly. Ninan would come back on Senin, which would give him today and tomorrow to investigate before tying himself down with a job.

Ninan pulled from his coat pocket Jesisca's drawing and stared at it. He meandered away from the warehouse district. What was her side of the story?

She didn't look like the type of person who'd want to be with Petre. For one, she looked entirely too young for him; she couldn't possibly be any older than eighteen anons.

The long hair cascading over her shoulders didn't seem consistent with other women who liked to sail. They usually opted for short hair on the windy sea.

The picture showed her smiling with full lips and perfectly straight teeth, also quite the opposite of Petre. What color were her large, almond-shaped eyes? The drawing was in black and white. He cursed himself for not asking Petre about her hair color either.

That ought to make things a little more complicated. Now that Jesisca's image was fresh in his mind, he folded the drawing up and put it back into his pocket.

He refocused his attention to where he walked and realized he had made it to the market district's center. It, too, was empty since conducting business on Sabtu didn't ever happen.

He noted the location of different wares and tried to decide what would be most regularly needed for a household. His ideas were to watch those vendors' stalls the most and maybe ask them some pointed questions about Jesisca or show them her picture.

I could tell them I'm her brother and that our parents are worried sick about her.

He grinned at that story angle. With his plan set, he returned to the boarding house. He'd try out his ideas the next day when there'd be people around to talk to. Maybe he'd get lucky and find Jesisca.

Ninan ate breakfast at the boarding house the following morning before venturing out. He figured people wouldn't be out shopping until after they'd eaten anyway. Ninan would wander through the crowds until lunchtime, and then he'd buy something from one of the vendors.

I should start building rapport with these people if I want them to help me. Maybe I should find somewhere in the open to eat, and then I can stare at Jesisca's picture as though I were sad that she's missing. Luck might be on my side; someone might ask me about it and tell me where I can find her.

Ninan did as he had planned, but he ate in solitude without interruptions. *So much for luck.* He gathered his lunch trash and his jacket. While he didn't garner any knowledge about Jesisca, he did overhear several people talking about the shipping warehouse being a great place to work. He was looking forward to going in the next day to see if he could get a job.

He spent the rest of the day walking up and down the neighborhoods' sidewalks near the marketplace. He hadn't realized there were just that many housing developments in Kirma.

This town wouldn't be a bad place to settle down and make a living. He admired the large houses in rows and the children playing in the yards.

He paused to watch two young boys and one small girl play with a couple of babies on a blanket in their front yard, smiling at them playing house. The girl was bossing around the two little boys while she spent all her time watching over the babies.

That's a typical woman's role. He started walking again to the boarding house.

Early the following day, Ninan arrived at the distribution warehouse before any of the workers. He sat outside the main entrance and watched as the employees trickled into the facility. Most of them smiled and appeared happy about coming to work on a Senin. He was more accustomed to people dragging their feet because their weekend was over.

This must be an excellent place to work.

A tall, older man with graying hair and a slender, young woman came toward the office entrance where Ninan sat. Ninan stood and asked, "I'm looking for the manager. Do you know when he or she'll be in?"

The woman replied, "The manager's name is Bryon, and he should be here within the next ten minutes or so. The warehouse doesn't open for another half an hour. Is there something we can help you with?"

"I heard I might be able to get a job here," Ninan said offhandedly with a shrug.

"Oh, well, you'll need to talk to Bryon about that."

The man spoke for the first time, "Do you want to wait in the office? The weather's not as nice today as it was this weekend."

"Sure, if I won't be in the way," Ninan responded hastily, eager for the opportunity to look around the office before meeting Bryon. Ninan followed the couple inside and promptly sat in one of the waiting chairs. Upon observation, he noted the sparse decorations and the complete lack of anything personal in nature.

A few minutes later, Bryon walked into the office and spotted a younger man sitting in the waiting area. He walked over to Frasnia, the receptionist, with a questioning expression. As she leaned forward, Bryon mimicked her and did so as well.

"He's looking for a job," she whispered.

Bryon mouthed the word, "Ah," and turned around with a smile on his face. He walked purposefully toward the shabbily dressed gentleman in the chair and extended his hand as he said, "Hi, my name's Bryon Kesh. I'm the manager here at the warehouse."

Ninan hastily stood, grasped Bryon's hand in a firm grip, and replied, "Hello, Bryon. It's nice to meet you. My name's Ninan Tigua."

Surprised at the strength of Ninan's grip, Bryon reassessed the gentleman before him. Getting straight to the point, Bryon asked, "I hear you're looking for a job. Is that right?"

"Yes," he replied simply and nodded.

"Come inside my office, and we'll see if there's anything we have here that'll suit your talents." He gestured for Ninan to follow him as he made his way across the lobby and into his private domain.

He closed the door behind Ninan, went around his desk, and then sat. He leaned forward with his elbows on the table in front of him. "In what line of work do you specialize?"

"Well, mostly, I've been a sea crew member up until recently," he began and then thought he should shift away from that for fear of answering uncomfortable questions. "I've also worked at the distribution centers at the Port of Cresdon. Captain Ahn would probably remember me if you needed to ask someone about my work."

"How long ago did you work with Captain Ahn?"

"Well, I didn't actually work with him," he said slowly. "When I was fifteen anons old, I apprenticed under Ceren as a clerk. I eventually worked my way out into the dock warehouse until my work caught the eye of one of the captains."

"Were you participating in Barla's apprenticeship program?" Bryon asked with genuine interest.

"You know about that?"

"I sure do," he said with a smile. "I've always thought that was a wonderful idea. Were you part of it?"

"Yes, I started at the school when I was just seven anons old. I was grateful for the opportunity to have a place to live. Then when I turned fifteen, and they asked me if I wanted to start to learn a trade, I jumped at the opportunity."

"That's wonderful. How long did you work in the dock warehouse?"

"After my apprenticeship ended, only about one and a half anons. When I turned eighteen, I went to work for Captain Issyn on his shipping route," he added.

"So you have experience handling cargo and sorting it, right?"

"Oh, yeah. I've loaded and unloaded more cargo than I care to think about," Ninan replied with confidence.

"Would you have any problem working in the receiving department for a week or so until I can see your skills and where they'll be put to use?"

"Sure. No problem. I'd appreciate any work right now."

"Well, the pay's not that great, but it'll get your foot in the door."

"You'll be happy with my work. I'm not worried about the starting pay, either. It's more than I came through the door with, that's for sure!" Ninan replied with a grin on his face.

"Perfect, let's go get you started then," Bryon said as he stood to lead the way to Ninan's new workstation.

This plan is working out better than I hoped. Ninan pushed himself up from the cushioned chair to follow Bryon out to the reception area.

CHAPTER 5

Ninan worked fast and hard, trying to prove his worth to Bryon. He fit in with the rest of the crew seamlessly since he regularly worked in close quarters on the shipping vessels.

Ninan entertained the other employees with stories of adventures on the high seas and some of the more difficult cargo they had handled, such as a herd of foxl.

During the first week, Ninan spent every lunch hour in the marketplace searching for Jesisca. Each day, he ordered lunch and sat at a different table with Jesisca's picture out in front of him. Ninan almost thought he was getting a lead when someone stopped near him to look at the picture.

"Boy, she looks familiar. Is she your girlfriend?" the old man asked.

"No, she's my sister, Jesisca," Ninan replied easily, glad he had already decided on that lie. "Have you seen her? Our parents have been worried sick about her."

The old man leaned closer to look at the picture and slowly

shook his head. "No, sorry. I don't think that's the same girl. What color is her hair?"

"Dark blonde," he replied, hoping it was the right answer.

"Nope, definitely not then," he said as he continued to scrutinize the drawing.

Ninan decided to fabricate a little more on his story and added, "Well, her hair changes color depending on sunlight exposure. Sometimes it's really blonde, and other times it's brown. You've seen that before, haven't you?"

For the first time, the old man looked skeptically at Ninan and replied, "Nope, can't say as I have seen hair color change that drastically. Eye color, maybe, depending on a person's mood or what they're wearing, but not hair color." He moved away from the table.

Ninan called after him, "I eat lunch every day here in the marketplace. If you see her, will you let me know?"

"Sure," the old man called over his shoulder as he walked away, melting into the crowd.

At the end of Ninan's first week in the receiving department, Ninan was surprised when Bryon asked him to come to his office at the end of his shift.

With a bit of trepidation to his step, Ninan walked to the front office, stopped at the receptionist's desk, noticed her nameplate for the first time, and said, "Hi, Frasnia. Bryon asked me to stop in and see him. Is he available?"

"Just one moment, and I'll find out," she replied cheerfully. Frasnia turned and typed a few strokes on her keyboard and then looked at the patil's screen while waiting for her answer.

With a smile on her face, she turned back to Ninan and replied, "Bryon said he's ready to see you. Please just go on into his office."

"Thank you," Ninan replied. He twitched with nervous energy, but he couldn't imagine the receptionist being so cheerful if he were about to be fired. Ninan crossed the lobby and paused for just a second to take a calming breath before opening Bryon's office door.

"Ninan, it's good to see you. Please, sit," Bryon said as he indicated the chair he occupied the one other time he'd been in Bryon's office.

Ninan sat and folded his hands over his knee to disguise their shaking.

"I've got good news for you, Ninan," said Bryon with a smile on his face.

"Really?"

"Yes, I've spoken with many people about you—including Captain Ahn, Ceren, and the crew you've been working with here at our facility. Everyone told me you're a hard worker who can learn new tasks with little to no instruction.

"I, too, have seen this trait in you, and I'd like to offer you a position which has just come available in the transfer department."

Ninan nodded during Bryon's speech, glad to know his hard work hadn't gone unnoticed. When Bryon got to the part about a promotion, Ninan was both surprised and thrilled and hurriedly replied, "That'd be wonderful."

Then he thought about all the other people who worked in the facility. He didn't want to create any hard feelings and asked, "Are you sure there isn't someone who's been here longer who might want it? I mean—I'm not saying I don't want it. I just don't want to upset anyone."

"No problem on that score," Bryon assured him. Bryon was inwardly glad to know Ninan was thinking about his fellow staff more than his own gain, which raised his estimation of Ninan tenfold. "I already spoke to the staff about the promotion, and they all agreed you'd be a good fit for it."

"Really? Nobody here mentioned anything to me about it," he said with more than a bit of wonder that the people could be so discreet.

Bryon was again more than a little smug in his employees' performance. He knew he could trust these people, but times like these proved he had a good work group.

"Well, if that's all settled, why don't you come by my office first thing next Senin, and I'll introduce you to your new department."

"Perfect!" Ninan enthusiastically replied as he stood to take his leave.

"Oh, Ninan," Bryon said as he just thought of one last thing.

Here it comes. Ninan paused, dread making it hard to breathe.

"Frasnia has your week's pay at her desk."

Relief washed through Ninan as he replied cheerfully, "Thanks, that's wonderful news."

"Now, don't get too excited, Ninan. Remember, I told you the receiving job's pay is dreadful. Your new position will pay better, I promise."

"Hey, money is money. I'll take whatever I can get!" he replied as he opened the door and returned to the lobby. He stopped at Frasnia's desk and said, "Bryon told me I can pick up my week's pay from you."

"Sure thing," she replied as she took a key ring from her pants pocket and unlocked her desk drawer. She pulled out a locked box and placed it on top of her desk. She selected another key, fit it into the box lock, and opened the lid, obscuring the contents from Ninan's view.

Frasnia sorted through the papers until she finally found what she was seeking, and then she handed Ninan a sealed envelope with his name written on the front. "Here you go. Have a nice weekend."

He took the envelope from her outstretched hand and said, "Thanks, you too." He put it into his coat pocket without opening the envelope and walked out of the office into the late afternoon sun.

Before heading back to the boarding house, Ninan needed to

write his weekly update to Petre. He went to the marketplace, purchased some writing supplies, and sat at his regular lunch table to compose his letter.

TAMMUZ 19, 3443

Petre,

I don't have much to write about other than I got a job working at the distribution warehouse as you suggested. My first weekend here, I also walked through the marketplace and all of the local neighborhoods. I didn't realize there were so many people living here.

Also, I look at Jesisca's picture while I eat lunch in the marketplace, hoping someone will recognize her, but I haven't had much luck yet. One old man said she looked familiar, but when he asked me what color her hair was, I told him it was dark blonde. He then said it wasn't the same girl.

What color are Jesisca's hair and eyes? I forgot to ask you, and it might help me locate her faster.

I guess that's all the news for this week. I'm staying at the Bedford Boarding House so that you can send my weekly payment there.

Until next week,

Ninan

HE READ THROUGH HIS LETTER, making sure he gave Petre enough information to know he at least tried. Satisfied it was sufficient, Ninan folded the letter in thirds, inserted it into the envelope he had purchased, licked the glue on the flap, and sealed it shut.

He took out the card Petre had given him and addressed the envelope. Ninan deposited the letter in the courier box at the edge of the marketplace on his way back to the boarding house.

Back in his room, Ninan ate his foxl stew in silence. He enjoyed the silence surrounding him, which allowed him to think about what direction he wanted his life to go. He hated the idea of working for Petre.

Should I just give up the whole thing?

More than once now, he regretted writing to Petre at all. He could have just sent back the money he initially received and then just enjoyed his new life here in Kirma.

Remembering his new job reminded him of his pay envelope. *How much much money did I make for this first week's work?*

He crossed the bedroom to where he had draped his jacket over the back of the second chair in the room. He rifled through the outside pocket until he could extract the envelope he had received from Frasnia.

He ripped it open and dumped out the five shills it contained into his other palm. Ninan laughed out loud at the paltry pay. He was even more thankful to know that starting on Senin, he'd be making better wages.

Ninan did the unthinkable the following morning. He slept in. If his old crewmates saw him now, they wouldn't stop razzing him until the next greenhorn came on board the ship.

He luxuriated in the feeling of sleeping until he was no longer tired. He rolled over onto his side and spotted the previous day's newspaper which he had picked up on his way back to the boarding house.

Now is as good a time to read what's happening in and around Kirma as ever.

He reached over and grabbed the paper. Ninan punched the pillows into order to be able to rest his back against them and settle the blankets across his lap. He unrolled the large bundle of papers and spread them flat across his outstretched legs.

He spent most of the morning browsing through each page.

Once again, the sheer number of activities available to the Kirman residents came as quite a pleasant surprise.

His stomach's growl forced him to check the time. It was already afternoon, and he'd missed breakfast. If he spent too much time getting dressed, he'd miss lunch as well. He pulled on his trousers walked through the bedroom door and into the hallway while still buttoning his shirt.

CHAPTER 6

Ninan entered the dining hall just as the last patrons were being served. He picked a table closest to the kitchen so he wouldn't have to inconvenience his waiter any more than he already would by his tardiness. He glanced through the paper menu on the table and was glad to see one of his favorite meals was the day's special.

His waiter came over and deposited a glass of ice water onto the table. "You cut it pretty close today; the kitchen's almost closed. Do you know what you'd like to have?"

"Do you have any of the au jus left?" Ninan asked politely.

"I'm sure we do; the head chef likes to have extra to take home on the weekends," he replied easily.

"Good! I'd like to have a shredded foxl sandwich with cheese and a big bowl of au jus, please," Ninan ordered.

"You got it," he said and then asked, "Would you like something other than water to drink?"

"No, water's fine," he replied.

"Very good. I'll be back with your order in a few minutes," he said as he hurried through the kitchen doors and yelled out his last-minute order to the chef.

Again, Ninan felt terrible for making the wait staff work later than usual. He contemplated asking the waiter to make his order to go but then realized it would only make them have to get out other supplies. He'd just eat quickly and be done before the staff cleaned the dining room.

True to his word, the waiter brought Ninan's meal within minutes of placing the order. Even though he ate fast and burned his mouth on the hot au jus, he appreciated the tasty foxl meat and the soft, buttery bread encasing it. He tipped the cup of broth into his mouth and washed it down with the rest of his water.

He stood and looked around for his waiter. He spotted him across the room, walked over to him, and said, "Thank you for the excellent meal. Will you also give my compliments to the chef? I'd appreciate it."

The rest of his day went without incident as he spent most of his time back in his room. He re-read some newspaper articles, and then he just stared out his bedroom window at the few people walking by. He still was not any closer to finding Jesisca.

More than anything, he wanted to meet this woman who had captivated his imagination. He wondered if she had a sense of humor or as wholesome and innocent as she seemed from the drawing.

Maybe I'm reading too much into the artist's rendition. He once again stared at the drawing.

Senin came all too soon. He took his breakfast early in the dining room and was surprised by receiving a letter from the waiter and his morning java. He ordered his morning oats, sat back in his chair when the waiter left his table, and opened the letter from Petre, which read:

.   .   .

TAMMUZ 21, 3443

Ninan,

I'm glad to hear you got a job. To answer your question, Jesisca's hair is a dark brown with some red and gold highlights. Her eyes are brown with a bit of green and gold mixed in.

I hope I don't have to remind you to be careful about asking too many questions or flashing her picture around to everyone who'll look at it. I'd rather it take a little longer and find her rather than scare her into running again.

I've included your five shills with this letter leaving a total of 8½ taj left owing.

I look forward to your next letter. I'm going back on my regular trading route so send your next letter care of the Harbor Master at the Port of Cerid.

Petre MacVeen

NINAN BALLED up the letter and set it on the table with renewed disgust. He dumped the five shills from the bottom of the envelope into his hand and put them in his pants pocket along with his last week's pay. He just couldn't believe Petre was chastising his style of garnering information when he couldn't locate his own wife.

His breakfast arrived, and he almost didn't have the appetite to eat it. Then he remembered he'd start a new job in about an hour. For now, he'd forget about Petre and concentrate on his latest adventure. As he did the week before, he arrived half an hour early to work and waited in the lobby for Bryon's arrival.

Bryon showed up for work fifteen minutes later and escorted Ninan to his new assignment. Bryon introduced him to his new supervisor and left them alone.

Ninan's new job was on the opposite end of the facility. His position's responsibility was to check inventory on the patil, print out orders to be placed, and then pull the stock and distribute it onto various pallets across the staging floor. The change of pace and the increased responsibility level helped.

His morning went by amazingly fast, and he was surprised when his supervisor tapped his shoulder and invited him to lunch. Still upset with the tone of Petre's letter, Ninan decided to abandon his regular lunch routine in favor of eating with his new work crew.

He alternated between going out with his co-workers and eating by himself for the rest of the week. Each evening he left work exhausted, too tired to do more than eat dinner and retire to his room. By the time Jumat arrived, Ninan was glad the week was over. With his shift done, he walked with several of his fellow workers to the office to get their pay.

Ninan entered the room first and overheard Bryon say Petre MacVeen's name. He paused in the doorway only to get pushed by the men coming in behind him. He stumbled into the lobby, causing more commotion than he would've liked.

To cover his astonishment, he jokingly said, "Sorry, I must've tripped on the way in." He turned to Bryon and said, "Remind me not to get in the way of the guys and their paychecks, will you?"

Bryon laughed, turned to Frasnia, and said, "We can talk about this later. It looks as though our crew is anxious to begin their weekend!" He turned and crossed the lobby to his office, shutting the door quietly behind him.

"Okay, boys," Frasnia said as she retrieved the weekly pay box from her desk. "Give me a sec, and I'll get you on your way." She hastily located each person's envelope and handed them over to their eagerly outstretched hands.

The men filed out as soon as their envelopes crossed their palms, leaving Ninan alone in the office with Frasnia. She held out his envelope and said with a smile on her face, "Here's yours."

"Thanks," Ninan said automatically, still distracted by Bryon's comment about Petre. Frasnia might shed some light on her conversation with Bryon. He innocently asked, "Did I hear Bryon mention Petre MacVeen when we came in?"

"Yes," she replied and then leaned forward to continue, "Bryon hates that man. He was just asking me if I knew anything about his whereabouts. I was just about to tell him I hadn't heard anything when you guys walked in."

"Boy, I can sure understand about not liking Petre. I don't like him much myself. When I worked for Captain Issyn, I heard more than one tale about Petre working outside the proper channels to move his cargo. Those kinds of activities give honest shippers a bad name."

He paused to consider how he'd present his knowledge of Petre's whereabouts without sounding suspicious.

He finally decided to say, "You know, I just spoke with Captain Issyn, and I recall he mentioned Petre being at the Port of Cerid this weekend.

"You could let Bryon know that you heard through shipping channels where Petre's located without mentioning that I told you, couldn't you? I really don't want any association with him."

"Sure thing," Frasnia said with some excitement. "Bryon will be thrilled to get any update whatsoever. He probably won't even ask me where I heard. He'll be so relieved to get any news. I'll wait a few minutes after you leave to let him know."

"Thanks," Ninan said as the front office door opened and more people filed in to collect their money. Ninan took this distraction as the perfect opportunity to take his leave.

Ninan opened his envelope, still clutched in his hand, to see how much better this job paid to keep from thinking about Petre for a few moments. He was pleasantly surprised to find it contained five taj and six shills.

The money hardly seemed worth it when he realized, with dragging footsteps as he walked to the marketplace, that he was now going to have to betray the good people he worked for to write his second letter to Petre.

TAMMUZ 26, 3443

Petre,

I have less to report this week than last. I often went to the marketplace and looked for Jesisca. I didn't see her or anyone who might resemble her. I'll spend some time this weekend walking the neighborhoods again.

Until next week,

Ninan

HE SEALED the envelope and addressed it in the care of the Harbor Master at the Port of Cerid. There was nothing more to do than put the letter in the courier box and feel as though another piece of his integrity just left him.

His mood darkened while he thought of Petre and his story about Jesisca. His steps dragged as he walked back to his dinner at the boarding house.

The one good thing about today was that I got to let Bryon know where Petre is currently. I wonder why Bryon even cares. Does Bryon know where Jesisca is? Is he helping her stay hidden from Petre?

That thought brought a little life back into his step. If it were true, which of course, couldn't possibly be, Jesisca couldn't be in better hands than Bryon's.

CHAPTER 7

Ninan did walk through the districts that weekend. On Sabtu, the first day of the weekend, he walked every neighborhood on the side of the city closest to the warehouse district. By the end of the day, he was exhausted and yet not a little bit discouraged.

One benefit to walking by himself was the ability to spend a lot of time thinking. The more he thought Jesisca was staying with Bryon, the more convinced he became. *I wish there were some way to ask Bryon without making him suspicious. I really would like just to get to know Jesisca and hear her side of the story.*

On the second day of the weekend, Minggu, Ninan continued his community search on the city's other end. He got an earlier start than the previous day, it was around nine o'clock in the morning, and most people were still in their homes. Ninan figured people would get out of their houses today, considering the sunny skies.

Within half an hour, he spotted a telepod in front of someone's house. It was the first one he'd seen the entire weekend. Ninan slowed his steps. He'd like to see if anyone was either already in the telepod or, if it were empty, maybe delay until the passengers showed up. People didn't generally have their telepods out unless they planned on using them shortly.

Just a few minutes later, Ninan's eyes rounded when he saw Bryon walk out of the house laden with a large basket and hurriedly get into the waiting telepod. When the telepod didn't leave right away, Ninan thought Bryon must be waiting for someone still in the house to join him.

Ninan stepped behind the neighbor's shrub to continue his surveillance. Seconds later, Ninan gasped out loud as the woman, whose picture he had looked at every day for the past two weeks, skipped out of the house and into the waiting telepod. He didn't have any time to react before the telepod blinked out of the front yard.

He could hardly credit that his outrageous suspicion was actually confirmed. He chuckled as he turned around to start the long walk back to the boarding house.

I don't have any reason to continue looking for her when I know where she lives. He continued to chuckle and shake his head in wonder.

Back in his room, Ninan conceived of various ways to talk to Jesisca. First, Ninan wondered if there were any way he could get invited over to Bryon's house for dinner to provide a valid reason to talk to her.

Then, he thought he could talk to Bryon about his telepod and maybe even go for a ride with him in it until he realized this train of thought wouldn't get him any closer to talking with Jesisca.

Abandoning that thought, he moved on to needing an excuse to see a wise-woman. He heard from his co-workers that Bryon's wife was a newly appointed wise-woman with a rising reputation for her successes.

Ninan gave up on this idea, too, since he was obviously in good health and without any reason to hang around their house to talk to Jesisca.

Maybe my only option is dinner. He'd talk to Bryon about it the next day at work.

During his first break, Ninan went to see if Bryon wanted to have lunch with him that day. He entered the lobby, walked over to where Frasnia sat, and asked, "Is Bryon in today?"

"Sorry, he sent in a sick message today on the patil."

"Do you think he'll be back tomorrow?" Ninan asked with concern. Bryon seemed fine the day before.

What could've happened to make him miss work?

"I imagine he'll be in. All the time I've worked here, he's never missed a single day."

"Okay then. I'll check back in tomorrow," he said and waved goodbye to Frasnia as he left the office.

The next day, Ninan received the same answer from Frasnia about Bryon being out sick and every subsequent day that week. On Jumat, Ninan took his time going to the office to pick up his pay.

He wanted to talk to Frasnia without anyone interrupting. His timing was perfect. The last employee was leaving the office just as Ninan entered. Frasnia looked as though she'd been crying, although she was valiantly trying to hide it.

"What's wrong, Frasnia? Has something happened to Bryon?"

"Bryon's physically fine," Frasnia began. "I just found out why Bryon's been out of the office."

When she didn't continue, Ninan prompted, "What happened?"

"He and a friend went hiking up in the Cresdon foothills. There was a sudden rainstorm which caused a mudslide. His friend got caught in it and died. Bryon's beside himself with grief and guilt.

"As I understood it, it was Bryon's idea that they go hiking. Can you even imagine? I feel so badly for him!" Frasnia started to sob again even as she pulled out the pay box and retrieved Ninan's money.

Ninan felt as though someone had punched him in the gut. He had the sickening feeling he knew that this friend of Bryon's was Jesisca. He just couldn't believe that she was dead. Ninan decided to ask, "Who was this friend? Was it a man or a woman?"

"That's what makes it even worse," she began, "it's the woman who's been staying at their house for the past few mesans taking care of Bryon's children while his wife went through her wise-woman training."

"Wow, that's rough," Ninan said absently as Frasnia inadvertently confirmed his worst fear.

Jesisca was dead.

He'd have to report this to Petre. Thoughts began to race through Ninan's mind.

Will Petre believe me? Will Petre still pay me even though she's dead? Maybe I should keep the dying part to myself for a few more weeks. Then I can get the rest of the money Petre promised me; there's no reason why something good shouldn't come out of this dire situation.

"Try to have a good weekend, Frasnia," Ninan said as he pocketed his pay envelope and walked out the office door.

He sat at one of the marketplace tables and pulled out his writing supplies to compose his weekly letter.

Ab 3, 3443

Petre,

I have good news: I saw Jesisca earlier this week. I didn't have an opportunity to talk to her as she got into a telepod and 'ported away before I could make my move. I never saw her return, but I will keep my eyes open to see if she does.

Until next week,

Ninan

. . .

HE READ through the letter to ensure it didn't contain anything that wasn't true. Satisfied with his report, he sealed the envelope and addressed it to Petre. With a bounce in his step, he deposited it into the courier's box and went to get his boarding house dinner.

With his new job, Ninan would begin saving some money. He'd like to find a house to buy and stay in Kirma permanently.

From what he'd seen on his neighborhood tours, the housing was reasonably priced. He was also impressed by the people, employment opportunities, diversity, and vitality the city offered.

He spent the next two days walking the neighborhoods. Rather than searching for Jesisca, he had an eye to purchase a house. Ninan found several places available that would be perfect starter homes.

At the home closest to his job and incidentally his favorite, he approached the front door and knocked. A few moments later, a young woman answered the door.

"I saw your house is for sale. Could I schedule a time to walk through it?" he said.

"How about right now?" she inquired with some excitement.

"Really? It won't put you to any trouble?"

"No trouble at all," she replied. "We just put the sign in the yard this morning, and we're quite anxious to sell quickly. You see, my husband just had his match day, and his new job is at the Old Soul Engineering Facility starting in just two weeks, on the twentieth of Ab."

She stood to the doorway's side and gestured for Ninan to enter.

Ninan stepped forward, hand outstretched, and said, "My name's Ninan."

"I'm pleased to meet you, Ninan. My name's Kanekoa," she

replied and shook his hand. She proceeded to give him a tour of the entire house.

Impressed with the layout and cleanliness, Ninan especially appreciated the backyard with the immaculate landscaping and the wide variety of fruit trees. He could easily see himself living here and enjoying a simple, laid-back life.

Before the tour was half over, he made up his mind. He wanted this house.

"Would you like something to drink?" she asked as they finished the tour.

"Sure, that'd be wonderful."

"Would pika juice be alright?"

"Perfect."

"Why don't you take a seat in the living room while I get the refreshments," she said as she walked away toward the kitchen.

Ninan already felt at home as he walked down the bright hallway back toward the living room. He paused at the doorway and smiled as he envisioned making this his home. He picked a chair facing the windows to appreciate the neighborhood view while waiting for Kanekoa.

Kanekoa entered the room with their drinks and passed one to Ninan. She inquired politely, "Do you have any questions about the house?"

He took a sip of the pika juice and nodded his head, "How much are you asking for it?"

"We had thought to ask thirty-five hundred taj," she began but then added hastily, "but we're willing to entertain offers."

Ninan visibly gulped at the asking price. He expected it to be high, but not that high. Inspiration struck, and he asked, "Would you be willing to carry the contract?"

CHAPTER 8

Kanekoa thought about his idea for a moment and then replied, "We might be able to do that. Our housing will be paid for through my husband's new job so we won't have to buy a house for several anons. How long of a contract were you thinking?"

"Well, if we could negotiate the purchase price to three thousand taj, and you could carry a two anon contract, I could pay you twenty taj each mesan with the lump sum at the end of the two anons," he replied more confidently than he felt.

He saw her wavering with a counteroffer, so he added, "You see, I just started a new job here in Kirma, and I haven't had a chance to build my reputation with the lenders."

"I see," she replied as she continued to consider.

"You don't have to decide right now," he supplied hastily. "Talk it over with your husband and let me know whatever you choose.

"You can send a message to me at my work at the distribution facility. The receptionist, Frasnia, can hold on to your message for me."

Kanekoa smiled at Ninan's idea of talking to her husband. "That sounds good."

Ninan downed the remaining pika juice and set the glass down on the table in front of him. He rested his hands on his knees and looked around the room once more.

He pushed his hands against his knees as he stood from the chair and said, "I should get going. Thank you for showing me the house. I look forward to hearing from you soon."

Kanekoa jumped to her feet and replied, "Thanks for stopping by. I'll talk to my husband tonight and hopefully have an answer for you tomorrow. Will that be okay?"

"That'd be perfect," he replied as he once again held out his hand to say goodbye formally. "Have a wonderful day," he said as he walked to the front door and let himself out.

Ninan sat down to breakfast before work on Senin. The day's prospects were more exciting than any other since arriving. The waiter handed him a letter from Petre. Even that reminder only put a minor damper on his mood.

First things first.

He opened Petre's letter and read:

AB 5, 3443

Ninan,

Excellent news! I knew she was still there. When you do get to talk to her, make arrangements to meet her somewhere, and I can go with you.

I've included your five shills with this letter leaving a total of 7½ taj left owing.

I'm anxious to receive your next letter. Send your next update to me at the Maiden's House at the Port of Cresdon.

Petre MacVeen

. . .

ONCE AGAIN, Ninan thought Petre's fascination with the brothel houses deeply conflicted with his desire to get back together with his wife.

If I were with a woman as beautiful as Jesisca, I definitely wouldn't be frequenting the houses of ill repute. I guess this does confirm my belief that Petre's not a very honorable man.

He carefully folded the letter and tucked it away into his jacket pocket just as the waiter brought his breakfast.

When Ninan arrived at work, he stopped by the office. "Good morning, Frasnia," he said as he approached her desk.

"Good morning, Ninan. Did you have a good weekend?"

"It was wonderful, but I need to ask you a favor."

"Really? What's up?"

"I made an offer on a house yesterday," he said with a broad grin of accomplishment.

"That's wonderful, Ninan. I guess this means you plan to stay for a while then?"

"I sure do. I think this city's great," he began and then remembered the favor he needed from Frasnia. "Anyway, the couple who own the house needed some time to consider my offer.

"I suggested they let me know their decision by sending you a message to get to me when I check in during my breaks. I hope I wasn't being too presumptuous by making that arrangement."

"Oh, no, Ninan. Not at all," she responded immediately and smiled enthusiastically, "A new house! How exciting! And to think, I'll have my part in it, too."

Just then, the front door opened, and Ninan turned to see an extraordinarily sad and downtrodden Bryon enter the building. "Hello, Bryon," Ninan said softly, not expecting a reply.

Bryon looked up from the floor and spotted the two people in the room. He seemed startled that he was in the office and belatedly replied, "Oh! Hello, Ninan, Frasnia."

He nodded his head to each as he continued his journey across the lobby and into his office, shutting the door quietly behind him.

"Wow, he looks terrible," Frasnia whispered conspiratorially to Ninan.

"You're telling me," he replied. "I guess I better head to my workstation. I'll check back in at first break to see if you've heard anything. Keep your fingers crossed. Oh, and, good luck with you know who," he said as he nodded his head toward Bryon's office and then took his leave.

"Thanks," Frasnia said out loud to a now empty room. "I think today will be very different." She looked toward Bryon's office.

Should I check on him and see if he needs anything, like a cup of java?

Then she remembered the distracted look on his face and thought he might appreciate some alone time to get adjusted to being back at work.

Maybe later. Sadly, it wasn't hard to convince herself.

CHAPTER 9

After a plane change in Dallas, Texas, Amanda's family arrived in Roswell, New Mexico, five hours and thirty minutes after leaving Miami, Florida. They collected their luggage from the baggage return and then hailed a shuttle to take them to the car rental facility near the airport.

Once they had their luggage in the back of the plush Toyota 4-Runner SUV, Chris handed the travel agent's paperwork to Diane in the passenger seat.

Diane leafed through the papers until she found the step-by-step directions to the Fairfield Inn, chosen solely for its proximity to the International UFO Museum Center. With Diane's instructions, Chris easily drove them to their hotel, where they checked in and took their luggage to their two separate rooms.

Amanda sighed as she set her luggage down on the king-sized bed and sat next to it with a sigh of relief at resting her aching body. While excited to see what this adventure could bring, physical exhaustion from her near-death experience made her wish to take a nap. Only four days ago, she'd been found unconscious on the Mexican beach.

This trip might've been a little premature since she was still bruised and broken from the mudslide, but she didn't dare tell her parents how much she hurt. Too much was at stake.

She didn't know what to expect here in Roswell. So far, a spaceship was the only thing keeping her hope alive of finding a way back to Tuala. She shook her head as the enormity of their task threatened to overwhelm her.

I don't know what we were thinking about coming to Roswell. It's not as if Tualan travel clues will be lying around for us to find. It's not like the spaceship replica will have a map on it. But I'll turn every stone to bring back my children.

Amanda looked up when someone knocked on her door. She swallowed a groan of discomfort as she pulled herself up from the bed, walked the short distance across the room, and opened the door. Her mother smiled at her and said, "Your father and I were thinking we should get something to eat. Do you want to come too?"

"Sure," she said. She was hungry, and she needed to keep her body fueled so her mind could remain focused on the task at hand instead of on her appetite. After adjusting the sling for her casted arm, she grabbed her purse from the bed and joined her mother in the hallway. "Where's Dad?" she asked as she looked up and down the hall for him.

"He went to bring the SUV around front for us." Diane tucked her hand around Amanda's elbow and smiled as she walked with her daughter. "I still can't believe you're back with us. And to think, if we're successful with this trip, we'll have you bring our grandchildren to us, as well. I can't say I'm too happy about you having to go back there. What if you aren't able to find another way back home?"

Amanda shrugged but hearing her mom use the word *if* set her on edge. She couldn't doubt her success, not yet anyway. "There's never any guarantee. But, nothing's going to stop me from trying."

"I know, honey. I know. I'd do the same thing for you or your sisters." Diane's hand squeezed Amanda's elbow.

They walked out of the hotel, the hot air blasting them even in the shade. Chris pulled up to the entrance with the SUV. He rolled down the passenger side window, and with a broad grin, he said, "Hey, pretty ladies, do you want a ride?"

Playing along, Diane replied, "Gladly, I always accept rides from handsome men."

Amanda shook her head at her parents' strange humor and climbed into the back seat of the SUV as her mother took the front passenger's seat. They drove through the main roads to see what was available. Diane spotted what she thought was a Denny's from a distance and said, "Let's go there."

They drove closer and discovered that the original sign was covered with a cloth which read 'Roswell Cover-Up Café.' They laughed at the sign's double meaning and then laughed some more when they spotted the light post with the black painted eyes on an alien-shaped head at the entrance.

Inside, Amanda commented to her parents, "This doesn't look like any Denny's I've ever seen." She noted that the central kitchen was shaped like a control center of a spaceship. The seating areas radiated out from the restaurant's center, and even the hanging silver metal light fixtures reminded her of little, floating spaceships.

The hostess seated them at a table near the kitchen entrance and brought them their menus and glasses of water. "Your server will be with you in a few minutes," she said as she turned away to seat another couple who entered the restaurant. They opened their menus in companionable silence and decided what to eat.

While eating their meal, Amanda and Diane talked about the rows of antique shops and alien-themed tourist traps they saw along the way to the diner.

Diane leaned against the table and said enthusiastically, "We're definitely going to have to walk a few of those streets to see the different types of antiques and souvenirs available. I just love the old-fashioned storefronts with recessed doorways all advertising unique alien memorabilia."

Chris groaned and said, "You guys'll drop me off at the hotel first, right?"

Diane rolled her eyes and smiled at Amanda. "If you insist, dear."

Amanda stifled a laugh and finished her fries. "I can't eat another bite!"

"You know, Amanda, I think we should stop somewhere to buy some comfortable walking shoes. I didn't even think about that while I was packing. Let's drop Chris off at the hotel and see if we can find a Wal-Mart."

"Sounds good to me," Amanda replied.

Chris paid the bill, and they returned to the 4-Runner. Chris parked outside the hotel's entrance and met Diane at the front of the SUV. He handed her the keys, gave her a quick hug and kiss, and said, "Please don't buy too much stuff. We'll just have to carry it all back home on the airplane."

Seeing her parents talking outside of the vehicle, Amanda got out of the back seat and went into the hotel lobby to ask for directions to Wal-Mart. As it turned out, Roswell didn't have a Wal-Mart yet, so she received instructions to another store instead. She thanked the hotel employee and returned to the vehicle just as her parents finished talking.

"I'll behave," Diane said with a smile as she walked away from her husband toward the driver's door. Diane slid into the left seat just as Amanda got into the passenger's seat. Amanda gave her mom the directions, and within a few minutes, they pulled into the parking lot and burst out laughing.

The store had a spaceship painted on the side of the building, with six-foot-tall green aliens painted on the windows of the cart return area. Shaking their heads at the absurdity of it all, they went into the store and began shopping.

After dark, they returned to the hotel. To their credit, they each only had two small bags of souvenirs from the dozen or so shops they browsed throughout the day.

Diane walked Amanda to her room and hugged her. She held Amanda's packages in the hallway while Amanda dug her room key out of her purse. When Amanda stood in her open doorway, Diane handed her the purchases, touched her daughter's shoulder, and said, "Get some rest tonight. Tomorrow could be a crucial day at the museum, but there's no point in borrowing trouble and worrying about everything until we know what we're up against. Okay?"

Amanda smiled a small, crooked smile and replied, "That's just it, Mom, I *know* what I'm up against. That's what has me worried. Every moment I spend here, my daughters are spending all alone in a strange world! I've got to get them back!"

Diane pulled her daughter into an awkward but fierce hug around her cast and answered sharply, "That's why we're here, honey. We'll get some answers at the museum, I'm sure of it."

She pulled back and grabbed her daughter's shoulders, looking her straight in the eyes, and said with conviction, "We'll do everything we can to see them back here safely! Put your faith in God, and things will work out as they should! I'll keep saying my prayers. I love you. Now go in and get some sleep."

At nine o'clock the following morning, they finally got to the museum. They drove their SUV down North Main Street until they saw the enormous blue UFO Museum and Research Center sign on the front of the building. They parked in the parking lot just past the location and got out of their vehicle.

Diane commented on the mural painted on the side of the building with a human hand reaching out to touch an alien hand with the words 'Be in Touch' written below it. They left the parking lot and walked along the sidewalk until they reached the concave covered entrance of the building, which could easily shade one hundred people from the harsh sun.

After paying their admission, they walked through the glass front doors to be greeted by a child-sized alien statue. The exhibition hall's lobby was enormous. The floor was set in a checkerboard pattern of blue and cream vinyl tiles last used in schools in the 1950s and never used again.

They chose the right-side corridor and looked at the many research and history displays. They examined the pictures of various crop circles and other items believed to have been created by aliens.

Amanda found the most disturbing item on display was a hospital room setting with two doctors surrounding a gurney containing a naked, child-sized alien. Amanda's heart went out to the little alien and hoped it didn't have any element of truth to it.

"This display is ridiculous, Dad. The people on Tuala don't look like this! They look just like us," Amanda whispered loudly to her father.

"I know, honey. They have to do it to keep people interested."

Neither Amanda nor Chris heard the older woman behind them gasp when she overheard the word "Tuala" nor that she watched as they moved on to view the next display.

CHAPTER 10

For the past fifteen years, Shemalla worked at the museum, and she had never heard anyone mention Tuala. She needed to find some way to talk to these people to discover how they came to know about Tuala.

She cautiously trailed them throughout the entire museum without losing sight of them. She had another thrilling moment when she overheard Amanda talking to her father.

"Look, Dad," Amanda said excitedly, "the telepod is over there."

"Let's get a closer look, shall we?" He responded with a hint of excitement in his voice. When they got right next to it, Chris disappointedly said, "This replica looks pretty dinky. Is there enough detail to help you remember something to help you go back? If not, maybe you can tell me more about the telepod's performance."

Receiving yet another shock from hearing the word "telepod," Shemalla moved quite close to eavesdrop on them discussing the replica. She just had to know what they'd say about it. Pretending to tidy up a nearby display, she leaned toward the pair and listened.

"Well?" Chris prompted Amanda while, at the same time, Diane leaned closer to inspect the ship.

"It's obviously too small, but it looks pretty good." She paused to consider what was wrong with the rendition and finally realized the difference and said, "The windows all the way around are a bit ridiculous considering the crystal drive would be at the back. It needs to be out of the sunlight to prevent overheating."

Amanda looked it over more intently and said, "I wish we could see inside it. You'd be interested in the way the pieces come together seamlessly to create a real work of art."

"Well, as you said, it's just a replica. I doubt they'd think anyone from Tuala would come and dispute its accuracy," Diane quietly pointed out as she led them away from the display.

Just as they were finishing their tour, Shemalla knew she had no other choice but to talk to them. Bursting with curiosity, she rushed up and touched Amanda's elbow and said, "I hope you enjoyed your visit to the museum."

Surprised, Amanda whirled around and nodded.

"My name's Shemalla," the woman in her early thirties said as she turned to include Chris and Diane in her introduction. "I work for the museum," she clarified as she registered their confused expressions.

"Oh," Chris said. "Yes, it's very well put together."

"Um, I don't know how to ask you this without sounding a little crazy," she started and then hesitated.

"What is it?" Amanda asked. Something about the eager glint in the woman's eyes made Amanda's heart begin racing. Was this the break they hoped to find? Could it possibly be this simple, or was this a trap?

"Well, I thought I overheard you say the word Tuala. I was just wondering what that word meant to you," she finished lamely.

Amanda looked around them to see how many people were nearby. Thankfully, they were relatively secluded at the moment, and she leaned forward to reply, "At the risk of sounding crazy myself, Tuala is an alternate plane of reality here on Earth."

Shemalla gasped, and her hands flew up to her mouth as she rocked back on her heels. *They know!* "Who are you?" she whispered through her fingers still covering her mouth.

"Are you saying you believe me?" Amanda asked, now suspicious herself.

"Yes, yes, of course, I believe you," she replied promptly. "Who sent you?"

"Nobody sent me," she defensively answered as she saw the look of disbelief on Shemalla's face. Then an inspired thought struck her, and she blurted out, "Are you saying there's a portal between the planes?"

Shemalla's eyes darted to each of the group before scanning their surroundings. Leaning in closer, she whispered, "We should talk after I get off of work."

She fished in her pockets for a pen. Coming up empty-handed, she said urgently, "Let me give you my address and phone number. I have to get something to write with from the desk over there."

She didn't want to leave them, but she had to give them her contact information. Excitement buzzed through her, making her hands shake and causing her to make several attempts to write down what they'd need to know.

"Sorry about my sloppy handwriting," she said as she shakily thrust the slip of paper into Amanda's outstretched hand. "My shift ends at five o'clock tonight. Would you be available to meet with me after that?"

Amanda took the paper with equally trembling fingers. Did this woman hold the answer to her quest? Or was she just some alien conspiracy nut? After all, the lady did work at this museum.

She looked at her parents, who nodded at her to answer in the affirmative. Amanda shifted her gaze back to Shemalla and said, "Sure. Do you want us to meet you out front at five?"

"That'd be all right," she replied. Her sudden nerves made her motions jerky and awkward. "I've got to get back to work now, but please come back this evening, okay?"

"Absolutely," Amanda replied almost breathlessly. She watched the slender woman go back the way they had come and turned to her parents to exclaim, "Can you believe this?"

Diane hugged Amanda and replied with a wide grin, "This is it, baby, just like I said last night! We're going to find a way back to Tuala so you can bring your girls back to us!"

The trio left the UFO Center, but they were too amped up to go back to the hotel. Amanda forgot all about her aches and pains; her mind whirled with the possibilities Shemalla presented.

They walked along Main Street and looked at the tourist shops again. Amanda didn't notice much of their surroundings, considering all of her unanswered questions. She mentally ticked off the minutes until they could return to the UFO Center.

"What time is it?" Amanda asked for the sixth time.

Patiently answering his daughter, Chris glanced at his wristwatch and replied, "It's 11:30."

"Good grief, this is going to take forever."

They walked across a parking lot and found a little white booth, the size of a small shed with turquoise trim. It caught their attention because it had snow falling around a spaceship on the side and an alien painted on the front.

Chris pointed it out to the two women and said, "It's kind of hot walking out here. Do either of you want to get a snow cone?"

Amanda couldn't remember the last time she ate one and eagerly replied, "That sounds wonderful. Let's see if they have my favorite blue raspberry flavor."

They stepped up to the small window, and each ordered a shaved ice. After taking their money, the employee handed out their flavored ice cones and said, "Enjoy your Alien Sno."

Walking down the road with snow cones in hand, Amanda

pointed out another oddity, "That's not your typical Mcdonalds'," she said enthusiastically. "Look, the children's dining room area is shaped like a huge, silver flying saucer."

Even the typical children's playground contained alien-themed toys. "I bet the children get a kick out of the lamp post, too," she said as she looked at the alien eyes painted on the glass globe.

Chris, as always, was hungry. "Let's stop somewhere and get something real to eat."

With a new mission, they walked a little faster, searching for a restaurant where they could get out of the sun to enjoy a meal. They found a small diner that didn't contain any alien themes and ducked into the interior's cool dimness.

They seated themselves in one of the booths just as a young woman in an old-fashioned poodle skirt brought them three glasses of water. "Welcome to The Diner," she said as she gestured toward the menus under the table's glass surface. "I'll take your order whenever you're ready," she said with a smile. "Can I start you off with something to drink?"

"I'll take a Mountain Dew," answered Chris.

"I'll just have water," Diane and Amanda said in unison and then started laughing.

"I'll be right back with your soda," she nodded to Chris and walked over to the soda fountain to pull his drink.

She returned a moment later with Chris' drink and straw. She set them on the table and said, "Do you need a few more minutes to decide?"

"I'm ready," said Amanda.

"I'm ready, too," added Diane.

"I'll have it figured out by the time the ladies place their orders," Chris replied with a grin.

"All right, you first, Miss," the waitress stated as she nodded her head toward Amanda.

"I'd like a Cobb salad minus the bacon."

"What kind of dressing would you like with that?"

"Bleu cheese, please."

The waitress nodded and wrote down the salad order on her small tablet. "And you, Miss," she said and looked down at Diane.

"I was going to order something else, but the Cobb salad sounds good. I'd like mine exactly the same as Amanda's, please."

"No problem," the waitress replied as she scribbled the number two next to the salad order. "Did they give you enough time, Sir?"

"Definitely! I'd like to order the ultimate double cheeseburger with fries and coleslaw, please."

"You got it. That'll just be a few minutes," she said as she finished the order ticket and walked back toward the kitchen.

Amanda couldn't wait to discuss their meeting with the museum employee. She leaned her chest into the table's side but fussed with placing her casted arm in a position that didn't hurt as much. Finally, she asked, "So what did you guys think about Shemalla? It's kind of an odd name, don't you think?"

"I don't know," started her father thoughtfully.

"It's an odd name, and I thought she seemed excited," Diane said as she looked across the table at her daughter, ignoring her husband's grunt at being dismissed so easily.

"That's what I thought, too. What do you think she meant when she asked, 'Who sent you?'" Amanda mused.

"That was curious, wasn't it?" agreed Diane.

"Do you think she's trying to find a way to Tuala, too?" Amanda asked. "She never did answer my question about any type of passage between."

"That's an idea. I wonder if she's from there or if she just wants to go there?" Chris asked.

Amanda felt even more anxious about their upcoming meeting. Initially, she wanted to believe Shemalla might hold the key to returning. But now, she thought it might be possible that the woman was in the same situation as herself: trying to find a way back.

Amanda sighed and sat back against the booth seat. She looked beseechingly at her parents and asked, "What if this's just a dead end?"

"Let's not think that way until we have a reason to," soothed Chris. "I can't stand seeing you in such turmoil. Ah, here's the waitress returning from the kitchen with our food. You know what I always say."

"A full stomach brings a better outlook on any of life's situations," the trio spoke simultaneously.

Amanda rolled her eyes, but she'd trust her dad for now. She loved how her dad always knew exactly what to say. It felt better to think positively, anyway.

Once the waitress deposited their food on the table and left, Chris prayed over the family meal. Then he picked up his hamburger with both hands, took a huge bite, and moaned in delight.

"Good food definitely makes life easier to handle," he mumbled around his bite.

Diane rolled her eyes at her husband's reaction to food. She enjoyed eating, but Chris positively lived for it. She picked up her fork and dipped the tines into her dressing before stabbing a few pieces of lettuce. She took the bite and chewed, all the while thinking about their upcoming meeting.

Amanda picked up her fork. She was hungry when she ordered her salad, but now she was too nervous to eat. She poked her fork at the lettuce, the avocados, the tomatoes, and then the eggs. Her mind wandered anywhere but on eating.

CHAPTER 11

"Come on, Amanda. You need to eat your meal," admonished her father. "We're all anxious about seeing that woman tonight, but we don't know what'll happen. What if she could get you back there tonight, but you hadn't eaten? We need to be prepared, even if it's just by keeping our stomachs full."

"Dad, that's the lamest thing I've ever heard," Amanda responded as she sighed and looked out the window. Regardless, her thoughts were distracted enough to let her brain register that her stomach's churning and growling could be hunger-related. She stabbed a decent mouthful and ate it.

"That's more like it," Chris said with a dorky grin as he took a forkful of coleslaw and watched his daughter actually eat her meal instead of playing with it.

With the salad's last forkful gone, Amanda set her utensil down on her plate and sat back with a satisfied sigh. "Well, that was the most effort I ever put into eating a meal!"

"It'll be worth it," Chris declared as he pushed away his empty plate as well.

Diane continued to eat her salad delicately. Between bites, she faced Amanda and inquired, "What are you planning on asking her?"

"I was thinking of first just finding out what she knows about Tuala. We can see where the conversation goes from there," Amanda replied with a shrug. *How much of my own story should I discuss with this mysterious stranger?*

"That sounds good to me," agreed Chris.

"What should I tell her if she wants me to talk first?" Amanda asked suddenly.

"Put it back on her," Diane replied. "After all, she's the one who wants to meet with us."

"Okay, well, what if she's trying to find a way back to Tuala as I am? What then?"

"Ask her what she's found out so far. Compare notes with her on how you both got there and came back," Chris answered.

"Do you think I should tell her about my girls?"

"I wouldn't, at first," Diane said cautiously. "Just say you left something significant behind and that you need to go back and get it."

"That sounds like I'm trying to bring back something that should be left in Tuala."

Diane finished her salad and pushed the plate away just as the waitress returned to put their bill on the edge of the table.

"Can I bring you any dessert?" she inquired as she picked up the empty plates and stacked them on one arm.

The three at the table looked at each other and shook their heads. Chris spoke for the family as he said, "No, thank you. I think we're all full."

"Okay. You can pay at the table or the register," she replied as she took the dishes back to the kitchen.

"Can we go outside, please?" Amanda's nerves started to act up again, urging her to do anything other than sit still.

"Sure. You two can go on out while I take care of the bill," Chris said as he took his wallet out of his back pocket and selected a credit card.

"Great. Come on, Mom," Amanda shimmied out of the booth and stood to leave. She grabbed her mom's elbow and almost towed her out of the restaurant in her rush to get moving.

They stepped outside and were soon joined by Chris. They walked up one side of the street without any plan, crossed the road, and strolled down the other side. They entered a few of the antique shops to look around, but neither Diane nor Amanda was in the mood to buy anything, much to Chris's relief, who would end up carrying anything they purchased.

Finally tired of being out in the heat, they found a bench in a nearby park and sat on it in the spindly tree's sparse shade next to it. "I know I've already asked you a million times, Dad, but what time is it?"

With an indulgent smile, Chris lifted his wrist, looked at his watch, and replied, "It's four o'clock."

"Oh, do you think we should start heading back to the UFO Center?" Amanda could hardly contain her excitement, fearing her father would tell her it was only noon. To hear the miraculous news that it was already getting so late, her nerves kicked into high gear, her pulse raced, and she rubbed her suddenly moist palms against her pants. In just a short time, what might they discover?

Chris looked up and saw the UFO Center at the far end of the street from where they sat. "Um, even if we walked at a snail's pace, it won't take us more than ten minutes." He shook his head and replied, "We could go, but just know that we'll be standing around outside the UFO Center for the next fifty minutes."

"I guess not," Amanda's gaze followed her father's. *Of course, he's right.* "Today has gone by agonizingly slow! Why couldn't that woman just take the rest of the day off?"

"She probably has bills to pay and couldn't," Diane admonished with practicality.

Amanda rolled her eyes and hugged her casted arm over her chest. She blew air out of her mouth loudly and let her head fall backward until she was staring at the bright blue sky.

She thought about meditating to bring peace and harmony to her mind, but her racing thoughts wouldn't allow it. The silence was killing her, and she finally blurted, "Somebody, please talk!"

"What do you remember about your last day in Tuala?" Chris asked.

"Bryon took me to the mountain lookout just south of the City of Cresdon. That's Cancun, as you guys would know it," she said as an aside.

"Are you sure it was a mountain?" Chris asked.

"Quite sure. It took us almost an hour to climb the steep trail to the lookout." Then she thought to ask, "Why?"

"Well, if I remember my geography correctly, there aren't any mountains along that entire coastline." Chris continued to trace his mind's map. "How can the topography be so different when the landmasses seemed to be the same but with different names?"

"Well, I'm sure that's where we were. I remember Barla showing me an atlas of Tuala where she wrote in Earth names, and she did say the landmasses were all the same, but the topography didn't always match. Given that as far as the rest of Earth is concerned, Tuala doesn't even exist, so I guess anything's possible."

"Okay, so what did you two do on the mountain?" Diane asked.

"We sat and ate lunch. I looked in on the girls through their crystals and saw they were happy with Alena and her children. Bryon and I talked about the twins. Mostly, we just enjoyed the view of the coastline until the clouds started to roll in and obscure it."

She paused. *Should I tell them what happened next?* Glancing over at their expectant stares, she added, "A dragon flew onto the mountaintop and spoke to me."

Diane laughed and slapped her knee. "Ha! You had me going there for a second. A dragon! Isn't that funny, Chris?" When nobody joined her chuckles, she stopped and stared first at her husband, then her daughter. "Wait. Are you serious?"

Amanda nodded. Seeing she had her father's avid attention, she added, "She was royal purple with a gold belly. I've never seen anything so massive and graceful in all of my life. I bet she was the size of three elephants."

"What happened then?" Chris asked.

"She leaned forward as if she were smelling me or inspecting me. I don't know, maybe both. But then she spoke into my mind."

"What did she say?" Chris asked, at the same time Diane asked, "Weren't you terrified she was going to eat you?

Amanda inhaled slowly, remembering the encounter. "I don't know why, but I wasn't scared at all. Neither was Bryon; only he didn't hear her." Shifting her gaze to her father's, she said, "She only said, 'Almost. Hmm. Interesting.' Then she turned and flew away into the low clouds."

Chris and Diane exchanged a strange look between them. It might have been Amanda's imagination. She continued her story and said, "Then Bryon announced it was time to get back to the telepod, and we headed down the trail."

"Then what happened?" Diane prompted.

"The clouds opened up, and the rain poured down. Everyone had talked about how late the rainy season was that year. I guess the time came for it to start. The small seasonal stream alongside the trail we were walking filled with muddy water. Bryon walked faster, and we slipped and slid along the path.

"You both know I'm not terribly coordinated, and I worried the entire time that I'd fall over my feet and take Bryon down with me. As it turned out, Bryon fell. But that was after we heard this loud noise behind us, and we saw a wall of mud coming straight toward us."

"Okay, that's officially terrifying," gasped Diane as she reached out and touched Amanda's casted arm in sympathy. "Then what happened?"

"We ran, and Bryon fell. I helped him up, and then I tripped and fell into the then raging water beside the trail. The water ran so fast that I couldn't keep my feet under me long enough to get over to the edge. It was all I could do just to keep my head from getting hit by the swirling debris.

"Then the wall of mud came around the bend and hit me full on. Luckily I took a deep breath before it struck, or I probably would've drowned. I was pushed under and carried for at least a hundred feet in just a matter of seconds. I surfaced again just before the creek poured into the ocean.

"The last thing I remember was hearing a loud explosion right behind me. There was a bright flash of light and pain all over my body. I must've passed out then because I don't remember anything else except seeing the man who rescued me in Cancun."

"What do you think caused the explosion?" Chris asked.

"I have no idea. There was so much earth moving along behind me; it could've been anything."

"Lots of earth moving, huh?" Chris repeated quietly to himself.

"What're you thinking, Chris?"

He looked at his wife and said, "I can't be sure without checking with a geologist, but I think," he paused to consider the possibilities, "maybe the weight of the moving earth caused shifting underground. There could've been a pocket of methane gas that released and exploded."

"So?" Diane asked.

"So, maybe, that triggered Amanda's crossing back over to Earth," he finished triumphantly. He looked back and forth from his daughter's face to his wife's. "Well, it's possible," he added with less certainty than before as both the women continued to stare at him with confused expressions.

"Hmph," Diane finally replied noncommittally.

Amanda continued to consider her father's theory. She vaguely remembered studying about the Bermuda Triangle in school. One of the theories for the ships disappearing was because of methane gas bubbles rising from the ocean floor and causing the vessel to become less buoyant in the water and sink.

The trouble with this theory was that the ships were never found. *What if they didn't sink but transferred over to Tuala?*

"Maybe Dad's onto something," she said aloud. "If this lady doesn't have the answers we need, then when we go home, we can research that angle."

"Speaking of that lady, let's head over to the UFO Center," Chris said as he looked at his watch.

CHAPTER 12

"Really? It's that time already?" Amanda asked with both amazement and excitement.

"If we walk slowly," Chris sternly answered, emphasizing slowly.

It took them fifteen minutes to stroll to the UFO Center, and they stood under the vast concrete canopy to wait. Amanda paced across the length of the area while the remaining five minutes passed. Every time the doors opened, Amanda flew to face them, only to be disappointed when it was just another visitor leaving the exhibit.

Finally, the last flurry of visitors exited all at once, followed by an employee who locked the door. Amanda glanced across the way at her parents. She frowned and returned to where they stood. "Where is she?" she asked anxiously.

"I'm sure they have some closing procedures to follow once all of the visitors leave. She'll be here in a couple of minutes, I'm sure," Chris answered, always the voice of reason.

Amanda resumed her pacing. She had just completed her third

circuit of the area when a woman's voice spoke up, "Sorry I'm a little late."

Amanda twirled around and spotted Shemalla standing next to her parents. She rushed over to their side, anxious to see what would happen next.

"The staff has to leave out the employee entrance at the back. I hope you haven't had to wait too long," she explained as she gestured behind her.

"Oh, just a couple of minutes," Chris answered.

Shemalla asked, "Where do you guys want to talk? I don't think here would be a good idea." She motioned toward the UFO Center.

"We're not from around here. Do you have any suggestions?" Chris asked.

"We could go back to my house. I don't live too far away. We could walk, if you like," she suggested.

"Sure, that'd be just fine," Diane said as she stepped closer. Even though they knew nothing about this woman, Diane felt good about her. Her instincts rarely led her wrong.

"It's this way." She walked toward the parking lot and away from the UFO Center. The group remained in relative silence as they all wondered what would come of this meeting.

Shemalla led them down the main street for a couple of blocks and then turned right. They swiftly left the downtown area and entered a small neighborhood of older homes.

They crossed the street and went to the fourth house on the block, which turned out to be hers. "It's not big, but I live alone and don't need much," she said as they walked up the gravel path through the cactus garden to the covered porch.

Shemalla unlocked the front door and walked inside. A blast of cold air hit them as they walked single file through the front door. "Make yourselves at home," she said as she indicated the living room to their left. "I'll just go get us some glasses of water to drink, and then we can talk, okay?" She set her purse down on the table in the hall and kept walking to the kitchen.

With no other options, Amanda led the way into the living room and picked the wooden rocking chair to sit in. Her parents sat next to each other on the old, red sofa.

Looking around the room, Amanda saw drawings of various people with odd little trinkets placed in front of them. Every corner of the small room had plants stuffed in them, some large, some small. Next to the doorway was a large potted jade plant. Amanda had never seen one quite so large except out in nature. It had to be quite old.

Shemalla swept into the room carrying a tray with four water glasses. She set down the tray on the coffee table in front of Chris and Diane and served each of them. She turned and handed Amanda a glass while picking up the last one for herself.

She turned back and walked over to the chair opposite Amanda beside the sofa. Her hand shook as she took a sip from the glass. When she finished her drink, she cradled the glass between her hands, resting in her lap. "Since it was my idea that we talk, I'll go first," she announced.

"My name is Shemalla Paramasivam, and I was born in Pantano on Tuala," she began and then paused before continuing, "Can you please tell me who you are?" She looked pointedly at Amanda.

"My name's Amanda Covington," Amanda began, gesturing at her parents. She continued, "These are my parents, Chris Covington and Diane Covington. We were all born on Earth, and we currently live in Florida."

Shemalla nodded even though she was now more curious than ever. She continued telling her story, hoping it would inspire Amanda to share as well.

"In Tuala, I became Elder Vargen's apprentice. He's always been very interested in all things to do with Earth, and he's one of the co-founders of the Old Soul Engineering Facility. He passed his interest along to his son.

"One summer, his son was showing off to his friends and performing his right of passage by creating a verifiable stunt on Earth. Well, his stunt was definitely verifiable since it went wrong, and his telepod crashed just outside of Roswell."

Shemalla paused to see if her guests followed what she was talking about. She smiled as, one by one, each person in the room put together the events to realize this was the 1947 flying saucer crash highlighted in the UFO Museum. "By your expressions, I can see you are starting to understand what has happened to bring me here."

"You haven't been here since 1947," Amanda protested. "You're not nearly old enough for that!"

"You're right, Amanda. I haven't been here that long. I've been here on Earth working at the museum for the past fifteen years. You see, Elder Vargen was ashamed that his son created such a mess on Earth, and he took it upon himself to clean it up."

"So are you saying, you know exactly what happened on that night in July of 1947?" Chris asked eagerly.

"Yes, I do."

"Are you allowed to tell us?" Chris pushed. Like most boys his age, he grew up fascinated with this whole scandal and was as anxious as a little kid to know the absolute truth behind the cover-up.

"We'll see," Shemalla replied cautiously. She continued her story by saying, "Anyway, since Elder Vargen's son was responsible, the Elder was highly embarrassed by the whole incident.

"He attempted to keep the entire episode quiet by filing a brief report with the Council of Elders with the promise to keep one of his employees on the case until all traces of it vanished from Earth's memory."

"That's going to take a while," scoffed Chris, "what with the museum and all."

"That's exactly what Elder Vargen thought, too," Shemalla agreed. "Because of the museum, he has assigned Tualans to the Roswell case ever since it opened. It's our job to make sure that all traces of Tuala remain hidden.

"Of course, when I heard you mention Tuala, you can imagine how much it startled me." She looked around the room at her three guests to emphasize her position.

Diane nodded and raised her eyebrows expectantly for Shemalla to continue.

"Anyway, when my predecessor reached his work contract's end and requested a return to Tuala, I was stationed in this position. During my briefing in Tuala, I was made to understand that the Roswell incident isn't common knowledge on Tuala, and Elder Vargen would very much like it to remain that way.

"When I left, I had to tell my family I was going to Earth to study Earth's technology, which, in a sense, is true."

"When is your assignment over?" Amanda couldn't resist asking.

"Not for another twenty-two years."

"Wow, that's a long time," Diane gasped. "Didn't you ever want to have a family?"

"Oh, I can still have a family when I return."

"Won't you be too old to start a family by the time you go back?" Diane was now more than a little confused.

"That's the wonderful thing about this assignment. When I finish, I'll only have aged thirty-seven months: one month for every year spent here, which was also negotiated in my contract," she said happily. "Elder Vargen will excuse the rest of my work life because of my service here."

"So you're saying the time difference isn't set in stone?" Chris inquired with interest.

"Oh, not at all," Shemalla replied with surprise. "The time difference varies for everyone. If they enter the Gate using the Elder's control and they agree to a timeframe. Or, if they transfer through a Gate unassisted, it can depend on what they're thinking.

"Some people control their shift to go forward or back in time depending on what they are trying to accomplish.

"Take teenagers, for example. They're trying to perform verifiable acts for their rights of passage. Since they have a strong talisman in their birth crystal and a solid desire to return to their friends, their focus is on a specific time and place. They tend to return to a time almost immediately after they leave.

"You can see why the Elders would want to try to curb the Tualans from shifting into Earth and leaving mischief in their wake. Imagine a Tualan going back in time and teaching advanced techniques to Earth's people before the proper foundation of understanding is in place. This interference would create havoc.

"Or imagine a Tualan going into the future to try to steal technological secrets and bring them back to Tuala. This, too, would cause an unfair advantage and possibly create unrest in Tuala, where the technology could be misused to the people's detriment.

"Because of these dangers to both worlds, the most powerful gates between the two worlds are protected by Elders. However, the gates on Earth don't have the same protection other than the simple fact that Earth's people don't know there's someplace they can navigate at those locations.

"Also, people here don't know what words to say or what talismans to carry to create a safe passage between the worlds. Without that specific knowledge, the gates are relatively harmless to Earth's people."

manda shivered at the thought of being lost between the worlds. She realized her engagement ring probably did act as her talisman, and she silently thanked Nealand for her safe passage even if she wouldn't spend the rest of her life with him.

Amanda glanced at her father to see if he would pursue this line of questioning. She knew he could go on for a very long time just to satisfy his curiosity for both new ideas and unfamiliar technology.

He gave her a shameless grin coupled with a slight shrug and motioned for Amanda to ask the next question. Trying to turn the conversation back to the current situation, Amanda asked, "Can you communicate with your family while you're here?"

"Yes, but rarely. I have to be very careful what I talk about since the amount of time I'm here isn't the same as what happens in Tuala."

"So what do you do? Write? Talk through crystals? What?" Amanda sounded more and more like her father.

"I can write through my patil," she said offhandedly, all the while wondering if they would know the significance of a patil.

"Really? How does your patil work through the veil?" Amanda asked with amazement.

"Elder Vargen arranged it. I don't know the exact mechanics of it myself," she said as she waved her hand. Seeing that Amanda's expression didn't show any wonder at her revelation of the patil demonstrated she was already familiar with the technology. "Now, may I ask you how you know so much about Tuala even though you claim to live in Florida?"

Chris and Diane both shifted their gaze to Amanda as she looked at them.

"I accidentally spent ten months there even though I was missing from Earth for fourteen months. Your explanation about the time differences explains that anomaly.

"While I was staying in Tuala, I also discovered that my mother's sister, Barbara, lived in the Port of Cresdon. I didn't find out she was my aunt until after I managed to return to Earth. She sent a letter with me to give to her family."

Too late, Amanda remembered that her aunt would be in danger of being taken by the Elders if any Tualan knew of her existence. She closed her eyes, took a deep breath, held out her hands beseechingly toward Shemalla, and murmured, "Please don't tell Elder Vargen about my aunt or her husband. She's been a good Tualan citizen for over twenty years. I don't want either of them punished for my indiscretion!"

"Oh," Shemalla exclaimed and shook her head. "Please don't worry about it. I've never agreed with the practice of holding Earth's people captive for questioning when we Tualans regularly come here to learn things."

Relief spread over Amanda's face, and she slowly raised her gaze to look at Shemalla again. Why did she suddenly overshare? What was it about Shemalla that made her speak so freely? Was she employing a compulsion to speak? Even as she looked at the woman sitting so calmly across from her, she knew this wasn't the case.

Shemalla stared at Amanda and considered her following statement before she hesitantly said, "You were very fortunate to survive the passages there and back through the gate without preparation or protection. Tell me, how did you accidentally end up in Tuala?"

In Amanda's mind, it all came down to one thing. This woman is connected with Tuala. Now, she could be evasive, but that wouldn't get her any closer to her daughters. No, she'd tell her everything and hope that Shemalla would take compassion on her and help her go back.

She took a deep breath through her nose and answered, "Somehow, the yacht I was in was transported through the gate. My fiancé and I found ourselves suddenly in a massive storm with high seas, thunder, and lightning.

"I don't really know or understand how the transfer happened since I was knocked out on the floor after I split my head open on a table. I was found and held captive for several weeks by a madman named Petre MacVeen—."

"Petre!" Shemalla gasped, "I've heard tales about him."

"It seems as though everyone in Tuala has heard of him!" Amanda exclaimed with amazement. Her eyes widened as she shook her head and looked at her parents in disbelief.

Shemalla said, "There aren't that many master deceptors born on Tuala. He has infamously used his gifts for mischief and personal gain instead of for the good of all. Typically, a person with that status would seek employment in either government, counseling, or teaching.

"In any of those positions, they'd be able to convince people to do good things with their lives with the least amount of resistance. But I digress, go on with your story, please." Shemalla prompted with a sense of dread as dire thoughts of what had probably happened to Amanda while being held by the notorious Petre MacVeen.

Shemalla speculated more about the girl's time alone with Petre as Amanda continued her story. Petre wasn't known for respecting women, and to have an unsuspecting, injured woman alone on his water craft for weeks, Shemalla shivered with ominous predictions about Amanda's journey.

"Well, after several weeks on his boat, I jumped overboard and got rescued by a passing ship. I still didn't know at that time that I was not on Earth anymore. I found out when my Aunt Barbara told me after getting a job at the Port of Cresdon. Her husband knew something about me reminded him of her, and he had her come and talk to me.

"Everything started to make more sense then. I had to move to a safe house because Petre was searching for me, claiming that I was his wife, and he wanted me back. I moved to a city named Kirma with a nice family that my Aunt Barbara knew. Several months later, I went hiking with Bryon, and I got caught in an avalanche and somehow ended up back on Earth."

"Wow, that's amazing," Shemalla began. She didn't have any reason to disbelieve Amanda's story since Amanda knew the names of so many people and places in Tuala. With her curiosity piqued, she asked, "So what brought you to the museum?"

"That was my idea," volunteered Chris. "Amanda needs to go back to Tuala, and we're trying to figure out how to make it happen."

Shemalla turned to look at Amanda again as she asked, "Why? Is it to get your Aunt?"

"Not exactly; although, I'd like to be able to tell her that we're related and to let her know that her family is happy to know she's safe."

"So if it's not for your Aunt, why do you need to go back?"

"I didn't know if I should share everything with you, but I guess since you've been so honest with us, it's only fair I tell you everything," she started and waited for her parents to nod their approval. Once received, she continued, "I need to go back to get my babies."

Shemalla's jaw dropped, and she stared at her. She didn't know what to say.

Concerned with Shemalla's silence, Amanda asked, "Can you help me?"

"I—," Shemalla paused and shook her head in concerned amazement and started again, "I don't know. Give me a few days to see what I can arrange."

CHAPTER 14

"I'm concerned about Amanda's accounting of her own demise. I think we should put someone in her room on suicide watch." Dr. Gascon looked up from the latest stack of notes from Dr. Medin.

"I don't think that'll be necessary. Amanda seems to be handling the situation. She's been discussing her time with her parents, and that shows me she's creating a support group for herself." Jasmine Medin felt conflicted about her decision to give Dr. Gascon the latest session notes.

The more she worked with her patient, the more convinced she became that the young woman had experienced something extraordinary. Of course, she wouldn't ever tell Dr. Gascon her true feelings, or he'd take the case away from her.

"I also don't like her saying that Nealand found another girlfriend and is denying that the children are his. These are classic signs of displaced feelings. She is hiding her guilt in his disappearance by creating a scenario where she is the wronged party and is, thereby, justified in keeping him out of her life. The Taivas family is paying good money for us to figure out what Amanda knows about their son's disappearance. We need to do more to get answers for them."

Jasmine held her tongue concerning the Taivas family's money. Dr. Gascon was more impressed with the amount of money the family paid to take Amanda's case than he was in getting to the truth of the matter. There was also the worry about Dr. Gascon's personal interest in Amanda's story in particular. Usually, he only took cursory notice of the patients except when he thought they might be able to increase his status in the psychiatric field.

Amanda's story was too consistent to be a complete fabrication. Each person Amanda came into contact with had individual personalities and desires to help her. A mentally ill patient could not create such an elaborate setting while also maintaining continuity with their tale. Usually, it was as though the patient was explaining a dream where disjointed parts made sense at the time, but when it was retold, it didn't make sense in the least.

"I think we're making progress. She's only been here for ten days. I think given a little more time, she'll come to terms with what happened to her, and she'll be able to tell us everything we need to know."

Jasmine still couldn't forget the hypnosis session with Amanda in her room before her medication. It had been a risk going against Dr. Gascon's orders, but one she felt had given her greater insight into Amanda's journey.

"Just so, I'd like you to push her a little harder during your sessions. We need to get to the truth soon."

"I'll do everything I can. I'm meeting with her this afternoon."

"Well, it's too bad I won't be able to sit in. I have a patient consult at Memorial Hospital just after lunch."

Pleasure bubbled up inside her knowing Dr. Gascon would be out of the building. This opportunity was just what she had hoped for since she first met with the young woman. Scheming ideas began to form in her head as she maintained a neutral expression.

"I think we're at a good point with Amanda since she's actively seeking a way back to Tuala. Maybe we can find out more about Nealand."

"I hope you're right. I'll read your notes when I get back into the office tomorrow morning. Good day, Dr. Medin."

Jasmine stood and replied, "Good day, Dr. Gascon." She turned and left the office. Without missing a beat, Jasmine walked down to the nurse's station and spoke with the attending nurse, "I'm going to be meeting with the patient in room 426 at 12:30 pm. I'd like to get her medicine dosage and take it with me so I can make sure it's administered at the proper time without interruption during her session."

She must have sounded authoritative enough as the nurse nodded her head and immediately turned to gather the cup already made ready for each room. Jasmine held out her hand and took the white paper cup containing three blue pills.

"Thank you. I'll be bringing the patient with me as I'm heading to my office right now."

She turned and walked confidently away from the desk and around the corner to get to Amanda's room. Once she reached her room, she briefly tapped on the door and waited for the invitation to enter.

"Hi, Amanda. Would you mind coming to my office right now?"

"Dr. Medin! I wasn't expecting you until after lunch. Is everything alright?"

"Absolutely. Let's go to my office, and we can talk freely, okay?"

Amanda stood from the bed centered in the room. She didn't have anything personal or any clothes to change into, so she was ready immediately. Her curiosity was piqued, and she had many questions to ask since their abruptly ended unorthodox session.

They marched to Dr. Medin's office, and Amanda watched with surprise as the doctor locked the door before she took her seat across from the brown leather couch. For the first time,

Amanda spotted the dreaded pills in the doctor's hand. She had thought something good might come from this meeting, but now she wasn't so sure.

Jasmine saw where Amanda gazed and rapidly reassured her, "Don't worry. I took these from the nurse's station so they wouldn't interrupt us. I told them I'd give it to you at the proper time." She balled up the paper cup with the pills still inside it and lobbed it across her office, where it made a perfect arc into the metal wastebasket.

"I don't think you'll be taking today's dosage. I'd like your mind to be clear during our session if that's okay with you?"

Amanda could hardly believe her eyes. Weren't all of the doctors of one accord when it came to medicating the patients? Obviously, not. For the first time in over a week, Amanda felt as though she could breathe freely. Dr. Medin was clearly on her side.

"I have a question for you, Dr. Medin."

Jasmine witnessed the change come over Amanda. She smiled reassuringly and said, "Feel free to ask me anything."

"Out of all the times we've met, I didn't remember anything except when you hypnotized me in my room. What was different about that time?"

Jasmine looked down at her now-folded hands and sighed. "Amanda, I'm always going to be completely honest with you." Seeing Amanda's nod, she continued, "At Dr. Gascon's insistence, I've given you a post-hypnotic suggestion to forget what we've discussed at each meeting except the one in your room. I lost track of time and abruptly ended the session when the attendant came to give you your pills. It's against the rules to treat patients in their rooms, so I couldn't let him see you hypnotized."

Amanda sat staring at the doctor as she processed the information. Not only did she admit to keeping information from her, but she also made herself vulnerable by sharing that she broke the rules. Amanda was unsure if she should be mad or relieved.

Finally, she asked, "If you'd paid attention to the time, would you have given me the post-hypnotic suggestion to forget?"

Jasmine considered before she answered, "I don't believe I would've. I think you'll make better progress if you remember what we've discussed. If you like, I can give you a post-hypnotic suggestion in our session today, which will negate any future suggestions. You see, when Dr. Gascon is here, he'll be expecting me to adhere to his rules. I'd like you to continue to remember. Would you like me to do that for you?"

"Absolutely! I'm desperate to remember everything."

"Okay, sit back, and we'll do that right now. Dr. Gascon said he'll be out of the office for the rest of the afternoon, but just in case—."

Amanda positioned herself on the couch, stretched out and as comfortable as possible. She took a deep breath and relaxed even more with the realization she wouldn't be seeing Dr. Gascon that afternoon. She was unaccountably relieved at this latest news.

The session seemed over almost before it began. Amanda opened her eyes and asked, "How long was I out?"

"Only about five minutes. I just gave you the new suggestion since I want to talk to you while you're awake. Tell me what you remember about our session in your room?"

Amanda took a moment before formulating her response, "I remember saying I had twins, which I left in Tuala. Is that true?"

"Why don't you tell me? Is it?"

After scanning her thoughts for a few seconds, Amanda nodded confirmation. "It is true! Can you help me?"

"My job is to help you, Amanda. What would you like to do next?"

"I'd like to get out of here and go home. I'm sure my family could help me."

"What do you think it'll take for Dr. Gascon to release you?"

"I think we should resume our hypnosis so we can get to the bottom of everything. Can we start right now?"

"If that's what you want, then that's what we'll do. Are you ready?"

"As ready as ever!"

"Take a deep cleansing breath and release it slowly through your nose…"

CHAPTER 15

Eight weeks passed since Bryon returned to work. He wasn't the same person anymore; he was haunted and distracted.

He always seemed formidable with his tall, muscular frame, but his current situation had him feeling less than confident, and it showed in his slumped shoulders and bowed head. Frasnia couldn't help but worry about his despondent condition. She looked for every opportunity to make him smile, but they were few and far between.

She never thought she'd look forward to the days when Bryon was out of the office, but she now found herself scheduling him out more often so that she could enjoy the work environment without his dark, oppressive cloud. What seemed almost worse was that Bryon didn't even notice he was out of the office more than he was in it.

Frasnia couldn't even bring herself to feel guilty about it. He never even commented that Frasnia re-assigned a warehouse worker to be his personal telepod operator. In his current mental state, Frasnia didn't trust Bryon to concentrate enough on his destination coordinates to arrive in one piece, if at all.

Frasnia just began working on the second quarter audit paperwork when the front door opened. Since it was between breaktime and lunch, she didn't know who to expect with the rarity of visitors.

She set aside her papers and folded her hands to wait. Frasnia could only make out the silhouette of a petite woman holding a small child against her hip with the sun shining behind the person.

The door closed, blocking the outside light, revealing the newcomers' identities. Frasnia looked at the curly-haired, blonde child with interest as she spoke, "Well, hello, Alena! It's been a long time since you've been down here. However, I don't think it's been long enough for you to have had this precious little girl, though!"

A slight grimace marred Alena's otherwise beautiful face as she replied, "No, this is Jena. She's been in my care since her mother died in the hiking accident with Bryon."

"Oh!" Frasnia exclaimed. "I didn't realize—" she let her sentence trail off as her patil beeped for her attention. "Just one moment," she said to Alena as she turned to take the call.

"Hi, Bryon," she said, and she looked up at Alena. "Let me check the inventory really quickly." She switched screens on the patil.

She carefully checked several pages and then switched back to the video screen. "You're right, Bryon, the Beewa Quarry should've already received that order, but our records show the shipment got quarantined at the Port of Cerid. Remember, that's the shipment that contained the thousands of beetlesnatch hatchlings. They have to wait until the life cycle is complete to make sure a secondary hatching doesn't take place."

"Are you kidding? How much longer until it's going to be released?"

"Our records indicate it'll be arriving here by the end of the week. If it were up to me, I'd tell them to wait for two mesans just to make sure. I'd be terrified to come to work if there were even a chance of a beetlesnatch infestation here!"

"Okay, I'll let Kenen know. He's going to be furious at the delay even though it's not our fault!"

"Sorry, Bryon. Do you want me to send something nice to Kenen's house? Maybe a box of sweets or something?"

"I think that'd be perfect, Frasnia," he replied with more enthusiasm.

"Have you thought about who you want to handle the transport? You do remember Cleon's scheduled out this entire week."

"Good grief, I forgot. Can we get a temp worker or something?"

"Why don't we let Ninan take it? He's been dying to prove himself."

"Fine. Can you arrange it? I gotta go. Kenen just came out of his meeting. Bye."

"Bye," Frasnia said just as the connection ended. "Well, I didn't even get the chance to tell him you were here," she said with some exasperation as she turned back to Alena.

"That's okay. I should've called first anyway. I just brought some paperwork in for him to sign, but since he's not here, I'll take care of it myself." Alena resettled Jena on her hip and looked at her watch. "Goodness, I've got to get going," she said and turned to leave.

"I didn't realize it was getting so late; the kids will be expecting lunch. Don't bother telling Bryon I was here. He's been so busy, and I don't want him to worry. I'll see him at home. Oh, and I'll send a beetlesnatch venom kit in with Bryon tomorrow, just in case. It certainly wouldn't hurt to have it on hand in any case!"

"Thanks," Frasnia called out as she watched Alena sweep out the door.

She had so many unanswered questions concerning poor little Jena. Different ideas raced through her mind as she tried to figure out whether or not Jena would be adopted into their family or if they were waiting for the baby's relatives to come and pick her up. Frasnia shook her head and wished she could've had more time to talk with Alena.

She wouldn't dare bring up the topic of Jena with Bryon for fear he'd backslide into a more depressed state. The old Bryon never would've forgotten the quarantined shipment, but the fact that he was starting to smile again gave Frasnia hope he was on the road to recovery.

Deciding to keep her eyes and ears open for any further news concerning the child, she turned her attention back to work. She contacted a candy caterer near Beewa and ordered a basket of goodies to be delivered to Kenen's house. She sent a message to Ninan's supervisor to have Ninan stop by the office a couple of minutes before his lunch break and then returned to prepare the audit records.

Nearly thirty minutes later, Ninan walked into the office. Frasnia could hardly believe it was almost lunchtime, but the clock on her patil confirmed it. "Hi, Ninan," she spoke cheerfully.

"Hi, Frasnia. I got a message from my supervisor that you asked for me to stop by."

"Yes," she said slyly.

"What's going on, Frasnia?" Ninan asked with a smile quirking his mouth.

"An interesting turn of events," she cryptically replied. "You know how you've wanted to try new jobs to see where your talents lie? Well, as it turns out, there's a shipment which needs to be 'ported to Beewa at the end of the week, and Cleon's out until next week.

"Bryon forgot about Cleon's absence and wanted me to hire a temp, but I suggested he let you give it a try!" She waited for Ninan to respond, but when his jaw just remained slack, and he still hadn't replied, she taunted him further by saying, "So, what do you think? Do you want to do it, or should I hire a temp?"

"No, no," he replied while fiercely shaking his head, "I'll definitely do it!"

"Great, now that that's settled, just be on the lookout for the order. It's coming from the Port of Cerid and bound for Beewa. It should be here on Kamis or early on Jumat. Either way, it needs to get delivered on Jumat. Kenen's really anxious for the order seeing as it's already been delayed for weeks."

"Sure thing," he replied enthusiastically. He turned to leave for lunch and then had an inspiration, "Do you have plans for lunch today?"

"No. Why?"

"I'd like to buy you lunch to thank you for suggesting me for the job."

"That'd be wonderful," she replied as she stood and picked up her purse. "Let me lock up everything, and I'll meet you outside."

"Okay," Ninan replied as he stepped out into the sunshine and thought the weather was a perfect reflection of his current mood. The door behind him opened and shut.

He turned and watched Frasnia lock the door and rattle it to ensure it was secured. The sun highlighted the gold and red streaks in her straight, auburn hair. She turned, and his attention was caught by how bright green her eyes were in the sunlight. He cleared his throat and managed to say, "All set?"

"Yep," she said with a quick nod.

"Where do you want to eat?"

"It's a nice day today. Let's get something from the marketplace."

They walked in companionable silence for a minute before Frasnia asked, "How do you like your new house?"

"Well, it's a lot better since I got my meager belongings out of storage in Cresdon. My furniture consisted of a couple of crates, and my bed was a pile of blankets on the floor. At least now I have a chair, a small table, and a cot."

"That's still not much," she said sadly.

"No, but it's more than I've ever had before," he replied with a smile. "You can't take much with you when you work on a shipping vessel."

"I guess not," she replied skeptically. She thought about all of the extra furniture cluttering her parents' house and wondered how Ninan would feel about hand-me-downs. She decided to ask her parents first and then broach the subject with Ninan later.

"So, how's Bryon doing these days? He's still not all there, is he?"

"No, but it has only been two mesans since that girl died," she said sadly and then turned to Ninan excitedly and said, "You'll never guess what I found out today!"

"Since I'll never guess, what is it?" Ninan asked, amused by her sudden mood change.

"Bryon's wife, Alena, stopped by the office today to see him," she began and paused dramatically.

"And," Ninan prompted as he guessed he was supposed to do.

"She brought a baby in with her."

"She has three children, doesn't she?" he asked with some confusion.

"Yes, she does, but she doesn't have a baby."

"So whose baby was it?"

"That's the amazing part, Ninan! The baby was the child of the woman who died."

"You're kidding, right?" Ninan suddenly felt nauseous, and he continued walking toward the marketplace with a sense of dread knowing he'd have to share this information with Petre in his following letter.

"Nope," she replied pertly. "Oh, you should've seen her. She couldn't have been much older than four mesans, but she had a full head of curly, blonde hair and the biggest, most striking, blue eyes. Her name is Jena, isn't that a beautiful name?" She paused long enough to glance over at Ninan and saw an odd expression on his face, "What's wrong?"

Not wanting to reveal his genuine sense of trouble over this news, he said sadly, "I was just thinking that Jena's now an orphan like me."

"Yeah, that's rough, isn't it?" she asked kindly and put her hand on Ninan's arm to show her support and offer what comfort she could for his unfortunate upbringing. "It wouldn't surprise me a bit if Alena and Bryon adopted the poor girl."

Ninan was happy they'd reached the market and changed the subject by asking, "So, what kind of food do you want to eat this fine afternoon?" He gestured grandly at the various stalls and allowed Frasnia to take the lead.

CHAPTER 16

Ninan couldn't concentrate for the remainder of the day. He was thankful when his shift was finally finished, and he could take a walk to help him think. He knew he should contact Petre and tell him about his daughter but was uncertain how Petre would react to the news.

Ninan didn't respect Petre or his lifestyle but wondered if maybe having a child would bring out Petre's better side and finally turn him into a decent and honest person.

No matter what, I'm going to have to talk to him in person.

He didn't desire being seen with Petre anywhere around town. He'd have to make arrangements to meet outside of town somewhere.

He made up his mind about what he'd do by the time he reached his house. Ninan retrieved his writing supplies from the kitchen and took them to the living room. He sat in his only chair and used the table to compose his letter.

Tishri 1, 3443

Petre,

I have some important news which must be delivered in person. I'd rather not meet with you in Kirma, but I'll be near the Port of Cerid on Jumat, Tishri 5th. I can meet you at the Southside Town Deli at noon.

Please write back to me to let me know you'll come to the meeting.

Ninan

HE SEALED the letter and walked it to the courier's box at the end of the street. Ninan sincerely hoped he was doing the right thing.

FRASNIA WAS EXCITED about her news to share with Ninan. She spoke with her parents the night before, and they were more than happy to give their extra furniture to her friend. Since they moved to a smaller house, they felt overrun with the excess.

She stood just outside the office door and waved urgently at Ninan when she saw him walk through the entrance gates. She smiled when he acknowledged her wave and changed the direction of his steps to come into the office. Holding the door open for him, she said, "I think I've got some really great news for you!"

"What's that?" He stepped into the office and faced Frasnia.

"I hope you don't mind, but yesterday you talked about your dismal furniture situation."

"That's true."

"Well, my parents just downsized, but they still have all the furniture from a much bigger home. I asked them what they wanted to do with it, and they said they'd give it away if it'd get them more space. Would you be interested in it?"

"Sure, that sounds perfect!"

"We could go over to their place after work tonight if that'd suit you." Frasnia could barely contain her excitement and grinned until her cheeks hurt.

Ninan smiled at Frasnia's enthusiasm. He realized then that he was more than willing to go somewhere with this lovely woman other than for something work-related. He could see himself in a relationship with her and thought the trip to her parents' house would be a good start. "Okay then, I'll stop by the office when my shift ends, and we can head over there!"

SHEMALLA DIDN'T KNOW what to do with the Covington family's information and plight. In the fifteen years since her Earth assignment began, she'd never had anything like this happen. Her training didn't prepare her for Earth's people trying to get into Tuala. Quite the opposite, she was supposed to keep the Tualans in line when they visited Earth.

She didn't know if she should talk to Elder Vargen about the situation or try to find a way to Tuala without the Elder's help. Luckily, she'd thought to ask for a few days to decide how to create a passage for Amanda. Now she just needed to figure out if she really could make that happen.

NINAN'S unexpected freight delivery to Beewa caused him to lose sleep with his excitement. He got up early on Jumat morning and went into the office to talk about the job with Frasnia before work began. Thankfully, she regularly got to work early.

He entered the office, smiling in Frasnia's direction as he could see she was talking on the patil. He walked up to her desk, rested a hip on the desk edge closest to her, and waited until her call disconnected.

"I'm glad you came in," said Frasnia, "I've got a change in plans for you."

"Okay," Ninan said with a bit of trepidation that his assignment might've been canceled.

"I just got off the phone with the transport agent at the Port of Cerid. It seems there isn't anyone there who's willing to bring that quarantined load to our facility. It looks as though you'll have to go there first to receive it before you can deliver it to Beewa. Is that going to work for you?"

"Sure, I don't see why not," Ninan replied, withholding his relieved sigh. He was still on the assignment. That brought him back to his original reason for coming into the office to talk with Frasnia. He then asked, "Can you do me a small favor, please?"

Frasnia smiled and said, "I'll do what I can. What do you need?"

"Well—," Ninan began hesitantly, and he dropped his head and rubbed his nose with his index finger.

"It's okay, Ninan. What do you need?"

"It's just that this shipment today is super important for me."

"I know that, Ninan. What's the problem then?"

"I've been to the Port of Cerid, so that's not an issue, but I've never been to Beewa, so I'm not sure how to visualize coordinates to get there. I know Bryon's anxious to get this there on time, and I want to do my best for him. Do you think you could help me with the coordinates?"

Frasnia's smile broadened by the end of Ninan's explanation and replied, "Of course, Ninan. That's what I do. Let me just finish printing out your plot maps as well as the verbal directions for both locations."

She turned to her patil and entered a few keystrokes before the printer began dispensing page after page. She gathered them up and slid them into a large manila envelope. She clasped it shut and handed it over to Ninan.

"Clear coordinates and maps," she declared with finality. "Make sure you look them over before you go."

Ninan sheepishly smiled as he took the proffered envelope. "Thanks," he said, "I'll study these during my morning break."

He turned the envelope over several times before he worked up enough nerve to ask, "I don't want to be difficult, but if I need anything more, would it be alright if I came in to ask for clarification?"

"Absolutely," Frasnia said with a bright smile, "we'd expect you to be confident in your delivery before we'd want you to travel. That's part of my job, so don't think of it as being difficult. It really is no problem, okay?"

"Whew, that's a huge weight off my shoulders, Frasnia," Ninan confided. "I'll get out of your way now and get to work. Do you need me to check in before I head out?"

"That'd be great! Bryon's been very anxious about getting this taken care of. I'll pass on word to him about its progress."

"Will do, then," Ninan promised as he crossed the room with a new spring in his step. He turned at the door and spoke the other thing on his mind since coming into the office.

"Frasnia, can you thank your parents again for the furniture? I can't tell you how much more pleasant it is to come home and be able to relax in comfort rather than just getting by with poor furniture substitutes."

Frasnia smiled with genuine pleasure that her conversation with her parents turned out exactly as she hoped. "Sure," she said, "They were grateful for all of it to find a new home since they moved now that all of us kids finally moved away from their house. They were starting to feel the walls closing in with all the clutter of the extra furniture jammed everywhere."

"Let them know if they need anything, and I do mean *anything;* I'll be over there immediately to help out."

"I'll be sure to let them know," Frasnia promised as Ninan left the office with the manila envelope carefully tucked under his left arm.

Her thoughts returned to the pleasant evening they'd spent arranging all of the furniture in Ninan's new house. More than once, she could imagine herself being the lady of his house. She just had to convince Ninan that it'd be a good idea!

Frasnia smiled after him as she turned to answer yet another urgent message coming across her patil.

CHAPTER 17

The all-clear code for the shipment being held in the Port of Cerid came as a relief for Ninan. It was still before lunch, and he'd be able to meet with Petre at the Southside Town Deli as arranged at noon.

He diligently studied the paperwork from Frasnia. He was confident he had it memorized by now. All of the reference points were duly learned, and he shouldn't have any issue landing at either of his officially designated landing spots.

Before Ninan left the shipping yard, he went into the main office to let Frasnia know he'd be leaving a few minutes early to eat lunch in the Port of Cerid. He couldn't contain his cheerful jaunt as he opened the office door. Frasnia was at her desk, and she returned the happy smile plastered on Ninan's face as he said, "Hello, Frasnia. Thanks for the heads up that the shipment's clearance."

"Are you sure of the teleporting coordinates?"

"Absolutely, thanks to your wonderful instructions," he confidently replied.

"Well then, when do you anticipate leaving? The beetlesnatch infestation's delayed it long enough."

"I'm leaving as soon as I'm done talking with you. I want to try the local cuisine in the Port of Cerid while I'm there."

"That sounds perfect. Just be sure to stay away from the raw seafood as I've heard it can be hazardous to your bowels in a multiple transfer telepod journey," she laughed as she started to rifle through her desk drawer and came out triumphantly with her lockbox key.

She turned and retrieved the pay box and said, "I might as well give you your salary before you go so you'll have lunch money." She found his envelope and handed it to him with a flourish.

Frasnia stood and walked across the room to a cabinet beside the front door. She unerringly selected a key from the many rows inside. She smiled and held out a key to him and said, "Here's lucky number thirteen freighter telepod for your first transporter assignment. Both the freighter and the personal telepod inside are keyed the same."

Ninan excitedly received the key that Frasnia dropped into his outstretched palm. He curled his fingers around the object and smiled at Frasnia when he said, "Wish me luck!"

"No luck will be needed as long as you follow my instructions," Frasnia jokingly replied. "Your telepod is located at the back of the fenced telepod area. It's just been serviced, so there shouldn't be any performance issues.

"Be sure to put the telepod back in that same space when you return. If you get back after closing time, just deposit the key through the dropbox next to the door here," she said as she pointed to the return location with her left hand.

"One more thing, Ninan," Frasnia said when Ninan turned to leave. "Try to be nice to Kenen at the Beewa Quarry. He's not the nicest guy to start with, and this shipment's already way overdue. Kenen hasn't been happy with the delay, and he might try to take it out on you. Just apologize a lot and try to get out of there quickly before he really gets going on his tirade!

"Oh, I almost forgot," Frasnia exclaimed as she bent down to reach under the desk. "Here's the anti-venom kit, just in case, since that shipment was quarantined for the beetlesnatch infestation. I wouldn't want you to have to worry about being in the telepod with a beetlesnatch on the loose."

Ninan accepted the kit, grinned, and replied, "Thanks for the warning about Kenen. I'll be my most diplomatic!" He was already out the door and down the first step before he remembered he probably wouldn't see Frasnia until the weekend was over and said over his shoulder, "Have a great weekend, Frasnia!" He glimpsed her smile and her farewell wave just as the office door slammed shut.

He jogged across the shipping yard to the waiting telepod. While he had limited experience with personal telepods, Ninan had never flown a freighter. He was more than a little anxious it'd be more complicated than he was equipped to handle, and something would go terribly wrong. Ninan found telepod number thirteen located next to the fence, just where Frasnia said it would be.

He used the key to activate the loading door opening and stepped onto the platform. Thankfully, nobody was around to witness his open-mouthed admiration of the freighter's internal size.

The space inside was three times greater than the size of his entire new house. He walked beyond the personal telepod near the exit and heard his footsteps echo across the empty expanse as he traversed the length of the cargo bay to get to the control panel.

With trepidation, Ninan sat in the left-side controller seat and palmed the dash control to close the loading door. As soon as the airlock sealed, Ninan let out a whoop of exhilaration that he was actually going to be operating this beautiful marvel of modern machinery. He set the anti-venom kit down on the floor next to his chair, keeping in mind he'd need it within easy reach should anything happen.

Ninan was especially conscious of his new position. He knew he needed to impress Bryon with this assignment because this was possibly his only shot at a promotion. He reached into his back pocket and took out Frasnia's folded well-read paperwork. He once again reviewed the directions on how to get to the Port of Cerid.

With more than a bit of apprehension, he keyed the start-up commands for the telepod and confirmed all was okay by noting every green indicator light on the control panel. His excitement level rose when he felt the colossal telepod hovering close to the ground. Next, he closed his eyes to visualize the destination coordinates before allowing his hand to rest on the activation module.

The few seconds of darkness overwhelmed his senses, and absolute nothingness took over. He was just on the verge of panic, but with the coordinates still clear in his mind, he reappeared in the air. He loudly exhaled, and his heart hammered loudly in his ears.

The coordinates teleported him to a location above the Port of Cerid, so it was simple to use the manual controls to steer the telepod into the right slot at the shipping yard and initiate the shutdown procedure. He carefully placed Frasnia's paperwork packet beside the anti-venom kit for when he'd have a full cargo load to transfer to Beewa.

As he exited the loading platform, Ninan noticed the port's shipping yard was bustling. People rushed to and fro with both paperwork and shipments. Not quite sure of where he was supposed to go to find out his cargo's location, Ninan stopped the first person who passed close enough to him and asked, "Where's the main office?"

"See that red building down on the left," the man hurriedly said and looked back to Ninan to verify he had the proper location and site, "just after that building, take the first right, the office will be across from that, it's got a blue door. You can't miss it." As soon as the man finished, he left abruptly.

Since Ninan was used to working in shipping yards, he knew these people were on a tight schedule, and he didn't take offense. He followed the directions exactly, and sure enough, the main office was right where the man said it would be. He walked through the door and waited in line until it was his turn with the desk clerk.

"I'm here to pick up the quarantined shipment bound for Beewa."

The harried clerk did a double-take and actually looked at Ninan for the first time. "Well," said the clerk, "it'll be a real relief to get rid of that load, I must say. Never in my life have I been so afraid to come to work every day. I've never heard of a beetlesnatch infestation during this time year."

"Yeah," said Ninan, "I'm not really thrilled about having the shipment in the telepod with me either. I've got an anti-venom kit in the 'pod just in case," Ninan chuckled.

"Smart," the clerk said as he typed the order request on his patil. "Ah," said the clerk, "this cargo goes to Kenen, right?"

"That's the one."

"In which dock did you land?"

"44," replied Ninan, glad he'd taken the time to look before he walked away from the telepod.

"Perfect, that's really close to where it's stored. Take a seat over there, and I'll have one of our loaders pull it from the warehouse and bring it over to your transport. I'll have someone come and get you when you need to head out there to supervise the loading."

"Thanks," said Ninan as he turned and sat in the proffered seat.

A couple of minutes later, somebody came through the office door and asked for the handler for the quarantine cargo. Ninan immediately stood and walked over and shook hands with the loader. "That was quick!"

"Can you blame us?" he asked with a smile as he turned to leave the office. "We'll be really glad to see the backside of this shipment. As it is, we had to draw short straws to figure out who'd be unlucky enough to have to load it into your transport."

CHAPTER 18

"I totally understand," replied Ninan as he followed the loader out the office door. The worker's nervousness started to transfer over to Ninan, causing him even more trepidation. Ninan shuddered and then gave himself a little shake to ease his tension. His whole future in Kirma rode on this single assignment.

The loader set a swift pace through the shipping yard's narrow corridors. Again, Ninan was used to this and had no trouble keeping up. Just as the desk clerk said, the shipment was not only close; it was stored in the building right next to the loading dock where Ninan set down the freighter.

The loader looked over his shoulder and said to Ninan, "If you wouldn't mind keying your cargo door open, we can start scanning the crates and getting them loaded immediately."

"I'm on it," Ninan cheerfully replied as he continued to the telepod, whereas the loader turned and walked into the warehouse. Ninan carefully watched as they loaded crate after crate for more than twenty minutes.

He noticed the loaders were very conscientious of weight and balance and appreciated that he wouldn't have to oversee that aspect of the loading as well. After the last crate was installed in the hold, Ninan stopped the final loader as he was leaving and shook his hand, saying, "Thank you for all your wonderful help."

"It's what we get paid to do, man," he replied with a smile, "but it sure is nice to be thanked every now and again. Have a great day!"

Ninan watched as the man walked away. He noted with a smile how nobody lingered near his telepod. He was about to turn around and go back into his telepod when he realized he recognized someone from his old cargo handling days walking across the shipping yard. He cupped his hands around his mouth and yelled, "Hey, Fordin!"

The man crossing the yard stopped midstride and turned. As soon as he recognized Ninan, a smile broke across his face, and he strode over toward Ninan's telepod. When he got within easy speaking distance, he said, "Well, as I live and breathe, I never expected to see you here."

"I never expected to see myself here either," replied Ninan with a grin as he reached to shake Fordin's outstretched hand.

Fordin used the handshake to pull Ninan into a bear hug and thumped him soundly on the back several times as was his custom. When he released Ninan from his embrace, he asked, "How long are you here?"

"I was just getting ready to get some lunch at the Southside Town Deli," replied Ninan as he looked down at his watch and noticed he still had another twenty minutes before he was supposed to meet up with Petre.

"It's been ages since I've been there," exclaimed Fordin, "Mind a little company?"

While Ninan really did want to have some time with Fordin, he was reluctant to let him know with whom he was meeting. He looked at his watch again and replied, "Yeah, I have a meeting with someone in about twenty minutes, but I'd love to chat with you while I'm waiting."

Fordin smiled and replied, "Yeah, it'll only take me a few minutes to down a couple of bruskins before I need to be on my way as well." He clapped Ninan on the shoulder as they walked out of the shipping yard together. Curiosity got the better of Fordin, and he asked, "Who are you meeting, anyway?"

Left with no other option, Ninan decided to tell Fordin the truth and replied with a sigh, "Petre MacVeen."

"What business do you have with him?" Fordin glanced at Ninan with disdain evident in his voice, a frown deepening the weathered creases around his eyes.

"It's a long story, but I can give you the short version over a bruskin."

It was only a three-minute walk to the Southside Town Deli. From the bright daylight, Ninan and Fordin strode into the deli's dim interior. Before their eyes could adjust to the difference in the light, they located the bar near the entrance and sat at two empty barstools.

The bartender greeted them with a smile and asked, "What'll you have?"

"Two bruskins," replied Ninan as he dug into his pocket to get a couple of shills to place on the counter. He took a deep breath and wondered how much he'd tell Fordin.

Ninan trusted Fordin and knew he could keep anything he was told in strict confidence. The lie he'd been living since arriving in Kirma weighed heavily on him, and he came to a quick decision.

"Look, man," Ninan began as the bartender put their two bruskins in front of them and swept up the money in the same practiced stroke. Ninan waited until the bartender was out of earshot and helping another customer before he continued with his story.

Stalling for yet another moment, Ninan took a swig of his bruskin, looked over at Fordin, and said, "Whatever I tell you today, you have to keep completely secret. Can you do that?"

"Sure," replied Fordin as he took a sip from his own bruskin. "You know, Ninan, you don't have to tell me anything if you don't want to."

"I know that. I really just need somebody to talk to about this business with Petre MacVeen."

"It's got to be pretty bad. Anything having to do with Petre is bad news."

"Oh, it's not as bad as that," replied Ninan and then qualified it with the statement, "at least I didn't think so." Ninan considered his following words as he continued to drink his bruskin.

He played with the condensation on the side of his mug as he turned to Fordin and said, "I've been taking money from Petre to find this girl, who he says is his wife, and in return, I mail him weekly updates. The thing is, I'm having a tough time believing she's his wife. I mean, if she really was his wife, why isn't she trying to be with him instead of just hanging out in Kirma?"

At the mention of the word 'wife,' Fordin's features turned from polite interest to absolute incredulity. "With as many brothels as that man visits, I doubt any sane woman would stay with him, let alone marry him in the first place."

"That's what I was thinking too. I mean, every letter he's had me send to him has been to a different brothel in a different city. Is it just me, or does that seem tacky to you?"

"So I take it you found her." Fordin's fist thumped against the bar, and his eyes drilled into Ninan's.

"Yeah, I found her, except there're complications." He sighed and took another long drink of his bruskin.

"What kind of complications?"

"The worst kind," replied Ninan as he lowered his voice and said, "She's dead."

"So, what's the problem with that then?"

"Well, for one, Petre still owes me half the money that he promised me for the weekly updates."

"So just tell him that she's dead and to pay you up. What's so hard about that?"

"If that were the only problem, I'd do just that," said Ninan, and he took yet another longer and deeper drink from his mug.

"So what else is there?"

"I found out earlier this week that the woman he was having me report on not only died, but she left behind a four mesan old daughter."

"Oh, I see what you mean by complication," said Fordin with meaning as he raised his eyebrows, and he too took a deep gulp of his bruskin as he considered the complex circumstances.

"If it were any other person, I wouldn't have a problem telling him that he's a dad. But we're talking about Petre MacVeen, man! Can you see him taking care of a little girl with the line of work that he does and the places he likes to stay?"

"Not at all," Fordin spoke emphatically.

"The receptionist at the company where I work said that my manager and his wife are adopting the woman's little girl. I think she'd have a much more normal life if she stayed with them, but isn't it kind of mean of me not to tell Petre that he's a father?"

"As you said, if it were any other person, you'd be able to tell him with a clear conscience. However, I wouldn't have any problem keeping that piece of information from Petre. I mean, what would he do with the girl while he's visiting all the brothels across the land? Knowing Petre, he probably put her to work in the brothel if it could make him some money.

"Besides, Bryon and Alena would have to petition an Elder if they wanted to make it legal. The Elder would ultimately be the person responsible in this matter, not you."

Ninan shuddered at the thought. "I can't wait to get this over with," Ninan confessed to Fordin, "I really just want to finish delivering this shipment from here to Beewa. Then I can go back to my new home and forget ever making a deal with Petre!"

CHAPTER 19

Petre was pleasantly surprised to arrive half an hour early at the Southside Town Deli. He found a booth near the front door and ordered a couple of bruskins so he could wait in comfort for Ninan's arrival. He just took a drink of his second bruskin when he spotted Ninan entering the deli with someone else.

Knowing he was planning on meeting with Ninan alone, he opted to wait to hear Ninan's business with the stranger. Petre leaned back into the booth's shadow and grinned to discover he didn't even have to strain to eavesdrop.

While he was first glad to hear himself be defended to this stranger that his assignment was not all bad, he was just as easily angered over Ninan's assessment of his choice of staying at the brothel houses. What did Ninan care about whom he slept with? His 'wife' wasn't available, so what was he supposed to do, be celibate? Not this man!

How could he use this against Ninan? His plots of revenge stopped cold when he overheard Ninan's following statement.

Jesisca was dead.

What the hell!

Now, what am I supposed to do to keep warm at night?

Shock quickly turned to anger. He didn't need to be dragged across the country to hear this news in person. A letter would've sufficed.

I guess I can't blame him for worrying about getting his final payment for the information. I probably wouldn't have paid him.

He schemed about getting out of the deli without being seen until he heard Ninan say there was something worse than finding out Jesisca had died. Petre couldn't imagine what could be worse, so he leaned forward to make sure he heard the news correctly.

A daughter?? Wow, really? A daughter?

A growing wonder coursed through him at the novel idea.

Finally, someone who'll have to do whatever I tell her to do! That girl is mine!

Did Ninan just say that Bryon and his wife are legally adopting her with the Elder's approval? No family or Elder's decision will keep me from my child! I'm not going to lose another child over a technicality!

I know for sure Bryon knew I was the father, what with him asking around about my whereabouts! As if he thought I wouldn't hear about it! This just confirms it!

I'm going to make him pay!

Petre ground his teeth and balled up his coat in his whitened fist. *Ninan can pay too for even questioning whether or not to share that information with me. Ninan's my employee. I'm paying him for information, after all!*

With self-righteous indignation, Petre slid out of the booth. Petre marched through the deli's entrance with one last glance at Ninan. He wished he could've confronted Ninan about his doubts.

I'm going to be a fantastic parent! Just wait, Ninan. I've got plans for you yet. Nobody ever talks that way about me and gets away with it!

Petre's feet slammed against the cobblestone street as he planned his next move.

~

NINAN GLANCED at his timepiece yet again. It was an hour past their scheduled meeting time, and yet Petre didn't show up. Having already eaten, he couldn't wait any longer.

He had a delivery to make.

As Ninan stepped outside the deli, he turned around to make sure the name on the storefront was the one at which he agreed to meet Petre.

As he stared up at the Southside Town Deli sign, there was no mistaking it. He could only assume Petre either got held up, or he forgot. Whatever the case, Ninan's delivery couldn't wait, nor could he mess up this opportunity to elevate his career path because of Petre.

He jogged the few minutes back to the shipping yard and navigated his way between buildings to the waiting telepod. As soon as he had it in sight, he keyed the cargo door to open and lengthened his stride. Anxious to finish this assignment, he stepped through the opening into the dim interior.

Just as he passed the personal telepod inside, several quick footsteps echoed on the ramp behind him. Turning to investigate, a solid object struck him across the side of his head.

~

PETRE LAUGHED.

That was way too easy.

He bent down and picked up the telepod's key from Ninan's slack hand. He dropped the crowbar as he hurriedly keyed shut the cargo door so no one would notice him stealing the freighter.

Moving Ninan seemed like too much work, so Petre rummaged through the cargo hold until he found some shipping tape and bound Ninan's hands and feet right where he lay.

With the necessary task completed, Petre wandered across the cargo hold to the control station. He sat at the operator's seat and issued the standard start-up commands. Petre navigated the telepod out of the shipping yard with his destination coordinates firmly in mind.

Petre didn't really have much of a plan beyond making Ninan pay for his unpleasant opinion of himself. Several seconds passed before Petre and his stolen telepod reappeared in the air at his chosen destination. He set the telepod down at an abandoned farmhouse near where Petre grew up.

Now that he wasn't in imminent danger of discovery, Petre had some time to plan. After issuing all of the shutdown commands, Petre pocketed the telepod key in his overalls and stood to survey his newest acquisitions.

How much profit can I make with my new inventory?

Petre wandered through the cargo hold to make his cursory inspection. At the nearest set of boxes, he tore open the top. He rummaged through the contents and grinned in satisfaction as he discovered these were replacement parts for standard mining machinery.

At the next stack, he opened another box containing a variety of complex mining equipment. With his luck improving by the second, Petre realized this shipment would be a cinch to sell on the black market.

Now to handle the problem of getting rid of Ninan.

He strolled back across the cargo hold and looked down on his informant-turned-hostage. Petre nudged Ninan with his foot but met with no response. Bursting with unvented frustration, Petre expelled his anger by kicking Ninan as hard as he could, once, twice, and then a third time for good measure.

Out of breath, Petre realized he should've moved him while he was still unconscious, but the beating had roused him enough to moan.

Petre was definitely not interested in having a hostage or having someone who could identify him as the thief. He would need to remove Ninan from the cargo hold and the general area as well. Petre speedily looked around to see what options he had at hand. Petre laughed aloud as he realized his best plan was right next to Ninan—the personal telepod.

He trotted across the cargo hold to retrieve the operator key and spent several precious minutes in a mad search for the key before remembering he had placed it in his own pocket. Shaking his head in disgust at the lost time, Petre returned to the personal telepod.

After keying open the side door to the small telepod, Petre dragged Ninan, with more than a bit of effort, into the personal telepod and left him lying in an uncomfortable heap on the floor behind the operator seat.

Petre palmed the sequence to open the freighter's main cargo hold door to allow him to fly the personal telepod out into the open. Once in the telepod's operator seat, Petre navigated the small 'pod out the cargo hold door and into the open field. After a few moments of contemplation, he visualized coordinates for yet another safely isolated spot, and within moments he arrived at his secondary location.

Once landed, Petre wasted little time and even less effort as he unceremoniously shoved Ninan out the door with the heel of his foot as he held onto the seatback for traction. Petre dusted his hands off and let out a loud sigh as he returned to the control seat. Keying the door shut, Petre hastily returned to the freighter telepod.

Petre sat slumped over at his seat for a few minutes to control his body's shaking. With so many teleportations in quick succession, Petre's body pulsated with queasy sensations. Thankfully, he wasn't going anywhere again for the next several hours since he needed to remove the cargo from the freighter.

Conscientious of the freighter's locator beacon, Petre rushed to offload all of the cargo into the abandoned farmhouse's barn. Wishing he had a partner to share the work or at least a couple of helpers, Petre took frequent breaks as he painstakingly removed the cargo.

Sweat soaked his clothing and made every movement unbearable. He almost regretted taking such a large haul. Although he was unused to such manual labor, he kept his spirits up by calculating the profit he'd make. In some ways, he didn't even mind manually working for this. He was getting even with Ninan and Bryon for deception regarding Jesisca.

If Jesisca had been returned to me, she'd still be alive! Every person who had a part in keeping me from my Jesisca and my daughter will be held accountable. They're going to pay dearly for letting her die!

Petre didn't have a clear plan for how he'd get his daughter. Assuredly, he couldn't just walk up to Bryon's house and demand to have his daughter. He'd have to watch and wait for an opportunity to take his daughter, which meant one thing.

He was going back to Kirma.

CHAPTER 20

First thing first. I've got to get rid of this telepod. I can't have that beacon alerting anyone that this delivery isn't gonna happen. Where should I ditch this pile of metal? Really the last place anyone would have a freighter telepod would be near the ocean.

Petre racked his brain for a suitable location. It needed to be both large enough to accommodate the telepod and remote enough so nobody would witness him leave it behind. Petre suddenly recalled a place just outside of Ishal near the Lookout Tavern where that bitch Hashma had filed her ridiculous sexual assault claim against him over an anon ago.

After all, she's a whore. What did she expect from me—a tender lovemaking session with a boyfriend? What a joke!

Elder Debbon had forbidden him from going near Hashma or her place of business, so it seemed the perfect location to lead an investigation that wouldn't point toward himself.

It's too bad I can't figure out a way to make it look as though Hashma was involved in this theft. That'd be just a perfect way of getting back at her!

Smugly smiling, Petre visualized the coordinates and the time of day to land the freighter in the cover of night. Timing the transfer made the teleportation take a few seconds longer which always unnerved Petre. He arrived almost at the desired location, which required only a few minor adjustments and several minutes to land the large telepod and perform the shutdown procedures.

Petre jogged across the cargo hold and entered the personal telepod before opening the large cargo doors. He wanted as little time out in the open as possible. If he were a skilled enough operator, he would've preferred to teleport directly from the cargo hold, but he was afraid of failing at this point in his plan.

He hurriedly moved the personal telepod outside into the open, visualized his final set of coordinates, and disappeared into the evening.

ELDER DEBBON WAS ONCE AGAIN thankful for the advancements created from the patil's invention. No longer did he have to endure the days of slogging through paperwork stacks from his petitioners, patrons, and citizens. While his staff still received the paperwork, they were diligently scanned in immediately upon receipt. He was reasonably sure the turnaround time for each document was a maximum of one day, which satisfied him very much.

Having already reviewed all of the day's district disputes, he was more than ready to move on to a different subject. It seemed adoptions were the next topic to address. While he was thankful to see every adoption go through smoothly, just the idea that the children were either unwanted or orphaned made him sad for his people.

Debbon was surprised to see an adoption application for a set of twins. Multiple births were relatively rare in Tuala, so it was doubly sad that these two girls had lost their parents. He reviewed the document for the accounting of why the parents were unsuitable or unavailable.

It appeared the mother was recently lost in a mudslide, and her remains weren't recovered. The father was also presumed dead in a water craft accident from before the children's birth. While the accounting of the birth parents' demise was undoubtedly interesting, it wasn't unheard of for these types of accidents.

He read the rest of the application to find out more about the people proposing the adoption. One significant item he noted was there was only the wife's signature on the application.

Why didn't the spouse sign the document as well? Again thankful for the resources available on the patil, Debbon effortlessly retrieved the statistics for each parent without leaving the page he was currently reading. A window popped up on the screen which read:

PETITIONER NAME: Bryon Kesh
    Birth Date: Heshvan 2, 3416
    Occupation: Manager at Kirma Shipping and Receiving
    Status: Married
    Spouse: Alena Bellen
    Marriage Date: Tishri 16, 3436
    Children: 2 birth children, 1 first-daughter
    Citizen Standing: Good

PETITIONER NAME: Alena Kesh, formerly Bellen
    Birth Date: Ab 26, 3417
    Occupation: Wise-woman
    Status: Married
    Spouse: Bryon Kesh
    Marriage Date: Tishri 16, 3436

Children: 2 birth children, 1 first-daughter
Citizen Standing: Good

DEBBON REMEMBERED TEACHING ALENA. She was a natural healer, but with her new practice, it surprised him that the new wise-woman would want to care for two more children with three of her own. He knew the amount of time and effort it took to take care of the citizens' medical needs as it was one of his own duties.

On the other hand, he knew the twins would be well cared for with someone so skilled living in the same house. It also bode well that they had a betrothal agreement in place for their son. Only families in good standing would get a betrothal petition accepted.

This case seemed open and shut in Debbon's mind. Without further consideration, he clicked on the button marked 'Accepted.' He watched as his signature was electronically entered onto the document and was immediately delivered back to the petitioners.

JUILA AND JENA still amazed Alena with how easily they adjusted to their mother's absence. Of course, they were just infants, but she would've expected them to at least get fussy because Amanda wasn't around. They remained perfect angels whom Alena adored with as much affection as if they were her own daughters.

She still held onto a spark of hope, which she dared not share with Bryon, that Amanda would be located even though with every passing day, the likelihood became slimmer.

Her husband, on the other hand, was another matter entirely. Guilt etched across his face every time he saw the babies doing something new; the first smile, the first giggle, the first time rolling over, each first was a dagger in his guilty heart. No matter how many times Alena assured Bryon it wasn't his fault Amanda died, he continued to blame himself since he took her to the fateful event.

He spent more time at work and avoided contact with the twins when he came home. Alena couldn't take his sulking any longer. An intervention was needed to retain both her sanity and her marriage.

According to Tualan law, children could be adopted if family members couldn't be found within two mesans of the parents' death. The two mesans had just passed, and Alena had petitioned the Elders for legal custody.

Her idea was that Bryon would be forced to take a more active role in the children's lives if they were legally his. He'd have to let go of his guilt when he discovered how endearing these girls were becoming. Alena was surprised at the quick affirmative decision of Elder Debbon in approving the custodial change.

She carefully planned their dinner that night, and as usual, Bryon arrived home just as she put the last dish on the dining room table. "Kids, get washed up for dinner! Your Papa just got home!"

She grinned at hearing the patter of three pairs of feet moving to the bathroom. She wished the kids were feeling better for the night's occasion. They all seemed to be coming down with colds.

Keeping the twins as close to Bryon as she could manage, she bent down and picked up the blonde, curly-haired girls who sat on the dining room floor watching her set the table. With one child in each arm, she greeted her husband at the front door and stood on her tip-toes to kiss him on the lips.

"Your timing's perfect as usual; dinner is just now ready. How was your day, honey?"

"The same as ever," he replied with a sigh as he removed his coat and hung it in the hall closet. "We found out today that we had a shipment get lost on its way to Beewa last Jumat, and the handler hasn't shown up anywhere."

"Who was the handler?"

"Ninan. He's the new guy we hired several weeks ago. I should've known better than to send him on that run," Bryon said as he brushed past Alena on his way to the bedroom without even acknowledging the twins in her arms.

Alena turned with a scowl on her face and followed after him, wishing he would've offered to at least carry one of the girls; they were getting heavier by the second. She gritted her teeth and followed him into the bedroom.

"But I thought he just bought a house here in Kirma. It doesn't make sense that he'd just take off," she said as she gratefully set the squirming girls down in the middle of the bed and tickled their tummies as she waited for Bryon to change his shirt for dinner.

Bryon paused to consider Alena's comment about Ninan's new house and then shrugged. "Maybe you're right. I might be jumping to the wrong conclusion. I'll give him another day to get that shipment delivered before I report it to the authorities. Maybe something happened with the freighter telepod, which delayed the delivery." With his shirt changed, he turned to leave the room.

Alena suspected he'd try to scoot out of the room without offering to help carry the twins, so she preempted his attempt by holding out Jena and saying, "Here, take Jena and set her up at the table, please."

Without wanting to sound surly, Bryon had little choice but to take Jena into his arms. "Wow, she's gotten so big in these past two mesans," he whispered loud enough that only Jena could hear. She grabbed his ear, and he turned to look at her. "I'd forgotten just how adorable babies are at four and a half mesans old."

Her blonde hair curled in ringlets, her eyes were a startling bright blue instead of the newborn dark blue, her chubby cheeks were rosy, and she had two perfect little teeth in her smiling mouth.

He couldn't resist reaching up and twitching her cheek as he said, "Careful with my ear, I've only got the one on that side." Jena giggled as Bryon teased her while they walked out of the bedroom together.

Juila flailed her arms to be held by Alena. She picked up Jena's identical twin and hugged her tightly as she whispered in her ear, "I think Jena will win him over yet!" Juila giggled, too, as Alena mimicked Bryon's teasing of Jena as she followed him to the dining room.

Alena noted that Juila seemed warm with a fever as well. She knew from experience that she'd be kept busy with cranky children and runny noses very soon.

Once everyone finished eating dinner, Alena cleared her throat and announced, "I have important news for our family." She winced as she realized Bryon would assume any good news would be related to Amanda's return.

She hurriedly continued by saying, "Elder Debbon has approved my request to adopt Juila and Jena legally. They are official members of our family now!" She smiled around the table.

Justan, Andera, and Kyelon smiled and clapped their hands with genuine happiness. Even though Justan was just four anons old, Andera almost four, and Kyelon nearly three, they were very active participants in the twins' lives. Kyelon was incredibly grateful that he was not the youngest in the house anymore, always teased.

Bryon, on the other hand, scowled and said, "Don't you have to have two signatures on the adoption contract?"

"Only if it's the husband requesting the adoption," she replied cheerfully. "Isn't it wonderful, children? We get to keep them forever now."

"Don't you think we should've waited a little longer?"

"No, I don't," Alena spoke more harshly than she intended. "These girls deserve to have both a mother and father they can call their own. I'm more than willing to fill that role even if you aren't."

"I never said I didn't want them," Bryon defended himself and then continued, "I just thought maybe we should give Amanda a little more time to make it back here."

Alena inhaled sharply through her nostrils as she replied through clenched teeth, "That's enough, Bryon, you know as well as I do that Amanda's not going to come back. She's gone, but her precious little girls are still alive and here, and they deserve to have our unconditional love!"

Their three small children looked at each other with concern. Were Mommy and Daddy fighting? Did they just say that Amanda was dead and not just visiting family?

Andera and Kyelon both looked to their oldest sibling, Justan, as though to find out what they should do with this new information. Any time they were confused, Justan always had an answer. This time, Justan slightly raised both his shoulders and mouthed the words, *"not now,"* to them.

They all looked from one parent to the other. They knew their Papa was unhappy ever since Amanda left. They wanted their family normal and happy again. They turned to watch their father.

As though the last thread of hope snapped, Bryon closed his eyes and then spoke quietly, "You're right, Alena. I've been holding onto a false hope so I wouldn't have to face the facts. I've been horrible these past two mesans, haven't I?" He looked into his wife's eyes and silently pleaded with her to understand his guilt.

Alena nodded and said, "Well, you've certainly left yourself a lot of room for improvement. Why don't you start right now by taking the twins and the other children into the living room for storytime? I'll take care of the dinner dishes while you get started." She stood and gathered the dishes.

Alena noticed a difference in her children as they smiled at one another, jumped up from their chairs, and clambered to the living room for their favorite time of the day. Bryon's fundamental shift vindicated her decision to adopt the twins; it was just the thing needed to bring her family back together again after the terrible tragedy.

Once finished with the dishes, Alena quietly stood leaning against the living room doorway to watch her husband's natural interaction with all five children. She smiled at the scene in front of her as Bryon's spiky, dark-haired head was leaning over the two blonde heads of the twins while the other three children nestled around them.

Alena always marveled at Bryon's natural ease with all ages of children. She liked knowing that his firm, muscular frame could be so gentle with the children. Alena watched his large hands as they deftly turned the book's pages as he read. She enjoyed the deep richness of his voice as he imitated different characters in the story.

The twins fell asleep in Bryon's arms, getting heavier as they drifted into their dreams. Should he read another story while they slept, or should he put them to bed and then return to the other children? He looked up from the girls while deciding and spotted Alena watching him.

Not knowing how long she stood there, he raised his eyebrows and nodded down toward the twins. He watched his slender wife shrug, make a decision, and then walk gracefully across the room to assist him.

"Wait here a few minutes. We'll be right back," Alena whispered to her three children, kissing Justan lightly on the top of his head as she bent over and picked up Jena from Bryon's left arm and gestured for Bryon to follow her with Juila. Her heart almost burst with joy to see Bryon's change of heart.

She was unsure if her adoption news would be received with understanding or anger, and apparently, she correctly guessed that he'd come out of his despair.

Placing each girl in her own bassinet, Alena turned toward Bryon and leaned into his chest to hug him. When his arms wrapped around her, and his lips brushed the top of her head as he held her close, she melted against him.

"Thank you, Alena," he whispered as he held the love of his life in his arms.

She leaned back far enough away from him to look into his face as she replied with a smile, "You're welcome." She kept her arm around his waist as they returned to the living room and said, "Let's give our other children a couple more stories tonight, okay?"

"You get to read the next one," Bryon replied with a smile as they walked down the hallway.

"Is there something you're not telling me?"

"Well, I kind of promised Justan that you'd read *Genero* tonight."

"Really? How kind of you," she replied a little too sweetly. "And here I thought you might like a little time for us tonight. I guess I was wrong since you offered for me to read such a long book."

"Hey, I didn't say you'd read the *whole* book," he replied hastily, all the while wishing he hadn't promised anything at all to Justan.

"I'd hate to deprive our children of any of our time," she said as she teasingly removed her hand from around his waist. With a bounce in her step, Alena entered the living room and smiled at their three little ones impatiently waiting for the next story. She announced, "Who wants me to read *Genero*?"

Justan jumped off of the couch to retrieve the book. He selected it from the many on the shelf without reading the title—since they all knew the book by its cover. He ran up to his mother, looked up at her with his big brown eyes, and gently handed her the book saying, "It's one of my favorites, Mama!"

"That's my smart boy," she said as she took the book from his tiny hands and continued, "Let's all sit together on the couch while I read." She gestured for Bryon to sit beside her and hold Andera and Kyelon on his lap while she situated Justan on her own.

She opened the brightly colored book and began, "Jehoban lived alone in a world called Tuala—," Alena read until all of the kids were limp with sleep, and she quietly closed the book. She looked over at Bryon and said, "I guess that's the end of tonight's story."

"Not if I can help it," Bryon whispered back with a mischievous grin.

"Did you want me to finish reading *Genero* to you, honey?"

"No, I was thinking more along the lines of making our own creation tonight."

"What did you have in mind, painting, cooking, or something else?"

"Definitely something else," he said as he easily stood while holding both Andera and Kyelon.

Alena stood while holding Justan and said, "I'm excited to find out what you have in mind." She followed him into the boys' bedroom and settled Justan down into his bed for the night.

She then took Kyelon from her husband's arm and tucked him into his own bed across from Justan's. Alena followed Bryon into Andera's room and watched as Bryon gently settled her in and covered her with the pink blankets. Alena kissed her first-daughter on the forehead just where Bryon had before turning out the light to leave.

Bryon took Alena's hand and said, "I can't wait to show you what I have on my mind." Alena giggled like a young girl as she snuggled closer to her husband. He led her back to their bedroom, firmly shut the door behind them, and pulled her into a tight embrace.

He kissed her with a passion she forgot he possessed.

AMANDA WAS BURSTING with anticipation over possibly finding an avenue back to Tuala. Her mind was in such a whirlwind that sleep proved somewhat elusive. She just had to get back to her girls. With all of her memories clear again, every moment spent away from the twins was an agony she wouldn't wish on her worst enemy.

What were her girls learning without her there to witness and cheer them on? Or worse, what if they didn't remember her when she did finally return? Amanda tried talking to her mom about her concerns, but her mom doggedly reminded her to keep faith that everything would turn out perfectly.

All Amanda knew was that her faith was being tested in the extreme. The only thing that gave her a moment's peace was that her children were safe with Alena and Bryon. They were excellent parents, and they'd love Juila and Jena as their own until she could bring them home.

How much time had passed on Tuala? Would her baby girls still be babies, or would they now be toddlers or even young children? She resigned herself to be thankful no matter their ages. Of course, she'd be sad for any missed time, but she'd be grateful for any future with her children in it.

Shemalla said it would be a few days before she'd be able to arrange transportation back to Tuala, but she also seemed hesitant even to offer that much support. Suppose the Elders denied the transportation request and instead decided to keep her children for testing in one of their facilities.

The Tualan people held onto the fear of *old souls* being among them. There were so many unknown aspects that Amanda could come up with that the frustration started to overwhelm her tiny shred of hope.

CHAPTER 22

Ninan's house in Kirma proved to be the best place for Petre to hide out. He knew nobody would be coming home for a while. He flew the personal telepod through the streets of Kirma, cloaked in the darkness of night.

Hovering outside of Ninan's house, he left the telepod running and exited the craft with the plan of breaking into the front door to get the garage door opened promptly. Once his feet hit the ground, however, the additional timed teleportations caught up to him, and he heaved the contents of his stomach onto the front lawn.

He staggered to the entrance without enough time to recover and clumsily forced it open. He fell several times as he went through the house and located the garage.

Pressing the button for the door opener, Petre continued through the garage into his awaiting telepod. At last, he maneuvered the machine inside and didn't relax until the door safely hid the stolen telepod.

Petre wandered miserably through the house, inspecting each

of the rooms. As he looked around at the luxurious furnishings, Petre's fury rose regarding Ninan.

He must be making a fortune at Kirma Shipping and Receiving. I don't know why he even took my money because he certainly didn't need it.

He just liked taking it from me. He probably laughed at every pitiful payment at what a loser I am to have to pay to find my wife. Just see if he gets another shill from me.

What a hypocrite! I should've given him a few more well-aimed kicks for trying to deceive me. ME!

His angry inspection of the house ended in the kitchen. He hadn't eaten much of anything since the bruskins at lunchtime, and even that was now residing on the front lawn. Having put in a lot of effort for the day, Petre's stomach churned and growled.

Who knew how much effort it took to time a teleportation? Putting together several foxl sandwiches, Petre sat at the kitchen bar and scarfed down his meal. Even if he didn't taste the food, he still enjoyed the idea of getting something back from that crook, Ninan!

Now that he had eaten and his nausea was settling, Petre wanted nothing more than to go to bed. The next day was Sabtu, so he knew he'd have a day of rest along with everybody else. He had big plans to figure out, and he wanted to get an early start.

He used the restroom and then turned into the bedroom. Again, Petre sneered with warped satisfaction that he was sleeping in Ninan's plush bedding while he imagined Ninan in an uncomfortable heap on the hard, cold ground. Stretching out on his back on the sleeping platform, Petre folded his hands behind his head and smiled at his day's accomplishments.

Now the most tedious tasks were still ahead of him. He would have to watch Bryon's house to work out their household routine. He'd wait for Bryon's wife to take the girl to the market, hopefully within the next two to three days. Somehow, he'd need to distract the woman so he could snatch his daughter.

Petre didn't have much time. His luck would have to hold out if he planned on taking the girl before anyone noticed Ninan's absence. Plus, he wanted to be well away from here when Ninan finally returned.

Luckily, the drop spot was pretty remote. Unless Ninan knew how to translate himself, Petre's confidence in having several days to work seemed pretty decent.

Petre fell asleep with a smile on his lips and the expectation of success.

ALENA EXPERTLY JUGGLED the duties of taking care of her five children. Three of them were sick with head colds, as Alena had suspected. The weather change came fast this year which always increased the likelihood of becoming ill.

She dosed them lightly with *epeny*, and they were finally resting peacefully. Now that she'd have a few minutes of peace, Alena called over to Tana's house. Once connected, Alena said, "Hi, Tana, could I ask you a favor?"

"Sure! What do you need?"

"Could you watch three of the kids for me while I get some supplies at the market?"

"Would you rather I went to the market for you?"

"Normally, that would be perfect," Alena replied but then continued, "However, I was hoping while I was out to check on one of my patients who's a vendor there. Plus, I need to spend a little quality time with Jena and Kyelon."

"No problem. When would you like me to come over?"

"Well, the children are sick with colds. I just gave each of them a dose of *epeny*, which thankfully made them comfortable enough to rest. Could you come over in the next few minutes?"

"Absolutely," Tana replied cheerfully, "although it'd be more fun if they were awake."

"Trust me when I say you'd rather they were sleeping! They're so cranky that they haven't been much fun to be around!"

"Okay, I'll be right over," Tana said as she disconnected the call.

Moments later, there was a knock on the front door. Alena smiled as she welcomed her neighbor into the house and said, "I really appreciate you doing this without any notice."

"Sure, no problem," she quickly replied. She took off her coat and hung it on the rack beside the door. They walked toward the living room when she asked Alena, "Do you have any instructions for me regarding your little patients?"

"I don't expect them to wake up, but if they do, then it would be just the usual dose of *epeny* for each of them. I left it on the kitchen counter should you need it."

Kyelon came around the corner just then, and he squealed with delight when he saw Tana. Somehow he had managed to escape getting the cold, and he was bored with inactivity.

He ran up and hugged Tana's knees. Then he turned his face up to her, raised his hands upward, and demanded in his cute baby voice, "Up."

Tana smiled as she bent down and reached under his arms to lift him onto her hip easily. She asked him, "Have you been your Mommy's helper with your brother and sisters while they've been sick?"

Kyelon smiled as he nodded his head firmly up and down. "I've been real good," he replied, "Mommy wants me to go to the market, but I want to stay home with you. Can I?" He snuggled into her side, very pleased with himself.

"Let's just ask your mommy, shall we?" Tana replied as she looked over to Alena.

Looking at the two of them settled together in the entryway, Alena shrugged with resignation and admitted, "It will probably go faster if I just have Jena in the stroller to worry about."

Kyelon smiled from ear to ear as his little legs kicked with glee on either side of Tana. "Yippee," he squealed, "Let's go play."

"Just one second, little guy," she smiled at Kyelon and looked over at Alena, "Do you need any help getting Jena ready to go?"

"No, no, go have fun with Kyelon. It'll just take me a couple of minutes to gather together everything I need to get out of here," Alena replied as they parted ways in the living room.

Alena continued to the kitchen, where she got the stroller and baby bag out of the kitchen closet and her shopping list off the counter. She retraced her steps with all her accouterments back to the living room, where Tana and Kyelon had joined Jena already playing on the floor.

Tana saw her coming and gathered Jena up with her play blanket. She took the two steps to where Alena settled on the couch to ensure everything she might need was already in the baby bag.

Tana placed Jena in the stroller and ensured her blankets were securely around the six-mesan-old little girl. Tickling her little tummy, Tana smiled and said to Jena, "You be a good little girl for your Mommy while you're with her at the market."

"Thank you," Alena said to Tana as she leaned over from the couch. She stuffed the baby bag into the basket under the stroller, and then she stood. Alena pushed the stroller through the living room.

Tana rushed ahead of her to open the door for both of them. She stood in the doorway and waved as she watched Alena wheel the stroller down the sidewalk. Kyelon joined Tana at the door and held her hand. "Take your time at the market," she called after the pair, "I've got everything taken care of here."

Alena waved back and said to the couple, "Thanks again. I hope I won't be too long. Be good for Tana, Kyelon!"

It had been too many days since she could last get to the market, and Alena desperately needed fresh food. She lengthened her stride and was grateful that she only had Jena to look after at the market. Kyelon was a well-mannered child, but he was a boy who tended to get his little fingers into almost everything.

Alena's trip took almost fifteen minutes at her brisk pace. The gentle roll of the stroller lulled Jena to sleep. Again, the timing was perfect since it was time for Jena's nap anyway, which was another reason Alena wanted to go to the market right away.

If delayed, Jena could become overstimulated, and then she'd have a more challenging time settling down. Alena didn't have to worry about the marketplace's noise as Jena was used to the racket of four other children in the house. As it was, once Jena was out, she slept so soundly that almost nothing could rouse her until she was good and ready to be awake.

With most of her concentration now on shopping, Alena began looking over the different vendors' products. She worked her way through the rows and haggled for most of the items on her list.

Within about ten minutes, Alena worked her way over to the vendor she sought, her patient. She smiled and called out to the woman, "Bistea, how are you feeling?"

CHAPTER 23

Bistea turned to the sound of her name and smiled when she realized it was Alena calling out to her. "Doing great," she replied and waved hello with her left hand as her other arm was firmly bandaged to her side. "I'll be happy to get this strapping off sometime soon," she added with grim resignation.

"If you have a few moments, I could take a look at it. You never know. It might be healed already." Not wanting to seem too overbearing, Alena settled her newest purchase into the baby bag and waited for Bistea's reply.

Relief washed over Bistea's face, and she said, "I couldn't think of a better time than right this moment!" She turned to her youngest daughter and directed, "Watch the booth for a few minutes while Alena checks my arm." She received a nod from her daughter, and then she moved to the back edge of her stall to allow Alena enough light and space to adequately inspect her arm.

Alena pushed the stroller to the front side of the stand since there wasn't enough room for both herself and the stroller in the space between the booths. She edged herself through the narrow gap. She smiled at Bistea as she gently unwrapped the bandages holding her arm immobile. With experienced hands, Alena spent a few minutes gently probing the entire limb for any signs of tenderness or of improper healing.

She ran her healing crystal up one side of Bistea's arm and down the other, looking for any blips which might indicate improper healing. Seeing a red area on Bistea's arm, she took some numbing cream from her front pocket and applied a small amount to the site where the bone had been exposed through the skin. Alena handed the ointment vial to Bistea and instructed, "Use this salve on the red area several times a day until the redness disappears."

Feeling satisfied with her patient's progress, Alena assured Bistea that she could resume her normal activities as long as her arm didn't start to hurt or swell. Bistea nodded and smiled with relief at Alena's diagnosis.

Alena patted the newly healed arm in farewell as she wedged herself back between the two booths. "Feel free to call me if you have questions," Alena said when she reached the stroller. She automatically looked down to check on the sleeping baby only to discover a pile of empty blankets.

Her heart stuttered to a stop, and she couldn't breathe. A moment later, her heart hammered so fast it sounded as if it were a frantic bird trying to escape captivity. Where was Jena? Surely, she was nearby.

"Jena!" she cried loudly. She looked around frantically for the toddler to see if she crawled on the ground. She turned to the girl watching the booth and shrieked, "Did you see where my baby went?"

The little girl looked terrified and shook her head mutely.

"Jena!" Alena screamed again. By now, people at the market realized there was a problem. They were looking in Alena's direction, and some of the other mothers began to move toward her.

"Has anyone seen a six-mesan-old girl? She was just sleeping in this stroller, and now she's missing! Please, anyone, please help me find my little girl!"

Panic rose inside Alena, and she had to stamp it down firmly to focus on finding Jena. *Of course, she has to be somewhere nearby. She just crawled away. Someone is bound to say they see her in just a few moments now that they know she's missing.*

There was a frantic but organized search of the entire marketplace, yet there was no sign of Jena. Someone had the foresight to contact the authorities. It wasn't until Alena was answering questions from two public officials that the desperateness of the situation started to affect Alena's thinking.

I've lost Jena. What'll I tell Amanda if she ever comes back? Here's the one daughter I was able to keep track of. I lost the other one at the marketplace.

She hadn't answered the last couple of questions, and she wasn't able to concentrate on anything except her misery.

The next thing she knew, Bryon drew her into his arms. She didn't even think about how he'd come to be there before she wrapped her arms around his waist and started sobbing uncontrollably, repeatedly saying, "I lost Jena! I lost Jena! I lost Jena!"

"It's okay, Alena," Bryon soothed as he held her tightly and stroked her back rhythmically, "We'll find her shortly. She's got to be nearby."

Reason slowly returned to Alena, realizing she didn't know how Bryon knew to come to the marketplace. She asked, "What are you doing here?"

"Bistea contacted my office while you were searching the stalls. She told me you needed me right away, and luckily I was in the office. If you can, will you please tell me what's happened?"

Alena described the events both before and after Jena's disappearance as best she could. Bryon nodded but never interrupted. He put his arm around her shoulder and steered her back toward the authorities, who were now questioning the people in the marketplace. They both listened as one person after another said they didn't see anything unusual.

Finally, one person seemed to remember an average-sized man leaving the marketplace rather hurriedly. The only strange thing about the man was that he was unknown to the woman who saw him. Nothing more was known as people came and regularly went from the marketplace.

Alena turned to Bryon hopefully and said, "Do you think that mystery man found Jena and wanted to take her to our home?"

"Maybe," Bryon replied without conviction but wanting to keep Alena calm. "Why don't I take you home, and we can see?"

Bryon turned to the authority and said, "I'm going to take my wife home, and then I'll return immediately."

The official curtly nodded as he finished writing his summaries in his notepad. He turned to another patron and started asking more questions as Bryon grabbed the stroller handle with one hand and kept Alena securely beside him with the other.

They walked even faster home. Alena kept saying she thought Jena was safe at home and needed to hurry. They were almost running by the time they reached their house. Together, they burst through the front door. Tana looked up in surprise to see the two harried-looking people in the living room doorway. Alena cried, "Where's Jena?"

Tana looked confused and answered, "She was with you, Alena. Remember?"

Kyelon looked at his parents' stressed expressions and started crying. He didn't like seeing the blatant fear on their faces. Tana pulled him into an embrace as he continued to sob quietly. "It's okay, Kyelon, we'll get this figured out," Tana said to him as she rubbed his back and returned the look of fear to both Bryon and Alena.

Bryon suddenly nodded confirmation of his suspicions, turned to Alena, and said, "You stay here in case anyone calls or comes over. I'll go back to the marketplace with the telepod and see if I can see anything from the air."

Alena nodded and sobbed, "Hurry, Bryon, bring Jena home!"

Bryon kissed her cheek and optimistically declared, "I'll be back before you know it!" He strode out the front door with purposeful steps. Bryon didn't like the train of thought his mind started taking. He definitely didn't want Alena to know he was reasonably sure that the unknown man seen leaving the marketplace would turn out to be none other than Petre MacVeen.

He needed to talk to the authorities to get a search underway immediately! Entering the garage, Bryon keyed the door to open. The start-up sequence never seemed to take as long as it did that time. Bryon was cursing under his breath at every delay. Within moments, Bryon concentrated on the marketplace's coordinates, hovering over the busy square.

He was thrilled to see several officials searching for Jena fanning out from the last known location. Bryon scanned the streets swiftly himself before he decided to land outside the general area and talk to an authority about his suspicions.

The telepod settled onto the ground just as Bryon keyed the door open and jumped out. Striding over to the official, he introduced himself as Jena's father. The official's expression changed from aggressive to comforting in seconds.

"I think I know who took Jena," Bryon declared.

"Really," the authority said noncommittally, "Do you have a name of the suspected person?"

"Petre MacVeen," Bryon replied dejectedly.

"Oh," was the authority's response as he wrote the name on his notepad. "Excuse me while I let my boss know." The officer turned slightly and raised his radio to his mouth, clicked the talk button, and said, "The suspect for the abduction of Jena is possibly Petre MacVeen."

"That son of a bitch," came the rapid reply over the radio. "We'll keep our eyes open for that son-of-a—. Thanks for the update. Carry on then."

"Will do," the official beside Bryon replied and hung the radio at his side as he turned back to Bryon. "We'll continue our search for Petre from the ground. There are several officials on every street leading from the marketplace. We don't take child abductions lightly around here, so we hope to have her found before dark."

Bryon nodded as he agreed with the officer's statements. Knowing the ground was being well covered, Bryon offered, "I think I'll do an aerial search in my telepod."

"Do you have a radio in your 'pod?"

"Absolutely!"

"Should you see anything suspicious, the authorities are using channel 7-4-6 for this search. Let us know your coordinates right away, and we'll get on the scene immediately."

"Thanks, I'll enter that into my 'pod as soon as I get back in there." Bryon returned rapidly to his telepod. Since he had left the door open, he could immediately enter the unit and settle into the operator's seat.

He issued the start-up sequence and waited for the communication devices to activate before entering the official search code. As he lifted up into the air, he heard the various authorities issuing the 'all clear' for each successfully searched street without finding any sign of Jena.

CHAPTER 24

Petre rushed away from the market square with Jena tucked awkwardly under his jacket. The last thing he needed was for the girl to awake and start crying. He lengthened his stride. Within fifteen minutes, he found himself in front of Ninan's home.

He couldn't believe there was no pursuit. Could his luck be changing? Everything seemed to be working out perfectly for him since meeting Jesisca. The only thing which hadn't worked out was keeping Jesisca as his wife.

Oh well, I guess I can't have everything!

Walking through Ninan's front door, he kicked it shut behind him. He figured he'd have some time before he'd need to leave. Besides, he wanted to get to know his daughter. Pulling her out from under his jacket, he first noticed the blonde ringlets sticking out every which way on her head. They were adorably cute.

Even though he'd never considered having children, just knowing this one was his, he was fascinated by every detail. Her eyelashes were unusually long as they rested on her plump, rosy cheeks. What color were her eyes? She had a cute little nub for a nose.

He reached out and touched her tightly balled fist, noticing the cute tiny buds of her fingernails. Her hand flew open at his touch, startling him into jarring her whole body. She slept through it all.

He smiled down at her and then realized he had a huge problem. In his one-track-minded obsession to acquire his daughter, he forgot to plan for after he had her. He needed baby supplies, and he'd need them as soon as she awoke. He didn't want to leave her. Reluctantly, he set her down on the couch and raced into the kitchen to see if there was anything in there that a baby might eat.

The icebox contained a milk jar that he set on the kitchen counter to let it get to room temperature. He didn't think a baby would want to have cold milk. Not really knowing what to look for, he opened the cupboards and found some crackers. *Those have possibilities.* He added them to the counter beside the milk. A bread loaf also found its way to the counter, as well as tomatoes and carrots.

He raced back to the living room to check on Jena. She hadn't moved from where he placed her. He walked across the living room toward the bedrooms. He looked in all the cupboards and drawers for anything useful for baby care.

Finally, he came to a cabinet containing towels. He realized then that he was going to have to change dirty clouts. His nose wrinkled at the nasty thought, but he shook his head, grabbed the entire stack of towels, and set them on the couch next to Jena.

He then checked the bedrooms for anything else which might be handy. Nothing more seemed appropriate for taking care of an infant. He walked back to the living room and picked up the towel stack. Then he changed his mind, took one towel off the pile, and put it back on the couch. He returned to the kitchen with the remaining towels, grabbed as much food as he could carry, and took them all out to the garage to put into the telepod.

He went back to the kitchen, picked up the remaining food, and moved it out to the telepod in a second trip. The milk almost spilled as he was setting it down, and he realized he would need some sort of cup or bottle for Jena to be able to drink out of. He didn't think she'd want to drink it straight from the jar like he was used to doing.

He rummaged through the kitchen cupboards until he found a small plasfilm cup. Thinking this was the better option than glass, he also took that out to the telepod.

Petre returned to the living room and sat on the couch next to his sleeping little girl.

Now what? This isn't so hard. Why are women always complaining about how much work children are? They seem pretty simple to me.

Now that he had all of his supplies ready, he couldn't think of any reason to hang out in this stupid little town. He had places to go, cargo to sell, and people to avoid! He gently picked Jena up and cradled her in his left arm.

Walking carefully, he made his way out to the telepod. He went to put her down when he realized he had no place to keep Jena without having to worry about her falling and getting hurt. With her heavy, limp body still in his arm, he went back into the house to look for something to put Jena in during the transport.

Finally, he found a laundry basket in the bedroom that would be a perfect vessel to hold her. He dumped out the dirty clothes with his free hand and carried it back to the telepod. He set the basket on the floor and awkwardly arranged several towels onto the bottom. He settled Jena onto the makeshift bed and fussed with it a little longer.

Satisfied that he could do no better, Petre palmed the side door shut and moved into the operator seat. He activated the telepod and then realized he couldn't open the garage door from inside his purloined transportation.

Leaving it running, he palmed open the door and jumped out.

He took the several steps necessary to press the garage door button and then hurried back to the 'pod. With alacrity, he gingerly moved the telepod onto the waiting platform outside. He concentrated on his destination coordinates, set his hand on the control module, and blinked out of Kirma.

Forever.

At least he hoped it would be the last time he stepped foot in that dreaded town filled with lying, cheating, kidnapping people.

AIRBORN for only a couple of minutes, Bryon spotted a telepod leaving a garage a few streets away from his current location. Typically, this wouldn't have been such an unusual sight. However, Bryon was reasonably sure he saw the number thirteen written on the roof of the telepod just as it blinked out of sight.

Personal telepods weren't numbered. Only corporate telepods were, like the one that went missing a couple of days before from his shipping yard. He directed his telepod to hover over the driveway where the telepod disappeared. He noted the address and called over to his office as he settled his telepod onto the ground.

"Kirma Shipping and Receiving, this is Frasnia. Can I help you?"

"Frasnia, this is Bryon. Can you look up Ninan's address for me?"

"Sure thing, Bryon, just one second." She came back a moment later and said, "His address is Thursto Block 43-3. What's going on, Bryon?"

Nodding confirmation, Bryon replied to Frasnia, "I think I just saw our missing telepod leave his driveway. Can you begin a focused search on the beacon signal from that telepod? Thanks, Frasnia. I have to go now."

Without waiting for a reply, Bryon changed the radio frequency back to 7-4-6 and said, "Officers, please initiate a search for Jena's abductor at Thursto Block 43-3. I just saw a stolen telepod leaving this address."

Within a few minutes, several authorities converged on the house where Bryon was waiting in the entry of his telepod. The officials confirmed that the front door was forcibly entered, which also confirmed Bryon's growing suspicion that Ninan was also in trouble. If Ninan had been a party to the abduction, he would've let Petre into his house without damage to the entrance.

He flagged an official and stated, "One of Kirma Shipping's telepods went missing last week as well as the shipment and operator. I now believe that Petre MacVeen somehow stole the shipment and either abducted or killed the operator. I have our office tracing the beacon signals for both the freighter and personal telepod that are missing."

"That's good information," the official stated as he continued to make notes on his scratchpad. "Can I have your name as well?"

"Sure, I'm Bryon Kesh. Jena's father."

"Okay," replied the official as he wrote the provided information and turned to his partner. "Let everyone know we're now looking for a stolen freighter with cargo, a personal telepod, an operator, as well as Jena. Kirma Shipping is tracking both of the telepod beacons and will let us know if they receive any information."

The officer looked significantly at Bryon, who nodded confirmation immediately. "Bryon, why don't you come down to the station and file an official theft report while my men search the house for any clues as to where the abductor might have taken Jena."

Bryon acquiesced and turned to enter his telepod. He had a sinking feeling he wasn't going to see Jena again that day, and he fervently hoped Petre wouldn't harm her. Visualizing the coordinates for the station, Bryon completed the start-up sequence and blinked out of the driveway.

CHAPTER 25

Jasmine knew what Dr. Gascon would make of her latest notes. She sat across from him in their daily consultation of Amanda's progress.

"It seems significant to me that Amanda would continue to villainize this Petre fellow. It seems he might be the key to finding out the truth. I'm also intrigued by the fact she feels the need to divide up her children as though she feels she's been left out of her own family structure."

Jasmine noncommittally nodded while she waited for Stephen to continue to psychoanalyze her notes.

"Also, Ninan appears to be working both sides, but Amanda feels as though he can be of help in her delusions. Make a note to follow up on him as well. What I find most insightful is that she's maintaining the stories of the people in Tuala when she's obviously safely home with her family. I think she displays a lot of guilt by insisting on returning to Tuala. She must really want to get Nealand out of what could possibly be a dangerous situation. Do you agree?"

"Absolutely, Dr. Gascon. My thoughts exactly." She could barely choke the words out. If Dr. Gascon were not so respected in his medical field, Jasmine would wonder about his sanity.

How could he not see there may be more truth to Amanda's story than any of them may know? What if Tuala really were a real place? Who were they to say that Amanda had to be delusional to have these memories?

"I have the rest of the morning free. Are you meeting with Amanda right now?"

"Yes, she'll be brought to my office in about five minutes."

"Good, I'll sit in on this session. Let's walk to your office now and wait for her. I'd like to get some answers today." Dr. Gascon stood from behind his massive mahogany desk and tapped the stack of paper notes before setting them precisely on the edge of his tabletop.

With no other choice, Dr. Medin rose from her chair and nodded affirmation at Dr. Gascon's request. She could hardly tell the Cannon Memorial Asylum Director of Psychiatry that she didn't want him interrupting her patient's session. Her only solace was that she had already programmed Amanda to ignore any further post-hypnotic suggestions. Dr. Gascon's visit wouldn't impede Amanda's progress; maybe just slow it down a little.

They met the attendant and Amanda in the hall on their way to the office. Jasmine thanked the attendant, and Amanda walked into Dr. Medin's office with the two doctors.

"Amanda, as you can see, Dr. Gascon has once again requested to participate in your session today. He has reviewed your file and has a few questions he'd like to have answered while you're under hypnosis. Please take a seat, and we'll get started right away."

Amanda trusted Dr. Medin to keep her safe from Dr. Gascon now, so she complied quickly. She closed her eyes and nodded her head.

"We're going to continue where we left off last time, Amanda. Please take a deep, cleansing breath and release it slowly. You are feeling warm, safe, and secure. Good. Now another deep inhalation..."

AMANDA SAT with her parents in Shemalla's living room for the second time within a week. She was excited to hear any news that Shemalla might have learned regarding her return to Tuala. Their host seemed hesitant to start the conversation. Amanda needed to break the tension. She asked, "Have you heard anything from the Elders about my being transferred to Tuala?"

"About that," Shemalla started but then paused as she looked first at Amanda, then Diane, and finally Chris before she hesitantly began again. "I haven't found a good enough reason to explain to Elder Vargen why you'd want to come without raising his interest in your journey. As one of the Old Soul Engineering Facility's founders, he'd be the first person to apprehend you. His questioning techniques are extensive, and I fear anyone who may have helped you in the past would be in danger."

She looked down into her lap at her clasped hands. "I may have given you false hope when I said I thought I could get you passage into Tuala."

"Oh," was all Amanda could come up with as a response. She understood the position in which she'd put Shemalla. Now that it was explained, she should've known it would be this complicated. "Are you saying that it's impossible except by accident?"

"I'm not saying it's impossible...just more challenging, possibly dangerous."

"Now, wait a minute," Chris interrupted, "We just got Amanda back from what we feared was death; we're *not* about to put her in danger so that she might be able to travel to Tuala. It's just not worth it!"

Amanda's mouth dropped open in disbelief. Her head whipped around, and her gaze locked on her father's. The sudden movement caused pain to course through her arm and abused muscles, but she ignored it all as anger surged inside her. "Not worth it? My children are still on Tuala, and they're worth everything to me!"

Chris raised his hands conciliatorily as he spoke, "I understand your feelings, Amanda. We need to find an alternative that'll pose the least amount of risk."

"That's right," interjected Shemalla, shifting forward onto the edge of the couch. "There are other possibilities which we should seriously explore."

"Okay," Diane finally spoke, her voice shaky, but her following words came out as though measuring the risk versus reward. "Let's talk about Amanda's other, less dangerous options."

"Right," Shemalla said, nodding and looking again at Amanda but addressing the trio. "Remember how I told you that there are many gates into Tuala here on Earth which don't need to be guarded since Earth beings have no understanding of how or where to cross over?"

Her guests nodded with renewed excitement evident in their expressions.

"This is where it'll get tricky," she continued. "We'll need to find a gate, closest to your children, which an Elder doesn't monitor. To do this, I'll have to conduct some covert research. I don't mean to offend any of you, but in good conscience, I'll only be able to share that information with Amanda since she's the only one of you who's been to Tuala. Actually, I shouldn't even be offering to help Amanda since she's an Earth resident and not a Tualan. You must understand?"

"I don't like it," Chris began after looking at his wife, "but I do understand." His hand snaked over and grasped Diane's in his.

"Would you like Chris and me to leave?" Diane asked quietly.

"I think that might be for the best," Shemalla answered with a sad shake of her head. "I'm so sorry," she said as the couple rose from the couch across from her.

"Don't think anything of it," Chris said. He thought he'd probably be able to talk to Amanda when she was through talking with Shemalla. Amanda never kept secrets from them. She'd need their help to get wherever she'd have to go anyway. He told himself it was just a minor inconvenience that he wouldn't be a participant in the fascinating conversation which was about to occur.

Shemalla walked them to the front door and bade them a good evening. She assured them that she wouldn't be too long talking with Amanda this evening. She'd bring her back to the hotel after they put together an initial plan.

Shemalla watched the couple walk down her sidewalk and then get into their vehicle. She waited on the porch until they drove away before she shut her front door. Slowly, she turned back to go into the living room, not knowing exactly what would happen tonight.

Amanda looked up expectantly when Shemalla entered the living room and sat on the couch, which her parents had just vacated. "What's next?"

"Well," Shemalla slowly began as she reached into the front pocket of her pants. Her fingers pulled a chain out, which contained a beautiful white crystal. She noted the expression on Amanda's face and asked, "Do you know what this is?"

"Sure, it's your birth crystal."

"That's true, this is the crystal that was given to me at my birthing ceremony, but it's also something more. Do you know what that is?"

"I guess not," Amanda said with some hesitation. "What is it?"

"As an adult, the crystal becomes something more than a form of protection. This white diamond amplifies my abilities even while I'm here on Earth. One of my abilities is to teleport without the aid of machinery." She waited a moment to see if Amanda could see any benefit of this ability for herself.

"I guess you'd save a lot of money on airfare then," Amanda

quipped. She still didn't understand how this would benefit her situation and said as much to Shemalla.

Shemalla continued as though she weren't concerned with Amanda's confusion. "It also gives me the ability to erase memories from people around me." Now she noted a look of fear on Amanda's face.

"Please don't make me forget about my children," Amanda begged.

"Oh, I'd never do that," she corrected immediately. "I'm sorry if I gave you the wrong impression, Amanda. I only meant to say that I'll have to take tonight's conversation back from you, so you won't be able to share it with your parents. I know your father's an inquisitive man, and I don't want you to be in an uncomfortable situation with his questioning."

"Oh," Amanda sighed in relief and continued, "That makes sense. Do you have a plan in mind for getting my children back?"

"I'm still working on it," Shemalla admitted. "This is a very complicated situation, and I really do care about your safety first."

"Okay, where do we start?"

CHAPTER 26

"First, you must allow me to condition your brain only to remember our conversation when we're together. That way, we won't have to start over every time we meet, but you'll be safe from your parents or any Elder who might question you."

"Wow! That must be powerful if it can override an Elder's questions. I'd been led to believe they're almost omnipotent."

"It only works if you agree to my conditions, Amanda," Shemalla replied with a smile. "I promise I won't take any other memories from you. Will you agree to let me continue?"

"I guess I have to if I'm going to get your help. I also don't want to put you in any danger with the Elders for trying to help me."

"Perfect," Shemalla smiled at Amanda and said, "Now if you'll just lie back on the couch and get comfortable." She waited for Amanda to comply before she continued, "Without moving your head, just watch the crystal as it swings on the chain. Do not take your eyes from the crystal. Good. Perfect."

Shemalla continued to gently turn the pendant in a circular motion as she concentrated on the elemy inside of her birth crystal. She'd had many years of familiarity with her crystal and understood its resources intimately. Shemalla focused the energy through her crystal and gently moved it into a section of Amanda's thoughts with practiced elegance. She saw a change in Amanda's expression and knew that her conditioning was successful. Now she'd be able to share anything with Amanda without fear of repercussions.

"Okay," Shemalla crooned as she used her other hand to cradle her necklace and set it down on the coffee table next to them. "You can sit up now if you like."

"That's it?" Amanda asked with incredulity.

"Yep, your cooperation made it very quick and easy."

"What else are these stones able to do?" Amanda asked with fascination as she leaned forward to look more closely at Shemalla's crystal on the table.

"Feel free to pick it up."

Amanda did so with enthusiasm. She was surprised that it was warm to the touch even though it was on a cool table. "Does the energy inside it keep it warm, or is it your own energy?"

"I think it's both, really," she answered, her expression thoughtful and her eyes unfocused. "It's not really crystal at all, you know. Those are white diamonds. All birth crystals are indeed gemstones, even though we call them crystals.

"There's powerful energy contained in each stone depending on the cut, the setting, and the wearer. The potential power is why it's so important that the correct stone is assigned to each person at their birthing ceremony."

"That makes sense. Alena had to request a particular stone for one of my daughters at their birthing ceremony."

"What stone did Alena require that she didn't already have? I've never heard of a stone needing to be requested."

"It was a black diamond," she replied offhandedly while still inspecting the crystal in her hand. She missed Shemalla's concerned expression.

"What was your other daughter's stone?"

"Juila's was a deep red ruby color, but Alena had that one in her ceremonial box," she said as she looked up at Shemalla.

"Still, that color is uncommon," Shemalla spoke softly before continuing, "Are you sure you want to bring your children back here? Maybe you could just watch over them with their crystals."

"I've tried that already. I can't see anything at all. Are you saying there may be some danger in bringing them home?" Shemalla's idea that they remain in Tuala caused Amanda to despair that they might not be able to come back. An element of anxiety began to grow inside of her mind.

"That's one way to look at it."

She considered her following statement before deciding she should probably just get everything out into the open. "The stones given to your children mean they'll face great danger. The deeper the color, the more protection is offered. The black diamond is the darkest possible for birthstones.

"It could mean that they'll be seriously hurt or killed if you attempt to bring them across to Earth. It may also mean that if they're left in Tuala, they'll be in grave danger all of their lives. It's a hard decision you must make and one that I don't envy you."

Amanda sat in silence as she thought through all of the repercussions of Shemalla's news. Was she going to bring danger to her children? Was it Petre? What about the Elders? Or maybe some unknown force or person? This was an impossible situation. She'd have to think carefully about this before making any decisions for her children.

"Would it be possible to modify my mental block to allow me to think about this situation while I'm by myself but remember nothing when I'm with other people?"

"I think I could arrange that modification." She shut the crystal in Amanda's hand and folded her own hand over Amanda's.

Amanda felt the crystal heat further. The warmth traveled up her arm, across her shoulder, snaked up her neck, and into her skull. It was a weird sensation knowing things were being programmed in her brain. Even with her full consent, it seemed a strange thing to allow.

Shemalla released her hand and gently removed the crystal. She returned it to her pocket and sat on the couch opposite Amanda. Now that the block was in place, reinforced with a second block, she felt confident that her part in this adventure would be safe from discovery. She asked Amanda, "Do you want to talk about options for travel, or do you want to tell me more about your time in Tuala?"

"Well, I think the more you know about where I was and what I was doing would make your job easier for getting me closer to my daughters, right?"

"That's a fair assessment."

For the next couple of hours, Amanda recounted everything she could remember about her time in Tuala. Shemalla asked very few questions to allow Amanda's story to unfold naturally. Amanda remembered many details that she'd previously forgotten to mention to her parents.

The more she talked, the more miserable she felt about leaving her daughters behind. She should never have gone hiking with Bryon. What had possessed her to think she needed time away?

Now she would do anything to just be with her daughters every second of the day. She was willing to risk her life to go back to get them. Was she willing to risk their lives for them to be with her, though?

Shemalla let the silence draw out as Amanda thought through her situation. After several minutes Shemalla asked, "It seems you were happy in Tuala. Would you consider staying with your children there?"

"But I'd miss my parents. And they'd never get to know their grandchildren!"

"But remember you have family there as well. Your Aunt Barbara and your cousins, whom you've never even met, are all there. You could make a life with them, maybe even work for Captain Ahn or your Aunt Barbara with her orphaned children," Shemalla paused to assess Amanda's reaction, then offered. "Just think about it for a while, okay?"

After a few seconds of hesitation, Amanda nodded and replied, "I guess that wouldn't be too bad for me, but I can't help thinking my parents would feel as though they'd lost me again."

"I understand, but it's an option. I think we've covered a lot of territory tonight, and it's time I got you back to the hotel," Shemalla said into the quiet. She stood and waited for Amanda to join her.

Together they left the house. Amanda remained silent with the multitude of scenarios playing through her mind. She continued her reverie in the car until they arrived at the hotel.

"When will we meet again?" Amanda asked before she opened the car door.

"I think we could get together again tomorrow night if that works for you."

"Perfect. Give me a call when you're ready, and I'll borrow my parents' truck to come over."

"Okay, I'll see you tomorrow then," she said as Amanda left her car and walked into the hotel.

AFTER A SLEEPLESS NIGHT and a restless day, Amanda was anxious to get back together with Shemalla. More than anything, she wanted to have a plan in place. She had a terrible feeling that she needed to go soon, or trouble would come to either herself, Shemalla, or her children. Her parents attempted to comfort her, but her agitation wouldn't abate. Amanda almost cried in relief when Shemalla called and said she was ready for her to come over.

Back in Shemalla's living room, she found herself looking at several maps laid out on the wooden coffee table. Each map contained locations of ley lines, natural sites such as canyons or caves, man-made structures such as pyramids and ruins, and also known gates operated by the Elders.

Amanda was fascinated by the dozens of gates available on Earth for people to just wander through without ever knowing what their true nature allowed.

Shemalla explained how the ley lines played a significant role in allowing the gates to function. She pointed at each of the Elder operated gates and showed that their locations were where multiple ley lines intersected, which made them stronger and therefore easier to navigate.

Next, the natural sites proved just as interesting. Shemalla told Amanda that the ancient people always knew about sacred sites and usually marked them with hieroglyphics. She said that the deeper caves near the ley lines were the best gates but also the most treacherous.

Amanda was interested in the man-made structures regarding their ability to function as gates. Shemalla said they were similar to the caves containing hieroglyphics. The ancient people understood that some locations were more sacred than others. They knew that strange things had happened to some people, such as disappearances or reappearances.

These locations were then marked with unique buildings such as pyramids or stone circles. The larger the structure, the more important the site regarding the gate's strength.

Shemalla insisted if Amanda decided to go back to Tuala, she should probably consider a site close to the last known location of her daughters. Travel in Tuala wasn't very easy for someone visiting; it wasn't as though Amanda could readily access a telepod.

Before, she'd been fortunate to find people sympathetic to her cause. She might not be so lucky the next time. If she fell into the wrong crowd, she could find herself sold to the Elders for research.

Amanda shuddered at the thought. Her only objective

remained to be with her children again. She didn't give much thought to the semantics of getting there. She never realized just how blessed she'd been on her first journey into Tuala.

Shemalla moved most of the maps off of the table and said, "I think we should concentrate on getting you through one of these gates." She pointed to several locations on the map and said, "Do any of these places seem familiar to you? Or do you have any impressions of any of these sites?"

Amanda looked up at her quizzically.

Shemalla clarified her statement by saying, "Gates are a very personal matter. If you have a better feeling about one over another, you'd have a better chance of success with that one. Do you understand?"

"That makes an odd kind of sense," Amanda said with a grin. She bent over the map and seriously considered the multiple locations Shemalla selected. She spent a few minutes studying the topography and geography of each area. One site did seem to stand out to her, so she put her finger on it and said, "This one!"

Shemalla bent forward and read the name on the map where Amanda's finger was still resting and said out loud, "Campeche. That's a little further from the ley lines than I would like to see you arriving in Tuala, but if the site speaks to you, then that'll be our target."

"Is it possible to have a portable gate?"

Shemalla grinned, her gaze meeting Amanda's, but it was short-lived. "They actually do exist, but only the Elders can operate them."

Amanda's shoulders slumped. Her voice sounded dull and flat as she asked, "Aren't there any Elders who might be sympathetic to my cause?"

"None who are available in my limited range of influence." Shemalla didn't glance at Amanda again but busied herself gathering the maps and placing them in a neat pile.

Amanda flopped back into the couch, grimacing at the twinges of pain from her bones and muscles. "Is anything about this going to be easy?"

"Sure, getting to your gate will be a cinch."

"How do you figure that?" Amanda asked with confusion.

"Easy! I'm going to teleport you there!" She smiled at the stunned look on Amanda's face. She continued, "I told you that was one of my gifts."

"Yeah, but I didn't know you were able to transport anyone other than yourself." Amanda remembered her excitement for her first trip in the telepod with Bryon. She wasn't sure how she felt about not having any mechanical protection around her while being teleported.

The idea seemed slightly unsafe to her. Then she chuckled to herself and thought that both modes used the same type of movement from location to location, so it shouldn't really matter the means for getting there.

"It's just a little trick of mine. Now, let's get back to planning your journey."

SHEMALLA SAT across from Amanda and considered the last problem she knew Amanda would face in Tuala. She asked, "When do you get the cast off of your arm?"

Amanda looked startled by the question, glanced down at her left arm, and replied, "Not for another four to five weeks. Why?"

"The answer should be pretty obvious, Amanda. Just think about your time in Tuala. How many people did you encounter with a hard cast?" She raised one eyebrow as she looked smugly at Amanda while waiting for an answer.

"None, I guess. I never thought about it, really." Suddenly, the next obvious question came to mind. "Are you saying I won't be able to go back to Tuala until my arm heals? That's too long!"

"I may be able to help out a little with this problem," she said as she removed her birth crystal from around her neck and held the stone itself between her thumb and ring finger of her right hand. She slowly moved the stone the length of Amanda's arm, first along the bottom and then along the top.

"Now, I'm not a wise-woman by any means, but each person can access the elemental energy, known as elemy, in the earth and direct it to the cells of a person's body. The extra energy excites the cells to invigorated movement allowing for faster healing. If I were you, I'd schedule an appointment with the hospital here in town and have it x-rayed sometime in the next few days. In my opinion, it should be completely healed by then."

Tingling sensations coursed through Amanda's arm. She could almost imagine the cells racing through her body and repairing the damaged bone and tissue. She smiled at her fanciful thought and looked up at Shemalla when she asked, "Can anyone with a crystal do this?"

"I suppose so, but I tend to think that the lighter the crystal, the easier it is to accomplish," she said with a self-deprecating shrug.

Amanda thought this over and realized she didn't know the crystal color of any adults she had had contact with in Tuala. Now she was becoming intensely interested in finding out to satisfy her own curiosity. She lightly snorted as she realized she really was her father's daughter.

But she couldn't shake the ideas rolling through her brain. Were there any books detailing the stones, their uses, and the abilities which they could enhance? She finally asked, "Is there any documentation on the stones? I'd love to read up on them just for my own education."

"I'm sure the Elders have such things, and I believe the wise-women are taught the basics for each color range. Other than that, the crystals themselves teach each individual wearer what they're capable of—." She let the sentence drop off as she considered any other information she might know without realizing it was not common knowledge. Her expression turned thoughtful but cleared when Amanda spoke.

"What do you mean by the crystal teaching the wearer?"

"It's hard to explain, but it feels like an intuition that something is possible, so you give it a try. Sometimes the idea works, and sometimes it doesn't. That's how you discover its limitations.

"I sometimes wonder if the limitations change with the wearer's need and maybe maturity level. Can you imagine a little kid asking for the power to do something outrageous just because they wanted to without an actual urgent need? That could get pretty scary!"

Amanda chuckled at the thought. "Do you think I'd ever be able to get a crystal?"

"I've never heard of an adult crystal ceremony, especially not someone from Earth. Part of the problem is the limitation with which your mind was raised. You see, there's no physiological difference between someone from Earth and someone from Tuala.

"The difference is mental. We're taught that the mind has unlimited potential, and we know it. People from Earth are taught that the mind has definite limitations, and you believe it. It's a matter of knowing versus believing," she ended with a rush.

The whole concept rang true with Amanda. She had always felt that there was something more out there. She always wanted the ability to do extraordinary things with her mind, but she'd always been told it wasn't possible. And she believed the lie. "So what if I believe, as you do, that the mind is limitless? Would that increase my chances of being able to work well with a crystal?"

"I don't know. Maybe." She considered thoughtfully, her eyes narrowing as she appraised Amanda as though she were a test specimen. "Let me think about that idea for a while, and I'll get back to you!" Shemalla's eyes sparkled with suppressed excitement.

"I can't say anything about it just yet, but I'm thinking about trying an experiment. I sincerely hope you're successful because I'm really starting to like you!"

CHAPTER 28

Bryon was exhausted by the time he teleported back to his house. He felt clumsy as he performed the shutdown procedures for the telepod in the garage.

There was a grave danger of being lost during transit when too tired to visualize landing coordinates properly. If he hadn't been so anxious to get back to Alena, he would have just walked home from the station.

Alena opened the door to the garage with an expectant expression which fell as soon as she realized Bryon was exiting alone from the telepod. As hard as it was, she waited until he was inside the house before she asked, "What happened?"

"I went down and filed an official theft report for Kirma Shipping and Receiving," he said as he continued through the kitchen, grabbed a glass out of the cupboard, and automatically filled it with water from the sink.

"What are you talking about? I don't care about a stupid shipment for Kirma Shipping and Receiving! I want to know what happened with Jena!" Alena snapped out her frustration. She folded her arms across her body and tapped her foot as she glared at her husband with the expectation of being answered immediately.

"That's what I was talking about," Bryon confirmed after he swallowed several gulps of water.

"Bryon, you're not making any sense! What does the one thing have to do with the other?" Alena was almost to the point of a nervous breakdown, and she couldn't connect A to B.

"Let's go sit in the living room, and I'll tell you everything I think is going on," he said as he stretched out his arm across Alena's shoulders and steered her toward his chosen destination. He wasn't looking forward to this conversation, but he knew he was correct in his assumptions.

They sat beside one another on the living room couch. Bryon set his glass of water on the coffee table to free his hands. He reached over and took Alena's hands in each of his own as he began to recount all of the details of the evening. It hurt his heart to have to tell Alena his theory about Petre abducting their beautiful little girl, and Alena was crying silently by the time he completed the recounting of events.

"But why would Petre want to take Jena? I know he was asking around for Amanda as though she were his wife, but how would he know anything about Jena? It doesn't make any sense, Bryon." She shook her head in negation.

"I don't know how it happened, but I think Petre may have found out that Amanda was living with us. He must have put two and two together and figured out that Jena was Amanda's child. Of course, if he called Amanda his wife, then he would imagine her daughter would be his in his sick and twisted mind," Bryon reasoned.

"Can you think of any way that Petre would have put the two people together? Remember, he said his *wife's* name was Jesisca, and Amanda said the name of her fiancé's yacht was the Golden Jesisca. Petre must have found the yacht and sold it to an Elder.

That could be the reason why you found the vessel at the Old Soul Engineering Facility."

"I can't think of any way he'd know," Alena despaired. She placed her head into her hands to try to rack her brain for any clues. She dug her fingers into the hair on the sides of her head. Finally, a thought came to her mind, "Oh, Bryon, I might have done it!"

"What are you thinking?"

"I brought Jena with me to your office. I introduced her to Frasnia, and I told her that she was Amanda's daughter. I had adoption paperwork with me that I wanted you to sign, but Frasnia told me you were out of the office.

"You even called in at that exact moment, asking about the missing shipment for Beewa. You didn't have time to meet with me, and I was already late picking up the other kids from Tana's house. I left right away but not until Frasnia knew the truth about Jena. Do you think Frasnia is in on this as well?"

"Frasnia has worked for me for almost ten anons. I don't think she intentionally had any part in the abduction, but she may have inadvertently told someone who did!" Bryon stood with agitation.

He paced back and forth, thinking about all of his recent interactions with Frasnia. From what he could remember, which was not all that much, their conversations seemed to be centered around work. He couldn't think of any personal conversations that he might have had with Frasnia.

"It's too late right now, but I think you should talk to Frasnia tomorrow about this."

"So, where are we now?" Bryon asked. "Somehow, Petre found out Amanda was living with us. He also found out we had Jena. Petre knows that I don't like him, so, of course, he wouldn't come to see me about getting who he believes is his daughter. That's not his style anyway. He'd instead take what he can get rather than ask permission first.

"So now, he may have taken the shipment bound for Beewa. Otherwise, how would he have gotten the personal telepod out of the freighter? Do you think that maybe Ninan was in on this, too? He's been missing since Jumat along with the shipment."

"From what you've said about Ninan's work ethic, I'd have a hard time believing he had any part of this. Besides, the people at the market all know Ninan since he eats lunch there every day. Also, he just bought a house here. Didn't you say that Frasnia helped get his house furnished with her parents' extra furniture? Oh, Bryon, that's it!" She jumped up and grabbed Bryon by the arm in her excitement.

"What, Alena? What does his furniture have to do with Jena going missing?"

"Frasnia and Ninan are friends, right? Frasnia knew about Jena, and she must have told Ninan about her as well. She seemed pretty excited about the whole idea when I told her. We really need to talk to Frasnia!"

"Okay, let's table that idea right now since it's too late to talk to Frasnia. So, let's assume Ninan knew about Jena. How does that news get to Petre? And do you think Petre wants to be a father? He doesn't seem the type, but he has gone through a lot of trouble to get Jena away from us."

"I think you may be right, Bryon! The only good thing about this whole mess is I don't think Petre would hurt Jena if he thinks she's his own daughter. Although how Petre came to that conclusion is a mystery. Amanda told us the girls were the children of her fiancé, Nealan." She freed one of her hands to reach for a tissue to blow her nose. "What are our next steps?"

"If we can get a solid lead on the telepod beacons, we'll at least have some clues to continue the search. Meanwhile, the authorities plan to send out bulletins to every port, letting them know that Petre MacVeen is wanted for questioning. They're going to wait to file the missing shipment report for a couple of days to see if we can recover it along with the lost freighter telepod."

Alena reluctantly nodded, knowing her husband wanted to keep a perfect record for safety and security with the company. This missing shipment report could raise unwanted investigations around the shipping and receiving facility.

The investigators were known for taking serious advantage of businesses in trouble. She still had a nagging thought that the filed report might aid in discovering the stolen shipment and maybe Jena. Alena had to leave the decision up to Bryon since he'd have to face whatever consequences came from the record.

"Alena, I'm sure you've already done this, but I have to ask—" Bryon started hesitantly.

"What is it, Bryon? You know you can ask me anything."

"As Jena's mother, you are best able to check in on her through her birth crystal," he started and was shocked when Alena's complexion first turned white and then immediately bright red. He continued swiftly, "What have you seen? Any detail may help the authorities in their investigation."

Alena stammered and then suddenly covered her face again with her hands while shaking her head. "I'm so stupid, Bryon! I can't believe I'm so stupid! At her crystal ceremony, I saw she'd have a tumultuous life, and she'd need as much protection as we could give her.

"I made such a big deal for Amanda to put protective charms over both girls because of the visions I'd seen. I was so devastated by Amanda's death that I didn't even think that those charms would be ineffective once Amanda was gone, and I never remembered to place those charms back onto the girls. Now Jena is missing, and it's all my fault!

"Here you are now reminding me to use her crystal to locate her, and I never even thought about it! What kind of a wise-woman am I when I can't even think to look in on my own little girl to save her life?"

"You're not stupid, Alena! Stop saying that! You've been under a lot of stress. It's not your fault." He stroked her back to comfort her as he spoke, "You're not acting as a wise-woman right now but as a mother! The one thing has nothing whatsoever to do with the other. Use what you know to look for our daughter. Why don't you try to take a look right now, okay?"

Alena took a deep, steadying breath and began the mental process of centering her thoughts around Jena's black crystal. She felt an immediate connection, and her first worry for Jena's safety was alleviated. She excitedly spoke, "She's alive, Bryon!"

CHAPTER 29

"Good! That's really good, Alena. What else can you perceive?" His hands hovered near Alena, but he dared not touch her, lest she lose her tenuous connection with Jena.

While waiting for an answer, he reviewed the information she had inadvertently revealed about what she saw during the girls' crystal ceremony. He wished to ask her more about it, but he knew she was bound to secrecy. His thoughts were interrupted when Alena started speaking again.

"It's dark where she is," Alena began, "and I don't hear any sounds around her." She pursed her lips and clenched her eyes harder to focus her concentration more on the birth crystal. Finally, Alena shook her head, opened her eyes, and exhaled loudly. She looked directly at Bryon and said, "I'm not getting anything else. She appears to still be sleeping; she's alone and in the dark."

Bryon reassured her immediately by saying, "The important thing is that she's alive and well. You would've felt if she were in any distress, right? That's excellent news!" He nodded his head as though he had made a decision.

He slapped both hands on his knees and said, "I'm going to send a message to Frasnia that I'll be taking a few days off. You're going to need help with the children if you're going to try to keep monitoring Jena's whereabouts. Also, I think Frasnia should come over here first thing tomorrow morning to ask her questions about Ninan and anything she knows about Petre. I'll be right back." Bryon stood and strode swiftly from the room to send the message through his patil.

Alena watched him leave the room. As soon as he was out of sight, she silently broke down into uncontrollable sobs. Her shoulders slumped forward, and she tightly folded her arms across her stomach to help comfort the ache inside. She rocked herself back and forth and settled into her misery for a couple of minutes.

Trying to keep herself hopeful all afternoon and evening had finally dissolved into despair. She continued to castigate herself for thinking that her patient's well-being in the market was more important than keeping an eye on Jena. Then she failed Jena again by not thinking of checking for her through the birth crystal. Maybe she wasn't fit to be a wise-woman. She certainly didn't feel wise at the moment.

Bryon paused in the doorway at the sight of his beautiful wife in so much obvious pain. He wasn't sure he'd be able to help her heartache, but he did understand the feeling of guilt at Jena's loss. He felt exactly the same way since he was responsible for Amanda's death.

Crossing the room rapidly, Bryon decided to use the same tactic his wife had used on him for his guilt. With a stern voice, Bryon stated, "Stop whatever line of thinking you're having. It's not helping, and we all need for you to be thinking clearly right now."

He sat on the couch beside her and pulled her into a firm embrace to show her that they were in this together now. "Let's put together an action plan," he stated with authority.

Alena took a deep, shuddering breath and asked, "What can we do? What do you have in mind?"

"I think we should start writing a log of what you perceive through Jena's birth crystal," he began, rubbing his hand in small circles across her back. "We should also write down all of the things we need to do, like talk to Frasnia. We need to keep organized, so we don't miss any details. Do you have any ideas?"

"Maybe you should learn to use Jena's birth crystal to look in on her as well. Then we could take turns," she offered helpfully. "It can be very tiring, even dangerous, to monitor a birth crystal for extended periods of time, especially if it's far away. I won't be able to do it alone."

"Okay," Bryon said with some skepticism, "you know I've never been very good at it. I'm willing to try anything if it means we can get her back sooner. Give me another tutorial right now."

For the first time, Bryon was an active participant in receiving the necessary training. He had always had a half-hearted willingness to learn since Alena was already proficient in the practice. He had never felt the loss of the skill until this very moment when he needed it to work so desperately.

Together they spent the next several hours going over the details of centered concentration. Bryon worked hard at following all of Alena's instructions. He had always respected Alena's easy use of the crystals and again admired Amanda's skill when she learned it so readily.

He mistakenly began to think of it as a woman's talent. He struggled to access their own children's birth crystals when they were in the next room over at their house. He never even thought to attempt long-distance monitoring.

After at least the tenth attempt, Bryon gasped and then exclaimed, "I saw the darkness around Jena!" Of course, his excitement broke the connection, but Bryon didn't care. He had finally been successful in using the crystal.

Alena smiled at Bryon's exuberance over his success but admonished him for losing the connection. She said, "Get right back to where you left off."

Bryon returned Alena's grin and then frowned in concentration again with his eyes closed. With tight control over this tone, he spoke, "Okay, I'm back in the darkness. What should I do now?"

"Concentrate on the individual details. Bring each item into focus. Listen for any sounds. They won't sound like they do around you here; there's a quality to it which almost echoes," she spoke in a measured, almost hypnotic, monotone. She didn't want her instructions to distract Bryon from his experience. She needed him to be good at this, too.

"Oh!" Bryon yelled suddenly, and then his eyes flew open as he turned his head to lock his gaze with his wife's.

"What did you see, Bryon?"

"I just saw Petre leaning over Jena!" He jumped up from the couch and spoke over his shoulder as he rushed out of the room, "I'm going to call the authorities."

"Wait!" Alena ordered as her expression took on the look of someone using their inner sight. Her voice changed as the connection was established, "Let me see if Petre says anything to Jena which might help us figure out where they are!"

Bryon hurried back to the couch and waited expectantly beside his wife. He found himself holding his breath as she continued her silent observance. As the minutes dragged by, Bryon left to retrieve pen and paper to start documenting their discoveries to stay as systematic as possible.

The ability to do something—anything—helped to alleviate the nervous tension building inside him. Within a minute, he was back in the living room writing down the few things they had already learned that evening and noted the time beside each item.

Alena shook her head to clear her second vision. She said, "I think Petre is planning to move Jena somewhere else right now. I expanded the field of vision around Jena and noticed Petre had stacked several boxes near where she was sleeping. I think they're both in the personal telepod. Petre picked up Jena and cradled her in his arms as though he really did care about her.

"He could've just as easily left her to sleep undisturbed, but he picked her up, Bryon. Let me think for a moment about what he said to her." She rested her elbows on her knees and rubbed her temples with her index fingers as she tried to recount what she had just witnessed.

"Okay, I think he said, 'You're mine, Jena. Nobody will ever keep you away from me now that I have you.' There was something else, too," Alena paused to consider her words carefully.

"Let's see, 'Jesisca had no right to keep you from me. I told her I always wanted a daughter named Jena. I'm glad she used the name I picked for you. She should've stayed with me. I would've kept her alive. Don't worry, Jena. I'll make everyone pay who kept me from your mother. Once I get some money together, we can sail away in my water craft, and nobody'll ever keep us apart or tell us what to do.' Then he set Jena back down and walked out of the birth crystal's field of vision."

Bryon was busy scribbling down every word Alena spoke. He reviewed what he wrote and then mused out loud, "So you saw boxes stacked near Jena. They were in a personal telepod. Petre needs money to get away. It sounds to me like he's planning on selling the cargo that he probably stole from Ninan. With the money from the cargo, he'd be able to be lost for a long while.

"We're going to have to get a message out to any potential

mining equipment buyers to report if Petre approaches them. Maybe we could work with them to trap Petre and force him to give Jena back to us." Bryon tapped his pen against the notepad, furrowing his brow as he contemplated his plan.

Alena reached out and stilled the pen when she covered his hand with hers. She waited until he looked up at her to say, "That sounds too dangerous, Bryon. He doesn't want to give Jena up. He made that pretty clear. What if he were willing to let her die because he didn't want anyone to have her but himself?

"He's obviously sick, Bryon. You heard him say that the name Jena was his idea! We were all there when you suggested that name for her, Bryon. He's delusional! We can't risk it!" Alena's alarm continued to rise as new ideas raced through her mind.

Bryon dropped the pen and turned his hand over to clasp hers when he felt her trembling. He'd be her rock. With a gentle squeeze, he said, "It's okay, Alena. We'll think of something else. In the meantime, I'm calling the authorities and telling them what we've discovered. If Frasnia can locate the telepod beacon before he gets back onto his water craft, we could end this whole ordeal swiftly!

"We should also notify the port authorities to be on the lookout for his water craft. If he doesn't have it as a means of escape, we could corner him somewhere. Somehow, we need to convince Petre that he's not Jena's father because we know Amanda told us that Nealan is Jena's father."

This time, when Bryon stood, he really did leave the room. Alena heard his half of the conversation with the authorities. Her head ached abominably, and she pressed her middle fingers hard against her temples, hoping for a small measure of relief but too spent to use her healing gift on herself. Monitoring crystals was a tiring task under ordinary circumstances, and they'd been at it for most of the evening, far longer than recommended.

She was going to have to get some rest, but she hated the idea that she'd be comfortable, safe, and sound in her bed while her beautiful little girl was in the hands of a psychopath.

Shaking her head in resignation, she'd have to make peace with it until they could get her back safely. At least it appeared Petre was concerned about Jena's well-being. She'd take comfort in that small mercy even as a hot tear slid down her cheek.

CHAPTER 30

Amanda sat beside Shemalla in a booth with her parents seated across from them. Chris and Diane didn't have a clue as to what they'd discussed since Amanda'd been unable to answer any of their questions.

Shemalla wanted to alleviate their concerns by having dinner with them before she'd meet again that evening with Amanda to continue their plans. "We've made some serious progress," Shemalla stated simply.

"Is there anything *you* can share with us?" Chris asked a little bit petulantly.

Shemalla nodded. "I understand your frustration. I can imagine it's maddening to be excluded from your own child's problems. We have a small complication with Amanda's cast. She won't be able to travel until the cast is removed."

"But that'll be weeks," Diane interjected suddenly. She looked over at Amanda to see how this news affected her. She frowned upon seeing her daughter's unconcerned expression. "Am I missing something?" Diane asked in the silence as she looked at each person around the table.

"I suggest you take her to the hospital tomorrow to have it x-rayed. I think she may not need it anymore."

Diane inhaled sharply but held her tongue when Chris squeezed her hand. Chris stated flatly, "I have the distinct impression this's one of those things that we should just go along with and not question." He remembered Amanda telling them that on Tuala, the wise-women could heal people immediately, so it stood to reason that Shemalla did something similar for Amanda. Apparently, Tualans's powers weren't limited to just Tuala but could be performed on Earth as well.

Shemalla flicked one eyebrow up at the astute man across from her, nodding her appreciation. "I like the way you think, Chris. Anyway, once the cast is removed, I believe we'll make the transfer as soon as possible. I won't be able to control how long Amanda will be gone. I want both of you," she paused and looked purposely at both Chris and Diane, "to understand the possibility that Amanda might not be able to return to Earth. She could be gone forever."

Diane gasped and shook her head. "I'm not okay with that at all!"

Shemalla replied, "With all respect, Diane, it's not your decision."

Chris opened his mouth to protest when Amanda raised her right hand and instantly spoke up, "Mom, Dad, please stop! This is my decision. I know the hazards. I'm willing to take any risk to be with my children. Rest assured, I *will* do everything in my power to stay safe, but ultimately this is about *my* children. If I can bring them back, I will. If I can't get them back, I *will* choose to stay with them.

"Also, remember I have family members who live there as well. I'd love to get to know Aunt Barbara better and finally meet my cousins. Barla expressed an interest in getting to know me better, and she didn't even know I was her niece. Barla and Ahn will do everything they can to help me, which they've already proven, more so when they discover I'm actually a part of their family."

Diane wasn't going to let this go easily and cried, "This isn't fair, Amanda. We just got you back."

Chris patted Diane's hand on the table and looked at Amanda intently before saying, "We'll respect whatever decision you make, Amanda. You're grown up now and have a responsibility to your children. We understand that responsibility which is why your mother's having such a hard time with this. She wants to be with you, too."

"I know, Dad, and I hate the idea of leaving both of you as well. It just can't be helped," she said with a sigh of resignation.

The waitress came up to the table during the awkward silence. She efficiently took their meal orders and topped off their beverages. When they were private again, the conversation resumed.

"Like I was saying before, I think the transfer should happen this week, given that her cast gets removed," Shemalla continued as though she hadn't been interrupted.

Diane swallowed a sob. Chris looked apprehensively at his daughter and then at his wife. Amanda smiled tentatively at both of her parents, willing them to understand and accept her choice. Finally, Diane reluctantly asked, "What can we do to help you get ready?"

Amanda sighed, relieved that they were finally accepting her decision. She smiled at her parents and said, "I don't think I'll need much after I get this thing off." She raised her casted arm and scowled down at the offending appendage.

"It's funny to think, the two bones I've ever broken and both have been healed almost instantly. I guess I'll never get to go through the full dreadful experience of belabored Earth healing. I can't say that it makes me overly sad."Her attempt at levity made her parents smile. She hoped that meant they'd also make an effort to be more helpful than selfish.

"Okay," Chris said. "We'll get Amanda in for an x-ray tomorrow. What next?"

"Amanda and I will go over our final plans for the transfer during tonight's discussion. Understandably, she's very anxious to get started, so I think maybe within the next two to three days, both of you should write notes for Amanda to take with her. Include all of the details you want her to remember."

"I'm confused," Chris and Diane said in unison. Chris continued by saying, "Why won't she remember without our notes? That doesn't make sense."

"That's understandable," replied Shemalla as she then tried to explain, "The gates aren't designed for people from Earth. To help protect Tuala from unwanted interference, the gates are programmed to erase the memory of any Earthling when he or she passes through, in either direction.

"Written notes, carefully protected in sealable plastic, are the easiest way to 'remind' a person as to why they're in a new place. *If* Amanda comes back to Earth, she'll have to make sure to write an explanation for herself, or she may not even remember her own children."

"That sounds like a serious risk! But how will she remember to look for a note if her memory is erased?" Chris asked logically.

"That's been my concern as well, so I think we should include something which crinkles or is uncomfortable so Amanda will check it out before she gets very far into her journey."

"That sounds good in theory," Chris continued, "but can't we make arrangements for someone to meet with Amanda? She has several contacts in Tuala whom she could trust."

"I would like nothing better, but there's the problem of contact. I'm afraid to use my patil here on Earth to contact someone other than my family. I have no idea if my personal communications are being monitored. I'd hate to put Amanda's journey in jeopardy even before it has begun." She raised her hands in resignation and set them on the table in front of her. "Do any of you have any other ideas which might be helpful?"

Each person shook their head in negation. Silence continued. Again, the waitress brought them their food during this silence. She looked around the table, probably wondering what was happening with these people. They surely appeared strange, but they'd leave a good tip since they'd already been seated in her section for a long time.

The group ate their meal with very sparse conversation. Usually, the things spoken were small-talk, such as passing the salt or pepper. Nobody really had an appetite. They were just going through the motions. After the waitress had picked up their empty plates and left them their bill, they resumed their prior conversation.

Chris asked, "How long should our papers be for Amanda to take with her? I know Diane would probably like to write a book so Amanda will remember everything. Should we limit it to just a couple of pages each?"

"That sounds about right," Shemalla agreed and then added, "It's not as though her memory will be erased. Think of it more like her memories will be covered up temporarily. Once she is reminded of key ideas, she'll be able to pull her previous ideas back into her conscious thoughts. Without the reminding guidance of your letters, her mind will be like a blank slate in a new world."

She then turned to Diane and said, "You might want to write a separate note for your sister. I'm sure some things have happened in your life or with your family that you think she might be interested in knowing. It's kind of one-sided, but at least there'd be some contact made."

"That's an excellent idea," Diane said, excitement making her voice rise above their previous low tones. As if realizing her mistake, she glanced around the diner before she leaned forward and quietly added, "I'm sure my sister would want to know all the family business since she went missing. Can we include pictures as well?"

"No, we don't have pictures like they're done here on Earth. You could have a drawing made, but that'd be the only thing that could pass for normal. Tualans use a plasfilm technology similar to photo processing, but the medium is quite apparently different."

This new tidbit of information intrigued Chris. "I wish I could see samples of their technology. Of course, that's not the reason we're meeting with you. Sorry. So, will Amanda be able to communicate with you once she's made the transfer?"

"Unfortunately, no," Shemalla admitted. "Honestly, I don't really like the idea of sending her through the gate without any real notion as to what'll happen to her on the other side. We'll take precautions as many precautions as we can, but I can't negate all of Amanda's risks."

"Maybe Amanda could become friends with your family and contact you through your patil," Chris offered hopefully.

"I can't imagine how that would ever happen. My family doesn't live anywhere near where Amanda's going. They live up near what you know as Alaska," she replied sadly.

Chris looked deflated for a few minutes, then another idea occurred to him, "What if Amanda were to establish a real reason to contact you through Captain Ahn's or Bryon's patil?"

"It's possible, but again, the risk of monitored communications would make me leery of trying it."

"I can look into it once I'm there," Amanda interrupted before they debated the issue any further. "If Shemalla gives me her contact information, I can assess my situation and see if there'd ever be an opportunity for me to establish contact. If that works out, then Shemalla can let you know."

"As long as you don't take any unnecessary risks, Amanda, I'm okay with that," Shemalla offered.

Chris patted Diane's hand and said, "I don't think we're doing anything here but stalling for more time with Amanda. We should let them get on with their plans. Besides, we need to spend the next couple of days writing our notes for Amanda."

He grabbed the bill and slid out of the booth. He offered his hand to Diane and looked across the table at Shemalla, "I know you want to keep her safe. Please try to think of every contingency so she'll have the best chance for success."

"I promise I absolutely will." She watched them pay the bill at the front counter and then leave the diner. She turned back to face Amanda. "I can't help but feel sorry for their plight. I promise that even after you use the gate, I'll continue to work on finding a way to create a two-way communication for your broken family."

"Thanks." Amanda elbowed Shemalla gently and said cheerfully, "Let's get out of here so we can continue planning without fear of being overheard."

"Sounds good to me!"

CHAPTER 31

Petre finished stacking as many boxes into the personal telepod as he could fit and still access the door. He also left enough room to reach Jena, an odd new consideration in his simple, selfish life.

Bending over her basket, Petre stared at his little girl and wondered if she'd wake up anytime soon. He contemplated picking her up but decided against it until he was ready to leave.

He walked away and went outside. Looking around the location where he stashed the rest of the cargo, he ensured there was no sign of him being there for anyone else to discover. Satisfied with what he saw—or more to the point, what he didn't see—he turned around and entered the over-packed personal telepod.

Palming the entry closed, he turned on the interior lights at the control console—a glimmer of light filtered back to where Jena slept. Finally unable to resist, Petre bent over and gently picked her up and snuggled her into the crook of his arm.

He smiled as he continued to stare at her face when he said, "You're mine, Jena. Nobody'll ever keep you away from me now that I have you. I may have lost my other child because of that whore, Hashma, but I'm not going to lose you. Your mother didn't have any right to keep you from me.

"I told her I always wanted a daughter named Jena. I'm glad she used the name I picked for you. If Jesisca had stayed with me, she'd still be alive. Don't worry, Jena. I'll make everyone pay who kept you and your mother away from me. As soon as I get some money together, we can sail away in my water craft, and nobody'll ever keep us apart or tell us what to do."

He stroked the soft hair on her head and wished he had more time to hold her. He really needed to get going if he were to sell this inventory. Gently, Petre settled Jena back down into the laundry basket and returned to the telepod's operator seat.

After entering the start-up sequence, Petre visualized his next coordinates. He gripped the activation module and felt the utter nothingness as the telepod moved through a void and finally entered into the air above his secret staging location.

He wished he could just go to his water craft and sail away. Land made him uneasy. It just seemed too stable and rigid. He preferred the water's constant movement and shifting; its unpredictability matched his lifestyle and personality.

Petre maneuvered the telepod next to the small shack he often employed as a trading post and temporary dwelling. Once the telepod rested on the ground and turned off, he palmed the door open and went outside. He gathered branches from the ground and threw them onto the top of the telepod to disguise the general shape from any possible overhead searches.

He thought about moving the cargo out of the telepod but decided against it when he heard a rustling noise coming from the laundry basket. He raced over to where Jena lay and picked up the whole basket. Petre rushed into the shack and set her on the only table in the center of the room.

He raced back to the telepod and gathered all of the food and supplies from Ninan's house. Of course, this took two trips to accomplish, and he did drop a couple of things on the ground in his hurry.

Jena's full-fury crying spurred him to move faster, all thoughts of stealth erased from his mind. He shouldered the door open, so it banged against the back wall before springing back to close. He danced out of the door's range just as it banged shut.

Startled, Jena stopped crying long enough to draw a deeper breath and renew her wailing with increased vigor. She had slept for a very long time, and she was both wet and hungry. She wasn't going to be satisfied until she had a dry clout and was being held in the comfort of her mother's arm with a bottle of milk to meet her hungry need.

Of course, Petre didn't have any idea what to do, so he leaned over Jena and spoke reasonably to her, "It's okay, Jena, I'm here now." He was impressed when she did stop crying and actually looked at him.

What he didn't expect was when her face screwed up, and her crying began again, impossibly louder than ever. "Hey, hey, stop that, Jena!" Petre said in a booming voice that didn't even register with Jena or decrease the volume of her screams.

Petre braved the child's wrath and picked her up from the basket. The volume of her screams did go down, but then she arched her back, and her whole body went rigid as she protested further. Petre was desperate to make her stop crying, so he jiggled her up and down awkwardly.

He went over to the counter where he had put the food, grabbed a carrot, and said, "Jena, do you want a carrot?" She didn't even open her eyes to see what he was offering. She just continued her screaming.

Reasoning with her wasn't working; he put the tip of the carrot into her mouth and was rewarded with her lips clamping down on the offering. She sucked on it vigorously and then used her hand to swipe it away. Her crying resumed. "Hey now, that wasn't very nice," Petre said as he stared in disbelief at the carrot on the floor. "What do you want, Jena?"

Using one hand, he opened the bread bag and extracted a slice. He held it to her mouth and saw her mouth clamp shut on it immediately, the same as the carrot. While she didn't throw it on the floor, she also didn't try to eat it. She gummed it around her mouth while her tongue pushed it out of her mouth. She did stop crying, but little residual sobs kept disturbing her eating.

Petre looked at her closely and realized she was a mess. She had bubbling snot dripping out of her nose, and tears were making wet trails from the outside corners of her eyes, where they dripped into her hair. Her face sported angry red splotches, and she wasn't nearly as cute as she'd been when she slept peacefully.

She managed to smear soggy bread bits all over her face, hair, and clothes. He didn't know how that happened so fast. He was just relieved she stopped crying.

The piece of bread was gone, and Jena's face screwed up as if she were about to erupt again. Petre grabbed another slice of bread and handed it to her with alacrity. She grabbed it in both of her hands and tried to jam the whole thing in her mouth. Of course, she wasn't very coordinated, and pieces fell all over. She smashed slobbery globs of bread in between her fingers as she crumbled the bread to bits without getting much of it into her mouth. She didn't want bread. She was thirsty.

She was getting angry that her thirst wasn't being addressed. She started to get herself worked up to cry again when Petre handed her another slice of bread. Jena immediately threw it on the floor right next to the carrot.

"What do you want, Jena?" Petre almost screamed. His tone

startled Jena, and she looked up at him with her big blue eyes wide. Large tears formed, and she took a deep breath to cry again.

"Are you thirsty, Jena?" Petre tried to control his tone because it dawned on him that he scared Jena. He clumsily removed the lid from the milk jar and poured it into the plasfilm cup. He held it out to her, not realizing she'd never used a cup before. She didn't know what to do with it, so she grabbed it with both hands and promptly poured it all over herself.

"Ugh," screamed Petre, and he immediately moved her away from his body to minimize the mess on his shirt. "Why did you do that? That was stupid! What a mess," he continued as he looked for a place to set her down where he could take off her soggy, filthy clothes. He grabbed one of the towels out of the laundry basket and unfurled it on the floor.

Bending over, Petre laid Jena on the towel and began unsnapping her onesie. He sat her up and pulled it over her head without caring for her ears or nose. His rough treatment made her cry louder. Not knowing what to do with the wet garment, he balled it up and threw it toward the sink. He looked around for something to put on Jena when he realized he didn't have another outfit for her. He'd have to wrap her in a towel until he could clean and dry her onesie.

He took another towel out of the laundry basket and started to wrap her up when he realized that her clout was soaking wet as well. He laid her down on her back and unfastened her clout.

Hastily, he pulled the disgusting diaper off before he realized she'd had a runny bowel movement. The poo smeared all along the length of her leg. The cold air stimulated her to have a strong stream of urine which just happened to flow right onto Petre's pants, where he kneeled next to her.

"Ugh," Petre screamed again as he scooted backward to get away from the gross mess. He was utterly at a loss for what he should do now that his perfect little girl was a completely naked disaster on the floor.

How did this all go so wrong, so quickly?

He looked around at everything he was going to have to do. He needed to wash Jena, both of the towels since they were now wholly soiled, her clout and onesie, and his shirt and pants as well. Thankfully, he'd grabbed the entire stack of towels since it appeared they'd all be needed shortly.

CHAPTER 32

Leaving Jena to her own resources on the floor, Petre stood and selected another towel from the stack. He took it to the sink and wet it down. He took the sloppy, dripping towel back to Jena and started to smear the messy poo around.

If only Jena would stop wiggling around while he tried to do a thorough job of getting her clean, he might get this done faster. He swore under his breath as he attempted again to grab both of her legs again to pick up her bottom to get the nasty smear that mysteriously found its way up her back. He managed on his third attempt and groaned at the sight. "How could this have gotten so far?" Petre desperately asked while he struggled to finish the unsavory task.

Relief and satisfaction rushed through Petre when he finally cleaned Jena's disgusting messes. He moved her naked body to a clean towel on the floor next to him. He scooped up the soiled towels and dumped the whole lot into the sink.

He ran warm water into the basin and picked up each article, washing them as best he could. After wringing them out, he draped each damp item on any place which looked likely to assist in drying.

Jena's crying resumed. He turned around and stared at her with wonder at his naivety. "What in the world was I thinking to take you with me now? I have no idea how to take care of a baby. I'm going to have to figure something else out to keep my sanity!"

Petre poured another plasfilm cup of milk. He folded the towel around Jena and picked her up, where he held her in his left arm and offered her the milk cup. This time, he didn't let her control the cup but instead, he held it for her and brought it to her lips. He tipped it slightly so the milk could wet her lips.

As planned, she opened her mouth, and he poured a little milk in her mouth. Not really knowing what to do with the milk, she let it dribble down her throat and immediately started choking on it. Petre instantly sat her up and started thumping her on the back. The new position did help, but her throat was still irritated, so the coughing continued for a few anxious minutes.

Petre didn't have any clue what to do. She obviously wanted to drink, but she didn't know how to drink out of a cup. When her coughing subsided, he lifted the cup to her lips again. This time he kept her sitting up and only poured a couple of drops inside her mouth. He took the cup away, and she closed her mouth and swallowed.

It worked. Petre congratulated himself and would've pumped his fist in the air if his hands weren't both full.

Together, they continued this way of drinking until the whole cup was gone. Most of it had gone into Jena's stomach, but some of it had dribbled down her chin, onto her chest, and soaked into the once-fresh towel.

Petre calculated that he'd be in trouble if every meal took four towels and two outfits.

Jena's crying and eating had sufficiently worn her out, and her eyelids drooped. Petre was incredibly relieved when she finally settled into sleep once again.

Hastily exchanging her dirty towel for a clean one, he settled her back into the laundry basket. He sighed with relief when he finished washing the milk out of the last towel and wrung out the excess water.

He didn't know how he'd continue to do this alone. Plans still needed to be made to dispose of the stolen cargo, and he had rounds to make in his water craft. How would he do that if Jena required all of his attention all of the time?

Wearily, he draped the towel on the back of a chair and then dropped his drained body onto the sleeping platform next to the table. Within seconds, he slept.

FRASNIA KNOCKED on Bryon's front door before the sun was up the next day. She didn't even worry about whether or not she would wake up the family. She figured they probably didn't get much sleep anyway with Jena missing. Bryon would want an update on what she'd found with the telepod beacons.

She came prepared.

Bryon answered the door within a few seconds of her knocking. "Come in, Frasnia. Thanks for coming over so early." He gestured for her to precede him into the living room. "Sit here while I get Alena." He rushed from the living room toward the kitchen.

Moments later, Alena and Bryon entered the living room and sat on the couch across from Frasnia. Alena spoke first, "Frasnia, how good of a friend would you say you are with Ninan?"

That question was about the last thing Frasnia expected. She sat in stunned silence for a moment before she stammered, "I think he's a really nice man. I don't really know what you want me to say. What's going on? You don't think Ninan has something to do with Jena's disappearance, do you?" Her gaze darted from Alena to Bryon.

"That's just it," Bryon spoke up briskly, "we don't know what to think. We've been racking our brains trying to figure out if there's a connection between Jena's disappearance, Petre MacVeen, Ninan, and yourself."

"You think I had something to do with this?" Frasnia asked with incredulity. Simultaneously, her spine stiffened, her cheeks blazed red, and her fists clenched. "I'm more than a little hurt to believe you could think so unfavorably about me."

"Not directly, Frasnia," Alena corrected immediately. "I think you may have passed on some information, completely by accident —mind you—but we can't figure out any other way it could've happened."

Frasnia's eyebrows furrowed at Alena's cryptic comment. "How *what* could have happened? I think you guys need to start explaining things before I get even more upset!"

"Calm down, Frasnia. Nobody's blaming you for anything. We think you were used just like we were," Bryon began. He spent the next few minutes going over all the details they figured out the evening before. When Bryon told Frasnia their theory about Ninan and Petre knowing one another, Frasnia gasped. "What is it?" Bryon asked immediately.

"I did tell Ninan about you two adopting Jena!" She said with a gasp of shame at her indiscretion. "Oh, and on Jumat when Ninan took that shipment, he said he wanted to go early to get lunch at the Port of Cerid. Do you think he met up with Petre?

"Oh, my goodness, all of this is my fault! If I'd kept my big mouth shut about your business, then Jena would still be safe and sound at home with you! Oh, Bryon, I'll clear my things out of the office as soon as I leave here! I'm so sorry!"

"Stop, Frasnia! I won't hear of you doing any such thing," Bryon yelled impatiently at Frasnia. After taking a calming breath, he continued in a quieter voice, "We all have our part in this tragic story, and we can all find ways to blame ourselves. However, right now, we need to work together to figure out what happened to all three people who're currently missing. Let's start with the most obvious lead we have, shall we? What did you learn about the telepod beacons?"

"I didn't find anything out yesterday," she said with some desperation. "The beacon tracking system crashed. I contacted a technician, and he worked on it all afternoon. He assured me he'd have it functional before the start of business today. If you have your patil on, I can probably access the data from here."

She looked desperately from Alena to Bryon and added, "I'll do anything to help after what I've done. I'm so sorry. If anything happens to the precious little girl, I'll never forgive myself for my careless indiscretion."

Bryon led them to his home office and turned on his patil. He moved from the seat and gestured for Frasnia to sit and take over. Frasnia typed a few commands and logged on to the main screen, which hadn't worked the previous day. She entered her security codes and then navigated through several screens before she got to the beacon location plot map.

Usually, she needed to have a general idea of which map to pull up to find any given beacon signal. She scanned map after map for any signs of interest. One after another, she dismissed them until she got to the map containing the coastline of Ishal. She almost didn't believe her eyes and stared at it for a second longer before she cried out, "I've got it!"

Frasnia moved to the side as both Bryon and Alena crowded close to look at the screen. "Let me zoom in so we can have a more accurate location," she offered as she typed a few more commands. "One more time," she mumbled to herself and then said, "Okay, here it is. It's on the coastline of Ishal near the Lookout Tavern."

Bryon looked for a second longer and then took over the patil's keyboard. Frasnia swiftly moved out of the way as the screen filled with the face of a bored police official.

"Kirma Authorities, how can I direct your call?"

"Lead authority for the missing person named Jena Kesh."

"One moment, please." The receptionist didn't wait for a reply before switching the screen to a holding pattern. Within a few seconds, the screen blinked once, then twice before the face of a familiar authority filled the screen.

"Mr. Kesh, how can I help you today?"

"We've located the missing freighter telepod. It's on the coastline of Ishal near the Lookout Tavern. Can you please contact someone near there to investigate right away?"

"Sure thing, Mr. Kesh. I'll get right on it. Anything else?"

"That's all for now, thank you," Bryon replied and then terminated the connection.

Bryon turned to Frasnia and said, "Good job, Frasnia. I'm staying home today. Can you please continue searching for the personal telepod at the office? It doesn't look as though it's near the freighter."

Frasnia didn't take offense. "Oh, of course. I'm already late, and I know you want to be alone with your wife." She nodded and said, "When I find the other telepod, I'll let you know immediately. Also, I'll think about any and all conversations I've had with Ninan to see if I can remember anything else. Again, Bryon, I'm so sorry for getting you into this mess."

She stood and walked around the desk, stopping to touch Bryon on the arm. With effort, she lifted her gaze to meet his. "I wish I could do more. I promise I won't rest until I've found the other telepod." She didn't wait for a reply before running from the room.

The slamming front door let them know they were alone again.

CHAPTER 33

Amanda found herself rubbing her left arm again and consciously removed her hand. She looked up at Shemalla and smiled in embarrassment. "I still can't believe my arm's healed. The x-ray technician told us that the break looked as though it healed quite some time before the doctor came in and told him to keep his opinion to himself."

Shemalla just smiled back at her, yet her eyes looked distant. Finally, she said, "I wasn't really thinking about your arm right now. I'm trying to think of any other complication that might arise when I transport you to the gate in Mexico this morning. Having never been there myself, I'm not sure what to expect, but I'm trying to anticipate every possible contingency."

That was a sobering thought. But it didn't deter Amanda from her resolve—nothing would keep her away from her daughters. She'd gladly face a little discomfort if it meant reuniting with her girls.

Amanda looked down at her non-descript, Tualan-style carry sack. Shemalla gave her the bag when she first arrived. "What is this?" Amanda asked as she accepted it.

"It contains some provisions that you might find useful until you can get to Bryon's house in Kirma."

Amanda opened the top of the sack and peered in to see the contents. She saw clothing, simple travel food, and a water bottle. "Thank you, Shemalla. I have a few things I'd like to add as well."

"Just make sure whatever you take would pass as normal in Tuala. I don't want you to make any mistakes that might get you in trouble with the Elders."

Amanda nodded, although Shemalla's caution was unnecessary. "I'll be selective. I'm more anxious than anyone to succeed at this journey!"

"I guess you would be," she agreed half-heartedly.

"Is there something wrong, Shemalla? You aren't acting normal."

"I've been trying to decide if I should have you try something first," she responded cryptically.

"What is it?"

Shemalla didn't answer right away and finally must have decided something. Instead of answering, she reached up and removed her birth crystal from around her neck. She held the chain out to Amanda and said, "Hold the diamond in your hand."

More than a little confused, Amanda held out her hand and allowed Shemalla to drop the warm diamond into it. She closed her fingers over it automatically. "What are we doing?"

"I want you to experiment with something before you go," she paused for a few moments, raising her eyebrow as she stared at Amanda's hand, and then continued, "I want to see if you can use my crystal the same way I can use it."

"Oh," Amanda said as she realized just how important this experiment could prove to be. "What do I need to do?"

"Keep your hand closed and concentrate on the warmth you feel coming from the stone. Really focus and try to imagine the heat source inside the rock. Keep breathing normally," Shemalla instructed.

Amanda could feel Shemalla's intense scrutiny even with her eyes closed. Was she seeing any sign that something was changing? Amanda thought she felt a subtle change.

As if confirming her intuition, Shemalla instructed, "Now that you feel the core, imagine pushing the elemy outside of the stone and beyond your hand. Keep breathing."

Amanda desperately wanted this to work not only for herself but also for her guide. She imagined she actually could move the energy she felt. Suddenly it worked, and Amanda gasped and said, "The power jumped from my hand!"

"Good, Amanda, keep focusing your thoughts on the elemy. I want you to open your eyes and physically move that energy and set it into my outstretched hand," Shemalla followed her own instructions and put out her hand, palm up about a foot away from Amanda's hand containing the diamond.

She waited patiently for the feel of the familiar energy. When it touched her hand finally, she almost cried out herself. "That's enough, Amanda. You can let go of your focus now." She reached over to Amanda's hand and gently retrieved her necklace. She felt relief when she put it back around her neck and sensed its accustomed energy pulse into her chest as it rested against her skin. The crystal seemed the same as usual, which also relieved her.

Amanda sat beside Shemalla with a look of wonder on her face. "That was incredible, Shemalla. Do you think that was normal?"

"I don't think anything about you is normal, Amanda!" She replied with a chuckle to take any sting out of her words.

"But what did that prove?"

"Only that someone from Earth is capable of using the elemy that Tualans take for granted. It's a shame I don't have another diamond I could send with you as a talisman for the gate," Shemalla murmured, almost to herself.

"You mean to say that the birth crystals are a talisman?"

"Yes, didn't I say that before?" Shemalla asked with a frown of confusion.

"No! That's kind of an important detail, don't you think?" Amanda's expression mirrored Shemalla's, but anger tinged her tone.

"Sorry, I told you before that some things are so commonly known that it doesn't seem necessary to mention." Shemalla fidgeted with the fringe on the decorative couch pillow.

Amanda reached out and placed her hand over Shemalla's, her chilled hand warming at the contact. Amanda was instantly contrite. "I'm sorry, Shemalla, that wasn't fair of me to snap at you like that. You're doing everything you can to help me. I'm embarrassed at my outburst. I must be more nervous about what we're going to do than I thought! I'm not usually this touchy."

"It's okay, Amanda, I understand," she patted Amanda's hand comfortingly.

They sat in silence for a few moments before Amanda's expression suddenly brightened, and she asked hurriedly, "Do you think any diamond would work as a talisman?"

"As long as it's good quality, any diamond would do the job," she said. "Why, do you have one?"

"I have a two-carat diamond engagement ring back in my hotel room," she answered with a smile. "At least it'll be good for something!"

"I didn't know you were engaged," Shemalla said, slightly confused.

"I'm not—anymore." It still stung to admit it, but she straightened her spine and continued, "He got another girlfriend when he thought I was dead. Now he just thinks I'm crazy because I told him what happened to me. He even had the audacity to deny that the twins are his!" Anger rose inside her as she spoke, heating

Amanda's cheeks. Nealand wasn't worth the trouble. She'd use his engagement ring to get herself back to their children.

"Oh," Shemalla said when Amanda finished her tirade. "Let's go get your ring, and we can experiment with it to see if you can access its elemy. If you can, then this is the last puzzle piece that had me concerned about your journey's success."

CHAPTER 34

Screams filled his dreams, and he wished it would stop so he could relax back into his magnificent fantasy. Rolling over, Petre discovered the screams weren't part of his nightmare; they were coming from Jena on the table. He fell out of bed, scraping both knees, in his hurry to rush across the room.

He glanced up from the floor just in time to see Jena leaning against the side of the basket. Watching in horror, he saw almost in slow motion the hamper tip and Jena tumble out of the carrier, across the table, and over the edge. Petre made a mad leap from his knees to catch Jena before she hit the flooring.

With supernatural speed, Petre managed to rescue Jena from the fall but at the expense of his jarred back, bruised elbow, and the lump growing on his head when he hit the chair. Jena was not any happier with her sudden fall or rescue.

She continued to scream at the top of her lungs and was not content to be coddled by Petre. Not knowing what to do with her, he set her safely on the floor. Groaning with effort, he picked himself up from the rough wooden planks and went to pour a cup of milk for Jena.

Petre kneeled in front of the girl and set the cup against her open, screaming mouth. She paused in her cry to find out what was being offered. He took it as an invitation to pour a few drops of milk into her mouth. He was wrong. She used her tongue to push the milk out of her mouth, and she used her arm to swipe the cup out of Petre's hand. He watched in disbelief as the cup flew from his fingers and spilled the milk across the cabinets and onto the floor. He looked back at Jena as she began a fresh set of screams.

"What do you want?" he cried in exasperation. Of course, he didn't receive any reply from Jena, so he picked up the cup and returned it to the counter. His eyes fell on the crackers, and he grabbed one. Kneeling again in front of her, he said, "Jena, be a good girl and eat this cracker." He held it out to her and was surprised when she actually took it from his hand.

He watched as she used both her hands to crumble it into small pieces. One or two crumbs actually made it to her mouth, but most of it fell to the floor. She leaned forward and patted the crumbs on the flooring with the flat of her hand. With pieces stuck to her hand, she started to lift her palm to her mouth. When Petre realized she was going to eat the filthy crumbs, he reacted instantly. "NO," Petre yelled and swiped her hand from her face.

Startled, Jena began to cry again. Petre felt terrible for overreacting and picked her up and held her in his arms. He spoke to her calmly even though he had to talk louder than usual to be heard over her crying and said, "I'm sorry I startled you, Jena. You can't eat dirty things off of the ground. Here, let me get you a new cracker, okay?"

He rubbed her back, and his voice did seem to have a calming effect as her cries lessened to whimpers. He took small steps toward the kitchen counter and managed to pick up another cracker. He offered it to her, and she grabbed it from his hand. She immediately threw it on the floor. Great, now she probably associated crackers with him yelling at her.

"That's not nice, Jena. Don't throw food on the floor," he said and looked around for something else for her to eat. "Let me get you a piece of bread. You liked that last night." One-handed, he wrestled a piece of bread from the bag and brought it to Jena's mouth. She tried to take it from him, but he held on. He was learning.

She managed to rip sections off of both sides with each hand, but some of what Petre still held made it into her mouth. She happily gummed the bread into a disgusting mush. She spread it around her face, down her chin, across her chest, and even managed to get some in her hair. Petre smiled with relief that she was not only eating, but she was also no longer screaming. He sat in the chair and continued to feed Jena.

Petre realized he needed to change his original plans. He'd have to hire someone to care for Jena while finding buyers for his newest inventory. Suddenly he was glad he hadn't removed the boxes from the telepod. His ability to pack up and leave immediately was increased immensely.

Now he just had to gather up all of the things Jena had messed up the evening before. While she was happily nibbling on the bread crust, he collected the towels and clothing and threw them into the now-upright laundry basket.

With everything piled high in the laundry basket in one arm and Jena in the other arm, Petre struggled out the front door sideways. Jena started to squirm at being held too tightly. Petre realized he was squeezing her, so he relaxed his grasp and continued toward the telepod beside the shack. He needed to set the basket down to free a hand to palm open the telepod door, and some of the basket's contents spilled out.

"Really?" Petre cried in exasperation as he stared at the mess all around him. He awkwardly kneeled on the ground, picked up the towels, and deposited them back into the basket, not wanting to set Jena down.

He managed to open the door, grab the basket, and enter the telepod without further incident. Then he realized he didn't know where Jena would stay in the telepod now that she was awake. He dropped the laundry basket in the hole left where he had kept Jena on their previous trip.

With no other option available, Petre decided Jena would sit on his lap during the teleportation. As he maneuvered toward the operator console, he asked Jena, "Are you ready to go for a ride?"

He sat in the operator seat and settled Jena on his left knee, careful to keep her curious fingers furthest from the activation module. As soon as he shut the exterior door and began the activation procedures, Jena started slapping the metal panel in front of her.

Petre found it hard to concentrate on getting the sequence correct to start the telepod. Maybe he should find another place for Jena to sit until after they arrived at his water craft. Inspiration struck. Petre shifted Jena from his lap up to his shoulder. She faced the other direction now and became interested in the seat's headrest.

Petre used her distraction to complete the start-up. The telepod rose from the ground, and Petre had to close his eyes to visualize the coordinates of the uninhabited strip of land where he had left his water craft. It took him longer than usual, and with a little less clarity, with Jena bouncing her legs up and down on his lap and her knees jabbing him in the stomach. With as much confidence as he could muster, he placed his hand on the activation module, and they were gone.

As soon as they blinked into the air above the ground beside Petre's water craft, Petre lowered the telepod toward the sandy ground. Jena had been startled by the sudden blanking of her senses, her legs lost all of their strength, and she sat hard on his lap. As soon as she sat, all of her breakfast spewed out of her mouth and dripped down the front of Petre's shirt and pants.

"Eehw," Petre screamed even though he couldn't move to escape the smelly mess. His hand jerked on the manual override navigation stick, and they crashed onto the hardpacked sand.

Petre immediately grabbed Jena harder as they struck the ground, and he heard cargo falling in the back of the telepod. He took a steadying breath and finished the shutdown procedures faster than he ever had before. He smacked the button on the console to open the cargo door as he jumped up from his seat.

He thought he'd be able to get outside swiftly, but the shifting cargo obscured the path he had left to the door. The odor from the vomit was becoming too much for Petre. He turned around and hurled all over some of the cargo boxes.

Of course, the smell didn't improve with his addition. Gagging, he moved boxes out of his way with a foot and one hand to escape the noxious stench in the telepod. When he finally reached the door, he inhaled the fresh air outside.

He strode down the ramp and set Jena on the ground. Quickly pulling his shirt off over his head, he walked over to the water's edge and dunked his shirt in to rinse it out. He then used the sopping shirt to sponge off his neck, chest, and pants as best he could. Petre rinsed his shirt again and wrung it out.

When he turned around to head back to the telepod, he realized Jena wasn't where he left her. Immediately he searched the area near the telepod, broadening his search to include the beach, then the dock where he saw Jena reaching over the edge, lose her balance, and fall headfirst into the water.

It all happened so fast he could hardly believe what he was seeing. Not only did Jena tumble into the water, but he also felt sure he saw a dark shadow push her from behind.

CHAPTER 35

"Jena!" Petre screamed and raced in a straight line to where she dropped into the water. In his haste, he threw his shirt to the ground and charged through chest-deep grass growing in the sand along the beach. The abrasive grass ribbons grass cut through the exposed flesh of his arms and chest, but he didn't care. Jena hadn't resurfaced.

After what felt like an eternity, he ran into the water and slogged through several slippery steps before he dove where he last saw her. Through the murkiness made worse by his abrupt entry, he made out Jena's white body, where she started to float back up to the surface.

Petre grabbed her arm and hauled her up. As soon as her head resurfaced, Jena took a great lungful of air and started screaming. It was the best sound Petre had ever heard.

He hugged her to his chest and said, "Jena, you scared me to death. Don't you realize you could have drowned? Why did you wander away from me?" He held her at arm's length and looked her over to ensure she was indeed okay. Her breathing sounded good, her crying sounded healthy, and her life was safe once again.

How did everything happen so rapidly? Good grief, he almost watched his daughter die right before his eyes. He was mortified.

He wouldn't be able to take his eyes off of her as long as she was awake. Twice, today alone, she was almost seriously injured on his watch; three times if Petre included crashing the telepod. Petre glanced back at Jena, tilting his head as he scrutinized her more closely. Was there something about Jena that brought danger into both of their lives?

Only then did he notice her black-stoned birth crystal. Immediately, he felt a kinship with her since it matched the stone in his master deceptor ring. Did she inherit his special gift? If so, he'd personally train her in the art.

Jena's feet kicked against the lapping water's surface, breaking his reverie. A cold breeze wafted past him, causing his skin to prickle and all his arm hair to stand on end.

Petre wearily pushed through the water to go back to the telepod. He needed to get Jena into something dry, or she'd catch a cold. A sick child was about the last thing Petre wanted or needed. Hugging her close to his bare chest, he hoped he generated enough body heat to prevent the little girl from going into shock.

Just as he reached the telepod's cargo door, a gush of warm fluid ran down his side, soaking into his already wet pants. All Petre could do at this point was laugh at how angry he would've been before Jena almost drowned.

Now, he was glad she was alive to even make a mess on him. Besides, he was already soaked through and through and needed to change his clothes once he got back on his water craft.

Petre hugged her tighter to himself as he entered the telepod. He reached over several fallen boxes to grab the blanket basket. With a dry towel wrapped around Jena, they crossed the beach and walked down the dock where his water craft was secured.

Finally allowing himself to relax, Petre stepped onto the water craft, looked down into the big blue eyes staring back at him, and said, "Welcome home, Jena." He hurried below deck to get Jena out of the wind.

Setting her on the floor, he shut the door behind him, so Jena had nowhere to go in the room. He was promptly learning his lessons that Jena was mobile and could get into trouble in mere seconds.

Feeling secure for the first time, Petre rummaged through his clothes pile until he found a new shirt and pants in which to change. He unbuttoned his pants but noticed Jena watching him from where she sat on the floor.

Suddenly mindful of his young audience, he took his dry clothes into the bathroom. He struggled to remove his wet shoes, socks, and pants in the small space with the door closed. He finally ended up sitting on the toilet to strip off his pants inside out. He was panting and cursing at the time and effort it took.

Petre grabbed a washcloth from the cupboard beside the sink to clean up the urine on his skin before donning the fresh clothes. Using some of the purloined soap from *The Golden Jesisca* he lathered up the washcloth and gave himself a quick sponge bath. After rinsing a couple of times, Petre felt clean enough to dress.

The silence inside the main cabin struck him as odd. What had Jena been up to while he was in the bathroom? Panicked, he flung the door open to investigate. As the door swung open, he felt a bit of resistance and heard a small thud just before Jena screamed. He stepped through the narrow opening and looked on the floor behind the door. Jena was lying on her back with bloody fingers balled up in her mouth.

"What happened, Jena?" Petre asked as he scooped her up from the floor. He noticed the tops of her fingers were all scraped up, and then he looked at her face and saw a lump forming on her forehead. She must have been crawling behind the door when he opened it.

The bottom of the door scraped her knuckles just before it

struck her head, knocking her over onto her back. Petre just injured his daughter. He felt sick.

"This is awful," Petre cried to nobody in particular. "I can't seem to get anything right with you, Jena."

Still holding her, he returned to the washroom and retrieved the wet washcloth. He gently dabbed the blood from her scraped knuckles. He rinsed the cloth out with cold water and then held the cool fabric to the lump forming on her forehead.

With light streaming down through the bathroom skylight, Petre looked deeply into her eyes. For the second time, she stared up at him during his gentle ministrations, and he realized her eyes were the exact unusual shade of blue as his own. If he needed any further confirmation that Jena was his daughter, he certainly had it now.

Petre realized he couldn't do anything until Jena slept, but he itched to get going. Now that he was on his water craft with all of his provisions, he concentrated on making a cup of warm foxl broth and laced it lightly with *epeny*.

He picked up the liquid-filled cup and held it to Jena's mouth. "You need to drink this, Jena," he encouraged by tipping the liquid into her mouth. She automatically swallowed, and, liking the new flavor, she leaned forward for more. Little by little, Petre fed her the drugged broth and sighed with relief when she finally drooped heavily in his arm.

Learning from past experience, he looked around for the lowest spot inside the cabin for her to sleep. Petre pulled a bottom drawer out from his chest of drawers. He removed several hand-fuls of clothes and unceremoniously dumped them onto the floor.

He nestled her into the open drawer with as much gentleness as he could and used a clean towel to cover her. He tucked the edges around her still form for warmth and hoped it would be enough.

Tiptoeing as quietly as possible, Petre left the cabin, latching the door behind him to keep Jena safely on board. He returned to shore to transfer the stock boxes onto his water craft.

Every several trips, Petre checked in on Jena. He cracked open the cabin door and peered inside. She slept peacefully and hadn't moved from where he settled her. He closed the door with a relieved sigh and resumed transferring the last few loads into the water craft's cargo hold.

When Petre grabbed the last box from the telepod, he wearily exited the cargo ramp and palmed the door shut. He set the box down and made a half-hearted attempt to gather nearby branches around the clearing to throw them on the telepod's top and sides.

He considered leaving the key with the telepod and then reconsidered that he may come back at some point and want to use the telepod. Petre picked up the final box with a grunt and trudged across the sand, over the dock, and finally onto his water craft.

He pulled the rope tying his water craft to the dock with one hand. He needed to get far away from the telepod as soon as possible. Concentrating on the ship's navigation system, he set a fast course across the bay to make it to the calm, open ocean water. He mentally set his newly purchased anti-collision system so he wouldn't have to worry about staying awake to navigate the waters.

The idea of making another trip into the cargo hold for just one box seemed like too much effort. Instead, he brought this last box into the main cabin with himself. Petre was so tired; he imagined he could sleep for a week. He carefully opened the cabin door, making sure Jena wasn't behind it, and clumsily dropped the box on the floor beside the door. He winced as the carton fell over onto its side with a loud thud.

He closed the door behind him, automatically looked over to ensure Jena still comfortably slept, and then took the remaining few steps to his sleeping platform. Petre dropped onto his back on the soft platform. He didn't even have the energy to cover himself up before he, too, was fast asleep.

CHAPTER 36

Amanda rubbed her moist palms against her pant legs. Shemalla declared their readiness to go. Every contingency was covered, they hoped. Shemalla praised Amanda's elemy skills progress using her diamond ring. Amanda stared down on her left hand and once again thanked Neal for the means of a safe journey to get back to their children.

Sitting on Shemalla's couch, Amanda once again patted her pants pocket to reassure herself that the packet of family papers stayed securely in place. She checked the top tie on the carry sack on the floor between her feet to ensure the contents couldn't spill out.

Shemalla entered the room and narrowed her eyes at each nervous motion Amanda performed. Clearing her throat, she said, "I totally understand your concerns. This trip has dire consequences if I fail. Amanda, I could be putting you in grave danger, possibly even death, if you're unsuccessful in passing through the gate. Are you still certain you want to go through with this?"

Amanda soaked in Shemalla's blatant explanation of her proposed trip. Rather than respond immediately, she paused to consider her options. She didn't have any. Each minute she delayed, she risked the possibility of her children moving or the time shifting farther than she was willing to accept.

She had already lost enough time with her children.

Her gaze flicked up to meet Shemalla's, and she nodded. "Yes. I understand the risks, and I'm ready." Amanda saw something flicker across Shemalla's expression. "Is there something you haven't told me?"

Shemalla pursed her lips before she grinned. "You're very perceptive. There is something, but I'd prefer to wait to tell you the last piece of the puzzle when we're at the gate. As much as I trust you, there's one piece of knowledge regarding the gates that can't be shared with a resident who remains living on Earth."

"That's fair." Amanda trusted Shemalla not to steer her wrong. She also didn't want to compromise Shemalla's standing here on Earth; she'd play by Shemalla's rules.

"Are you ready to go now?" Shemalla asked, infusing her voice with confidence.

"As ready as I'll ever be," Amanda replied with a weak smile plastered to her lips. Her stomach churned, making her wish she'd eaten a lighter breakfast.

"Okay, let me tell you what to expect from the first part of our journey," Shemalla spoke slowly. "I know I've already told you before, but I want it fresh in your mind, so you don't create a ripple in our transfer with your fear."

Amanda nodded solemnly. Excitement and fear of teleporting without a telepod warred for dominance of her thoughts. "You know, I always wondered if this type of travel were possible after watching science fiction shows on TV; now I'm going to experience it first-hand."

My dad would be thrilled to do this. Her speech merely delayed the inevitable. She looked up at Shemalla and said, "Go ahead, I'm ready to listen."

"We're going to drive out to the hills. Once we get there, we'll have to hike until we get to a particular cave I know. It has the type of hieroglyphics indicating a special status to the ancients.

"From that location, I'll have the most earth energy to be able to translate both of us to the gate at Campeche. You'll have to keep your mind clear of fear or confusion during the translation, no matter what happens. I'll need all of my concentration to ensure we both get there alive. Do you understand?"

"That sounds pretty straightforward to me." Straightforward and almost unbelievable. Her throat went dry just imagining it. How would she feel in the middle of it all?

Shemalla plastered a smile on her lips and clapped her hands with nervous energy. "Okay then, pick up your bag, and let's get going."

They silently went out to the car. Amanda woodenly sat in the passenger seat with her bag perched on her lap. She fastened her seatbelt and stared straight ahead out the windshield.

Should I go through with this? Bryon and Alena will be good parents to the girls. Really? What am I thinking? I'm their mother, and they need to be with me. I'm going to do this. I have to do this.

The car ride lasted only about twenty minutes. Shemalla turned off the engine and said, "There's the trail over there." She pointed out Amanda's window to the clearly marked trailhead.

Amanda opened her door, put both her arms through the drawstring ropes, and slung her carry sack onto her back. It was a little awkward, but she didn't have to worry about dropping her bag if she lost her balance and fell. Hiking had never been her forte.

Shemalla took the lead on the trail. "I hope you don't mind the brisk pace. I want you to have as early a start as possible when you finally get to Tuala," she said, glancing over her shoulder as if making sure Amanda remained close behind her.

She continued along the path until they came upon the cave.

She carefully walked into the cavern's dim interior and followed the left-hand wall until she reached the back of the cave.

Amanda paused at the opening giving her eyes time to adjust to the interior dimness. She took a few quick steps to catch up when she noticed Shemalla was still moving away from the entrance. Only a few more moments passed before she stopped beside Shemalla at the cave's rear wall.

"Do you feel it, Amanda?" Shemalla whispered.

"It's not as cold as I thought it'd be in here. The air almost feels charged with electricity. Is that what you mean?"

"Yes. That's an excellent sign for our success."

She focused on calming her nerves. This was the point of the journey where she'd have to stay relaxed and centered so she wouldn't interfere with Shemalla's concentration. This had to work. She couldn't wait to take a flight to Mexico; it had to be now or never.

Shemalla drew Amanda close until she was hugging her. Amanda put her arms around Shemalla's waist.

Shemalla whispered in Amanda's ear, "I know I should make the transfer swiftly, but I want to be careful that I'm clear on my coordinates before I initiate the process. Keep taking calming breaths. I'm going to begin the visualization of our destination. It might take me a few minutes to gather the elemy needed for both of us to go, so don't worry. Okay?"

Could Shemalla hear Amanda's heart hammering away as if trying to escape the confines of her ribcage? Drawing in a shaky breath, she said, "I'm okay. Do whatever you need to do. I'll wait."

"Oh, wow. The elemy almost seemed to leap up out of the ground to surround us."

Shemalla spoke so low Amanda almost missed it. Amanda imagined Shemalla using that elemy to center around the bright, clear birth crystal nestled on her chest right beside Amanda's head. The shock of it caused Amanda to draw in a sharp breath

Shemalla said, "It's time, Amanda. Remember to concentrate solely on holding onto me. Keep any fear away from your thoughts. We might take a few seconds in the void before we arrive at our destination: this is normal. Ready?"

Amanda nodded and whispered, "Yes." Tightening her hold on Shemalla, Amanda clenched her eyes and reveled in the all-embracing elemental energy surrounding them. She maintained her focus through the void even as the seconds passed by slowly. Suddenly they arrived at their destination, surprised by the sun's brightness after the dimness of the cave.

Letting go of Amanda, Shemalla stepped back and smiled at their success. "I wish I could accompany you through the gate, but I'm sure that my presence in Tuala would be noted by an Elder and reported back to Elder Vargen. I wouldn't have any way to keep my participation a secret from the Elder, and that would jeopardize your opportunity to reunite with your daughters.

"We only have a few minutes left for me to instruct you with the final procedures before I have to return to the cave. Already, I can feel the excess energy melting back into the earth. Let's get to the gate, Amanda," she said suddenly, startling Amanda out of her amazed reverie.

"Right," Amanda replied automatically. "That was miraculous, Shemalla. Does it always feel that way?"

"No," she said and paused to consider her reply. "The extra energy from the multiple ley lines gave it a touch of primal excitement not typically felt." She looked around their new setting.

"There's the ruin that contains the gate," she said as she pointed with her finger. She headed toward it; obviously, confident Amanda would follow her lead.

They walked up to the structure and climbed the giant steps. Shemalla told her they were looking for the opening on one of the sides, which they found when they rounded the corner. They both paused at the entry to see what was inside. Looking up, Amanda saw bats hanging upside down in the darkened interior.

Shemalla took out a flashlight and shined it around the opening. Amanda followed Shemalla as they took two steps through the entrance, turned to the right, and followed a narrow corridor for about fifteen paces. They turned left at the end of the first passageway and found an area one step lower than everywhere else.

Shemalla shined her flashlight on the wall about chest height and saw the symbol she wanted, a swirling circle, indicating the gate. She sighed.

"See this swirling circle design?" Glancing back toward Amanda, Shemalla waited for a confirming nod.

"Yes, does that mean this's the gate?" If Amanda thought she was nervous before, it paled in comparison to the reality of what she was about to do. She was willingly leaving Earth—to go to an alternate dimension. This trip was absolutely insane, yet, she wasn't about to back down.

Not now.

"It does. When you're ready to come home, make sure any location you pick to return to Earth has this symbol. Otherwise, you can't guarantee that the gate will return you here," she cautioned.

"Okay, I have the map we made of potential gates still in my carry sack." Amanda unconsciously lifted one hand to touch the strap of her makeshift backpack, and the other patted the notes in her pants pocket. Her fingers trembled. Somehow, this leg of the journey was even scarier since she would be going alone.

"Why don't you get that map out right now and write a notation on it, so you'll still remember it after you've passed through," Shemalla offered.

"Good idea," Amanda said as she shrugged her arms out of the straps for her carry sack. Maybe she was glad for the excuse to delay the inevitable. She dug her hand through until she felt the map and again for a pencil.

She kneeled on the ground, drew the symbol, and wrote, *Make sure the gate contains this symbol before trying to go through.*

"While you have that out, write down the phrase 'Outside Ascension.' That's the phrase you'll have to say to get back. Say nothing more and nothing less if you want to arrive on Earth successfully."

Amanda froze, her head tilted up to see Shemalla.

CHAPTER 37

Shemalla instructed, "Since you're traveling with a proper talisman and key phrase, you should enter into Tuala on this same date or maybe a couple of days earlier. It won't be like when you came back to Earth, and you had lost months. Preparation will make it easier."

Amanda nodded agreement, fervently hoping this would be true, and wrote the new instructions next to her other notation. She had wondered about the time change. She wouldn't lose any more precious time with her children.

Satisfied, she refolded the map and returned both items to the sack. As she stood, she swung the bag around onto her back and adjusted the straps until they were moderately comfortable again.

"You aren't supposed to know how to get into Tuala, and I didn't want to tell you the phrase for entering Tuala through the gate until after you finished writing. Once you go through, you won't have access to the memory of the words anymore, leaving Tualans 'safe' from further 'invasions' as they are termed. This is the only way I can justify breaking the rules by helping you,"

Shemalla looked at her with a pleading expression. "I hope you don't mind my saying this."

"I totally understand your position, Shemalla." Amanda touched Shemalla's arm to add sincerity to her words. "You've done more than I ever expected. Don't worry about trying to keep your people safe; it's understandable."

Shemalla nodded and then continued her final instructions, "Once you step down to the gate, clear your mind at once. With your mind, focus the energy you feel from the gate and place it into your diamond ring. Then say the words 'Inside Ascension.'

"The transfer should be almost immediate. You won't have to worry about coordinates because the gate is already set to open and close at this same location. This building, however, will not be on the other side."

Amanda immediately repeated the instructions aloud to fix them firmly in her mind. She nodded and asked, "Is there anything else I need to know?"

"Can you feel the energy from the gate from where you are?"

She took a moment to assess the sensations around her before she replied, "I can."

"Good, start to gather the elemy before you step down in there. It can happen fast, and I want you as prepared as possible," she instructed.

Amanda's heart raced, and she stared at the innocuous space that would change her whole life. She drew in a ragged breath, readying her mind to follow Shemalla's instructions. More accessible than she imagined, she processed the gate's energy field.

Shemalla moved to back away. "Don't step in there until I get clear. I don't want to be accidentally caught in the transfer. Are you ready?" Shemalla asked once she reached the corner.

"I am."

"Go ahead and step down. Remember to say 'Inside Ascension'

as soon as both feet touch the ground. Concentrate on the elemy!" Shemalla was yelling from around the corner now.

Amanda inhaled deeply, focused the gate's energy into her ring, and first lowered her left foot down the ten inches. As soon as her right foot hit the ground, she cried out, "Inside Ascension!" Bright light filled the dark cavern, but everything surrounding Amanda turned black.

Frasnia rubbed her eyes again. She had never stared at her patil screen for so long in her life. True to her self-imposed promise, she didn't take a break from searching for the missing personal telepod since arriving at work more than five hours before.

While she may have been getting frustrated, she wasn't giving up hope. Unless the telepod crashed into the ocean and sunk more than five thousand feet, nothing would keep the beacon from staying operational.

Starting with the areas nearest to Kirma, Frasnia loaded one map after another and scanned each for the unique beacon code for telepod number thirteen. Each time she opened a new map, it seemed to take longer and longer to load.

She couldn't worry that the system would crash again before making the final identification. She widened her search to the next nearest set of maps. Did she miss the code on any of the previous maps?

Now that she doubted her ability to maintain her usual standards of perfection, it was easier to lose hope. More than once, she wished the authorities could help in this aspect of the search, but the company's proprietary system made that impossible.

Realizing she was more prone to miss the code than to see it, she closed her dry and scratchy eyes and rubbed her aching temples with her index fingers. She couldn't shake the feeling of being responsible for her part in talking about Bryon's personal business with Ninan.

Tears formed in her eyes, burning against the dryness. "I will not start crying," she said out loud, startling herself out of her self-pity. She wiped the moisture with angry swipes of the backs of her hands. After wiping the wetness onto her pants, she resumed scanning for the missing telepod.

Only moments after searching again, her screen blanked out, and the patil registered an incoming call. More than a little bit frustrated, Frasnia answered the call with less than her typical good cheer, "Kirma Shipping and Receiving. What do you want?" she barked out the question.

Immediately realizing how unprofessional she sounded, she was instantly sorry she hadn't taken a second to compose herself before answering the call.

Too late now.

Trying to make up for her rude reception, she said, "I'm sorry. How may I help you?"

"I'm looking for someone named Frasnia. I was told she'd be at this code," the female voice inquired politely.

"This is Frasnia," she replied. "May I ask your name, please?"

"My name is Copa. I'm the wise-woman for the district of Desio. I have a patient who's been insisting that you be reached immediately."

With piqued interest, Frasnia smiled and asked, "And who might your patient be, Copa?"

"His name is Ninan. Do you know anybody by that name?"

"Ninan!" She screeched at Copa through the patil. "Let me talk to him immediately!"

"One moment, please. He needs to be moved carefully because of his head injury," she said as she stepped out of the patil's view.

Shuffling sounds and a couple of grunts came from the patil before she saw the bruised and bloodied face of her friend and coworker. Frasnia gasped, and her hand flew to cover her mouth at how horrible Ninan looked.

How could Ninan even be conscious, let alone talking with the colossal lump protruding out from the side of his head? She looked past the dried blood on the side of his face and caked in his hair and spoke the first thing that came to mind, "What happened to you, Ninan?"

"The best I can remember," Ninan began with some effort, "was when I picked up the shipment in Cerid. I went to lunch with my friend, Fordin, and then returned to the shipping yard to take the cargo to Beewa.

"When I was back on the freighter, I thought I heard footsteps behind me, and when I went to turn around, I got bashed in the head. I didn't see who hit me, but whoever it was, they tied my hands and feet and dumped me out in the middle of nowhere outside of Desio."

"Ninan, that's terrible! How come that wise-woman hasn't looked to your injury yet?" Frasnia couldn't keep the tone of disgust for lack of professionalism out of her voice. She knew people could die from injuries not even as severe as Ninan's looked.

"Don't blame her, Frasnia. I refused any help until I could talk to you. She said her healing would put me to sleep for several days, and I couldn't wait that long. I needed to talk to you first."

With a pained expression, he continued with, "The shipment, Frasnia. I'm afraid it was stolen. I'm so sorry. I'm pretty sure Bryon will fire me now, and I'd completely understand. Do you think you can track the locator beacon? I'm hoping the cargo can still be salvaged!"

"Don't worry, Ninan, we've already located the freighter tele-pod. This morning, we notified the authorities, and they're sending troops out to investigate. When you didn't show up for work yesterday, we knew something went wrong."

"Yesterday?" Ninan asked plaintively. "How long have I been gone?"

"You went to make that delivery five days ago. We've been very anxious. At least one missing person has been found today!" Frasnia exclaimed with a little bit of satisfaction.

"One person?" Ninan repeated. "Who else is missing?"

CHAPTER 38

Frasnia said, "Bryon's newly adopted daughter, Jena, was abducted yesterday. We think Petre MacVeen took her. The personal telepod from your freighter was seen leaving your house yesterday.

"At first, we thought you might have had some involvement, but when they investigated the house, they found somebody had been broken into it. We still aren't sure why Petre would want to take Jena, but I'm certain we'll find out soon. I've spent all day searching for the missing personal 'pod, but so far, I've come up empty-handed."

"Petre MacVeen," Ninan said thoughtfully, "I seem to recall something about him." He squinted his eyes as if he tried to remember something important.

He shook his head slowly to reduce the pain from the lump and said, "Ow! I can't remember right now." His hand covered one of his eyes to decrease the pain shooting through his eye socket.

Suddenly the patil was turned to frame Copa's face again, and she said, "I really must insist on treating Ninan now. He's in a lot of pain, and I can see he's getting confused."

"I'm sorry for keeping him so long. It's just he's a vital part of our investigation of an abducted six-mesan-old girl. If he should remember anything about Jena, please contact me right away, okay?" Frasnia spoke hurriedly.

"If you need to contact me, feel free to use my code through the patil. I'll obviously be busy for the next several hours while I treat Ninan. I'll give you an update once he's resting comfortably. I just hope I'm not too late," she said with a sorrowful shake of her head.

"He was injured several days ago, and this should've been treated immediately. There's no telling how much permanent damage has been done with all the swelling in his brain."

"Oh, I'll let you get back to it then," Frasnia replied with a bit of fear in her voice. "Goodbye, Copa." Frasnia promptly disconnected before Copa could scare her anymore with her dire prognosis. She closed her eyes and silently prayed that Ninan would make a full recovery.

While the conversation with Ninan was fresh in her memory, Frasnia contacted Bryon on his home patil. After a few anxious moments, Bryon connected the call, and his face filled the patil's screen.

"Did you find the 'pod?" Bryon blurted as his first statement of greeting.

"Sorry, Bryon, not yet," Frasnia replied with a grimace. "I have other news about Ninan, however. He just called from Desio, where he's being treated by their local wise-woman named Copa.

"He suffered severe head trauma to the point where Copa's afraid he might not have a full recovery. From what he told me, he was inside the freighter at the shipping yard when his attacker blitzed him on the head; he never saw it coming."

"Did you happen to ask him about Petre?"

"I did mention Petre, but he couldn't remember. He said he ate lunch with someone named Fordin. I guess I was wrong when I said I thought he would meet with Petre at lunch. I'm sorry, Bryon. I keep saying the wrong things. You must just hate me!"

"I don't hate you, Frasnia. You're a genius!" Bryon replied earnestly. "Did Ninan happen to mention Fordin's last name? Maybe he knows something about what happened."

"I'm sorry, Bryon, he didn't say. Would you like me to call his previous employer to see if anyone working there is named Fordin? I don't think that's a prevalent name," Frasnia offered helpfully.

"That's an excellent idea, Frasnia, but I'll do that myself. It would be best if you kept searching for that missing 'pod,'" Bryon told her with a bit of desperation in his tone.

"I'm on it!" Her optimism renewed with news of Ninan's whereabouts. She hated loose ends and unsolved mysteries. She liked her simple, small-town life, ordinary and predictable every day! Frasnia disconnected the call and resumed her ever-widening search of the maps with renewed vigor.

Snapping her fingers with inspiration, she checked the area surrounding Desio next. Her previous search hadn't reached that far, but she thought it might be the most logical place to resume with Ninan being discovered there. As the map slowly loaded onto her patil, she had a few moments to think about the changes in circumstances surrounding Ninan.

Frasnia smiled at herself because she realized Ninan was no longer complicit in Jena's abduction. She hated to think she could've been so wrong about the friendly new employee. After seeing Ninan's injuries, she felt confident he couldn't have been a willing participant in the cargo theft either.

～

BRYON MADE several calls resulting from his newly acquired information. What seemed like a promising lead rapidly turned into another dead end. Nobody had ever heard of Fordin.

How did Ninan know him?

He wrote down Frasnia's conversation with Ninan on the list of clues. He didn't know how it would fit into the whole scheme, but he felt it was valuable information nonetheless.

Having nothing further to do, Bryon tried to check on Jena. He took several deep breaths to center his concentration. Using the locating techniques, he felt the energy from Jena's birth crystal. Instead of the clear picture he saw yesterday, everything was blurry and shifting like shimmering water. He ended the connection abruptly as his head felt like it was going to explode.

Bryon knew something serious was wrong. Without much experience with the crystals, Bryon ran out of his office yelling, "Alena!"

"What is it, Bryon?" Alena rushed around the corner from the kitchen. "Did you locate Jena?" She wrung a cloth between her hands, her knuckles white with the effort.

"Have you checked her crystal lately?"

"No. Have you?"

"Try it right now," he spoke without answering her question again.

"Okay, give me a moment," she replied as she walked toward the living room. "This is usually easier to do when a person is sitting," she said as she took her favorite spot on the couch.

Bryon sat beside Alena and watched her breathe deeply, composing herself for the connection. Immediately, he knew when she had looked through the crystal. Her reaction mirrored his.

"Something's wrong!" Alena cried out.

"I hoped it was just me. What can we do now?"

"Nothing! We can do nothing, Bryon! If anything has happened to Jena, I'm going to kill Petre MacVeen with my bare hands!"

Alena burst into tears that she could not care for her daughter when she so obviously needed her mother.

"We can take turns checking on Jena to see when the blurriness subsides. I don't know about you, but my head is killing me." He stood and offered, "I'll go get us some pika juice. I think we're going to need some sugar in our systems if we're going to keep monitoring that crazy-feeling birth crystal."

Alena just nodded as she silently leaned back on the couch. "I know you're right; if Jena were close to dying, the stone wouldn't have given us any image. Jena must've been drugged for the crystal to have that bad of a connection with her vital essence. It'll just take time to wear off. Darn it! We don't have time!"

Bryon brought back a full glass of pika juice in each hand. He handed her a drink and resumed his seat. asking, "What happened?"

Immediately ashamed at her outburst, Alena replied with resignation, "Nothing happened. It's just me feeling sorry for myself." She took a long drink and then sighed as she began thinking about any drug which could cause such a disruption between Jena and her birth crystal.

Finally, she had it and spoke urgently, "*Epeny*! That's it, Bryon, he must've given her *epeny*! I don't know if she's hurt or he's just trying to keep her quiet, but I'm certain that's what he used on her!"

"That's good, right?" Bryon asked with concern.

"As long as she isn't hurt, then the *epeny* should wear off in a couple of hours," she responded hopefully. "We can keep checking on her and see if the fuzziness lessens. Don't try to look through the murkiness; it will only make your head hurt.

"As soon as you make contact with the stone, if it feels wrong, disconnect immediately. That will lessen the hazy effects on your own brain. We're going to have to check often, I'm afraid." She sighed with resignation.

"Let's set a timer; we'll check on her every twenty minutes. Does that sound okay to you?"

"That sounds perfect," she replied with her first smile of hope.

Bryon stood from the couch and left to get the timing device. The smile he had shown Alena fell as he turned away from her. He wasn't nearly as optimistic as Alena about this new turn of events. If Petre were drugging her, then he was probably moving her too. They needed to find him soon and get her back before he could find a way to harm her permanently with his selfish neglect.

I'm going to make him pay for this!

Bryon thought about all the dire things he could do to Petre as he angrily grabbed the timer from the kitchen counter.

CHAPTER 39

Jena awoke in a strange place. Her chubby hands gripped the side of her drawer to lift herself to a sitting position. Her unsteady core didn't help her coordination, nor did her blurry vision; she was even less coordinated than usual. With both hands on the front of the drawer, she pulled herself over the edge and thumped awkwardly onto the floor. At least the drugs in her system kept her from registering the fact that the fall probably should've hurt.

On hands and knees, Jena scooted away from the boring bed. A shimmering stream of light coming from near the front door made her want to investigate. She loved shiny bits and pieces; the pull to touch it was intense.

The floor tipped from side to side, making her compromised balance even more precarious. She stumbled into the chair legs and fell over more than once. Still, the shiny thing kept her attention.

Finally, she was next to the fist-sized metal and crystal object. She sat beside it and clumsily stretched out her hand to grab it off of the floor. Immediately, she deposited the item into her mouth.

She liked the metallic taste, and drool ran down her arm and dripped off of her elbow. Both hands held the piece, and she stared at it again before returning it to her mouth to scrape her teeth and gums along each new surface.

Something moved beside her. The movement caught her attention. She focused on the big, brown object with a bit of struggle. She dropped the metal and crystal item to free her hand to explore. Her vision cleared, but her coordination remained terrible. Her fingers touched the object, but it skittered away.

She turned and used her other hand to slap the thing onto the floor. Jena's fingers closed around the wriggling body. She sat back on her rear and used both hands to bring it to her mouth for further investigation. This time, her aim fell short, and she brought the item up beside her mouth.

A burning sensation radiated across her cheek. This thing wasn't nice—she threw it back onto the floor.

The pain issued from where it began and became so intense it overcame the *epeny's* drugging effects. Jena screamed where she sat. The pain spread, and the shrieks turned into agonized piercing wails.

ONCE AGAIN, screaming roused Petre. He knew instantly that this wasn't a cry of unhappiness but one of pain and terror. Even his dull sleep senses could hear the difference.

He looked immediately at the drawer where Jena was supposed to be, and, of course, she wasn't there. His fuzziness evaporated as he spotted Jena sitting by the front door and the beetlesnatch skittering away from her.

He leaped from the bed, thankful that he still wore his shoes. Stomping on the offending beetlesnatch, he bent over and picked up Jena.

He unerringly spotted the disgusting bug bite on her face. Knowing the severe deathly nature of the beetle's venom unless treated immediately, Petre was desperate to get help for Jena.

Still carrying her, Petre opened the cabin door and ran up the stairs to the main deck. He had to know his location before he could steer his water craft somewhere for help.

Realizing he must have been asleep far longer than he planned, he noticed they were nowhere near where they had started. With the dawning sun just above the horizon, he had difficulty seeing any signs of land.

There it was! Just to the left of the bow, on the skyline—a smudge indicating land. As best he could with a screaming baby in his arms, he concentrated on increasing the water craft's speed to the maximum. Not knowing what landmass was ahead of him, he only hoped there was an experienced wise-woman to keep his daughter alive.

Minutes slowly passed as Petre rubbed Jena's back and repeatedly said, "It's okay, Jena, I'm getting help for you. It's okay, honey! We're almost there. It's okay!"

Jena arched her back, making it difficult to keep her in his arms. She didn't pay any attention to his ministrations while large tears rolled down her cheeks and snot dripped from her nose.

After what seemed an eternity, but was in actuality only about five minutes, Petre made out the island's harbor. To his utter dismay, he was going to be docking at Elder Debbon's islet.

Petre said a silent prayer of thanks as he realized this might be the best scenario possible since the Elders taught the best wise-women.

As his vessel drew near the islet, Jena's screams echoed off of the water and drew the people's attention on the dock. The people recognized the shrieks of pain; they, too, could hear the difference. Someone broke free from the crowd and ran toward the Elder's Residence.

Petre noted the runner and was relieved to know there would be advance notice for his daughter's arrival. He spotted many people at the edge of the dock, where he maneuvered his craft. As he came near the pier, he threw a rope at a young man while jumping from the water craft.

Without waiting to see if his vessel were tied up properly, he too made a straight line for the Elder's Residence. He was more thankful than ever that he had already been there once and knew exactly where to go.

The guard at the front gate waved him and the screaming Jena through without asking for his signature. He followed the path up to the massive wooden door.

Just as he reached for the doorknob, the doors flew open. Petre came up short when he realized he nearly ran directly into Elder Debbon himself.

Elder Debbon held his hands out for Jena. Elder Debbon shook his hands when Petre paused and said, "Hurry, give the child to me, Petre!"

Petre thrust his screaming daughter into Elder Debbon's hands without another thought. "Elder Debbon will heal you, Jena. Be brave!"

Petre stared in disbelief when Elder Debbon suddenly turned and ran down the hall with Jena.

Everything happened so fast; Petre was in a stupor. Then it clicked. Petre should be with his daughter! He hurried after the sound of his daughter's screams.

ELDER DEBBON FELT a jolt of energy as his hands came near the youngster. Few things in life surprised him anymore, but this child was a revelation, more so since Petre was the giver of this naked youth.

An odd sense of déjà vu washed over Debbon as he held the girl. He knew this matter required investigation, but for now, he needed to find out what was causing this little girl to scream in so much pain.

Debbon took in the angry, bleeding puncture wound on the small girl's cheek and the even more insidious red streaks emanating from the injury. Only one thing could cause these marks coupled with this much pain: a beetlesnatch!

Where had Petre been that there were beetlesnatch hatching at this time of year? Only a new hatchling could carry enough poison to cause this much damage.

He ran into his surgery. He set the little girl on a padded bench and kneeled on the floor beside her to use his healing powers without falling over. This healing was going to be tricky.

Seeing the black birth crystal around the child's neck, Debbon focused his healing energy through that stone. He then moved the elemy up and over the screaming girl's head.

Immediately, he felt her power rise and mingle with his own. The mixture was so potent, and he was almost overwhelmed.

Wanting desperately to explore the new sensation, he was then made aware of *epeny* coursing through the toddler. He swept the drug out of her system with a single thought, eliminating the fog of confusion that surrounded the little girl.

Her screams intensified as the drug dissipated, allowing the wound's full pain to register. Belatedly, Debbon realized he erred in removing the *epeny* first. His desire to feel her uninhibited power made him forget to use his common sense. The drug would help her more than hurt her at this point.

Too late now. I just need to get this done.

Debbon reached up and touched the girl's skull to both heal the large lump on her forehead as well as to draw away her pain from the bite on her cheek. Her screams turned into whimpers and then finally subsided to deep gulping breaths. Now that she wasn't feeling the pain, Debbon could get up from the floor and get his beetlesnatch ointment.

Once applied, he felt confident that the poison wouldn't continue to break down the muscles under the skin. He then spent a few moments drawing the poison from the red streaks and out of the opening.

Knowing the scarring that such a bite could leave, Elder Debbon did something he normally wouldn't do; he used their combined energy to heal the wound completely.

Such a beautiful child shouldn't live her life disfigured by such a prominent scar on her face. It was unthinkable. The healing was now complete, and Elder Debbon rested back on his heels and took a deep, cleansing breath.

It had been a long time since he'd performed such a rushed healing. To his utter amazement, he wasn't even the tiniest bit tired. Thinking on this oddity, it occurred to Elder Debbon that the child's energy must have played a much larger part in the healing than he had even realized.

Who is this girl?

With sudden insight, he recognized this child from the vision he'd had mesans ago when he interrogated Petre. He could hardly believe that the dream had come to pass and that Jena was the child in danger being handed to him.

CHAPTER 40

A shuffling noise off to Debbon's left side caught his attention, and he turned his head. He hadn't seen Petre follow them into his surgery.

I must be dazzled by this child not to realize Petre was here!

He chastised himself for letting his keen interest in this girl get in the way of his perceptions.

To deflect attention away from his excitement, he asked Petre, "Whose child is this?"

"She's mine," Petre proclaimed proudly, not bothering to hide his smug smile of satisfaction.

"Yours?" Erupted Elder Debbon before he composed himself and asked more calmly, "Who's her mother?"

"Her mother was Jes…" he started to say and then paused awkwardly.

Debbon's eyes narrowed at Petre's hesitation. *What is Petre withholding?*

Petre cleared his throat and said, "Her mother was Jessa." He hung his head as though he were grieving

"Where did you meet this Jessa?" Elder Debbon asked with suspicion dripping from his tone.

"We met at the docks."

"How did you happen to have a daughter with her?" Elder Debbon continued his quick questions.

"The usual way, I suppose. I slept with her, and she got pregnant," he answered blithely.

"Don't get cheeky with me, Petre. It's not smart," he cautioned. "Tell me how you ended up with custody of this child."

Petre thought for a moment, then replied, "When Jessa and I met, we fell in love at first sight."

Elder Debbon's eyebrow rose to show his skepticism.

Petre quickly added, "It was bound to happen for me sometime." He added a theatrical shrug for good measure.

"Go on," prompted Elder Debbon, wanting to see how far Petre would go with this obviously fabricated tale.

"Well, Jessa said she wanted to sail the world with me. So she came with me on my water craft. After a few weeks, we knew it was meant to be forever for us, so we got married."

"Who married you?" Elder Debbon jumped in to ask, hoping to trip Petre up.

"We married ourselves. We can do that since we were officially living on the water. It was a civil ceremony between just the two of us."

Debbon didn't say what he really thought. Instead, he lifted his hand and flicked his fingers. "Okay, so you married yourselves. Go on."

"One thing led to another, and before you know it, Jessa was pregnant with little Jena there." Petre pointed at the little girl, who was now happily discovering her feet flying above her as she lay on her back.

"So, where is Jessa now?" Elder Debbon decided to cut to the question at hand.

"A few mesans ago, there was a sudden squall," Petre temporized immediately. "Jessa was worried about me on the deck, so she came to check up on me. I held on to the center mast as the wind whipped so hard. Jessa didn't stand a chance. As soon as she came on deck, the wind swept her overboard. I never saw her surface again." Petre hung his head.

"I see." Elder Debbon half expected Petre to try to squeeze out a tear or two for good measure. Then he had a brilliant thought to try to trap him in his lie, "I assume you filed a swimming report?"

"No, but you can ask at any port that I was searching for my wife. I've spent every waking minute looking for her. My life would be over if it weren't for little Jena here."

"I see," repeated Elder Debbon. He was going to have to look into this matter later. First, he wanted to have some time alone with little Jena.

There was something special about this girl's powers that warranted further consideration. He wasn't about to let Petre take her away until he had his chance to find out more about her.

Elder Debbon took a single step to reach the small table next to a side door. The Elder picked up a little bell, rang it two times, and softly returned it to the table. He turned and contemplated Jena for a moment while waiting for something to happen.

There was a gentle knock on the door just before it opened. A young girl walked in and asked, "What may I get for you, First Elder?"

"Please take Jena here to give her a bath, dress her properly, feed her, and then see if she'll settle for a nap," he replied with authority.

"Right away, First Elder," the girl replied as she bent to scoop up the naked baby girl in her arms. She tucked her into the crook of her arm and left immediately out the same door from which she entered.

It had all happened so fast, Petre shook his head and frowned.

"Now, wait a minute. Where are you taking her? She's mine! I want her back!" His voice rose with each statement.

Elder Debbon made a cutting motion with his hand, and Petre found himself unable to utter another syllable even though many more phrases tried to leave his mouth. Petre's face turned red, he crossed his arms defiantly, and he tapped his foot on the ground in frustration.

"Are you quite through yet?" Elder Debbon asked reasonably.

Petre looked like he had many more things he wished to say but only nodded his head instead. Elder Debbon raised his finger and released Petre.

He said, "That wasn't very nice."

"Neither was your vulgar display of manners in my Residence," Elder Debbon reprimanded Petre.

Petre cast his gaze down to the floor and simply said, "I'm sorry, Elder Debbon, please forgive me."

Elder Debbon gently probed Petre's usually obscured mind and found that Petre meant his apology. Dumbfounded, Debbon belatedly realized he infiltrated Petre's unusually thick skull and sent another probe to investigate further.

No matter how unethical, this opportunity couldn't be squandered. Debbon's barely managed to withhold his shocked intake of breath that Jena indeed was his daughter, whom Petre loved very much.

Debbon also received the very barest glimpse of whom he supposed was Jessa, but the whispy thought was gone too soon to be sure. Petre's mind clouded and became unreadable within the thud of a single heartbeat.

Elder Debbon went on as though nothing strange or miraculous just happened and responded with, "It's understandable that you're protective of your daughter."

Petre nodded and said, "I'd do anything for her. She's extraordinary. She deserves nothing but the best this life has to offer now that her mother's gone. When will Jena be ready for me to take her back to my water craft?"

"I understand you want to be on your way. However, a beetlesnatch bite isn't something to mess around with. I want to keep Jena here for a few hours to ensure she doesn't have a secondary reaction to the bite.

"You know how the secondary reactions can be much more sudden and severe than the initial poison. It's very serious. I'd be remiss in my healer duties if I let her go before I was confident of her good health. I'm sure you'd agree?" Debbon nodded as he spoke, encouraging Petre to agree with him subconsciously.

"Absolutely," Petre responded, nodding in time with the First Elder. "I'd like to be with Jena."

Elder Debbon leaned his formidable skills on Petre when he said, "Why don't you go get something to eat in the village. Take this chit." He removed a small talisman from his front pocket and held it out to Petre.

"Let the vendor know that I'll take care of the charges. You've had a very trying day. It would be best if you rested; regained your strength. Then in a few hours, you can return to get Jena. I should be through evaluating her condition by then, and you can both be on your way."

"Okay," Petre replied as his hand lifted to take the chit from Elder Debbon. Petre turned around with the object in his hand and sauntered the way he had hurriedly come before.

Elder Debbon watched Petre leave his surgery, rushing after him to watch his progress through the window.

As though in a daze, Petre passed through the open front doors, down the garden path, and past the guarded gate. Debbon maintained his spell, leveraging his newfound foothold of Petre's love for Jena.

Petre would never suspect that Elder Debbon might have

spelled him into doing as he wished. Nobody was able to do that to Petre MacVeen.

It never has before. He really must've been rattled by Jena's accident.

He smiled at successfully getting rid of him. He turned on his heel and left the surgery through the same door the young woman took Jena. Debbon knew he'd find Jena in the kitchen, so he went directly there.

He hesitated in the doorway, watching as Jena finished her milk bottle. Debbon drifted over and looked down into her face. The thought struck him that her eyes were the exact shade of blue as Petre's.

As though she knew she was admired, Jena shifted her gaze and looked directly at Debbon. She continued to stare in a way that suddenly made Debbon uncomfortable enough to look away first. He realized her power grew as she became more content with a full stomach.

Without the pressure to perform in any way, he grappled with the notion that Jena was the same girl from his vision so long ago. He took a moment to retrieve the events of that day and recall the name of the girl who he questioned alongside Petre.

Amanda.

And she was an *old soul* visitor from Earth.

How does Amanda play into this scenario?

CHAPTER 41

Debbon's infatuation increased when Jena pushed the nearly empty bottle away from her mouth and reached her hands up to himself. Without thinking, he lifted her and cradled her close.

Her power was a physical presence surrounding her body. Why didn't anyone comment on it? Was she reflecting his power? He'd have to test her abilities to determine where her strengths were strongest.

He carried her over to a chair by the window and settled himself down to admire this bright little child. He positioned her to sit up on his knees so she could face him. She excitedly waved her arms while she smiled and cooed at him.

This little mystery clearly enchanted Debbon. He leaned forward and smelled her freshly washed hair.

She appeared to be ready to go with him for observation. He lifted her against his shoulder and carefully passed through the kitchen, down several hallways, and ended up in his study. He laid her on the plush rug in the middle of the room, and he sat on the floor beside her.

Now that she was comfortable, he drew a ball of energy and let it hang from his hand just out of her reach. He wanted to know if she'd recognize it but was surprised when she created her own ball and merged hers with his.

Expanding the scope of the energy, Debbon made an object appear within the ball, leaving it suspended inside. Jena giggled and continued to stare at the floating object. Her hands were flailing to try to reach it, but she was lying down.

Inspiration struck, Debbon got up from the floor. He went to his desk, retrieved several small objects, and set them near Jena on the floor, but not close enough for her exploring hands to grab.

Pointing at one of the objects, he said to Jena, "Move one of these into the ball, Jena. Can you do that?" She didn't appear to understand what he was talking about. To demonstrate, he used his mind to transfer an envelope off of the rug and move it into the ball of energy.

"Now you do it," he encouraged. Before he knew it was happening, all of the objects were gone from the rug. He stared in disbelief at the empty space beside Jena. She was waving her hands and giggling again.

He returned his gaze to the energy ball and saw every object turning in circles around each other. Debbon clapped his hands, and with a grin wide enough to hurt his cheeks, he exclaimed, "Well done, Jena! Well done!"

Jena seemed encouraged by his praise, and she also started to giggle.

"Can you take them out of the orb now?" He demonstrated this by taking the ball of twine from the sphere and dropping it onto the rug. Jena's eyes followed the progress of the orb, and Debbon saw comprehension register in her eyes.

In the next instant, all of the objects, including the original thing which Debbon had placed there, were lying on the rug beside the twine ball. Again, Debbon encouraged her ability by clapping and exclaiming, "That was perfect, Jena."

Imagining all of the things Jena would be capable of under his tutelage, he was more confident now than ever that Jena belonged with him instead of Petre. He racked his brain to develop a plan where Petre would willingly give Jena up to him. He laughed out loud as the most brilliant idea came to mind, a plan Petre couldn't possibly refuse.

Picking Jena up, he returned to the kitchen and handed her back to the young woman who had initially taken care of her. "Make sure she gets a nap for the next couple of hours," he instructed.

He practically ran back to his study. At his patil, he performed a quick search of any records on a female with the first name of Amanda. He wanted to find her right away if she had anything to do with this child.

There were very few entries on anyone with a matching first name, but one, in particular, caught his attention.

A death notice.

He pulled up the record for further review and noticed that Bryon Kesh was the person who had reported the accident and the missing person report. He assumed it was the same Amanda since Bryon accompanied her when Debbon first became aware of the girl from Earth.

With that avenue turning up a dead-end, his thoughts swiftly turned to his next plan of action. Through his patil, he contacted his legal advisor. "I need you right away," he spoke excitedly when Miorlen's face appeared on the screen.

"I'm at your service whenever you require," Miorlen answered politely.

"I'd like to 'port you to my office right now."

More than a little surprised at his request, Miorlen responded with the only possible answer, "As you wish, First."

Not waiting for another second, Debbon teleported Miorlen right from where he sat directly in the chair opposite Debbon in his office. He gave Miorlen a few moments to readjust himself from the rapid transport by disconnecting his call from the patil. "Thank you for coming here so unconventionally. I have an urgent matter that must be attended to right this moment," he spoke in a rush.

"I gathered as much. What would you like me to do? I've never seen you so flushed with excitement, and I'm intrigued. This must be something big." Miorlen leaned forward, eyes wide with anticipation.

Debbon turned to face the counselor, weighing his words. "I'm going to need a birth certificate and a betrothal agreement drawn up."

"That seems pretty standard. I can get those written within the next couple of days. Do you need anything else?"

"No, you don't understand me, Miorlen. I need these documents completed within the next two hours."

"But that's—."

At Debbon's glare, Miorlen choked off the word 'impossible' when he realized to whom he was speaking.

Miorlen coughed into his hand and said, "Let me know the names for the birth certificate and the betrothal agreement. I'll have them done within two hours." He grimaced as the words left his mouth.

Debbon nodded, pleased that Miorlen wouldn't fail him in this. "There's just one small problem," Debbon started, and then an idea occurred to him.

"I'll give you what I know. I'll find out the rest in a couple of hours, and you can enter it when I receive it and print it immediately. I don't have to remind you that the betrothal agreement must be air-tight and rock solid. There can't be any loopholes in it!"

"Of course," Miorlen answered, although his expression showed barely concealed curiosity.

Debbon handed Miorlen a notepad and a pencil and instructed him to write. "The birth certificate is for a girl child named Jena MacVeen. As you can guess, her father is Petre MacVeen. Her mother's name was Jessa. I don't know her last name. I also don't know Jena's birthday yet, but I do know she's approximately six-mesans old, which would make her birth year 3443. As I said, I'll get the exact date when Petre returns from town."

Miorlen scribbled rapidly on the pad of paper, but his face registered disbelief. "Wait, Elder Debbon. Are you sure this is what you want to do? I mean, are you honestly going to betroth your son to *Petre MacVeen's* daughter? No offense, First, but what could possibly drive you to this crazy idea?"

He looked around, relief making his shoulders sag. "Am I being pranked?" His gaze rose to Elder Debbon's. "Oh, by your look of pure excitement, I assume this is real. How amazing!"

Debbon rapped his knuckles on this desktop and said, "Okay, now for the betrothal agreement. I want it between Jena and Willian. Effective immediately," he mused in thought for a minute.

"What does Chelesa think of this match?" Miorlen asked innocently.

"What?" Debbon rhetorically asked as he came out of his reverie. He then understood what Miorlen asked and replied absently, "Oh, Chelesa doesn't know about it yet. I'm sure she won't mind."

"I'm not so sure about that," Miorlen replied under his breath as he continued to write.

"What was that, Miorlen?"

"I just said that I thought you should probably let her know about it before you sign the documents with Petre. As you said, it will be irrevocable. An unhappy wife lasts forever just the same," he said as diplomatically as possible.

"You could be right," Debbon conceded, much to Miorlen's relief. He hated to think of the paperwork, not to mention the expense if his wife contested the betrothal. A person in his position couldn't afford to have discord in his home made known to the public. This betrothal would definitely make the news circuits!

"Okay, I'll take care of discussing this with Chelesa while you draw up the documents. Where were we?" He mused for a second before he snapped his fingers and continued, "The betrothal document must contain an abandonment clause. Make sure it's buried somewhere deep within an exceptionally boring paragraph. Make it the standard three days. I'll have to be fair, even if it makes me cringe to think Petre might actually read the document just for the pure enjoyment of getting one over on me!"

Miorlen grinned at Elder Debbon's verbal musing. "I must say, I've never seen you this agitated before, and I'm starting to wonder what this Jena must be like to make you go to so much trouble. She must be alluring."

Debbon grinned sheepishly. "You have no idea." He steepled his fingers under his chin, imagining how much fun he would have teaching her bright new mind.

"Okay, the last thing to discuss is the bride price. It must be enough to satisfy Petre's greed but not enough to seem as though I'm buying the child from him. What would you consider an acceptable price without being ostentatious?" Debbon looked directly at Miorlen for the first time since he had brought him to his office.

CHAPTER 42

Miorlen spoke slowly at first, speeding up as he warmed to the idea. "Well, your status could be part of the price, so it wouldn't have to be as high a taj amount as if you were a person of lower status. That's significant to people like Petre, bragging rights that *his* daughter is betrothed to an Elder's son.

"Let's see, he probably doesn't have much means, being the deck hopper that he is, so I believe we could offer him five thousand taj and not bring criticism from your constituents," he reasoned out loud.

"Perfect, make it happen." Debbon gleefully clasped his hands. "Feel free to use my office to get the documents drawn up. Leave them on the patil so when Petre gets back, you'll easily be able to add the details as I receive them from Petre. I'll set up a one-way voice device so you can hear our conversation without the worry of interrupting us with your typing."

He signed off of his patil, got up from his chair behind the desk, and offered the vacated seat to Miorlen. "Thank you," he said to Miorlen as he left the office.

Thinking about what Miorlen said about talking with Chelesa, he agreed it might be a good conversation to have in person. As he stood in the hall, he gathered elemy to his birth crystal and translated himself the several gania away to his private estate.

He materialized in the front entryway hall and surprised several maids with his sudden appearance. "Sorry to startle you," he said to nobody in particular. "Does anyone know where I may find Chelesa?"

"She's in her study this time of day, Elder," replied one of the older maids shyly.

"Thank you," he replied as he took the left-side hallway to go to her office. He took long strides in his excitement to deliver his news. Never thinking she might not be expecting him, he opened the door to her office and walked in before realizing she wasn't alone.

"Excuse me," he stammered as he came to an abrupt halt. "I didn't know you had a visitor." He started to turn around when his wife's voice stopped him.

"What is it, Debbon?"

"I need to talk to you privately," he stated promptly. "Let me know when you're available. I'll be in my office." He turned around, shut her office door, and walked across the hall to his own private office.

For some reason, he felt deflated that Chelesa wasn't immediately available. Then he scolded himself for being so assuming of her time. Of course, she had other things going on; she was an Elder's wife.

She had responsibilities to the community. She also was a co-founder of their enlightenment program. He sat wearily in his desk chair and sighed at having to wait at all.

About ten minutes later, Chelesa appeared in his office doorway with raised eyebrows and a smile on her face. "To what do I owe the honor for your mid-day visit?" She walked through the office and seated herself in the other office chair across the desk from Debbon.

Relieved that Chelesa could get away to meet with him so soon, he blurted out, "I found an amazing girl today, Chelesa! She was absolutely stunning; you're going to love her!"

"What are you talking about, Debbon?" Chelesa asked with a considerable amount of confusion evident on her face.

"I met this girl, her name is Jena, and I think she's a perfect match for Willian. Just wait until you meet her. She's—no, wait, I want to get your opinion of her without me telling you."

"Are you talking about a betrothal?"

"Yes, didn't I just say that?"

"Yes, but I didn't believe you were serious. What happened today? I think you have some serious explaining to do!" Chelesa folded her arms across her chest, which was never a good sign.

"Come with me back to the Residence. We have at least an hour before he returns. You can meet her. She's just amazing!" Debbon jumped up from his chair; excitement and nervous energy made it impossible for him to remain seated.

"Before who returns. Debbon, what is going on?" Chelesa's voice verged on anger. "You seem to have made up your mind on something as important as a betrothal without even consulting my opinion. I don't like this at all!"

Miorlen's words haunted him, but Debbon wasn't deterred. "Do you trust me?"

"Most of the time," she conceded.

"Then let me teleport you to the Residence. Meet Jena and then tell me she's not perfect for Willian. Okay?" Debbon fairly pleaded with her. He held out his hand to her, imploring her to trust him.

Energy started to build up around him. He would leave without her if she didn't decide immediately. Not that he wanted to, but he needed to spend as much time with Jena as he had available.

Chelesa frowned. "I've never seen you in this type of mood

before. I guess I'd better go with you now or forever wonder what you wanted me to see for myself."

Chelesa stood suddenly and thrust her hand into her husband's outstretched one. Mere moments later, they found themselves standing in Debbon's office with a startled Miorlen looking at the two of them.

"Sorry to interrupt you. This was the only room I knew wouldn't have anyone standing right here at this time. It seemed safest. We're going to go see Jena," he explained as he pulled Chelesa out of the office by the hand he still held.

Not knowing exactly where Jena would be at this time, he returned to the kitchen to make inquiries. Another of the servants told him she was resting upstairs, where a young maid was tasked to monitor her sleep. Thanking the kitchen servant, Debbon rushed through the corridors, up the stairs, and down the hallway until he came to the first guest room's closed door.

Breathing heavily, he turned to Chelesa. His eyes brimmed with excitement, and he reached across her to grab her other hand. He said, "Close your eyes and tell me what you feel?"

Chelesa frowned with confusion, but she complied with his request. She let her other senses take over and jumped when she encountered an unexpected energy. She gasped, and her eyes flew open. "I think I'm beginning to understand why you're so excited. Let's go in there. I want to meet her."

"Good, that's what I hoped you'd say!" His smile positively beamed as he quietly opened the door.

Motioning for Chelesa to precede him into the room, he whispered, "Feel the energy around her."

She walked over to the bed where the little girl was asleep. Chelesa instantly glanced at Debbon and whispered, "Is it my imagination, or is energy pulsing around her body?"

He smiled confirmation.

Chelesa leaned closer and looked carefully at the girl's features.

"Oh, Debbon, even while she's sleeping, she's stunning. What does she look like with her eyes open?"

After studying her for a few minutes, Chelesa sucked in a ragged breath as though reminding herself to breathe. She straightened and turned toward Debbon. She motioned for him to leave the room with her.

Debbon smiled big enough to hurt his cheeks as they exited the room. Without preamble, he asked, "You felt it too, right?"

"I'd be surprised if the neighbors didn't feel it," she confessed with a grin to match his. "I can't wait to meet her parents to begin the negotiations. Did you say they were coming back in an hour or so?"

"That's the only problem," Debbon's smile faded as he turned to the serious matter of her parentage.

"What could possibly be the hangup? Who wouldn't want to betroth their daughter to an Elder?"

"Well, first it appears as if her mother's dead," he began and then rushed on with, "and that her father's Petre MacVeen."

"*What?*" She grabbed his arm and yanked him further down the hall, away from the sleeping girl's door. "You can't be seriously thinking of tying our family name with a master deceptor? Have you lost your mind?"

"Do you remember feeling the power surrounding that child? She'd be a perfect match for our son. Can you imagine how she'd turn out if Petre raised her? She'd be ruined at best and dead at the worst!"

He grabbed both of her arms and gave her a little shake. "She needs us to rescue her! Do you know she arrived here an hour ago almost dead from a beetlesnatch bite, and she had a massive bump on her head?

He continued to shake his wife by the arms as he made each of his arguments. "He drugged her with *epeny* sometime before the beetlesnatch bite. She wasn't wearing a stitch of clothing, not even a clout! Can you imagine Petre actually being able to raise her to adulthood? She probably wouldn't even survive his stupidity!" Debbon had to stop to take another breath.

"Okay, okay! I see your point. But there has to be another way other than making her part of our family. Let's just think about this for a second, alright?"

Debbon shook his head. "I don't need any special mind-reading skill to see that you're frantically searching for another solution to extricate Jena from Petre's terrible influence. Even so, Chelesa, I want her."

She motioned for Debbon to follow her, and together they went to the end of the hall and entered the master room reserved for themselves. She closed the door behind Debbon and paced the room.

"I have Miorlen writing up a betrothal contract," he said and held up his hand to keep her from interrupting as he continued, "I insisted that he add the abandonment clause to the document and bury it in the middle somewhere.

"If Petre doesn't attempt to visit her within three days of the contract's signing, he loses all rights to Jena. That would legally protect us from any future visits from him." He shrugged noncommittally and said, "It was the best I could do to protect us as well."

Chelesa didn't pace. She held her ground with her arms tightly folded across her chest. "What I don't understand is how could you get this started without even discussing it with me?"

Debbon abruptly stopped, his gaze cutting over to meet hers. "That's what Miorlen pointed out as well. I just got so excited about Jena's power I wasn't thinking straight. Anyway, it wouldn't hurt anything to be prepared in case you said okay to it. We need to get her away from Petre and train her ourselves!"

She inhaled loudly through her nostrils and exhaled quickly. "Can't we wait a bit to see if we can come up with another solution?"

"It's now, or never, I'm afraid. If Petre realizes her power, he could do anything with her. I don't trust him at all to care for her for another day," he mused. Remembering his tests with her in the study, he recounted them to Chelesa and finally saw her last reservations break down.

Her hands dropped limply to her sides. She shrugged and said, "Okay, Debbon. I'll trust you on this matter. You just better hope he doesn't come to see her within that first three days, or our lives will be made miserable for the next eighteen anons!"

CHAPTER 43

Chris and Diane waited anxiously to find out from Shemalla what had happened with Amanda. Together they sat at the diner booth and spoke in hushed whispers.

"Do you think everything went okay, Chris?"

"I'm sure of it!"

"But why would Shemalla want to meet here instead of at her house? Could she want to avoid a scene, so she decided it was best to talk in a public place?"

"Diane, please have a little faith. Shemalla was doing everything she could to ensure Amanda would have safe passage. She probably wanted to meet here because she just got off of work, and she'll be hungry!"

Diane slapped Chris's arm at his last statement. She desperately wanted to believe it was just as simple as his explanation. Another worry came to Diane's mind, and she decided to voice it to her husband. "We only have two weeks off from work. What happens if Amanda hasn't returned by the time we need to go home? We can't just abandon her here!"

"We wouldn't be abandoning her. We have obligations of our own, so we'll go back home as planned. Amanda will contact us when she returns, and we can figure out the logistics of getting her home at that time."

She knew he spoke the logical sequence of events, but her heart screamed at her to stay in New Mexico and wait for her daughter's return. Diane didn't know how that would be possible, but she was sure she'd have to remain right where she was until her baby girl came back. On the verge of telling Chris her decision, she spotted Shemalla entering the diner. She tugged on her husband's sleeve and tipped her chin up to signal him to look up to see.

Chris stood from the bench seat as Shemalla neared their table. He smiled and said, "I'm glad you were able to meet with us. Are you hungry?"

"I'll probably just have a cup of coffee," she replied as she sat on the opposite side of the booth from Amanda's parents. "I'm sure you just want to hear about what happened, so I'll get right to it."

The waitress chose that moment to come over and ask to take their orders. Each occupant ordered either a coffee or a tea and declined to get any food at this time. The waitress said she'd be back shortly with their beverages and turned so sharply that her shoe squeaked loudly against the linoleum flooring.

Diane leaned forward against the table, barely breathing with anticipation of the journey's details. "Have you heard from Amanda? Is she safe?"

Shemalla mirrored Diane's pose and looked directly at her when she replied, "We went to Campeche just as planned. We found the gate, and Amanda activated it. I can't say for sure whether or not she made it to her intended location, but I can say that everything appeared normal with her transfer. I haven't heard anything from her since she left." She rested her hands flat on the table between them when she finished her recitation.

Diana sputtered, her gaze shifting from Shemalla to her husband and back. "But what about Amanda? Is she safe?"

Shemalla pursed her lips and exhaled. With a slight shake of her head, she said, "I don't know."

"That's not a good enough answer!" Diane's voice rose loud enough that several patrons and their waitress looked over at them.

Chris reached across Diane's shoulders and addressed her in a low voice, "That's enough, Diane! Shemalla did everything we asked. We knew there wouldn't be any news until Amanda returned."

He shifted his gaze to Shemalla, "Thank you for everything you've done. I know there's a considerable risk to yourself by getting involved with our predicament. Hopefully, Amanda will return soon. We have to head back home at the end of the week."

"I'm not going!" Diane exclaimed adamantly.

Both Chris and Shemalla stared at Diane. Chris opened his mouth to argue, but Shemalla spoke before he was able, "You won't have to stay, Diane. If you leave me your contact information, I'll let you know if I hear anything or if Amanda returns. Rest assured, I am very curious to see her succeed as well, and I can't wait to meet her twins!"

"You see, Diane? You can come home as planned since Shemalla can contact us anytime, day or night. It'd just be a waste to have you languishing here when you could occupy your mind with work instead. There's nothing you can accomplish by worrying while waiting here in a hotel room."

Diane understood his point, but her mind refused to be reasonable right at that moment. She crossed her arms defiantly and refused to look at either person at the table. Her daughter could be in danger, and what mother would walk away from that?

Chris pointedly ignored Diane and addressed Shemalla instead, "Did everything go as planned then?"

"Yes. It couldn't have gone any smoother. Amanda's a fast learner, and I'm sure she'll succeed. I just want to remind you that Amanda might decide it's too risky to bring the children back. She may opt to remain in Tuala permanently."

Chris saw Diane's lower lip start to tremble as she held back tears. He rubbed her shoulder to let her know she was not alone in this. "We know. We just hope everything will turn out as we expected and that she comes back with our grandchildren right away."

The coffee and tea arrived, and they sat in contemplative silence while sipping their beverages. There wasn't much more to be said. Everyone wanted Amanda's safe return to Earth with her children.

TANA WANTED to do more to help Bryon and Alena other than just watching their children while they were going through this terrible time without Jena. Her heart ached for their pain.

She looked down on Juila. Did she have any kind of special connection with her identical twin? She had heard that twins sometimes knew things about their other twin, but these two girls were too young to talk.

Her musings were interrupted by Justan asking, "Tana, read us another story, please!!!"

With a smile, she nodded and replied, "Go pick one out and bring it back to me."

Nodding thoughtfully, he turned around and walked over to the bookcase. He looked so serious as he contemplated the book spines. She knew he'd pick the one with a black cover and a picture of a star on the spine.

Almost the last book in the line, Justan smiled as he carefully pulled the book off the shelf and carried it respectfully over to where Tana sat on the couch with Juila held in her left arm. He handed her the book, careful of Juila, and sat on her right-hand side, snuggling close so he would have the best view of the pictures in the book.

"Andera and Kyelon, come sit on the couch while I read *Genero*," she called to the two quietly playing with blocks on the floor. They were all extra quiet these days, and it saddened Tana that the awful events of the past couple of mesans were affecting their naturally energetic exuberance. She kept things as normal as possible in her house so they could forget about their problems at home, even if it were only temporary.

The older girl and smaller boy both set down the blocks they held. Andera got up first and took two steps toward the couch when Kyelon tripped over a toy he hadn't noticed. "Ouch," he cried as his knee came down painfully on another block.

Andera turned around and rubbed his knee and said, "There, now it's all better!" She offered him her hand to help hoist him up onto his feet. She kept ahold of him until they reached the couch. Andera waited for Kyelon to sit next to Tana on her left-hand side before she went to sit on Justan's other side.

Tana noticed Andera's mothering of her brother, and she smiled inwardly. Did Andera subconsciously use the energy from her birth crystal to soothe away Kyelon's pain? With Alena as her mother, anything was possible.

She'd have to contrive a way to ask Andera some questions to see if she had figured out there was more to the stone than being a pretty necklace. Andera was young for the knowledge, but the crystal would limit Andera's use until she was old enough to be responsible with the power.

With the children settled, she nestled the book between her knees and allowed it to open to the beginning. Before she began reading, she asked, "Do you want us to sing the Unity Song together?"

The children adored the song, making them feel closer to one another. The kids solemnly nodded, so Tana began the simple tune, and the children immediately chimed in:

Crystal around the neck,

Follow the next step,

Changes today,

Changes tomorrow,

We all become one.

They ended the song by each finding someone else's hand to hold. They smiled up at Tana, and she asked, "Do you want me to start from the book's beginning, or do you have somewhere else you'd like me to begin?" Unsurprisingly, Tana saw the children look toward Justan for an answer and suppressed her knowing grin.

Justan looked at Andera and then Kyelon before lifting his index finger to his chin while he considered the question. "Maybe, this time, we could start reading at the part where Jehoban goes off on his own to start a school..." he mused and then reconsidered, his hand jutting out with his finger pointing toward the ceiling as if the most fantastic idea popped into his head.

"No! Let's read the part where he lives with the wild animals and talks to them like they're his best friends." He smiled at this idea and looked to both his siblings for their agreement.

"Okay, friendly animals it is," Tana said as she flipped through the book's pages to reach the requested section. Suddenly Juila stiffened in her arms.

Tana peered down at the previously quiet girl and saw that her eyes were wide open as well as her mouth. Juila made a strange face, and then her arms and legs flailed. Juila wasn't breathing, and her face turned an angry shade of red.

CHAPTER 44

Without wanting to alarm the other children, Tana hurriedly moved off of the couch and said to the other children, "I'll be right back. Juila needs her clout changed." She couldn't think of another excuse, so she raced out of the room toward the spare bedroom she reserved for the children.

Once in the room, Tana unwrapped the blanket from around the small girl. She flipped her over her arm so she could thump her back with the palm of her other hand. Tana thought she might have swallowed something and was choking, but she knew she had been sleeping empty-handed. She flipped her back over to see if she was breathing again. Juila suddenly gasped a big breath of air and then closed her eyes and peacefully slept again.

"That was very strange," Tana murmured. She fussed over Juila for a few more minutes to ensure she would stay breathing right. With nothing more to see and three children waiting for a story, Tana carried Juila back into the living room.

She smiled at the children, pretending nothing was wrong, but Justan's and Andera's eyes mirrored concern. It may have been a brief look but there nonetheless. With exaggerated motion, Tana snuggled down onto the couch between Justan and Kyelon. She then brightly said, "I think we were just about to read about Jehoban living with the animals—."

Tana was still troubled by the strange event from the day before with Juila. She spent more time looking after her than usual because she was worried about a repeat episode. The children already had lunch, played outside, visited with their parents, and were now taking naps on the living room floor. Tana and the children made tents for indoor playtime, and the little ones fell asleep while playing house.

Tana enjoyed the simplicity of children's lives. As long as they had food and play, they were content with their existence. They lived in the moment and didn't expect anything of the next hour, let alone the next day. She sat on the couch overlooking the happy mess strewn about the living room while, once again, holding Juila while she slept.

Tana found herself staring at Juila's face while she slept in the quietness of nap time. Suddenly a bright red spot appeared on Juila's cheek at the same time as Juila started crying. Tana was startled out of her reverie by the suddenness of the onslaught.

She sat forward and stared in horror as the spot started radiating red streaks onto her cheek. Her crying turned more frantic. Should she take Juila back home to see Alena, or should she wait to see if it would pass like the earlier breathing incident?

Could this be what she imagined? Yes—it had to be! Juila was feeling what Jena was living! With this idea in mind, Tana stood and rushed to the kitchen. She got some ice out of the freezer and wrapped it in a cloth from beside the sink. She gently pressed the ice pack to Juila's cheek. That seemed to quiet her crying.

She sat in a chair at the kitchen table and rocked Juila back and forth while humming a soft crooning tune. Just as she started to think that maybe she erred with the twin connection, the crying softened to whimpers and then just deep breaths. Amazingly, Juila stayed asleep throughout it all.

When Tana removed the ice pack from Juila's cheek, she only saw a healthy pink cheek; the angry red spot and streaks were gone as if they had never been there. Even as she stared in wonder at the little girl's face, Juila smiled in her sleep and even blurted a little giggle.

Definitely strange. Should I say anything about this to Alena, or would that just make her worry all the more?

A BRIGHT FLASH blinded Amanda and, immediately after, she found herself in a cave's dark, oppressive gloom. She only had a moment to notice her surroundings before everything turned black. She passed out in a heap on the ground.

Sometime later, Amanda groggily opened her eyes, confused by the rough, cold surface under her cheek. She pushed herself up to a sitting position and continued to blink her eyes like a waking owl.

"Where am I?" she whispered out loud. Her voice echoed off the cave's stone walls surrounding her, and it was dark except for the bright shaft of light from somewhere in the distance.

Not knowing what else to do, Amanda struggled to her feet and headed toward the light. The closer she came to the cave's opening, the more her eyes adjusted to the increased light. By the time she reached the entrance, her vision had cleared, but her confusion about herself was increasing. She spotted a boulder beside the cavern's opening, and she thought it looked like an excellent place to sit to figure out what was happening.

As she sat, a crinkling noise came from her pocket. She discounted the noise as the pack on her back scraped against the cave wall. She hadn't even realized she wore the bag. Shrugging out of the straps, she pulled the pack around to her lap and carefully opened the strings to discover what it contained.

She first encountered a water bottle, realizing how incredibly thirsty she was. She pulled out the bottle and removed the cap speedily. Eager for the moisture, she tipped the liquid into her mouth and luxuriated in the feel of it coursing down her throat with each swallow.

Now that her thirst was assuaged, she continued looking through the bag's contents. She saw unfamiliar clothes, a pencil, and a folded piece of paper. Curious, she removed the paper and unfolded it. She turned it around and found a map with a whole bunch of marks. Peering more closely at it, she saw a swirling symbol drawn on the bottom edge and handwriting that said these were the gates' symbols.

She closed her eyes and concentrated on the symbol. It seemed familiar to her. She turned around and looked at the cave's entrance. At the top of the opening, she saw that same symbol etched into the stone.

Interesting. That cave is considered a gate. A gate to what?

She stood to get a better look at the symbol and heard the crackling sound from her pocket again. Now that she stood, it was easy to reach inside her pocket. Something plastic brushed against her fingertips, piquing her interest enough for her to pull it out to investigate. Strangely, it contained several folded pieces of paper on which was written on the outside 'Open Immediately.'

Amanda dropped back onto the rock. *What a strange mystery.* Biting her bottom lip, she opened the bag and carefully removed the papers. The handwriting on the first one she opened seemed familiar. She read:

LET'S START WITH THE BASICS:

1. YOUR NAME IS AMANDA.
2. YOU ARE NOW IN TUALA.
3. YOU ARE SEARCHING FOR YOUR DAUGHTERS, JUILA AND JENA, WHO ARE PROBABLY AROUND 6-MONTHS OLD. THEY CALL MONTHS 'MESANS' IN TUALA.
4. YOU CAN USE THE BIRTH CRYSTALS ON JUILA AND JENA TO CHECK IN ON THEM. JUILA'S CRYSTAL IS A DEEP RED RUBY, JENA'S IS A BLACK DIAMOND. CONCENTRATE ON THE ENERGY FROM THE EARTH TO TAP INTO THEIR CRYSTALS.
5. YOU NEED TO TRAVEL NORTH TO A TOWN CALLED KIRMA.
6. YOU WILL NEED TO FIND BRYON OR ALENA KESH. BRYON WORKS FOR KIRMA SHIPPING AND RECEIVING. ALENA IS THE LOCAL WISE-WOMAN (HEALER).
7. IF YOU CAN'T FIND BRYON OR ALENA, GO TO THE PORT CITY OF CRESDON. LOOK FOR CAPTAIN AHN (HE'S THE HARBOR MASTER). AHN IS MARRIED TO YOUR AUNT BARLA.
8. ONCE YOU FIND JUILA AND JENA, DECIDE IF IT WOULD BE SAFE TO RETURN HOME TO YOUR PARENTS (CHRIS AND DIANE).
9. READ THE OTHER NOTES FROM CHRIS AND DIANE.
10. THE GATE OBSCURES YOUR MEMORY. IF YOU CONCENTRATE ON EACH DETAIL, YOUR MEMORIES WILL RETURN. IT MIGHT BE EASIER TO REMEMBER AFTER YOU PUT SOME DISTANCE BETWEEN YOU AND THE GATE.

GOOD LUCK!

WITH THE LAST remark about getting away from the gate, Amanda slung the pack strap over her shoulder, looked up at the sun to determine her course, and walked in what she hoped was a northerly direction. As she walked, she kept glancing at the pages still clutched in her hand.

Could this be for real? Let's assume this is real, and I have two daughters? Wow!

She traveled on foot for about half an hour before she came to a cluster of trees on the banks of a small creek. The shade looked more comfortable than the hot sun currently beating down on her head. She desperately wanted to read the other notes from the bag. Amanda changed her course to head straight for the shaded area. Once out of the hot sun, she wearily sank to the ground and rested her back against a tree.

She closed her eyes for just a moment, sighing as she relaxed. After what seemed seconds, she felt a tickling sensation on her arm. A moment later, something crawled across her other arm. Her eyes popped open only to discover there were hundreds of beetlesnatch swarming all over the ground around her. They climbed on her pants and moved across her shirt. She jumped up and screamed with equal parts fear and disgust as they crawled on her arms' bare skin.

Amanda thought she had them all removed from her when suddenly one of them bit into the tender flesh on her forearm. The pain's intensity was almost impossible to register. She slapped the offending bug away from her and stomped on the beetle-like body with unholy satisfaction, knowing she had at least killed one of the dreaded insects.

CHAPTER 45

The first stages of poison coursed through Amanda's veins. She felt light-headed and stared in wonder as streaks of red radiated out from the initial bite wound.

Well, that's just great. The insect is probably poisonous. How long do I have before the venom kills me?

Amanda shrieked, all of her pain and frustration venting in a primal scream.

The next thing Amanda knew, a gorgeous man with kind-looking brown eyes looked down at her where she lay on the ground. Relief washed through her at the luck of having someone nearby.

"Who are you? Where did you come from?"

"My name's Riccan, and I was taking a walk from work when I heard you scream. Are you okay? What happened?"

"A disgusting beetle bit me." With as much effort as she could muster with her uninjured arm, she waved halfheartedly toward the bite mark.

"A beetlesnatch? Oh my goodness!" He scooped up her slight

frame and held her tightly against his muscular chest, and he ran. The jarring from his breakneck pace made her nauseous.

She passed out.

When her eyes opened, she was again leaning against the tree. She looked around to search for the beetlesnatch on the ground. Nothing but grass and dirt surrounded her. It had all been a dream —a nightmare, really. The man in the dream, though—he seemed extremely familiar, but she couldn't place where she might've seen him before.

Amanda shook her head and then remembered her reason for sitting in the first place. She still held the first note in her hand; she refolded it and returned it to the bag. She unfolded the second letter and read:

My sweet baby girl,

You are so brave to take this journey. I have loved you from the moment you were put in my arms after you were born. Even though you are my third daughter, you have brought me more joy than the other two combined. Your quick wit, insatiable curiosity, and eager mind for learning have always been fun to witness as a parent.

I know you're facing a difficult situation with Juila and Jena being where they are. I also know that, as a mother, you'll do whatever you can to protect them from harm. You'll also have to decide if it's safer to live with them or come home to be with your father and me. We'll honor whatever you choose but know we desperately wish you all would come home.

I do envy your ability to reunite with your Aunt Barbara and get to know her children. In that regard, you'll be able to do something I never thought possible as we believed she had drowned before you were born. Let Barbara know we love her. Remember to give her the letter I wrote if you do happen to see her again.

Safe travels, my beautiful daughter. I love you!!!
Mom (Diane)

Tears blurred Amanda's vision. She felt terrible that this woman was struggling with her decision to come here to find her daughters. Amanda was glad to have some insight into Diane.

She had one more note to go, so she refolded the one from Diane and returned it to the plastic bag. She also noted the envelope addressed to her Aunt Barbara and returned that to the bag, as well. With the final note in hand, she unfolded it and read:

Hi, Amanda, this is your father, Chris. I'm sure your mother covered all of our love for you, so I'm going to be more practical. Think very hard about what these notes have told you. Believe everything as soon as possible to speed up the recovery of your authentic mind.

You are on an alternate plane of reality on Earth. Tell nobody that you are really from Earth. The people who matter already know who you are; everybody else could potentially turn you over to the Elders. You do not want to go to the Elders!

Find Bryon and Alena as fast as possible. Find your children. Bryon and Alena don't know you're from Earth, but they are Barla's friends. They are supposed to be caring for your children as you were living with them before you accidentally returned to Earth.

Open your mind to their technology and learn as much as you can. They have many abilities which we don't have at home. Believe them all! Don't doubt your instincts; they are your first and best resource.

We hope to see you soon, and we hope to meet our granddaughters for the first time!

I love you, my adventurer!
Your dad,
Chris

EACH NOTE POINTED to the same story. It was hard not to believe their writing, even though it stretched the bounds of plausibility. "If it's all true," she spoke out loud, "then I have quite the journey ahead of me! Okay, I'll follow the advice of 'my father' and say this is my real mission. I need to get myself to Kirma and locate Bryon and Alena right away!"

Amanda refolded the last note and stuffed it alongside the other papers in the plastic bag. She stood and jammed the packet into her pants pockets.

She confidently walked along the river with renewed vigor until she encountered a road. She checked the sun's location and chose to walk left on the path as that seemed the most northerly direction. Hoping to find some sort of sign indicating she was going the right way, she was disappointed as mile after mile of road unfolded ahead of her.

Just as doubt clouded her mind over her chosen course, she encountered some farmers resting for their afternoon break alongside the road. Her steps involuntarily slowed.

Should she talk to them or keep walking? If she never asked for directions, she could continue walking for a long time on the wrong path. Casting her pride aside, she made the bold decision. As she got closer, she waved her hand and yelled, "Hello."

The couple looked up and said in unison, "Hello." They stopped talking to one another and looked up expectantly at Amanda when she stopped in front of them.

"I'm wondering how much further it is to Kirma?"

"Oh, I'd say it's about five gania more," the man replied, then turned to the girl beside him and asked, "Don't you think?"

She didn't speak, but she nodded her head solemnly in agreement.

"Yep, about five gania," he repeated with more certainty this time.

"About how long do you think that'll take?" Amanda asked, unsure of a gania's measure.

"Well, if you step quick, it should be about two hours," he said as he continued to nod.

"That's perfect," Amanda replied with a smile. "Have a nice day!" With a jaunty wave to the couple, she turned and continued down the road at a quick pace. She hoped to make it to wherever she was headed before it got dark. Sleeping out in the open of a foreign land didn't seem very appealing.

As she walked, Amanda reviewed the information from the notes. This adventure exhilarated her, but she'd feel better about it once she truly remembered choosing to take this journey. And Chris's advice to believe everything—well, she was trying. But it was difficult.

"How do you believe something you don't remember," she muttered out loud. Amanda looked around her hastily to see if anyone were around to hear her talking to herself. *All clear.* She sighed heavily.

Smudges of buildings appeared on the horizon. Hopefully, that meant she was nearing Kirma. Her legs felt like wobbly rubber bands, and her feet were agonizingly abused and sore. The sun dipped toward the horizon on her left.

"Please let Bryon and Alena live on this edge of town!" The mere idea of traversing the whole city to get to their house seemed daunting after the distance she'd already endured that day.

As she neared the town's edge, many people walked on the same road as she. She thought to talk to some of them but then realized she wouldn't have much to contribute to a conversation. She opted to limit her speech to polite greetings until she got into the town proper. Once there, she hoped she might be able to see the Kirma Shipping and Receiving building, where Bryon worked. If she found the building, she'd inquire inside for Bryon's whereabouts.

Her plan didn't pan out. The road she traveled led her into a neighborhood. She'd have to ask for directions to the Kesh household. She made a complete circle where she stood before she realized she was alone on the street.

Are you kidding me right now? Ugh. It must be dinner time.

She struggled with the decision to continue walking or take a break and wait for someone to come along.

It seemed as though fate were finally stepping in to help her. When she came around the corner and spotted the bench only fifteen feet away, she imagined hearing choir music playing, exalting her choice to rest.

She unslung the bag from her back and set it down heavily on the bench before bonelessly dropping next to it. Almost too weary to move, Amanda remembered the food and water in her pack. Since everyone else was eating, she may as well too!

With a supreme effort, she dragged the bag closer, opened it, and pulled out a sandwich and the half-full water bottle. She took a drink first to remove the road's dust from her mouth. She set the glass down on the bench and opened the sandwich bag.

Never in her life did a peanut butter and jelly sandwich taste so good. She closed her eyes as she chewed and luxuriated in the luxury of eating while sitting down. Life was good!

"Amanda?" A woman's voice asked nearby. "Amanda, is that you?"

Amanda looked up and saw a stranger. Her mouth was full, so she answered by nodding as she modestly covered her mouth with her hand.

The stranger rushed up and awkwardly hugged her, where she remained seated on the bench. She pulled back from the embrace and said, "Where have you been? Bryon and Alena have been worried sick about you. Have you been to their house yet?"

Amanda shook her head from side to side.

The lady suddenly looked mortified and spoke urgently, "What are you waiting for? Get your bag and follow me; we're going to go there right now. This is the best news since—." She waved her hands to rush Amanda along in stowing the stuff back in her bag.

Amanda stood and tried to clear the peanut butter from her mouth to talk finally. The woman had curiously stopped in the middle of her thought. Amanda finally asked, "Has something happened?"

The woman looked sharply at Amanda and replied, "You don't know? Oh, do hurry! Their house is just around this next corner."

The woman set a brisk pace, and before Amanda felt ready, they walked up the sidewalk of a house that looked vaguely familiar to Amanda. It was the first thing to register as anything special in Amanda's clouded memory. They paused at the front door for the lady to knock several times. Within a few moments, the door opened.

Alena stood still in the doorway, her mouth hanging open and her eyes flaring wide. "Bryon!" She screamed over her shoulder, and then she rushed forward and grabbed Amanda in a big hug. "Amanda, I can't believe it's you! I'm so happy to see you!"

Just as she turned around to usher Amanda into the house, Bryon rounded the corner. Amanda watched his eyes widen the same as Alena's, and then he ran toward her. She braced herself for another hug but was surprised when he stopped short and said with some skepticism, "Amanda, is it really you?"

Amanda only nodded again.

Bryon looked up at the sky and moaned, "Thank you, Jehoban! Oh, Amanda, we thought you were dead!" He turned to the lady still standing beside Amanda and said, "Thank you for bringing her home. We obviously have a lot of catching up to do. I'm sure you understand."

"Oh, of course. I'm just glad to have helped. I need to get home to my dinner anyway," she replied. She turned and walked back toward her own house.

Amanda was ushered into the residence. All was silent when she sat in the living room. Bryon and Alena sat on the couch across from her and looked at her expectantly. She wasn't sure what she should say, so she started with, "I appear to have lost my memory. Can you help me?"

They looked at each other with bewildered expressions and then back at Amanda. This question wasn't what either Bryon or Alena expected. Bryon recovered his composure first. He cleared his throat and started with, "Do you remember the last time we were together?"

Amanda shook her head. Then she offered, "I found a note on myself saying you two could help me find my twin daughters, Juila and Jena. Unfortunately, I don't remember them either."

"Who wrote the note?" Bryon asked logically.

"I think I did."

"Bryon, can you run next door and get Juila? Sometimes memories can return with strong emotions. What's stronger than a mother's love for her child?"

"Why is she next door?" Amanda asked with confusion.

"Tana's watching all of our kids for a couple of days while—we get things sorted out," she ended lamely.

Bryon stood and declared, "I'll be right back."

Amanda simply stared. Even without recognizing these people, it appeared as though Bryon wanted to delay the upcoming conversation. Bryon practically ran from the room in his haste to follow Alena's instruction.

The front door opened and then clicked shut. Amanda and Alena stared at one other across the coffee table, probably wondering what the other was thinking. The door opened again a few minutes later, and footsteps crossed the front entryway. Bryon held a beautiful girl with blonde curls and piercing blue eyes.

Once Amanda made eye contact with Juila, all of her memories flooded back. "Oh," she exclaimed as her eyes rolled back into her head. She felt herself slumping sideways into the chair before her whole world turned black.

CHAPTER 46

Petre basked in the respect everyone showed him as soon as he presented Elder Debbon's chit. This was the life he deserved.

When he stopped at the first restaurant, he doubted the power of using the voucher—until he set it on the table while waiting for the server to take his order. He saw the man's gaze fall upon it as he walked over. His eyes widened, and his expression changed to one of admiration.

"How may I serve you, sir?" the waiter asked in his most polite tone.

Petre could get used to this type of service! He was unfamiliar with this establishment's meals as it was much nicer than he could ever afford before, so he just said, "Please bring me your most popular dish."

"As you wish," replied the waiter. He made a small formal bow, backed away one step, and then turned around and strode swiftly to the kitchen.

The meal arrived, and Petre spent no time appreciating either the presentation or the taste. He scarfed the food down as he did with every meal.

All he could think about was what would happen in his next meeting with the Elder. He hoped it would be short so he could be on his way to finding a caretaker for Jena. That little girl caused him more worry in such a short time than he would have thought possible. Also, the constant attention for Jena drained his nerves.

Petre ignored the waiter's horrified expression about how Petre disposed of the fancy plate of food. The waiter was immediately ready to remove the dish when his plate was empty. He politely asked, "Would you like me to bring you our special dessert?"

Petre merely nodded as he leaned back in his chair and folded his hands across his distended belly in satisfaction while he waited. A loud belch erupted from him, and he smacked his lips together with joy.

Oh, yes, I can definitely get used to this type of living. Everybody catering to my needs suits me just fine!

He consumed the dessert with the same sloppy haste as the main course. He scooted his chair back and looked around for the waiter when he finished. Spotting him just coming out of the kitchen, Petre held up the chit and yelled across the crowded dining room, saying, "Are we good here?"

The waiter frowned and nodded sharply. Petre loudly pushed his chair farther away from the table as he stood and strode out of the restaurant.

Petre went to the marketplace and gathered food and supplies for the next leg of his journey. He was equally delighted to find Elder Debbon's voucher worked with each vendor. Nobody questioned his use of the chit. Nobody cared about the number of purchases he placed on the counter. His arms were fully laden when he was ready to return to his water craft.

For the first time since arriving on the islet, Petre wondered if someone had tied down his water craft from his rushed entry onto the islet. He quickened his pace and loudly exhaled when he saw his beautiful water craft securely tied to the primary docking station, usually reserved for the Elder's guests of honor.

Another jolt of self-importance washed over him as he stepped onto his vessel. He scanned the dock to see if anybody noticed that he was the Elder's special visitor. Nodding to several people staring in his direction, he lifted his chin, squared his shoulders, and proudly descended the steps into the main cabin of his craft.

He spent considerable time putting all of the supplies away in the cupboards. Petre would have to change his ways in the cabin with little Jena would be crawling around. There was no telling what she'd get into next. He surveyed his living quarters with the eye of a concerned parent for the safety of his child and realized there were quite a few hazards he had never noticed before.

He groaned when his gaze fell on the box from the stolen cargo shipment. Where there was one beetlesnatch, there were bound to be more. Not wanting to take any chances, Petre ascended the stairs, crossed the deck, hopped onto the dock, and hastily retraced his path to the marketplace to get materials designed explicitly for exterminating beetlesnatch.

It took him some time, but eventually, he located the materials needed for fumigation. He returned to his water craft and first went into the cargo area. He detonated several devices in the hold and shut the door immediately to contain the sulfurous smoke to the cargo area. He then went to the main cabin and repeated the process.

Only then did Petre realize that his plan to rest in his cabin for a few hours was now impossible. He jumped back onto the dock and returned to the town. After asking a few people walking down the street, Petre discovered to his great disgust that there were no brothels on this islet.

Finally, he contented himself with a hostel highly recommended by several people. He found the building, went in, displayed the chit one more time, where he was ushered into their best private room with its own attached bath.

Petre walked through with an eye for the chamber's elegance. The sleeping platform looked utterly luxurious, but a nice hot bath sounded even better. After the day's trials, he was ready to relax with a nice long, hot soak.

As the steaming water swiftly filled the tub, Petre removed his clothes. He admired his fine reflection in the mirror. He appreciated his lean arms but frowned a little at how his midsection was a little less firm than it had been in the past.

Oh well, I'm sure running after Jena will fix that shortly.

He turned some cold water on so the bath wouldn't be scalding. After a minute or so more, he turned off the faucet and carefully stepped into the tub. Holding onto both sides, he eased himself into the bath up to his neck. He leaned his head back onto the edge and closed his eyes in relief. Within minutes, Petre slept.

DEBBON READ through the betrothal document, more than satisfied with all of the contingencies set in place. Each item was subtly written so Petre wouldn't take offense, but it severely curtailed his involvement in Jena's life even if they couldn't activate the abandonment clause.

As he finished reading each page, he handed them to Chelesa to review as well. Taking the advice of his legal counsel to heart, he wanted to make sure she was comfortable with this document as well. He was surprised each time Chelesa giggled as she read through the contract.

"Oh, this is good," she finally said, "This speaks to Petre's arrogance even while it takes away his rights! He'll be so busy preening over the flattery that he won't notice what he stands to lose."

"That's just what I intended," Miorlen spoke up. He sat across from the Elder and his wife, a pleased smile pasted on his lips. "This is my kind of art, my specialty, really. I love creating an irrevocable document with such skill and finesse. My only regret is that I wasn't given more time to polish it to perfection."

Miorlen sighed. "I'll have to content myself that it's good enough for whom it was intended. Besides, anything more would've probably been lost on the likes of Petre MacVeen anyway."

Elder Debbon looked up from the pages and asked Miorlen. "Do you also have the birth certificate started?"

"I sure do." He paused and then asked, "Would it be possible—."

"Ask what you will, Miorlen," Debbon prompted when Miorlen hesitated.

"I hate to presume to direct your meeting with Petre, but it would be helpful if you could ask him the mother's full legal name and birth date right away. Next, I'd need Jena's birth date to complete the document. After that, you could discuss the betrothal document while I finish the birth certificate. That way, I could have all the documents ready in time for everybody's signatures," he finished in a rush.

"That sounds good to me." He was genuinely looking forward to setting Petre up to lose Jena. A niggling worry tugged at him. What if Petre already realized what a prize Jena was and refused to negotiate a deal with him?

It had been a long time since Debbon doubted his success. With his high-ranking position, success was usually a certainty; however, nothing was ever sure with a master deceptor like Petre MacVeen.

"I think it'd be best if you met with Petre alone, my dear," Chelesa suddenly spoke into the silence. "I don't think I could keep the contempt from either my voice or my face if I had to sit with him for any length of time."

"That's okay, Chelesa. I understand your feelings entirely," Debbon replied. Inwardly he felt the same feelings. However, he had more experience dealing with difficult people since his elevation to First Elder status. He couldn't allow his thoughts to be distracted from the final outcome.

His family must raise Jena. She'd be utterly wasted anywhere else.

What was keeping Petre so long? Not that he minded the extra time, but he left three hours ago. The guard hadn't alerted them to the greatly anticipated visitor.

He hoped to get this matter squared away before dinner since his appetite was non-existent while he worried over the agreement's outcome. However, once it was all finalized, Debbon was sure to be ravenous.

Success had that effect on him!

CHAPTER 47

Seemingly ready to abandon all of his personal rules today, Debbon called up the elemy to extend a search for Petre throughout his islet. Once a target was known, he could hone in on the signal and then get a clear picture of a person's location. With the signal sent and identified, Debbon saw that Petre had fallen asleep in the bathroom at the hostel.

He returned the elemy immediately back to the earth and angrily turned on his patil. How could Petre sleep at a time like this? Debbon anxiously paced his office while waiting for a visitor who slept! The nerve of the man! He called up the hostel and requested the owner to knock on Petre's door. The blasted man was late for a meeting.

The hostel owner sputtered and stammered once he heard Elder Debbon identify himself. He became tongue-tied trying to explain his honor to do as the great Elder requested. Right away, the man had assured Debbon.

About fifteen minutes later, the guard finally notified Debbon that Petre MacVeen wished to meet with the Honorable First Elder Debbon. Debbon smiled at the formal phrasing used by the guard. He only spoke that way when he was trying not to take offense at a visitor's officious manners.

"Please send him into my private office," Debbon replied politely into the patil. He thought Petre might feel a false sense of importance by being invited into the Residence's inner sanctum. He smiled to himself at the many ploys enacted for Petre's benefit.

Debbon stood in his office and took a few paces while inhaling deeply through his nose and exhaling slowly out his mouth to calm his nerves. This meeting was possibly the most important one in his family's lives. He had to ensure he did everything possible to play to Petre's personality to sway him to give up his daughter.

After a few moments, loud slapping footsteps sounded in the hallway near his office. He concentrated on holding an expression of both concern and friendliness. If he displayed any desperation about Jena, Petre would surely pick up on it and use it to his advantage.

A sharp rap on the door followed immediately by the door opening was his cue to begin the most crucial game of his life. Debbon's personal guard, Gatson, walked through the entrance and said, "Petre MacVeen is here to see you, sir." He elaborately waved Petre into the room. Gatson bowed formally to Elder Debbon, turned on his heel, and left the room while softly closing the door behind himself.

Debbon noted Petre's smug expression and ensured his own didn't display the same. He continued Gatson's lead and said, "Petre, please take a seat."

He didn't wait to see if he sat. Instead, Debbon turned and walked around his desk. He spent a few seconds composing himself as he settled into his own chair across from Petre.

"I trust you were able to get a good meal as well as the opportunity to get some rest while I was monitoring Jena's recovery," Debbon inquired without actually making it a question. He was already well aware of the vast expense of items purchased with his personal chit. Debbon chalked it up to an investment in Jena's future, her future living with himself!

"Yes, I did. Thank you very much. Your generosity was beyond compare. How's my daughter doing? Did she have a secondary reaction?"

Debbon refrained from raising his eyebrow. At least Petre's first concern was about his daughter's health. Debbon's estimation of this man was raised by a single point. "No, fortunately. She's been sleeping peacefully upstairs. As I'm sure you're aware, she's a very charming little girl. You must be very proud," Debbon said in his most flattering tone.

Petre positively beamed with the compliment. "Thank you, I am aware."

Debbon began again with chit-chat and asked, "What was her mother's last name?"

Petre looked down as if he were hesitant to speak about Jesisca, and finally, he said, "Keeper."

"That's an unusual last name. When was her birthday?" he asked promptly. There really wasn't any easy way to get that bit of information.

"Elul 22, 3424. Why?" Petre asked suspiciously.

"I just have to fill out some paperwork for my healing records. Oh, that reminds me—what's Jena's birthday?" Debbon continued as if it didn't matter.

Petre seemed content with Elder Debbon's explanation for asking questions. To his credit, he only paused for a couple of seconds before he answered, "Sivan 15, 3443."

"That's good. I should be able to complete my paperwork with that information," Debbon stated with satisfaction. He thought for a moment how to move the conversation over to betrothals without seeming desperate. "How's it been, raising Jena, since Jessa died? I know infants can be very frustrating."

Petre nodded emphatically. "You can't believe how fast they

move once they learn to crawl. I've had to actually spend time going over the water craft to make sure she doesn't get hurt on anything. And as you already saw, even those precautions sometimes aren't enough!

"After this last incident, I'm seriously thinking about finding a caregiver for her since I can't be awake all the time to keep her out of trouble. Right?"

"For sure," Debbon agreed instantly. He couldn't have planned for a better opening, so he carried on, controlling his nervous energy and excitement. Maybe Jehoban was helping him in this matter. It certainly felt like it. "A caregiver, hmm? That gives me an idea, Petre."

"Do you have someone in mind?" Petre leaned forward until his elbows rested on his knees, his hand falling forward, outstretched as if grasping at this unexpected lifeline.

"Something like that. Have you considered making a betrothal for her? She's a charming child. I'm sure someone would be amenable to a match. She'd then go live with their family, and you can carry on with your own life as usual," Debbon suggested helpfully. Unabashedly, he pushed immense concentrations of elemy into Petre to make him more agreeable to the suggestion.

The way Petre's eyes rounded and he fell back into his chair showed that this idea never occurred to him. "Well, no. I can honestly say that's never crossed my mind. I'm afraid my reputation might be a hindrance." His gaze turned down toward his onyx ring, and his fingers clenched into a fist.

Debbon remained silent, waiting for Petre's thoughts to turn toward the final resolution to his problem. He had to know that a betrothal came with compensation. If there were one thing predictable about Petre, it was his uncanny ability to discover a way to profit in any circumstance.

Petre nodded his head suddenly and said, "I think a betrothal might be the best solution. Thank you, Elder Debbon. I'll have to make some inquiries once we are on our way. Is Jena almost ready to go?"

Debbon refrained from smiling as he could see Petre was eager to be on his way now that he could have someone else take care of Jena, and he'd get paid to be still able to see her. It was the perfect solution.

"As long as we're waiting for Jena to be readied to go," he started as though he were just coming up with the idea himself. He said, "What if I said I might be interested in Jena being betrothed to my son Willian. Is that a match you might consider?" He looked at Petre as though he might be granted a favor if Petre accepted his offer.

Petre's gaze riveted to Elder Debbon, his mouth hanging open unbecomingly. From his reaction, it was clear he never expected such an offer from the Elder himself. This was working out better than Debbon could have ever hoped. Jena would have a fantastic home, and Petre himself would be free from the parenting burden.

Petre snapped shut his mouth, composing himself to answer calmly even as his heart raced. "I think we could look at that as an option."

"I've been looking for someone for Willian for a while now. I've had my legal counsel draw up a betrothal agreement in case I might find someone who we thought might make a good match for him," he said as though this had been a thought for a long time. "Of course, there's also the betrothal price which would need to be agreed upon. I'm sure you know I'd be fair with that as well."

Nodding hurriedly, Debbon could practically see Petre add up just how much he'd be willing to pay to marry his son to someone special like Petre's daughter. Unethically, Debbon used his mind-reading ability to read Petre's thoughts. The sum was astronomical in Petre's mind the longer he mused.

Petre imagined sitting down to dinner with Elder Debbon regularly, visiting his private house, walking through the town beside the esteemed Elder Debbon. These images made Petre smile, even as Debbon cringed that this might become his reality. Petre thought his life had finally made the turn toward fortune as he had always imagined.

Debbon used this opportunity to have Petre sign the paperwork. He pushed back his chair and opened one drawer after another. In each drawer, he pretended to rummage through them to look for the betrothal agreement and murmured as if to himself, "I think I have a copy of a betrothal agreement somewhere around here."

He shuffled a few more papers for good measure before he suddenly ripped a wad of paperwork out and flourished it with a sense of triumph and said, "Ah, I knew I had a copy somewhere."

Debbon briefly glanced at the document to ensure it was the blank copy without Jena's name and then passed the papers across the table for Petre to read. He saw Petre's eagerness to read the document. Debbon cleared his throat and asked, "Would you like something to drink while you read through the agreement's terms?"

"Sure, sure," Petre said as he was already distracted by this unexpected turn of fortune. "Water would be good," he added offhandedly.

Debbon rang a small bell and requested two glasses of water from the maid who appeared at the office door. While he wanted to make it seem as though he wished Petre to read the document, in actuality, he was just anxious for him to sign it and leave. Creating minor diversions would interrupt Petre's concentration, so he'd probably miss the abandonment clause.

Less than a minute later, another diversion came in the form of the maid returning with a small tray containing two glasses of water and a full carafe for refilling. She bent over the desk next to Petre and deposited the tray closest to Debbon. She picked up one of the glasses and offered it to Petre first.

"Thank you, miss," Petre replied as he leered at her shapely figure so close to him.

"You're very welcome, sir," she replied sweetly.

Debbon hid his smirk by picking up the other glass and taking a quick sip. *Petre is a very predictable man. He must have gotten to the agreement's part with the monetary terms—ah, now he has!*

CHAPTER 48

Petre's eyes widened perceptibly, and he quickly reached out and grabbed his water glass. He took a huge gulp. In his distraction, he misjudged the swallow and set the glass down clumsily when he coughed uncontrollably. Tears streamed down his cheeks as he doubled over in his chair.

"Are you going to be okay, Mr. MacVeen? Do you require my assistance?" Debbon needed to at least act concerned. He stood from his chair as if prepared to spring into action if required.

Petre continued to cough, but he shook his head to indicate and held up one hand in a stay motion. A few minutes later, Petre's coughing subsided. He wiped his eyes with the backs of his hands and rubbed them on his pants to dry the moisture. "Sorry," he croaked, "the water went down the wrong way." He coughed a few more times and then picked the papers back up to resume his reading.

Debbon felt Petre had had sufficient time with the documents, so he cut right to the chase, "As you can see, I'm willing to pay five thousand taj as a betrothal price for the proper companion for my son. I think you'll agree that this sum is more than fair."

Petre nodded solemnly and said, "Quite fair."

Debbon saw Petre's expression change when he realized he'd agreed too readily. Petre was used to haggling for a price. Indeed, in his mind, Petre figured he could've raised that figure by at least half. Clearly, it was too late now to backtrack.

Debbon didn't want to give Petre any more time to create additional concessions to throw in. This discussion had already gone on long enough. He stood from his chair and thrust his hand out toward Petre, and said, "Do we have an agreement for our children?"

With how quickly Petre popped up from his chair, he didn't want this offer to pass him by. Belatedly he thrust his hand forward until it clasped Elder Debbon's. His satisfied look made Debbon grimace inwardly.

Debbon knew he'd provided Petre with the most favorable solution to his problem with Jena. Now he'd be free to pursue whatever illegal ventures he had planned without having Jena as a witness or a distraction.

"I think it's worth noting that Jena's a magnet for trouble. I'll check in with her often to make sure she's happy with your family."

"Great! I look forward to Jena joining my family," Debbon announced happily. No matter what objections Petre employed now, he couldn't care less. "Let me just have my legal counsel fill out these documents to make them official. Then we can take care of the money matter. We should finish within a few minutes."

He sat back down and called up his counselor on the patil. "Miorlen, please draw up an official betrothal agreement for me," he requested as if this were an everyday occurrence. He spent the next couple of minutes answering each of the lawyer's questions about items unique to the documents. He watched Petre's expression as he spoke with the counselor and was delighted to see he appeared content with the transaction.

"I have the documents ready for teleportation, sir," Miorlen said a moment later.

"Very good, thank you!" Debbon ended the connection just as a stack of plasfilm appeared on the desk beside the patil. "Here we are, Petre."

He shoved the plasfilms in front of Petre and personally handed him a pen. The side flags indicated each spot the documents required a signature. Debbon walked around the desk and sat on the table's corner to flip the pages while Petre signed. When Petre finished his last signature, Debbon took the stack and returned to his side of the desk. Debbon then added his name to each page and removed the flags as he went along.

When the papers were complete, he entered the stack into his replicator and waited a few seconds for the duplicated set of documents to generate. He took the copies, tapped them on the desktop, clipped them together, sealed them in an envelope, and handed the packet to Petre. The originals were treated similarly and then put into a locking top drawer of his desk.

Debbon removed a large bag containing five thousand taj from the next drawer down. With a flourish, he deposited the bag into Petre's eagerly outstretched hands. "It's been a pleasure doing business with you, Petre," Debbon added for good measure and offered his hand to shake Petre's again.

Debbon looked at his timepiece and then exclaimed, "Is it really that late? Wow, I need to be getting home! My wife will kill me if I'm late again!" He walked toward the door expecting Petre to follow after him.

Petre belatedly realized that their meeting had ended. He grabbed the envelope and stood with the money still clutched in his other hand. He strode over to the door to join Elder Debbon. "Am I going to meet your wife now?"

"Oh no, Petre. I'll be heading home with Jena immediately. The betrothal agreement states that you mustn't contact Jena for at least twenty-four hours from when the document's signed. We must be sure to follow all of the directives so as not to create a breach of contract. I'm sure you understand," he answered quickly. This was the part of the conversation he'd been anticipating the whole evening.

"Oh, sure, sure," Petre replied with a troubled look on his face.

Debbon took advantage of his confusion and walked out of the office and into the hall, saying, "Right this way, Petre." He glanced beside him to ensure Petre stayed beside him and then hurried through the double doors, out along the garden path, and up to the guard station. Here he stopped and turned to Petre to say, "I guess this is goodbye until we meet again." He smiled at Petre for what he hoped would be the last time.

Petre smiled back and said, "It's been good doing business with you." He held up the bag of coins and nodded his head meaningfully.

As if it were an afterthought, Debbon snapped his fingers and said, "I'll need to have my chit back."

So began the night's most entertaining dance for Debbon. Petre didn't want to release either precious package to retrieve the chit from his tunic pocket with the envelope in one hand and the money bag in the other.

His attempt to balance the heavy taj pouch on the flimsy envelope caused it to fold in half and dump the money onto the ground. Upon impact, the coins bounced out of the top of the sack and rolled in every direction, much to Petre's dismay.

Petre dropped the envelope and scurried after each coin. After a few minutes, he recovered the money. He tied the top with a solid knot and left the bag on the ground next to the envelope.

Digging in his pocket, he retrieved the Elder's voucher and slapped it into his outstretched hand. Petre picked himself up from the humiliating position on the ground and grabbed up his two items with as much dignity as he could muster.

"I really must be going now. Goodbye," Debbon said one last time and then turned on his heel and walked back through the Residence. He didn't bother restraining his grin from the vision of Petre scrambling after the money, but he did manage to keep his shoulders from shaking from his contained mirth.

Once he got to the kitchen, where Jena was being entertained by several of the kitchen staff, he addressed everyone in the room. "I want to thank all of you for your help regarding this matter. Jena is officially ours!" He raised his hands in thanks and happily heard the genuinely joyful cheers from his employees.

Debbon walked over to where Jena sat on the floor. He kneeled in front of her, held out his hands, and said, "Are you ready to go home, Jena?" He was delighted when she immediately raised her hands to go with him.

Debbon lifted the little girl and tucked her close to his side. The hairs along his arms and neck prickled with the elemy crackling around her body. He backed up a few steps and said to his staff, "Sorry for my bad manners."

With that scant warning, he hurriedly raised sufficient elemy, augmented significantly by Jena's power, and translated the two of them to his private estate.

CHAPTER 49

D r. Stephen Gascon pursed his lips as he read the case file. "It seems as though Amanda is once again using the father-figure of the Elder to protect her inner child. Her account of Petre being taken advantage of tells me there's some discord among the people who know Nealand's location."

"How can I use Amanda's ability to move between these two worlds to my advantage? As disorders go, the multi-dimensional disorder seems to meld both the rational and irrational mind together to create order out of chaos." Dr. Gascon pressed the stop button on his hand-held recorder as he responded to the knock on his office door. "Come in!"

"Dr. Gascon? I'd like to discuss Amanda Covington's case with you." Dr. Jasmine Medin asked as she entered the office.

"Sure, I was just going over her notes." He pointed to the stack of papers on his desk. "What are your thoughts?"

"I'd like to suggest a medication change."

"You know where I stand on this issue, Dr. Medin." Stephen sat back and crossed his arms, irritated at having this conversation yet again with the hypnotherapist.

"I know, Dr. Gascon. I'm not asking for Amanda to be taken off the medication, only for a dosage reduction. She's lost weight since she's been here, and I think a lower dose would be just as effective without having any harmful side effects." Jasmine rushed through her explanation, hoping to encourage the Director to agree with her summation.

Dr. Gascon pursed his lips as he pretended to consider the doctor's request. He didn't need to take any advice from someone subordinate to him.

"I'll consider that. Speaking of Amanda, I've received yet another phone call from the Taivas family asking about our progress in locating their son. I wasn't pleased to report we have no further news. I'd like you to push Amanda harder in your sessions. She must divulge where Nealand is. Soon."

A pained expression crossed Dr. Medin's face, but she managed to smooth it into neutrality almost instantly. "I'm not sure pushing her harder will yield better results. Our sessions are already lasting almost four hours, and that's longer than I'd typically keep anyone under hypnosis in any situation. Please consider her dosage reduction as the next step to speeding up her recall."

Oh, this woman was going to drive him to distraction. If he didn't already have so many irons in the fire, he'd take Amanda's case on himself. As it was—. "Fine! I'll put in the order right now."

He turned to his computer and typed a few notes on Amanda's chart. He jammed his finger down on the enter key and turned back to Jasmine. "No more excuses, Jasmine, get me results!"

JASMINE'S PULSE raced as though charged by the thrill that she'd managed a minor win over Dr. Gascon. She smiled at Amanda, sitting on the couch across from her.

"I've convinced Dr. Gascon to decrease your medication

dosage. I'm sorry I couldn't get him to banish it altogether, but he has a definite affinity for drugging all patients. It was a small victory, but more than I've achieved in the past. Shall we get started?"

Amanda smiled as she prepared herself. The medication entered her bloodstream and increased her heart rate. Chills and heatwaves washed over her, making her squirm uncomfortably.

Dr. Medin watched over her patient, knowing her discomfort and wishing she could do more. She'd always look out for her patients' best interest. Focusing on the task at hand, she instructed Amanda to relax and guided her thoughts back to Tuala...

AMANDA WOKE in a state of disorientation. She lifted herself back into a sitting position. *What happened?* She surveyed her surroundings, immediately recognizing Bryon and Alena's living room.

"It worked," she whispered to herself as all her memories flooded back with breathtaking speed.

"Amanda?" Alena asked quietly. "Are you okay now?"

Amanda turned her head toward where Alena kneeled in front of her. She smiled at Alena and said, "I think I'm perfect now!"

She leaned forward and embraced Alena as if her life hung on this contact. She pulled herself away and asked, "Didn't I see Juila before I passed out?"

"Yes, Bryon's holding her just behind you," she replied and signaled with her hand for Bryon to bring Juila over for Amanda to hold.

Bryon rushed around the chair to kneel next to Alena and held Juila out for Amanda to take into her lap. Even as his lips smiled, it didn't reach his eyes. Amanda ignored this conflict for the moment as she reunited with her daughter. Whatever Bryon was withholding could wait for a few more minutes.

"Oh, she's gotten so big! How old is she now?" Amanda asked in wonder as she looked intently at the daughter she hadn't seen for two and a half months of her time. How could she have changed so much in such a short time?

Juila's big blue eyes looked into her own with comprehension and curiosity. She attempted to sit up on her own. That was new too.

"She's six mesans old now and crawling everywhere," Alena replied but didn't move from where she sat protectively in front of Amanda.

"I can't wait to see Jena! Are they even harder to tell apart now that they're moving around?" Amanda smiled at Juila. Neither of them answered. The silence in the room caused Amanda's heart to race. Did this have something to do with Bryon's cryptic look? Amanda looked directly at Alena and asked, "Where's Jena?"

"Oh, Amanda, I wish I didn't have to tell you this," she paused to measure her words.

"Just tell me, Alena. Otherwise, I'm going to think the worst." Amanda's mind raced.

"She was abducted the day before yesterday. We're relatively sure Petre MacVeen took her."

Her heart faltered. This news was completely unexpected. What was she missing? How did Petre find out about Jena? Yesterday! If only she'd hurried, she could've prevented any of this from happening.

Amanda hugged Juila close to her chest and stared uncomprehendingly at Alena and Bryon. She desperately wished that she'd misheard what Alena said.

Seeing the apparent fear and sadness in their eyes, she despairingly concluded she'd heard correctly. She refused to lose focus—her daughter deserved better from her. With her eyes closed and her cheek resting on top of Juila's head, she asked in a whisper, "What's been done to try to find her?"

Bryon said with some hope in his voice, "We've had a hit on the beacon from the stolen freighter telepod. The authorities are checking it out as we speak.

"Frasnia's continuing to search for the beacon signal from the freighter's personal telepod. She promised not to sleep until she found it."

"Okay," Amanda said slowly. Opening her eyes, she addressed Alena, "Have you checked her birth crystal?"

Alena looked guiltily at Bryon before she returned her gaze to Amanda and said, "Yes, we've both been checking it. Most recently, there was a disturbance with the connection—."

"What does that mean?" Amanda interrupted with rising concern.

With as much assurance as he could convey in his tone, Bryon said, "We think it means Petre drugged Jena, either for transport or because of an injury. We're not sure which yet, but we were about to try again when you came knocking on the door."

Alena offered, "Why don't you try to connect with Jena's birth crystal? As her mother, you would have the best connection."

Amanda paused for a moment before she thought to say, "Why don't you lead me through the steps again. This is too important to mess up, and I've been out of touch for the last two mesans."

"Absolutely," Alena instantly replied while nodding her head in agreement with Amanda's assessment of the situation. "Let Bryon take Juila for a few minutes while we get this sorted out."

Bryon instantly bent forward and offered his hands for Juila. With only a moment's hesitation, Amanda lifted Juila from her lap and into Bryon's waiting grasp. She eagerly watched Juila snuggle into Bryon's arms and felt relief that her daughter would be safe while she tried to locate Jena.

"Okay," Amanda said to Alena, "I'm ready to begin." Amanda closed her eyes, took several deep breaths, and slowly exhaled as she settled back into the chair to relax her body and let her mind roam free.

"First, picture the deep black color of Jena's birth crystal. As you breathe deeply, imagine the elemy surrounding Jena's crystal. Focus on the energy's colors, which are unique to Jena. Can you see the colors?"

"Yes," Amanda slowly said as the details appeared surrounding the colors distinctive to Jena. "The connection seems as clear as I last remember it. She's in a small room. The shades are drawn, making the room darker, but it's obviously daytime outside.

"A woman is sitting in a chair beside the bed where Jena's sleeping. She's reading from a book in her lap, and I can only see the top of her head." The strain of using the crystal from such a distance became too much, and Amanda broke the connection.

She took another deep breath and slowly opened her eyes as she exhaled. The strangest feeling of having seen that room before assaulted her, but that was impossible since she'd only been in a few Tualan homes. "Maybe you should check in on her and see if you know the location where she's sleeping."

"Okay," Alena agreed. She spent only a few moments to confirm that the fuzziness from before was now noticeably gone. Unfortunately, she didn't know where Jena was sleeping, nor did she recognize the woman seated beside her.

Breaking the connection, Alena said to her avid audience, "Jena appears to be fine now. Whatever affected her before has either passed or was taken away by a powerful healer. I think I'll contact some of the best healers I know to ask if they've treated a baby today. This might be our best lead yet!" Alena jumped up with renewed hope, rushing from the room to make the inquiries on the patil.

"I can take Juila back now," Amanda said to Bryon. Thankfully, Bryon didn't hesitate to comply. Even with Juila returned to her lap, an emptiness threatened to overwhelm Amanda, knowing that her other daughter was among strangers and possibly hurt.

She didn't know what to do now other than hold on to her

remaining daughter and pray that Frasnia would find the personal telepod swiftly to give them another lead on which to follow up.

CHAPTER 50

Petre hoped Elder Debbon wouldn't remember to ask for the chit back. *Oh well, in the end, I got the better deal!* With a snap to his step and a smile toward each person he passed on the way back to his water craft, he imagined everyone would soon know, if they didn't already, that he was now a part of Elder Debbon's family.

When he took Jena, this scenario never even occurred to him. He never anticipated that this would work out so favorably for himself. Even better, someone else would have to deal with all of the messes Jena would get into.

Just thinking about the trials he endured, he didn't think much about Bryon's child-rearing skills since Jena wasn't very cooperative with anything, especially eating.

By now, he strode up the wooden dock, almost at his water craft. Had enough time passed for the beetlesnatch bombs to eradicate any infestation on his ship? It was more than a little concerning to think those critters might be loose on his craft while sailing out on the vast oceans.

He stood at the dock's edge, looking down onto his vessel. Pursing his lips, he concluded he'd rather not risk it. He turned around and returned to the vendor's square to procure an anti-venom kit from the vendor who'd sold him the extermination bombs.

After a few negotiations, Petre owned the kit and hoped he'd never need to use it. He tucked it under his arm and returned to the dock. He noted the sun's location near the horizon's edge from this vantage point. If he hurried, he'd be well away from the sand-bars, coral reefs, and riptides before sunset.

He hopped over his craft's railing and descended several stairs to the main cabin door. Smoke no longer escaped from the cracks around the door, so Petre felt reassured that enough time had passed to clear out the malodorous fumes.

He opened the door and walked in. While the smell inside wasn't exactly pleasant, he'd leave the cabin door open to allow the salty sea breezes to clean out any remaining stench.

Petre dropped the anti-venom kit, the bag of money, and the precious envelope onto the table as he passed by on his cabin inspection for any beetlesnatch bodies.

Back up on the deck, Petre unfastened the tie-down ropes from the dock. He concentrated on navigating his vessel away from the pier and the surrounding water crafts. As he continued to navigate from the deck's bow, a satisfied grin crept across his lips over how his prospects were finally turning to his favor.

Only the unfortunate incident with the spilled money put any type of damper on his mood. With the fortune supplied by Elder Debbon, Petre could take his time selling the stolen cargo. He could stay out at sea for an extended time, courtesy of Elder Debbon's voucher in resupplying his craft.

Petre didn't have any monetary worries for the first time in his life.

He called out his joy, exhilarating in how his voice carried over the open waters. He relished the waves shifting below him as he swiftly sailed away from the islet and out into the expansive sea's open water.

Today marked the beginning of Petre's new life. A life of riches, respect, and long-deserved rewards.

~

ELDER DEBBON proudly offered Jena over to his wife. Debbon delighted in seeing Chelesa's reaction when she felt Jena's crackling energy as soon as she took the girl into her arms.

"Is there anything we can do to dampen her abilities? It's quite distracting," she said with a massive grin as she lovingly caressed Jena's blonde curls.

"I'm almost loathe to discourage any of her ability," Debbon said. Then, seeing his wife's frown, he added, "I can teach her to hold it in. She's a fast learner!"

"Must we wait three days before we can perform her ceremony to switch her crystal from Petre to us?"

"I think it'd be wise. We don't want to have Petre come back with exclusion accusations should he make an appearance within the three-day visitation clause."

Chelesa pursed her lips thoughtfully but let the conversation drop. "Fine, I don't want to put any thought out into the universe, which might encourage Petre to read the document more closely and show up at our home."

Jena's eyes locked onto hers. Chelesa said, "No matter what happens with Petre, I'm going to love this wonderfully powerful little girl. Plus, I have total faith that my brilliant husband can teach Jena all the skills necessary to harness her massive talent through her black crystal."

With effort, she managed to break eye contact to look up at Debbon. "Do you think she'll receive a new crystal color at the ceremony now that Petre isn't raising her? I'm hopeful that Jena's life troubles are now at an end since we'll watch over her."

"It's possible. We'll just have to wait and see," Debbon replied. He sniffed the air and asked, "Is that dinner I smell?"

"Yes, let's go sit and enjoy our family meal." Chelesa turned around and preceded Debbon into the dining room. She handed Jena to a waiting nursemaid and watched while Jena was settled into a highchair positioned next to her place at the table.

Chelesa sat, and with a contented smile at her now-expanded family, she said, "I've prepared all of your favorite dishes. Thank you, Debbon, for our new first-daughter."

Debbon smiled at Chelesa, Willian, and Jena as he, too, took his seat at the table. Did Willian realize that the little girl seated across from him was his betrothed?

Debbon watched as Willian stared at Jena and then glanced at his mother, trying to figure out how they suddenly had a new baby in the house.

Finally, he addressed his son. "Jena is your betrothed, Willian. She'll be living with us forever, and when you both grow up, you two will be just as happy together as your mother and I have been. Isn't that exciting?"

Willian's shoulder raised almost to his ear. "I guess," he replied, "Can we eat now?"

Chelesa and Debbon erupted in laughter. The awkward moment passed without incident. They ate in silence while staring at the newest family addition, where the nursemaid expertly spooned strained carrots into Jena's mouth.

"She has perfect manners," Chelesa commented.

Debbon never doubted she would. Jena was perfection personified. He closed his eyes and prayed, *Thank you, Jehoban, for showing me this future and blessing me with the beautiful first-daughter.*

⌇

BRYON ENDED the connection on the patil and loudly exhaled his frustration. They needed a win for once. They expected better news regarding the personal telepod's discovery. When Frasnia excitedly told them that she'd located the vehicle, Bryon immediately contacted the authorities to investigate.

Even with the search completed, the outcome didn't result in Jena's imminent return. On the contrary, they'd have to search for Jena by other means with the recovery of both telepods.

Gripping the edge of his desk, Bryon leveraged himself from his chair. He felt a million anons old, but he had to stay strong for the women.

He composed himself to tell both Alena and Amanda the unsatisfactory outcome. He strode as his mind whirled with different scenarios of how this conversation would turn out. In any event, Jena wasn't coming home again tonight; that was evident.

Alena looked up in anticipation when Bryon came out of his office. "What did the authorities discover? Are they bringing Jena home?"

Bryon couldn't stop his crestfallen expression. Alena had her answer without him having to say a single word.

"I'm afraid not," he replied slowly. He turned to address Amanda when he continued, "The authorities investigated the site where the personal telepod was found. There *is* some good news, however. They discovered evidence of Jena having been at that location.

"Apparently, while Petre walked back and forth from the telepod to his water craft, he set Jena down on the ground. They found hand and knee prints from her crawling in the sandy soil. Unfortunately, that was all they discovered.

"Now they're launching a search for his water craft. We must assume that he's still using the same one where you were held captive, Amanda. Eventually, he'll have to dock for supplies at some port. Before that happens, every port official will be notified to contact the authorities immediately. Petre will be detained for questioning, and his water craft will be searched. We'll get Jena back. I just don't know how soon it'll be."

Amanda hung on his every word. Bryon knew she tried to keep herself hopeful, but she'd been on that vessel with Petre. He shared her concern, especially if they were out on the ocean.

Amanda cried out, "Now that she's crawling, what's to keep her from falling overboard and drowning in the sea? Ugh, I'm starting to sound like my mother." She held a fist against her lips as if trying to prevent any further words from escaping.

Alena asked, "How long will it take the local authorities to notify all of the port masters?"

Bryon jumped at the opportunity to give some positive news. "They told me it'd be done before the end of the day. I'm sure with all of the shady dealings Petre's had with most of the port masters, they'll be more than ready to repay Petre by turning him in.

"Meanwhile, the local officials instructed us to continue monitoring Jena's birth crystal to see if we can get any more clues as to her whereabouts. When was the last check-in? Whose turn is it now?" He looked from Amanda to Alena questioningly. He wanted them to feel like something was being done to locate Jena.

Bryon badly wanted to punch something. He cringed at the idea of Jena being alone with Petre for the past four days. Each day was worse than the one before as all of their leads turned into nothing but one dead end after another. Even though it was nearly impossible, he wanted to keep positive thoughts.

Alena sighed, mirroring Bryon's sentiment over the monotonous and most likely fruitless task.

"It's Amanda's turn."

CHAPTER 51

Elder Debbon wasn't about to question how he could be so lucky that the third day since Jena's betrothal had come and gone without Petre making an appearance at their estate. He hadn't realized how much strain his whole family had been under during the waiting interval.

Readjusting the ceremonial supplies next to him, Debbon looked up as his wife entered the room, holding a freshly bathed Jena in her arms. Debbon couldn't contain the smile that spread from his lips to his eyes at how happy his wife was carrying Jena.

Even though it was unorthodox for him to perform this ceremony himself, Jena's powerful aura would be best served with his touch. He waited until his wife and son were seated on the floor in front of him before beginning the ceremony.

"We have gathered here today to mark the special bond between our son, Willian, and his newly betrothed, Jena. As their parents, we must demonstrate the importance of a loving relationship and teach our son and our first-daughter to respect one another unconditionally. Each union blessed in this manner is held in the highest regard.

"Chelesa, as their mother, do you promise to watch over both of these children? Will you teach them to the best of your ability the rewards of a loving relationship?"

Chelesa responded before Debbon finished the last syllable. "I will."

"And I, as their father, do promise to guide both of these children throughout their lives into becoming productive citizens of our world. I also have the responsibility as an Elder and representative of Jehoban to teach them to use their skills to benefit society and make us proud to call them our son and first-daughter.

"I understand the task of teaching them in the ways of Jehoban will become my first priority so they'll know the importance of following His ways. As they mature, I'll ensure they understand their position in society. And I'll prepare Willian also to become an Elder when he's ready. I'm equipped to undertake these tasks with love and devotion."

Debbon reached down, mixed several ingredients into a bowl, and added a few dollops of liquid to make a paste. He thoroughly mixed the contents with his finger until it was smoothly blended. With the green paste on his fingertip, he drew a line across Willian's forehead and then Jena's. He redipped his finger into the bowl and then drew a circle on the backs of both of the children's hands.

He set aside the bowl and wiped his finger on a small towel. Next, he opened his ceremonial box and pulled out two small rings, each with a clear diamond set flush. He placed one band on Willian's right-hand middle finger and then guided Chelesa to put the other ring on the middle finger of Jena's left hand.

"These rings symbolize the everlasting bond between them. If, at this time, a new birth crystal should be required for either Jena or Willian, I ask that it be made clear that this is Jehoban's will."

Debbon waited only a moment before he received a definitive answer. The lid to his ceremonial box slammed shut. Everyone jumped at the unexpected noise in the quiet room. Debbon grinned and said, "I guess we have our answer. Their crystals shall remain unchanged."

Although he kept his expression light, he swore he saw an ominous shadow behind the box just before it closed. It had only been there for a split second. Even so, he wouldn't take any chances. As soon as all of the ceremony witnesses left, he'd perform a blessing ceremony on their house.

"By the power vested in me by the name of Jehoban, I declare these two children bonded for life. I also decree that since Petre has enacted the abandonment clause by not visiting Jena within the last three days, and in the absence of any other parental guidance for Jena, she is now in the sole care of myself and my wife, Chelesa.

"I have marked Jena's forehead to be able to divine the thoughts and intents of this being. I have marked each of Jena's hands to be able to divine the actions for which she will be responsible in her lifetime.

"Chelesa, rest your hand over Jena's crystal and say, *Saya memberikan ini untuk Anda dengan cinta.*"

Chelesa smiled.

Debbon knew she translated the phrase. *I give this to you with love.* She wasn't the original giver of the crystal necklace of protection, but she'd gladly assume the motherly duty for her first-daughter.

Chelesa spoke the required phrase and watched as Debbon took a warm, wet cloth and wiped the green liquid from Jena's forehead and hands.

He rinsed the cloth in another bowl of clean water. Debbon removed the fabric, picked up the cup, and gave it to Chelesa. She didn't hesitate.

"I give you this water to drink. By the drinking of the liquid which contains your first-daughter's essence, you will seal the bond between your life and her's."

Having participated in this ceremony once before for her son, Chelesa brought the liquid to her mouth and drank it down hastily. She shivered, and her face contorted as if she'd swallowed something bitter, but she managed to hand the empty cup back to Debbon.

Debbon would have to ask her about her strange reaction after the ceremony. Right now, he had to conclude this ceremony, forever sealing Jena into their family.

Debbon then spoke to everyone in the room, "With this child, Jena, safe and protected from harm, we can all celebrate." There was an eruption of applause from the house staff who had attended this sacred occasion.

Debbon reached over, smoothed the blonde curls away from Jena's cheek, and smiled at his beautiful wife, who tenderly held the child.

As Chelesa and Debbon stood at the front of the room waiting for the compliments from each of the spectators, she turned to her husband and said, "I can't believe she's really ours!"

Chelesa turned Jena forward as the first guest from the crowd came forward and kissed Jena's forehead in a welcoming to the family. Chelesa smiled at each person and graciously accepted their congratulations for their first-daughter.

Debbon grinned foolishly at everyone, but inside he was troubled that Jena's crystal assignment hadn't changed with her new life. He knew a dark crystal color denoted a hard life for the wearer.

Thinking about this caused a twinge of concern for his son and wife, wondering if Jena's adoption into their family would somehow bring about danger or sorrow. There was nothing he could do about it now. He'd set extra protection wards around Jena and hope for the best.

PETRE WAS IN HIS ELEMENT, surrounded by the open ocean. He enjoyed every aspect of the water's smell, breezes caressing his skin, and the uncertain sway of his water craft when it shifted with the gentle waves.

Never had he enjoyed doing nothing all day more than he did now. Not only did he have a pile of money sitting on his table in the cabin, but he also had enough supplies stored on his vessel to allow him the luxury of sitting idle for better than two anons.

Three days passed since signing the betrothal contract with Elder Debbon. Only a couple of times since then did Petre feel a twinge of regret for not spending more time with Jena.

Each time one of those thoughts blossomed, he comforted himself with the idea of showing up at Elder Debbon's private estate and the warm, welcoming greetings he'd receive before several maids presented Jena to him for his inspection. Never again would he be defecated on or have to worry about Jena getting into something harmful.

Petre went inside his cabin and sat at the room's only table. He picked up the betrothal agreement. If he wanted that dream visit to become a reality, Petre needed to know when he could visit. Elder Debbon explicitly said he wasn't allowed to see Jena for the first twenty-four hours but never gave a clear answer about when he should return.

The light wasn't very good in the cabin as the sun was setting, so Petre stood and retrieved a candle from the cupboard. He lit it with a thought and resumed his seat with the plasfilms in hand.

As he had before, he skimmed through the document. This time, he specifically sought any visitation timelines. Suddenly his eyes caught the phrase *abandonment clause,* and he slowed down to read the passage, which was tucked in the middle of a particularly dull paragraph on daily care.

Should the birth parent be unable or unwilling to visit with the child after the first twenty-four hours have elapsed, but before the expiration of seventy-two hours from the signing of this document, then said parent will forego all future visitation and rights to said child. It will then be assumed that said parent will have abandoned the child in the best interest of the betrothal and henceforth will have no recourse to future contact with the child.

Petre looked at his timepiece, dreading what he already knew in his heart. He only had half an hour before the seventy-two hours expired. Even if teleportation were an option, he was nowhere near landfall to make that happen. By feeling overconfident in his newfound wealth, he had missed his only opportunity to a better life.

Now, more than anything, Petre wanted to forget about his life. He got up and opened the cupboard containing his newly stocked liquor supply. He selected a large bottle of the most potent alcohol and sat at the table.

Tearing off the cap, Petre stared at the thick bottle brimming with bronze-colored liquor. He didn't need a glass. He wasn't planning on having anything left in the bottle when he finished.

He lifted the bottle in a toast to nobody and said aloud, "To the wonderful life I could've had!" He brought the bottle to his lips and guzzled the liquid for several seconds.

After swallowing, he took a deep breath before chugging the foul liquid again. Numbness pulsed through his body on his way to becoming exceedingly drunk.

<h1 style="text-align:center">CHAPTER 52</h1>

Amanda leaned back in the living room chair to compose herself for seeking the crystal's energy. She was intimately familiar with the process since they'd performed it every hour on the hour.

As was her usual, Jena spent most of her time sleeping. On the few occasions where she was awake, she'd been eating and too busy examining her food to help reveal her surroundings.

The elemy rapidly built as Amanda focused on the black diamond. Each detail became distinct as her heart raced at finally seeing a different scene. A woman held Jena, who looked down at her with a loving smile.

In the next few seconds, Amanda heard the woman say, "I can't believe she's really ours," before her connection with the crystal shattered. Amanda gasped, and her eyes popped open.

"What is it, Amanda?" Bryon and Alena both asked in unison.

"The connection just ended! I can't feel Jena anymore. I don't understand. How could this have happened, Alena?"

"I don't know. Just a second, let me take a look."

The room was utterly silent. Bryon and Amanda held still while they waited for Alena to connect with Jena's crystal. Seconds dragged like hours as they continued to wait. Alena shook her head and finally opened her eyes before saying, "I can't find her either."

"How can that be?"

"It's almost as if her crystal's been reassigned. Exactly what did you see before the connection stopped, Amanda?"

"A woman held Jena. She smiled down at her and then—." When she replayed the woman's words, Amanda exhaled, deflating as fast as a balloon pricked by a sharp needle. In an ominous tone, she continued, "the woman said something like 'I can't believe she's ours.' What did she mean by that, Alena?"

"That's what I was afraid of. Somebody performed a new crystal ceremony to reassign Jena's crystal. This's actually a blessing, Amanda. Only wise-women or Elders can reassign a crystal.

"And we can discount an Elder doing it because they only perform them on infrequent occasions. We need to contact every wise-women and find out who performed the ceremony and who requested it."

Juila chose that moment to cry from the other room. Amanda immediately left the room with a heavy heart. She picked up the upset infant from the cradle and hugged her close.

Could Juila tell something had happened with her twin? The timing seemed a bit suspect. If only Juila were old enough to talk about what she felt! Amanda desperately wanted Jena with her as well, and she spoke intently to Juila, "We'll get your sister back! I promise!"

THE MAGIC OF TIME
BOOK THREE OF THE CHOSEN ORIGINS

CHAPTER 1

Amanda held Juila on her lap while Bryon and Alena discussed their latest progress on finding Amanda's other daughter, Jena. It had been almost sixteen mesans since Jena was taken from the marketplace where Alena had been shopping.

While they knew Jena was well-cared for, they didn't know where she lived. Amanda's original belief that she could find Jena immediately and return to Earth vanished long ago.

She was sure her parents were worried sick about her while she was gone. Every day that passed felt like a fresh failure and a disappointment to the family she willingly left behind on Earth.

Her heart ached for their sorrow; she knew the feeling intimately. Unfortunately, there wasn't any way to get a message to her folks letting them know of her safe arrival to Tuala, so they were left not knowing if their daughter still lived.

Her parents didn't have the luxury of looking in on her birth crystal. Although, Amanda lost that ability as well with Jena.

One consolation Amanda held on to was she knew what Jena

would look like even though she hadn't seen her since she was two mesans old. Her other daughter, Juila, was Jena's identical twin.

Amanda spent considerable time studying Juila closely while awake and sleeping. Her beautiful curly blonde hair just now touched her shoulders. Her eyes were a striking shade of blue surrounded by thick, dark, long eyelashes, which almost everyone commented on when they first met her.

At almost two years old, or anons, as they called them here in Tuala, her baby teeth were nicely spaced in her mouth. She still had her rosy cheeks and a small nose that tipped up slightly.

Amanda reverently touched the deep red birth crystal pendant resting on Juila's chest as it hung from the ornate chain around her neck. She thought about the pendant adorning her other daughter's neck.

While they were identical twins, their stones were very different as Jena's birth crystal consisted of black diamonds. She marveled at the seemingly magic elemy surrounding the pendant, which prevented its removal until a child turned eighteen.

Juila's intelligence and precociousness for her age seemed to be the norm for children in Tuala. Every time Juila talked, she seemed to have an incredible insight into her surroundings.

She was very helpful around the house, which was also a drastic change from children her age on Earth. Just after the twins were born, Amanda had commented on this strange ability when she was alone with Alena.

While Alena was a native Tualan, she didn't know any other way for children to behave and had looked at Amanda strangely for the remark. Alena must've seen something in Amanda's expression since she shared with Amanda what she had learned during her wise-woman training about the birth crystals' abilities.

"The children change when they receive their birth crystal. The massive amount of elemental energy, called by its shortened term 'elemy,' which surrounds the crystal, matures them more rapidly.

Their motor skills enhance along with their abilities to think, reason, and speak.

"Parents are taught this's important for the children so they'll more readily understand the concepts of their world in a manner which will be safer and more productive. Without the crystals, the children would be at risk for many more dangers.

"There'd be a greater mortality rate for innocent accidents. Not willing to risk this for their children, parents almost always have the child's crystal ceremony performed within the first twenty-four hours from drawing their first breath."

Amanda didn't expect such a lengthy explanation but gratefully consumed the information just the same. It definitely answered some of her previous thoughts about Alena's three children.

Since arriving at their house, before even knowing about her pregnancy, Alena's very young children impressed Amanda with their abilities to help around the house and how they expressed their opinions so succinctly.

At first, Amanda believed the children were exceptionally bright, but she witnessed the same traits in all the other children at the marketplace.

Amanda looked back at Alena and Bryon sitting on the couch across from her—once again struck by the handsome couple. Alena was a small woman with shoulder-length brown hair. Black eyelashes framed her dark brown eyes, accented by very expressive, narrow eyebrows. Her delicate nose and well-shaped, full lips almost made Amanda jealous. Alena nearly always had a smile on her face, which showed her straight, white teeth.

Bryon was Alena's opposite regarding size as he was tall and extremely muscular. He kept his dark hair short and, since he usually ran his hands through his hair, left it spiked up.

When he was with Alena, he usually was close enough to touch her as he was doing right now. With his arm slung across the couch back, his fingers played with her hair as he listened to her progress report on finding Jena.

The account went the same as all their weekly reports since Jena went missing. Another lead discovered only to find it was, again, a dead end.

The typically optimistic Alena ended her update with, "She was the last wise-woman in Tuala. She was hard to locate, but she insisted she hadn't performed a crystal-changing rite for anyone matching Jena's description. She maintained she would've remembered a child with a black diamond birth crystal.

"You remember how rare it was when Jena received her stone. I needed to ask for it directly from Jehoban. It's not something to be forgotten by any wise-woman. So I'm sorry to say I've reached a dead end. There aren't any more people to question. Oh, Amanda, I feel as though I've failed you again."

"That's nonsense, Alena! I couldn't have asked any more from you. We've been searching every lead almost to the exclusion of everything else for almost two anons."

"It's true, but if it weren't for my inattentiveness at the market-place and letting Jena get taken by Petre MacVeen, we wouldn't be in this situation in the first place."

Bryon squeezed Alena's shoulder and chided, "We know how devious Petre's always been. You can't keep criticizing yourself over the actions of a known master deceptor.

"Honestly, you never stood a chance to keep Jena once Petre decided he'd abduct the girl he believed to be his daughter. We were just lucky Petre only knew about Jena. Imagine what would've happened if he'd been aware of Juila as well."

Amanda hugged the squirming Juila to her chest protectively. She shuddered at the idea of losing both her daughters and never seeing either of them again. Before returning to Tuala from Earth, she thought she might never see either of the girls grow up.

The harrowing experience to cross through the Gate between

dimensions from Earth to Tuala still haunted her dreams. She still wondered at her luck in receiving help from a fellow Tualan who just happened to be on assignment on Earth.

Would she ever attempt to pass through the Gate again with her remaining daughter? Should she risk the passage even though she didn't know how it would affect Juila?

If she did cross over, was she admitting she wouldn't ever see Jena again? She might have been rash in her promise not to return to Earth unless both daughters came with her. As more time passed, the hope of finding Jena diminished.

Because their last clue of finding the wise-woman who could have reassigned Jena's crystal didn't pan out, they'd need to figure out a new direction for searching. Short of locating the woman who held Jena in Amanda's last glimpse through Jena's birth crystal, what choice remained?

She could find a job and stay in Tuala. Did she want that for herself or Juila? It was grossly unfair for her parents not to know their granddaughter.

The decision didn't have to be made right away, but Amanda would choose soon.

Alena's brows furrowed as she concentrated on their problem. "There's got to be another way to trace Jena. Maybe something regarding the power imbued in her crystal. I wonder—" She paused and looked over to Amanda. Her face lit up in a way Amanda hadn't witnessed since Jena disappeared.

"Let me see your birth crystal, Amanda. I want to try something unusual. I might be able to use your stone to bond with the residual energy of Jena's to create an alternate connection other than the usual mother-daughter link." Alena spoke in her wise-woman's authoritative voice.

Amanda stammered. What valid explanation could she have for not owning a birth crystal? Finally, she said as close to the truth as possible, "I don't have a birth crystal. I lost it in the water when I escaped from Petre."

A look of utter disbelief contorted Alena's usually pleasant expression.

Amanda's muscles tensed at what her admission could mean. Would she have to admit that she was an *old soul*? Would Bryon and Alena throw her and Juila out on the street or turn them in to the authorities? Amanda should've added more details, but Alena recovered from her stunned silence.

"Why didn't you say something before, Amanda? We need to perform a formal procedure to get you a new one. I can't imagine how you managed without it for so long.

"I must say, I wondered why I never saw you use or wear it. Even the mudslide accident might've been avoided if I knew you were without protection. I'm so sorry this conversation didn't come up sooner."

She should be pleased to have a chance at receiving a crystal but fear filled her instead. What if the ceremony exposed her as a foreigner?

Amanda arranged her expression to one of relief without a valid excuse for refusing the opportunity. After all, this would answer Shemalla's question about *old souls* sharing Jehoban's blessing.

"Honestly, I've never heard of a crystal being lost except when a person died and then it'd simply disintegrate into dust. It's good to finally have something positive to concentrate on since Jena's disappearance. Also, the added power of a crystal might assist you in locating Jena."

FINALLY, Alena could do something to benefit someone. Lately, she worried that she'd failed in her calling as a wise woman. Having made so many mistakes since receiving her license made her question whether she should petition to get more training.

Usually, there'd be a party for a birth crystal ceremony, but it didn't seem entirely appropriate because this replaced a lost one. It was essential to have the rite performed immediately. Just the idea of going a single day without her crystal sent a shiver of fear skittering over her spine.

"I think we'll have the service as soon as everyone gets dressed. There should be at least one witness who isn't family. We should invite Tana; she loves any gathering. Although, I'm not exactly sure how elaborate the service will be to replace a missing crystal. As far as I know, this hasn't ever been done before."

She waved her hand as if to dismiss the matter from further consideration and nodded to affirm the decision in her mind.

Alena smiled brightly at her husband and patted his knee. "Let's go dress up, shall we?"

"First, I'll call Tana to ask if she's available and wants to attend, and then I'll meet you in the bedroom," Bryon answered as he stood from the couch and went to his office.

Alena's watched him leave. With the way his shoulders slumped, she knew he felt her same depression at their lack of progress in locating Jena. Bless him; he didn't want to show his concern to herself or Amanda.

Would she learn something about Amanda's origin today? The missing birth crystal was another piece of Amanda's puzzle. Maybe the ceremony would reveal Amanda's true heritage after all.

If Amanda did come from Earth, as her husband suspected, then the crystal ceremony wouldn't work. Amanda would finally be forced to tell her true story. At least something important would be revealed today.

CHAPTER 2

Amanda picked up Juila and retreated slowly to her bedroom. She knew just the outfit to wear as it was the same one she wore to Juila and Jena's birth crystal service. Unexpectedly, Bryon and Alena kept all of her clothing after she disappeared with the hope that she'd return.

She wanted to receive her own birth crystal. Right? But, what would happen if anything went wrong? Maybe it was a mistake to invite Tana. Without her, there'd be one less witness to her shocking revelation of being an *old soul.*

She blew out an exasperated breath, which Juila immediately copied. Amanda grinned at her, thankful for the cute distraction from her unexpected problem.

Never in her wildest dreams did she imagine this day would come. She couldn't come up with a valid excuse for excluding the helpful and friendly neighbor without raising undue suspicion.

Besides, what if it all turned out in her favor? She'd want Tana there, especially after all of the neighbor's help during this trying time.

Setting Juila down in the middle of the bed, Amanda opened

her dresser drawer and pulled out the fanciest outfit she owned. It was a loose-fitting dress to which she added a shiny gold belt.

She hastily pulled off her plain, everyday clothes and set them on the bed next to Juila. She dragged the dress over her head and fastened the belt loosely around her waist. Amanda looked herself over in the full-length mirror at the end of her bed.

Amanda was disappointed in her appearance. Smoothing the wayward strands of long brown hair back into position did nothing to improve it, as the static electricity made it jump even wilder than before.

If only she could sleep better, she wouldn't have the dark circles to match her brown eyes. She held out her arms, disgusted at how pale and skinny they'd become. The constant strain of worrying about Jena was wreaking havoc on her whole body.

There used to be a time when she would've done anything to be this thin, and now she'd gladly accept being plump if it meant having Jena back.

Nothing was worth the loss of a daughter. While Amanda was thankful Jena was simply missing and not dead, she wanted her home and safe in her arms.

Recognizing the dark direction of her thoughts, she shook her head, cleared her mind, and turned around to face her toddler on the bed. "What do you think, Juila? Is Mommy ready to get her very own birth crystal?"

Juila sat staring at Amanda as though she were considering the questions. Suddenly her lips pulled back to display her beautiful, infectious smile, and she held out her hands as she said, "Mommy pretty! Hold me, pretty mommy!"

Unable to resist smiling in return, Amanda laughed at her daughter's audacious comment. She flopped down on the bed beside Juila, grabbed her up, and rolled the giggling toddler over onto her stomach, hugging her tightly.

"I love you, Juila. I'm so glad I have you back in my life!"

Without any further excuse for delay, she finally got off the bed. She carried Juila back into the living room to wait for Alena to prepare for her service.

Once again, Alena transformed her workroom into a bright and cheerful area for the occasion. She set out a bowl of green liquid alongside her ceremonial box containing many things, including the birth crystals.

Alena wore the official wise-woman's garb, which consisted of a red tunic, a yellow belt embroidered with scenes of nature, a black pair of pants, and soft-soled shoes. Her hair was pulled up into a bun secured tightly to the base of her head to keep it from interfering.

Amanda's heart raced, and her palms grew sweaty. The next few minutes could change everything. For better or worse, she hoped she was ready.

ALENA WATCHED the procession of attendees enter the room. Bryon looked handsome, dressed in his best suit, holding their youngest son's hand. Kyelon also wore his most formal khaki slacks and a red tunic. At almost four and a half anons old, he understood the solemnity of the ritual and was on his best behavior as his father settled him in the seat next to him.

As they walked in together, Alena didn't try to contain her pride in her oldest son, Justan, and his betrothed, Andera. Nearly the same age of five and a half anons, they looked adorable as they held hands. Justan's curly dark hair was almost tamed, and his outfit was practically a duplicate of his little brother's.

Andera's long, blonde hair fell freely down her back as she wore her best full-length dress. She almost looked like a little bride in how she carried herself with poise at being asked to attend this important ritual. The little couple sat beside one another across the aisle from their father and brother.

The next-door neighbor entered the room with her sunny smile and bright personality. Tana didn't make any fuss as she swiftly crossed the room and sat behind the two kids so she'd still have a clear view of the formal procedure.

Amanda entered the room last, carrying Juila in her arms. Even though Amanda smiled, the joy didn't reach her eyes. Did Amanda look nervous? What would make her anxious as this should be a happy occasion to replace her crystal?

She watched Amanda step forward and offer Juila to be managed by Tana. It wouldn't be appropriate for Amanda to hold Juila during the service, and she approved of Amanda's awareness to approach the formality alone.

With so few people attending, everyone would have an easy time witnessing the entire process. Alena hoped she could successfully recover Amanda's birth crystal.

Since there wasn't already a precedent for this, she'd perform a modified birth crystal ceremony. She gestured to a spot on the floor directly in front of her. Once Amanda kneeled, the room went completely silent while waiting for the rite to begin.

"Friends and family, we have gathered together for the important task of replacing the protective crystal that Amanda lost during a tragic time in her life. Amanda, do you agree to allow me to look into your mind for me to assign a unique crystal?" Alena waited for a reply before continuing.

Amanda swallowed, hesitating for only a second before she replied, "Yes, I do."

Alena dipped her finger into the bowl of green liquid beside Amanda's knee. She marked a line across Amanda's forehead and chanted, "I mark your head to be able to divine the thoughts and intents of your being."

Dipping her finger again into the bowl, she marked a green

circle on the backs of Amanda's outstretched hands, chanting, "I mark each of your hands to be able to divine the actions for which you'll be responsible in your lifetime."

The room was utterly silent as Alena held each of Amanda's hands. With her eyes closed, she rocked back and forth with a thin smile on her lips as she spoke, "*Allah dari langit, silakan me panduan dalam penyelidikan. Membuat saya benar bacaan dan kristal tugas tepat.*"

Even as she spoke them, Alena's mind translated them, "Jehoban of creation, please guide me in the quest. Make my readings true and the crystal assignment precise." Alena felt the tremor in Amanda's hands along with the dampness forming on her palms.

They all sat in silence as Alena continued to rock silently. Probing an adult mind in this manner was a unique experience. She found it complex and fascinating as she shuffled through Amanda's consciousness while trying to peer into her future.

Alena finally spoke. "You have a full life with wonder and pain in the future. Pureness is apparent in your very nature as well as a strong sense of right from wrong," Alena finished and released Amanda's hands.

The wondrous things in Amanda's past and future were more than a little alarming. But this wasn't her secret to share, and it wasn't her decision regarding the gifting of the birth crystal. Jehoban would decide.

To hide her sudden apprehension, Alena opened the hinged lid of the box on the floor. It was a beautifully ornate container with many gemstones set into an elaborate design of leaves and flowers.

The raised lid obscured the onlookers' view of the contents, but everyone knew the box contained the protective crystals. Alena took her time, needing this to be the right choice for the situation. She glanced over the box to where Amanda squirmed uncomfortably on the floor. Alena understood her apprehension and didn't want to prolong her agony.

After a few moments of concentration, Alena didn't hesitate as she reached into the open coffer. She brought forth a thumbnail-sized deep blue stone that seemed to shine with a light of its own.

She purposefully closed the lid as she deftly threaded the tree-of-life pendant crystal onto a delicately ornate chain that she retrieved from an almost hidden pocket in her tunic.

She then handed the necklace to Amanda and started giving her instructions when Amanda cried out when the crystal turned to dust in her hand. At that same instant, an oppressive darkness passed between Alena and Amanda. Alena's eyes flared with concern at this sudden departure from the usual ritual.

What was she to do now? A sparkle caught her eye on the lid of her ceremonial coffer. A beautiful, flawless, diamond-encrusted pendant rested as if waiting for attention where nothing had been before.

Alena took the chain back from Amanda and strung the new crystal on its length. With a moistened towel, she wiped the dust from Amanda's palm. She hesitated for only an instant before she placed this new crystal into Amanda's open hand.

For a tense moment, everyone watched with anticipation to see if the second crystal would suffer the same fate as the first. The crystal remained in Amanda's palm. Amanda's face lit up with joy and relief. Her gaze moved away from her palm to meet Alena's.

Continuing the formal procedure, Alena said, "As you place this crystal of protection on yourself, say, *Saya memakai ini dengan restu dari Tuhan.*"

Amanda repeated the phrase as she placed the necklace around her neck.

Translated as 'I wear this with the blessing of Jehoban,' Alena knew with certainty this was true. Her heart warmed, and a prickle of tears blurred her vision as she realized Jehoban accepted

Amanda. He even provided her with a particular crystal in her moment of need.

Alena took a new, warm, wet cloth and wiped the green liquid from Amanda's forehead and hands. She rinsed the fabric in another bowl of clean water.

Alena removed the cloth, picked up the cup, handed it to Amanda, and announced, "I give you this water to drink. By the drinking of the liquid which contains your essence, you'll seal the bond with your new birth crystal."

Amanda brought the cup to her lips, drank, and then returned the cup to Alena. To conclude the service, Alena spoke to the room's witnesses, "With Amanda safe and protected from harm now that she's reunited with her birth crystal, we can all celebrate."

AMANDA STOOD and turned to face everyone in the room, the water's minty taste still on her lips. She smiled as each person came forward to kiss her cheek, compliment her crystal, and offer blessings.

Never before did she feel so wanted and loved as she did at that moment.

Tana stepped up last with Juila propped up against her hip. She kissed Amanda's cheek and murmured a blessing before returning Juila into Amanda's waiting grasp.

"It looks beautiful, Mommy. It matches what I see in you," Juila said cryptically.

Amanda beamed brightly at her daughter. What did Juila mean by that? She'd have to remember to ask Alena about it once everything settled down.

CHAPTER 3

"What happened during the service?" Bryon asked Alena as they got ready for bed that night. Maybe she'd let something slip if he caught her casually off-guard.

She sighed and pulled her nightgown over her head. The fabric muffled her voice as she said, "I wish I could tell you! I was just as surprised."

"So you've never heard of that happening before?"

"Never."

Bryon sat on the edge of the bed, silently contemplating whether or not he should bring up his idea of Amanda being an *old soul*. He didn't want to add to his wife's stress, but he wanted to know.

Would Alena wish to consider the ramifications of providing a crystal for someone not from Tuala?

Wait! What about the second crystal?

"Alena, where did the second crystal come from?"

Alena swiftly looked up at the intensity of Bryon's question.

She only considered the query for a moment before she replied, "From Jehoban. Only He can provide the rare crystals."

"Didn't you think it odd that you didn't even have to ask Him for it? It was almost as if He were watching the service."

"Of course, He was watching, Bryon. I petitioned Him for His blessing at the beginning. Did you think those were just empty words?" She crossed her arms and scowled at him to accentuate her disapproval.

Clearly, she was appalled that he'd even consider Jehoban involvement. He knew crystal ceremonies were one of the most sacred acts of a person's lifetime. He agreed that the mere act of thinking it might be an empty ritual seemed sacrilegious.

"That's not what I meant, Alena. I know it's His formal procedure to bless each of His children. I was trying to say, very poorly, that there wasn't any delay from the time the first crystal disintegrated to the other one appearing on your box. Do you think Jehoban changed His mind on the crystal assignment at the last second?"

Alena's scowl turned thoughtful, and she lowered herself onto the edge of the bed beside Bryon. "There was something strange—something dreadful. I don't know if I should say anything. But, whatever it was, it happened the moment my fingers touched her palm with the first pendant. It had all arose so fast—oh, I don't know what I'm saying. I'm not sure, Bryon. I *do* know that the second crystal was accepted.

"I should've asked Amanda about her original crystal's color. The visions I saw of her life demonstrated a need for a darker crystal, but who am I to argue with Jehoban's choice?"

Bryon didn't want to move or distract Alena in any way. Should he attempt prying any further information out of Alena about the visions she saw? Already, she said more than she probably should've since, as a wise-woman, those visions were meant to be strictly confidential; the protection of intimate secrets was part of the reason wise-women were so respected.

"Where do you think Amanda comes from?" Bryon asked quietly. He hoped he could be subtle enough to get Alena to disclose something more if he didn't seem too eager for the answer.

Alena stood and flipped the covers back on her side of the bed. She plopped down on the mattress and said, "I don't know; I never thought to ask. When she was pregnant, I inquired about her parents, but she said they were both gone, so I didn't try to pry any further. Why do you ask?"

Bryon mirrored his wife's movements, but he couldn't lie down just yet. He pursed his lips and said, "I don't know. Sometimes I think there is something extraordinary about Amanda.

"Remember when she first came home with me? I never asked Captain Ahn or Barla any questions since she needed protection from Petre and our house seemed the safest option. When they wanted us to take Amanda in, I never hesitated, but the trip home was so strange.

"She asked me the oddest questions before she got bit by the beetlesnatch. Then, when the wise-woman treated her, I could've sworn she disappeared. It was only for a split second, but I promise, she was gone. The wise-woman seemed surprised, too.

"Amanda's wounds healed way faster than anything I've ever seen. Her wrist was clearly broken, and then it was perfect. Do you think maybe she's Jehoban's representative?"

Alena stared slack-jawed at Bryon. "I'll never know where you come up with these things, Bryon. But, this time, you might be onto something.

"So many times, I wondered at Amanda's strange ways. She never used the elemy to prepare meals or take care of menial tasks. I'm ashamed to say I always assumed she wasn't very talented."

She shrugged, pushing her spine against the headboard. "Perhaps it was simply because her crystal was lost. But your question has some genuine potential." She grasped Bryon's arm, startling him with her sudden movement. "Do you think Jehoban is testing my talents? Oh, please don't listen to me. That's just ridiculous.

"I don't know, Bryon. I'll have to think about it later because right now I'm too tired to think straight. The service took more out of me than I realized."

"Of course! Rest on the bed, and I'll rub your feet," Bryon offered solicitously.

Alena smiled and scooted herself down the mattress, so her feet neared the end of the bed.

Bryon took his job as an expert foot masseuse seriously, and she wouldn't ever turn down an opportunity to be pampered. She fell asleep before he finished the first foot.

PETRE DOUBLED OVER, his stomach knotting and roiling worse than he could ever recall. Bile rose into his throat, and he raced up the stairs from his cabin, barely making it to the water craft's railing before losing the liquid in his stomach.

Each day he made a new promise that he'd stop drinking. But once his mind cleared enough to remember how much he lost, his resolve vanished. The liquor bottle appeared in his hand with nothing but a thought, and the stopper left just as quickly.

He only forgot his problems once he reached the bottom of the bottle. Where he sprawled on the deck, the sea spray soaked his bearded cheek along with his grimy clothes. He should have put the alcohol back in the cupboard, but that sounded like too much effort.

He couldn't recall the last time he ate actual food. Where he had thought he started to develop a gut, his midsection was now spongy and sunken in on itself. The wind whipping his lanky, brown hair into his eyes reminded him that he was long overdue for a haircut.

The clean smell of the sea breeze masked his offensive body odor. Petre couldn't remember the last time he bathed.

Leveraging himself up from the deck was a chore in and of itself. The swaying deck didn't improve his already precarious balance. He clung to the railing until he was too far away from it, and then he hastily grabbed for the water barrel beside the main mast in the middle of the vessel.

For one terrible moment, he feared he might be sick again, and he waited a few seconds until the nausea passed. He inhaled a few deep breaths and descended the stairs to the main cabin.

Once he opened the door, the room's foul odor rushed out to greet him. He swallowed down the threatening bile several times to keep from vomiting.

How did everything get so terrible? It was time he made some serious changes and got back to his life.

Yes, he lost Jena to Elder Debbon. Somehow the Elder tricked him into giving up his rights. Petre was sure the Elder either befuddled his brain or purposely rushed him into signing the betrothal document.

The Elder's unscrupulous actions were the reason he could no longer see his precious girl or even have the right to call her his daughter anymore. He missed the three-day deadline to visit her, which enacted an abandonment clause buried within the betrothal contract.

He needed a clear mind to plan how he'd get even with Elder Debbon. It'd be a tricky matter since the Elder was a Jehoban's representative.

Jehoban was responsible for creating the universe and wasn't someone to find yourself on the wrong side. Yes, he'd have to be very clever when he finally figured out how to get even with Elder Debbon.

JENA PRACTICED her ability to move objects with the elemental energy focused through her birth crystal while Debbon watched. Her talent to pick up an idea when he just gave her the merest hint of what he asked fascinated him continually.

After explaining what he wanted, he'd start to demonstrate the skill. She'd take over the energy he began using each time and then put her gift into completing the task. Unbelievably, she had already mastered the crystal skill levels to control elemy, fire, and wind. And she was only two anons old! Her talents exceeded that of someone who trained for anons with Jehoban Himself.

Since adopting Jena when she was six mesans old, Debbon spent at least an hour every day working with her on harnessing her fantastic capability to use the elemy. His wife insisted on immediate instruction because she fairly buzzed with the wild and untrained energy.

Even though formal training usually began around three anons old, he never regretted starting her lessons so early. She was an eager and fun student, and she continually stretched his abilities to keep up with hers.

He watched her dance across the room with her blonde curls bouncing softly against her shoulders, her arms raised toward the toy she suspended midair with her thoughts. She turned to smile at him with her perfect little teeth and her bright blue eyes alight with joy and wonder at what she was able to accomplish.

Debbon smiled in return and clapped his hands in approval. He loved the elegant turn of her mind. It was so easy to forget that Petre fathered her.

"We've practiced enough for today, Jena. You were supposed to go down with your momma more than fifteen minutes ago. She's planning a surprise in the kitchen. Do you want to go down there now?"

Jena, always eager for a surprise, immediately withdrew her elemy and let it soak back into the earth. Without her continued assistance, the ball dropped to the floor as she turned to grab his hand to leave the room. She smiled sweetly at him and said, "Let's go!"

Trying to be stern with the precocious child, Debbon purposely looked from Jena to the dropped ball and back to Jena. "Are you sure you're ready to go?"

Jena sighed, and with almost no energy expenditure, the ball disappeared from the floor and almost instantly reappeared in the basket beside the desk. "Is that better?" she asked with a bright smile.

"Much better." He grinned down at his first-daughter as he led her from the room.

CHAPTER 4

Three weeks. That's how long Amanda owned her very own birth crystal. She found herself touching it again as it dangled from the chain around her neck.

Never before was she so conscious of a piece of jewelry, especially since she knew the pendant's special meaning. This talisman granted her immunity while crossing through the Gate between her two worlds.

Jehoban thought enough about her to grant her greatest wish. Were there any particular implications with this gift? After all, she wasn't even from Tuala.

Alena spent considerable time with her, attempting to link her new crystal with Jena's. So far, they weren't successful, but they were far from giving up hope. Each day they worked on advancing her skills enhanced by the powerful pendant.

Amanda went so far as to make a glass of pika juice appear in front of herself in the kitchen. Alena seemed pleased with this progress, while Amanda curbed her amazement in making it happen at all.

Juila sat with a silent but intense interest in their activity during every lesson. Amanda didn't know when the Tualan children began learning how to use their crystals, but it made her happy to have her nearby.

CAPTAIN AHN COULD HARDLY BELIEVE his ears while listening to Captain Issyn recounting his tale. In almost two anons, nobody made any report of seeing Petre. Now Captain Issyn emphatically stated that he saw Petre's water craft on one of his more minor sailing routes. Even though the sighting lasted for only a split second, it was more than enough time for Issyn to identify Petre's uniquely shabby vessel.

"How long ago did you see him?" Ahn asked sharply.

"Well, now," Captain Issyn said, scratched the well-trimmed beard, and continued, "I'd say it was almost two weeks ago now."

Ahn's fingers paused over his keyboard. He leaned closer to his friend and asked, "What direction was he heading?"

Issyn frowned and pursed his lips. "I don't think he was going anywhere. It looked as if he were sitting still in the middle of the bay."

"Show me exactly where you think he was." He smoothed out a map of the Gulf of Thulen in front of Issyn and gestured for him to indicate the exact spot.

With almost imperceptible hesitation, Issyn pointed to the little-used waterway.

Ahn nodded confirmation and looked up at his friend. "Thanks for letting me know. There are very few people I can say I despise, yet Petre's one of them. He's long overdue for questioning in Jena Kesh's disappearance."

"I feel the same way about the man! There's no need to thank me. We've been friends for a long time, and I'm glad to be of any assistance in this matter."

Ahn watched Issyn's limping gait as he left the harbor's headquarters. Should he contact the authorities or Bryon first? Placing himself in Bryon's situation, he decided it was more prudent for the parents to know.

If only Amanda could've been alive to hear the news, then—gah, it was pointless to go down that sad path. Since her disappearance in the mudslide so long ago, both he and his wife were heartbroken over her untimely and senseless demise.

He moved through the reception room to reach his patil in his private office. He spent a moment composing his thoughts and then tapped in the coordinates initiating the call with Bryon. After only a short wait, Bryon answered the call himself.

"Captain Ahn! To what do I owe this pleasure? It's been a long time since we've talked!" He grinned, but the joy didn't reach his eyes.

Man, he looks so much older! Ahn smiled with true joy, knowing his news would be welcome. "It sure has! I'm finally able to report there's been a sighting of Petre MacVeen's water craft."

Bryon leaned forward, his expression shifting to an almost feral grin. "Really? How fantastic! Where is he? Have the authorities been notified?"

"I'll send the coordinates right now."

The only noise in either room was the tapping keys through the patil connection as Ahn entered the exact coordinates.

"There, you should have them now. I haven't talked with the authorities yet as I thought you'd be the most interested in this new development," Ahn replied with a smile wide enough to show his molars.

Bryon's eyes lit up when the new window popped up on his screen. "So, this blinking red dot on the map of the Gulf of Thulen indicates where Petre was last seen, right?"

Ahn nodded. "As you can see, he's nowhere near where you live."

Bryon nodded in agreement and said, "There's little danger of the deranged man showing up to steal Juila. When was this sighting? Was it from someone we can trust?"

"Most definitely! Captain Issyn saw the vessel himself. Unfortunately, he confirmed it was almost two weeks ago because it took him that long to get back to port."

"Hmm. That's good. At least we can trust him not to be after the reward offered. It's too bad this lead's as old as it is.

"There's probably not much the authorities can do with it now, but I'll contact them and give them the update. Both Alena and Amanda will be thrilled to hear there's any news at all! Are you okay, Ahn?" Bryon leaned forward toward the patil's screen.

Ahn's heart very nearly stopped, and his eyes widened. "Amanda's with you?" Ahn whispered.

"Oh, Ahn! I'm so sorry we didn't think to let you know. Amanda showed back up at our house almost sixteen mesans ago. She lost her memory, and then we spent all of our time searching for Jena through our active leads. We never even thought to tell you about her return."

Ahn's heart slowly returned to regular pumping, and then he smiled. "Barla and I would love to see her again. Barla was especially heartbroken when she heard of Amanda's death. Is there any chance you might 'port her over to our house sometime soon?"

"I think it might be just the thing we need to do right now. Amanda would be thrilled to see both of you, I'm sure. How does tomorrow sound?"

"That sounds perfect. Even if Barla has plans, I'm sure she'll rearrange them for another chance to see Amanda!" He imagined his wife's reaction to this. She'd probably break into tears and throw herself on him, hugging him until he felt like he could no longer breathe. He could hardly wait to get off the patil so he could head straight home.

"All righty then, it's all set! If anything comes up, I'll let you know. Otherwise, we should probably plan on meeting in the morning, say eleven o'clock?"

"We'll be in the landing square!"

BRYON BLINKED in confusion at how abruptly Ahn ended their call. The way Ahn grinned from ear to ear was a good indication that he wasn't going to be in his office much longer.

It felt nice to get to deliver good news these days. Although, guilt assaulted him that he hadn't shared Amanda's return with Ahn and Barla much sooner.

Bryon sat back from his patil and pulled his keyboard close to contact the authorities. He typed the connection code from memory and forwarded the information to the official in charge of his case. Since the evidence about Petre's whereabouts was somewhat old, he was told they'd send a patrol, but there wasn't a lot of hope of finding him still there.

"I understand completely," Bryon replied for the third time. They weren't telling him anything he didn't already know. "It's just good to know Petre is still out there somewhere. Since he slipped up this once, he'll probably do it again. I'll let you know if I hear anything else. I'm sure you'll do the same."

He stood as soon as the call disconnected. This new development was definitely great news to share. Rushing out of his office, he immediately spotted Alena and Amanda together in the living room practicing crystal techniques. "Just the two women I wanted to see! I have news about Petre!" He sat across from the pair as they stared anxiously at him.

"Has he been caught?" Amanda inquired into the silence as she leaned forward and set the squirming Juila down on the floor at her feet.

Bryon held up his hands to forestall more questions. "I just got off the patil with Captain Ahn," Bryon said with less enthusiasm since he should've prefaced his first statement more carefully.

"Captain Issyn saw Petre's water craft two weeks ago. I then spoke with the authorities, and they're going to send a search party to the last known coordinates.

"I can't imagine how he wouldn't have come to any port for this long. Since we haven't found any trace of the cargo he stole from Kirma Shipping and Receiving, he couldn't have gotten any money from that angle. How has he been able to stay at sea for so long without money or resupplying his water craft?"

"Maybe he sold something besides the stolen cargo," Alena offered.

"Like what? His water craft?" Bryon asked with a touch of irritation. "Where would he live then?"

AMANDA'S STOMACH churned over where this conversation was going. How come this idea didn't occur to her before now? She wished her following statement wouldn't be true with all her heart but believed down to her soul that she finally unearthed the only answer possible.

"What if Petre sold the most valuable thing possible? What if he sold Jena?"

The silence in the room was deafening as each person looked at one another in horror. Amanda's truth bomb registered on their faces. It would explain the unknown woman Amanda saw looking at Jena with love and adoration in her final view of her daughter through the birth crystal.

"The bright side would be that Petre wasn't keeping Jena

anymore," Amanda offered. Amanda knew firsthand Petre's manipulations when he wanted something, having been his captive herself.

"So," Amanda said, hoping her question wouldn't raise their suspicions, but she forged ahead anyway. She'd gladly give up her secret if it helped bring Jena home. "If he put her up for adoption, wouldn't there be some sort of record?"

CHAPTER 5

"Good thinking, Amanda," Bryon jumped up from the couch and jogged back into his office across the hall from the living room.

Alena looked intently at Amanda as they listened to Bryon's keyboard keys clacking under the onslaught of his forceful typing. "You're right, Amanda. An Elder would have to approve a formal adoption request. We also have to consider the people who have Jena might not have formally adopted her. However, if there is a record, Bryon will do his best to find it."

Amanda's eyes remained fixed on Juila playing on the floor. Juila had already lost so much time with her sister. If only she'd thought of this angle so much sooner.

"I know. I have to believe this idea will lead us in the right direction." Amanda tried to remain hopeful even while she worked on how she'd return to her real life on Earth. She spent so much time searching for Jena that she neglected to go back to the first people who had helped her after escaping from Petre.

Amanda stood from the couch, suddenly nervous about the implications of their latest theory. Juila played quietly with her set of blocks. Amanda asked, "Would you mind watching Juila while I go to the office with Bryon?"

"Not at all, go ahead!"

"Thanks," she replied and rushed from the room.

She paused at the office door. Bryon typed on his keyboard and stared at the patil screen. Work stacks and books littered the surface of his big, mahogany-colored desk. Shelves filled with books covered three walls of the room. Some of the books were for research, she knew, but some of the others looked more used.

At some point, she'd like to spend some time looking through the selection to see what else she might learn about Tuala. More than once, her questions about daily life created awkward silences, all the while the answers may be just a few steps away.

Bryon must have felt her presence. He glanced up and waved her into the room. His watchfulness made her even more self-conscious about how much weight she'd lost. Was he thinking the same thing about her as he looked her up and down, noticing how her clothes hung from her slight frame?

Bryon finished his query and turned off the patil. "I made arrangements for us to visit with Captain Ahn and Barla. He seemed most insistent on seeing you. I can't believe we forgot to tell them about your return. I felt so bad when he discovered you weren't dead and living with us again; he looked like he was almost ready to pass out."

"I was just thinking the same thing. I came in here to ask if we could get together with them. I'd like to visit with them for a while. I'm sure they'd like to meet Juila as well," Amanda agreed.

"We're scheduled to meet tomorrow at eleven o'clock. I hope that'll work. I imagine Barla will come and pick you and Juila up to go back to their house for lunch. Ahn and I will go down to the local deli to grab lunch and catch up on all the latest news. I hope that's okay. I know you wanted to talk to Ahn as well."

"Oh no, it's perfect. I hate talking about Petre, so it works perfectly for me to let you do that. I'd love to spend some time with Barla. I haven't had a chance to thank her for making the arrangements for me to come live with you and Alena in the first place."

Bryon looked slightly embarrassed by Amanda's comment.

Amanda shook her head and sighed. "Bryon, I know exactly what you're thinking. It wasn't your fault that I had my little accident. Nor is it anyone's fault that Jena was taken. Well, it's certainly Petre's fault, but that's on him, not you."

As if to cover his confusion over how to respond to Amanda's blatant statements of truth, he said, "I've entered a query for any formal adoptions matching Jena's age and description for any time between when she was taken and today. My best guess for the timeline would be four days after she was abducted since that's when you lost access to Jena's birth crystal."

AHN'S exuberant mood and unexpected return home at such an odd hour piqued Barla's curiosity.

"What's going on, Ahn?" Barla asked, wiping her hands on her apron and leaning forward to kiss Ahn's cheek when he leaned close to her.

"The best news ever!" Ahn shared his miraculous news.

Barla's hand blindly groped for a barstool. Was she dreaming? She and Amanda shared a special bond. Their connection couldn't be spoken of in public as they were both displaced from Earth, known in Tuala as *old souls*.

Over the anons, the Elders cultivated the idea that *old souls* posed a danger to the Tualan people. Their nurtured fear caused the populace to turn over for questioning to the Elders anyone suspected of being an *old soul*. The people taken into custody were seldom, if ever, seen again.

Barla dearly loved her husband, and even though she hadn't been born in Tuala, she was a Tualan at heart. Their children were born in Tuala, and their youngest daughter, Rasa, was even being trained by Jehoban Himself. She would do anything for her husband, which he knew, and returned her love more than she ever hoped for herself.

As soon as the initial shock wore off, Barla's arms flew out and pulled Ahn in for a crushing hug. "Oh, Ahn. This's incredible. I've missed that girl since the moment she left with Bryon. I can't wait to meet Amanda's daughter since we didn't even know she was pregnant when she left."

Only a few minutes remained until she and Ahn would leave their house to go down to the open square where the telepods landed. People didn't like teleporting too close to the ocean-side community. The unpredictable offshore wind gusts made the manual guidance challenging to control in the telepods. She glanced at her timepiece again and wondered where her husband had disappeared.

As if on cue, Ahn rounded the corner of the house. She stood from the front porch bench and impishly grinned at Ahn. She loved his confident stride and his air of authority.

He was tall and muscular but lean in his build. She suddenly noticed his short, dark hair graying at the temples, but his full beard was just as dark as ever. Though they'd been married for over twenty-five anons, she never noticed that they were both getting older.

Ahn took the porch steps two at a time before he lifted Barla in a huge hug and kissed her soundly on the mouth. He never had any problems with public displays of affection, for which Barla was pleasantly thrilled; she eagerly returned the warmth. "Are you ready to go?"

"I've been ready all morning!" She smiled up at him as she snaked her arm around his waist. They descended the stairs together, and she added, "This's been the slowest morning of all time! I sure hope Amanda will let me spend a lot of time with her daughter."

"I'm sure she'd be more than happy to let you watch over her toddler. She's probably running herself ragged keeping up with her!"

Barla's mind whirled with the activities they could do together. "I can't wait! It's been forever since we've had a little one running around!"

"I don't think it's been all that long," Ahn replied. "While I love having children around, I've discovered in my old age that there's joy in some quiet time at home when I finish a long day at work."

Barla looked sharply up at Ahn but refrained from speaking as they walked up the pathway toward the landing square. She did notice a few anons back that Ahn was getting worn down from the burdensome workload of being the Harbor Master.

While she was the founder of the orphan training program and the children usually lived in their house, she started fostering the younger kids at the women's houses who volunteered with the program. Now she spent more time working with the children in other homes only to return to her own empty house.

Their son, Gravin, came home for a short time after finishing his post-study program, but now he enjoyed his retirement with several of his school friends. She wanted to become a grandparent sometime soon, but Gravin appeared to be having too much fun in his travels even to consider finding a girlfriend. At twenty-three anons old, he still had plenty of time to find the right woman to settle down with before beginning his career.

Their daughter, Rasa, was two anons younger than Gravin, but her life took another path entirely when Jehoban's representative requested she study with Jehoban directly. While Barla and Ahn visited with her whenever possible, Rasa was extremely busy with her schooling. Rasa had matured beyond her anons, and she took her training so seriously her interest in the opposite sex wasn't a consideration.

Barla hadn't realized her musings over her children took so long. She gasped and shook herself as they stopped at the landing site. Was she so consumed with her musings that she missed the telepod's arrival? Her gaze raked over the expansive field, but the area was empty of any vehicles.

Ahn directed her over to the shaded seating area, but they felt a burst of elemy emanating from the open grassy area before they turned. Barla never tired of the electric feeling and sudden sight of the vehicle popping into existence where before had been nothing but empty air.

She knew how the technology worked, yet she never dared to ask for lessons on mastering the technique. Barla held onto Ahn's hand tightly. Her anticipation rose as they waited for the door to open.

CHAPTER 6

Alena sat, fascinated by Juila playing with her blocks. What started as an everyday activity promptly turned into an unusual occurrence. She considered calling for Amanda to come and witness it, but she didn't want to disturb Juila's concentration.

Juila quietly played with her block pile when she suddenly jumped up and called out, "I want to try it too!" Without any guidance on Alena's part, Juila pulled elemental energy through her birth crystal and used it to lift one of her blocks to her head height. She ran around the room with her arms raised and laughed at the new game she had created.

This activity shouldn't have occurred to Juila until after her crystal training began in approximately another anon. Yet, most surprising was Juila's phrase before she even started. It sounded like she was having a conversation with someone even though Alena was the only other person in the room.

Did Juila still have a connection with her sister? Maybe Jena was being trained to use her birth crystal. This brought another thought to Alena, causing her to whisper in wonder, "Who'd be powerful enough to train her so young?"

The activity only lasted for a few moments before she let the block drop to the carpet. She turned to Alena and beamed delightedly with her newest achievement.

Alena smiled at her and clapped her hands. The block disappeared immediately and reappeared with the other blocks at Alena's feet. Alena didn't hide her surprise at this other new demonstration. She held out her hands to the precocious little girl and said, "Come to Alena."

Juila grinned and happily skipped over. She was such a good cuddler. Once she was comfortably settled into Alena's lap, she asked, "Can we make something special in the kitchen?"

Alena blinked blankly at the abrupt change in subject and replied, "Sure, but first can you tell me where you learned to do the trick with the block?"

Juila cocked her head to the side as she considered her answer. She furrowed her brow and pursed her lips before she finally answered, "I saw myself doing it in the other room."

"What other room? The kitchen?"

"No, the big white room with the desk!" She answered indignantly.

"We don't have a big white room with a desk," Alena said with more than a bit of confusion.

"It's not here, silly," she said with a grin, "It's at the other place!" She exhaled, and her bangs flew up to hit Alena's chin.

"Have you ever been to this other place?"

"I'm there every day." Juila pressed her fingers together like two spiders climbing a wall.

"I see," Alena answered as she contemplated the implications of this newest revelation.

Now more than ever, Alena was convinced Juila was intimately tied with her twin sister. Even though Juila didn't remember having a sister, their minds were seeing what the other was doing. This revelation was going to take some serious consideration. She'd wait until Juila napped to discuss her ideas with Amanda.

"Let's go to the kitchen and make a snack. We can put together a basket of goodies for you to take when you visit with Barla and Ahn later this morning."

She carried Juila into the kitchen and set her down on the counter while gathering supplies to make quick snacks. Alena liked to manually prepare food during stressful or confusing times as she found it a relaxing activity, even though most Tualans used their mental abilities to create dishes instantaneously. With all of the unrest currently plaguing her mind, she welcomed the distraction.

She turned to peer into the refrigerator only to discover the juice jug was missing. When she turned back, the pitcher was on the counter right next to where Juila sat with a big smile on her face. "Did you get this out, Juila?"

The little girl nodded with exaggerated movements. "I love pika juice."

"Well, let me get a cup then," she replied and reached up into the cupboard when a cup appeared beside the jug. Alena jumped at the sudden appearance, but she wasn't surprised to find Juila enjoyed this new game. "Aren't you a smart girl!" She poured the juice into the cup and offered it to Juila.

With Juila distracted with her drink, Alena gathered the remaining supplies without further displays of budding power. Alena thought about training Juila early since she could connect with the energy source and apply it responsibly. Now Alena needed to guide the little girl in the appropriate usage of the skill so Juila wouldn't find herself in trouble in school or public with any inappropriate displays of power.

Having decided to begin her training, she was pleased when

Amanda walked into the kitchen. She smiled at her and asked, "Would you like me to make you something?"

"No, nothing to eat, but the pika juice looks good. I wouldn't mind a cup."

"Why don't you ask Juila for one?" Alena said with a mischievous grin.

"Okay," she replied quizzically and turned to address her daughter sitting on the counter, "Juila, could I have a glass of pika juice?"

In the next instant, a brimming full cup of juice was sitting on the table in front of Amanda.

"Oh!" She exclaimed at the event's suddenness. She smiled brightly at her daughter and said, "Thanks! And so fast!"

Amanda glanced meaningfully at Alena and said, "I think we have some things to discuss when we return!" She looked back at Juila as she carefully picked up the over-full glass of pika juice and took a sip.

"My thought exactly!" Alena grinned in agreement with Amanda. It would be exciting to find out the extent of Juila's abilities since she showed an interest in using them.

Bryon walked into the kitchen in time to hear Alena's last comment and playfully asked, "Do I even want to know what you two are concocting?" He glanced first at his wife, then Amanda, and watched them exchange a secretive glance. He groaned. "When you both get that look, it usually means trouble for me."

"Juila was just demonstrating how skilled she is at serving a drink," Amanda said as she lifted her glass and took another sip of the cold juice.

He looked meaningfully from Juila to Alena and solemnly asked, "Did she use her crystal energy?"

Alena nodded confirmation and watched Bryon mouth the word 'wow.'

"Isn't it a bit early?"

"I guess she's ready since she's already demonstrating her ability with remarkable accuracy. We can discuss it some more once you all get back from visiting with Ahn and Barla. Mention it to Barla and see if she's had any early development experience with her orphans." Alena finished preparing the snack and tucked it in a sack.

"Good idea. I think she'd love to talk about it," Amanda responded. She fidgeted in her chair, and her foot bobbed as if it had its own heartbeat. "Speaking of our visiting, will we be leaving soon?"

"I was just coming in here to say we can go whenever you're ready. The telepod's waiting out front."

Amanda hastily gulped the remaining juice from her cup and set it down with enthusiasm. "I'm ready right now!"

Bryon chuckled at her eagerness and said, "It looks like Alena's putting together a snack basket for our journey. Do you need any help, honey?"

Alena took advantage of the few moments when the two talked and created the entire basket of snacks by using her creation skill to assemble and wrap the sandwiches in foil instantaneously. It wasn't her original intention, but she understood Amanda's eagerness to get going.

Alena held the basket up toward her husband and said, "All set!" She leaned toward Bryon to give him a goodbye kiss and giggled like a schoolgirl when he held the basket out from between them and pulled her into a body hug, and kissed her full on the lips.

"I love you, Alena! I imagine we'll be back late, so don't wait up for us. If it gets too late, we might stay over with Ahn and Barla."

"Okay, I won't be worried. Although I'm keen to hear if there's any new information regarding Petre's whereabouts." She tried to ignore how Bryon's hand turned into a fist against her back. She knew exactly how he felt.

AMANDA STOOD from the chair at the table and went to Juila at the kitchen counter. She scooted her forward, so she rested easily on her hip. Her little girl was getting bigger and heavier, so she was grateful for not having to lift her from the floor.

"Are you ready to meet your Aunt Barla and Uncle Ahn?" She asked Juila as she led the way from the kitchen to the front door. She looked back to find Bryon and jumped with nervous energy to see him practically on her heels. Maybe he was just as eager to get going.

Bryon leaned forward and grabbed the door handle for Amanda to precede him outside. He waved goodbye to his wife, who remained in the kitchen but still had a clear view of the front entry.

Amanda turned just in time to see Alena's loving smile and returned wave as Bryon shut the door. The telepod already had its door open, so Amanda herself settled into the right front seat at the control panel. She fastened her seatbelt before she lifted Juila to sit on her lap.

Bryon entered the personal telepod and palmed the door closed. He joined Amanda at the control panel and took the left pilot seat. Once he was also fastened in, he began the start-up procedures and confirmed all was okay by nodding at every green indicator light on the control panel.

The process was supposedly quite simple but still magical in Amanda's mind. Bryon activated the crystal drive with the key, but from that point on, Bryon's thoughts and elemental energy focused from his birth crystal operated the vehicle. Bryon tapped his power through some mysterious process into the powerful crystal drive located at the telepod's rear.

CHAPTER 7

For some people, the mere idea of traveling at the speed of thought was scary, but Bryon always found it exhilarating. From the expression on Amanda's face, he believed she felt the same. Once he activated the crystal drive, the telepod would hover several inches above the ground leaving the occupants floating.

He took a few quick, calming breaths to center his mind. He focused only on their destination coordinates, ensuring they arrived at their landing location with plenty of air space between their telepod and the unforgiving ground. It wouldn't be very professional and embarrassing to pop into existence halfway in the ground.

He let his hand rest on the activation module with the coordinates firmly in mind. Several seconds of darkness overwhelmed his senses, and absolute nothingness took over.

He squinted from the sudden daylight at the port city of Cresdon and then grinned with childish delight at their successful flight. Bryon swiftly switched over to the manual controls to safely steer the telepod to the proper landing location in the open field and performed all of the shutdown procedures.

Amanda hugged Juila close and smiled over her head as she told Bryon, "This kind of travel never gets old!"

"I know what you mean!" He pointed out the window and said, "There're Captain Ahn and Barla now. It looks as though they just got here, too. Perfect timing!" He used the remote door switch on the control panel and unlatched his seat harness simultaneously. "Let me take Juila so you can get up." He lifted the child from her lap and tucked her into his side with the ease and skill of someone who had three other small children of his own.

AMANDA APPRECIATED the offer since she didn't know how Juila would react to her first telepod ride. Apparently, the travel didn't disagree with her as it did with others.

Some people became violently ill upon arrival at their destination, a condition believed to be caused by the abrupt change in equilibrium. Luckily Juila didn't seem at all fazed with the change of scenery or the transport mode.

With her seatbelt unlatched, she stood and joined Bryon at the telepod's side in front of the open door. She considered asking to hold Juila again, but once she saw how eagerly Barla advanced toward them, she bolted from the telepod and raced into Barla's open arms.

"It's so good to see you," they said in unison, which then caused them to laugh. Amanda released her hold on Barla to back away from the hug when another set of arms wrapped around them both as Captain Ahn expressed his delight in her visit as well.

Once the joyous greetings ended, Amanda reluctantly broke free of their arms and rushed over to where Bryon stood off to their side and held out her arms for Juila.

He handed her over, and Amanda turned around to Ahn and Barla and introduced her daughter, "This's my daughter, Juila!" Fully expecting to see accepting smiles, she frowned, confused by their shocked expressions. "What's wrong?" she asked swiftly.

"Nothing, really," Barla began. "It's just that Juila looks exactly like our Rasa did at that age. They could be twins, Amanda!" Ahn just nodded with confirmation as he continued to stare unblinkingly at Juila.

"Oh, if that's all. I can explain all about that when we get to your house," she said almost offhandedly. "I also have a letter from your family, Barla. There's just so much I need to share. I can't believe it's been more than two anons since I saw you both last."

"My family—" Barla began and then suddenly looked at her husband. "I think Amanda, Juila, and I will go directly home, Ahn. Why don't you two come home at dinner time, and we can all catch up then." So eager to hear Amanda's news, Barla bordered on rudeness.

Ahn instantly understood what Amanda's news meant to her. He gave Barla a quick hug, then tweaked Juila's cheek and said, "I guess this means we men are excused. We'll be home in time for dinner. Do you think you'll remember to make it, or should I pick something up from the deli on the way home?" He couldn't help but tease her, but Barla's response surprised him into barking laughter.

"Oh, Ahn, that would be wonderful! I don't think I'd be very good at cooking tonight, what with all the excitement of Amanda's visit!" Barla tugged on Amanda's free arm as she turned to leave the landing square. "It's not very far up the way, Amanda. I can't wait to hear the news from my family!"

Amanda glanced over her shoulder as she walked away. The two men grinned like fools after them. She waved farewell and then promptly turned forward as Barla set a brisk pace to get home. Amanda wanted to kick herself for leaving this visit for so long.

"Barla, I'm so sorry we didn't come to visit sooner," Amanda started, stopping only when Barla waved her to silence. She kept her counsel for the next few minutes until they arrived at the Harbor Master's house.

Once settled in the family room, Barla asked, "Would you mind if Juila played with the toys over there in the corner while we discussed my family?"

"Not at all." She shifted to rise when Barla swiftly stood and offered her hands to Juila. Juila instantly lifted her arms to Barla. Amanda watched as Barla took several toys from the box on the floor and offered them to Juila.

Barla returned to her chair, perching on the edge in anticipation. "What did you find out? And how?"

"Well, let me start with the how," Amanda said and settled back into her chair to tell her story swiftly. "After I had the twins, Bryon and I went hiking. A sudden rainstorm caused a mudslide, and I got caught up in the flow.

"Just when I thought I was going to die, there was an explosion around me, and I found myself back on Earth somewhere in Mexico. The hospital contacted my parents, and they came and took me home to recover."

Barla's concern over Amanda's near-death experience morphed into relief. "Your account of the accident makes so much more sense than the one Bryon shared. Now I feel like I can relax and listen attentively."

Amanda patted Barla's hand sympathetically. She could hardly wait to get to the good parts. But she needed to do this right. Her father would be proud of her methodical delivery.

"As I promised you, I had your letter in my pants pocket when I went hiking. I never went anywhere without it. Anyway, while I was recovering, my mom found the notes.

"Imagine how my parents felt when I tried to tell them about being transported to another realm on Earth. They feared I sustained an undiagnosed brain injury until my mom found the letters. Barla, you're never going to believe what I have to share!"

Barla's hands clasped together so hard that her fingers turned white. "What is it, Amanda? The suspense is killing me!"

Amanda leaned forward, eager to impress the importance of her following statement. "My mom recognized your handwriting. When she read your letter, everything started to make sense.

"Remember when I saw the picture of Rasa in the hallway? I said then she and I could be twins. Then you said Juila looks just like Rasa did at her age. There's a good reason for both of these things, Barla.

"My mother is your sister. You're my aunt. Rasa is my first cousin! Are you okay, Barla?" Amanda rose with concern at Barla's ashen complexion.

Barla sat back suddenly and shook her head in silent amazement and a bit of disbelief. "Amanda, are you sure? Not that I wouldn't be excited to have you as my niece, but what are the odds of us meeting in Tuala?"

"Here," Amanda said as she stood and dug in her pocket for the letter from her mother to Barla. "Read this letter that my mom wrote." The envelope shook from Amanda's outstretched hand.

Barla hesitated for only a moment before she accepted the letter. She looked down at the closed envelope and ran her fingers over the handwriting on the outside. Her hands trembled as she tore the flap open and took out the single sheet of paper.

BARBARA,

I can't believe you've been alive this whole time! We all thought you drowned, and I've been afraid of the water ever since.

I wish we could meet your husband and children. Amanda has

told us all about them. We'll have to be content with that unless you can figure out a way to come home. Amanda said you found your soul-mate with Captain Ahn, so I guess it'd be selfish of us to want you to leave the life you've built for yourself.

Our parents divorced right after I finished high school. Mother was much happier afterward. Father died of a massive heart attack in 1981. As he always feared, he died alone. Amanda can tell you all about our family.

I can't express how happy I am to know you're alive and well. Write back to me if possible. I'd love to let Mom know how you're doing.

With all my love,
Diane

BARLA READ through the letter a second time before letting it drop into her lap in awe. "It's true. You're my niece. Diane's handwriting is almost the same as my own. I'd know it anywhere.

"I should be sad to hear about my father passing away, but somehow I can't describe my current emotion. I never trusted, loved, or respected the man who gave me life. He was a difficult man with strange ideas about family and business."

Barla leaned back in the chair, her head tilted back to rest against the fabric. She contentedly sighed and opened her eyes once again. "It's all so incredible. And my mom's still alive?"

"Yes, Grandma Ellen and Uncle Saul are alive and well. They live in Oregon, where Grandma is now retired. Uncle Saul lives with Grandma, and he's never been married. My mom married Chris in 1968 and had us three girls. I'm the youngest.

"I was only nine when Grandpa Sydney died. I only met him a couple of times, but he was kind of weird, so Mom didn't take us to visit very often. Plus, he lived across the country in California, and we were in Florida, so it made it a little more difficult."

Barla nodded understandingly. "It's surprising to hear that Saul never married. But then again, he'd actually have to talk to a girl to form a relationship. He was always so painfully shy around girls. It'd be easier for him to just live with Mom rather than attempt to converse with the opposite sex."

Barla then looked over at Juila, and her face lit up. "That means your beautiful little girl really *is* my grand-niece.

"Since accidentally arriving in Tuala when I was eighteen, I've never had a blood relative until I gave birth to my two children. It's a strange concept actually to have family in Tuala. I love it!

"Tell me everything." Barla leaned forward and grasped Amanda's hands, and waited for Amanda to begin her family story from the beginning.

CHAPTER 8

The hours passed like minutes while Amanda talked about their mutual family and answered Barla's innumerable questions. When the front door slammed shut, they both jumped.

"It can't be dinner time already!" Barla cried.

They smiled at each other as they both gingerly rose from their chairs. So much time spent in tense conversation made easy movement a painful concept at present.

Amanda glanced toward the hallway and back to Barla. She leaned close and whispered in Barla's ear, "Do you think it'd be alright if we told Bryon about our relationship?"

Barla's face radiated joy at the idea and rapidly replied, "I can't think of anything I'd rather do!"

Amanda crossed the room and picked up Juila from among the pile of toys. She turned to face Barla, expecting to join the men in the kitchen or dining room.

Barla stepped closer and touched Juila's hair. "You know, I've always admired your long dark hair and brown eyes. And now, they're such a contrast to Juila's blonde curls and blue eyes. What does her father look like?

Amanda stiffened. She'd told Barla about her missing fiancé, Nealand.

As if she read Amanda's mind, she asked, "Did you ever find Neal? I'm sure he's worried sick that you and the twins haven't returned to Earth."

Barla hooked her hand around Amanda's elbow. "Oh, my goodness! Where are my manners? The men have brought food, and I've done nothing but monopolize your time since you arrived. We can discuss this later after our bellies are full."

They walked arm in arm out to the entry, where the men noisily removed their coats and shoes. Barla smiled brightly at her husband and nodded conspiratorily at him.

Amanda saw Ahn's answering smile. Those two were so perfectly in sync with one another; it made her heart painfully constrict for what she'd lost with Neal.

Barla released her arm to rush forward and grab the delicious-smelling food bags. She kissed Ahn on the cheek and said, "Thank you for picking up dinner. Just wait until you both hear the wonderful news Amanda has brought to us!"

Everyone followed Barla as she turned around and moved purposely toward the dining room. The men sat at the table as Barla and Amanda continued down the hall into the kitchen and got plates, glasses, and silverware to set up in front of each person's seat.

Barla pulled each entrée from the bags and set them up buffet style in the center of the table. She returned to the kitchen and retrieved serving utensils. With everything finally ready, the women sat at the table, and Ahn said the blessing.

When the initial rush of eating ebbed, Ahn said, "So whose news do you want to share first?"

"Oh, definitely yours first! There will be way too many questions with my news. Plus, mine's a much more cheerful way to end the evening," Barla reasoned.

"Okay. My news won't take any time at all as there's not much to share. We followed up on today's lead regarding a sighting of Petre—it turned out to be a false report. Once people heard there's a reward for any news of his whereabouts, anyone looking to make a quick shill is coming out of the woodwork. So, that's it, really.

"We're no closer to finding Petre, but we do know he'll have to come ashore at some point to restock. Hopefully, it won't be too long before we have reliable information.

"So, since I'm done, why don't you share the news which is fairly buzzing from you, Barla? It's a wonder you were able to eat at all."

Barla blotted her lips with her napkin and balled the cloth in one hand. Her eyes sparkled with glee as she looked at each man at the table to ensure they were paying proper attention. "Okay! While Amanda was away, she met with my sister!"

Ahn's gaze cut to Amanda at this newest revelation. He knew what this meant. She'd gone back to Earth and somehow returned to Tuala.

"Now I'm really intrigued to hear how this came about. But, do you want to wait for another time to discuss this?"

Amanda knew they'd never shared Barla's true heritage with Bryon, but they knew they could trust him as an *old soul* sympathizer.

Ahn looked at Barla and then purposely back to Bryon.

Barla took the hint and shook her head. "Before I go any further," she turned to address Bryon, "I must ask that anything we discuss tonight is kept in the strictest confidentiality.

"I hope this doesn't offend you, Bryon. I know you've always been someone we could trust intimately. It's just this is the most important part of my life, and you'd be holding my future in your hands."

Bryon fidgeted uncomfortably under Barla's gaze. "I'm honored that you want to include me in this sensitive conversation. But, just because I arrived with Amanda doesn't mean I need to be included in your private affairs. If you'd rather I go back into town so you can speak privately with Amanda, I'll completely understand. I won't be offended in any way, I promise!"

Barla dismissively waved her hand and said, "No, don't be silly. You have a stake in this as well, what with Amanda and Juila living in your house. Besides, there might be something you can do to help us once all of the facts are known."

"Okay, but only if you're certain. I just don't want to be included at the expense of our long-time friendship." Bryon scrutinized Barla intently as if ensuring she wasn't just placating him. "I'll stay if you really want me to know your family business. I'll keep whatever I learn here completely private. I won't do anything to betray your trust."

Barla nodded and then continued with her original story. "Amanda and I are both from Earth."

Amanda watched Bryon swallow purposely as he digested this fantastic piece of news.

"As it turns out, Amanda's my sister's daughter." Barla turned to Ahn and said, "Which explains why I felt such a deep connection with her from the start. Initially, I believed it was because she was a swimmer and displaced as I'd been. However, now I know it was more than that. It also explains why Juila looks so much like our Rasa, Ahn. They're cousins!"

Ahn seemed less shocked by the news than Barla had been. He sat quietly and contemplated the meaning of these new revelations. "Hmm. We ought to have Amanda and Juila come and live with us. It only seemed right since they're family. I'm sure you would want to get to know your nieces and catch up on family news."

"It's like you're reading my mind, Ahn!" She playfully slapped his wrist. "I'd love to have the two of them come live here; I just don't know how safe it'd be until Petre's apprehended."

Amanda looked hastily at Bryon. What did he think about Ahn's idea about her moving? More than once, she'd felt as though she'd overstayed her welcome with Bryon's family. She never intended to live with them for two years.

Bryon answered Amanda's unspoken question when he rapidly voiced his opinion, "I'm sure it'd be better for her to remain with us. As Ahn said earlier, it can't be too much longer before Petre comes ashore. Besides, teleportation is a quick means of travel. Amanda can come to visit as often as you'd like."

Amanda didn't know if she should be glad or disappointed that Bryon wanted her to continue living with them. She wanted to get to know her long-lost aunt, but she also needed to consider Juila's safety while Jena was still missing. It appeared Petre didn't realize Juila existed, and they'd all like to keep him ignorant of that fact.

"I'm sure we can make those arrangements," Barla agreed. A contented smile lingered on her lips as she looked from Juila to Amanda and then her husband. "My life feels complete now that I finally have a link to my past. I thought I was okay with my decision never to return to Earth, but now I see how much I missed out on with my extended family. This's my opportunity to get some of the histories back.

"I don't want to bore you with my story, Bryon, but you should know how I came to Tuala. A few months, mesans, as they're called here, after my eighteenth birthday, my friends and I went swimming in the Gulf of Mexico, known here as the Gulf of Thulen, between Cuba and Cancun, or Reesun and Cresdon. Wow, it's a mouthful when you have to use two different names for everything!

"Anyway, we were out sailing when we decided to go for a swim. The ocean was refreshing but still warm. I swam out farther than my friends when suddenly all of these bubbles rose around me.

"In an instant, I couldn't stay afloat, and I sank. The bubbles vanished as soon as they began, and I returned to the surface. I remember gasping for air as I came out of the water, relieved to have survived the bizarre incident.

"I turned to go back to the sailboat only to discover I was very much alone in the water. I'm not quite sure how long I tread and stared in disbelief at the emptiness around me, but I knew I'd have to start swimming to make landfall.

"Not long after, Ahn came sailing along in his water craft and picked me up out of the sea. I say it was love at first sight; however, I was also very relieved to be rescued."

Ahn reached over and patted Barla's hand. "I vividly remember rescuing Barla. She was the first swimmer I ever picked up when I still operated my own shipping vessel before becoming the Harbor Master and retiring from active service. Lately, I've been missing those days of freedom on the seas, yet I've enjoyed our married life much more than I ever dreamed possible."

CHAPTER 9

"Y ou've had an incredible journey, Barla. I didn't have any idea how the two of you met. One of these days, we'll have to sit and talk about Earth. I went there once as a young boy. It was one of my rights of passage," Bryon said. "I've heard about people from Earth being in Tuala, but I didn't know I was actually living with an *old soul.*"

He quirked an eyebrow at Amanda and winked conspiratorially. "Remember when we first met? I questioned your true identity, but then I doubted myself because you learned our ways so rapidly."

Bryon simply nodded as though this were an ordinary fact to let Barla know to continue. "Earth fascinates me, more so after I went there. I know it's a normal place and not the dangerous habitation some of the Elders teach people here in Tuala."

"I did wonder about that," Barla admitted. "It seems that most of the *old soul* sympathizers have had some interaction with Earth, even though I never felt comfortable asking directly. I thought it might seem odd or inappropriate somehow."

"I wish you had. It would've been nice to have someone to talk to about it. There have been several times I started to tell my wife about it, but then we were always interrupted. She seemed eager to hear about it, but it's never been a subject we finished."

"Speaking of finished," Barla brought the conversation back to Amanda and her news. "Amanda needs help getting herself and Juila back to Earth. She told me about a Tualan who lives on Earth, working on behalf of Elder Vargen. She helped Amanda return to Tuala after the unfortunate hiking incident."

Barla looked sympathetically over toward Bryon. "Since Amanda's back, you no longer have to carry any guilt, but I know you think it's your new responsibility to find Jena and reunite Amanda's small family."

Bryon looked stunned. "Really? There are Tualans living on Earth? Sent by an Elder? And to think of all the negative things I've heard about their opinions on the matter."

He leaned against the table's edge and tapped his index finger on the hard surface to emphasize his point. "You're not suggesting that Elder Vargen's a sympathizer, are you? I mean, he's one of the founders of the Old Soul Engineering Facility, where they detain people from Earth for questioning.

"Somehow, I doubt Elder Vargen has a good reason for sending someone to Earth permanently. Now you've piqued my curiosity. When I get home, I'm going to look into the matter to see how long Elder Vargen's held an interest in Earth."

Barla cleared her throat, drawing attention back to her. "Be careful, Bryon. Don't draw unwanted attention with your research. If you must research something, think about this. Amanda needs to get a message back to her parents, letting them know she's doing okay.

"Obviously, we don't know how and we certainly don't want to put the woman who helped her in jeopardy. Does anyone have any ideas on how we might get in touch with my sister and her husband?"

Everyone sat in silence. Barla so casually asked the room at large to implicate themselves in illicit activity, and, bless them, they wanted to help.

Bryon said, "I remember my teenage rights of passage. Each boy created a verifiable incident on Earth and then returned to show it to the other boys. There never seemed to be any risk of discovery, but then we tried to stay away from the people on Earth. Barla's suggesting actual contact be made."

Barla pursed her lips, nodding to encourage Bryon to continue. "What has your wheels turning so intently, Bryon?"

He blinked and smiled in embarrassment as though he'd been caught out and replied offhandedly, "I don't know. Our teenage pranks on Earth were to prove how grown up we were. How did we all go from daring to cowardly in the face of the Elders?"

Amanda blinked several times as she focused on Bryon's last statement. She'd been thinking so fiercely about solving her problems that she wasn't paying sufficient attention. "Bryon, you might be on to something. How'd everybody get to and from Earth without being seen?"

"Some of us used the special places in the caves outside of town, and some of the richer kids used their parents' telepods. It depended on opportunity more than actual planning."

"I've seen some of those caves," Barla interrupted with excitement. "It always felt like there was something special about them, but nothing ever happened when I was there. Are all of the caves the same, or is there something which needs to be done to have them work properly?"

Bryon visibly flinched at the direct question. "I shouldn't say. As a young boy, I was sworn to secrecy about triggering the Gates. We were warned that the secret must be kept from Earth or that the dangerous foreigners would overrun Tuala.

"I've always kept the secret. But, then again, nobody would ever ask me about it." He chuckled and glanced from Amanda to Barla, and his gaze came to rest on Captain Ahn. "Now, here I'm faced with two people from Earth who want to know the very thing that's supposed to be kept from them."

Amanda hated Bryon feeling as though he needed to go back on his word. She said, "It's okay, Bryon. I already know how they're activated. Don't share anything that might put you in a precarious position."

Bryon sighed, and his shoulders relaxed, but his face showed incredulity that the decision was taken from him. "How many others know the secret?"

Amanda continued her explanation, "The Gate's activation is specifically designed to allow Tualans to come and go from Earth, but it also limits us who live on Earth. Even though we can use the Gate, it's designed to hide our memories from ourselves.

"As you've said, Bryon, you went through the Gate as a teenager but didn't suffer any memory loss on either side. If we," she gestured to herself and Barla before continuing, "go through in either direction, we have to be sure to write down everything we want to re-remember when we get to the other side. Even with the notes, it's difficult for us to accept the truth. Your world goes against all of our beliefs about reality."

"So that was the note you wrote to yourself when we first saw you back at our house? How come I've never heard about those aspects of the Gates?" Bryon asked.

"Based on what Shemalla taught me, I don't think it's common knowledge. The Gates are all supposed to be monitored by the Elders, right? The most powerful ones actually are watched, but the caves outside of town are ancient and not nearly as powerful, so they're left untended."

Barla interrupted with an abrupt question as she asked, "Amanda, do you have the ability to go back anytime you want?"

"In a manner of speaking," she replied hesitantly. "I was told it might be dangerous for my daughters based on the color of birth crystals they received.

"Since Juila's is dark red and Jena's is black, they indicate perilous lives. We don't know if the danger's posed by me taking them through the Gate or if it's because of their lives should they remain living here.

"I'm uncomfortable with either decision, although I'm not going anywhere until we can find and question Petre. If everyone's correct that he can't stay gone too much longer, then hopefully we'll have Jena back soon, and then I can decide what'll be best for all of us."

"I'd love the opportunity to get to know the three of you better, Amanda," Barla said. "Especially now that I know you could potentially leave any day."

"Me, too. You're one of the reasons I have for remaining in Tuala. But I'm not going anywhere without Jena. I'd also like to see how Juila's power manifests."

Barla looked at Amanda with a confused expression, and then she spoke hesitantly, "What makes you think the girls will have any powers?"

"Because I've seen Juila demonstrate them for me just today," Amanda answered with a healthy dose of smugness in her voice.

"I'm confused. Isn't their father, your fiancé, from Earth?"

"Yes. What's that got to do with their potential powers?"

"It's just that if both parents are from Earth, the children wouldn't have any powers. It's not the land that imbues the power in the person; it's the parents. Neither of your children would inherit any elemental power unless either you or Nealand is really from Tuala."

"You must be mistaken, Barla. You know where my family comes from; we are Earthlings to the core. Nealand comes from an affluent family in Florida, which can trace its heritage back forever.

"And yet I saw Juila manifest a glass of pika juice for me right before we teleported over here." She looked over to Bryon for affirmation. "You heard what Alena said about wanting to teach Juila since she's shown an interest, right?"

"I did," Bryon began, "but what if what Barla says has merit? Since your crystal ceremony, I finally believed you were from Tuala, so it'd make sense for your children to use their power.

"But using Barla's interpretation on the matter, then maybe Nealand isn't the children's father as you thought. He drew in a sharp breath and snapped his mouth shut. He cast his gaze down to the table, his fingers suddenly busy caressing the rim of his plate.

Amanda saw Bryon's troubled look. "What is it, Bryon?"

"What if Petre MacVeen truly has a valid claim to Jena. Since Juila undeniably has crystal power, it stands to reason that while Petre held you captive on his water craft, he probably took advantage of you while you were recovering from your head injury. I think Petre might be Juila and Jena's real father."

Dead silence permeated the room. Amanda's stricken expression said everything to each adult in the room. She reviewed every thought and deed she could recall from the time she was held against her will by Petre so long ago.

She remembered being appalled at seeing the massive bruises on her inner thighs and breasts the first time she was allowed to go to the bathroom alone and away from Petre's overprotective presence.

Also, every time he gave her the foxl broth, which must've contained *epeny*, she'd fall into a deep sleep so he could have his way with her. In horror, she recalled asking Petre for his special broth to sleep and have more dreams, which aided in recovering her identity.

Amanda believed her head injury caused her memory loss, but now she knew it was the transfer into Tuala that erased her memories.

CHAPTER 10

The more she thought about what Petre most likely did to her, the more her stomach churned. Petre couldn't be her children's father. Nealand was their father, yet he adamantly refused to admit sleeping together.

Was she wrong? Or did she merely convince herself otherwise because she just couldn't believe such a monster fathered her beautiful little girls?

Did Petre have a legitimate claim to her daughters? Would she have to share custody with him? Was the reason the girls had such dark birth crystals because they'd interact with Petre for their entire lives?

Amanda's gaze darted to Ahn desperately and implored, "If Petre's their father, will I be forced to share the children with him?"

"No, Amanda. If it's against a woman's will, laws prohibit what he did."

"Obviously, it was against my will!" How could Ahn think otherwise? She wouldn't ever consent to be with someone as dishonest as Petre.

"I know, that came out wrong, Amanda. Rape is a serious crime, and obviously, he took advantage of you while you were unconscious with your head wound. If it can be proved that he's their father, he'll be charged with rape. Of course, he doesn't have to be told anything.

"Once Jena's back, you could just take both girls and return to Earth. But then he'd be free to do to other women what he did to you. It's up to you, though.

"You'd have to live with whatever the Elders decided. This would also bring you to the attention of the Elders, which you might want to avoid if you're trying to go back home."

Amanda scowled at her options. There wasn't any good answer, and it frustrated her that she even needed to consider the possibilities. "Oh, what a mess! It makes me ill. Just the idea of Petre touching me at all in that way is disgusting!"

She scowled as the unwanted memories flashed through her mind. Why couldn't these scenes remain lost when she passed through the veil to get here? Her vision blurred with unshed tears when she recalled Neal's twisted, angry expression with her claim that he fathered the girls.

Her voice came out like a broken whisper as this new reality kept hammering against her tortured soul. "No wonder Petre kept telling everyone I was his wife when he searched for me after I jumped overboard to get away from him. In his sick and twisted way, he felt as if he had a claim on me because of what he did!

"Excuse me; I need a moment to clear my head." Amanda abruptly rose from the table, the chair falling backward in her haste. She tightly wrapped her arms around her middle as if to hold herself together as she ran from the room.

"I'll go check on her," Barla said to nobody in particular as she stood and ran after Amanda. Barla took the stairs two at a time and jogged down the hall to the guest bedroom. The door stood slightly ajar. She pushed it open and scanned the room until she noticed the terrace doors were also left open.

Barla tiptoed across the bedroom and through the terrace doors. Amanda clutched the balcony railing and gulped deep, ragged breaths.

Barla hesitantly touched Amanda's shoulder in reassurance. Amanda flinched under her touch. An instant later, Amanda abruptly turned and buried her face against Barla's shoulder as she sobbed uncontrollably.

"It's going to be okay," Barla comforted Amanda as she stroked the back of her head softly and held her tightly with her other arm. "We'll get this all sorted out, Amanda. Please don't cry so. It's going to work out." Several minutes passed while Barla continued to croon nonsensical but soothing words.

"Although I've never suffered the abuse that you're just now processing, I have spoken with enough victims to know you need someone to listen to you and hold you if you want the comfort of a friend. As your aunt, friend, and fellow swimmer, I claim my right to console you."

Amanda finally pulled away from Barla and sniffed deeply to clear her nose. She abruptly brushed the tears from under her eyes and apologized, "I'm sorry, Barla. I don't know what overcame me. It shouldn't matter how the girls were conceived; I'm just thankful I have them. I need to keep my mind clear to figure out a way to find Jena.

"Ahn was right; I need to get both girls back to Earth as soon as I have them together again. I can't risk Petre being part of their lives, and I can't risk drawing attention to any of us concerning the Elders.

"I don't want to bring any danger to you and Ahn or Bryon and Alena. I'm sorry I won't get to know you and your children better, Barla. This drama has gone on long enough. We need to get home!"

Barla brushed her hand over Amanda's hair, "I'm glad you're over the worst of the shock. Please don't try to bottle up any of these emotions. They need a time and space to get processed."

"I'm fine. I promise," Amanda said, feeling anything but fine.

Barla sighed. "I know from experience that once you're alone and without any pressing concerns, you'll relive this moment of shock and horror. Amanda, you're going to have to come to terms with what had happened in your past.

"I won't lie and say it's going to be easy, but you'll have to learn to forgive Petre, not for himself, but for yourself before you truly heal."

Amanda's abruptly turned to face the ocean view. Could she ever forgive Petre? Her fingers clenched the railing and imagined how she'd like to use her hands around Petre's throat.

She swallowed down the unwanted bitterness. She wasn't a violent person, but her pain clouded her thoughts. She closed her eyes when Barla continued reasoning with her.

"You have two beautiful daughters who need all of your love and none of your hurt or anger at how they came into existence. I firmly believe everything happens for a reason, and you'll come to the same realization in your own time.

"We still have some time to visit since we haven't discovered Jena's whereabouts yet. Let's just promise one another that we'll take full advantage of whatever time we have left together," Barla said.

She put her arm around Amanda's shoulder and steered her back into the bedroom. "Why don't you all spend the night tonight? You've had some terrible shocks, and I think a nice warm bath would do you wonders. Don't worry about Juila; I'd love the opportunity to spend some time with my niece."

Amanda mutely nodded as she allowed Barla to lead her into the en suite bathroom. She fondly recalled the luxuriously hot bath from before, and she imagined it being just as welcoming this time.

"Do you think Bryon will mind the change of plans? He told Alena that we might stay over if it got too late with our discussions. Certainly, I never imagined the evening would end up quite like this!"

Barla patted her on the hand and replied, "Don't worry about Bryon. I'll let him know our decision. If he needs to return home right away, we'll make different arrangements to get you home later. It's no bother, really. Let's get this bath started."

She leaned over and opened both fixtures to allow the water to gush freely into the waiting tub. Barla pulled out a plush towel and a robe from the cupboard and set them on the chair next to the bathtub. She shut the bathroom door and left Amanda alone while the steam rapidly obscured the room.

PETRE FINALLY SOBERED up enough to navigate toward land. He devised a scheme for getting back at Elder Debbon, but he needed to recruit help from some additional people to make it work.

His first action plan was to meet with his usual partners. Never one to trust anyone other than himself, he knew he'd have to enlist others so he could carry on as usual and eventually get his daughter back from the devious Elder.

He originally planned to use his natural charm to convince people to help him with his cause against the Elder. But then he decided this issue was too important to take the chance.

After removing the several items obscuring his prized possession, he lifted the crystal skull down from the upper cupboard. The power emanating from the stone was palpable in the room, even more so when his skin came in direct contact.

Petre found himself staring intently at the depiction of a skull in his hands, and he was disgusted with himself for letting the crystal's thrall overtake him. He hastily set the object on the table in the main cabin and forcefully turned his back on it.

He left the cabin and went upstairs onto the deck to check for land. After scanning the horizon and noting the sun's position, Petre groaned. The powerful crystal held his mind captive for several hours instead of the few minutes it felt like.

During his mesans of intoxication, he spent many weeks conversing with the crystal skull. In his drunken stupor, he swore he received answers to his questions; however, now he knew it was just the alcohol and not the object that created the illusion of a two-way conversation.

Now he remembered why he'd put the crystal into the cupboard so long ago—he lost too much time when it was exposed.

Shaking his head and swearing under his breath, Petre made a few mental adjustments to his tacking course and slowed the water craft down so he could sleep for the night. He'd need to be well-rested before he met with Rualin.

Come morning, he'd be near his planned destination.

CHAPTER 11

Diane's hand shook with frustration as she hung up the phone. This call from Shemalla didn't make their choice to let Amanda go any better. They needed actual news.

Instead, they received the same two sentences, "I'm sorry to say I haven't heard anything. I'll call next month as scheduled unless I find out anything before then."

They assumed no news was good news because to think otherwise would crush Diane's spirit. With eighteen months elapsing, it appeared as though Amanda decided to stay in Tuala instead of risking the journey home with her girls. She didn't have any choice but to be content with her daughter's decision, even if it did break her heart.

A few minutes after the phone call, Chris arrived home from work and immediately asked, "Did I miss the call?"

"Yes, but you didn't miss any news. Same as ever: nothing to report."

"Hmm, I guess it's still good news."

Diane turned her back on her husband to hide her deep emotions.

Naturally, her husband wasn't fooled. He knew her too well. He stepped behind her, enfolding her within his arms, and said, "I'm sure we'll hear something soon. Please don't be upset."

Diane twisted around in his embrace until she faced him and said, "I'm tired of waiting. I'm sick of being so far away and having to wait a whole month for any updates at all. I want to move to New Mexico, Chris."

"Okay."

Diane stared open-mouthed at her husband. She anticipated hearing dozens of reasons why they should stay in Florida. Never did she imagine such an easy agreement. This wasn't a new conversation, and she expected the same rational response.

"Do you mean it, Chris?"

"I do! Nothing here in Florida means more to me than your happiness. We've discussed this before, and I was selfish to think only about my job and how this move would affect me. After the terrible day I had at work, I'm ready to make whatever change you want."

Diane's eyes brimmed with tears, and her smile positively beamed as she flung her arms around Chris's neck. She kissed his cheek repeatedly. "I love you so much! Thanks for understanding!"

DEBBON STRUGGLED to concentrate on the petitions in front of him. His thoughts repeatedly returned to the conversation between himself and his wife, Chelesa. She saw Jena's progress with her lessons and innocently asked if Debbon should direct her to continue her schooling with Jehoban. Jena's extraordinary talent was pretty obvious.

Debbon secretly wanted to take credit for her skills because of his love for teaching. Losing his best student, even to Jehoban, seemed unbearable.

If she were anyone other than his first-daughter, he would've been the first to petition for her to be instructed by the Creator Himself. Was Jehoban testing this prideful streak against his First Elder position?

The Elder never taught such an eager student possessing so much natural ability. He wanted to see how far she'd go in her studies. If he contacted Jehoban now, he would surely lose her as a student and possibly as the betrothed for his son.

There must be some way to keep her with his family. Yes, a loophole he should've realized mesans ago. Jena was still too young to be formally trained. He'd wait until after she was three anons old before saying anything.

When he got home that evening, he'd let Chelesa know of his decision on the matter. If nothing else, it'd give him several more mesans to figure out what he'd do with his favorite student.

ARRIVING at Rualin's port was a simple matter of a few directional corrections when Petre awoke at first light. He noted the neat and orderly dock as he occasionally staged stolen items at this isolated location. Since no other vessels appeared along the horizon, he felt relatively confident their conversation could be held without interruption from incoming shipments for disbursement.

Petre carefully wrapped the crystal skull before he tucked the small yet weighty object under his arm as he mounted the steps to the upper deck of his water craft. He hoped to convince Rualin to go along with his plan without the stone's added power. More than likely, he'd also be caught up in the stone's thrall and waste another entire day staring at the dumb thing.

He stepped across the salty deck and bent over to pick up his securing line. As he straightened, he spotted Rualin exiting his front door to see who was tying up to his dock.

Petre didn't have a hand to wave a welcome, so he shouted, "I hope it's not too early!" Petre stepped across the open expanse of water onto the dock with rope at the ready and secured his water craft.

The tie-down would've been more straightforward with the use of both hands, but he couldn't risk revealing the crystal skull before the right time, especially if the covering came undone and exposed its sheen to the open sunlight.

Petre couldn't have Rualin spotting the object before sharing his story. With a secure grip on his package, he finished with the rope, stood, and strolled along the rickety dock to the house.

Rualin didn't look entirely pleased to see Petre. What's wrong with him? They hadn't seen one another in almost two anons. Petre couldn't imagine why he'd be upset by his presence. Mentally shrugging, Petre disregarded the fleeting expression and held out his hand when he came near enough for a greeting.

"Did you bring something to sell?" Rualin gestured toward the bundle in Petre's arm.

"This? No!"

"What's your business then?" Rualin's question came out clipped and unfriendly.

"I have a favor to ask."

Petre removed his hand from Rualin's grasp with more than a bit of force. He turned slightly, moving past the man to enter the house. Not bothering with the fact he wasn't invited, Petre moved with quick steps until he was in front of the small table in the room's center.

He set down the stone with a gentle thud. Making himself at home, he sat in one of the two chairs while waiting for Rualin to enter the building and take the other seat.

Rualin's recalcitrant attitude would require using the skull's power to garner his cooperation. Hopefully, he could shield his view of the crystal so only Rualin would become entangled in the skull's emanating energy.

"What's wrong with you, Rualin?"

"You're putting me in a hard position, Petre."

"What're you talking about? I haven't even told you why I've come."

He turned and spit onto the uneven, dirty floor. "I don't care why you've come! Did anyone see you heading this way?"

"Certainly not! What's that got to do with anything?" Petre may have been out of touch for a while, but he'd never allow himself to get sloppy. His livelihood depended on staying out of sight.

Rualin barked rudely. "As if you don't know!"

Petre scowled, wishing Rualin would get to the point already. "Know what? What are you talking about, man?"

"I don't know. Maybe the warrant for your immediate arrest has something to do with it! Now you've put me in danger of being apprehended just because you decided to tie up to my dock. Did you ever think of what this could do to me, or are you honestly only concerned about yourself?"

Rualin glared across at Petre, lounging insolently in his favorite chair.

Petre's face completely blanked. What was this all about?

Rualin's expression softened, but he continued to scowl. "You really didn't know about the warrant?"

"Of course not! I've been at sea for almost two anons, and this is the first landfall I've made in all that time. What are they claiming I've done this time?"

"Kidnapping."

"Kidnapping! That's ludicrous! Who was I supposed to have taken?" His mind immediately went to Jesisca, but he dismissed it just as quickly. Jesisca was dead, confirmed by Ninan.

"A baby girl named Jena," Rualin said, doubt now lacing his tone.

Petre swore under his breath. He slammed his fist onto the tabletop, making the skull jump, and threatened to expose the crystal before he was ready. "It's not kidnapping if she's my own daughter. I had every right to her since her mother died."

"So you admit you took her?"

"Certainly! She was mine, but who'd ever believe me?"

Rualin jumped up from his chair and stabbed his finger toward the door. "I think it's time you left, Petre. You confess you took the girl. I don't care if you think you had a valid claim; you should've gone through legitimate channels to get her. You can't just go around taking children, Petre. It's just not right."

"Well, I don't have Jena anymore! Not since Elder Debbon tricked me into signing away all my rights to her."

"Elder Debbon? What does he have to do with this?" He sank back into his chair, eagerly awaiting an explanation.

Petre spent the next few minutes detailing how Jena was bitten by a beetlesnatch and subsequently healed by Elder Debbon. He told him about the betrothal agreement containing the deviously buried abandonment clause.

By the time he finished the story, Rualin was seated across from him with a hard expression in his eyes. Petre knew there was only one person who despised Elder Debbon more than himself, and that man was now just as furious as himself.

"So Elder Debbon got away with it! Why didn't he report finding the missing child? There can't be too many girls missing with the name Jena. He must've known but kept her for himself anyway. What's this favor you need?"

"I want to force Elder Debbon to reinstate my parental rights. She's my daughter, after all!"

"I don't see how I can help with this. Have you tried negotiating with Debbon?"

"No. Like I said before, you're the first person I've talked to in forever! Besides, Elder Debbon didn't hide the clause in the document to renegotiate the terms later.

"I'm going to have to take my rights back by coercion rather than diplomacy. He hurt me by taking my family; now I will have to hurt him by taking his family."

"What do you have in mind?" Rualin laced his fingers together on top of the table. He leaned forward, ready to hear Petre's plan.

"I want you to gather as many people as you know who have a grudge against the Elder and start organizing a planned threat to his wife and son."

"That's insane, Petre. Their residence is heavily protected. If we got caught, we'd have to forfeit everything. Going up against Jehoban's representative is more trouble than I want to entertain no matter how much I hate the despicable Elder."

"I was afraid you'd say that, so I brought along a little enticement." Petre leaned forward and unwrapped the skull.

Rualin leaned forward to see the mysterious bundle. He gasped in recognition and said, "Petre, is that what I think—is that one of the thirteen legendary samaras—"

Petre stared intently at Rualin's face to ensure the crystal absolutely entranced him. He crookedly smirked when he realized he now possessed full power over this man to make him do anything he asked.

Keeping his eyes averted from the samara on the table, Petre spoke his plan for revenge in great detail. It pleased him to see Rualin merely nodding acceptance to everything he said. His scheme would work flawlessly!

CHAPTER 12

Morning came quickly, and Amanda had to get herself together. Juila deserved a stable mother, which she planned on providing.

Taking some time to get herself ready to go downstairs, she blessed Barla for insisting on taking care of Juila for the night. Amanda didn't notice the strain she'd been under until she didn't have any responsibilities and could completely relax for an entire night.

Amanda left her room and descended the stairs with her morning routine accomplished. The sun shone low on the horizon; however, her daughter typically rose with the sun.

Her best bet would be to head for the kitchen and see what was happening. Her instincts proved correct when she entered the doorway and found Barla offering Juila small bites of fresh fruit.

Barla swiftly glanced up at the movement caught from the edge of her vision, "Good morning, Amanda! Did you sleep well?"

"Very well. Thanks. I hope Juila wasn't too much trouble."

"Oh, no trouble at all. She's just an angel, and I've thoroughly enjoyed spending time with my little niece. As I told Ahn yesterday, it's been a long time since we've had a little one in the house. I'd forgotten how much fun they can be.

"Are you hungry? Would you like me to make something?"

"Do you have any pika juice?"

"Sure," she replied as she moved toward the icebox.

"Wait a minute, Barla. Let's see if Juila can get it for me. Are the glasses in the cupboard over there?" Amanda pointed to the cabinet right next to the icebox.

"Mmhmm," Barla replied with a grin. "I've never attempted mastering the use of elemy since I wasn't born here. But it never ceases to amaze me to see someone else access it so effortlessly."

Amanda bent over the chair in front of her daughter and asked, "Juila, please get me a glass of pika juice from the icebox. The glasses are in the cupboard right next to it. Can you do it for me right now?"

The requested juice appeared on the tray between Juila and Amanda within a moment of the question. Amanda clapped her hands together with a squeal of delight and praised her daughter, "Perfect, Juila. You're such a smart little girl!"

She picked up the juice and held it out in a celebratory toast to Barla before taking a sip. Amanda saw Barla's shock from the quick response, which inordinately pleased her with how well Juila used her powers.

"Barla, Alena wanted me to ask if you've ever had any children this young display such raw talent?"

"No, I haven't! I think I'm kind of grateful, too! Imagine the trouble they could've gotten themselves into if they had." Barla continued smiling to take the sting out of her words.

"Let's sit down. I'd like to hear stories about my cousins growing up."

Nodding, Barla seated herself across from Amanda and next to Juila and talked about her children. "Gravin was such an inquisitive little boy. He could find trouble in a cardboard box.

"There was one time he and the neighborhood boys wanted to build a telepod, but they didn't have anything to make it with. Gravin got the brilliant idea that they could use the steps of our back porch.

"When Ahn fell into the yard after they went missing, Ahn tried to have a stern talk with him about destroying property. Gravin said he didn't think there was a problem since we never used the steps anyway. Ahn had difficulty keeping a straight face when he told little Gravin he'd have to help rebuild the stairs.

"Naturally, it wasn't any punishment since Gravin loved working with tools and his father. I'm surprised he didn't pull more stunts like it to work alongside his dad.

"Then there was the time I caught Gravin cutting Rasa's hair. It just got long enough to curl into ringlets, and I teased her about having unruly hair. Gravin took it upon himself to help me.

"When the children were quiet for a bit too long, I went to investigate. Imagine my surprise to see Rasa sitting in the middle of the backyard with all her beautiful ringlets resting on the ground around her.

"Gravin just cut the last one off and saw me standing on the porch. He held it up proudly in his hand and said, 'I got them all, Mommy! Now you won't have to worry about Rasa's hair being unruly!' How could I get mad with his reasoning?"

"Oh no! Didn't you worry he'd keep cutting her hair?" Amanda's hand automatically went out to caress Juila's long ringlet, cringing at the idea of them all getting cut off.

"Ahn talked to him about it. He told him cutting hair was a woman's job, and he should leave it up to Mommy from now on. It's not exactly how I would've approached it, but he never did anything with her hair again."

"When Gravin was a teenager, he got into several fights with one of our neighbors down the street. The other kid used to bully

Gravin every day after school, and we always taught him to turn the other cheek.

"If he'd told Ahn what was going on, he'd have talked to the kid's parents, but he decided to retaliate differently. One night, he snuck out of the house and took some of our weed killer from the gardening shed. He went over to the kid's house and used the poison to kill a message in their front lawn."

Amanda stifled a giggle by covering her mouth with her hand. Through her fingers, she asked, "Oh, no! What did he write?"

"He wrote, 'Jonan is a foxl.'"

"Is that bad?"

"Yes, we'd say he's a sissy. It was nearly a week before the lawn died enough to show the message. Since nobody saw Gravin do it, they couldn't very well retaliate.

"The only reason we found out about it was that Gravin insisted on taking a stroll by their house every day so he could look into their yard to see how it was coming along.

"Once the message was very apparent, he stopped going up the street. The last time he walked over there, he returned with the biggest grin, which was a dead giveaway to me that he'd done something.

"I never said anything to him or Ahn about it. I hoped the feud between the two boys would end, and it basically was. A couple of anons later, the family moved out of town, and Gravin enjoyed school much more after their departure."

"Tell me about Rasa. What was she like growing up?" Amanda picked up a piece of fruit and offered it to Juila, and then took a second piece for herself. Juila appeared just as interested in hearing Barla's stories as Amanda.

"She was such a quiet little girl," Barla said, staring off into the distance of her memories. "I used to worry something was wrong with her since she hardly ever spoke. She watched everyone intently but didn't want to interact with anyone other than Gravin. They even spoke to one another in their own unique language.

"Neither one of them remembers it now, but it was something to hear when they were little. People used to ask me what they were saying, but I'd just shrug since I didn't have any clue either."

Amanda's eyebrows rose. What if they channeled a foreign tongue? They only spoke English in all of Tuala, except during special ceremonies.

"You said she left when she was about seven to be taught by Jehoban. How did that come about?" Amanda sat forward and quickly sipped her pika juice.

Barla's expression changed as she thought over her answer. "It was both a surprise and a scary time for our family. Although thinking back on it, we should've known she'd be okay.

"I raised both kids here at home until they were old enough to go to school. Usually, children are taught the basics about using elemy by their parents. We have an unusual situation here at home since I'm from Earth. I didn't know what the children were supposed to know before starting school, and Ahn was too busy with his new position to notice the problem.

"So, as you can imagine, Gravin didn't have any knowledge of accessing his birth-crystal abilities until after he went to school.

"Gravin had it the worst since he was the first to enter the school system. His teacher was appalled at his utter lack of knowledge, and she made no bones about telling me how terrible I was in not teaching him his elementary education.

"Ahn told me to ignore the teacher's insults, and for the most part, I could. But I did ask Gravin to demonstrate what he learned for me when he got home every day, and I ensured Rasa played nearby so she'd learn from him as well.

"I couldn't tell if she picked up anything because she was so quiet, but we kept at it until she was ready to go to school three anons later. It obviously worked because I never heard anything disparaging from her teacher.

"Children in Tuala start school after they turn six, and one of the first things they do is take a placement test to find out where their skills excel and where they need help.

"Evidently, Rasa learned quite a bit more from her brother than I guessed because her test scores caught the school administrator's attention. They didn't say anything to us until she started her second anon of school.

"Her scores were again off the chart at the beginning of the anon. They called both Ahn and myself in for a conference. I was afraid they'd scold me for her lack of education, but I was swiftly disabused of that notion when we found a couple of people we didn't know also in attendance for the meeting.

"Rasa's teacher introduced both gentlemen as Jehoban's representatives. After the introduction, the instructor sat and gestured for the men to conduct the meeting. They got right to the point and said that Rasa was too gifted to continue her education without Jehoban's personal guidance.

"They posed it as a request for Rasa to come with them for this great honor, but it was apparent we wouldn't really have a choice in the matter. Nobody ever says no to the request.

"We told them we appreciated the offer, and we'd have to discuss it as a family before we made any decisions. They said they'd stop off at our house in two days, and they expected a response at that time. When we got home, we gathered everyone and told them what had happened."

CHAPTER 13

Amanda could hardly imagine how she'd react in Barla's shoes. "Oh, man! I bet you were so scared. I mean, here you are, trying to live your life under the radar, and then Rasa brings you to Jehoban's attention. What did you do?"

Barla hummed her agreement. "Gravin was jealous. He thought he should've been offered the opportunity since he was older and because he taught Rasa everything she knew. Rasa patted his hand and told him he was an amazing brother.

"She always knew how to handle him in his worst moods. She went on to tell him as the oldest, it was his responsibility to take care of their mother while their father was at work. He was the second man of the house, and his role in the family was very important.

"I remember Ahn looking at me with his eyebrows raised in amazement at Rasa's careful wording. Then Rasa continued talking to her brother, saying she wasn't very useful around the house and it'd be easier for their mother to take care of all of the orphan children if she had one less child at home.

"I started to tell her it wasn't true when Ahn's hand squeezed mine, and I looked up in time to see him imperceptibly shake his head. I realized Rasa was only saying these things to convince Gravin he was more important than herself, and if she went away to be taught, things would be easier at home.

"After a few minutes of consideration, Gravin finally nodded agreement but then told Rasa he'd miss her company. Rasa hugged him and said she'd learn how to contact him using the elemy so they could talk whenever they wanted. Gravin seemed placated with her solution to the problem, and he finally agreed she should go.

"I think that conversation was the most I ever heard Rasa say all at one time. It was also the most excited I ever saw her become. Since she worked so hard to get Gravin's approval, we also consented to her wishes."

"Didn't you worry about Jehoban finding out about you not being from Tuala?" Amanda shook her head in puzzlement. She still found the whole process bazaar, to put it mildly.

"That was a daily concern for us until we remembered one important detail—" Barla paused and seemed to have an almost mischievous smirk on her face.

"What was it?"

"We were afraid of Jehoban. He's the Creator, so He already knew who I was and obviously didn't care. Or maybe it was because I was from Earth that made Rasa's gifts even more power-ful. He takes on so few students; maybe He's looking for mixed-race pupils. I should ask Rasa about it the next time we talk."

"What happened when she left? Why didn't the family go with her?"

"Oh, we were allowed to accompany Rasa, but Ahn was just promoted to the Harbor Master position, and he felt as though he'd found his calling as well. Gravin made many friends and enjoyed his studies, and we knew it wouldn't serve him well to move to a new location.

"While I knew I'd miss Rasa terribly, she was right in reminding me of my orphaned kids to look after. If I left, I wasn't sure the children would still be cared for in the way they deserved.

"We had two days to get everything in order. We told the school we'd allow Rasa's education to be reassigned to Jehoban. I'm sure they expected no less at the school. The administrators practically beamed that one of their students was selected. Of course, they took all of the credit even though Gravin was probably more instrumental than anyone in her achievements.

"Rasa virtually blossomed in those two days, and I couldn't bring myself to say anything that would make her regret her decision to go. I was also curious to see what she'd do with the unique opportunity. Although I've never regretted allowing her to leave, and she has surpassed my expectations in her education, I missed the chance to see her grow up."

Amanda reached across the table, patting Barla's hand sympathetically. "I can totally imagine how bad it was. I only lost about four months of Juila's life and almost two years of Jena's, and it has just about broken my heart. Since Rasa's so close to Jehoban, do you think He might help me find Jena?"

Barla looked up at Amanda in surprise, but her expression changed to sadness as she slowly shook her head from side to side. "I'm afraid it doesn't work like that, Amanda. Jehoban may decide to instruct some of His children, but He promised not to interfere with their lives."

Juila started slapping her hands on the table before her, which startled both women from their silent ruminations. They grinned at one another when Juila suddenly used her untrained powers to attempt propelling several pieces of fruit into her open mouth. Only one piece actually made it into her mouth while the other two fell to the floor.

"That's what I get for ignoring her appetite," Amanda sighed and bent over to pick up the mess. As she did so, her crystal pendant slid out from under her shirt to bounce off of her chin. When she straightened up, it fell to nestle between her breasts on the outside of her shirt.

Barla gasped and pointed toward Amanda's chest and whispered urgently, "Is that what I think it is, Amanda? Do you have your own birth crystal?"

Amanda self-consciously grasped the pendant in her hand, looked into Barla's eyes, and simply nodded.

"How did you get it?"

Amanda explained how Jehoban gifted her this crystal in the strangest manner for the next few minutes. She ended with, "Bryon mentioned it last night during dinner."

Barla could barely contain her rising excitement. "I must've misunderstood Bryon, or I wasn't paying proper attention. Don't you understand what this means, Amanda?

"Jehoban has already given you the one thing you needed to find Jena. Earth people don't have their own crystals, and yet there you sit with one of your very own! Jena must be significant, or else Jehoban wouldn't have interfered. Now we just need to figure out what His gift means."

"What're you saying, Barla? I've already tried using the crystal to locate Jena, but it hasn't helped at all. What more could there be?"

"I don't know right now. Let me think about this." She shook her head, her gaze never leaving the necklace. "I can't believe you have your own crystal. Are you able to do anything with it? Can you access the elemy?"

Barla's intense interest shook Amanda. She still clutched her diamond-encrusted, tree-of-life pendant and silently nodded.

"Wow," Barla breathed in wonder. "What was it like? It was totally amazing, wasn't it? Oh, you've got to show me. What can you do?"

"I used Shemalla's birth crystal on Earth before coming back here, so I already knew what to expect. Looking back, I guess it was a good thing I'd had practice so Alena wouldn't be shocked by my fascination with the process.

"To answer your questions in order, it's unlike anything I've ever experienced, totally amazing, and other than searching for Jena, I've only pushed the elemy around through the stones."

"I always wished I could use the elemy, but I never thought it would be possible because of my birthplace." She sadly exhaled. "Oh, well. Even if it is possible, there's no way for me to obtain my own necklace without drawing unwanted attention to my family."

"Here, do you want to try mine?" Amanda reached up to remove her necklace.

Barla instantly raised her hands with her palms toward Amanda as she spoke in an almost shrill voice of alarm, "Oh no! That's a gift from Jehoban. I wouldn't dare touch it for fear I might damage it somehow!"

Amanda frowned slightly at Barla's rushed explanation, but then her expression cleared. Even though Barla might wish to have her own birth crystal, she was also terrified of the power accessed through the stones. She couldn't blame her since she'd felt the same trepidation with Shemalla.

Thank goodness her first experience was with someone who knew who she was and didn't try to judge or condemn her for her origins. Although she doubted Alena would turn against her, the residual fear of being turned over to an Elder for questioning was too upsetting to contemplate.

Barla broke into her reverie with an inspired thought, "Maybe Rasa could teach you to use your crystal to its full potential? I don't think it'd be considered interference from Jehoban if one of His students were to teach you different techniques."

Hope swelled inside Amanda's chest. Could this be the break she needed? Would it be wise to pursue? "Well, I certainly don't want to get Rasa into any trouble. But, I'll take whatever help I can get. It's already been so long since Jena went missing, and I'd do just about anything to hold her again!"

At the lull in their conversation, Bryon walked into the kitchen. "Did I interrupt something? I can come back." He pointed his thumb over his shoulder and swiftly turned on his heel to leave.

Barla looked up and smiled at him, waving for him to come to join them. "Nonsense. Come join us."

He grinned back at her as he changed course again and crossed the room.

"I can't help but think I've interrupted your discussion," Bryon apologetically said when he sat at the table across from Juila.

Barla spoke before Amanda could. "Oh, not at all, Bryon. I was just telling Amanda stories about Gravin and Rasa growing up."

Amanda spoke when Barla paused to take a breath. "Barla noticed my birth crystal, and she thought that maybe Rasa can help me locate Jena if I use more advanced techniques with the pendant and the elemy."

Bryon's eyebrows rose nearly to his hairline. "Wow. You're appearing and sounding so upbeat today. After last night—." He let the sentence drop like rotten fruit into the sudden silence.

"Great idea!" He stared pointedly at Barla and said, "When can we go see her?"

CHAPTER 14

After what felt like forever, Barla answered Bryon's question. "I'll have to ask her about it during my weekly call. She hardly ever has a moment to herself, and it's impossible to contact her. I can't imagine she wouldn't want to help considering Jena's a family member, even if she doesn't know it yet!"

Amanda wanted to jump up and demand action, but she couldn't do any of that. Instead, she remained seated, crying a little on the inside and wishing Jehoban would tell Rasa to call that very moment.

Bryon, Alena, Ahn, and Barla already spent a considerable amount of time helping her during her two visitations to Tuala, and she could hardly expect them to drop everything at her whim. As frustrated as she might be, she learned the importance of patience very well.

Bryon spoke again into the silence, "We should think about heading back to Kirma. Unfortunately, I have to go to work today to meet a new buyer that can't be rescheduled. We won't have to rush out of here since the meeting is right before lunch. I'm sorry, Amanda."

"Don't worry about it, Bryon! I got to stay longer than I thought. Plus, I'm thrilled to think we might have another lead to follow up on since everything else seems to have run dry."

Amanda picked up her pika juice and swallowed the contents of the glass before she pushed her chair back to get her things together. "I'll be ready to go in a few minutes. I just have to gather the few items we brought for Juila."

Barla pulled Juila out of the high chair and hugged her close. "I'm so sorry that you have to leave so soon, but I understand."

She reached into her tunic pocket, removed an envelope, and held it out to Amanda. "I wrote this letter for Diane last night after you went to bed. I wasn't sure how much time we'd have today, and I wanted to be prepared in any event. With your luck, you might pop back over to Earth unannounced." She playfully wiggled her eyebrows to take out any sting from her statement.

Amanda chuckled, "I know I'm prone to accidents and general clumsiness, so I'm not offended in any way." Reaching out, she took the offered envelope and tucked it carefully into her pants pocket. Her only hope was the next time she went to Earth, it was at a time of her own choosing and with a daughter in each arm.

Amanda walked over to the sink and rinsed out her glass. She set the glass in the sink, turned around, and looked for anything of hers or Juila's to gather.

Patting Barla's arm as she walked past, she said, "I'm going to get our stuff together." She walked to the living room, picked up a few toys, and put them in the diaper bag that she still used for Juila's many accouterments even though she hadn't used a clout for almost a year.

She went upstairs to her room and gathered her outfit from the day before out of the bathroom. Amanda searched the bedroom for anything else of hers. No matter how short of a stay, she never lost the feeling that she was leaving something behind. The compulsive need took over to look in each place several times before she felt confident she had everything she came with.

ON HER WAY down the stairs, Amanda saw Bryon standing in the hall, accompanied by Barla, holding Juila on her hip. If only she could've spent more time with her aunt.

Once again, regret washed over her for not getting together with Ahn and Barla sooner. She'd wasted so much time searching empty leads for Jena when she could've gotten together with Rasa much sooner and probably already been home with both children.

Amanda unconsciously patted her pants pocket to ensure Barla's letter was still there. The paper crinkled loudly. She walked up to the trio and announced, "I believe I got it all. I'm ready to go whenever you are." Her voice sounded more cheerful than she felt.

"I can take Juila now," Amanda spoke to Barla and held out her arms to her daughter.

Barla hugged Juila a little tighter. "It'd thrill me to carry her back to the telepod for you. I really miss having a little one to care for; they're so innocent and trusting. They just make me feel younger when they're around."

Amanda shrugged. "Suit yourself; I don't mind at all. Just yesterday, I thought that Juila's starting to get too big to be carried all of the time. If she gets too heavy, let me know, and I'll take over."

Barla smiled at Amanda and whispered to Juila, "I don't think you're heavy at all. You're just perfect!"

Bryon walked ahead of them in the hallway and opened the front door. He made a gallant gesture for the women to precede him and carefully closed the door behind him as he followed the ladies. "It's too bad Ahn had an emergency at work. It would've been nice to say goodbye to him."

"I didn't realize Ahn wasn't home. I just thought he was upstairs sleeping." Amanda looked at Barla with some confusion. "Is everything okay?"

"Oh, sure. I told Bryon about Ahn's early departure while you were getting your things together. These kinds of things happen pretty often, so I don't even worry about them anymore." Barla shrugged, clearly not bothered by the matter.

They leisurely strolled toward the telepod landing ground. Their conversation remained light-hearted as they neared the grassy plateau.

They rounded the last corner and encountered the unusual sight of several other telepods surrounding their own, including a bright red one that stood out from the others. Something big must've happened for so many to be parked there simultaneously.

Barla reluctantly handed Juila over to Amanda as they stood in the telepod's open door. Without hesitating, Barla pulled Amanda close with Juila sandwiched between them.

She whispered into Amanda's ear, "I'll let you know what I find out from Rasa. I'm so glad to know you're my niece." She pulled back and squeezed her arm gently in farewell.

"Feel free to come to visit or stay anytime. We have so much more to catch up on. I love you." She stepped backward, trying unsuccessfully to stem the flow of tears.

Amanda already missed Barla's physical touch. Tears threatened, and she smiled back, "I love you too, Aunt Barla. We're only a patil call away. We'll talk soon." She turned and walked up the ramp to get them both settled for the return trip.

Bryon entered the small telepod and palmed the door closed. He joined Amanda at the front of the craft in the left controller seat. He initiated the start-up procedures and noted the green indicator lights on the control panel. Once the crystal drive was activated, the telepod rose several inches to hover.

On the way to the Port of Cresdon, Amanda paid more attention to the flight; this time, she watched Bryon. He closed his eyes, probably visualizing the coordinates for his house, and then his hand moved to rest on the activation module. Darkness overwhelmed her senses for several seconds while absolute nothingness took over.

A moment later, they hovered over the landing pad at his house. Bryon manually steered the telepod to the ground and performed numerous shutdown procedures.

"Since I'm leaving shortly, I'm leaving the 'pod outside," Bryon announced.

"I'm looking forward to seeing Alena's reaction to your stunning news," he said.

"Are you sure we should? I mean, what if Barla doesn't—" Amanda said but stopped when Bryon held up a hand.

"Barla granted permission to tell Alena anything I felt she should know about what was going on. She thought it might aid in finding Jena, so full disclosure was imperative."

Amanda nodded, but her stomach churned. What if Alena freaked out and told her to leave immediately? Surely, not everyone was so blasé about *old souls* living in their houses with little children around.

Bryon followed Amanda out of the telepod. He carried the baby bag since Amanda held Juila, and she was enough burden for anyone. He rushed ahead to open the front door before Amanda reached the opening and gallantly gestured for her to enter the house ahead of him.

Before the door shut behind them, Alena pounced on them as if she were waiting for their arrival. "How was the trip? Have you two already eaten? Let me put something together." Alena didn't even wait for any answers. She turned and headed toward the kitchen.

Due to the early hour, she correctly assumed they'd want breakfast. She used the elemy to scramble eggs, fry foxl slices, and make toast on four different plates already set onto the table before Bryon entered the room.

Amanda's eyes widened at Alena's powerful display, and she smiled up at Bryon as she settled Juila in her highchair at the table. "That power sure does have its uses, doesn't it, Bryon?"

Bryon nodded and looked swiftly toward Alena for her reaction to the odd statement. Predictably, Alena looked quizzically at Amanda and then toward Bryon. Bryon grinned at his wife and said, "Sit down, Alena, we have a lot to discuss. We might as well eat while we're talking."

Alena scoffed, "You're always hungry." She sat next to Bryon and across from Amanda. "Why do I get the feeling that you two have something cooking? Did you discover something while you were with Ahn and Barla? Whatever it was, you two are mightly pleased with yourselves."

After ensuring Juila started on her breakfast, Amanda finally faced her plate, inhaled, and said, "This smells heavenly. Thanks for putting this together so fast. Why don't you tell Alena what you discovered from Ahn, Bryon?"

Amanda picked up her fork after a quick prayer of thanks and ate the succulent meat while it was still quite warm.

CHAPTER 15

B ryon cleared his throat and said, "We thought we had another lead on Petre, but it turned out to be a false report. It's been so long now since Petre's last sighting; I'm surprised people are still thinking about him even with the reward.

"Maybe there's been a resurgence of interest since Captain Issyn saw him. He must've said something to his crew about it and got them talking in the bars once they went ashore. Anyway, we know Petre's still out there, and he'll eventually have to make landfall. The only trouble is we don't have any idea of where or when it'll happen."

Amanda woodenly nodded and swallowed her bite. Quickly covering her mouth with her hand, she added, "Barla thought of another search avenue. Her daughter, Rasa. I don't know if you know she's a student of Jehoban and very talented with her skills. Barla thinks she can teach me some advanced techniques to aid my search using my crystal."

"But why would she do it? I've heard Jehoban's students guard

730

their time jealously. It seems odd for her to want to help a stranger." Alena looked from Amanda to Bryon and gasped. "There's more to this story. Don't keep me in suspense! What am I missing? Spill it already!" She glared from her husband to Amanda, clearly impatient.

Bryon said, "I recognized that look. Hurry, Amanda, we only have a few more seconds before she loses her patience!" His lips curled up on the side, and his eyes sparkled mischievously, enjoying the moment and drawing it out even longer. "We discovered that Barla is Amanda's mother's sister."

Alena drew in a quick breath and said, "Really? How'd you find that out?"

Amanda interrupted before Bryon could continue, "I learned about the connection while I was gone for those mesans when everyone thought I was dead. I wasn't just missing, Alena. I was gone."

Alena's brows furrowed, and she frowned. She set her fork down on the table and folded her hands beside her plate with exaggerated care.

"I'm from Earth." Amanda let those three words sink in for a few moments before continuing. "As you probably figured out, Barla is also from Earth. We'd appreciate it if you'd keep that part to yourself.

"When she was eighteen, she experienced an accident similar to mine in the sea and ended up here in Tuala. Neither of us had any advance warning or idea of what had happened. She fell in love with Ahn when he rescued her from the water, and she decided to stay in Tuala and live with him rather than try to find a way back to Earth.

"When I went missing from here, I found myself returned to Earth. With my girls both still here, I didn't have much choice but to return. However, while I was in my world, I got back together with my parents. Barla sent a note with me, and I always kept it in my pocket for such an occasion as I found myself in.

"At home, my mother recognized Barla's handwriting, and then we discovered she was my mother's long-lost sister. I'd never met her as she went missing before I was even born, so I was just as stunned."

Alena simply stared at Amanda in open-mouthed shock. "I can hardly believe any of this. I mean, I know people from Earth exist, but I imagined they'd somehow be dissimilar enough for me to tell the difference. Now you're telling me that I know two people from Earth, and I never even had any clue!

"Well, not exactly true," Alena added, as though to herself. "There were times when you did or said things that made me wonder where you came from. But not this!"

She sat silently for a few seconds. "Wait! I performed the birth crystal service for you! It's not possible!"

Amanda unconsciously reached up and wrapped her fingers around her prized possession. She nodded and replied, "Remember how odd the ceremony turned out to be? The first crystal evaporated to dust and the second one appeared before you even asked Jehoban for it.

"Barla seemed to think that Jehoban's helping me in my quest to find Jena or at least to protect me while I'm in Tuala. It was because of this crystal Barla got the idea that, while Jehoban probably wouldn't give me more assistance than He already has, His student—my cousin, Rasa—would most likely be more than willing."

"I see," Alena replied. She grabbed the sides of her head and said, "I have so many questions whirling through my brain. I can't even bring a single one to the forefront to vocalize."

Another minute went by. Bryon kept eating during the lull in the conversation. Amanda broke off crumbs of her toast and nibbled sparingly. Alena took the news even better than Amanda hoped.

Finally, Alena exclaimed, "But both of your children have birth crystals."

Bryon said, "I wondered how long it would take to get around to that situation."

Amanda kept her gaze glued to her plate. She could guess where the conversation would go next. If there were any way she could escape the truth, she'd take it. But Bryon was right. Alena had to know the whole truth. She opened her mouth to speak, but Bryon beat her to it, and instead, she popped a dry piece of toast into her mouth to avoid talking.

Bryon said, "We think Petre may have had his way with Amanda while holding her captive. That means her children are half-Tualan and eligible for birth crystals. When Amanda returned to Earth, Nealan adamantly denied any intimate relations, so the children are most likely Petre's."

"Like hell they are!" Alena's outburst startled everyone in the room. All eyes stared at Alena.

Alena's hands dropped to the table with a thud, and her fingers curled together so tightly they turned white. "Rapists don't have any claim to the products of their sin! He may be their biological donor, but they're not *his* children!"

Bryon reached over and covered one of her fists with his large hand. "Alena, I'm sorry, it was a poor choice of words on my part. We all agree he doesn't have any claim on them, but it does explain why he took Jena.

As Frasnia said before, she didn't think Petre knew Juila even existed, or he probably would've tried to take her as well." Bryon picked up his fork and continued eating until the room's tension dissipated.

Alena seemed somewhat mollified with Bryon's apology. She

folded her arms defiantly and declared, "Those children are Amanda's alone. As far as I'm concerned, they don't have a father!"

Amanda smiled at Alena's stubbornness on the matter and said, "I've always known that! When I thought Neal was their father and still on Earth, I raised the children alone. That hasn't changed because of what Petre most likely did." She looked toward Juila, who busily pushed her food all over her plate and chair tray.

She noticed how Juila's blue eyes starkly contrasted Neal's brown eyes for the first time. While two brown-eyed parents could have a blue-eyed child, it wasn't very common; something like a twenty-five percent chance if either one of Neal's or her parents had blue eyes.

She vividly remembered Petre had the same bright blue eyes as those staring back at her right now. While Petre's eyes were filled with wicked imaginations, Juila's were full of curiosity and wonder. There was no comparison when she thought of it that way.

Amanda snapped back to attention. She said, "Another curious matter to consider is Rasa herself. Her mother's from Earth, but her father's from Tuala. Rasa's crystal talent was so impressive that it caught Jehoban's attention.

"It stands to reason since Jehoban is the Creator of everything, then He already knows who Barla is, and Rasa's more than she appears.

"Does the mixing of the two races create a more powerful talent? Juila's already shown advanced skills for her age, don't you think?"

Alena considered these new revelations carefully and finally nodded. "You've given me a lot to think about, starting with my perception of *old souls* being in Tuala. Jehoban obviously doesn't mind if they're living in Tuala.

"Why would the Elders make such a big deal about them?

Aren't the Elders supposed to be representatives of Jehoban? There's something not right about this situation."

Alena's body shook as though she felt a chill. She turned her absent gaze from the tabletop over to Amanda. "When will you find out if Rasa will be able to help?"

Amanda said, "Barla said she'd hear from her at the end of this week. I'm sure she'll let me know as soon as she has an answer."

Alena's expression lightened. "That's good. We'll have a few days to see what Juila's capable of." She looked over at Juila and smiled at the mess she had made.

"Your girls never seemed different than any other child I've known, but now I wonder if Juila and Jena are going to be so much more than anyone can imagine.

"I sure hope I'll be able to see how they grew up. If not, I'm certainly going to take advantage of evaluating Juila's skills in the time I have left." She picked up her fork and resumed eating. Her eyes gleamed.

Bryon looked down at his timepiece. "Good grief, it's later than I thought." He stood, and both women looked up at him with questioning gazes. "Sorry, ladies, I've got a meeting."

"Is it that late already? Where did the time go?" Amanda gazed across the room to where Juila played on the floor quietly by herself.

"We should probably make a snack for Juila," Alena offered as she stood and gave her husband a farewell kiss. "We'll see you later this afternoon."

Bryon looked down on his wife with love and adoration in his eyes. "I never get tired of gazing into the depths of your soul through your gorgeous eyes. I'll try to make it as short as possible," he promised as he turned and left the room.

He strode down the hall to their shared bedroom. He called over his shoulder, "You could help me get ready."

"You wish. But then you'd end up being late," Alena teased.

Amanda scooped up Juila and went to the kitchen with Alena. The two women couldn't help but giggle at the playful banter with Bryon. Amanda's heart ached to have someone in her life like that. She wanted a role model like Bryon for her children, too.

CHAPTER 16

It only took Bryon a few minutes to power up the telepod, navigate to Kirma Shipping and Receiving, and walk the short distance to his office.

Under his breath, he said, "Man, I'd rather spend my afternoon enjoying this beautiful weather than meeting with Kenen right now."

Once Bryon opened the office door, he paused at the threshold to let his eyes adjust to the dim interior in stark contrast to the outside's bright sunshine.

Enough stalling.

Bryon took the final step into the office and let the door close behind him. He smiled at his secretary, Frasnia, just as she finished a call on her patil.

Frasnia's shoulders dropped, and she sighed. "Good, you're back! That was Kenen's office on the patil just now; he's running a little bit late.

"How was your visit with Captain Ahn? Was Petre arrested? Were there any leads for locating Jena?"

Bryon sat on the edge of Frasnia's desk to wait for her barrage of questions to end before he answered each one in order, "It was a great visit, we haven't found Petre, and we do have a new idea for locating Jena!" His smile grew as Frasnia's big green eyes widened with anticipation over the last bit of news.

"What is it? Can I help?"

"Unfortunately, no." Seeing Frasnia's gaze fall away and her smile falter, Bryon added, "This one's all on Amanda."

She pushed her straight, dark hair behind her ear as she did when uncomfortable. She desperately wanted to make herself useful to make up for her perceived involvement.

Unquestionably, her feelings were misplaced, but no amount of consoling convinced her she was not complicit. Bryon leaned closer and spoke, "Really, it's true. Barla's daughter might help Amanda locate Jena through her birth crystal. It's the mother-daughter link that's the key."

Frasnia looked up at Bryon through her lashes as if trying to decide Bryon's truthfulness. "Okay, but if anything comes up where I might be able to help, please ask."

Plastering on the most cheerful grin he could muster, he said, "Absolutely, you've been invaluable throughout everything. We won't know anything for sure until after this Jumat since that's when Barla will talk with Rasa."

"This will be exciting."

He pushed his hip off of the desk and straightened. "That's what we think, too. Back to business—how was Kenen's mood?"

"I didn't speak to him but his secretary. She seemed pretty relaxed, so I think he can't be too bad today."

"That's good," Bryon mused, and then another thought came to mind, "You've been dating Ninan, right?"

Frasnia seemed confused by Bryon's sudden subject change and hesitantly answered, "Yes. Is that okay?"

"Oh, fine, fine. I just wondered if he might have mentioned any new memories from his kidnapping. If we could just find the stolen shipment, it might go a long way toward repairing our relationship with Kenen."

Frasnia's guilty expression cleared, and she shook her head sadly. "I'm sorry, Bryon, he hasn't recovered any memories from that time. It's been so long; I'm starting to think he may never remember. After all, his head trauma was pretty severe."

"You're probably right. It was worth asking, though. I guess I should review what I'm going to go over with Kenen. Once he arrives, make sure to let me know immediately, so he doesn't feel as though we're brushing him off. His business with us is critical, as you already know."

Frasnia folded her hands and rested them on her desk as she leaned forward to keep Bryon in her sight as he walked toward his office. "Sure thing. I put all of their work requests on the right-hand side of your desk. They added a few new things yesterday."

"Okay, thanks," Bryon said over his shoulder as he entered his private office and shut the door. Would they ever recover the lost shipment? Probably once they located Petre and questioned him, they'd solve several mysteries. Until then, everything would remain business as usual.

Dr. Gascon thrust the latest session notes back onto his dark, mahogany desk. "Amanda's weaving an intricate tale to keep us distracted from our goal of finding Nealand!" He glared at Dr. Medin over the rims of his glasses. "And please don't tell me you believe all of this bullshit because that's exactly what it is. I've decreased Amanda's medication dosage, yet the story seems to be getting more involved rather than less."

Jasmine watched as the Cannon Memorial Asylum Director of Psychiatry's face turned several shades of red as his anger increased over Amanda Covington's case. She knew he wouldn't be happy with her latest case notes, but now she was worried he'd do something drastic to prove his point.

"I'm encouraged by the fact she feels it's okay to move on. I think she's on the verge of telling us what you want to know."

Dr. Gascon glared harder and leaned closer to Jasmine. "What *we* want to know, you mean?"

"Yes, Dr. Gascon, what *we* want to know."

"But now Amanda claims she has the same powers as the other people!"

"Exactly my point. Amanda no longer feels helpless; she can play a more important role in society. I just need to direct her to feel powerful enough to tell us Nealand's location, and then we'll have news to share with the Taivas family. We're on the right path, Dr. Gascon. I'm sure of it!"

He jabbed his index finger into the pile of Jasmine's notes. "You better be right, Dr. Medin. That's all for now. I need to think." He raised his hand and waved it impatiently to encourage Dr. Medin to leave immediately.

Not needing any further encouragement, Jasmine stood from the leather chair and left the Director's office without looking back. As it had become her routine, Jasmine collected Amanda's afternoon medication from the nurse's station and then proceeded down the hall to Room 426 to retrieve the patient herself. Amanda exited her room and followed the doctor to her office at the quick knock on her door.

They entered Dr. Medin's office, and Amanda watched as the doctor balled up the paper cup containing her pills and threw it into her wastebasket.

Amanda sighed and sank onto the couch. "I was getting worried that you weren't coming to get me." Nodding toward the garbage can, Amanda added, "I can't tell you how much better I feel without that dreaded medication."

Jasmine turned and smiled at Amanda sitting in a patch of

sunshine cascading through the office window. For the first time, she noticed Amanda wearing a crystal necklace. Jewelry wasn't permitted in the Psychiatric Ward, so of course, she asked, "Amanda, where did your necklace come from?"

Amanda's hand reached up and gently touched the ornate pendant of crystals. She almost seemed surprised to find it there herself as she replied, "I don't know. I didn't even realize I was wearing it." Her fingers continued to stroke the gems.

Jasmine checked the visitor's record and noted that Amanda hadn't received any visitors. She was just as astonished by the new addition. Since she didn't have any explanation and neither did Amanda, she decided to let the matter go until she could think on it further.

"Amanda, how do you explain that you've been in Tuala for two years, yet you're still living with Alena and Bryon? Why haven't you gotten a job?"

Amanda cocked her head to the side as she considered the question. "I don't know, really. I guess each day just slipped by. Alena was busy with her wise-woman practice, and Bryon had his work to do. I spent my days around the house with the children, cooking, cleaning, and taking care of any errands to make life easier for the Kesh family."

"Do you think it was a fair trade: their hospitality for your services?"

"I hope so. I'd hate to think they may have resented my staying there so long."

"Why do you think it took so long for you to remember to go see your Aunt Barla? I would have thought you'd have tried to get in touch with her immediately."

"Yeah, that was bad. It just seemed as though one thing after another happened, and it just slipped my mind."

"For two years? Don't you think that's a little long for 'slipping your mind?'"

"When you put it that way, it does. I can't explain it; I was distraught with worry over finding Jena."

"What about finding Nealand? Was that important, too?"

Amanda looked up in confusion. "I looked for Neal; everyone looked for Neal. But when I came home, I found out he'd been looking for me. He'd been fine the whole time here on Earth."

"Are you sure about that?"

"Of course, I'm sure! Dr. Medin, just what are you asking me? Has something happened to Neal?"

"Why don't we start your hypnosis session, and we can explore that a little further, okay?"

Amanda hesitated and then haltingly stretched out on the leather couch. "Something doesn't feel right about your questions today, but I trust you'll do what's best."

Jasmine bungled her line of questions. She should've waited until Amanda was under to ask those pointed questions. As soon as Amanda closed her eyes, Jasmine began the session, moderating her tone to induce hypnosis. She'd get Dr. Gascon's answers today.

CHAPTER 17

Amanda felt an unexplainable urgency to tie up loose ends before the end of the week. She didn't know about Rasa's cooperation, but she had decided no matter the outcome, she'd have to make plans for her future here in Tuala. She'd never give up looking for Jena, but she wanted Juila to have a stable place to call home.

The idea of leaving the people who loved her like family made her stomach churn. But she also knew there was a limit to how long a person should stay with family before it was just too long. Indeed, two years just about maxed that limit.

After gathering all of her clothes and Juila's, Amanda left her room and wandered into the kitchen to grab a bite to eat. She stopped short in the doorway as soon as she realized Alena was holding an impromptu birth crystal skills lesson in the kitchen with all of the children. That answered the question she'd left unvoiced.

While she addressed the kids at the table with the directions for pulling energy out of their individual birth crystals, Amanda noted Alena's evaluation of Juila's limits.

Amanda imagined these tests were similar to those administered to children when they entered school. Since Juila didn't mind the tests, Amanda eagerly awaited seeing what would happen.

Alena glanced up when she noticed movement from the doorway. She smiled at Amanda and continued talking with Juila while setting an object down in front of the child. "Can you lift this spoon from the tray, Juila? No, not with your hand. Use your mind."

Within moments the spoon hung in the air between them.

"Very good, Juila. Now set the spoon down gently." Alena chuckled when the spoon clanged loudly back onto the tray. "We can work on that!" She then gestured for Amanda to come into the kitchen and sit at the table where they practiced.

Amanda hesitated, but her heart raced in anticipation of hearing the lessons herself. "Are you sure? I don't want to interfere."

"No problem. While my children worked on the first skill required for school, I discovered what Juila was interested in doing with the elemy. We're just learning her limits, not teaching her anything new."

Amanda's gaze took in the children quietly sitting in various states of concentration. "I still find the whole thing fascinating."

"It certainly has gotten more interesting for me as well!"

"What have you found out?"

"Well, we already knew she can bring items from out of sight, and that's a pretty advanced skill. I've determined that she can do it as long as Juila understands what I'm asking her to do.

"So far, we've only worked on moving physical things. The next lesson covers mental manifestations of something such as wind or fire. We've worked a little out of order on the skills since Juila seems to like to move objects around the kitchen."

Amanda imagined the havoc her daughter could reek if she

learned too much, too soon. "Won't it be kind of dangerous to teach her?"

"I won't teach her anything. I'm just asking if she can do something. You may as well participate, too, since you haven't been assessed in these things either."

Amanda smiled at the idea. How many mothers could say they learned something alongside their toddlers? She eagerly jumped at the opportunity. She always thought this was possible, even while living on Earth.

Thinking back on her time with Shemalla, she remembered using the borrowed crystal to push energy outside of it. How much more could she accomplish with her own tuning crystal and using the original energy source here in Tuala?

"Okay, push the energy out of your crystal and into my hand." Alena directed Juila's hand to touch her own dark red birth crystal. "Juila, can you feel the energy living inside these stones?"

Juila solemnly nodded.

Justan and Andera paused in their efforts to see what Juila would do with their mother's instruction. It looked like they silently cheered Juila on since they had just completed this task mere moments before.

Kyelon sat with his arms crossed and his chin resting on his chest in a dejected posture.

Amanda playfully nudged him and asked, "Hey, buddy. What's wrong?"

Grumbling, he answered, "I'm older than Juila, but Mom told me I was only allowed to watch. It's not fair."

She leaned closer and whispered in his ear, "If it makes you feel any better, I'm older than both of you, and I still don't know how to do what she's doing. I've got a lot to learn, so I'll be paying close attention. We can learn together, okay?"

Kyelon's eyes widened, and he nodded in the exaggerated way

that young children did. His mood lightened, and he grinned at Amanda.

Alena continued the lesson that Amanda and Kyelon missed while they talked. "Good girl. Push the energy out of the stone and into my hand."

Amanda saw Juila's concentration on the task. Luckily, Amanda already learned this from Shemalla. She waited her turn to demonstrate. A moment later, pulsing energy moved from Juila's crystal to land on Alena's outstretched palm.

"Excellent, Juila. Now put it back into your crystal." When the energy returned flawlessly, Alena turned to Amanda and said, "Now it's your turn."

Amanda easily complied.

Alena's eyes narrowed at Amanda. "Have you done that before?"

Amanda smiled and said, "Shemalla showed me before taking me to the Gate to come back."

Alena nodded and looked down at the sheet of plasfilm on the table. She made a short notation and then moved her finger down to the next item on the list:

1. Pull energy out of the birth crystal
2. Move energy to a noted location
3. Put energy back into the birth crystal
4. Create a breeze
5. Boil water
6. Freeze water
7. Extinguish a flame
8. Create a flame
9. Move an object
10. Memorization
11. Heal

12. Create
13. Distance notation
14. Navigation
15. Aura detection / Matchmaking
16. Intuition
17. Deception / Illusion
18. Health detection
19. Teleportation
20. Push
21. Light source without flame
22. Mind read / Mind swipe
23. Extrasensory perception
24. Levitation
25. Time jump / Timewarp
26. Invisibility
27. Adaptation

AMANDA LEANED FORWARD to see the page. As she read each item, she appreciated that there was much more to these birth crystals than she ever realized. Her original perception of them as skills for convenience in making dinner, teleporting, or monitoring their children, was sadly mistaken.

She didn't know if each citizen tested for all of these items. Even if it were only a portion of the list, her appreciation for her pendant snowballed as she understood these were things now available to herself as well.

Amanda couldn't resist asking, "Are children tested for all of these items when they enter school?"

"Oh, no. Schools only evaluate the first four items for their first anon. By the second anon, they're assessed for items five through ten.

"Once they enter middle school, they have mandatory classes

on crystal energy to learn to heal, create meals, write notes at a distance, intuitive navigation, detect auras in people, and develop concise intuition.

"The rest of the skills are usually only taught to people who need to use a particular talent for their occupation."

Amanda nodded along with each explanation, her eyes never leaving the list. Would she ever learn more than the first few skills? Now, she wished she had more time with Alena to learn.

Alena sat next to Amanda and spoke low enough for only Amanda to hear. "I'm curious to see what Juila's limits are because of her heritage. I promise I won't push her beyond what she wants to do.

"I think that if I show Juila how to do something and then ask her to repeat it, I'll know if she possesses the skill. She won't have to try to perfect any of it, just demonstrate the ability to perform it at all. Most people never learn many of these things, but that's what makes us each unique."

Amanda tore her gaze away from the page to look at Alena. "I wasn't worried about it. I know you think of her as your daughter, too.

"I'm curious, though. Are you able to do all of these things?"

Alena chuckled ruefully but shook her head. "I've never mastered aura detection, and deception is something I've never even ventured to try since it goes against my beliefs."

Alena looked down at the list for a moment. "I'm not very good at pushing, which entails making someone agree with what you're talking about as it feels like deception to me. Let's see, hmm, I can't read minds, but I'm very good at reading body language, so it almost seems as though I'm reading someone when I'm not."

Amanda studied the list again and finally asked, "Can you teach me all of these things?"

Alena's eyes sparkled with the challenge. "I'll do my best. We should spend as much time as we can to catch you up. If Rasa helps you, you need to know a lot more than just the basics! I'll push you as far as you can go if you want."

The magnitude of the task ahead of her almost took her breath away. Talk about a crash course! Luckily, the subject matter was fascinating. "Whew! I have *a lot* to learn. It's a good thing I'm a motivated student."

Justan asked, "Why don't you already know how to do these things? Didn't your mom teach you before you went to school?"

Amanda's wide-eyed gaze cut over to Alena. Their free speech in front of the children didn't go unnoticed. Not sure how she should answer, Alena luckily was one step ahead of her.

"I'm sure her mother taught her many things, Justan. Do you remember when Amanda first came to live with us?"

Justan nodded solemnly.

"Right before she came here, she had hit her head in a really bad accident. Because of the injury, she lost her memory. She's a lot better now and has asked me to teach her how to reaccess the elemy. Since she has her birth crystal, it'll make it a lot easier."

Wanting to avoid any more questions the children were sure to dream up, she turned and grinned at Amanda and then said, "Okay, we've established the first three basics for both of you. Now we need to concentrate on creating a breeze."

She addressed her oldest two children and said, "I'd like you to face each other and work on the second and third skills we just went over while I move ahead with Amanda and Juila."

The trio worked on the following several talents on the list until it was apparent Juila needed to go down for her nap. Amanda gladly took the opportunity to rest her brain from the constant strain of trying to make the elemy bend to her particular wishes.

Her attempts were getting better as she started to get a feel for how the elemy functioned. It almost seemed as though the less she concentrated on molding it, the easier it bent to her will.

Somehow she needed her intuition to take over the task instead of her conscious mind. She felt as though she were right on the cusp of a breakthrough.

CHAPTER 18

As Amanda carried Juila to her crib, she cuddled her close. Amanda could hardly contain her pride in Juila's blossoming crystal talent. The only thing Juila stumbled with was freezing water.

Amanda almost helped Juila a few times. But, she consciously restrained her energy and looked away until Juila finished her attempt.

Amanda settled the covers over the now-sleeping toddler and smiled at her adorably content expression. If only her life were as simple as her daughter's. Amanda left her daughter's room and returned to the kitchen to continue her lessons with a sigh of resignation.

"Can you get us each a glass of pika juice?"

Out of habit, Amanda's feet changed direction, and she walked toward the cabinets. Alena corrected her by saying, "Use your power."

"Right. Of course." Juila performed this task effortlessly. Shouldn't she be able to accomplish as much? She relaxed and formed the thought to complete the request.

A moment passed. Nothing happened. Then suddenly, two glasses of pika juice appeared on the table. The glasses wobbled a little, and some of the liquid spilled onto the table, but Amanda smiled at her success as she grabbed the glass nearest her seat. She took a drink and sighed with satisfaction.

Alena snatched the other glass mid-tilt and smiled as she said, "Well done, Amanda! Let's go into the living room to continue our lessons."

"That sounds good, but where are the other children?"

"While you were putting Juila down, Tana came over and asked for the kids' help planting flowers in her back yard. I thought they looked ready to do something else, and poor Kyelon was just miserable with not being able to participate. I felt bad telling him he couldn't work on the skills, but he's about an anon too young. They're only little for so short a time, and I want to keep him 'my baby' as long as possible."

They strolled shoulder to shoulder into the adjacent room and settled onto the couch. "How does your progress feel so far? Are you too tired to continue?"

Amanda tucked her feet up under her as she leaned against the couch's arm. "No, I'm good. I was starting to think there's more to these skills than just manipulating the elemy.

"It feels as though the harder I try to make it happen, the worse the results are. When I relax and just let impulse take over, then it seems to work easier. Does that make sense?"

Alena nodded as Amanda spoke, pressing her lips together thoughtfully. "Perfect sense, and you're right; the elemy does work better with the subconscious mind. Let's take a look at the next skill of extinguishing a flame. With this one, you have two options: either create a breeze that blows it out or remove the oxygen from around it, making it go out on its own."

Alena leaned forward and thought a flame into existence on the candle resting on the coffee table. She gestured toward it and said, "Go ahead and put out the flame."

Amanda couldn't decide if she wanted to use the wind or snuffing method. She already used her ability to create a breeze, so it might be better practice to snuff it instead. This time she tried using her subconscious by imagining the flame snuffed out instead of concentrating on the elemy doing a specific task. As the flame went out, she squealed in delight at her success. She beamed a smile at Alena, who smiled just as broadly.

"Wonderful! I believe that's the fastest you've been in learning something new. Now reverse the process and create a flame in the same spot."

This task seemed more dangerous to Amanda than the others. *What if I light a flame on something other than the candle? Shouldn't we try this outside first? Alena wouldn't ask it of me unless she thought I could do it properly.* Once again, she visualized a flame on the candle, and even faster than before, the flame surged to life.

"Excellent, now go ahead and put it out, and we'll try moving an object. Which reminds me, remember when Juila prepared the glass of juice?"

Amanda nodded.

"Just before she did that amazing feat, she was playing in the living room. Out of the blue, she suddenly jumped up and said she 'wanted to try it too.' She made several of her toys fly through the air while she danced underneath them.

"So I know she already knows how to make an object move under her direction. The question I have is how she learned it in the first place. Do you have any ideas?"

Amanda uncurled her legs and slid closer to Alena. "None whatsoever. That's amazing! What are your thoughts about it?"

"I asked her, and she said she saw herself doing it in the white room. The only thing that makes any sense is she's somehow still connected to Jena and that her sister's learning how to access the elemy through her birth crystal. I could be wrong, but it made sense at the time."

Amanda cupped an elbow with one hand while tapping her lips with the other. Her eyebrows furrowed and then released. "No, you could be on to something. Man, I wish Juila could help us find Jena. If she still has a twin connection with her, she might be the key to locating her sister."

Alena scratched the back of her neck. "Let's not get ahead of ourselves. I could be totally wrong. I wish I could talk to other wise-women about this, but I'm afraid it would draw unwanted attention.

"Just watch Juila and see if you ever notice anything strange. Let me know right away, and we'll compare notes."

Amanda nodded thoughtfully, keeping her composure calm despite her racing heart. "Okay. Now, you said the next thing I need to accomplish is moving an object. What does that entail? Can you explain the process?"

Alena snapped back into teaching mode. "Let's see, moving an object is kind of like getting a glass of juice, but without making it appear from a separate location."

She scoffed and added, "I often move objects when I see where one of the kids will trip over something and get hurt. In such instances, I just move the offending object out of the way. Try moving this candle across the table."

Amanda grinned at her explanation about keeping her kids safe. This skill would be beneficial to master to help protect Juila from unnecessary harm. Looking at the candle, she concentrated on shifting it across the table without making it disappear and reappear; she wanted to get this right.

Nothing happened. Immediately, she recognized her error and adjusted without thinking. She relaxed and just imagined it slowly moving across the table. To her relief, the candle shifted in the direction she envisioned.

Alena nodded when Amanda capably performed the task. "You pick up these skills without much guidance. Do you think all people from Earth could learn these things so rapidly, or are you an anomaly?

After all, your daughter seems to have the same capability, but then again, she's probably half-Tualan. It's too bad we don't have a lot more time to figure out all these mysteries you pose!

"I'll have to content myself with today and tomorrow to work with you before Barla arranges for you to meet with Rasa."

She reached over and patted Amanda's knee in a motherly gesture. "Ever since I was little, I heard stories about *old souls* and the dangers they posed in our society. I always thought the Elders were a bit too judgmental since Jehoban was the Creator of all, including the *old souls*.

"That reminds me—Bryon mentioned something about how he once went to Earth as a teenage prank. I think it's way past time that we heard the details of his unauthorized adventure when he gets home from work. What do you say?"

Amanda eagerly nodded. "He mentioned that at Ahn and Barla's, too. I guess it's a good thing we'll be having a quiet evening with all of the kids having a sleep-over at Tana's house. We won't have any interruptions or have to worry about being overheard."

Thankfully, Alena wanted to hear the stories. Amanda looked forward to the evening's entertainment. Hopefully, Bryon would humor them by regaling his adventures.

CHAPTER 19

Preparing all of Bryon's favorite dishes, Alena set the table for the three adults. Amanda took a nap after their arduous training session, which ended about an hour before Bryon was due to be home.

Alena didn't mind preparing meals alone; in fact, it was preferable to having four little children underfoot while she tried to concentrate. As she set the last dish on the table, she smiled at the click of the front door opening.

True to his usual manner, Bryon set his telepod key on the table by the front door strode down the hallway and into the kitchen to greet his wife. He smiled as he caught her setting the last dish on the table and said, "Perfect timing again, I'd say!"

"Yep," Alena agreed as she leaned into his chest while turning her mouth up to receive his welcoming kiss. With all the kids absent, she'd gladly let dinner get cold to continue their romantic mood in their bedroom. The kiss cut short when they heard Amanda's bedroom door open.

She arrived in the dining room the next moment, rubbing her eyes and blinking furiously. "Did my nap hold up dinner?"

Alena moved until her hip brushed against Bryon's thigh. She slung her arm behind his back to hold him close beside her. "Nope. Your timing's getting to be as good as Bryon's!"

Amanda stifled a yawn, holding her hand up to cover her mouth. "Hi, Bryon. How was work today?"

"Hi, yourself. It was a typical day. I did work up an appetite. Let me get changed and washed up, and I'll be ready to sit and talk about anything you want!"

Alena slapped him playfully on the rear as he turned to leave and said, "Hurry up, dinner's going to get cold!" She mischievously grinned at Amanda at Bryon's fortuitous opening. "Are you hungry, Amanda?"

"I'm so hungry I could eat a horse!"

Alena cocked her head to the side and then laughed loudly, "If you'd said that a few days ago, I would've wondered about your sanity. Today, however, I can only assume it's an Earth phrase."

"I guess it is. I never really thought about it. We don't eat horses on Earth; it just means we're famished. You know—because horses are big animals."

"It's still a strange saying," Alena commented and then gestured for Amanda to sit while she walked around the table to take her usual place.

A cleaned and changed Bryon returned to the dining room and took his place beside Alena. His gaze traveled over the food selection and nodded his pleasure. "This spread looks good enough to entertain an Elder!"

Alena preened at his compliment. Even though it didn't take a lot of energy to create the dishes, she still appreciated the praise for her thoughtfulness. She took up each person's plate and served helpings of each item.

After Bryon spoke the prayer, everyone silently enjoyed their food. Once their initial appetites were satiated, Alena spoke up,

"Amanda and Juila have both demonstrated admirable elemy skills."

"Really? How far did you get in the assessment?" Bryon looked meaningfully from Alena to Amanda.

Alena recognized the look Bryon usually reserved for indulging a child's display of hideous artwork. He didn't expect great results, but he wanted to appear supportive.

Alena continued, her eyes sparkling with unspoken joy and purposely drawing out her news for maximum effect. "Juila's proficient through the first five elements and is having trouble freezing water."

Bryon's eyebrows rose almost to his hairline. "Really? That's unheard of for a child so young!"

Amanda blushed prettily at his compliment but remained quiet.

Alena's gaze darted to Amanda and back to Bryon. She said, "Tell me about it. She's a fascinating little student, so eager to try everything. I decided to start training Justan and Andera as well. They only have about six mesans before they begin school, and they're going to need to know the core skills anyway."

Bryon nodded in agreement and said, "How far did our little ones get? I can hardly believe they're almost old enough to begin their education. It seems like yesterday I was holding Justan for the first time."

"I know, I feel the same way," Alena agreed with a sigh of regret for how fast they were growing. "They both completed the first skill with relative ease. I had them working on the second and third elements on their own. They're going to take a little while to master them.

"Since I've been formally trained as a wise-woman, I'm afraid our children might be held to a higher education standard. I hope they'll be intrigued with Juila and Amanda learning and want to learn quicker than other children usually do."

Bryon pursed his lips. "I agree with your assessment of other people's expectations for our children." He took his last bite of dinner and swallowed. He set his fork down and said, "Knowing how well Juila did with her lessons makes me curious about Amanda's progress. How far did you get, Amanda?"

Alena answered for Amanda when she looked at a loss for words. "Amanda made it through the first nine levels. We were working on memorization for several hours until it was clear we'd done enough for the day. Her hour-long nap proved I ended the session at the proper time, and it gave me enough time to get dinner ready."

Bryon's mouth dropped open. He snapped it shut and coughed. "I'm glad I swallowed that last bite before you told me about Amanda's progress. I'm utterly flabbergasted." He stammered, "All in one day? Imagine what you'll be capable of achieving with more instruction."

Alena beamed her pride in her student's success. She wished she could take all of the credit for being an excellent teacher, but Amanda's desire to learn everything she could to bring Jena home enhanced her skill. Desperation served itself well in times like these.

She turned to Amanda and said, "As you said earlier, you're a very eager and capable student. I wish everyone had as much desire to learn as you do."

Amanda's voice remained quiet, "I'm just glad you're willing to teach me even though you know who I really am."

Alena patted her hand and turned purposefully toward her husband. "Speaking of that...Bryon, weren't you going to tell us about your adventures on Earth? I can't think of any better time to tell us than tonight while all of the kids are gone for the evening." She batted her eyelashes playfully and smiled at him.

"Sure, although the actual adventure probably won't be as good as what you imagine it to be. We should retire to the living room for storytime." Bryon pushed his chair back and rested his hands on the chair arms to leverage himself up.

"Sounds like fun!" With a final thought, Alena cleared the table and stacked the dishes in the sink to take care of later.

Amanda jumped back, pulling her hands off of the tabletop. "That's a skill I want to learn right away. It's so efficient, although shocking to the uninitiated. Do you think I'll ever be able to use the elemy as effortlessly as what I just witnessed?"

Alena nodded, "With plenty of practice, I don't see why not."

They left the dining room and regrouped in the living room. Bryon took his usual seat on the loveseat. Likewise, Alena tucked herself under Bryon's arm draped across the back of the couch with her body touching Bryon's side. Amanda seated herself in the chair across from them and sat in silence to await the tale.

Alena poked her finger into Bryon's ribcage and said, "Start talking! We've waited for more than two anons to hear this story. You better add a few details if it's not interesting enough!"

"Ouch! How can I think of anything with you bruising me so?" He laughed down at his wife's upturned face and rubbed his ribs for dramatic effect. He pursed his lips as he gathered his thoughts.

"Let's see; I think I was about fifteen, and school had just let out for the summer. About six of us guys, ranging in age from fourteen to sixteen, were sitting around a campfire telling stories of other boys and their pranks that they supposedly performed on Earth. Each tale seemed more extensive and unrealistic until we started scoffing and saying Earth was just a myth that didn't exist.

"One of the sixteen-anon-olds, Lindon, insisted his story was true because it was his older brother who'd gone to Earth. So we asked him to tell the story again to see if we could point out any discrepancies with the telling. Once again, he recounted what he'd been told and promised he could go and do the same thing if he wanted to.

"That sounded enough like a challenge for each of us to egg

him on until he agreed to ask his brother how it was done so we could watch him do it as well. He agreed to find out that night about the secret details, and we'd meet the next night again to set up a plan."

"It sure sounds like a whopper of a tale on the other kid's part. What made you think he'd go through with it?" Alena asked humorously.

"We didn't," Bryon insisted, "we just thought we'd meet the next night and tease him for having made up the whole thing."

"So, what happened next?" Alena demanded.

CHAPTER 20

Bryon stretched out his long legs and drew in a deep breath. "Everyone arrived except Lindon. We thought for sure he wasn't going to show up, but just as we were getting ready to leave, he arrived pale as a ghost and dripping with sweat. He was obviously scared, and naturally, we were all madly curious about what happened.

"He said if we wanted proof, then one of us would have to accompany him on the journey. There was considerable debate among us as to who that person would be. Eventually, we drew straws, and I got the short one. Once we agreed I would go, he turned around without saying a word and walked away.

"We looked at one another, shrugged, and silently followed him. His direction wasn't back toward town but deeper into the wilderness. We never ventured this far from home, and the adventure seemed to get better even if we didn't know how it would end.

"After several gania, we finally arrived at a rocky outcropping. Lindon didn't stop at the base like we thought he would. Instead, he ducked into a cave opening that we overlooked. We all moved to go in after him, but he turned around and said, 'No, only Bryon can enter.' So now I was to go in alone with him, and I'm not ashamed to admit I was terrified."

Amanda sucked in a breath, leaning forward with her face animated. "Bryon, I know that cave! It's where I came back!" Amanda could hardly contain her excitement. "Was there a swirl carving above the entrance?"

"Yes, there was. I didn't notice it when I went in, but the other boys had plenty of time to poke around and investigate while we were inside, and they told me about it several days later."

Alena asked breathlessly, "So, what happened next?"

"We walked for quite a while in a tunnel and then turned a corner. Lindon created a sphere of light to see, so we weren't left in the dark. Once we went around the last corner, there was a curved space with a depression in the ground. There weren't any other places to go in the cave except where we ended up. Lindon stepped down into the depression and gestured for me to do likewise.

"Once I stepped beside him, I turned around to see if anything had happened. Suddenly he wrapped his arms around me from behind and spoke two words before everything changed."

"What did he say?" Alena could barely contain herself as she grabbed his leg and leaned forward eagerly.

Bryon shook his head. "I'm not allowed to say." He grinned down at his wife's eager expression.

"I already know what he said, Bryon, if that's the problem. I said something similar getting here, and I'll have to repeat what he said to return. I've already used the Gate, remember?" Her eyes widened, and she held up a finger. "Hold on. I'll be right back with proof."

Alena and Bryon exchanged confused looks. "What got into her? What could she possibly have that we haven't seen?" Bryon asked.

Alena shrugged. "We'll know in a minute."

Amanda returned only moments later, clutching a scrap of paper.

"Let me show this to Bryon first," Amanda requested as she gestured for him to come to stand beside her.

Bryon's curiosity rose; intrigued, he hastily left the couch. Taking two steps to be in front of her, he looked down at where she pointed on the page.

"Well, I guess it's okay to tell, seeing as you've already done it." He turned and looked down at his wife and said, "Lindon said, 'Outside Ascension.'"

"That's it? It doesn't even make sense!" Alena said. "It should be something more meaningful." Wrinkling her nose, she thrust out her hand and said, "Can I see what you're both looking at?"

"Sure, this's the map I brought with me when I got here to remind myself how to get home safely." She handed the paper to Alena and returned to her seat across from them.

Bryon sat next to his wife, and they both looked over the document with wonder on their faces.

"Does this mean you plan to return to Earth with the girls once we've found Jena?" Alena's tone sounded flat, her expression matching her tone. "If you take the girls home, I'll never see them grow up. And even worse, they won't get to learn to use the elemy as is their birthright."

Bryon knew the question upset both women, so he interrupted the tense silence by asking, "Don't you want to hear about what happened to me on Earth?"

"Just a minute, Bryon," Alena dismissed him offhandedly as she continued to stare at her friend. "Amanda, are you?"

Amanda looked beseechingly at Alena. "I don't want to deceive you in any way, and I honestly don't know if it'd be possible or even wise to attempt to take the girls through the Gate."

She sighed, her shoulders drooping, and spoke quietly, "I don't know, Alena. When I first remembered my girls were here in

Tuala, my first thought was to bring them home. But after I spoke with Shemalla about their crystal assignments, I just don't know if it'd be safe to attempt it."

Alena frowned and asked, "What are you talking about, Amanda?"

"Think about it, Alena. Both girls have dark birth crystals. Could it be because I might put them in danger by trying to take them out of Tuala through a Gate? Am I their danger, or is it something else? You saw into both of their futures, were they living here or on Earth?"

"You know I can't talk about anything I saw."

Bryon shifted away from his wife so he could see her face. He knew she mentally reviewed the images she witnessed during the children's crystal ceremony from the way she sightlessly stared across the room.

Alena's body shook all over, and her attention returned to the present, but she didn't make eye contact with anyone. "I can say this. It's unlikely I'll ever forget the vivid and confusing pictures outlining your girls' lives. There are so many people who'll influence their lives, some of them I even recognized, which comforted me at the time; now I'm less certain."

She looked directly at Amanda and said, "I'll have to concentrate on what I remember, and if I can be any help in deciding whether you stay or go, I'll do my best."

Amanda sighed. "I guess I'll have to be content with your answer since it's the best I can hope for right now. I wish I could find a way to stay and have my family get to know the girls simultaneously.

"I feel such a connection with your family and your way of life. And, just as you said, because Juila and I are learning how to access the elemy, I'm even more drawn to stay and see what we can each accomplish with its power."

Alena turned back to her husband and asked, "Since we'll have to wait to get a definitive answer from Amanda, why don't you tell us about your adventure, honey?"

Bryon eagerly jumped at the opportunity to change the subject. He could tell the idea of Amanda leaving with her little girls upset his wife. Alena's attachment to Juila over the past two anons was clear. She thought of the girl as her child. It would be a sad time around their house if Amanda did decide to leave.

"Okay, where was I? Oh yes, we just stepped down, and the phrase was said to get us through the Gate. I felt a tremendous amount of elemy coursing through my body, more than I ever experienced before or since.

"Just when I thought the energy was too much to bear, it disappeared along with everything else around us. The next thing I knew, I was waking up in a different location.

"I don't know how long we were unconscious, but I imagine it was some time since it was dark outside. Once again, we used an elemy sphere to light our way from a man-made structure."

Amanda pointed over at Bryon, her face alight. "That's an ancient Mayan pyramid in Campeche, Mexico," Amanda declared.

"I always wondered about the history regarding the structure. It was massive and definitely didn't look natural or anything like the cave we entered in Tuala. Anyway, we walked out of the building and down gigantic steps. We didn't have any plan together once we used the Gate, so we just sat on the last step and looked at each other in shock.

"I remember asking Lindon what we were supposed to do. I was always told we needed to do something verifiable, but at that moment, I couldn't think of anything which would be more remarkable than simply being on Earth.

"We decided to go for a walk to find something to bring back as proof of our success. I expressed a concern about not finding the Gate in the dark. Lindon reminded me he mastered the navigation level of his training, so my excuse to stay put disappeared.

"I think we probably only took about two steps before several men came running up to us and kneeled on the ground at our feet. There wasn't any time to extinguish the elemy sphere, so Lindon opted to keep it lit. He looked at me in confusion, and I glanced back at him and shrugged. Lindon asked the men what they were doing.

"There were a few minutes of difficulty as they didn't appear to speak the same language as us. We knew for sure, at that point, we weren't in Tuala. Suddenly one of the men jumped up and ran away. We didn't know what to think about his startling behavior until he came back practically dragging a woman with him."

"'Can you understand me?' The woman looked up at us expectantly. When we nodded, she continued, 'We've been waiting.'"

CHAPTER 21

"'I don't understand. We just decided to come,' I said back to the woman as Lindon seemed disinclined to speak at all.

"She didn't acknowledge my outburst. 'We've been waiting two hundred years.'

"I shook my head at her admission, wanting nothing more than to get to the bottom of this strange mystery. 'You can't be that old!'

"'Not us, but our people. We are watchers. We've been watching for someone to come back to us, and now you are here. Come, we want to share a meal and give you a gift.'

"Lindon and I once again regarded at one another. We said we wanted to bring back verification; maybe their gift would be sufficient proof. Both of us nodded in agreement. The men still kneeling at our feet stood and smiled when the woman told them in their language that we'd come with them.

"The place they took us wasn't very far away, as it was a straight line from the pyramid entrance. We didn't even see it until someone opened the curtain at the entrance, and the light from inside poured out enough to light the rest of the path ahead of us;

at that point, Lindon let the sphere of light dissipate back into the earth.

"Several men entered the building and lined the entryway. They encouraged us to continue into the shelter by nodding and smiling, following the woman who spoke our language. While we were slightly scared about what awaited us, I was also thinking about what we'd tell our friends when we returned home. This experience would be a story to remember.

"The woman stopped in front of us, and she turned around and told us to be seated. Several low chairs were arranged in front of a fireplace, and we picked two side-by-side. The woman gestured for someone to bring us refreshments, and we were quickly served a slightly fermented juice that she said was made from guava."

"The woman held her cup between both hands, resting lightly on her lap. She regarded us with intense interest. 'My name is Maria. Is there a message for us?'

"We didn't know what she wanted us to say. I finally said, 'Tell me about the last visitors.'

"'There's only been one. She called herself Lillia, and she left us with something that she instructed should be given to the next visitors. We have kept the crystal in our family line over the generations and have diligently waited for another visitor.

"'As we told you before, it has been two hundred years. Since you've come, we'll give you the crystal. We'll be relieved to have someone finally take responsibility for the gift. When you see it, you'll know what we are talking about.'"

Amanda interrupted to say, "Why would Maria say that only Lillia had come through that Gate? Didn't Lindon's brother use it?"

Bryon shook his head. "No, they moved to Kirma a few mesans before our excursion to Earth. He used a different location but knew the password would be the same. Lindon took so long getting to us because he and his brother were locating this new Gate for us to use. Of course, he failed to mention that little detail until after we returned. I almost gave him a black eye for with-holding that little gem."

Alena clutched Bryon's arm and gave it a little shake. "Get back to the story. What happened next?"

"Obviously, we didn't have any idea what she was speaking about, but we nodded like fools. She continued chattering about what happened to their family while waiting for someone else to come through the Gate.

"We were shocked to discover that they knew a Gate existed. When I asked her about it, she told me the location was sacred to her people for thousands of years. She said her people built the temple around the Gate to show its importance and protect people from accidentally stumbling into it.

"That made sense—even though the Gate wasn't secured or warded in any way in Tuala. We knew the Elders guarded the more powerful Gates. This was obviously a lesser Gate to be left utterly alone.

"The family served us corn patties filled with shredded meat, rice, and a tomato-based sauce. They passed around platters of fruit. As young boys usually are, we were both curious and hungry, and we ate happily with the family. After the meal, several people picked up instruments and played songs about their history as Maria translated the words for us.

"When the music ended, I asked Maria how they knew we were the visitors they sought.

"Maria smiled and pointed to Lindon and said, 'He had a ball of light in his hands the same as Lillia did. She said it was special and all future visitors could do it. Your clothing is similar to hers as well. We knew you were the ones.'

"I tried to think of something profound to tell her that would make it seem worth the wait, but I couldn't think of anything, so I just nodded. I kept thinking the name Lillia should mean some-thing to me, but again I was at a loss.

"My stomach was full, seated in a comfortable chair with the warmth of the fire lulling me, my eyelids grew heavy, and I was afraid I'd fall asleep. I looked over at Lindon and saw him experiencing the same predicament as myself.

"'We need to go back. Thanks for your hospitality.' I stood, and Lindon mirrored my movement almost instantaneously. Maria looked alarmed and said, 'Let us get the gift. You can't leave without it; Lillia was very insistent.'

"She practically ran from the room and returned within moments. She carried a wrapped bundle that she carefully held away from her body in her hands. Maria stopped in front of Lindon and said, 'You were the one to hold the light in your hands. I give this into your safekeeping.'

"Lindon took the gift from her, and his expression changed. He told me later that he didn't want to make a scene and just wanted to get back to Tuala. Lindon nodded solemnly and immediately turned around to leave.

"I hurriedly thanked the family for the food and drink and rushed out the exit to catch up to my only link home. He, once again, made a sphere of light in front of him as he ran toward the pyramid.

"'What's wrong?' I asked, but he shook his head slightly and continued to stare straight ahead. We ascended the tall pyramid steps and entered the passageway to the Gate. I was bursting with curiosity regarding the crystal in his hands, but I wouldn't get anything out of him until we were back in Tuala.

"We turned left into the tunnel and stepped down into a square depression at the end of the hall. There was a swirl design above our heads on the wall that I remember thinking seemed familiar.

"Lindon thrust the crystal into my hands, and then he wrapped his arms around me. He spoke the phrase 'Inside Ascension,' and once again, the energy built up around us, and everything went even darker until we felt nothing, just like in a telepod.

"I woke up with someone roughly shaking me and crying my name. I didn't know where I was or who was calling out. I felt something in my hands. I didn't remember what it was, yet energy pulsed from it.

"Finally, I came to my senses and opened my eyes where Stavin looked relieved because I was finally coherent. I remember asking what happened.

"Stavin said we'd been gone for a full day and night. They were scared we weren't ever coming back since they'd never heard of anyone missing for so long. He asked me where we went, but since we never asked the name of the place where we ended up on Earth, I just shrugged.

"'What's in your hands?' Stavin asked.

"I looked down and tried to dredge up the memory of what Maria called it. I told him, 'It's just a crystal a woman named Maria gave us from Earth. She said we were supposed to have it and take care of it.' At that point, I unwrapped the cloth covering and almost dropped it as I realized it was a crystal skull.

"Stavin fell over backward in his haste to get as far away from it as possible. 'That thing's evil! Get rid of it quick!'

"Lindon spoke up for the first time, startling both of us since we didn't know he was awake. He said, 'It's not evil, but it doesn't belong in our possession either. It came from this Gate, and I think it should stay here to guard it.'

"He looked around for a suitable place before discovering a niche in the rock behind the Gate, almost shoulder height from the ground. He took the skull out of my hands and shuddered continually as his flesh remained in contact with the hard crystal. Colored light power streaks coursed through the skull, which, of course, made us all nervous.

"Lindon set the crystal down in the niche and took his hands away. The crystal started to glow a soft blue color and issue a moaning sound no sooner than he was done. That was the last straw. We screamed and ran as fast as possible to get out of the cave.

"I have no idea what happened to it after that day. All of us made a pact never to return, and, as far as I know, none of us ever did."

Amanda said into the silent room, "Well, somebody must've been there since I didn't see any skull when I came through!"

Bryon stared thoughtfully at Amanda. He assumed all of these anons that it was still there. What happened to it? He still recalled the immense power in just his brief encounter with it. If it ended up in the wrong hands—he couldn't finish that thought.

CHAPTER 22

Alena shuddered. She asked Bryon, "Was the skull life-sized?"

"No, not quite. It could easily fit in the palm of my hand. Is there something about it?"

"During my wise-woman training with Debbon, I read a passage in an obscure text about thirteen matching crystal skulls, called samaras. The master held one samara, and the others conveyed messages and power to the holders of the other twelve. I thought it was just a legend, but if what you're saying is true, I have to believe there're thirteen of them. Who's the master, and what messages are being transmitted to the twelve other owners?"

There was something ominous about Bryon's story. Alena never wanted to encounter one of the skulls if they were as powerful as Bryon believed them to be.

"I still can't think of why the name Lillia bothers me so much," Bryon mused.

"I had the same feeling when you first spoke her name," Alena commented. "It's almost as if the answer is on the edge of my thoughts—oh, I think I got it!" In her excitement, Alena gripped Bryon's arm in an abrupt gesture.

"What is it?" Bryon smiled at her enthusiasm.

"When I was a little girl, my mother told me a story about Jehoban and his angels. Lucinden was the leader of the rebellious angels, and the biggest problem came when Lucinden began a relationship with a woman from Tuala. Bryon, her name was Lillia!"

"I know the story, too! My parents told me the tale when I was little."

"If it's the same Lillia, maybe the skull was something evil," Alena spoke ominously.

"I guess we'll never find out now since Amanda just confirmed the crystal's gone."

"BRYON, I know some things about where you arrived on Earth. Do you want me to tell you about it?" Amanda asked.

Bryon's eyes sparkled with interest. "Sure, it'd be fun to have one part of the story solved."

"You were in Campeche, Mexico. The language they spoke was a dialect of Spanish. The pyramid is an ancient Mayan temple used to worship the star gods. I imagine the people you met were Mayan descendants, even though those people disappeared hundreds of years ago."

Bryon frowned. "Just what is a year?"

Amanda waved her hand dismissively and said, "Oh, it's the same as an anon."

"Good, that's kind of what I thought, but I was never sure. So who were these star gods?"

"They were probably people from Tuala. It's said that the gods brought knowledge to the Mayan people and taught them how to build massive structures and how to write.

"My guess is that the Tualan people showed them how to use the elemy to move the massive stones to build the pyramids around the Gates. Indeed, to uneducated people like the original Mayans, it would appear magical, and they'd readily believe them to be gods.

"It was said the people came from the stars because some of them arrived in their telepods. During that time in Earth's history, we didn't know how to navigate the skies, so, again, it would seem magical. Are there any legends of Tualan people going to Earth and teaching people?"

Bryon and Alena looked appraisingly at one another. Bryon shook his head and said, "None that I've ever known. Have you ever heard anything during your post-study or training with Elder Debbon?"

"No, I haven't, but that's not to say it didn't happen. I always wondered what the Old Soul Engineering Facility did with the knowledge they acquired. Maybe they sent people back in time to find out what people from Earth could learn and if they would carry on with the knowledge. It sounds as though the Mayans didn't, though."

"It's said the whole civilization disappeared. Nobody knows what happened to them. Maybe they were all brought to Tuala. I don't know."

"You should ask Rasa about it when you meet with her," Bryon offered.

"I doubt there'll be an opportunity to satisfy our curiosity, but I do hope Barla can arrange for me to meet with her. It's still not certain she'll have enough free time."

"You're her family; I'm sure she'll find a way to help!" Alena insisted.

Amanda clung to Alena's hopeful lifeline. "That's what I keep telling myself!"

Bryon leaned forward until his elbows rested on his knees and his hands hung limply. "Remember when you told us about Elder Vargen's involvement with the museum on Earth?"

Amanda nodded. "Yes, did you find something out about him?"

"On the contrary, and it sure is interesting. I had some time after my meeting at work, so I researched the Elder. There's very little published about him. As a matter of fact, he doesn't even have a public record regarding his involvement in the Old Soul Engineering Facility. Everybody knows he's a co-founder."

Alena tilted her head at her husband's summary and said, "They must want to keep him clear of anything related to Earth since it's already a pretty taboo subject. There must be so much more happening behind the Elders' closed doors than anyone might guess."

"Some things we may never know." Amanda smiled at the couple across from her. They'd probably appreciate having some time to themselves with all of the children gone for the night. "I'm exhausted. I think I'll head to bed now. Goodnight."

She stood, grinning at Bryon and Alena as she passed their couch. With the map still in her hands, she made a detour to the kitchen, where she located a pencil. She hastily wrote 'Inside Ascension' on the edge of the paper and then 'for passage to Tuala from Earth' so she wouldn't have to guess what the new phrase was supposed to do once she lost her memory returning to Earth.

Now, if only she could figure out a way to preserve her memories as the Tualan people did when they passed through, she'd feel much better about the whole thing. It seemed unfair that she should have to struggle through the Gates when everyone living here didn't have the same issue.

Bryon didn't know how helpful his story was to her strange situation. She'd forgotten the phrase he so casually shared. Shemalla might not want her to remember, but now she had the passwords for both directions. It relieved her to know she could travel in either direction should something unfortunate happen before she finished her quest to find Jena.

Amanda made her way to her room without any other reason to delay. She tucked the map away in her pants pocket that she'd wear the next day. She wanted to be fully prepared to go back to Earth more than ever.

Everything would be perfect once she found Jena. Then would come the hard part of deciding if she'd stay or go depending on how she could mitigate the dangers to her daughters in the crossing. Maybe Rasa would have an answer to this new question as well.

CHAPTER 23

Petre basked in the memory of meeting with Rualin. His plan confidently moved forward with his friend in charge of gathering everyone together. The idea that Elder Debbon thought he could keep him away from his own daughter with a stupid piece of paper was ridiculous. He'd teach him a lesson and be able to have access to Jena again.

His smile widened as he neared the Elder's Islet. Nothing would stop him from meeting with Elder Debbon since he set his mind on the course.

In all his righteous indignation, he imagined himself confronting the Elder and letting him know he was Jena's father, and there was no way around the fact. He'd demand to see her immediately, and, indubitably, the honorable Elder would have to know the truth in his words. Regardless of his master deceptor status, he had the facts on his side this time.

A smudge on the horizon indicated his destination's small spit of land. The sun just rested on the horizon behind him as he concentrated on the final course corrections to make landfall just after full dark.

With everything on track, he turned to go below deck. The wind ceased blowing around him as he entered the staircase, forcing him to acknowledge his foul body odor. He mentally added a bath to his list of things to get done before landfall.

Heading straight for the washroom, he grinned at the mental picture of holding his precious daughter in his arms again. The troubles he experienced with Jena were a distant memory, and he only considered that she was his daughter.

Nobody had the right to keep him away from his legal property. After so long, Petre imagined Jena probably grew up quite a bit, possibly even talking. He regretted missing so much time with her simply because he felt sorry for himself.

More than anything, he stupidly fell into the trap Elder Debbon set for him. He should've known the old foxl was up to something.

That day's whole scenario replayed in his mind. At the time, it didn't seem strange that the Elder kept a betrothal agreement and five thousand taj in his desk drawer.

Upon reflection, it appeared a bit too convenient. How long was the Elder planning to take Jena away from him? His mind seethed with righteous indignation as he whispered fiercely, "I'm going to make you pay!"

BARLA COULD BARELY CONTAIN herself while waiting for the designated call time she and Rasa arranged anons before. The week dragged by agonizingly slow. Knowing she could help her niece find her daughter, it all hinged on this one point of contact.

She was confident of Rasa's willingness. But, what would her busy daughter do to assist in the toddler's recovery?

Sitting in Ahn's home office, Barla stared at her timepiece until the appointed time finally arrived for her to activate the patil. She entered in the call sequence and waited what seemed to be an unbearable amount of time before the image of Rasa's face materialized on the screen. Barla smiled with motherly pride when she said, "Hello, Rasa! I've missed you!"

"I've missed you, too, Mama. What's going on? You seem more excited today than usual."

"Oh, I am! I have some amazing news and also a favor to ask."

Rasa tilted her head. "You've got me so curious now. You've never asked for anything in all the time I've been here. Whatever's going on must be pretty spectacular! Well, tell me! When you're done, I've got some news of my own to share."

"Okay. Do you want to go first?"

"No, no. It can wait. Start talking, Mom."

"Alright! Remember the swimmer Ahn hired down at the dock almost two anons ago?"

"The one who died after she went into hiding?"

"Yes, she's the one! Well, guess what? She didn't die after all!"

"Oh, Mom, that's fantastic! I remember how upset you were when you found out about the accident. Tell me what happened?"

"I'll get to that part later. First, I have to say she and I met earlier this week, and she had news about my family."

"I don't understand, Mom. I thought your family wasn't from around here."

Barla should've known Rasa would remain mindful of her secret. She used the code words they had worked out anons before since Elders could intercept patil conversations.

"True, but Amanda actually visited with them. Do you know what else she found out? You won't guess, so I'll just say—Amanda's mother is my sister!"

"Wait, are you saying that Amanda's your niece?"

"Yes, that's exactly what I'm saying! Isn't it amazing? Amanda brought her daughter to visit with us, and she was just the spitting image of yourself at the same age. Can you imagine how startled

Ahn and I were when we first laid eyes on Juila? We didn't know yet that we were all related."

"That's truly amazing, Mom. I have a blood cousin. But, wait, I thought Amanda had a set of identical twins when she went missing, yet she only brought one child with her to visit. Where's her other daughter?"

"That's the favor I spoke of earlier. Her other daughter, Jena, was abducted by Petre MacVeen just a few days before returning to Bryon's house. That was almost two anons ago now. Amanda's been training with her birth crystal to locate Jena, but she hasn't had any success. Could you meet with her and help?"

Rasa pursed her lips and scowled. "Oh, Mom, I wish I could, but I have news of my own, as I said. Jehoban has decided to complete my schooling. In two days, I'm moving to Durseni, and I have no idea how long it'll take me to finish."

Barla grimaced. "Oh, I'm so happy for you, but the timing couldn't be worse! I can't believe you're finally going to graduate! Does this mean you'll get to come home soon?"

Durseni was nearer to where Barla lived, which was also a blessing. However, it frustrated her to think Amanda would have another disappointment. Finally, she asked, "What if Amanda could come to Durseni and meet with you during any free time?"

"It could probably work. I don't know how busy I'll be, but I'm eager to meet a blood relative from your side of the family as I never thought I'd get to. It sounds exciting!"

"Once you get settled in Durseni, let me know your new contact information, and I'll forward it along to Amanda. She'll get in touch once she makes arrangements to get to the island.

"I sure hope you can figure out a way for her to find her daughter. I can't imagine how terrible this whole thing's been for her, especially knowing Petre's responsible."

Rasa nodded along with Barla's statements. "I'll do what I can,

Mom, but I can't make any promises with either my time or her skills."

"Oh, that's the other thing—Amanda has her own birth crystal given to her by Jehoban Himself. Alena's been teaching her some advanced techniques, so she'll be ready for whatever you may ask of her."

Rasa's mouth dropped open. "How's that possible? I mean, I heard what you said, but that's incredible. I've never heard of that happening. Jehoban's usually so reserved when it comes to matters of His children.

"Obviously, there's more to Amanda than we know if Jehoban's involved. This tantalizing bit of information alone makes me want to meet with my cousin right away.

Rasa leaned forward, her chin resting on her palm and fingers tapping her cheek. "I'll start working out some things that we might use to find Jena. The birth crystal should help the search immensely. I've got to get going now, Mom. I'll call you on Minggu when I get settled in my dorm. I love you."

"I love you too, sweetie! I'll let Amanda know what you've said. She'll be thrilled! I'll talk to you in a couple of days."

"Okay. Bye."

"Bye," Barla echoed as the screen went blank. Her dreams were coming true; her daughter might finally come home soon! Ahn would be so pleased about this turn of events.

Logistical details formed in her mind: Amanda would travel to Durseni, find a place to live while she trained with Rasa, and maybe even get a job.

Without delay, Barla connected with Bryon's home patil. She only had to wait through three beeps before Amanda's face showed on the patil screen. "Good afternoon, Amanda!"

"Good afternoon, Barla. Please tell me there's good news!"

Barla's lips split into a wide grin. "I have the most excellent news! Get packed and ready to move to Durseni."

CHAPTER 24

"Durseni?" Amanda repeated, utterly baffled. "I don't understand. I thought Rasa was on Acaim!"

Barla's face remained animated as she said, "She's being reassigned to Durseni starting this Minggu. As soon as she gets settled into her dorm, she'll give me her contact information to forward to you. She's going to start a new training session, so she's unsure how much time she'll have to meet, but she's agreed to try to help."

Amanda's heart raced. Finally, she'd do something proactive to locate her daughter. "Oh, Barla, that's fantastic. How can I ever thank you?"

Barla cocked her head and grinned. "Just finding Jena will be thanks enough. She's been gone too long, and I want to meet my other niece!"

"I can't agree more!" Amanda stated emphatically. Then she considered this new turn of events. Her joy dissolved into panic and uncertainty. "What am I supposed to do in Durseni? Where will I stay? How will I support myself and Juila?"

"I'll talk to Ahn about it this evening. I'd suggest you do the same with Alena and Bryon. I'm sure among the four of us, we can come up with something that'll work."

"Oh, I hope so. It's exciting to think I'll finally be able to do something on my own to find Jena. I've felt so helpless all this time." Amanda clung to Barla's optimism.

"I know, honey. But think about this—Jehoban appears to be helping. With Him on our side, we have to succeed!"

"You're right, Barla. This's going to work! I can't wait to meet Rasa. She sounds so amazing. I can't even imagine the life she's led living with the creator of the universe. It just boggles my mind."

"I know what you mean. If I didn't live through it, I'd hardly believe it myself. I'll call you on Minggu. I've got to get going."

"Okay, Barla. Thanks again for everything."

"You're welcome, Amanda. We'll talk again soon."

"Okay, goodbye."

Amanda jumped up from her seat and rushed out of the confining room. Her heart was bursting with joy, making her feel like she couldn't stay in the house for another minute.

With news this wonderful, she'd go down to the marketplace to find Alena. Maybe they'd even celebrate by going out to dinner.

Petre's water craft silently brushed against the dock just after the last glimmers of light faded from the sky. The late hour accounted for the absence of people on the waterfront, which suited his scheme perfectly.

Knowing about the order for people to turn him in to the authorities regarding Jena's abduction, he used extra caution with his land dealings. This visit was essential, or else he would've stayed out at sea until exhausting all of his supplies.

After tying up his vessel, he stepped lightly onto the rigid dock planks taking a moment to adjust to land legs again. He reviewed each of his statements in his head as he strolled toward the Residence. This meeting had better end well, or Elder Debbon would pay a very steep price for his deception.

In short order, Petre reached the guard shack at the edge of the Elder's Residence. The man in the booth seemed surprised to see someone arriving at this time of day and hurriedly set down his cup of soup.

"How may I help?"

"I'd like to meet with Elder Debbon. It's a matter of some urgency," Petre replied with more than a bit of self-importance added to his expression.

"I'm sorry, the Elder is not in right now," he replied reasonably. "Can you step aside so I can identify you?"

Petre didn't move; remaining backlit and anonymous suited him perfectly. "When will he be in?" Petre's patience wore thin. He wouldn't be dismissed so easily.

"I'm not sure when he'll be back. Would you like to meet with another Elder?"

Petre's vision turned red, his voice dripped with sarcasm and disdain, "What do you mean, 'I'm not sure when he'll be back'? This is his Residence; he should be here." He jabbed his finger on the shack's ledge for emphasis. "How's he supposed to help the people when he's not here?"

"I'm sorry to upset you, sir—Elder Debbon's teaching this anon's wise-women. The class begins next week, and he's already left. As First Elder, it's his responsibility to teach the healers. I'm sure you can understand.

"There are other Elders who'll assist his people where needed. Would you like me to arrange a meeting with another Elder?"

How was he supposed to see his daughter if the Elder insisted on galavanting around the country? This was not his plan! "No! Only Elder Debbon can take care of this matter! How can he abandon his post and his family? How irresponsible can he be?"

"I'm sorry, sir. If you leave your name, I can try to contact him," he said.

Petre's fists clenched to keep himself from reaching out and throttling the neck of this impudent guard. Was this stupid man not listening to what he said?

"No, I don't wish to leave my name. I'll take care of the matter on my own. He'll be sorry he didn't help me!" Petre whirled around on his heel and stomped back toward the dock.

Each step made him more livid as he realized he wouldn't be seeing Jena again any time soon. He hated being thwarted. Was the *Honorable* Elder taunting him? Elder Debbon would regret making him wait even longer.

EVERYTHING CAME TOGETHER SO FAST. Amanda could hardly fathom she was leaving Bryon and Alena's house for good. All of her belongings, as well as Juila's, were packed in the telepod.

Bryon and Alena's children gave both her and Juila a tearful send-off before they went over to Tana's house for a distraction. They were more than a bit upset at how soon their guests were leaving, and they tried to think up numerous ways to delay the departure until Tana offered to entertain them.

Alena didn't fare better in the tear department. "I'm going to miss both of you. I didn't get nearly enough time to discover Juila's limits, which seemed non-existent."

Amanda hugged her. "I'm so thankful that you could find me housing on such short notice. Just think, if I hadn't insisted you go to your wise-woman training, you never would have met the woman who provided this house. It's all working out so perfectly."

Alena pouted, and Bryon held Juila while Amanda rushed around, checking for last-minute things she might have forgotten. Finally, there was no other reason to stay, and Amanda turned to

Alena, pulling her into another heartfelt embrace. "Thanks for making this whole thing possible, Alena. I already miss everybody, and I haven't even left yet!"

Alena sniffled. "I don't know what I'm going to do without you. It will seem so lonely during the day without another adult to talk with!" She tried to make light of the conversation to stem the imminent fresh round of tears.

"Let's head out," Bryon announced from the open front doorway. He knew the women could stall their departure until the next day unless he intervened. "We want to get everything settled in before it gets dark."

"Okay, okay. I know you're right. It's just scary thinking about leaving the only home I've known in Tuala!"

"We'll have the patil set up in the new house so you can call us whenever you feel like it," Bryon consoled.

"You'll probably change your call sign because I'll call too often." Amanda joked as she pulled away from Alena to follow Bryon and Juila. Her heart ached as she stepped through the front doorway for possibly the last time ever.

While she wanted to go home to Earth, she hated the idea of leaving these wonderful people forever. Wasn't there some way to stay in touch? Rasa might have an answer to that problem as well.

She trailed behind Bryon and went up the telepod ramp. Waving one last time to Alena, who had taken a few steps toward the telepod yet remained near the house, Amanda turned and stepped through the telepod to her co-pilot seat.

With practiced ease, she fastened her seat harness and extended her arms to receive Juila from where Bryon waited patiently beside her. Settling Juila in her lap, she watched Bryon go through the telepod's start-up procedures.

The telepod lifted from the driveway and hovered in place while Bryon checked all the controls, verifying green lights and clearing them for departure. Bryon moved his hand for manual flight and shifted over to mental power. He shut his eyes.

Amanda knew he concentrated on the coordinates over Durseni moments before the telepod disappeared from Kirma. In the seconds where they were neither here nor there, he'd maintain a solid picture in his mind of their final destination, trusting explicitly in the engineering built into the telepod to translate them to their planned destination.

They popped into the air over the Durseni flight field, where Bryon used the manual control to fly the telepod to their designated landing area. He reversed the procedures for shut down until the telepod rested effortlessly on the ground. He palmed the door open using the dash control with all the systems turned off.

"Ready?" Bryon asked solicitously.

"As ready as I'll ever be," Amanda replied after gulping nervously. She looked around the airfield. How would they get all of her stuff to her new house? She thought they'd park the telepod in the driveway as they'd done in Kirma. She turned to Bryon and asked, "How come we didn't land at the new house?"

"Durseni doesn't allow residential flying. The people here value their privacy too much to let people fly randomly overhead.

"Once we get to the flight office, we'll arrange for private transport to take your belongings. Let's go." Bryon unbuckled with ease and moved to leave out of the telepod's side door.

CHAPTER 25

Amanda held Juila and stepped from the telepod's coolness into her new hometown's oppressive, moist heat. She stood at a standstill on the ramp.

Kirma's more temperate weather didn't prepare her for such a climate difference in Durseni. Thinking an island would have ocean breezes, she assumed it'd be cooler.

"Is it always this hot here?" Amanda cringed at the sheen of sweat building between herself and where Juila rested against her side.

Bryon smirked at her discomfort. "No, it cools off marginally during the rainy season."

"This already feels like liquid sunshine. I can almost drink the air." She fanned the collar of her shirt, hoping to get a little bit of relief from the oppressive heat.

"You'll get used to it. Come on, let's get into the shade of the office."

Amanda stepped off of the ramp allowing Bryon to palm the door closed. Together they rushed toward the main building and hopefully a cool reprieve. Without too much effort, they organized the transport of Amanda's belongings to her new house.

The tiny cottage's neighborhood felt similar to the one she had become accustomed to in Kirma; only the lots were significantly smaller. Also, the slatted windows allowed cooling breezes to circulate throughout, which would've been impractical in Kirma.

Bryon helped unpack the numerous crates. Fortunately, the house came furnished, or Amanda would've been living in barren comfort. They did bring Juila's crib from Bryon's home since they didn't expect the rental to have one.

With the last of Amanda's items put away, they relaxed on the couch and drank cold glasses of water. Amanda looked around and said, "I can almost see the entire living area from this one spot."

The living room was at the front of the house by the main entrance, the kitchen was at the back, the dining room to the left, and the bedroom and bathroom side-by-side to the right. She'd once again share a room with Juila with only a single bedroom.

Bryon interrupted her musings when he said, "I have a surprise."

Amanda turned to face him, almost spilling her water. "What is it?"

"I brought a recommendation letter from Captain Ahn."

"Oh? That was very thoughtful of him. I'll have to figure out how to look for a job while waiting to meet with Rasa."

Bryon wiggled his eyebrows playfully. "Well, Ahn also made arrangements for a job interview the day after next at the Telepod Engineering Company. He knew you'd be worried about supporting yourself and Juila, so he talked with one of the engineers who said they have an opening right now."

This move happened so fast Amanda's head started spinning. Doubt crept up unbidden, and fear quickly followed. "What'll happen with Juila? I can't leave her alone, and I don't know anyone here I can trust."

"They have on-site daycare. You can even drop her off there during your interview."

She took a sip of her water, processing Bryon's information. "It sounds as though everything's already been thought of and now all I have to do is show up. Do you think I'll be able to get a job? I'm sure there are people who're way more qualified than I am."

Bryon patted her knee in almost the same manner Amanda's father did. If only she were home right now!

"Don't worry about it. You have a great personality, just be yourself and be confident in your abilities."

"Sounds like a great pep talk! Where's the place located?"

He lifted his chin over his shoulder and said, "It's just two streets over from here. This location couldn't be more perfect since you can easily walk to work even with Juila."

"Can we go there today? Otherwise, I'll worry about finding it."

"Sure, I'm ready whenever you are."

Amanda stood and nodded nervously. Her adventure was genuinely beginning with this latest turn of events. Just days ago, she promised herself that she'd get a job. Now the perfect opportunity presented itself almost as if divinely ordered. Hmm. Was Jehoban's hand in the mix?

They strolled through the neighborhoods at a leisurely pace. During the day's heat, it appeared that nobody moved with any amount of urgency, and Amanda understood why. She turned to Bryon and asked, "What time is my interview?"

"Right after lunch at one."

Amanda hitched Juila higher on her hip and wished she'd brought the stroller Alena offered. "What type of job is it? What should I wear to the interview?"

"It's a desk job. Just wear the same thing you wore to the crystal ceremony. Yes, I think that'd be perfect." Bryon seemed pleased with his answer. "To be perfectly honest, I don't generally don't pay much attention to what anyone wears."

Amanda nodded as she chewed on her lower lip. What was she thinking? How could she uproot her family on the slim chance that Rasa'd have time to meet with her? Was this a fool's errand?

She hadn't considered the money aspect of moving to Durseni. She assumed she'd meet with Rasa right away, find Jena immediately, rescue her and then head home.

How could she have been so naïve?

It was an unrealistic plan. She knew that now and forced herself to grin at her simplistic scenario. Once again, her circle of family and friends looked out for her welfare on this journey.

Before she returned to Tuala, she thought she had a better handle on managing herself. She felt strong and in charge. How did she fall back into the old habit of relying so heavily on other people? Well, she'd be on her own as soon as Bryon left.

She wouldn't let herself or Jena down again.

Just as they rounded the last corner, Amanda got her first view of where she could potentially be working before the end of the week. It was an impressive office building, many stories tall with glass windows sparkling iridescent blue in the sunshine.

They arrived at the main entrance, and Bryon remarked that the manufacturing portion of the company was at a different location. This building housed the conference rooms, support personnel, engineers, and executives. The building was state of the art with crystal-supported ventilation to maintain a constant, comfortable temperature inside and designed to be an integral part of the business' image.

Amanda never even thought about air conditioning since she had been here. It wasn't necessary at Kirma or the Port of Cresdon.

Wow! What other applications might require crystal energy? There was much more to Tualan life than her previous exposure shared in her limited travels.

With nothing more to see of the building, they turned around and walked back toward Amanda's new home. They talked about the decorations in people's yards and the lack of outside activity during this time of day.

Amanda knew she was stalling for time with Bryon. She wouldn't have a single person in this town who'd care if she lived or died once he left. It was a scary proposition to be alone, solely responsible for a toddler, in an unfamiliar city.

"Is there a wise-woman close by?"

"Yes, Alena's friend is here. I'll write down her contact information and leave it by the patil."

Amanda nodded and racked her brain to think of other things she might need. "Where's the marketplace here?"

"It's one street over in the opposite direction from your cottage. I'm sure there'll be a stream of people coming and going from there. It shouldn't be too hard to find. Trust me, Amanda, you're going to be fine here."

He patted her arm. "Remember, you can contact us through the patil any time day or night. You won't be left without resources. We'll be here to help whenever it's needed."

"I keep forgetting that you're only going to be a telepod ride away." Amanda tried to cheer herself with that thought, but it didn't keep her heart from racing.

CHAPTER 26

Tears stung Amanda's eyes, but she refused to let them come. She wasn't being abandoned. This was the obvious next step to finding her daughter.

She inhaled a deep, calming breath, knowing she had to be strong right now. Her hand flew to her neck as she attempted to pull herself together. The form of her pendant pressed against her fingertips, reminding her of Jehoban's support.

She wasn't alone. Jehoban was on her side. If He supported her, then who could go against her? Heck, just being back in Tuala was a testament to how she could do anything she set her mind to.

Amanda straightened, and she squared her shoulders. "I'll be okay, Bryon. I'm just feeling a little bit insecure with the barrage of changes in my life. I think I've become too complacent living with you and Alena.

"All along, I've known there'd be a time when I wouldn't be with you anymore. It's just your family feels like a part of my family now, and I've never been very good at saying goodbye."

Bryon lifted his hand to her arm and gave her a friendly squeeze. "This won't be goodbye, Amanda. This's just a new chapter in your life. I have a sneaking suspicion that you'll enjoy the upcoming changes. You have a lot more in life to offer than just staying at home watching children."

Amanda quirked her eyebrow and grinned. "But they're so much fun! I never know what they'll do or say next." She lowered her voice so she wouldn't be overheard by anyone even though the street was empty. "Did I ever tell you how different Tualan children are from those on Earth?"

"No, how so?"

She leaned in closer and said, "Alena confirmed it's their birth crystal that changes them. The children I've known take a lot longer to speak well or be very helpful around the house. Actual sentences and conversation usually happen between four and five anons, and learning to clean up after themselves is even longer, like eight or nine anons."

His face showed his dismay. "Wow! That sounds frustrating."

"Oh, it definitely can be. We also have hundreds of different languages, and if children are taught when they're learning to speak, they pick it up easily. Otherwise, they usually end up learning a second language in high school when it's a lot harder to learn."

"How do people communicate with one another if there are so many languages?"

"Well, English is the primary language where I come from, and almost everyone speaks it. Different countries speak different languages. We usually need to hire a translator or learn a few key phrases if we travel there. If people move to America, where I live, they usually learn English."

"That sounds complicated. I'm glad our whole world has just one language. Life's hard enough without throwing language barriers into the mix."

"I agree, yet we still manage." They arrived back at Amanda's new house and out of the scorching sunshine. The relative cool-ness inside had them both sighing with relief.

Amanda prepared three glasses of water and brought them into the living room. She handed the small plasfilm cup to Juila and instructed her to be careful not to spill while she played with her blocks on the floor. She sat on the couch and handed a glass to Bryon.

They gulped the water down and sighed in unison, making them laugh. Amanda knew Bryon would have to leave soon, even as she wished she could delay the inevitable.

She appreciated the clean accommodations, the patil resting on the dining table ready for use, and knowing the locations of key places outside her house. There wasn't much more to do now other than wait for Rasa to arrange a meeting time and to go to the unexpected job interview.

Seeing the patil reminded Amanda of Bryon's earlier comment. "Oh, where's the letter from Ahn?"

"Oh, yes! It's a good thing you reminded me! Let me get it before I forget." He walked over to his jacket, which was draped over the seat at the dining table. He removed the envelope from the inside pocket and placed it next to the patil.

Using the pencil and pad of plasfilm on the table, he wrote down the name and contact information of Alena's wise-woman friend should Amanda have any emergency requiring a healer. "Well, I think that's everything then. I should probably head home now. Can you think of anything else that you might need?"

"Don't ask, Bryon; I can be just as bad as the children in stalling for time. As you said, you're just a patil call away if I need anything." She couldn't dwell on missing those sweet children.

"Thanks so much for helping me get here and settled in. I'm definitely scared, but I'm sure this's exactly what I need to do to find Jena."

Bryon nodded toward Amanda as he sat at the patil. "That's

right, Amanda! Think positive thoughts, and this'll all come out right!" He punched in a few keystrokes and contacted the transport service to pick him up. "Okay, all set. The transport should be here in about five minutes, and I'll get out of your way!"

"Bryon, you're never in the way! You could stay here forever as far as I'm concerned!"

Bryon shook his head and sighed dramatically. "I think Alena would get jealous!"

They laughed, and Bryon returned to the living room and pulled Amanda up from the couch to embrace her in a bear hug. "I'm going to miss you with all of your amazing stories."

Mischievously smiling as he released Amanda, he bent down, scooped Juila up from the floor, and tossed her in the air. She giggled as she landed back into his arms, and he gave her a big hug in farewell.

"I'm going to miss having you around, too. For someone as itty-bitty as you, you've carved out a definite spot for yourself in my family." He tweaked her nose.

She threw her little arms around his neck and loudly whispered into his ear, "I'll take good care of Mommy."

"I know, sweetie," Bryon conspiratorily replied as he set her down on the floor.

Hearing a knock on the front door, Bryon grabbed his jacket from the chair and crossed the room. As expected, his transport arrived, heralding his departure.

Amanda raced across the room to stand beside Bryon, holding onto the edge of the doorframe as if to support her legs. "Thanks again, Bryon. I'll let you know how the interview went."

"Can't wait to hear about it! Remember, contact us if you need anything." Bryon cheerfully spoke even as he shut the door behind himself.

Amanda looked down at her daughter and said, "It's just you and me, kid!"

"Let's play with blocks, Mommy."

Amanda smiled at her daughter's resilience. Juila was the perfect distraction for her nerves; she couldn't think of anything she'd rather do right at that moment than play blocks with her precious little girl.

CHAPTER 27

At times like this Debbon wished the title of 'First of the Elders' on anyone other than himself. More than anything, he hated leaving his wife and children because of his training obligation to the next group of wise-women.

The skills and questions posed by the eager women to learn their new trade usually intrigued him, but this anon seemed more of an inconvenience.

If he were completely honest with himself, he just didn't want to spare any time away from instructing Jena how to master her new skills. She was such an exceptional, eager, and capable student.

Her ability to anticipate his questions mesmerized him. He often wondered if she could read minds since she was incredibly astute in her learning.

Once again, he found a reason to think about Jena rather than his current task at hand. He needed to focus solely on his newest students since he'd be doing them a disservice to be distracted and rushed when they were pursuing their life's work.

He sent up a silent prayer for patience as he entered the auditorium full of women. Only two steps into the room and Debbon was surprised enough to stop before taking the third step.

Jehoban's favorite student sat in the back of the classroom. He nodded in Rasa's direction and then forced himself to look around the room at the other ladies before he continued moving toward his desk.

He rested a hip on the table's side and grinned at all of the eager students awaiting his instruction, yet he couldn't help but wonder why Rasa came. She already possessed relatively proficient skills in the arts of healing, yet she never expressed an interest in advanced learning.

"Ladies, welcome to your first day of training to become wise-women. If anyone is here for any other type of training, please let me know right away so we can get you directed to the correct classroom." Debbon stared directly at Rasa, thinking she must be in the wrong place; however, she remained seated.

"Okay, since we all seem to be here for the same reason, let's begin. I'm hoping everyone received plasfilm work and a stack of books when you first arrived on the island."

All the women nodded, so he continued, "Let's open the Healer's Teaching Guide to chapter one on page sixteen, and we'll begin discussing the ethics concerning healing—"

Several hours and two breaks later, Debbon sufficiently prepped the class to assess their individual skill levels. This was Debbon's favorite part of the class.

The women poorly hid their nerves in front of him, wanting to impress him without seeming to be showing off in front of the other students. He wished he could convince them just to relax in their knowledge and be natural, but they never were comfortable enough.

The students were all pretty average in their evaluation, with only a couple of women standing out. Since this was the last portion of the day's instruction, each student left the room to study in her dorm privately as soon as she finished.

As he could've guessed, Rasa waited in line for assessment, which allowed him to talk with her alone.

"I didn't expect to see you in my class, Rasa."

She grinned ruefully. "I was just as surprised when Jehoban asked me to attend this anon's session. Healing hasn't ever been my forte, but Jehoban insisted I learn the basics to complete my studies with Him."

"So this was a last-minute decision?" Debbon guiltily wondered if this had anything to do with keeping Jena to himself.

"Nothing is last-minute for Jehoban," Rasa smiled, "but He doesn't always share His plans with His students."

"Certainly," Debbon replied. "Shall we begin?"

THANKFULLY, Alena's gifted food supply would tide Amanda over. She found and toured the marketplace the day before without worrying about buying anything for a few more days.

Her breakfast was the usual fare of scrambled eggs and fried foxl. Wanting to take up as much time as possible, Amanda carefully prepared the two meals by hand rather than attempting anything using elemy.

After cleaning the breakfast dishes, Amanda spent a couple of hours playing with Juila before it was time for her daughter's nap. Amanda still needed to shower and get dressed for her interview, which was only a couple of hours away. Her outfit was already set out on the bed, and she'd have at least an hour of uninterrupted time to get herself ready.

As she washed her hair, she went over the questions they'd likely ask during the interview. In all honesty, she didn't have very much work experience, just with Captain Ahn.

During high school, she never needed a job, allowing her to concentrate solely on her studies. Now she was lamenting her lack.

"Just be myself," she murmured. "Let them decide if I'm were right for the job."

If only she knew more about the job duties of the open position. Maybe then she wouldn't be so stressed about the questions.

After her shower, she had plenty of time and opted to sit outside to let the sunshine dry her hair before getting dressed. She absently ran her fingers through her hair, her mind busily thinking about her current situation.

Would Rasa have time to meet with her? After Bryon left, she sent Rasa a message letting her cousin know her contact information in Durseni. She hoped to connect before now, and she struggled to remain patient even though she agreed to work around Rasa's busy schedule.

Juila made some noise, so Amanda picked up her towel and headed inside. She dropped the cloth off in the bathroom on her way over to the bedroom.

Standing in her crib, Juila smiled when she saw her mom enter the room, arms raised and waiting to be picked up. Amanda couldn't resist kissing her rosy cheek as she cuddled her.

"Mommy has an important meeting today, Juila." She spoke as she sat on the bed beside her outfit.

"Do I come, too?" Juila asked with a serious expression.

"Sort of," Amanda said and tried to think how to explain daycare to a two-year-old. "You and I will go to the building together, but then I'll leave you to play with other children while I meet with some people about getting a job."

"What's a job?"

"It's like what Bryon does most days of the week. I need a job of my own because we aren't living with Bryon and Alena anymore."

Juila wrinkled her nose and frowned. "Why did we have to leave?"

"We left so I could meet with a woman here on this island who can help me find your sister."

"Where's Andera?"

Amanda was torn between smiling and crying. Didn't she remember Jena anymore? "No, Juila, not Andera. We need to find your birth sister, Jena."

Juila's face animated once again and said, "Oh, Jena's fine."

"What're you saying, Juila? Can you speak with Jena?" Amanda held her breath while waiting for Juila's answer. Did Juila hold the answer to finding Jena after all? She wished she would've thought to have this conversation a long time ago; however, Juila probably wouldn't have been able to articulate it this well even a few months before.

"I speak with my other me all the time," Juila said indignantly.

Amanda moved Juila until she could easily look into her daughter's eyes. "Is she called 'my other me' because you both look the same?"

She put her hands on her cheeks as if assessing her appearance. "Yes, we do look the same. Why is that, Mommy?"

"It's because you both are what people call identical twins. You both started from the same egg inside mommy, but then split apart and became two girls who look the same."

Juila looked up at Amanda with a funny expression and giggled when she said, "Mommy, you're funny! We're not chickens! Only chickens have eggs, not people."

"I'm being serious, Juila. People have eggs, too, just not the same kind as chickens. Can you tell me where Jena is?" She grinned at Juila's explanation.

Juila cocked her head to the side, her eyes staring at nothing. "She's usually in a white room, but today she's playing with a woman."

Amanda wanted to grill Juila but forced herself to remain calm. "Have you ever seen this woman with your own eyes?"

"No."

"Who else is usually around Jena?"

"There's a man I see every day with her. He makes up fun games for us to play. I like to copy those games."

"Is there anyone else around her a lot?"

"Yes, there's a boy, but he's jealous of her. He glares at her with his arms crossed. Why do you think he wouldn't like her, Mommy?"

"I don't know, baby. Maybe you should ask Jena sometime. Also, ask her the names of the people around her.

"Wouldn't it be nice to visit with Jena sometime? We could do it together if you can tell me where she is." Amanda didn't want to pressure Juila into getting information; however, at this point, it seemed Juila was her best hope for locating Jena.

"Okay, Mommy, but I can't because she's sleeping right now."

"Does she seem happy when she's awake?"

Juila nodded thoughtfully and said, "We make each other happy."

"That's good, honey. Keep making her happy." Amanda widened her eyes and breathed deeply to force the threatening tears to recede. She hugged Juila to her chest and prayed for a breakthrough to come soon.

She finally pulled away when Juila squirmed and said, "Sit here while I get dressed for my meeting."

Juila crawled onto the middle of the bed and plunked her rear down to face her mommy. She intently watched as Amanda changed her clothes. "You look beautiful, Mommy."

"Thanks, sweetheart. I just hope the people in my meeting think so, too."

"One will, for sure!" Juila replied emphatically.

Amanda did a double-take at her daughter. What did Juila mean by that?

She glanced at the time and noticed she would have to get going soon to arrive early for the appointment. She had a recurring fear of being late or lost on the way, so she'd make sure neither thing became an issue.

CHAPTER 28

Amanda picked Juila up from the bed and jogged to the dining room to retrieve Captain Ahn's recommendation letter. His endorsement for her qualifications was imperative since she didn't feel she had anything else to share with her interviewers.

Amanda strolled up the street. She didn't want to sweat through her clothing because of the day's heat or her nerves. "I think you're going to have fun playing with some new kids. What do you think?"

"Okay." Juila smiled up at her mother.

Amanda loved how Juila was never scared around other children. Amanda smiled down at her daughter.

What was Juila thinking? Maybe her connection with Jena made it so she always had someone to comfort her in new settings.

After this meeting finished, she'd find out more about her link with her sister. How much did they know about one another?

They arrived at the building with more than twenty minutes to spare. A gust of cold air washed over her heated body when she opened the door. She walked into the reception area and to the main desk, a young woman eagerly waiting to assist.

"Hello, my name is Amanda Covington, and I have a job interview at one o'clock. I was also told there's an on-site daycare for my daughter to attend during my interview. Can you please direct me to the daycare?"

"Absolutely, Amanda. Simply go through those double doors on the left of the main entrance. Sign your daughter in when you drop her off, and sign her out when you're ready to leave. When you're done, come back to my desk, and I'll have your interview details available."

"Thanks." Amanda turned around, walked back toward the entrance, and then turned toward the side door as directed. She fervently hoped Juila wouldn't be the youngest one there; however, her worries were unfounded now. Luckily, the large daycare site had many children around Juila's age already happily playing.

A middle-aged woman greeted Juila immediately upon entering the room, "Well, hello, young lady. Have you come to play with us?"

Amanda grinned, feeling superfluous since nobody seemed even to notice her holding Juila. At least these people genuinely loved children. Amanda's tension about leaving Juila in an unknown play place disappeared.

Juila stared at the woman and nodded.

"We're going to have so much fun. What's your name?"

"Juila."

"What a beautiful name, Juila. Let's go this way while your mommy signs you in," she gestured toward Juila to come through the gate just the right size for Juila. Squirming to be set down, Amanda hastily complied and watched Juila toddle away with the stranger.

A younger woman behind the desk spoke to Amanda for the

first time, "If you just sign right here, then you can be on your way."

Amanda had mixed emotions about relinquishing her daughter to the older woman. She shook her head to dismiss her momentary dismay at being left without a second glance but then had to smile at her daughter's confidence.

She stepped over to the check-in desk, signed her name on the appropriate line, and then wrote 'interview' in the spot designated for the department. "I guess that's what's needed."

The woman looked at her entry and then smiled up at her. "Good luck with your interview. This's such a great place to work. I hope to see you again soon."

Amanda glanced one more time to see how Juila took to this new area and saw she was busy with introductions to three other little girls who appeared to be similar in age. As she didn't seem needed here anymore, she turned around and retraced her path back to the receptionist.

The girl glanced away from her patil and said, "The interview's being held on the second floor in conference room three. Take the elevator behind me and turn to the right. There's a bank of seats outside the conference room where you can wait to be called into the interview. Good luck."

"Thanks again," Amanda replied as she walked around the reception desk to the indicated elevators.

Hmm, they use the same word for elevator here. I didn't expect that. The technology between the two worlds must've been shared more than she previously believed.

She pressed the button and waited a few moments for the doors to open. The ride to the second floor was as short as expected, and she found the conference room easily. More nervous than ever, she sat in a chair, hoping her hammering heart wouldn't become so loud that even a deaf person could hear it.

While she waited, several people came and went from the

conference room. Without meaning to, she overheard several people talking about one more interviewer named Riccan, who appeared to be missing.

Amanda looked at her timepiece, which Alena gifted to her, and realized the interview should've begun five minutes earlier. Did something go wrong?

Finally, a man came rushing from the stairwell toward Amanda and the conference room. She was both pleased and slightly flustered to see the missing person was none other than Riccan Stel, whom she saw at the telepod races two anons before.

Not knowing what came over her, Amanda spoke teasingly to Riccan, "They're looking for you."

"I'm so sorry I'm late. Give me just a minute more, please." He turned into the conference room and sat at the head of the table. "Sorry, an emergency came up from the manufacturing department. This's our last interview for this position, right?"

"Yes. The candidate's name is Amanda Covington. Would you like me to bring her in?" a woman asked.

"Please do. I'm sure she's waited long enough."

An older woman appeared in the conference room doorway and smiled at Amanda as she asked, "Amanda Covington?"

Amanda nodded politely.

"If you're ready, we can begin the interview."

"Thanks." Amanda stood and followed the woman into the room. The space was relatively small, consisting of a table and six chairs, four of which the interviewers occupied. Amanda chose the seat directly across from Riccan.

Clearing his throat, Riccan introduced himself. "Hi, my name's Riccan Stel. To my right is Gilora and Kendon and to my left is Gwenda. I'm the department manager, and everyone here is a member of my team and will be working directly with the person we hire for this position."

Amanda nodded at each person as they were introduced.

Gilora brought her into the room. She repeated each name silently in her head several times to keep them firmly in place, instantly thankful to Alena for teaching her the memorization skill.

"Let me share a little bit about this position, and then you can tell us how you're a good fit for the job. We're looking for a person who can take vast amounts of information and compile them together to create various reports.

"This person will have to work well with diverse people both within and outside the company. We expect this person to operate a patil with ease, learn new programs, listen to customer needs, and deliver results promptly.

"Does this sound like something you'd be interested in doing?"

"Sure, it doesn't sound too complicated. What types of documents need processing?"

"Mostly process change orders with various invoices, bills of lading, as well as a few other odds and ends."

Amanda grinned, barely withholding a guffaw. "I've had a lot of experience with invoices and bills of lading with Captain Ahn."

Riccan nodded and made a notation on the plasfilm in front of him. "That's right; you came highly recommended for this position by Ahn. Did he provide a letter for us?"

"Oh, yes. I have it right here," Amanda reached into her pocket, pulled out the envelope, and handed it across the table into Riccan's waiting hand.

"Thank you. Just one moment while we read through the letter." He ripped open the envelope and reviewed the two pages. When he finished, he ensured each interviewer perused the contents before continuing the interview.

Amanda restrained herself from squirming under Riccan's intense scrutiny while the others read the letter. He didn't seem at all embarrassed to be caught looking at her but instead smiled when she made eye contact. She grinned back and hoped the letter didn't exaggerate her skills too much.

"Do you have any questions for us?"

"When will a decision be made, and when will I be starting?" Amanda decided to pose the question as though she were the obvious choice, hoping to demonstrate confidence rather than arrogance in her qualifications.

"We hope to have a decision made before the end of the day, and we'd like the person to begin as soon as possible."

"That sounds good," Amanda said lamely. What did Captain Ahn's letter say? The interviewers didn't have any more questions for her, so it must've been pretty comprehensive. If they had any concerns, they would've addressed them before she left.

Riccan tapped his pencil on the tabletop. "Well, Amanda, thank you for your time. If you haven't already done so, please leave your contact information with the front receptionist on the way out. Once we've made a final decision, we'll contact all of the applicants to let them know." Riccan stood, and everyone around the table did as well.

Amanda made it to her feet almost as fast and managed not to knock over her chair in her haste. Each person leaned forward and offered their hand in a farewell shake, and Amanda grasped each one and thanked them for their time. She just turned to leave when Riccan surprised her.

"Let me walk you out of the building." Riccan took several long strides and stopped right beside Amanda.

"Thank you, but it's not necessary." Amanda's face unaccountably heated at his proximity.

"I know, but please allow me anyway." He gestured for her to precede him from the room.

Amanda nodded woodenly. "Okay, if it makes you happy." She wasn't about to offend him before he offered her a job. But she also couldn't fathom why he'd want to walk out with her.

The other interviewers filed out of the conference room and turned in the opposite direction from the elevator. Seconds later,

Riccan and Amanda walked alone, and Amanda couldn't think of anything intelligent to say in the deafening silence.

Finally, she spoke the first thing that came to mind. "I met you a couple of anons ago at the telepod races. I'm sure you wouldn't remember, but the races were very exciting."

Good grief, what a stupid thing to say. He probably thinks I'm brown-nosing by talking about his passion for racing.

Her praise was sincere, but she should've kept her inane commentary to herself.

CHAPTER 29

"I'm sorry to admit I didn't remember you specifically at first. However, now that you mention it, I'm pretty sure I do recall seeing you outside my pit area. I find the racing quite exciting, and I'm glad you enjoyed the show."

Upon first seeing her sitting in the hall, he had a nagging suspicion they'd met before, but at the time, he couldn't remember where. He convinced himself it was a mistake. They reached the elevator, and Riccan pushed the elevator call button.

He frowned when the doors immediately opened. Since when did that happen? Oh, that's right. Never!

Amanda entered the elevator first and turned around to press the button just as Riccan reached out to do the same. Their hands bumped together, causing Amanda to pull hers back as though his touch burned her.

She wore the most curious expression. Riccan couldn't figure out what about her was so different from anyone else he'd ever met. He stared at her, unwilling to let even a second pass without soaking in her presence.

She laughed nervously and mumbled, "Sorry."

"No problem," he assured her as he stood close to her for the short ride down. The doors opened, and he gestured for her to exit first.

He wanted more time to talk with her. The interview was too short, but further questions seemed unnecessary after reading Captain Ahn's letter. He was reasonably confident the other interviewers felt the same way, too.

As if reading his mind, Amanda said, "I thought the interview would've been longer. I imagine some internal candidates would have more experience. Thanks again for humoring Captain Ahn's request to interview me. I appreciate the consideration."

Riccan cocked his head, considering Amanda's statement. "You don't know what Ahn wrote, do you?"

"No. Why would I? The envelope was sealed when I got it." Now her expression turned puzzled.

He grinned, glad for the excuse to extend his time with her. He crossed his arms over his chest and stood with his feet shoulder-width apart.

"His letter thoroughly detailed your experience while working with him. Going over the same questions seemed redundant when we just read all of his answers. Believe me, you have just as good, if not better, of a chance as the other candidates."

Amanda smiled up at Riccan and said, "Thank you for telling me. I was nervous you'd ask me a bunch of questions I wouldn't know how to answer. Then I felt almost as bad when there wasn't anything asked. Well, I guess all I can do now is wait until everyone decides which person is best for the job."

Riccan leaned on the receptionist's desk as Amanda faced the girl and said, "I'd like to leave my contact information if you don't mind?"

"No problem at all. Go ahead; I'm ready."

"My patil call sign is +amandacov.tua."

"Okay, I've got it. I'll send it up to the Engineering Department so they can contact you later today."

"Thank you," Amanda said and turned from the desk to get Juila from the daycare.

Riccan followed her, expecting to open the front door for her. He was slightly confused when she turned and went to the side door instead. Belatedly realizing she must have a kid, he rushed forward and opened that door instead. "I didn't know you had a child. Is it a boy or a girl?"

Amanda quickly inhaled as if he'd asked a painful question. Just as soon as the strange reaction registered, it disappeared.

She said, "I have my daughter, Juila, to pick up."

"What a pretty name. How old is she?"

"Almost two."

"Wow! I wouldn't have guessed."

Amanda signed her name in the check-out column. The woman at the desk then went to the back room and returned a minute later, holding Juila's hand as they slowly walked to the front room. Juila saw her mother, giggled with glee, let go of the woman's hand, and ran the rest of the way.

Amanda leaned down, caught her daughter mid-leap, and cuddled her into her hip. "Did you have fun, honey?"

"Yes. We played with blocks."

"That sounds great. Are you ready to go home now?"

She nodded as she spotted Riccan waiting beside Amanda. "Who's he?" She pointed her finger at Riccan.

"His name's Riccan. He's the one needing a new worker."

Juila smiled and said, "He's the one I told you about!"

Amanda blushed and looked around as if to see if anyone had heard her daughter's statement. She swiftly looked toward him.

Riccan smiled, his eyes narrowed, and his head tilted as he considered the cute little girl's announcement.

Amanda turned around to leave, but Riccan hurried ahead to

open the door. She smiled as she walked through the opening and said, "Thank you again!"

Wishing for more to say, Riccan pushed the front door open for her and watched her walk down the sidewalk toward the marketplace. Where did she live? Hopefully, not too far, considering the afternoon heat and the added burden of carrying a small child.

With nothing left for him to do in the lobby, he turned around toward the stairs, eventually sitting down in his office to resume work. He needed to review all of the candidates and their qualifications, praying that Amanda would end up becoming the obvious choice.

AMANDA CHECKED her patil first thing when she arrived home. It was ridiculous to think a decision might've been made in the time it took her to walk home. However, she also knew herself well enough that she'd continue to dwell on it until she satisfied her curiosity.

Her patil took forever to start. Or maybe her imagination made it seem that way. Eventually, all the programs popped up on the screen. It took her a moment to register the unread message on the screen, which she eagerly tapped with her finger to open.

An unknown woman's face, which seemed vaguely familiar, filled the screen and spoke, "Amanda, hi! My name's Rasa. We haven't met yet, but I'm your cousin. I'm sorry I missed you at home. I had a few minutes between classes, and I thought I'd try to get in touch with you.

"Anyway, I should have about an hour this evening if you want to get together. I was ecstatic to hear my mom finally found some of her family, and I'm eager to get to know you, too.

"Okay, I don't have much more time right now, but if you do

want to meet with me, send me an instant message, and we can meet on the north end of the marketplace by the cucumber vendor at six o'clock.

"I'm hoping you've at least had a chance to go there since relocating. I found a few benches where we can sit and have relative privacy to discuss your problem. Talk to you soon! Bye!"

The screen blanked, and then another box popped up asking Amanda if she wanted to send a video reply. Amanda declined and then selected the instant message option. She typed up a quick affirming message and then hit send.

The day's surprises kept coming. She looked over at Juila playing on the living room floor—no time like the present to get to the bottom of Juila's mysterious remark about Riccan.

She walked over to Juila and kneeled next to her.

"Juila, honey, what did you mean about Riccan being the one you talked about?"

The little girl turned her big blue eyes up to meet her mother's gaze and smiled as she said, "He's the one who thought you were beautiful at the meeting."

Amanda ignored the heat rising in her cheeks. "But how did you know it was going to happen?"

Juila's shoulders raised nearly to her ears, and she said, "I don't know. I just know sometimes."

"Is it something like you do when you talk with Jena?"

Once again, she shrugged, "I don't know."

Deciding to leave it alone for the time being, she asked, "Do you want to practice playing with the elemy?"

Juila's eyes rounded with eager delight. She broadly smiled as she nodded enthusiastically.

Amanda picked up a toy and said, "Put this block on top of the other blue one." Immediately it disappeared from her fingers and reappeared on the blue block.

The next instant, all of the other blocks from the floor were arranged in matching color pairs. Impressed with her daughter's skill, Amanda clapped her hands in delight and praised, "That's amazing, Juila. What else can you do?"

Juila squinted her eyes in comical concentration. "Oh, I know! Jena's dad loved it." After only a moment of thought, she surrounded a block with a sphere of elemy to float across the room. Juila jumped up and, with giggles of unabashed glee, ran around the room chasing after the energy ball.

Once again, Amanda marveled at her daughter's great control. Did she hear Juila say something about Jena's dad?

When Juila finally allowed the sphere to pop and release the block next to her mother, Amanda asked gently, "Where did you learn to do that?"

CHAPTER 30

"I saw Jena's dad teach her, and I wanted to do it, too, so I just did it. It's okay, Mommy, isn't it? You don't look happy. Did I do something wrong?" Juila asked.

Seeing her daughter's enthusiasm wilt, Amanda hugged her daughter tightly to her chest. With a tickle, she pulled her back far enough to look her straight in the eyes as she said, "It's more than okay. It's wonderful. I want you to do everything that makes you happy. This game made you laugh, and I loved it."

She tickled Juila's belly a second time, making her giggle all over again. "Show me some other things you've learned. I want to know everything!"

They played their new elemy game for several hours. Juila's enthusiasm to show off seemed inexhaustible. As soon as Amanda heard the patil's dinging of an incoming call, she exclaimed with excitement, "Oh, Juila, there's the patil! Please be super quiet for a couple of minutes; Mommy needs to take this important call."

Amanda raced over to the screen and saw it was from the Telepod Engineering Company. With her future on the line, she was inexplicably nervous to answer it for fear they may tell her no thank you. Without waiting for another instant, she touched the accept button on the screen and went speechless when Riccan himself appeared on the other end.

"Hello, Amanda. I hope this's a good time."

"Never better, Mr. Stel." She smiled, hoping to disguise her nervousness.

Brief confusion crossed Riccan's face, but then he smiled in return and said, "I'm pleased to say we'd like to offer you the job of Engineering Resources Analyst if you are still interested."

"I'd be very pleased to accept!" She could barely contain the happy dance that threatened to burst forth.

"Wonderful! We're willing to pay 546 taj per anon. We pay weekly, so it'd amount to ten and a half taj. Are you willing to accept the offered wage?"

Amanda managed to keep her jaw from dropping at the proposed earnings. It was fully two hundred more taj per year than she expected. After only a moment's pause, she managed to say, "I think I could work with that."

"Great! The last thing to be agreed upon would be the start date. We'd love for you to start tomorrow, but I'm sure you'll need a little longer than that, so how about next Senin?"

"Actually, tomorrow works perfectly, if you don't mind." Could this be happening? She couldn't have planned it any better.

Riccan leaned closer to the patil, his grin widening. "Really? Are you sure it won't be an imposition?"

Amanda shook her head. "None whatsoever. I just moved here two days ago, and I need to start making money as soon as possible."

"Well, okay. I guess I'll let everyone know to expect you tomorrow at eight o'clock!"

"Thank you so much for the opportunity. I appreciate it. See you tomorrow!"

The screen blanked, and Amanda screeched with delight. She

rushed over to Juila, scooped her up from the floor, and twirled around in circles until she fell onto the couch with dizziness.

"Did the man tell you something good, Mommy?" Juila put a hand on each side of Amanda's face.

She placed her hands over Juila's and grinned wider. "That man just made Mommy very happy, Juila! I got the job, and I start tomorrow. You'll get to play with those little girls at the daycare every day. Isn't that exciting?"

Juila nodded with exaggerated movement and smiled broadly. "You look so happy. I'm glad to play with new children."

Amanda checked her watch. Only an hour before the meeting with Rasa. She'd have just enough time to put together their dinner before leaving for the marketplace.

"Let's practice our cooking skills, okay?" She stood and held out her hand to take Juila's. They walked the short distance to the kitchen, where Amanda picked her up and set her on the counter next to the sink. "What would you like to eat?"

Juila didn't hesitate. "I want a chicken salad sandwich."

Thinking fast about the necessary ingredients, she murmured, "Okay, we'll need bread, chicken, mayonnaise, mustard, celery, salt, and pepper."

Each item appeared on the counter.

She should've known Juila would love the opportunity to use her powers to help. "Well, I guess we do have everything after all! Thank you, that was very helpful, Juila."

She started to cut up the raw chicken to cook faster when suddenly all of the chicken was cubed. Amanda pulled her hands back in surprise, glanced swiftly over to Juila, and asked, "Where did you learn to do that?"

Juila merely shrugged and replied, "I just thought about it, and it happened."

"Hmm." She glanced at Juila and asked, "What if I wanted the chicken cooked? Could you do that as well?"

"I don't know. I can try." Juila's face stilled as she concentrated on the chicken. Within an instant, each piece of meat was perfectly grilled.

"Wow, Juila! Very impressive!" Amanda picked up a cube and broke it open with her fingers to ensure thorough cooking. Satisfied, she moved the chicken into a bowl and sprinkled it with salt and pepper.

Amanda looked up at Juila and said, "Now I need a large scoop of mayo and a small squirt of mustard on top of the chicken. Do you want to try to do that?" An instant later, both ingredients were in the bowl.

"Can you chop the celery into small chunks and add it as well?" As soon as it appeared, Amanda smiled at Juila's easy ability and picked up the spoon to stir the mixture together.

Taking four slices of bread from the bag, she laid them out on the counter and scooped a generous amount of the salad onto two pieces. She smoothed the mixture and set the other pieces of bread on top of the sandwiches.

She found a knife and cut her sandwich in half and Juila's into four pieces. After plating the meal, she scooped Juila off the counter and set her down on the floor.

They went to the dining table and sat. Amanda set Juila's meal down in front of her. They said a prayer over their meal and ate. After eating the first half of her sandwich, Amanda noticed she overlooked getting any beverages.

"Oops, I forgot the water!" She scooted her chair back to get up when Juila took the matter into her power by producing the requested drinks on the table.

"I got it, Mommy!"

Amanda sat back down and smiled at her daughter, "I see that! Thank you." She began to think these new powers could make life very lazy or convenient after a long and tiring day at work.

The initial prospect of getting a job warred with the idea that she'd be working in Tuala. Her first real job should've been on Earth. Every tie she made to this world would be one more thing that would keep her from returning to her parents.

The thought disturbed her since she knew they'd continuously worry about her. If only she could get word to them to ease their fears and distress. It was unfair to keep them guessing about her health and safety, life or death. Amanda added this to her mental list of things to talk to Rasa about when they finally met.

Once again, she checked her watch, calculating approximately another half an hour before she'd have to leave the house. Gathering the empty plates, she strolled to the kitchen deep in thought.

She washed the plates, dried them off, and placed them in the cupboard without concentrating on the task. She turned around to go into the living room and stood in stunned silence. What was Juila doing? Was she having a conversation with herself?

Rushing into the living room, Amanda kneeled beside Juila and asked quietly, "Juila, are you talking with Jena?"

Juila stopped talking, refocusing her eyes on her mother before she replied in an earnest tone, "Yes."

"Can you ask her what the woman's name is who you see with her all the time?"

Juila nodded and did as requested. She answered a moment later, "She says her name's Mommy."

Amanda's heart sank. Obviously, Jena would know her as Mommy and nothing else. She wouldn't expect Juila to call her by her given name, so why would Jena? Another idea struck her, "What does she call the boy who glares at her?"

A moment later, Juila finally answered, "His name's Willian."

Finally, an answer that might be helpful! Another thought occurred to her, and she asked, "What does her daddy call her mommy?"

"Honey," Juila answered with a smile. "That's a funny name, isn't it, Mommy?"

"It's a nickname, but, yes, it is silly. Thank you for asking Jena all those questions for me. Tell her I said hello, and I miss her."

Juila returned to her conversation with Jena, and Amanda couldn't do more than listen to Juila's end of the exchange. Naturally, their talk consisted mainly of kid activities and problems that tended to be nothing major.

The conversation didn't last very long. Amanda didn't want to interrupt the exchange, but they were now running late. They'd have to rush if they wanted to meet with Rasa on time.

CHAPTER 31

While Juila conversed with her sister, Amanda took the opportunity to send a message to Bryon, letting him know she got the job. She asked him to thank Captain Ahn for the letter as it was instrumental in the interview's success.

Amanda stood, held out her hand to Juila, and asked, "Are you ready to go meet your cousin?"

Juila enthusiastically nodded as she took hold of her mother's hand.

Heading toward the marketplace, Amanda opted for Juila to independently walk as she was too heavy to carry in the sultry, motionless heat. Moving slightly faster than sauntering, mother and daughter entered the marketplace on the south end and weaved through the vendor stalls until they reached the designated rendezvous point.

Amanda stopped and glanced around expectantly, worrying that something prevented Rasa from coming. She saw the same woman's face from the patil waving at her from a bench near a cluster of trees behind the booth.

Amanda maneuvered around the stall and smiled at this cousin whom she had never personally met. She saw Rasa's expression change to astonishment when she recognized Juila's resemblance to herself at the same age.

It was the same look both Barla and Ahn showed when they first saw her. Amanda's grin widened, and she asked, "It's kind of spooky, isn't it?"

"I guess! If I needed any further proof, I just got it! It's just unbelievable that you found my mother! What are the chances you'd both come here?" Rasa stood from the bench and came forward to hug Amanda. "Welcome to the family."

Rasa pulled back and added, "And we're almost exactly the same height. I always wanted a relative near my own age but never thought it was possible since Dad was an only child and my mother's family is—well, you know. You're the honest to goodness answer to all of my childhood wishes."

What could Amanda say to that? Flustered, she said, "I'm sorry we're a little bit late. Juila was having a conversation with Jena, and I didn't want to interrupt them. It was the first time I've witnessed them talking."

Rasa's eyebrows rose, and she looked more appraisingly at Juila. "That's okay; I just got here myself. It's actually a good sign that they're still connected. It might make our task a little bit easier."

Amanda seated herself on the bench and pulled Juila up onto her lap. "I've been practicing different skills with my crystal with the hope that you could teach me something more advanced to re-link with Jena. Have you thought of something that might work?"

Rasa pressed her hand against Amanda's knee, leaning closer to answer. "I'm still working on it, but I'm even more amazed by the fact that your crystal was given by Jehoban Himself.

"I'm beginning to believe there's more to my assignment to

come here than just learning how to become a wise-woman. I'm certain Jehoban wants me to get to know you and help find Jena."

"It's what I've been praying for as well!" Amanda settled herself more comfortably on the bench and rested her chin on Juila's head while wrapping her arms around her.

Rasa beamed with encouragement. She rested her elbows on her knees and said, "Tell me what you know, and I'll see what I can do to help further."

Amanda spent the next twenty minutes going over all of the facts of Jena's disappearance, also sharing how all of their leads turned into dead ends. Then she revealed the recent discovery that Juila could use her skills because someone was teaching them to Jena.

Rasa straightened with surprise at this last statement. "You realize the training you've spoken of is way more advanced than normal parents teach their children. This news gives me a good idea about the people who have Jena.

"They're probably higher up in society, and either has access to the best tutors or are instructors themselves. We should keep this information between us until I can verify a few more things."

Amanda mutely nodded, practically holding her breath to prevent interrupting whatever Rasa might be divining.

Tapping her fingertips against lips, Rasa suddenly spoke, "It's a lot to take in all at once. I'll have to mentally go over everything again to determine what avenue we might take to locate Jena. For right now, I'd like to hold Juila if you don't object."

Juila stared at Rasa and flung out her arms to be taken. Both Amanda and Rasa laughed at the precocious child's actions.

"I guess we both have our answer on that count. I don't mind, either, if it makes any difference!" Amanda laughed as she lifted Juila onto Rasa's lap.

Rasa leaned forward and whispered in Juila's ear, "You look exactly like me when I was your age. We're going to have fun getting to know one another. Someday soon, you're going to have to show me what you've learned from Jena.

"I'm sure it's been enjoyable getting to know how to use your powers. Please don't show anyone outside of the family what you've learned, or it could get your mommy in trouble, okay?"

"Alena taught me some new things. Is it okay to show her what I know?" Juila's eyebrows pulled down as far as she could, and her bottom lip trembled.

"No, no, Alena's fine too. She's almost like family since you've known her your entire life. Just keep it between you and the people you've always known, okay?"

Julia's expression cleared as fast as a cloud moving away from the sun. Her smile beamed wide. "I'm happy I can keep practicing the new skills because they're a lot of fun. I wish I could share them with my new friends at the daycare, but it's still okay. Besides, I always have my connection with Jena. That's the most important."

With her arms wrapped around her, Rasa gave Juila a light squeeze and said, "I hate to end this meeting, but I do have to get back to the dorms and study for tomorrow's class. I'll call again when I get the chance so we can set up another meeting, hopefully soon."

"Oh, about that—I got a job today that starts tomorrow."

Rasa put Juila down, pausing to ask, "Really? That's great! Where at?"

Amanda practically burst with pleasure to announce, "The Telepod Engineering Company."

Rasa's eyebrows rose. "Wow, that's fantastic. I've always heard it's a great place to work. Okay, well, I'll have to call after five or leave a message, knowing I won't hear back until after work lets out.

"I'm so crazy busy with these classes. You can't imagine the piles of books we need to memorize! I was afraid you'd be sitting around waiting for me to call. I felt so guilty about not having enough time to devote to this cause."

Amanda's heart jumped for joy, knowing that Rasa was eager to help, but she didn't want to pressure her in any way. The latest confirmation about Jena lightened her heart.

"Oh, Rasa, don't worry about me. I know you'll do everything possible to help with Jena. I also understand you have your commitments to take care of.

"We'll do everything we can to find Jena. At least I know she's well taken care of in her new home. It's a relief she's not still with Petre.

"I just wish we could find him. He'd certainly be able to answer many unanswered questions about where Jena might be." Amanda twirled one of Juila's ringlets around her finger, imagining that Jena's hair would look the same.

Rasa reached over and touched Amanda's shoulder. She waited until Amanda looked at her to whisper, "I hate to say this, but it might be better if you don't find Petre. What if he found out about Juila? He might start making trouble all over again, and then what would happen?"

Amanda stared at Rasa, blinking like a wide-eyed owl, knowing what she spoke was more than true. She shivered. What if Petre pushed for shared custody of Juila?

The man was so deceptive; he wouldn't think twice about stealing Juila away as he'd done with Jena. Amanda looked down at her daughter and just couldn't imagine her life without this precious little soul in it.

"You may be right, Rasa. I'll have to talk this over with Bryon and Alena and see how they think we should proceed."

Rasa clasped her hands tightly together, looking anywhere but at Amanda. "That's a good idea. Well, it's probably good you've moved to Durseni and started a life here. Do you plan on staying once we find Jena, or will you go home?"

"I don't know. Shemalla pointed out their dark crystal assignments might be because I'd try to take them home and put them in danger. I'm torn between going or staying.

"My family still doesn't know what's happened to me. And I hate the idea of putting my mom through the torture of the unknown. She already went through that with Barla's accident. It's just not fair."

Amanda paused, not wanting to push her luck but unable to stop herself from asking, "Can you think of any way I can get a message to my parents to let them know I'm safe?"

"I believe the danger of going through the veil would be lessened if you used a sanctioned Gate. I'll have to think about the best option for communicating with your parents. I don't want to put Shemalla in any danger, but there might be another way. Have you heard of distance communication?"

Amanda nodded. Was it strange that she just read about the skill on the list Alena had put together to test them against?

Rasa spoke slowly, "I might be able to send them a message, but I've never tried it at the distance we're talking about. It might be possible. Let me work on it, okay?"

Rasa's words came faster as more ideas came to her. "Go ahead and write up what you want them to know and instant message it to me once you've got it done. If I can get it to work, I'll send it right away."

Amanda leaned forward and hugged Rasa with happy relief. "This means so much to me. I've worried every day about my mom. She didn't want me to make this trip because she feared losing me again. Now she can know I'm okay! Oh, I'm so excited! Thank you!"

"Don't get too eager, Amanda. I said I'd try. I don't know if it'll work."

Amanda's heart raced with renewed hope. "I believe in you, Rasa. You'll make this work; I just know it!"

CHAPTER 32

Rasa just shook her head and smiled at her cousin's blind faith. Amanda couldn't know how nearly impossible the task was she asked. Jehoban saw something in her skills, and she always tried to please Him. Maybe if it could be done, she'd be the one to make it happen. Anything was possible, especially if Jehoban wanted it.

She didn't want to admit to Amanda that while Juila spoke, Rasa probed Juila's mind for her sister's mental bond. She saw Jena in her room sleeping and knew the tie was not only real but extremely powerful. This was an essential factor in re-establishing the link between Amanda and Jena. The child wasn't lost to the family, but the crystal connection was severed for some reason.

She stood, wishing time allowed for a more extended visit. "I do have to get going. Thanks for meeting with me. It's exciting to have a relative near my own age finally. I want us to get to know one another well, especially if you plan to head home soon. I don't want to miss out on anything!"

Amanda rushed forward and hugged Rasa. "I'm delighted, too. I felt a connection between us from the moment I saw your picture in Barla's hallway. I didn't even know then that we were family, yet I still felt the pull. I'll send the message for my parents tonight, even if I have to burn the midnight oil to put it together!"

"Don't stay up too late. You have work first thing in the morning," Rasa playfully admonished. What in the world was midnight oil? She imagined it must be a familiar term on Earth, something she would've known about if her mother remained on Earth and raised her there.

"Yes, mother! I'll be a good girl. Hopefully, we can talk again tomorrow evening. Have a good night."

"You too. See you tomorrow!"

They parted ways and walked back through the marketplace to return to their separate houses. Rasa's thoughts were whirling about what would happen next.

Everything depended upon her skill and Amanda's ability to execute any directions. A lot or nothing could happen in the next few days, but she refused to think about the latter possibility. She would make it work!

Everyone who held a grudge against Elder Debbon or his wife gathered at Rualin's request. He still wasn't sure exactly why he was doing this favor for Petre. He just felt an overwhelming desire to get it done.

Rualin cleared his throat, and every eye turned to him, and the last of the conversations stopped so they could hear him.

"Thank you all for coming. I know everybody is busy. A matter has come to my attention that cannot be ignored regarding the *Honorable* Elder Debbon.

"I'm sure each of you has experienced some issue with him or his wife in the past, and I want you to know we're now able to do something about those problems. Are you all willing to help?"

A unanimous roar of assent echoed in the confines of his cottage, which pleased Rualin immensely. "First of all, I'd like to take a few minutes for everyone to share with your neighbors here in the room what has transpired between you and the Elder."

The volume in the room raised to a roar as each person began to share tales with one another. Rualin intended to get everybody riled up enough so they wouldn't question the ethics of the plan he had put together.

Once he felt everyone was sufficiently upset, he clapped his hands loudly several times to regain their attention before detailing the plan he and Petre concocted. After about an hour of questions, assurances, and answers, he felt sure everybody was clear on their part in the plot.

He raised his voice to the crowd and said, "Okay, everybody, it's time we made the Elder feel the same pain his unwarranted attention has brought on our people. Go out now and do your part so we can make him pay!"

The conversation once again rose in volume as each man cheered and stood. They began milling around the room and walking out toward the dock. When the last man finally left, Rualin felt all of the energy drain from him, and all he wanted to do was take a nice long nap.

It didn't matter that it was the middle of the day; he was too tired to even think about staying awake. Maybe tomorrow, he'd concentrate on what he could do to help advance Petre's plan, but today he'd go to sleep.

THE QUICK PROGRESS of his students after the first day of teaching pleased Debbon. This session might not last as long as some of the others had in the past. Each woman possessed skills in her own right, except for Rasa. She might actually be the sticking point in his goal of going home soon.

Maybe I could continue her training at my home. He immediately dismissed the idea of taking Jehoban's student home to his Jena.

His Jena.

He missed her something terrible. Guilt mixed with sadness immediately overtook him since he never felt that way about his son. Willian never seemed interested in learning to use his ability until Jena started getting all the attention.

Now it appeared as if a battle for attention among the three of them had begun, which was not at all what Debbon wanted to happen between his first-daughter and his son. They were supposed to grow up loving one another, but he felt just the opposite was happening.

He'd have to start devoting more time to his son if he wanted the relationship between the children to improve. Once he worked out what he'd do when he got home, he turned his attention to the incoming students.

He'd cover life-lines today. This was always one of his favorite lessons since it dealt with the inner workings of elemy in the body. So much could be done to heal the body by accessing the life-line.

This also happened to be one of the more difficult subjects to learn. It wasn't a physical thing they were searching for in the body, merely an element of vitality that could only be felt with the mind. Once the students learned the skill, their abilities would increase ten-fold without enhancing any skill levels.

He enjoyed watching the students' initial struggle. When they finally figured it out, the physical change in their expressions always looked the same.

He smiled at the waiting class and began. "Today's lesson will be on finding and using a person's life-line. Has anyone experienced accessing it themselves? Or has anyone had yours used by a healer?"

His gaze traveled over each student in the room. Surprisingly, three hands lifted at his two questions. He pointed to the first woman and asked, "Which one was it for you?"

"A healer used mine."

Debbon nodded and pointed to the next woman and received the same reply. The third woman indicated she accessed it on a patient quite by accident. Debbon smiled at the woman and said, "That's usually the case, but it's never forgotten, is it?"

The third woman nodded emphatically as the other students stared at her in wonder. Debbon could feel the jealous tension enter the room. Nobody wanted to feel like they were entering a lesson at a disadvantage. They knew that because she'd already used this part of the training, she'd have an easier time with it.

When the actual training began, Debbon would have her go first to be dismissed. It wouldn't do for her to watch the other students struggle. This wasn't meant to be a competition, but, somehow, it usually ended up becoming one.

He looked over toward Rasa. Why would she react so strangely to this lesson? What does it mean?

He couldn't dwell on the matter right now as he needed to explain the life-line's purpose and function.

"Each person is born in Tuala and establishes a connection to the elemental energy of the world when they receive their birth crystal. The service that you'll perform to assign the crystal is the one that ties the person to the energy.

"It's imperative to take the ritual seriously as the connection with the elemy is one that cannot be redone if it's not performed correctly in the first place."

Several women in the classroom nodded seriously. "Some of you might have met people who've had bad experiences with the crystal ceremony." He made a mental note to have private discussions with those women to see if he might help the people they knew.

The connection wouldn't ever be made perfect once it was botched, but it could be improved. Every person had the right to use the elemental energy freely, and he wanted each person to have equal opportunity.

"The life-line is a direct connection with a person's soul and his or her ability to tap into the elemy. Since each person discovers a unique method to access the power, there are innumerable ways a life-line can be established.

"It's your duty as a wise-woman to gain entry to their connection to deliver assistance to the patient. The more skilled you become at finding their link quickly, the more patients will seek out your particular services.

"Since each patient will only need you when there's a problem, some of which can be life-threatening, your speed will be vital in easing their pains and possibly saving their lives.

"The easiest life-line to find is your own. We're going to spend a few minutes right now where you're going to access the elemy and then trace the link from the source into the core of your own being.

"This isn't something that can be rushed, so don't feel bad if you take longer than someone else in the room. I shouldn't have to remind any of you that learning the art of healing isn't a competition; it's a collaboration.

"Once you've found your own life-line, turn to your neighbor on your right and try to find theirs. If you're at the end of the row, I want you to find the person's directly in front of you."

He moved his gaze to the student who puzzled him the most. Maybe he'd learn something about Rasa that would clue him in to why Jehoban put His special student in this class.

"Rasa, since you're at the end of the front row, I want you to find my life-line once you've found yours."

CHAPTER 33

Rasa seemed surprised to be called out in such a fashion. After the initial shock wore off, she seemed hesitant to link with him. Of course, Rasa had no way of knowing that he already knew about her parentage.

Her link would probably be different from everyone else's, and he was curious to feel her mental touch and how it differed. He smiled reassuringly at her even as he instructed them to begin the exercise.

The energy in the room increased until it became a palpable buzz that left the hair on his arms standing. He relished in the feeling of the power and eagerly watched his students' faces as they traced their own power.

The third student suddenly gasped as she found her core. Her eyes regained focus, and she smiled up at Debbon as understanding formed in her mind. He nodded encouragement and then gestured for her to turn to the student next to her to complete the exercise.

Surprisingly Rasa was next to indicate her success. Debbon smoothed his expression, not wanting to give away his surprise.

For some reason, he entertained the notion she'd have trouble with this exercise, yet he should've known a woman with her skill to learn advanced techniques from Jehoban would probably have an innate ability to access a life-line. He crooked his finger at her to let her know she should come over to sit up front to locate his own life-line.

Once again, she hesitated, and he chose to ignore it. She rose from her seat and slowly advanced across the room until she stopped in front of his desk. He stood and gestured to the chair he vacated. He said, "Go ahead and get comfortable here. I'll sit on the edge of the desk and monitor the class while you continue to practice on myself."

He sat in front of her so she'd have relative privacy from the other students. He stiffened with the powerful energy surge entering his mind a moment later. It took all of his skill to keep his mind relaxed from the onslaught as she searched.

Other students had used him before, yet this was definitely a different experience. Did Jehoban have any part in which seat Rasa picked today?

Over and over, he resisted the urge to nudge her in the right direction. He wanted her to succeed in her own right. Otherwise, she'd never build confidence in herself until she could do it on her own.

Finally, she touched the right spot in his mind. He felt his student's satisfaction when she achieved the goal.

Her potent mind hurried away from his own, leaving him once again alone but wishing he could repeat the exercise to feel her incredible power again. Surprisingly it was more captivating to him than teaching Jena.

Finally, he fully understood why Jehoban kept her so long!

"Thank you, Rasa. You may return to your seat." Debbon turned back to the class and watched as Rasa rushed back to her seat, seemingly relieved to conclude the task.

He considered talking with her about his knowledge of her, however, then he'd potentially have to explain how he came to find out, and he wasn't ready to divulge that information anytime soon. No, he'd keep his own counsel since her connection with Jehoban was too close for comfort.

Debbon's opinion of Rasa's prospects in healing shifted dramatically based on her competent demonstration with him. Maybe Rasa could make a good healer after all. She certainly seemed able to learn whatever he asked of her. He still wished he knew why Jehoban decided she needed this training after all this time.

Was Jehoban planning on promoting her to Elder status? It all made sense! An Elder needs to be skilled in all things to be an effective leader. This was the last thing she needed to allow her elevation.

As soon as he convinced himself of this answer, he dismissed it. Women didn't become Elders. There was no way the Council of Elders would ever accept her, not to mention the fact that she didn't have anyone to become the successor for, as was the custom.

His thoughts turned to all of the Elders, none of which would stand down anytime soon. Was Jehoban going to take someone down? Or was He going to create a new location for Rasa to take charge? Was he supposed to keep this knowledge to himself, or should he call together the Council of Elders to discuss the implications?

He chuckled at his own audacity. If Jehoban wanted this, then who was he to argue against it. Jehoban always wanted the best for His children, and Debbon would enjoy seeing how this all unfolded.

The other Elders would be up in arms about the new situation, and he'd be calm knowing what he knew about Rasa. He was almost re-convinced of Rasa's future, yet only time would tell.

This new idea distracted him for several minutes causing him to miss many of his students achieving their latest level. Putting Rasa's possible future out of his mind, he refocused on the remaining students in the class. Nearly half of the women found their own life-line and turned to find their neighbors'.

He mentally noted the students who still worked on finding their own to see if he could offer any pointers. This skill was paramount to their success, and nobody would move past this level until the entire class succeeded.

The three students with previous encounters quickly finished, just as he anticipated. He walked over to each pair of students who completed the task and quietly said, "You're excused for the remainder of the day."

Rasa seemed relieved to have this exercise over and couldn't exit the room fast enough. Debbon smiled at her hasty retreat, more than a little grateful to have her distracting power leave the room so he could concentrate on the struggling students. Only eight women remained, and they were all still working on their own life-line.

"Okay, students, please stop for right now, so you don't tire yourselves out unnecessarily." He saw them all come back to awareness and look around the room in surprise that most of their classmates were missing.

"Don't worry about the others; this step is important, so I'll give you additional lessons which they won't have to make you even stronger when you finally succeed."

Several students smiled at this newfound and unexpected advantage. Debbon couldn't implicitly vouch for the accuracy of his last statement, but if they believed it, it would enhance their efficiency and bolster their flagging confidence.

～

CHELESA MISSED her husband more than ever before. Having a second child was a blessing and a curse as it created twice as much work and distraction.

She loved having Jena and was grateful the little girl learned to curb her raw power. She was a joy to hold now that she no longer unintentionally caused physical discomfort.

As a mother, she noticed Willian's jealousy of his betrothed. His behavior was unacceptable and would have to be addressed soon.

She tried her best to give Willian just as much attention as before Jena came into the picture, but it was hard to keep Willian from seeing her pleased smiles at Jena's progress with her husband's expert instruction.

She took the day off for the three of them to get outside and enjoy playing in the park. It had been a long time since they were together without any distractions of business getting in the way.

The staff was instructed to give them privacy and keep any petitioners from knowing where they headed. Her mission for the day was only to be a devoted mother.

With her plan in action, she picked up Willian and held him close to her side, and then she pushed the stroller containing Jena in front of her. She maintained physical contact with Willian to make him feel more wanted than Jena—at least until he was old enough to understand that she had enough love for both of them equally. Siblings should never compete for the parents' limitless love, but Willian was still too young to appreciate the concept.

The day's warmth caused Chelesa's shoulders to relax, but she squinted against the brightness. With a thought, she retrieved her sunglasses from her room. She put them on without missing a step along the groomed pathway.

Chelesa looked forward to a peaceful and tranquil day away from work. Willian spent the entire walk looking behind her, and she assumed he didn't want to see the stroller pushed in front of them. Jena entertained herself, babbling contentedly with her 'other self' as she always called her imaginary friend. Chelesa exalted at the serenity of her family.

The park was usually quiet at this time of day since most children were either in school or taking their naps. She chose a spot partially shaded by the trees near the lake. She could see the children playing in the water or on the playground from this vantage point.

After setting Willian down and removing Jena from the stroller, she sat on the bench and said to the children, "Feel free to play with anything that looks fun. When you're hungry, I have a snack for us all to eat."

As usual, the children screamed in jubilation at being free to do whatever came to mind, and they ran toward the swings.

Thankfully, Willian seemed warmer toward Jena as he lifted her into a swing before hoisting himself up into the swing beside her. They pumped their legs and leaned their bodies backward while gripping the chains with white knuckles as they raced to see who could swing higher.

Chelesa kept a close eye on them to see if any intervention would be needed should they lose their grip on the chains. Luckily they tired of the game before any assistance was required, and Willian helped Jena down when she slipped forward and landed on her own. They raced toward the slide and took turns going down.

Finally, the children raced back toward Chelesa and demanded food. Just as she planned, their hunger forced them to take a break. She had already set out the food on the picnic table. The kids eagerly grabbed sandwiches and ate quietly.

Everything was perfect until Willian asked, "Why are those men watching us, Mommy?"

CHAPTER 34

Alarmed, Chelesa's eyes moved, but her head remained still. She discovered at least six men surrounding the park who didn't have any reason to be there that she could identify.

Not wanting the children to do anything out of the ordinary, Chelesa shrugged and answered calmly, "They probably work in the park. Who's ready to go to the marketplace and get some ice cream?"

Just as she planned, the children eagerly nodded in their cute exaggerating way. She packed up the remnants of their meal and settled Jena back into the stroller. Picking up Willian, she again glanced around to see if the men moved any closer.

One or two of them advanced, so Chelesa hurriedly left the park's seclusion to get to a location where there'd be people to come to her rescue should it be required. She accessed her crystal's power to be ready instantly but maintained her calm exterior for the children's sake.

The men didn't seem inclined to follow them to the marketplace, and Chelesa relaxed marginally. She did maintain a vigil for any other suspicious people watching them. Nothing seemed out of the ordinary as they stopped and bought ice cream for everyone at the refreshment stall. Her peaceful day was ruined, but she would make sure her children still had a pleasant day.

They wandered aimlessly through the marketplace, viewing the vendors' different wares. Probably more to ease her guilty conscience more than anything, Chelesa eagerly bought the few items in which the children expressed an interest.

Her mind whirled with an attempt to discern the men's intentions in the park. Should she or shouldn't she mention something to Debbon about it? After quite a bit of internal debate, she concluded she must've been mistaken, and Debbon would only worry about her over nothing.

After all, he bragged about his class making good progress. Maybe he'd return home within a mesan or so. She'd keep up her guard until then.

Really, what could go wrong? She was the wife of an influential society member, and nobody would even dream of hurting her or her family.

She turned the stroller toward home with her newfound confidence and set a leisurely pace. The afternoon was warm, and she set Willian down to walk independently. She held his hand, and her other hand rested lightly on the stroller. Without any warning, a burly man emerged from the crowd ahead of them and ran right into Willian, knocking the stunned little boy to the ground.

Chelesa immediately activated a protective shield around the three of them as she bent to pick up her now-crying child. She held him close and told him everything would be okay.

With Willian safely tucked against her chest, she cast her gaze around to find the dreadfully thoughtless man. He needed to apologize, but he was nowhere in sight. Wanting to avoid any further incidents, she kept the shield firmly in place and rushed home the rest of the way.

Not until she shut herself inside her own house did she begin to feel safe again. The nursemaid met them at the door, and Chelesa gladly relinquished both children. Holding on by a thread, she rushed into her office to have a minor, private meltdown.

Never before was she so scared for her children, but today everything changed. Something was different, forcing her to rely more on her maternal instincts. She'd figure out what was going on, preferably before Debbon got home. She could just imagine his wrath if someone attempted to hurt his family.

Petre sat motionlessly in his cabin, his water craft drifting with the swells in the middle of the ocean. The crystal skull presented itself like an altar resting on the table in front of him, keeping him mesmerized.

Time had no meaning with the crystal exposed to his view. He had no idea he spent more than three days entranced by the samara's powerful pull. Without warning, the crystal released its hold on Petre. His exhausted body slumped forward, asleep before his head thumped down, unresisting to rest on the table.

Dr. Medin spoke up at the meeting's beginning, "We've made some definite progress. Amanda has started to integrate herself into society by getting a job and meeting new people."

"Yes, and she's also feeling more empowered since she learned how to use the powers of the crystal. It's also interesting that her inner child is also becoming empowered." Dr. Gascon read through the accounts of Juila learning to use her skills.

How come Dr. Gascon refused to believe Amanda may have

delivered a child? His insistence on referring to Juila as Amanda's inner child made her grit her teeth, but she held her tongue.

The more details Jasmine heard about Amanda's story, the more convinced she became that she had somehow experienced living with these people during the fourteen months she was missing.

Dr. Gascon insisted everything Amanda spoke of related in some way back to the disappearance of her fiancé, Nealand Taivas. She understood his one-track mind on locating the ultra-rich family's missing son.

Before entering Dr. Gascon's office, she overheard him speaking on the phone. Apparently, the Taivas family set a time limit for Dr. Gascon to give them results with Amanda. Otherwise, they'd withdraw both their finder's fee bonus and their annual contribution to the Cannon Memorial Asylum.

Jasmine heard the unpleasant man's tone on the phone remind Dr. Gascon of the three-week deadline. Amanda had been hospitalized for fifteen days.

Dr. Gascon dropped the file and slammed it shut. He steepled his fingers under his chin, and he leaned back in his chair. The hinges squeaked alarmingly as if in protest of his new posture. "I think we've indulged Amanda's fantasies long enough."

The fanatical look in Dr. Gascon's eyes scared Jasmine. She could only imagine what twisted things he'd do to make Amanda progress faster. They were already meeting with her for more than four hours per day; it was unethical to do any more than that.

The chair continued to squeak as Dr. Gascon rocked gently. His gaze remained trained to a spot on the ceiling. "I'm going to switch Amanda's medication to something stronger and more compelling."

Jasmine shook her head, trying to form a coherent argument to keep him from this dangerous path. "But, Dr. Gascon, I really think she's getting ready to tell us what we need to know. Please hold off changing her medication for two more days. Two days, it's all I'm asking!"

His gaze flicked to Jasmine as if he just realized he wasn't alone. His brows lowered, and his lips curled down in an unpleasant snarl. "It's not your call, Dr. Medin. I'm the Director of this facility, and she's under my direct care. She's young and resilient, and I'm sending in the order today."

"Please, just one day then! Let me have my afternoon session today, and I'll switch my schedule to bring her in first thing in the morning. If I can get her to talk, you won't have to put her at risk!"

His chair dropped forward, and he leaned heavily against the front of his desk. Spittle flew from his lips as he said, "I think it's worth the risk." He inhaled noisily through his nostrils. His glare held Jasmine's eyes, and he added, "But I'll give you until lunch tomorrow. Don't disappoint me!"

Jasmine jumped up from the leather chair across from Dr. Gascon and said, "Thank you! I'll get her right now."

She grabbed Amanda's next dose from the nurse's station before rushing to Room 426. She didn't waste time knocking and burst into the room. "We don't have any time to waste, Amanda. Come quickly!"

Amanda's back straightened where she sat on her bed. One hand reached up and clutched her necklace as if it comforted her. "What's going on, Dr. Medin? Is something wrong?"

"Not yet, but it soon will if we don't get busy. Dr. Gascon gave me until lunchtime tomorrow to get to the bottom of your case. Please hurry."

Jasmine was close to tears with desperation to help Amanda. But she didn't exactly know what she was going to do differently. She didn't believe Amanda knew anything about Nealand's disappearance.

If only she could get Amanda to finish her story. She needed to hear it all before Amanda's rational mind was ultimately lost with Dr. Gascon's new plan.

They entered Dr. Medin's office, and the doctor turned and locked the door behind her. "Make yourself comfortable; we need to get right to business."

Amanda hesitated in front of the couch. "I still wish you'd tell me what's going on. I might be more helpful if I knew what you needed to know."

Jasmine shut her eyes for a moment before she nodded, deciding in that instant to tell Amanda the whole truth. When she opened them, she spoke rapidly, "Nealand Taivas has been missing since you two went sailing. His parents believe you know where he's been taken.

"They've given Dr. Gascon three weeks to find out before they withdraw their financial support for the hospital. You've been here for fifteen days. If I know Dr. Gascon, which unfortunately I do, he'll give you what amounts to truth serum and heavy-duty narcotics to get you to divulge whatever information you know."

Amanda shook her head, her hair flying out in all directions with her intensity. She held out her hands toward Jasmine, imploring her to believe her. "But I already told you Neal's at home. He came to see me at my parents' house right after we got back from the hospital in Mexico. How can he be missing this whole time if we all saw him at my house the day after I returned?"

Jasmine crossed her office and placed her hand on Amanda's bicep. With a gentle squeeze of her hand, she tilted her head and formed a tight line of her lips. She wouldn't keep the truth from Amanda anymore. She deserved better. "I don't know, Amanda. We can only go with what the Taivas family has provided for information. According to them, you're the key."

"Why would they do this to me? I thought they liked me? I was going to marry their son for Pete's sake. None of this makes any sense!" Amanda's fists clenched the cushion's edges as she tried to process this new, bizarre information.

"I'm sorry this news upset you, Amanda. However, now you know what we're up against, so let's get started."

Amanda nodded and wilted onto the couch, her expression desperate and sad.

Jasmine took her place across from Amanda. Modulating her tone, she said, "Relax and take a deep cleansing breath…."

CHAPTER 35

Amanda arrived early for her first day of work. Because her nerves were working overtime, she struggled to sleep all night. She gave up at first light and began getting ready.

Luckily Juila didn't have any trouble sleeping. She was bright and fresh for her day of playing with her new friends. After dropping Juila off at the daycare, she checked in with the front desk receptionist.

The woman's eyes lit up, and she leaned forward with a broad grin. "I'm glad to see you're back!"

Amanda grinned before stating the obvious, "I'm a little bit early. Is there paperwork I need to fill out?"

The girl looked at her strangely and shook her head. "We don't use plasfilm for that anymore. Once we get you to your desk, you'll be able to log in to your patil, where everything you'll need to fill out will be available.

"Riccan's your point of contact for assistance or if you have any questions. I'm sure another office person will be assigned as a back-up, but for now, it's just Riccan."

851

Amanda nodded and wanted to bite her tongue for making yet another stupid mistake. She should've asked Bryon more detailed questions about how business was handled. Hopefully, it would be her last blunder, but only time would tell. "Is Riccan available? I'd love to get settled at my desk and start my job?"

The receptionist shook her head. "No, he got tied up in an off-site meeting, but I can take you to your assigned location. Just one moment while I lock my patil."

Amanda waited while the receptionist tapped out a few keystrokes before she stood. She was taller than Amanda imagined; her shoulders were at the same height as the top of Amanda's head.

"Do you want to take the stairs or the elevator?"

"Stairs, please. I have a little extra energy to burn off before I sit at a desk all day." She looked at her watch, not to mention how much time she had to kill as well.

"Right this way then." She walked briskly toward a side door and held it open for Amanda. She caught up to Amanda on the stairs and continued talking, "Your security badge will be in the top, middle drawer of the desk. It'll give you access to the office area and your patil.

"Your security clearance is pretty broad since you'll be interacting with almost everybody in the building. If you encounter any difficulties accessing any location, simply bring it to me, and we'll get it straightened out right away."

They reached the second floor, and again the woman opened the door for Amanda. Walking past the conference room where Amanda had been interviewed, they continued past several more doorways until they reached the end of the hall.

The receptionist used her security badge to unlock the door, and they entered together as the door slid sideways. Several turns later, Amanda stood in front of her workspace.

Surprisingly, she had a window office with a pretty spectacular view. Eventually, she'd have to find out if she could see her house from here. She realized she didn't know the receptionist's name and felt ashamed of the oversight. To rectify the situation, Amanda cleared her throat and said, "I'm sorry, I never did get your name."

"That's okay; I'm Lana Gurdin. I'm glad to have someone else working here who's near my own age."

"Thanks, Lana. I appreciate all of your help."

"No thanks necessary as it's my job and all." She grinned impishly then continued into Amanda's office. She switched on the patil and opened the desk drawer to show her the badge.

Amanda picked up her first-ever official badge. How in the world did they get her picture on it already? She glanced up at Lana with a puzzled expression as she held out the badge. "How did this happen?"

Lana smiled broadly and said, "We have a state-of-the-art security system that took your picture yesterday when you entered the building and met with me at the receptionist's table. I sorted through each shot until I found one that looked good enough to use on the badge.

"Of course, if I didn't find one good enough, I would've arranged a separate time to get a presentable one. It's one aspect of my job that I love; surprising the recipients with my expediency.

"Go ahead and sit at the desk since the patil's ready for your input. Put your badge up to the screen and wait until it turns green. Okay, now follow the directions on the screen to go through all the forms that need to be filled out and submitted today. Don't let anyone put you to work until all of them are complete, okay?"

Amanda tore her gaze away from the screen to look up at Lana. A grin crossed her lips, and she said, "I can do that; if they want anything from me, I'll send them to you!"

"I like the way you think!" Lana nodded and moved away from the desk. "I'll leave you to it then while the office is still quiet. I'd hurry if I were you. These people have wanted this position filled for quite a while now, so they've got a lot of things for you to do."

"Thanks for the warning! I'll begin right now. Thanks again." It would've been nice to have more time to get to know Lana, but she saw the wisdom of her words. She filled out the biographical form that popped up first.

RICCAN GROANED. He should've been at work when Amanda first got in so he could welcome her properly to the company. With as much dissension as he'd received over his final selection of Amanda, he worried that the other staff members could make her feel less than comfortable.

He insisted that the best-qualified person be hired for the job, rather than just somebody who already worked for the company who wanted the position. He hoped she found the welcome note he left on her desktop. He could do nothing about this emergency meeting other than solve the problem quickly and return to the office to begin her training.

He rushed through the design flaws. He pointed out how to create workarounds so the machinery could at least function until a permanent fix could be made. He should've been consulted over these designs before they went into production.

The design error was so fundamental that it should've been caught by even the most novice engineer at the company. He made a mental note to put in new safeguards because of this incident. At least something good would come of the issue.

Finally, everyone agreed there wasn't anything more to be done at present. He excused himself with the barest courtesy and ran up the stairs to the rooftop where his telepod awaited him. After palming the exterior door, he activated the telepod, verified each green light, and then moved to initiate the processor for mental steering. Within moments he was back in Durseni.

Now more than ever, he was grateful for the ability to land on the top of the office building. He didn't have the inconvenience of waiting for ground transport.

Special flight concessions were made for the Telepod Engineering Company when they opted to build their headquarters in Durseni. Each pilot was skilled enough to pop into existence just above the rooftop landing field, which meant they didn't have to fly over anybody's house to park.

Riccan rushed through the shutdown procedures and left the telepod faster than ever before. He almost wished he had learned to translate himself so he wouldn't waste time taking the elevator down to the second floor.

He scolded himself for the errant thought since it was considered extremely rude to display the talent except in extreme instances. Wanting to greet his new hire hardly constituted a valid excuse to discard his manners. The elevator took forever to get to the rooftop, and he contemplated taking the stairs just as the doors slid open.

He stepped into the elevator and simultaneously pushed the button to the second floor. Riccan tapped his foot and sighed as the elevator car stopped on three other floors before reaching his desired destination. The doors opened slowly, and Riccan escaped with barely enough room for himself. He strode purposefully down the hall and badged his way into the secured section.

Without stopping in his office, he made straight for Amanda's cubicle. He slowed his pace when he saw her alone at her desk. He assumed she was filling out the new employee forms. She didn't seem confused by anything. Riccan let out a relieved breath. Amanda was obviously still at work and had not been made to feel unwelcome.

Once he reached her office, he paused and tapped quietly on

the open door. He smiled when she looked up. "I'm sorry I wasn't here to get you started properly. Did Lana show you everything you needed?"

"I think so. Don't worry about it. I've been busy filling out so many forms! Who knew there'd be this much information needed just to work?" She looked down onto her desktop, picked up the Riccan's note, and remarked, "I got your message. It was a nice touch since you couldn't be here."

Riccan's smile widened, and he took a seat in her office. He pulled the guest chair around the desk until he faced her patil. "Which form are you working on now?"

"Let's see," she said as she scrolled to the top of the page, "this one is for insurance and dependents." She looked over to Riccan and saw him grinning. "What? Did I do something wrong?"

His gaze burrowed into hers. "How long have you been here, Amanda?"

She looked at her timepiece and replied, "Just over an hour. Why?"

"I should've known you'd be early. That's the final form, by the way. It typically takes a new employee until at least lunch to get through them all. Captain Ahn was right about you."

"You're going to have to let me read his letter. These forms aren't hard; there are just a lot of questions. Anybody could fill them out fast."

"That's where you're wrong. Go ahead and finish that one up. When you're done, I'll give you a building tour." He sat back in his chair and watched Amanda carry on with the final form.

CHAPTER 36

Amanda fumbled self-consciously about having an audience while she worked. She may as well get used to it now. It was safe to assume some of them would watch her work while they anxiously awaited the results since she'd interact closely with just about everybody in the building.

Luckily she only had two more questions to answer before finishing with a final tap on the screen to submit the form. The screen flashed green, and then the icons for regular work appeared for the first time. She blew out a long breath and announced proudly, "Done!"

"Perfect, let's take a tour." Riccan stood and waited for Amanda. "Be sure to use your badge to lock the patil every time you leave the desk. We have very sensitive information, and it only takes a second to lock it down."

Feeling as though she'd made her first blunder, she hurriedly held her badge in front of the screen and saw it go blank. Thankfully, she'd seen Lana lock her patil so she wouldn't look like a complete novice in front of Riccan. She turned toward him and followed him out of her cubicle.

He immediately guided her out of the department and to the elevator. "I thought we'd start with the roof," he said as he turned to see her confused expression. He smiled mischievously and pushed the button to call the elevator. "I assume you found out right away about the ban on telepod flight over the island?"

Amanda nodded, "Yes, I was a bit concerned about getting all my stuff from the landing pad to my house. It wasn't as though I wanted to carry everything and Juila, too!"

The elevator came, and they shot up to the rooftop. The doors opened, and Amanda gasped as she saw a fantastic telepod parked. "Wow," was all she could think to say. She looked over at Riccan and noticed his smug expression.

Her reaction was exactly as he planned, and she smiled at his audacity. She moved toward it ahead of him to satisfy her curiosity about the telepod's structure. This design was nothing like any other telepod she'd seen.

If only she could take a ride in it—but that'd be a bit presumptuous to ask. Wishing to see inside, she raised her hand to the palm switch and looked back at Riccan to make sure it was okay with him. After receiving his nod, she reached the rest of the way up and rested her palm over the switch.

The door came forward and rested on the ground to create a convenient ramp to enter into the craft. She peered inside. Several rows of seats covered with expensive fabric, maybe leather, were spaced throughout the open cabin.

She stepped into the interior, ran her hand along the back of one of the seats, and nodded approval at the smooth, soft texture. The interior walls were covered in either fabric or plasfilm, so none of the metal framework showed, even on the floor.

Amanda continued through the cabin until she got to the control panel. It came as no surprise none of the panel looked even remotely familiar. This craftsmanship must be the sort of work Riccan created that made him excited to go to work each day.

She turned around to address him, only startled to find him directly behind her. She stammered and looked away from him quickly. She asked the first thing that came to mind, "I take it this telepod is your own design?"

"Yep, she's my pride and joy. She has all of the latest technology, most of which has yet to be seen by anyone outside of our company."

"I'm honored to be counted in the elite group. This is pretty spectacular." She ran her fingers over the sleek dashboard.

What would Dad say about all of this? He'd be brimming with questions. Her heart constricted just thinking about how much she missed her parents.

Bringing herself back to the present, she tried to focus. Riccan liked to race. She asked, "How fast does she fly?" Her dad would want to know the answer, and she was also curious about it.

Riccan's face lit up as he answered, "Faster than anything out there commercially. I haven't had the opportunity to test her paces, but I imagine she'd surprise everyone.

"I discovered a new way to align the crystals, so they're more responsive even when a lesser crystal is used. The control panel is mainly handled the same way as the conventional telepods, but the displays are all located within the plascreen.

"On other telepods, each function has its own light on the board. This one integrates them all to one screen, so there's less chance of missing something vital. There's even a built-in safeguard against pilot error almost equivalent to an auto-pilot."

Riccan suddenly stopped and swiftly looked at Amanda as though he had said something wrong. His brow furrowed when Amanda continued to look at him as though nothing were amiss.

He cleared his throat and looked away for a second. He shook his head and stammered, "I'm sorry to carry on so about this telepod. I just love talking about her to a new, appreciative audience.

Maybe you can keep that last part to yourself. It's not exactly common knowledge."

Amanda smiled reassuringly back at him and said, "Your secrets are safe with me. Besides, I liked hearing about it even though I didn't understand most of what you described. It doesn't take anything away from how exceptional this telepod is."

She purposely turned away from him to lean toward the front window to envision the pilots' view from the operator seats. "I imagine she must be a dream to fly," Amanda mused as she turned to check out the rest of the interior.

Riccan crossed his arms and leaned against the sidewall. He raised an eyebrow playfully and asked, "Would you like to fly it sometime?"

Amanda turned away from him, knowing her fair complexion betrayed her. She wanted to jump up and down with excitement and take a seat immediately, but that would be inappropriate on her first day of work. She answered, "I've never learned to fly. Although I've enjoyed every flight I've taken."

Riccan replied almost instantly, "I could teach you if you want to learn."

This time Amanda did turn around and look at him thoughtfully. Flying this telepod would be something she could hardly imagine but would love to try. Before receiving her birth crystal and learning to use it, she never would've contemplated the idea. Now, maybe it was within her reach.

She could just see herself telling her father all about learning to control the most advanced aircraft in Tuala. "I'd love it, but I'm sure you have better things to do than teach me. I'd be a dunce for all we know, which would surely be a disappointment for both of us."

Riccan shook his head. His eyes danced with delight as he said, "With what I already know, I'm confident you'd be an excellent student. The offer stands. Just let me know when you want to start.

"As much as I hate to leave my favorite topic," he looked at his timepiece meaningfully, "we should probably continue our tour. Do you want to meet some people and find out who you'll be working with directly?"

Amanda nodded a little less enthusiastically. She preferred just spending time with Riccan, enjoying his easy manner. There was no way around the upcoming meetings, so she was at least grateful for Riccan's introductions rather than blundering through new acquaintances on her own.

They took the stairs down to the thirteenth floor to visit the Executive's offices. Since they were all in a meeting, Amanda met their secretaries, but none of the executives themselves. Amanda was both relieved and disappointed at the same time. Riccan showed her the office of Ela Nena Dunless, the Executive Vice President of Customer Operations—and Riccan's boss.

The next floor down housed several departments, but the most important was Accounting. Riccan described the department's functions as a whole and said, "You'll only be working with the heads of this department since all of the other people report to them anyway. Oh, Teden, I'm glad you're around. This is our new analyst, Amanda. Amanda, this is Accounting Manager, Teden."

Amanda shook his hand and said, "I'm glad to meet you."

The tour continued down to the eleventh and tenth floor, which housed the Business Continuity and Corporate Security and Purchasing departments. Riccan told Amanda she'd most likely not have anything to do with anyone in the first department, but he thought she should at least know its location should anyone ask her for directions. Amanda was happy to meet many people in the Purchasing Department since Riccan had told her they worked closely with Engineering.

They then visited the ninth through the sixth floor in

descending order that housed the fitness center, the cafeteria, Business Development, and a giant conference room where Riccan said they held company-wide meetings.

The fitness center came as a surprise since she hadn't seen one since coming to Tuala. There were many pieces of equipment that she didn't recognize. What could they possibly do? Eventually, she'd have to find out.

Equally impressive was the cafeteria, especially after Riccan told her all of the food was available at no charge for employees. Apparently, the company believed a well-fed employee would be more productive. Amanda agreed with the concept's merit.

The fifth floor held their equivalent to Information Services, while the fourth floor contained both Human Resources and Payroll, both of which Riccan agreed she'd spend a lot of time creating reports for. The third floor had Customer Account Services and Billing, neither of which held any interest in Amanda's job.

They skipped over the second floor since Riccan pointed out they would end there anyway. They took the elevator down to the basement, which was considerably smaller, housing the Receiving Department and their Office Services. Riccan said Amanda's only interaction with Office Services would be to pick up the engineering plasprints and get office supplies.

Together, they returned to the elevator, where Riccan rechecked his timepiece. "Wow, it's lunchtime already. Let's go up to the cafeteria and get something to eat."

Amanda jumped at the chance. "That sounds great. I was afraid you could hear my stomach growling earlier!"

"First test—which floor has the cafeteria?" Riccan pointed to the buttons for her selection.

CHAPTER 37

I t only took her a second before Amanda pressed the button to the eighth floor.

Riccan nodded approvingly and asked, "How did you remember?"

"That one was easy since it's a play on words; floor eight is where you ate."

Riccan laughed out loud at her unexpected answer. "That's a good one!"

The elevator doors silently slid open to reveal a nearly empty room. Amanda looked questioningly at Riccan before asking, "Where is everybody?"

"I thought we should be a little bit early so you could look over the food options before there's a large crowd in the way. Plus, it'll be a bit quieter for us to talk." He walked over to the first buffet line and picked up a plate.

He strolled beside Amanda as she took her time making selections. She asked him what some entrees were but stopped when she recognized his puzzled expression. As far as she knew, they were pretty common and well known. The last thing she needed was for Riccan to suspect her of being an *old soul* and firing her on her first day.

Finally, with full plates, they chose a secluded table for two tucked behind a pillar next to a window. Amanda sat and turned to lean forward to admire the view. "We traveled so much around each office; I'm not sure which direction is which anymore, not that it really matters much, because the view's spectacular."

Riccan said, "You can see the best sunrise on this side and sunset on the other." He picked up his fork and speared a vegetable.

Amanda turned to look at him and said, "Hopefully, you don't see both in one day when you're here!"

His eyebrow quirked as he chewed and swallowed. "It happens quite a bit for me, but I don't mind. I love my job, and the people who work for me are great."

Amanda shook her head. She never understood why people became married to their jobs, especially when they were married. Maybe he was single. She glanced down to his left hand but didn't see a ring. "I'm sure it helps, but surely a family is waiting for you at home."

Riccan grinned, but he glanced down to his plate as if suddenly interested in selecting the perfect bite next. "Nope, no family for me yet. I still have to find the right woman."

Letting out a bark of laughter, Amanda said, "You never will if you spend all your time at work."

Riccan snorted, covered his mouth, and looked sheepishly over to Amanda. "That's the same thing my mother tells me. She's been bugging me for anons to settle down so she can have grand-children."

Amanda raised her eyebrows and pointed her fork at Riccan. "You should listen more to your mother."

"Not you, too! It seems like everyone is ganging up on me late-ly!" Riccan's expression showed mock horror, only partially as a joke by the way his shoulders stiffened, before he started eating his lunch.

Amanda tried to maintain a stern motherly look but rapidly gave it up in favor of sampling the new dishes. Riccan seemed like a lovely man who had a great job. Why was he still single?

Amanda suddenly recalled her daughter's declaration that Riccan was the one who thought she was beautiful. Could he have been waiting for her?

She shook her head at such a ridiculous idea since she planned to go home once she found Jena. Besides, Riccan would want someone closer to his age as he appeared to be around a decade older than herself.

"Is something wrong with your food? You look very serious all of a sudden."

Amanda almost choked at being caught thinking about him. She shook her head and covered her mouth. Once she swallowed, she temporized, "The food was just hot; it's okay now." To add credence to her words, she picked up her glass of water and took a long drink.

Riccan looked dubious, but luckily he didn't press her for the truth. There would be plenty of time to get to know him since she would be working with him so closely during her training period.

She'd only known him for one morning, yet she was eager to see how he worked with the rest of his employees. With Captain Ahn's letter, she wanted to prove herself as the best person for the job, but she also had to prove that she was worthy of Ahn's praise.

"I should probably tell you that there was someone from the office who also applied for this job. There was some tension in the office because I picked you and not her, but as I told my team, I want the best-qualified person for the job. You were that person, and don't let anyone tell you otherwise." Riccan leveled her a long stare.

Amanda almost wished Riccan hadn't told her about the office drama to form her own opinions about the people. However, she supposed it was best to be forewarned of any animosity aimed at her. She was nervous enough about starting her first real job, but now he added the pressure of proving her worth and ensuring she didn't disappoint Riccan or his team.

"Thanks for the warning. I'll do my best to show you were right!" Amanda smiled at Riccan and then resumed her eating. Since she didn't know what she'd be working on, she hoped she was telling Riccan the truth.

Time would tell. Amanda smiled inwardly at how insufficient the phrase seemed in light of her upcoming task.

Riccan set down his fork and leaned against the table. His suddenly serious expression seemed out of place. "I don't know if Lana told you, but I'm going to be your main point of contact in the office. Feel free to ask questions of anyone in the department, but if you get held up on anything, please come and ask me.

"I'll be doing most of your training, but I'll also have Denana show you the final details of working with the standard forms. She wasn't the person who wanted the job, so it should go smoothly."

Amanda's heart raced. She nodded, not trusting her voice until she could compose herself. What was it about working closely with Riccan that excited her so? He was her boss. She couldn't be having feelings for him.

"Lana told me you'd be my contact person, but she didn't say you'd be training me. I hope I learn everything fast, so I don't take up too much of your time. I'm sure you're very busy."

He quirked his eyebrow, and the left side of his mouth turned up. "Don't worry about my time; I'll still get everything done. Are you ready to start learning your job?"

Was he flirting with her? The way Amanda's breath hitched sure made her think it was so. Amanda set down her fork and replied, "As ready as I'll ever get."

They picked up their dishes and deposited them into the automated wash booth before going back to the elevator. Riccan pushed the button on the wall and asked, "So what do you like to do for fun?"

Amanda didn't expect any personal questions. To make matters worse, she suddenly realized she hadn't done anything simply for fun since arriving in Tuala the second time.

Riccan looked at her expectantly, so she hastily replied, "Juila takes up all of my free time. She's just learning how to do everything, and it's been pretty entertaining to watch."

Riccan nodded. "I should've realized that. Where's Juila's father? I don't think I've ever heard you mention him."

Amanda wished she could fall through the floor of the elevator. How could she explain her situation? She looked anywhere but at Riccan, searching frantically for something to say.

Riccan reached out and lightly touched Amanda's arm. "I'm sorry, Amanda. I shouldn't have asked something so personal—especially on your first day. Forget I said anything."

Amanda just barely caught herself from flinching at Riccan's touch. His warmth raised chill-bumps up and down her arm. She managed a weak smile and hoped she didn't just ruin everything.

They rode the elevator down to the second floor in silence and walked side by side down the hallway to their department. Riccan badged the door open and led the way to Amanda's office. "Did Lana show you around the department?"

Amanda shook her head.

Instead of heading directly into her office, he turned to the right and pointed out the department's essential features. She took note of Riccan's office location, thinking it was good for it to be relatively close to her own.

Another important place to know was the bathroom, just beyond Riccan's office. He also showed her the desks of the team members. Luckily, they were eating lunch at this time, so she didn't have to meet anyone personally. The final spot on tour was the break room, where there was a small kitchenette if she wanted to make steena tea or have a cup of java.

They worked their way back to Amanda's office, where she placed her badge in front of the patil screen, bringing it back to life just as she had left it. Riccan sat in the chair on her left-hand side, making Amanda overly conscious of his proximity needed to read her screen also. She'd get used to it once she got to know him better, but she wasn't quite there yet.

"Okay, let's do a quick tutorial through the different programs on your screen. Go ahead and click on this first one."

ALENA HATED the house's loneliness without Amanda and Juila. She actively sought out new patients to keep herself occupied. As a relatively new wise-woman, she should've earned a more extensive client base long before now.

However, she didn't regret the time she spent searching for Jena. Nor did she begrudge her time teaching Amanda and Juila how to use their birth crystals.

As if to compensate for the loss, she spent a considerable amount of time training her children with the elemy. *They needed it to be ready for school*, she rationalized.

The training should've started several mesans before, but again she'd been preoccupied. Alena finally broke down and allowed Kyelon to participate in birth crystal training with Justan and Andera, mainly because they weren't advancing as swiftly as Juila.

Alena didn't want her children to be so far ahead of the other students to make them stand out and feel awkward. Kyelon's exuberance at being included made her feel guilty for denying him the opportunity in the first place.

The children missed Juila almost more than Alena since they had spent so much time with her since birth. Alena ashamedly used the distraction of learning to use their skills to keep them from asking when Juila was coming home. It still hadn't occurred to them that their guests wouldn't be returning.

Dinner seemed to be the second most challenging time for the family. The two empty places at the table were an ever-present reminder, yet nobody wanted to talk about it. Conversations were awkward, mainly consisting of the progress in the children's training and anything interesting going on with either Bryon's or Alena's work.

Not surprisingly, the hardest part of the day came during storytime after dinner. The children stood in front of their parents and sang the Unity Song:

Crystal around the neck,

Follow the next step,

Changes today,

Changes tomorrow,

We all become one.

Andera cried as the song ended. "We're not all one anymore."

Alena held out her hands for her daughter. She hugged her close on her lap, offering both of them comfort. The boys then looked at one another. Alena knew that look. Juila usually sat on Bryon's lap.

Now the spot was conspicuously empty, and they didn't know who should fill it. On the first night of their absence, all the children cried themselves to sleep. Alena couldn't do anything to ease their pain.

After brooding over the idea for several days, Alena sat to employ her memory recall techniques to replay the images she'd seen during Jena and Juila's birth crystal ceremony. She had promised to review everything to see if the images seen were those on Earth or Tuala.

Each image flashed through her relaxed mind as she carefully noted the scenery. Finally, she admitted there were some troubling pictures. She could no longer deny the scenes from Earth and knew both children would one day return to the land they'd never known.

Her heart was heavy with the idea of them leaving. She needed to make arrangements to visit Amanda. Soon. Amanda needed to know.

She imagined Amanda was settled into her house and probably feeling lonely as well. Alena already felt better simply from deciding to visit them.

CHAPTER 38

Rasa pondered the unusual situation about getting a message to Amanda's parents. She couldn't let go of the idea of her unique qualifications to send something through the veil since she was half-Tualan and half-Earthling.

The best possible chance would be to send the message to Shemalla. Thanks to Elder Vargen's confidential, approved plan for the Roswell cover-up, she knew Shemalla's exact location.

Rasa's unlimited security clearance as one of Jehoban's students gave her access to the file. Also, the file contained a picture of Shemalla so Rasa could visualize the recipient as she was sending the message. Everything came together perfectly.

Too perfectly.

She would use distance notation. It was the best method for communicating—untraceable and relatively secure. Now, the only consideration was how to get the message to Shemalla without anyone noticing its appearance.

Shemalla worked at the museum until five o'clock. Rasa figured she'd most likely be home by six. After calculating the time difference between their locations using an advanced formula on the patil, taking into account the possible shift in time between the worlds and Shemalla's particular agreement for slowing time, she determined she'd be able to send the message in approximately two hours.

With so much time left before she'd send the message, she worked on tracing her life-line. Once Elder Debbon explained the process, the actual procedure of finding the life-line was relatively easy. When she started the wise-woman training, she feared that she'd always be the furthest behind since healing had always been so difficult for her to grasp.

Her hope renewed since Elder Debbon expressed the importance of the life-line—the class might not be such a trial after all.

Suddenly Rasa gasped. She made an intuitive leap from her own life-line to Jena's. If her idea worked, she'd be able to link with Juila's life-line and trace it to Jena.

She wasn't sure if linking to a life-line with a distance factor was possible, but she was certainly willing to try. She may find Jena's life-line; however, it still wouldn't tell her the child's location. Her shoulders sagged, and her fingers drummed on the tabletop as she realized her newest idea still wouldn't get Jena home, yet she couldn't let the idea go entirely.

She looked at her timepiece and saw it was late enough to reach Amanda at home. It was well after she would've gotten out of work. Rasa touched her patil screen to initiate a video connection with Amanda. After about thirty seconds, Amanda opened the link on her end, and her image popped up on the screen.

"Hi, Amanda." It still amazed her she had a cousin her own age, and she stared at the screen in pleased wonder.

"Hi, Rasa. How was your day?" Amanda's grin matched her own.

"So tiring! How was yours with the new job?"

A strange expression crossed Amanda's face but cleared almost as fast as it appeared. "My head's still spinning from everything they expect me to learn. I'm sure I'll eventually get it, but I don't want them to lose patience before I do!"

"I'm sure you're doing fine. Hey, did Alena and you get to work on the memorization techniques using the birth crystal?"

"We started it, but I kept getting tired and having to stop. Do you have any suggestions?"

"Sure, we can work on it when we meet again. I think it should be soon since I imagine you'll want to use it for work!"

"That'd be wonderful! I hate having to ask Riccan the same question all of the time. So, what's going on?"

"Well, I wanted to let you know I'll be sending your message to Shemalla in a little over an hour. Hopefully, your parents will have it soon after that."

Amanda leaned forward, her face lighting up. "That's amazing news, Rasa. Thank you for working it all out."

"I still don't absolutely know it will work, but I have a pretty good idea it will. Also, I had another idea I'd like to test." Rasa didn't want to get Amanda's hopes up, but she just had to give this idea a try.

Amanda cocked her head as if weighing the risk before hearing the plan. "Okay, what is it?"

Rasa breathed deeply, deciding where to start her theory to make sense to Amanda. "We were learning about life-lines today in class, and I got to thinking that I might be able to trace Jena's. I'm not sure how it'll help, but I don't want to leave any stone unturned."

Amanda's face brightened again, and she asked, "How far have you gone in the levels of birth crystal training?"

Rasa chuckled before replying, "I've completed them all."

Amanda's eyebrows raised in surprise. "Wow! That must've taken forever. I saw Alena's list of twenty-seven levels, and I only got to ten! And those were the easy ones."

It was Rasa's turn to laugh as she asked, "And how long did you train to get to level ten?"

Amanda blushed as she grasped what Rasa was saying and replied with a chuckle, "We only had a chance to train for five days."

"My point exactly! Many people train for more than twelve anons, and they don't even get that far. You're definitely a natural at it. I think it might have something to do with our heritage, but that's for another time.

"And just so you know, Alena's list is the one given to teachers and wise-women. With Jehoban's class, more than forty items are to be learned. Why were you asking?"

"Oh!" Amanda's surprised expression shifted back to serious, and she replied, "I thought if you could trace the life-line, then you could use the navigation skill to determine at least in which direction she's located. Am I right?"

Rasa considered Amanda's idea for a moment and then slowly nodded. "I think that might just work. I'd like to try an experiment with you first if that's okay."

"I'm at your service, Rasa. Experiment away!" Amanda sat still, staring into the patil.

Rasa nodded and then closed her eyes. At first, Rasa just sat there but then she felt a tickling sensation inside her skull. Rasa knew the exact moment Amanda understood she was trying to access her life-line to determine her location. The tickling dissipated a few minutes later, and Rasa opened her eyes.

"Did it work?"

"Sort of, I felt something. I think I'll have to practice this a little more before trying it on Juila or Jena."

"I'm available whenever you need me."

"Thanks, you know I'm going to take you up on your offer!"

"I know. It makes me feel better about asking for your help. It's the least I can do since I'm taking time away from your studies."

"I'm not even sure if anyone has tried accessing life-lines from a distance. Who knows, maybe I'm inventing a new level for training. Jehoban always said my brain didn't work like anyone else's, which is why He took me on as a student!"

"Were you terribly scared to go train with Him?"

Rasa tapped her lip, considering the question. "I was more curious than scared. I've always craved learning, and I certainly have been able to take advantage of my talent with Jehoban.

"Obviously, I missed home and my family, but Jehoban always made me feel welcome and loved. I'm pretty sure my childhood was as perfect as it could get. I was always safe, loved, cared for, and challenged mentally."

"Have you ever told Barla? She's always wondered if she did the right thing by letting you go."

Rasa's eyes widened. She never would've guessed such a thing. "Really? How crazy! Well, pretty soon, I'll be able to tell her in person. Once I finish my wise-woman training, my studies will be complete."

"Oh, Barla will just love having you home. She's missed you so much, and she always talks about wanting to see you."

"My only regret with my education choice was missing my family. Anyway, it's almost over now. It turns out I'm not as clumsy with healing as I once believed. Maybe it'll be over sooner than I thought." Just saying the words out loud gave her a thrill.

"What're you supposed to do once you're done with school?"

"Jehoban told me I'd have many anons before I have to worry about that part of my life. He wants me to take my time getting to know my family again and doing whatever makes me happy. Once I get tired of the retired life, then Jehoban told me to come back, and He'd give me my life's assignment."

Amanda's eyes widened. "Life's assignment? It sounds so serious! Aren't you scared?"

"No, I'm sure He'll pick something that suits me perfectly." She never doubted Jehoban's plans. He knew what was best for her, and she trusted Him implicitly.

"I hope you're right!"

Rasa grinned, wishing she had more time to speak with her cousin. She glanced at her timepiece and quirked her eyebrow. "Okay, it's almost time for me to message Shemalla, so I'm going to sign off to get prepared."

"Alright, call me again whenever you want to talk."

"I will. Maybe even tonight after I send the message."

"Okay, sounds great. Good night."

"Good night." Rasa disconnected the call and pulled out the sheet of plasfilm containing Amanda's message to her parents. She appreciated Amanda's concise wording without actually telling them there was a problem.

Rasa stood and crossed the room to her sofa. She wanted to be as comfortable as possible to send this message. She couldn't afford any mistakes. This message just had to end up at its intended location and at the right time.

Once she was calm and centered, Rasa practiced pulling up several spheres of elemy. She inserted an object from her room in each globe and then imagined each in another living space location. The globe reappeared where she intended with each effort, with the contents still intact.

Satisfied her control was sufficient, she made a larger globe than her practice ones and inserted Amanda's note. She concentrated on Shemalla's face, location, and time and then sent the sphere on its way.

Usually, there'd be a delivery confirmation, but it felt different going through the veil. She wasn't as confident about the outcome.

CHAPTER 39

Shemalla sat in her dining room, poised to eat dinner alone in the silence. A strange sound came from behind her, and she turned just in time to see an elemy globe appear. More than a little surprised, Shemalla jumped from her chair and reached into the globe to retrieve the piece of plasfilm.

With shaking fingers, she unfolded the note and read:

HI MOM & DAD,

I MADE IT SAFELY. I'M LIVING IN COZUMEL, AND I'M STILL WORKING ON THE DETAILS FOR COMING HOME SO I'M NOT SURE HOW MUCH LONGER I'LL BE GONE. PLEASE DON'T WORRY.

I LOVE YOU!

AMANDA

. . .

SHEMALLA WHOOPED WITH JOY. Finally, there was news to share with Chris and Diane. Since they were moving to New Mexico, maybe this update would make them decide to remain in Florida.

Without another thought for her dinner, Shemalla raced to the phone and dialed the Covington phone number. After what felt like an eternity, Diane picked up the phone.

"Hello?"

"Diane! This is Shemalla." She gripped the phone until her fingertips were white.

Diane inhaled sharply and asked, "Shemalla, what's wrong? This isn't our normal day. Have you heard something?"

"Yes! I just received a note from Amanda!" She read the contents to Diane and waited for a response that seemed a long time coming. "Diane?"

"I'm still here. I'm just processing what Amanda said. I think there's something wrong, Shemalla."

Shemalla frowned, and her gaze traveled over the words on the page. It seemed pretty straightforward to her. "Why would you say that? She said she's coming home; she just doesn't know when."

"It troubles me where she said 'I' instead of 'we' every time. Maybe she hasn't found the girls or maybe something even worse!"

Shemalla sighed before wilting into the chair next to the phone. This call wasn't going at all as she hoped. "Diane, please don't borrow trouble. We don't know anything of the sort except Amanda's safe. Is Chris home?" Maybe he could talk some sense into Diane.

Diane breathed into the receiver. "Yes, let me go get him."

Shemalla winced at the loud clack of Diane setting the phone down and calling for Chris. After a bit of rustling, Chris picked up the phone.

From his heavy breathing, Chris must have come running. Shemalla couldn't understand people who insisted on seeing the bad side of things. Chris must have his hands full with his wife.

"Hi, Shemalla. Diane tells me there's something wrong."

"I was afraid she'd say that. Let me read you the note I just got from Amanda." She paused while Chris whooped with joy. Again Shemalla read the contents of the short note and then said, "I think this's good news. Please talk some sense into Diane. She always looks for trouble even when there isn't any."

"Don't I know it! Thank you for letting us know, Shemalla. This news is a blessing. Have a good night."

"Good night, Chris."

Shemalla hung up the phone and sighed in resignation. Before the call, she had been so excited to get proof of Amanda's health, yet as she considered Diane's comment, she did wonder what went wrong with the twins. They had waited this long to hear any news.

Time would tell what would happen.

CHELESA WAS NOW OFFICIALLY CONCERNED. She refused to let the children leave the estate's grounds until she could be convinced there was no longer any danger.

Since the incident in the marketplace, each time she left the house to conduct her regular business, she had been followed. She valiantly ignored the intrusions, but that became impossible when she was physically attacked.

While not seriously hurt, the message the man whispered to her before he let her go chilled her to the core. She could still feel the man's whiskers on her cheek as he spoke, "Tell the Elder to step down, or your children are next."

She couldn't keep this from Debbon. With how close Debbon felt to the community, he'd understandably be hurt by the violence. Naturally, he'd never step down.

His position was part of his family line, not to mention this was his life's calling, that he'd train Willian to follow in his footsteps.

Of course, being First among the Elders held more responsibility, but Debbon absolutely loved his job.

There was no choice now but to tell Debbon what had happened since he left. She anticipated his anger that she'd waited so long to inform him, but she honestly thought it would subside over time.

Now she was scared. And she didn't want to leave the house for anything. This wasn't any way to live.

Alone in her office, she touched the screen to make the dreaded call. Unsure of Debbon's teaching schedule—he could be in class—she cried out in relief when his face filled the screen.

He smiled brightly and said, "Hi, Chelesa. I'm surprised to hear from you. Is everything okay?"

She blinked, trying to stop the tears from forming. She shook her head and bit her lip. "No, Debbon, we have a serious problem."

Debbon's smile vanished. "What's going on, honey? How can I help?"

Chelesa rubbed a hand over her mouth, and she breathed deeply through her nostrils. "I thought I could handle this situation at home, but today I was attacked—"

"What?! Chelesa, are you okay? I'm coming home this instant!" He didn't bother disconnecting his call on the patil; he immediately translated himself into Chelesa's office.

Debbon rushed forward and pulled Chelesa from her chair into his strong embrace. She melted against him, unable to hold back the tears. He held her tighter and rubbed her back in small circles.

Debbon rested his chin on her head and said, "Start from the beginning and tell me everything."

After quite some time, Chelesa finished recounting everything that had occurred since he left. He remained quiet during her recitation; however, Chelesa felt his anger rippling inside as his muscles tensed against her.

With a deadly low tone, he said, "It's one thing for people to be upset with me for my decisions as Elder, but to resort to hurting my family is the work of cowards.

"Unquestionably, I have to deal with this dreadful problem, but first, I have to ensure my family's safety. We have to send the children away for a while, Chelesa."

She shook her head. This wasn't what she wanted. How could she convince Debbon to change his mind?

Debbon hurriedly continued, "If I can ensure their safety and yours, I can address this problem properly. I can't do anything until everyone who's a potential target is removed from the equation. You know what I'm saying is true, Chelesa."

She hated it when her husband was right, yet she admitted the wisdom of his words. How quickly she agreed only reaffirmed how scared she felt. She pulled away from Debbon to look up at his face. "Where will you send them?"

"Now, don't get upset, but I think the best place for the children will be on Earth."

Chelesa's eyes widened. What was he thinking? "No, Debbon! I won't be able to monitor them there; the link doesn't work the same across the veil!"

Her heart broke just with the idea of losing contact with her children for even a moment, let alone the days or weeks it would take to get this problem resolved.

Debbon held tightly to her arms, shaking her slightly with each word he spoke. "We need them to be safe, and any people trying to hurt them here on Tuala won't have access to a Gate to harm them on Earth. It's the perfect solution."

"Well, then I want to go with them." Chelesa crossed her arms. She'd stay with her children regardless of Debbon's plans.

"You can't go, Chelesa. It'd raise too many suspicions." He paused for a second before adding, "Besides, you always wished you'd learned wise-woman skills, but there were too many demands on your time. Come back to Durseni and train with the rest of the class.

"We haven't gotten too far ahead of where you couldn't catch up. I can keep you so busy you won't have enough time to worry about our children." Debbon slid his hands down her arms until he held Chelesa's hands entreatingly.

"That's not fair, Debbon, to play on my deepest desires."

Pressing his advantage, he added the final touch, "I think you'd make a wonderful wise-woman."

Chelesa's always wanted to have more to offer the people other than her ability to negotiate well. She could help the community as a healer if she learned specialized skills.

Maybe the community would embrace her even more if she could heal them too. She sighed and said, "Okay, Debbon. You can have it your way this time. How long do I have to get the children prepared?"

"I'm going to make the arrangements tonight. The children will be gone by midnight because we'll need to return to Durseni before class starts at eight o'clock in the morning."

Chelesa's expression instantly shifted from resignation to horror at the speed of Debbon's plans. Her whole world would be turned upside down in only a few short hours. Panic enveloped her, and she cried harder than before.

Debbon pulled her onto his lap and wrapped his arms around her. He rocked her back and forth and repeatedly told her it would be okay. For once, she doubted he spoke the truth. This decision hurt too much.

"Chelesa, we have a lot to arrange. Pack some things for the children, just enough for each of them to carry. Then contact all of your appointments and let them know you'll be unavailable for at least two mesans."

She pulled away from his embrace, horror making her voice

sound shrill. "Two mesans! No, Debbon, that's too long. I can't go that long without seeing or hearing from them."

Debbon continued as if she didn't object. "I'll talk with the house staff and let them know the changes that'll be occurring. Then I'll call Elder Vargen to arrange the children's transfer."

Chelesa forgot her initial objections and asked, "Why Elder Vargen? Why can't they go through our Gate?"

CHAPTER 40

Debbon didn't hesitate with his answer. "Because it would be a little bit too obvious. Think about it, if we send them through another Gate, the children will be even farther from danger."

With one last sniffle and several angry swipes of her hands across her cheeks to get rid of the tears, she nodded curtly. "I can't believe people could do this to our family. I'll make them pay for every missed moment with my children."

Debbon inwardly smiled at Chelesa's mood swing. Even though she detested the plan, she finally came to terms with it. His wife was beautiful and intelligent, and he could always count on her doing the right thing even if she didn't like it.

He was asking her to do the ultimate horror of letting her children go, and he thanked Jehoban that he didn't have to do a lot more talking before she agreed. Her easy capitulation only emphasized the level of her fear.

Chelesa stalked out of the room. Debbon didn't have to hold back his grin at her defiance in the face of danger. He switched seats and turned toward the desk to access the patil.

He touched the screen to activate an emergency code to Elder Vargen. As he suspected, Vargen picked up the call almost immediately.

With a smug grin on his face, Vargen said, "Elder Debbon, how may I help?"

Debbon weighed his words. "I'm requesting a confidential transfer for two citizens to Earth."

Elder Vargen's eyebrows rose. "I never thought I'd hear such a request coming from you, First. Are there any special instructions?"

"Yes, they'll need to have caregivers on Earth. I also need the timing to be altered, so they arrive on Earth two mesans from now."

Vargen made notes as the First talked and asked, "What kind of caregivers will be required?"

"Parental guardians. The two citizens being transferred are my children."

Vargen's mouth dropped open before he could stop it. He forgot all protocol as he exclaimed, "Debbon, what are you doing?"

"My family's being threatened, and I'm not able to address the situation at this time since I just started the new wise-woman class for the anon. I need to know my children are safe until I get everything settled.

"Tell me you can make the necessary arrangements before midnight." Debbon didn't ask but demanded that Vargen get it together, or there'd be trouble.

"I understand, First Elder Debbon. I'll take care of everything."

"We'll come to your Gate at midnight." Debbon disconnected the call before Vargen thought of any more questions to ask. He didn't like this solution any better than Chelesa did. However, he couldn't conceive of an alternative in such a short timeframe.

Debbon left the office and asked the head maid to gather all staff for an immediate meeting. Every employee lined up in the grand foyer within ten minutes, wondering what had transpired to bring the Elder back home without warning.

"We have a serious situation on our hands, and I'm going to need everybody's cooperation. Chelesa has notified me there have been threats against our family, which can no longer be ignored. We have decided to take drastic measures to ensure everyone's safety.

"Before midnight, both children will be sent to a safe house. We won't be disclosing their location for obvious reasons. Furthermore, Chelesa will be returning with me to Durseni, where she'll enroll in the wise-woman training for this anon."

Several of the staff were clearly stunned at the suddenness of the Elder's plans. They exchanged glances nervously as they comprehended the danger must have been much more significant than Chelesa led them to believe if the Elder were willing to break up the family.

The head maid, Crysta, asked, "What can we do to help, Elder Debbon?"

Debbon was again grateful to see how flexible his staff could be and simply replied, "Keep all visitors out of the house. Cancel all engagements planned for Chelesa or the children.

"Ask Chelesa what she needs help with and do it immediately. She's already upset enough and probably about ready to break with the stress. Please don't take anything she says tonight personally; she's not thinking rationally. That is all for now."

Each staff member looked over at the head maid for their next assignment, and Debbon appreciated her efficiency in delegating tasks to each person. Within moments the foyer emptied of everyone except for Crysta. "Are there any special instructions for me, Debbon?"

Debbon felt an easy friendship with Crysta and was thankful she was in charge of all details. She had worked for his family for over twenty anons, and he knew he could trust her implicitly.

He gestured for her to follow him into the office, and he shut the door behind her. "I'm sending the children to Earth. I know it's extreme, but it's the only place I could think of where they'd be out of the reach of the hoodlums threatening us here on Tuala."

Crysta hid her shock quite well as she just nodded in agreement. "How long do you think they'll be gone?"

"I just don't know, and that's what kills me! Hopefully, it'll only be a couple of mesans, but it could take up to an anon to get this mess taken care of after I'm done training this blasted class!"

The more he thought about this situation, the angrier he became. He didn't want to lose a moment more than he had to of training time with Jena, and now this!

"I'll go check on the children and see what Chelesa needs." Crysta curtsied and let herself out of the room soundlessly.

Debbon watched her leave and wished he were in his own office so he could throw something. He hadn't resorted to physical violence since he was a teenager, yet he could feel the desire creeping up on him.

To calm himself, he performed the exercise of tracing his lifeline and linking directly with the elemy. When he felt the connection, he knew he possessed nearly limitless power.

Somehow it was enough to know he could do anything yet keep himself restrained. After inhaling a deep breath and letting it out slowly, he felt centered again, ready to take on the world.

He left the office and ascended the stairs. Debbon wanted to spend as much time with the children as he could before sending them away. His head ached. How could they create a link between themselves and the children that would work well across the veil?

Debbon cursed the situation. He'd make these hoodlums pay for forcing his hand in taking such drastic measures without adequate time to perfect the arrangements. The plan needed to be enacted tonight, or their unknown 'enemy' would have a chance of finding out their strategy.

The peacefulness of Tuala was shattered. This threat created a foreign tension for his family.

Debbon's steps were heavy on the stairs. His children were the innocent victims in this mess. How were the children supposed to understand why these changes were made so fast? Debbon hoped the experience wouldn't permanently scar them.

Debbon stood in the playroom doorway and watched Chelesa pick out toys for the children to take with them. Both Willian and Jena watched their mother with concerned expressions on their faces.

Chelesa had obviously been crying, but she was trying to put on the bravest face for her children, but it looked like it didn't fit too well. The children were unconvinced.

He walked into the room and announced, "Daddy's home!"

As expected, the children ran squealing over to Debbon. He scooped them both up into his arms and announced, "You two are going on an adventure tonight!"

"Where are we all going?" Willian asked seriously.

"This is something only children can do," Debbon made up on the spot. "Willian, protect Jena since you're older. We're going to take you to a special place where you'll be going to another place to live for a while."

Willian's brows furrowed low over his eyes. "This doesn't sound like an adventure. It sounds like a punishment. I don't like it already."

"You two aren't in trouble, Willian, so don't scowl like that. Mommy's going to come to school with me. And you two are going to learn some new things in another house for a while."

"How long?" Willian demanded.

"We're not sure. Wise-woman classes can take several mesans." Debbon struggled to keep his tone light since his son was noticeably not buying his cheerful act. Jena just looked back and forth between her father and brother with a concerned expression and a trembling chin.

Willian said, "Why do we have to leave tonight?"

"So your mother won't get any further behind in class. We started at the beginning of last week, so she's already missed several days of important training. She has to catch up."

Chelesa stalked out of the room to gather clothing for the children in their bedrooms. Even though Debbon could no longer see her, he heard her slamming clothing into Willian's small bag.

Moments later, she crossed the hallway and performed the same task in Jena's room. As she left Jena's room, Debbon sauntered toward her from the playroom, still carrying both of their children. Chelesa announced in a forced cheerful tone, "I've finished packing for them."

Debbon nodded and said to the kids lightheartedly, "Let's play in the living room for a bit. I've missed you both!" He turned toward the stairs, looking back over his shoulder, his gaze imploring his wife to follow soon.

CHAPTER 41

Elder Vargen's unexpected and outlandish request shocked Shemalla to the core. Nobody ever sent anyone to Earth for protection, let alone two children.

One thing was sure; the children couldn't stay with her, which meant she would have to make other arrangements immediately. Racking her brain, she realized she still needed to call Chris and Diane for their regular monthly update.

She picked up the phone to make the call. She snapped her fingers with glee and dialed faster than ever before. Not only would these two children be the perfect distraction for Diane, the Covington family already knew about Tuala.

There wouldn't be any need to explain why the children might do odd things. This had to work since she didn't have any other options.

Diane picked up the call on the second ring, "Hello?"

"Hi, Diane, it's Shemalla." She didn't have to pretend enthusiasm while addressing Diane.

Diane spoke immediately, "Is there any news?"

"Nothing from Amanda, but I do have an interesting problem that you might be able to help me out with."

"Color me intrigued. You've never asked anything of us in the two years we've been working with you. What do you need?"

"Elder Vargen just told me there are two children from Tuala who require protection. He's sending them to Earth and asked me to find parental guardians for them. Do you think you and Chris could watch them until it's safe for them to return?"

"Wow, that's different! Let me ask Chris, just one moment." She set the phone down and left the room.

Shemalla heard their muffled, yet animated, conversation in the background.

Diane returned to the call and breathlessly said, "We can do it! When will we get them? How old are they? Are they boys, girls, one of each?"

Shemalla laughed at Diane's eagerness and answered, "One of each. The boy is approximately four years old; the girl is almost two. Once the children arrive, I'll bring them to Florida by tomorrow." Shemalla held her breath, hoping the rushed timeline wouldn't scare Diane out of accepting.

"So soon? Wow, okay! What're their names?"

"The boy is Willian and the girl—now don't get excited, Diane —her name is Jena. It's a pretty common name, and this brother and sister are both children of Elder Debbon and his wife, Chelesa."

Diane inhaled sharply and exhaled loudly in the receiver. "I'm glad you forewarned me of the coincidence. Okay, I'll have everything ready. This house has seemed so big since all of our kids grew up and flew the coop. I'm so glad we didn't downsize now!"

Diane paused, then lowered her voice to ask, "What exactly is the story about these kids? Are they okay?"

"I don't really know. I've never heard of an Elder going to such drastic measures to keep his family safe, so it must be pretty bad. Hopefully, the children don't know anything about the danger."

"I hope so too, but I'll be gentle with them just in case. I'm sure they'll be scared enough as it is—being taken away from their home so abruptly."

"You're probably right. Okay, I'll see you tomorrow."

"Thanks, Shemalla."

"No, thank you, Diane. You're doing me a huge favor!"

Juila fussed, refused to play with her toys, and didn't want to go down for bedtime. She ignored all of Amanda's distraction attempts. Even though exhaustion had set in long ago, Juila remained awake but unresponsive.

Amanda was at her wit's end as to what could keep Juila from sleeping. She was usually such a good girl with bedtime. Tonight something was obviously bothering Juila, but she refused to talk about it with her mother.

Finally, Amanda rested on her own bed and snuggled Juila down next to her in hopes she'd eventually tire enough to be put into her crib.

Midnight rapidly approached, and Debbon mentally prepared himself to translate his family to Elder Vargen's Gate directly. He wasn't about to take any chances with public transportation; everything would happen under their own power in their own home.

He held Jena in his left arm, and Chelesa held Willian in her left arm. They both had a small satchel slung over their other shoulder containing the children's clothes and toys that would be their only comfort from home while they were on Earth.

Debbon and Chelesa faced one another in his office, moving together until their whole bodies touched with the children sandwiched between them. Debbon put his arm around his wife as she did the same to himself.

They both nodded their readiness when the elemy rose to enfold them all. Debbon sensed Jena's curious touch and hoped she wouldn't learn how this was done until she was older. Knowing her penchant for anticipating his action, he decided to quickly perform the transfer before she could get any more ideas.

Three seconds later, they arrived at Elder Vargen's Gate.

Debbon glanced around and spotted Vargen hovering near the room's entrance they now occupied. Lifting his chin, he addressed his fellow Elder, "Is everything ready?"

He gave a curt nod. "Yes, First. Leave the children where they are and quickly exit so they can be transferred immediately."

Debbon set Jena down as Chelesa did the same with her son, placing the satchels onto the children's backs. As they kneeled on the floor, Debbon said a quick prayer to keep the children safe on their journey.

Debbon double-checked the satchel's straps on Willian's back, fussing to hide his doubt about his plan as he spoke to his son seriously, "Please take care of Jena until you come home. Promise?"

Willian's lower lip trembled even as he nodded and reached over to hold Jena's hand. His fingers turned white as he held her tightly.

Debbon placed his finger under Willian's chin, tipping his face up until his son's eyes met his. "We'll see you soon, don't cry. We love you both! You're going to go through this Gate and begin an adventure. When everything's ready, we'll bring you home."

Taking hold of Chelesa's arm, he pulled her up and away from the children. They rushed away from their children, Debbon holding onto Chelesa's elbow to keep her from turning back to the kids.

It took all of Debbon's reserve to prevent himself from doing the same. They passed Elder Vargen in the doorway and heard a whooshing sound just before a bright light lit up the corridor.

AT MIDNIGHT, Juila screamed uncontrollably, causing Amanda to check for any physical injuries on her daughter. Nothing! Horror filled her heart. She kneeled in front of her daughter, holding both of her arms in her trembling hands. "Juila, did something happen to Jena?"

Juila continued crying, even as her terrified gaze didn't leave Amanda's. After several minutes, she finally caught her breath. "She's gone. I can't feel her anymore."

Amanda couldn't breathe. Her heart lurched painfully in her chest with her daughter's simple yet profound statement. Only one scenario came to mind that could possibly sever the bond the two girls shared, yet it wasn't anything she ever wanted to contemplate facing.

She held Juila close to her chest. Her hot tears soaked into Juila's hair, but her whole body felt cold.

JENA WOULD'VE BEEN SCARED if she weren't so intrigued by the power she felt in the Gate. Why did Willian insist on squeezing her hand so hard?

The brightness diminished, and the children blinked like owls caught in a spotlight. A woman came toward them.

She kneeled in front of them and smiled. "You must be Willian and Jena. My name's Shemalla. It's time to begin your adventure."

She looked from one set of big eyes to the other and finally took the little girl's free hand and stood. "Let's get going. I'm sure you're both exhausted."

She took them to her car, where she tried to take the bags from the children. Willian clung to his with all of his strength. "No, it's my responsibility to watch these!"

"As you wish," she easily replied as she buckled them into the back seat. Shemalla imagined the boy probably liked to feel the last connection with his parents by maintaining contact with the bag.

She walked around the car and got behind the steering wheel. "There're going to be many things that'll seem unusual at first. Feel free to ask me any questions if you want." She started the engine and drove them to the airport. Their flight left in less than an hour, so she needed to hurry.

The drive was relatively short, and Willian asked, "What kind of telepod is this?"

"This isn't a telepod, honey. It's what we call a car. In this part of the world, we don't have any telepods, just cars."

"That's not true, lady. Telepods are everywhere on Tuala!"

"True, but we're no longer on Tuala. We're now on Earth. We don't have telepods anywhere on Earth."

"Where's Earth?"

"It's hard to explain, but let's just say it's the same place where you were, but once you went through the bright light at the Gate, it made it different."

Willian didn't have any questions to refute her strange statement, so he asked, "Where are we going?"

"We're going to take a ride in an airplane, which is sort of like a telepod but much slower, and I'm taking you to some people who'll care for you until you can go back home."

Willian nodded. "I'm glad you know we're going to return home. I was worried my father lied to me, and we were being sent away forever." He looked over at Jena and said, "Don't cry, Jena. It's okay, Jena. I'm going to keep you safe."

Jena's tears streamed down her cheeks, and she whispered, "I can't hear my other self anymore. She's gone!"

Shemalla watched the exchange in her rearview mirror. Willian's eyebrows furrowed at Jena's bizarre declaration before he turned to look out the side window and let her cry in peace.

CHAPTER 42

Diane paced and fidgeted as Chris and she waited for Shemalla to call and say they landed safely. The children would be exhausted and need to go to bed right away. She fussed with their bedding until Chris made her stop.

Diane rounded on her husband. "Maybe something went wrong. Why hasn't she called yet? Should we go down to the airport to wait for them?"

"I'm sure everything's fine. They probably haven't landed yet. If we go to the airport, we won't be here to get her call. Please sit."

The last thing she wanted to do was sit, but once she really looked at her husband's furrowed brow, she knew he was just as nervous. She sat next to him and held his hand. He squeezed it while they smiled at one another.

They never imagined they'd take in two children, yet here they were doing just that. Not just any children either. These were kids from where their daughter's adventure began. This experience would be perfect practice for when Amanda brought their grandchildren home.

The phone rang. Diane jumped up as though spring-loaded.

897

She picked up the receiver before the first ring finished and said, "Hello?"

"Hey, this is Shemalla. We've arrived safely, and I think we'll just grab a cab to your house. These two are exhausted, and I think it'd be faster."

Diane clutched the phone tighter and swung around to face her husband. Her heart raced. In a few minutes, they'd have these two mysterious children. From Tuala. A place she hardly even dreamed could be real. "Okay, do you have our address?"

Shemalla's voice sounded tired and almost impatient. "Yes. We'll be there in twenty minutes. Bye."

"Bye."

Diane turned to put the phone back on the receiver. She breathed deeply, restraining the impulse to jump for joy. Having these children was filling a void she'd carefully disguised.

Feeling marginally composed, she turned back to her husband and said, "They're taking a cab. Oh, Chris, they're going to be here in twenty minutes. Do you think we have everything ready?"

Chris's mouth tipped up on one side. "Diane, everything's been ready since about half an hour after you got off the phone with Shemalla yesterday!" His grin morphed into a full-blown smile to take the sting out of his words.

He grabbed her hand and pulled her down into his lap. He snaked his arms around her waist and pulled her close. With his chin tickling her neck, he said, "I imagine this'll be the last time we have any privacy for a while."

Diane couldn't let herself get distracted. "I hope I got everything Willian will need. I've never raised a boy before. I'll need your help with him!"

Chris leaned back and cocked his head to the side. "We aren't raising them, Diane. We're just watching them for a little while until they can go home. You can't think of them as ours to keep. You'll remember that, right?"

Diane bit her bottom lip and gave a curt nod. "Of course, Chris, but they'll need to feel safe and loved while they're here. I'll treat them like they're family until they get to go home."

Chris continued looking at her with concern. "I hope you're not using these children as substitutes for our lost grandchildren; this could go wrong on so many levels.

"It's too late now to change our minds. But I'll watch and keep you safe from more heartache."

Diane cocked her eyebrow before looking away. She couldn't face Chris's scrutiny. He knew her too well.

After what seemed an eternity, the unmistakable growl of a car's engine sounded from their driveway. Diane practically ran to the front door, opened it, and stepped outside into the night's warm weather.

Even though he professed reticence, Chris practically tripped over her heels in his haste. Diane wasn't fooled; his actions spoke louder than his words.

Chris rushed over to help Shemalla extract the sleeping children from the cab. He pulled out his wallet and paid the fare to stay until Shemalla was ready to return. She had already told them she'd have to go straight back to the airport for her return flight.

Chris took the little boy's limp body from Shemalla's arms. He leaned toward Shemalla and whispered, "Wow, he's pretty heavy despite how small he looks. You made him look light as a feather."

Speaking even quieter, even though Diane blocked the driver's line of hearing, he asked, "Do your people have a denser body structure than people from here? Will it become a problem if they have to go to the doctor?"

Shemalla reached into the cab and brought out a couple of duffle bags and a little girl with blonde hair curled in ringlets. Diane gasped in surprise at the sleeping girl's beauty, not to mention how eerily similar she appeared to her own daughters.

She looked down at the boy and couldn't discern much resemblance between the two kids. Willian's dark hair and olive-colored skin were so opposite to Jena's coloration.

They entered the house, with Diane leading everyone into the little girl's room first. She turned down the sheet and gestured for Shemalla to put the girl into the bed.

Diane fussed with arranging the covers over the sleeping child in the dark room. A few moments later, they went to the next room down the hall and did the same thing for the boy.

Diane could hardly contain her questions until the door shut. "Will there be a problem if we need to take the children to the doctor or hospital?"

Shemalla looked back and forth between Diane and Chris. "No, why should there be?"

Chris tipped his head toward the driveway and said, "As I said, the boy's way heavier than someone his size should be. There must be something different with people from Tuala, and I don't want to bring unwanted attention to either of them."

Shemalla placed her hand on Chris's arm and shook her head. "Physiologically, our bodies are identical to yours. There won't be any problem with that count. There may be some difference mentally since they can probably access the elemental energy in the earth through their birth crystals. You may see them do some strange things, but it's normal."

"Normal for you! What if they do something in public that we can't explain? Can't you keep their birth crystals for them until they're ready to go home?" Diane already imagined the predicaments the children could get them into.

Shemalla edged closer to the door, clearly eager to head back to the airport. "That's another thing; their birth crystal can't be removed until they turn eighteen. It's their protection. Nobody can remove them, not even the children themselves."

Chris's tone was laced with sarcasm. "Oh, that won't seem

strange at all. Shemalla, is there anything else we're going to need to know?"

Diane could imagine all sorts of strange conversations stemming from these two fosterlings. She kept her mouth shut, not wanting to aggravate Chris further.

Shemalla's hand rested on the doorknob. "No, Chris, other than a few things seeming odd at first, they're just scared little kids who've been suddenly removed from their loving family and moved to a strange place with strangers taking care of them. I'm sure you'll do fine!"

Chris's aggressive stance melted away. "I'm sorry, Shemalla. I wasn't being fair. We'll do our best for them, and hopefully, their home situation will get resolved soon so they won't have to be separated for very long."

Diane rushed forward and hugged Shemalla before she could turn to go back to the cab. "Thank you for bringing me these children. I'll keep them safe until they can go home again. I'll love them like they're my own grandchildren!"

Shemalla said, "I'm sure you will. That's why I asked in the first place. I've got to go. Call me if you have any questions." She walked out the door and let herself into the back seat. She waved just as the cab pulled out of the driveway.

ONCE THEY REACHED Durseni and finally went to bed, Chelesa cried herself to sleep. Debbon rubbed her back comfortingly until her sobs finally subsided into the heavy breathing of deep sleep.

Going against his own rules, he used the tiniest amount of elemy to help his wife fall asleep faster. She probably hadn't slept very well from the moment he left the house to begin the training session.

Finally, time slowed, allowing him a blessed moment to think. How well would Chelesa learn to become a wise-woman? She always wanted to train for it when she first finished her post-education.

Because she never actively pursued it, he questioned whether or not she possessed the right aptitude for healing. He'd certainly find out shortly. Grinning at the new challenge, he rolled over on the bed, preparing to get what little sleep was still available before morning.

AMANDA TOSSED and turned more than she slept, eventually giving up altogether when the first light touched her bedroom window. If only she didn't have to work. Her mind was too sluggish to think straight.

One thing she absolutely must do was leave a message for Rasa to find out what Juila's statement at midnight had really meant. She refused to believe her daughter could have died during the night; there must be another explanation.

After turning on her patil, she walked into the kitchen to get herself a cup of java while she waited for the patil to boot up. Her mind wasn't clear enough to use the elemy to create the java, so she employed the old-fashioned method of making it by hand.

Knowing she could go home soon, she'd no longer have the luxury of using elemy to create anything since her powers would be nearly non-existent. She reasoned Shemalla could still access the power because she was a Tualan native, but she'd return to nothing as a native Earthling.

As soon as Amanda realized her abhorrent line of thinking, she banished it from her mind. Jena wasn't dead. She wasn't lost forever. And Amanda certainly wasn't about to admit defeat.

She strolled back to the patil with the cup held directly under her nose. The stimulating scent helped her gather her thoughts. Good, the patil was ready.

She carefully sat and took a sip of the java. "Ouch, ouch, ouch," she said as the liquid burned her tongue and the roof of her mouth. She set the cup down next to the keyboard to cool.

Amanda pushed the instant message icon and spoke, "Rasa, something strange happened last night. Juila lost her connection with Jena. I'm not sure what it means, but I hope you'll have some suggestions. I'm terrified. Please get back to me soon. I love you! Bye."

She finished her cup of java slowly as she considered all of the possibilities for Juila's reaction the night before. She really couldn't convince herself of anything concrete. Maybe a shower would help to clear her mind. Amanda rinsed out her cup and headed to the bathroom.

The shower proved nearly as effective as the java. She woke Juila and got her dressed.

Hand-in-hand, they strolled silently toward the Telepod Engineering Company building, both too preoccupied with their thoughts to attempt small-talk. Juila's brow furrowed, making her look upset. Maybe she was trying to re-establish a connection with her sister.

Amanda resisted the urge to pepper her with questions. Maybe she didn't want to know the answer—not if it meant –nope, she wouldn't even consider that possibility.

CHAPTER 43

Amanda should've stayed home. Her job seemed even harder to navigate that day. She figured out how to access her home account from her work patil, and she checked it often to look for Rasa's reply.

Riccan took one look at her and scowled. Amanda cursed her easily read face. What if Riccan asked her about her distraction? What could she possibly say that would make sense?

Amanda did her very best to avoid making eye contact with Riccan, and he must've gotten her message loud and clear since he shied away from her.

She struggled with items she breezed through the day before. If she didn't get her act together, she might not have to worry about returning the following day.

When Amanda finally appeared in his office, he didn't beat around the bush. He said, "What's going on, Amanda?"

Amanda twisted her fingers until the skin turned white, but she kept Riccan from seeing how hard they were shaking. Her gaze remained fixed on the front edge of Riccan's desk. He gave her the perfect opening, but the words were harder to speak than she expected.

"I have a family emergency. Would it be okay if I took the rest of today off?" She asked in a rush before she chickened out. Her problem was too significant to let go until later.

Riccan's chair squeaked as he hastily leaned forward. "Sure. Can I help in any way?"

"Sorry, no. I have to go. Thank you, Riccan." Amanda raced out of his office and down the hall to the back stairway Riccan showed her the week before. She knew she'd have to answer for her abrupt departure, but she'd worry about that later.

She couldn't wait for the elevator. Rasa's message said she had time to meet with her and Juila right away if she could manage it. Amanda would've quit her job if they didn't let her leave. She'd be there no matter what.

She rushed into the daycare and signed Juila out. The surprised attendants handed the little girl over to her.

"Is everything okay?" the woman asked.

"Yes, thank you," Amanda said, tucking Juila onto her hip as she retreated from the noisy playroom.

Amanda carried Juila down the street as fast as she could without running. The last thing she needed was to draw even more attention to themselves.

Rasa suggested they meet at the rental house as Juila would be most comfortable there. She must have found a solution to what Juila had gone through the night before. Amanda wouldn't let herself think otherwise.

They rounded the last corner and spotted Rasa just arriving at their house. Whew, she hadn't kept her waiting. Amanda jogged the last little bit to meet up with her cousin.

"Thank you for agreeing to come," Amanda said as she unlocked the front door and threw it open. The cool air rushed out to greet them, practically inviting them inside. Amanda gestured for Rasa to precede her into the house. Once inside, Amanda set Juila on the floor and headed straight for the kitchen to get three glasses of water.

"I hope you didn't have trouble getting away on such short notice," Rasa said from where she sat on the couch.

"Riccan was confused, but he didn't hesitate to grant my request. He's pretty amazing, considering how little he knows about me." Amanda set the glasses down on the coffee table within easy reach and sat on the couch beside Rasa. Unable to contain her curiosity, Amanda asked, "Did you find out something?"

Rasa reached over and clasped Amanda's knee. "No, but I wanted to be in physical contact with Juila to check if I can feel the same thing I felt before when holding her in the marketplace. My abilities are much stronger, so I might feel something even if Juila doesn't anymore."

Thinking Rasa's explanation sounded reasonable, Amanda picked up Juila and set her in Rasa's lap. Juila's unusual quietness and withdrawal hurt. Amanda hated seeing her bright little girl so listless. Rasa just had to feel something. Anything! She sat quietly and watched as Rasa began her examination.

AT FIRST CONTACT, Juila's fathomless sorrow almost kept Rasa from delving any deeper, but her intuition insisted she keep going.

She located the child's life-line and traced it to the earth's core energy. She kept following the line of elemy for what felt like forever, further than she even thought possible.

Suddenly there was something else, a separate spark that was Jena. It wasn't powerful, but she couldn't feel any sickness or danger, just separation. A vast distance separated them, and Rasa hoped she could re-link the two girls again.

Rasa came back into Juila's mind showing Juila the faint spark.

Instantly, Juila responded to her sister's energy, and the bond visibly grew.

How did Juila manage it so effortlessly? Rasa could only assume it was her desperate need to have her sister with her that made it possible. Finally, Rasa left Juila's mind and smiled with relief at Amanda.

"Jena's okay! She went somewhere last night that moved her really far away—farther away than I can even imagine. The link was still there. It was just weaker than they were used to. When I showed Juila where Jena was, she strengthened the bond all on her own. I think she'll be much happier because she has her sister back."

Tears of joy sprang to Amanda's eyes as soon as Rasa confirmed Jena was still alive. Amanda flung her arms around Rasa and let the tears flow. "I'll keep searching for her. Thank you so much, Rasa.

"As soon as I have both girls again, I'll do whatever's humanly possible to get them back home to Earth right away. Too many crazy things have happened to my kids here in Tuala, and I'll only feel safe once we're all home with my parents."

WHEN CHELESA AWOKE the following morning, she tried to access her children's birth crystals. She fought back the threatening tears; they wouldn't help, and they wouldn't bring back her kids. The empty feeling almost undid her resolve to carry on as though everything was normal.

Nothing would be normal until her children were back in the safety of her arms. She missed them more than she ever imagined possible.

She couldn't do anything for her children, but she could take advantage of this unexpected opportunity. She'd learn everything she always desired but never believed within her reach. She showered and dressed in record time and surprised Debbon with her cheerful greeting.

"Good morning, Debbon. Did you get me the set of books I'll need for class?"

Debbon blinked twice before he managed to form an answer. "They're over on the table. Are you really doing okay, honey?"

"Don't look at me like I'm about to fall apart. I won't. I'm making the best of this horrid situation. I'll devote all of my energy to being your best student. If the class graduates together or not at all, I have some serious catching up to do.

"I still have a little time before class starts, show me the topics you've already covered, and I'll read through them."

He jumped up from his chair and met his wife at the table. Opening the top book in the stack, Debbon flipped to the table of contents and pointed to the first two subjects. "We started class with healing ethics and responsibilities. Then we switched to this next book—" He pushed the first book away from the stack and opened the second, "where we covered chapters three and six on diseases and mental illness." The second book was shoved aside, and he opened the third book covering anatomy and physiology.

"We've covered the first four chapters on anatomy. The last thing discussed and practiced in class was regarding the life-line." Debbon pulled the last book from under the anatomy book and flipped to the section discoursing the benefits of healing using the life-line.

Chelesa glanced from the books to Debbon, laughed, and asked sarcastically, "Is that all?"

"I know it's a lot to cover, but you can do it. I just wish we could've started you with the class so you wouldn't feel such pressure to get caught up. We can still call this off if you want." Debbon stepped back and looked at Chelesa with a strange expression.

Chelesa knew that look. He wanted to give her the option to

bow out, but he didn't really want her to. She didn't intend to let this opportunity slip past her.

Besides, what would she do all day if she didn't go to class with him? Her options were to sit around the dormitory or return home to an empty house with some unknown people carrying out a nefarious plot against her family still lurking in their community.

"No, I'm not going to quit now; I've had a lot of experience reading through boring contracts. I can tackle this project even easier since it's at least interesting. Don't worry; I'll be fine.

"Now, leave me alone for a bit so I can get started. Come and get me when it's time for us to leave."

Chelesa picked up the first book Debbon opened and sat in the chair at the table. Using the speed reading techniques she developed over the anons, she rapidly turned the pages as she read through the ethics section.

She finished reading the portions of the first book and forced herself from continuing to the next section.

Closing the book with great reluctance, she picked up the second book, thumbed over to chapter three, and flipped through the pages with equal speed. She had just begun chapter six when Debbon cleared his throat to catch her attention. Chelesa looked up with a frown and said, "Is it time already?"

"Yes. I see you've made some decent progress. Do you have any questions so far?"

"None about the reading, but I'm sure I've missed some pretty important class exercises. When do you think we'll have time to go over those?" Would her new class resent the fact she was getting special treatment by starting late in training? She wanted her skills to prove that she was worthy of the honor to the other women.

"We can work on those in the evenings after class. Sometimes students will come over and work on things they still have trouble processing, so it won't be any special benefit if that's what you're thinking."

Debbon knew her mind so well she sometimes wondered how often he was using his mind-reading skill. He swore he never used it on her, but she thought he might not even know he was doing it during times like this.

She smiled at him and said, "You know me too well, Debbon. Let's go so that we won't be late. Which books will I need for today?"

Grabbing the anatomy book from the table, Debbon offered his arm to her. She was in high spirits to be with Debbon. Being away from him was the most challenging part of teaching these classes. Since they were together, she was instead looking forward to letting the course take as long as it would.

Chelesa took hold of Debbon's arm to keep herself from trembling for her first day of class. Her mind raced through the many things she had just read and prayed the rest of the reading would go as easily.

She hoped she wasn't too far behind. She didn't want to hold up the class—if she could've finished the assigned reading. That was a futile thought, and it didn't help soothe her tattered nerves.

She would stay focused on what she could do, not what she hadn't done yet. Chelesa smiled at her husband as they left their apartment to begin her new adventure.

CHAPTER 44

Diane awoke from her abbreviated night's sleep, refreshed and eager to begin this new journey. She anticipated and prepared for the children, hoping to alleviate their confusion over waking up in their new surroundings.

Before showering, she checked on both kids. She opened first Willian's bedroom door and peered around the door's edge to the dim interior. He was fast asleep. Quietly closing the door again, she moved down to Jena's room.

Diane peered in on the little girl she had barely seen the night before. Her hand flew to cover her mouth, muffling her surprised gasp. The light from the window just touched her blonde curls and gave enough light to highlight Jena's delicate and beautifully familiar features.

Without even realizing it, Diane found herself in the room right next to the bed. She kneeled and intently studied the little girl's face.

She couldn't shake the nagging feeling. This child was her granddaughter, as impossible an idea as it may seem to everybody else. The fact that she shared the same name probably didn't help the matter either.

One of her children had had blonde hair, although Amanda's had been almost black. She recalled Amanda's description of her children—blonde hair and vibrant blue eyes.

Diane could hardly wait for Jena to wake up. Chris might deny it, but if this child's eyes were blue—well, she'd wait and see.

Exhaling with resignation at the delay, Diane quietly left the room. She went back through her bedroom to enter her bathroom. As she showered, she kept seeing Jena with blue eyes and prayed it would be true.

She'd have to keep her thoughts on this matter to herself, or her husband would most definitely find a way to send the kids somewhere else. These children would stay with her if it were the last thing she ever did.

She finished rinsing her hair and body before turning the water dials off. Today would be a new beginning for their family. After quitting her job, she'd balked at the delay in moving, but now the timing seemed perfect.

They'd have to delay moving until the children could go back to their own home. Secretly, Diane hoped it would be a very long time before the situation in Tuala was resolved. She wanted to get to know these Tualan children and discover the differences Amanda spoke of herself.

Diane's motherly instinct told her to check on the children. She dressed hurriedly and went again to Willian's room first. She opened the door—the bed was empty. She hastily scanned the room and found it too was abandoned.

Not bothering to shut the door, she raced to Jena's room and flung the door open. The little boy sitting on the bed looked up, eyes wide with fear.

"I'm sorry to startle you, Willian. My name's Diane. We didn't get the chance to meet last night since it was late and you both were sleeping when you arrived. It must've worried you to wake up and not know where Jena was. Am I right?" She used a gentle tone with the little boy. She could have kicked herself for scaring him before they even had a chance to meet.

"Jena's still sleeping," Willian stated as he looked over at her. "I'm supposed to keep her safe until we get home."

Diane's heart almost shattered at his sad tone, but she nodded and said, "That sounds like a perfect job for a big brother. I'm sure you'll be very good at it."

Willian nodded seriously.

"Are you hungry? We can get something to eat while Jena finishes resting." Clearly, Willian didn't want to leave her alone now that he was awake. She quickly changed her mind and said, "Or, I could go get us something, and you can eat in here to keep an eye on her. Does that sound better?"

Again, Willian nodded and replied, "I like that idea. Thank you."

Diane smiled warmly and left the room. She didn't like leaving him alone since he was awake, but she supposed she'd have to get used to it. The children were bound to have slightly different sleeping schedules given their age difference.

She went to the kitchen before realizing she didn't know what they usually ate for breakfast. Making up her mind, she pulled out a box of Apple Cinnamon Cheerios and poured them into a bowl. She added milk and a spoon and rushed back to the bedroom.

She handed him the breakfast bowl and watched while he tasted the Cheerios for the first time. His face showed comical expressions as he tried to decide if he liked or hated the food. Deciding it was good enough, he hastily ate the rest.

"Thank you," he said as he returned the bowl to Diane. "What was that?"

"It's called Cheerios. Is it something you'd want to eat again?"

Willian hesitated as he considered her question. "I'm not sure yet, but I think so."

Diane leaned against the dresser and asked, "What do you normally eat for breakfast?"

Willian brightened immediately. "Usually fried foxl and eggs with toast. Do you have anything like that here?"

His expression was so hopeful Diane hated to have to tell him no. She recalled Amanda's description of foxl and thought beef bacon might be a comparable alternative. "I think we might have something similar. I'll have to call Chris to pick some up on the way home tonight, though."

Diane hadn't considered the food the children would eat. She assumed they'd eat what all her children had eaten growing up.

Now she realized she'd have to find out what types of food they preferred from the children. Maybe a trip to the supermarket sometime in the next few days would be in order. She'd have to see how well they settled in before planning an outing with them.

Willian interrupted her thought by asking, "What should we call you?"

"I guess you could call me Grandma or Diane. Whichever you prefer." Secretly, she hoped they'd pick Grandma since she already felt as though they were hers—well, at least Jena. She didn't quite understand how Willian fit into this picture. "My husband's name is Chris, but you could call him Grandpa."

Willian thoughtfully nodded as if considering his choices. "I'll decide after I have the chance to talk it over with Jena." He looked down at Jena as if willing her to wake up. He squirmed where he sat, obviously uncomfortable.

Diane knew the signs of a youngster needing to go potty, but she gathered he didn't want to leave Jena alone. Thinking rapidly, she said as offhandedly as she could manage, "I have to take care of your dish. It'll take me a few minutes. Jena can stay asleep alone if you want to use the bathroom down the hall."

"I'm fine, thank you."

Of course, he didn't want her to know he'd leave her unattended. Diane left the room without looking back. She took her time in the kitchen and smiled when she heard the toilet flush, followed by the patter of tiny feet racing back into Jena's room.

Some things never change with children, no matter what world they were born on. However, based on their conversation, Diane understood what Amanda said about how advanced their language and motor skills were even at a young age. How would Jena fit the description since she was even younger than Willian?

Diane puttered around the house, cleaning various items while giving Willian a chance to relax in his new surroundings. She kept her ears perked for any whispers from Jena's room. Eventually, she heard the two children murmuring with one another.

Desperately wanting to go in and see Jena, she restrained her urge to allow them some privacy. This first day must be so difficult for the displaced kids. Bless their little hearts.

Indeed by now, Jena would be getting hungry. She knocked quietly on the door and let herself into the room. "Good morning, Jena. I hope you slept well. I'm glad Willian was here when you woke up so you wouldn't be scared.

"Is everyone ready to get up and see the rest of the house? Willian, why don't you show her where the bathroom is so she can take care of her needs?" Diane tamped down her excitement when Jena looked up at her with vivid blue eyes, exactly as she suspected.

Willian's gaze cut to hers when he realized she knew he'd taken a bathroom break from his vigil with his sister. He helped Jena off of the high bed and led her by the hand out of the room. Willian stood guard outside the door until he heard the toilet flush. He opened the door and helped her reach the sink to wash her hands.

From watching the two children work with one another, Diane realized she had forgotten how short children were and their need for stools to reach things like the bed or the bathroom sink. She made a mental list of things they'd need to buy to make the kids' stay more convenient. Willian wouldn't always be around to lift her to reach the faucet, or maybe he would!

Diane led the way to the kitchen with the children following like sweet ducklings behind her. She lifted Jena to the chair at the bar. "Do you need help, Willian?" she asked, even as he scrambled up to the seat by himself.

"I gave Willian a bowl of cereal for breakfast. What would you like to eat, Jena?"

"I like oatmeal," she said quietly.

Diane's heart almost burst. Hearing Jena speak for the first time was music to her ears. She turned to the pantry and opened the door to see if they still had any oatmeal.

Just when she was almost ready to admit defeat, she saw it on the top shelf behind another box. On her tiptoes, she caught the canister's edge and brought it to the front of the shelf. She carried it into the kitchen and showed it to Jena. "Is this what you want?"

Jena nodded enough for her precious curls to bob. She didn't keep eye contact but swiftly looked down at the counter. Her shyness was exactly like Amanda's at that age.

CHAPTER 45

Diane hid her concern for these poor children by reaching down to get a saucepan out from under the stove. If only they were already settled in and happily running around, yet she knew it would take time—time she didn't want them to have to endure.

Once the water was set to heat on the stove, she measured out the portion needed for one child and then asked, "Willian, do you want some oatmeal as well?"

"Yes, please."

These children's manners made all the other kids she knew look really bad.

She leaned her elbows on the counter to bring her to eye level with the kids and asked, "What do you like on your oatmeal? Fruit, milk, honey?"

Willian didn't hesitate to answer, "I like mine plain, and Jena likes hers with honey. Why does it take so long to make?"

She looked over her shoulder to the pot. The burner was red, but the water was still far from boiling. "I imagine it's the same amount of time as at your house."

Willian adamantly shook his head and declared, "Ours is ready as soon as we ask for it. Mommy makes it with the elemy. Why don't you?"

Diane's mouth formed an oh as she realized what Willian was suggesting. It sure would be nice to do it, as he said, but she answered, "We don't know how to use the elemy here, Willian. Do you know how to use it?"

He shrugged. "A little."

She pointed toward the pan and said, "Do you want to show me what you know?"

Willian nodded toward it and said, "Your water's boiling."

Diane opened her mouth to deny the possibility when she turned and saw steam pouring out from under the lid. She whipped her head back to face him, her eyes wide with astonishment. "Did you do that, Willian?"

He frowned. "You asked me to show you."

Her lips drew back, and she winked at him. "I guess I did! That's wonderful and so helpful, too!"

She knew at that moment she would have to talk to the children about keeping their powers only inside their house. She could just imagine the trouble created if anyone found out what these children could do so effortlessly.

If the children could use the elemy so easily on Earth, was it possible anyone from Earth could learn it as well? She knew this was a topic that Chris would be eager to learn and terrified others would find out.

She took the oatmeal and poured it into the hot water, set the timer for six minutes while moving the pot to a cool spot on the stove with the lid back on to finish cooking the hot cereal.

She resumed her position in front of them and asked, "What do you two like to do for fun?"

Willian's expression turned hard, and he glared at Jena as he said, "I used to play with Mom and Dad until Jena started training with Dad. Then I hardly ever got to see him. Now both our parents are off to school, and I won't get to spend any time with them."

Diane was surprised to see the jealous look he gave his sister. As much as she wanted to ask Jena about the training, she thought it might be wiser to ask, "What did you usually play with your parents, Willian?"

He smiled brightly and replied, "We played lots with blocks, cards, telepods, and pillow fights."

Diane smiled back at his renewed enthusiasm and said, "I think we can play those things, too. Well, we don't have any telepods, but we can probably improvise something else."

Finally, the children ate their oatmeal which Willian seemed to think tasted much better than the Cheerios. It didn't take them long to finish, and they watched as Diane washed their dishes and set them in the sink to dry.

"Since you're done eating, let's take a tour of the house!" Diane helped Jena down from the chair and watched Willian launch himself from the tall stool. The children didn't say much as she showed them each room and explained their uses.

The tour ended with them going out into the backyard's bright sunshine. Thankfully, they never removed her children's playset and joyfully watched as both children raced toward the swings. This was the first time she saw their real personalities. Hopefully, they'd keep feeling free enough not to be scared.

RUALIN'S continued lack of updates irritated Petre beyond measure. Didn't that man understand the importance of maintaining harassing actions against Elder Debbon and his family?

Petre changed his ocean course to arrive at Rualin's port before the day's end. He needed some good news about how well their plan was working. He'd either have his custody returned when it was finished, or the Elder would have to step down from office. Either scenario pleased him.

Ensuring his concealment cloak was secure around his water craft, Petre tied up to the dock and hopped onto the worn pier planks. He strolled up to the house and knocked loudly.

Expecting a quick answer at the small hovel, Petre's impatience spiked when nobody answered the door. He knocked again, louder this time, and continued to wait with rising anger.

"Rualin! Answer the door!" Petre hollered. What if Rualin spotted him coming up the walk and simply ignored him? No, he refused to be dismissed so easily.

Without waiting for an invitation, Petre turned the knob and found it unlocked. He thrust it open hard enough to hit the wall behind it. The hinge cracked, and the door hung at an odd angle, but Petre dismissed it entirely.

Rualin was nowhere in sight, but it looked as though he had recently eaten a meal.

Petre stalked out of the house and around the corner, yelling, "Rualin!"

A bush rustled behind the house, and Rualin came forward, his face reddened and his fists clenched tightly. "Shut up, Petre! What are you doing here? I'm sure everyone within half a gania could hear your bellowing. I thought I made myself clear the last time you came here that you're not welcome at my home!" His toes nearly touched Petre's, and spittle flew from his mouth with every word.

Petre ignored it all, not allowing himself to get distracted from his goal. "I came for an update, and then I'll be on my way." Petre calmed considerably since finding Rualin. He used his vast manipulation skills to make Rualin cooperate with his pleasant request.

"Ha," Rualin scoffed, "your plan fell to pieces once Chelesa and her brats went away!"

The sound of Petre's pulse rushed in his ears. Indeed, he didn't hear Rualin correctly. "Went away? What are you talking about? She can't leave her post, and one of those 'brats' is my daughter, so I'd be careful if I were you!"

Rualin's shoulder hit Petre's as he rudely brushed past him. "Whatever, it doesn't matter now, they're gone, and there's nothing more to be done."

Petre whirled around and stalked after him. He grabbed Rualin's arm and roughly turned him around to stop him from going into his cabin. "Where did they go? Have any of your men talked with the house staff?"

Rualin's eyes narrowed as his gaze traveled from Petre's hand to his face. "Yeah, but it won't do you any good. Chelesa sent the children somewhere safe, and she went to Durseni with her husband to train with the wise-women."

Petre's grip tightened as his desperation grew. "Where did they send the children?"

"I don't know. One of the men said some garbage about them being sent to Earth, but nobody honestly believes it exists. I've told you everything I know, so get out. It's time you left!" He pulled away from Petre's grasp and crossed the threshold. He attempted to close the door, but the broken hinge protested. Rualin growled.

Petre's heart sank with the statement about Earth. He, for one, believed in its existence, yet he didn't have any way to get there, nor did he know where to look if he could go.

Without wasting any more time on Rualin, Petre turned back toward his vessel. He would pay Debbon a visit on Durseni. If he sent the children away, he could certainly bring them back.

CHELESA'S ARRIVAL with Elder Debbon shocked the entire class, even more so when Rasa heard she'd be joining their elite group.

She looked around the classroom, judging the sentiment in this new twist to their cohort.

She saw a mixed reaction ranging from joy because the students would forever have a tie with Elder Debbon's family and jealousy that Chelesa was offered a special dispensation to join the class quite late. Rasa hoped Chelesa could catch up, or she could find herself among a group of resentful women at being delayed in their education.

Chelesa chose her seat with all eyes watching her. She looked worried about something. If both Elder Debbon and Chelesa were here, where were their children? Had something happened to the kids to make her look so sad?

Rasa dragged her gaze away from Chelesa to study Elder Debbon. He seemed as composed as ever, maybe even slightly excited to have his wife attending the class, and they didn't have to be apart.

What an unusual turn of events. Rasa sat back in her chair, her mind working overtime. Would she ever find out the real reason for Chelesa starting the class in such an unorthodox manner?

CHELESA SPENT every waking moment catching up with the missed classes. Her hard work paid off since she was now on track with the other students, if not slightly ahead.

Debbon took time in the evenings to test her skills and ensure she achieved the same competencies as her contemporaries. She no longer felt undeserving of being included in the group, and she believed her cohorts felt the same way toward her.

After so many weeks of studying in the confines of their apartment, she felt she had earned herself a break. She'd treat herself to an outing to enjoy the heat and crowds at the marketplace.

The sun neared the horizon, but at least an hour remained

before darkness would force her to return home. She looked forward to the ocean breezes cooling the land. She strolled along the sidewalk and appreciated the scenery.

Since her abrupt arrival on the island, this was her first opportunity to see the landscape, buildings, and population. She missed her regular public interactions. Her shoulders relaxed, and the tension seeped out of her as she encountered more people closer to the marketplace.

She took particular notice of a woman ahead of her who carried a small child. Chelesa yearned for her daughter, who would be the same size as this little one—they even shared the same curly blonde hair.

She watched more intently and wished the girl would turn around to get the crazy idea out of her head that she saw her daughter in the stranger. As if her thought was broadcast, the little girl turned to look directly at Chelesa.

Chelesa gasped aloud and rushed forward to confront the woman carrying her child. Debbon insisted her children were sent to Earth, yet Jena was right in front of her. "Excuse me," Chelesa harshly spoke as she neared the woman.

CHAPTER 46

The woman stiffened, and her hold on Jena tightened. Chelesa wanted to rip her daughter from the stranger's grasp, but she restrained herself by sheer willpower. The lady turned and said, "Yes, may I help you?"

Directly in front of the woman and child, Chelesa realized that this girl wasn't hers. They appeared identical in looks, but this child politely smiled at her as though she didn't know her.

Jena would've been enthusiastic about reuniting while this child just held on to her mother and stared at her. She tried to come up with something to say and finally asked, "How much farther is it to the marketplace?"

The woman's wary expression cleared when she smiled and replied, "It's just down the next block. You're almost there. Have a great evening."

Chelesa watched the pair walk down the sidewalk and turn to go inside a house. She couldn't shake the unsettling idea that there was something very wrong with this situation.

The relaxing and peaceful evening she promised herself was now full of questions. Who was this girl, and is she somehow related to Jena? Was it just a coincidence she saw her or was something else happening?

Once she got some much-needed supplies from the vendors and returned to the apartment, she'd discuss this disturbing matter with Debbon.

JUILA'S deep depression now seemed like a distant memory, which lightened Amanda's heart and allowed her mind to clear. She didn't know what it was like to have a twin, but she could imagine how difficult it would be to lose one.

She'd be forever grateful for Rasa's ability to re-establish the connection for Juila. Juila blossomed when she communicated with her sister.

Amanda returned to work, slightly embarrassed at making such an abrupt departure the previous day. She didn't regret doing it since it made a difference for Juila.

Riccan politely nodded at her and said, "Is everything okay with your family?"

She nodded, her cheeks heating. Please don't ask me anything more, she pleaded without words. Thank goodness he didn't push to get an explanation, yet she should probably tell him something even though nothing came to mind that would make any sense to a stranger. She let it go.

He didn't press for more but continued to train Amanda at her desk.

More times than she could count, they talked about things other than work during her training sessions. They had quite a lot in common. They both enjoyed learning about alternative power types, although Riccan was considerably further ahead in his learning than Amanda could imagine. She looked forward to their conversations and eagerly awaited him strolling over to her desk every day.

The weeks sped by, and although she required Riccan's assistance less in getting her job done, she found Riccan still came to her desk just to talk. What were the other office personnel thinking about his attention?

She didn't really care. Let them say whatever made them happy; it didn't affect her.

Since she began working, more than one person gave her the cold shoulder, and she didn't have time to worry about their petty games. She enjoyed her job, and she was pretty adept at it.

Eventually, although grudgingly, she won over all the Engineering Department staff. Her cheerful attitude and ability to get all of her work done even without her co-workers' assistance, who should have helped her, let them know she was the best person for the position.

Each day she was more and more thankful for allowing Rasa to program her mind to remember details. They both agreed it would take too long for Amanda to master the skill on her own to be of any benefit for learning her job.

Then one day, everything changed.

Riccan leaned against the doorframe to her office, his arms crossed over his chest. "Do you want to go out to dinner?" he asked.

Amanda's initial response was to refuse, but she paused before answering. Would it be a bad idea? She enjoyed his company, and it'd be nice to have a friend closer to her own age. "I'll have to bring Juila, of course."

A smile lit up Riccan's face as he realized she agreed to go out with him. "That's perfect. I love little children." He clapped his hands as though her answer surprised him. "Great, let's go after work tonight. Does that work for you?"

Seeing his nervous energy made Amanda feel better about

agreeing to go. "Sure, I don't see why not. I don't have any other plans."

The workday flew by, and Amanda's curiosity about where they'd go to dinner plagued her thoughts. She'd never eaten at a restaurant in all her time in Tuala.

The question of whether Amanda should go to Riccan's office was answered when he showed up at her desk just as she badged her patil off. She grinned at him and said, "I'm ready to go whenever you are!"

"Great! Let's go pick up Juila and get out of here! I'm so hungry I could eat a horse!"

Amanda looked at Riccan with a strange expression. Typically she would've thought nothing of him using the phrase, but she remembered Alena's reaction to her saying the exact same thing.

Where would Riccan have heard such a thing if not from Earth? When the opportunity arose, she'd ask him about it. She smiled up at him, and they walked down the back stairs to the daycare.

With Juila in Amanda's arms, she said, "The three of us are going out to dinner. What do you think?"

"Riccan has the same color as you, Mommy," Juila whispered loudly.

Amanda hastily glanced over toward Riccan to see if he overheard while also wondering what her daughter was talking about. Riccan spoke with one of the daycare staff and missed the comment. She shrugged and turned to leave the building with Riccan. Sometimes her daughter said strange things, yet she hoped they'd start making sense one of these days.

Riccan playfully wiggled his eyebrows at Juila and asked Amanda, "Do you want me to carry Juila?"

Amanda's heart stuttered. It was so lovely to have a man offer to help her. She shook her head. "No, I've got her. It feels good to hold her after being apart all day."

Riccan just smiled at the two girls and led the way down the street. "I hope you like the restaurant. I come here pretty often. The offering of a great place to sit and eat or go to the bar to get a drink is a good combination for any mood I might find myself in. Today's definitely a sit-down dinner night, preferably in a nice quiet corner booth."

He clapped his mouth shut, but the definite spring in his step spoke volumes. Amanda nuzzled Juila and hid her grin. He was just as nervous as she.

Maybe this was a lot more than just a simple dinner. She envisioned settling down with Riccan, and she hoped he felt the same. As this idea finally formed in her mind, she recognized she'd have to talk to his boss at work.

This situation might get more complicated than she wanted or needed. After all, it wasn't like she was planning on staying in Tuala forever. Her life was on Earth. Was it fair to let Riccan think there could be anything between them?

Was she reading too much into this dinner invitation? Did he have any intentions toward his employee? It'd be bad business if he started dating her while she reported to him. She reeled herself back to reality. She'd enjoy the dinner and good company and let the rest work itself out.

Once they arrived at the restaurant, Riccan held the door open for Amanda and Juila to enter ahead of him. Amanda appreciated the gesture and liked how he could take care of them both. Riccan walked around Amanda to the hostess station and requested a particular booth he preferred.

The girl set them up without any delay where he wanted to sit. Juila was given a booster seat so the tabletop wouldn't be at her mouth level. As this was Juila's first time eating in a sit-down restaurant, Amanda hoped she'd be on her best behavior.

Amanda's evening went nothing like she'd planned when she went to work that morning. Unlike other evenings, this one included laughter and entertainment. Riccan was very solicitous of Juila. He wasn't doing it just to impress Amanda; he was genuinely interested in the things Juila thought and said.

The meal was as excellent as Riccan had promised, and Amanda was full even though Riccan pulled out the dessert menu. "Oh, Riccan, I'm quite certain I can't eat another bite."

Suddenly, a commotion in the bar caught just about everyone's attention. Along with most of the other dinner patrons, Amanda looked to investigate and then froze. Fear and apprehension made her skin grow cold, and her heart galloped hard enough that Riccan could probably hear it.

Her first thought was Juila. She could hardly believe the commotion's cause was none other than Petre MacVeen! How could he possibly be here on Durseni when so many people were looking for him? With alarm, she looked toward Juila and announced, "Riccan, we've got to leave right now!"

The easy and relaxed mood from the entire evening evaporated in an instant as Riccan acknowledged Amanda's fear. Without waiting for the waiter to bring their final bill, he took a handful of taj and dropped them on the table. "Let's go!"

Amanda went to grab Juila, yet Riccan was faster. She thought she should try to take her back, but then realized Riccan and she could exit faster if she just followed them. She raced out the side door and into the night with a final glance over her shoulder toward Petre.

Her heart thumped erratically in her chest as the tendrils of terror raced through her at how close she and Juila had been to Petre. If that wretched man discovered anything about Juila, she was at risk of being abducted. Nothing would make her feel safe at this point except the sanctuary of her own home.

"Where do you want to go?" Riccan asked as they walked briskly down the sidewalk back toward their work.

"Home! I just want us to get home."

He nodded. "I'd give Juila back, but I think you need to work through whatever scared you. Plus, we'll make better time if I keep her with me."

Amanda opened her mouth to reply but just as quickly shut it. If he still had Juila, then she'd have a great excuse for him to go with her to her house. Even though her mood shifted so suddenly, she hoped she hadn't ruined her friendship with Riccan. He deserved an explanation, and she desperately didn't want to be left alone until she knew Petre didn't follow them.

Amanda's fear drove her instinctively to take the lead. Riccan kept pace with her, and they nearly jogged along the neighborhood streets with only their footsteps and heavy breathing to break the silence. Okay, only her heavy breathing; Riccan didn't appear winded even though he carried Juila's extra weight.

After about ten minutes, they reached the quiet, older neighborhood. On the doorstep, Amanda paused. "I hope our evening isn't over. Do you want to come inside?"

Riccan grinned and brought Juila through the doorway.

Did she just make a huge mistake by letting Riccan glimpse inside her world? Until Rasa could do more to locate Jena, she didn't know how long she'd need her job. But, at this moment in time, she didn't care about the job. Riccan could help keep them both safe if Petre came calling.

CHAPTER 47

Amanda was distracted enough she didn't even consider asking him to leave. She was grateful to have another adult in the house with her for protection; just the thought of Riccan leaving for the evening made her panic. She took Juila from his unresisting arms and announced, "I need to get her changed for bed."

"Would you like me to go now?" Riccan took one step toward the door, clearly intent on leaving as soon as she turned her back.

"No! I mean, please stay." She hurried from the room, knowing her cheeks blazed red at her sudden outburst.

Juila spoke for the first time, "Riccan will stay if you ask him to." She didn't appear alarmed at their flight from the restaurant or through the streets to get home. Strangely, her calmness was almost unnerving.

"Juila, sometimes you scare me with your insight. I love you." She hugged her close before setting her down on the bed to retrieve her pajamas from the dresser drawer.

It was only a few minutes before she had Juila changed and settled into her bed; bedtime was usually a long ritual of stories and glasses of water. She seemed relatively acquiescent, which alarmed Amanda as well.

Juila's gaze managed to hold Amanda's with its intensity. "I love you, Mommy. You can trust Riccan."

Amanda's head tilted. In nearly a whisper, she said, "What are you saying?"

True to her strange ways, Juila grinned and rolled over onto her side. Tucking her fists beneath her pillow, she said, "Goodnight, Mommy. Riccan is waiting for you."

Amanda gave Juila another hesitant glance for being intentionally obscure. Juila's statement rang true—Riccan was waiting for her.

She'd stalled long enough. She turned out the light and shut the door quietly behind her as she returned to the living room.

"Do you want a glass of water or pika juice?" Amanda asked as she approached Riccan.

He stood directly in front of her patil at the dining room table and swiftly looked up at her question, "Pika juice would be great. Hey, it looks like you have a message on your patil."

Maybe Rasa had thought of some new way to track Jena, yet how could she explain it to Riccan? While she was intensely interested in checking her patil, she instead used the elemy to get two glasses of pika juice and have them appear at the table in front of them.

"Thanks," Riccan said as he picked up the glass and took a sip. "The brisk walk made me thirsty. Do you want to talk about what just happened? You don't have to if you don't want to, but I'm a safe person to talk with."

Thinking of Juila's last statement about trusting Riccan, she decided to come clean—at least where Petre was concerned. "Let's go sit and be more comfortable; this is a long story."

Riccan raised an eyebrow, clearly interested, and he moved over to the couch as requested. He took another drink of the juice before setting it on the coffee table and looked patiently at Amanda.

"A couple of anons ago, I had an accident that left me stranded in the ocean. Luckily I was rescued from the water and nursed back to health after my head injury. I had lost my memory, and nothing seemed to make sense.

"After quite a few weeks, my memory returned, and I found myself being held against my will. Eventually, I managed to escape, and then I was rescued again by a shipping vessel.

"When I was brought to shore, I was introduced to Captain Ahn. He gave me a job until I could get back on my feet and agreed to help me find my missing fiancé."

"I did wonder how you came to know Ahn."

Amanda noticed how Riccan tensed at her mention of her fiancé. She hurried on with her story before she talked herself out of finishing.

"Well, I didn't get to work for him for very long because we found out the person who held me captive on his water craft was then telling everyone I was his wife. He wanted me back.

"It was a lie, obviously, and Captain Ahn helped me go into hiding. I went to live with Bryon and Alena Kesh. It was at their home where I found out I was pregnant." She paused to gauge his reaction to her story so far. His shocked expression told her that her story took a different angle than he'd expected.

"Anyway, to make a long story short, I had identical twin girls."

"What happened to your other girl?" Riccan blurted.

Amanda sighed and said, "She was kidnapped. I've been looking for her ever since."

"So what happened at the restaurant?"

"Before I answer your question, let me tell you one more thing. My fiancé swore we never had sex, and the children couldn't be his.

"It was quite a while after his declaration when I had to admit I was raped while held captive and incapacitated with my head injury."

"What? Who did that to you, Amanda? I'll kill him!" Riccan started to rise from the couch and stopped when Amanda gripped his forearm.

"Please stay seated, Riccan; there's more."

Riccan was undecided whether he should sit or rush into action. He stared at her for a few seconds before loudly exhaling through his nostrils and sitting again. His muscles remained tense, but he nodded for her to resume her story. "I'm sorry, go ahead."

"We're not sure, but we think the man who abducted Jena, that's my other daughter's name, doesn't know she has a twin. I'd like to keep it that way as well."

Riccan looked confused. He said, "Let me see if I have this right. You don't want to deal with the man who kidnapped your daughter to save your other daughter from him? How are you going to get Jena back without confronting the man?"

Amanda sighed as she realized this was rapidly becoming a more complicated explanation. Almost as though she were changing the subject, she asked, "What do you think about what people say about the *old souls*?"

It was about the last thing Riccan expected her to ask based on his startled expression. "I believe wholeheartedly in them. Why?"

Relief rushed through Amanda, but she had to push him a little further. "What makes you believe, Riccan?"

He sighed and nodded. "You must promise not to share what I'm about to tell you, okay?"

It was now Amanda's turn to be surprised by the unexpected shift in the conversation. "Okay, I promise."

"My grandfather's from Earth."

"Is that a bad thing?"

Riccan looked at her strangely and said, "Some people would say so. Their son, my dad, was chosen by Jehoban to train with

Him. My dad is now an Elder. If people knew he was partly an *old soul*, they'd probably have him ousted from his office."

"I'm pretty sure Jehoban would have something to say about it since He's the one who would've appointed your dad as an Elder. If it didn't matter to Jehoban, why should the people care?"

"The people have some strange ideas about *old souls*. There's a lot of fear where they're concerned, which, strangely enough, is fostered by the other Elders. Anyway, now you know why I believe in the people from Earth. Why did you need to know?"

"Because that's part of the complication I'm running into in getting Jena back."

"What's the complication?"

Amanda sighed and finally said in a rush of words before she chickened out, "I'm from Earth."

Riccan stared at her and then pointedly down at the glass of pika juice. "You have to be mistaken; I saw you use the elemy to get us juice. People from Earth aren't able to do those things. I don't understand, Amanda."

She pulled the crystal up from beneath her shirt and watched as Riccan's eyes widened. "Jehoban accepted me by giving me this crystal. Alena performed the service, and this crystal appeared without her having to ask for it.

"I've learned how to access its power with the elemy. I've done it all to do my part in locating Jena. I can't go to the authorities because of who I am. I can't go to Jena's abductor because of Juila."

"That's amazing, Amanda. You must be exceptional to get Jehoban's attention. Is there anything I can do to help you with Jena?"

"I've been working with my cousin, Rasa. She's one of Jehoban's students as well. I think the message on my patil is from her, but I couldn't listen to it when you didn't know who I was or what I'm trying to do to find my daughter."

Riccan scowled. "I've got so many questions."

"Go ahead. I'll answer them if I can."

Riccan held up a finger for each of his questions. "If you're from Earth, how can you have a cousin here in Tuala? If Rasa's Jehoban's student, how does she have time to help you? Who was the person responsible for abducting Jena? What happened at the restaurant this evening?

"You've piqued my interest, and we have all night to get to the bottom of it. But first, let's find out what Rasa has to say. Maybe she's discovered something."

Amanda's hands clenched the edge of the couch cushion, hardly believing he suggested the very thing she wanted the most. "Really? You don't mind?"

"Mind? I insist! Get up." He sprang from the couch and offered Amanda assistance up.

She laughed for the first time since arriving home and took his hand, feeling a tingling sensation at their touch. They walked over to the patil, where she touched the message icon on the screen.

Rasa's image smiled from the patil as she delivered her message. "Hi, Amanda. I have some mixed news for you. I think I've discovered why the link between your girls became so weak. I'm pretty sure Jena's on Earth.

"I don't know how or why, but the link felt almost exactly like the distance I had to send the message to Shemalla. I don't know why it took me so long to make the connection, but there it is. I could be wrong, but I don't think so. I hope you have a great night. I'll talk with you again tomorrow. Bye."

Amanda turned to stare at Riccan with a sense of wonder. If her daughter returned to Earth, she didn't have any reason to stay. She could go home with Juila and continue searching for Jena in more familiar territory.

Riccan tapped his lip and said, "That's an interesting turn of events. But what if she's wrong?"

CHAPTER 48

Atendril of doubt rose in Amanda, yet she tried to ignore it and said, "I hope she's not!" As if she were sleepwalking, she returned to the couch.

Riccan sat next to her. In a quiet enough voice that she could choose to ignore him, he asked, "Amanda? Who raped you?"

She slowly looked at him and felt her face heat as she whispered, "Petre MacVeen." She watched Riccan's face pale and then flushed bright red. His reaction alarmed her.

"He was in the bar tonight, wasn't he?" Riccan asked through clenched teeth.

"Yes, but we can't do anything about it right now. Remember Juila, Riccan. I have to keep her safe from him."

"More like you have to keep Petre safe from me. I'm going back there right now to strangle him until he tells us what he did with Jena!"

"Riccan, stop! I don't think that'll work with him. He's too smug, and he's been hiding for almost two anons. Besides, he doesn't have Jena anymore.

"I lost my connection with her about three days after she was taken. Another family has her, and she's safe and happy." She considered her last statement. Is that still true? If she were safe, then why was she suddenly sent to Earth?

Riccan's hands clenched into fists as if he were ready to punch something or someone. "Give me one good reason why I shouldn't go back to the restaurant to beat a confession out of him?"

Amanda bit her bottom lip and looked Riccan straight in the eyes. "Because I am asking you not to do it, Riccan. Please trust me to handle this. I don't want Jena or Juila to get hurt in this problem."

Amanda's expression was so genuinely pleading he couldn't help but give in and let her have her way on the matter. "Fine! Although, if I find myself alone with Petre, I'm not so sure I can promise not to do anything to him." He nodded and said, "Okay, I'll leave him alone tonight. What's your plan then?"

"I'll contact Bryon and let him know I've seen Petre. He can follow up on it since he's the person who originally filed the abduction charges against him."

She got up and returned to the patil. She spent the next few minutes going over the evening's events with Bryon. They were both grateful to have a solid and current lead on locating Petre. He promised to keep her apprised of any news, and they disconnected the call.

Amanda excused herself for a bathroom break. What else should she share with Riccan? He certainly seemed to be someone she could trust, just as Juila had promised.

His parentage put him in as much danger as her own, so they had reason to keep one another's secrets. She wanted to get to know Riccan better, yet her need to find Jena was even more vital.

If Jena were already on Earth, she needed to start her search there as soon as possible. Then she realized she'd forgotten to tell Bryon about Rasa's suspicion over Jena's whereabouts. She'd tell

Bryon during their following conversation, which would be pretty soon since they had a new lead.

She returned to the couch and curled her legs underneath her to get more comfortable. She asked, "Tell me about your grandfather and how he ended up here."

To Riccan's credit, he didn't even pause before replying, "Well, let's see. I'm not sure how much you know about Tuala's interaction with Earth, but a long time ago, there was an incident that caused one of our Elders to send representatives from Tuala to Earth to monitor the situation—"

Amanda brightened immediately and asked, "Was it Elder Vargen's son in Roswell?"

"You do know about it!" His eyes narrowed as he appraised her. "You're quite the mystery, Amanda. Okay, well, I won't have to give you as much history other than my grandmother was sent over to the museum right after it opened.

"She fell in love with one of her coworkers who was an engineer. Eventually, she knew she wanted to be with him, but there was the problem of getting him back to Tuala without Elder Vargen knowing about it. He tends to collect people from Earth to help in his research."

Amanda nodded in agreement to his last statement with a shiver of fear. That could've been her own fate.

"Anyway, she eventually discovered a way to bring him home, but she didn't know he'd lose his memory when he crossed through the Gate. Once they were here in Tuala, she had to make him fall in love with her all over again. Eventually, he regained his memory, and they got married.

"They had my father and were very content with their quiet lives until they sent my dad to school. His test scores caught the attention of Jehoban's representatives, and they all moved to Acaim so their son could start his education.

"My grandparents gratefully lived with their son because there wasn't any concern about my father's heritage being discovered as long as they lived with the Creator.

"Since they had access to a Gate, they visited relatives on Earth. Jehoban made it so my grandfather wouldn't lose his memory on the transfers anymore, making things a lot less complicated. My dad got to experience both worlds as he was growing up, which pleased Jehoban greatly.

"Eventually, when my dad finished his education and retirement, Jehoban promoted him to Elder status. My grandparents chose to remain living on Acaim until they died about ten anons ago.

"My dad trained me to follow in his footsteps. I've also been to Earth more times than I can count. I spent about two anons there once while I went to school to learn about engineering. It's come in handy integrating both types of technology to spark innovative ideas."

"Like the auto-pilot on the telepod?" Amanda remembered how flustered he became when he mentioned that aspect. He changed the subject immediately at the time, and now Amanda understood the reason.

"I should've wondered at your lack of reaction at the time, but I just couldn't believe I slipped up so badly in front of someone.

"But yes, like the auto-pilot. I probably never would've thought of it had I not become a pilot on Earth. The two flying styles are nothing alike, but both are quite exhilarating."

"So you're an accomplished pilot on Earth as well, huh? Any other hidden talents?" Amanda couldn't help teasing him and was grateful the evening was turning out to be pleasant after all, if not more than a little unexpected.

He laughed out loud. "I'll let you know as I think of them!"

"What are your parents' names, and where do they live now?"

"My dad is Elder Daven, and my mom is Nena. She's a teacher. They live in Pantano."

Amanda reviewed her memory of Barla's map. She knew the name was significant somehow, and suddenly it hit her: Pantano was where her journey started with Nealand so long ago—Boca Raton, Florida. "Your parents live in Florida?"

It was now Riccan's turn to be shocked. "I'm impressed that you know the location so readily. Have you been there?"

She shook her head and replied, "Only on Earth, and it's where all of my problems began. It's an amazing coincidence, don't you think?"

Riccan hummed. "Are they really coincidences? Jehoban's involved, remember?" He smiled and shook his head. "So many strange turns of events. There's so much more to you than I originally believed, and I'm utterly fascinated with you."

What could she say to that? Flustered, Amanda looked at her watch. "Wow, is it really that late? We have to be at work in a few hours."

She looked up at him. Would he stay if she asked? There was only the couch as another bed, but she needed to sleep, yet she didn't want to be alone with Petre so close.

"I can see what you're thinking, Amanda. I can stay on the couch tonight if you want me to."

Amanda sighed as she answered, "I hate to even ask it of you, but I am scared to be alone."

"I understand. Don't worry about it. I'm sure I'll sleep fine."

"Thank you, Riccan. You have no idea what this means to me!" She leaned over and gave him a quick peck on the cheek before she got up and took their glasses to the kitchen to rinse them out. "I guess I'll head to bed then after getting you a pillow and some blankets."

"Sounds good, Amanda. Sleep tight! I'll keep guard out here."

"Thank you."

～

Without a doubt, Petre saw Jesisca leave the restaurant. It was impossible, of course, based on Ninan's conversation he overheard so long ago. She was dead, but now he wasn't so sure.

If Jesisca lived, he could get her back after concluding his business with Elder Debbon. He would've followed after her had the loud-mouthed guy at the bar stopped yelling that Petre was a wanted man.

He hastily left the bar, not wishing to get arrested before confronting Elder Debbon. It was too late to locate the Elder, so he returned to his water craft and sat at the table to think.

People now knew he was on the island. He could've kicked himself for his carelessness. There were many considerations to take into account to restore his custodial rights, and being careless wasn't part of the equation.

Using all of his mental strength, he added an extra layer of protection around his water craft to avoid discovery. He would have to wear a disguise on the island because people now knew to look out for him.

Again he cursed his bad luck since a disguise would be dreadfully uncomfortable in the island's heat. He shrugged and imagined the result would be worth the discomfort.

CHAPTER 49

Bryon contacted the authorities immediately after disconnecting from Amanda's call. This was their best lead in over an anon. Amanda was obviously a credible witness, but rightfully, she couldn't be brought into the investigation. The Kirma authorities assured him they'd get in touch with the appropriate people in Durseni.

With all of the things that went wrong over the last two anons, Bryon wouldn't wait to see what happened this time. He rushed into the living room, where he found Alena telling stories to the children.

As soon as she looked up at him, her expression shifted. She shut the book she held and said, "Okay, kids, go get your pajamas on and brush your teeth for bed." As soon as the children were out of earshot, she stood and asked, "What happened, Bryon?"

"Amanda saw Petre in Durseni."

Alena gasped. "If both Petre and Amanda are on the same island, it's only a matter of time before Petre finds out about Juila." She covered her heart with her hand and paced the room. "I feel like someone just kicked me in the gut."

Bryon continued, "I'm going over there to see what I can find out. I won't let the authorities lose him again."

Alena's pacing stopped when she whirled around to face him. "I'm coming with you, Bryon. I have a feeling Amanda's going to need me as well."

Bryon didn't want Alena anywhere near Petre. Frantically, he searched for a reasonable excuse to leave her behind. "What about the children?"

"I'll go over to Tana's house immediately. I'm sure she won't mind having them over for a few days until this situation is sorted. Besides, she wants this investigation resolved as badly as we do!"

It was a lost cause, and Bryon knew it. Rather than delay the inevitable, he said, "Okay, I'll pack a few things. I'll also let Frasnia know we'll be gone for at least the next day or two."

With their game plan sorted, they went their separate ways. In under twenty minutes, they boarded their personal telepod, ready to leave town.

He palmed the bay door closed while simultaneously activating the crystal drive. Within moments the console displayed an array of green lights, and the telepod levitated inches above their driveway.

Bryon visualized Durseni's landing port coordinates, taking into account the evening sun's position, and moved his hand from the manual control to shift into mind control.

Everything blanked out for a few moments while he held their destination's image fixed firmly in his mind. In seconds, they saw what he visualized. Grateful for the quickness of travel, he sped through the shutdown procedures. Soon, they were unbuckled and standing in the stifling heat as the cargo door opened into the twilight.

Bryon said, "There's not enough room at Amanda's house for us to stay with her. We'll have to go to a hostel for the night and call on Amanda tomorrow.

"Besides, she'd be beyond terrified if we knocked on her door tonight. After spotting Petre here, I'm sure she's a bit spooked." Bryon touched Alena's lower back to comfort her as they left the telepod ramp.

"Oh, Bryon, wouldn't it be amazing if we catch Petre before he causes any more trouble?"

Bryon held her tightly to him with his arm around her waist as he answered, "Yes. With Jehoban's blessing, that's exactly what we'll do. I want this whole nightmare over so we can go back to our quiet lives. Do you remember when we thought life was a bit boring?"

Alena leaned back to look up at her husband. "I can't say as I do, Bryon. Life is never boring around our house!"

Bryon grinned at her comment as he directed them toward the flight office to arrange for housing and transport.

He planned to head down to the dock, searching for Petre's vessel. If he knew Petre as well as he believed he did, the pompous man's water craft was probably tied up in a prominent location. However, he was also smart enough to have his vessel cloaked from view.

Bryon would locate any empty spots large enough for his style of water craft and, using a stick, he'd probe the sites for any solid surfaces. While the invisibility cloak worked on the eyes, it didn't work on something physical. He was determined to find Petre tonight with or without the authorities.

Once they were finally at their hostel, Bryon announced, "I'm going for a walk. I'll be back shortly." His nonchalance didn't fool her for a second.

Alena looked at him with a knowing expression, but she came forward, kissed him, and said, "I love you. Be careful."

"I will. I love you, too." Their hug lingered longer than he had planned before he left the room.

As soon as the hostel door shut, Bryon broke into a run. He

made straight for the main port. Since he lacked a stick to probe the seemingly vacant berths, he used his foot instead.

By the time he completed his search of the upscale marina, he was still no closer to locating Petre. Did he get spooked and leave? Was this whole trip a waste of time? No way. His instincts screamed at him to keep looking.

Contrary to his original idea, Petre's vessel wasn't located in a prime spot. Next, he searched a short, ill-maintained wharf. Once Bryon's foot encountered a solid surface that appeared empty, Bryon took a leap of faith from the dock.

With stealth uncommon for a man his size, he landed silently onto the vessel. Entering a water craft unannounced was never a good idea; however, Bryon believed the element of surprise would be an essential advantage. Feeling secure with his shield, Petre wouldn't expect any visitors.

As soon as Bryon breached the shield, the ragged materials making the water craft were clearly visible. He headed directly toward the main cabin. Descending the stairs two at a time, he burst through the cabin door.

Without hesitation, he walked straight in and grabbed Petre by the throat. He picked him up from the chair until his feet dangled inches from the floor.

"Where's Jena, Petre?" He shook him for good measure before realizing Petre wouldn't be able to answer if he couldn't breathe. Bryon let go of his hold on Petre's throat and punched him in the gut to incapacitate him further. "Don't mess with me, Petre. Where's Jena?"

Petre slumped to the floor, hands held to his neck as he gasped for breath. Glaring at Bryon, he spoke with a raspy voice, "What're you doing here? How did you get past my shield? Nobody comes aboard my craft without my permission."

Bryon took a menacing step forward, fists clenched to deliver another round of justice. Petre's eyes widened, and he held his hands out for mercy.

"I don't have Jena. That little brat was more trouble than she was worth. But you won't have to worry about her either since I sold her to Elder Debbon."

Bryon looked at Petre as though a horn had grown out of his head. *Elder Debbon? What was this man talking about?*

Then it all made sense. Alena said only a wise-woman or an Elder could perform the crystal-changing rite. They'd only questioned the wise-women, overlooking the Elders entirely. Now he'd have to approach Elder Debbon to get Jena returned, and he wasn't pleased with this new turn of events.

Petre's smug smile became too much for Bryon to handle. Bryon smashed his foot into Petre's face without even forming the thought. He watched as blood poured from Petre's nose and upper lip. Petre slumped to the cabin floor with his eyes rolled up into his skull.

Not waiting for another instant, Bryon bent over and slung Petre over his shoulder. Because Petre was unconscious, the shield surrounding the vessel disappeared, and Bryon could no longer see the shield's fuzzy haze.

He hopped onto the dock and jogged to the Durseni Authorities Office. The journey took nearly ten minutes, and Petre's body twitched as though he were starting to wake. He quickened his pace and reached the office just as Petre regained partial awareness.

Bryon burst through the front doors of the Authorities' Office and slammed Petre down into a seat next to the intake window. Petre's head thumped noisily against the wall.

An armed guard immediately confronted Bryon. "Who's this man?"

Bryon stood with his arms crossed and his feet shoulder-width apart. If Petre moved a single muscle, he'd take him down again.

"This's Petre MacVeen. He's wanted for kidnapping my daughter, Jena. There's also the matter of him stealing a shipment from Kirma Shipping and Receiving, which has never been recovered. Please arrest him and have him extradited to Kirma for processing."

The guard was taken aback by Bryon's confident request but swiftly regained his composure and grabbed Petre by the arm. "Come with me."

As Bryon watched Petre be hauled into the waiting cell, he was still disappointed with the outcome. Before turning him in, he should've spent more time alone with Petre to vent his anger.

The two blows he delivered didn't go very far in alleviating the frustration built up over the past two anons. Bryon was also seething with rage when he thought about Petre calling sweet Jena a brat. The man had no limits to his stupidity.

With nothing further to be done that night, Bryon returned to the hostel. He walked into the room and surprised Alena.

Alena whirled around; her hand raised to her chest as she caught her breath. "You're back early. I expected you to be gone most of the night."

"Yeah, well, I found Petre." He turned and shut the door.

Alena gasped and said, "Bryon, you're bleeding. Tell me what happened." Her fingers touched his side as if trying to find his wound.

Bryon looked over his shoulder to see what Alena was talking about. He forgot all about Petre's blood drying on the back of his shirt from carrying him. Realization dawned, and he replied, "It's not my blood; it's Petre's. His nose bled after I kicked him in his lying face. I carried him to the station and had him booked."

Alena stared at her husband's simple explanation. Seconds later, she asked, "Where's Jena?"

Bryon sighed and ran a hand down his face. He wanted a

shower and rid himself of any reminder of Petre, but his wife deserved answers first. "Alena, you won't believe it."

She stepped back, and her complexion paled. Her voice dropped to a whisper, "What won't I believe?"

He told her straight and fast, "Petre sold her to Elder Debbon."

Alena's knees gave out, and she dropped into the chair beside the table. "Obviously, it had to be an Elder. Why didn't I talk to them as well? We could have had this resolved a long time ago if I'd just followed up on all the leads and not just the most likely ones. I'm so stupid!"

Bryon stepped forward to console his wife but stopped as she raised her hands.

Alena's expression hardened, and she glared up at Bryon. "Take that shirt off and get in the shower; even the idea of Petre's blood in here makes me ill. On second thought, take a shower with your shirt on so the blood will rinse out. I don't want to have to scrub it clean."

Bryon smiled at his wife's practical advice. His initial fear over her taking it personally was soon alleviated once she began giving orders. He went into the bathroom with a confident step to get himself cleaned up.

Someone knocked on Amanda's front door. Her heart raced, and her hands trembled. The early-morning hour made it impossible to think anyone other than Petre stood on the other side.

How did Petre discover where she lived? Was he going to force her to leave with him?

Before she moved to her bedroom doorway, Riccan stood from the couch. In her fearful state of mind, she had forgotten about Riccan spending the night. Relief course through her that he had offered to stay.

"I'll get the door. You stay there," Riccan ordered as he took the few steps to open the door.

Bryon and Alena stood outside, staring in disbelief because a man was answering Amanda's door. Almost instantly, disbelief turned to recognition as Bryon recognized Riccan. "Riccan? Is that you? What are you doing here? Is Amanda okay?"

Riccan's fierce expression changed to one of curiosity. "Yes. And you might be?"

"Oh, sorry, I'm Bryon, and this's my wife, Alena. We came to see Amanda. Is she here?"

Hearing her friend's voices, Amanda rushed forward to greet them. She pulled them inside and hugged them before asking, "What are you doing in Durseni?"

"Let's sit," Bryon said as he led his wife to the couch.

Amanda and Riccan sat on the coffee table facing the new guests. From the blank stares they gave each other, neither knew what would bring these two to the house so early.

Bryon frowned and looked deliberately from Amanda to Riccan and back.

Amanda understood and quickly added, "Feel free to speak. Riccan knows everything."

Bryon and Alena both flinched. Alena whispered, "Everything, everything?"

"Yes. It's okay. Riccan won't tell anyone. Please, Bryon, tell me what brings you here so early." Amanda glanced over to Riccan, and he nodded.

"We wanted to get here before you left for work. We thought you'd want to know that Petre was taken into custody last night. I know it's true because I took him there myself. You won't have to worry about running into him on the streets."

"Oh, Bryon, thank you!" Amanda flung herself forward and hugged her friend fiercely. She had always admired Bryon, but she could kiss him now with her appreciation of him taking the matter into his own hands. She pulled herself away and continued, "I was so worried about it all night. I asked Riccan to spend the night to make sure we stayed safe."

Bryon looked at Riccan meaningfully.

Amanda blushed. "After running into Petre at the restaurant, Riccan deserved an explanation. He's going to help us get Jena home."

"What do you mean by 'everything,' Amanda?" Alena asked again.

"I told him my whole story last night. He's fine with me being from Earth. It's going to be okay, don't worry."

Bryon couldn't keep the skepticism from his expression.

Amanda grinned.

A squeal erupted from behind them. Juila hurled herself onto Bryon's lap and hugged him tightly a moment later. He smiled at Juila's exuberance, lifting her to say hello and give her a proper hug.

Petre was in custody. It was almost too hard to comprehend after so long. Amanda asked, "Did you find out what Petre did with Jena?"

Bryon's expression turned hard. "Yeah, the scum said he sold her to Elder Debbon."

Amanda gasped. All the clues clicked into place. Elder Debbon was teaching the wise-women's class on Durseni right now. The Elder had access to an Ascension Gate. Rasa believed Jena was now on Earth. Elder Debbon had sent her to Earth. It all made sense.

"What're you thinking, Amanda?" Alena leaned forward with concern as she touched Amanda's knee to draw her attention.

Amanda detailed Rasa's message from the night before and her belief in Jena being on Earth. "I need to talk to Elder Debbon to discover the whole truth. I'm just not sure how to make an interview happen."

Alena leaned forward and said, "Elder Debbon was the teacher for my training as well, you know. If you want, I can go today to ask him to speak with you."

"Oh, Alena, that'd be perfect. Thank you so much." Tears pooled on her eyelashes, and she brushed them away before they could fall down her cheeks. This day was turning out so perfectly.

She looked at her timepiece and said, "I've got to get ready for work. Excuse me, please." Amanda left the room with anticipation that she'd soon have her daughter back in her arms. All of her dreams were coming true.

~

BRYON LOOKED AT RICCAN. Where should he start? The most obvious question came to mind, and he asked, "How do you know Amanda?"

"She's my employee at the Telepod Engineering Company."

Bryon seemed baffled by the explanation before he remembered Riccan was more than just a famous racer; he was also a well-known engineer. It made perfect sense he'd work for the best company.

With his first question answered, he asked the second most pressing question. "How do we know we can trust you with Amanda's secret?"

Riccan cleared his throat as if the question made him uncomfortable. He replied, "Because I'm a sympathizer like yourself. The people from Earth are no different than we are. They deserve to have the same consideration as Tualans."

Bryon couldn't dispute his answer, so he had to be content with Amanda's assessment. Besides, she couldn't have picked a better ally than someone as well connected as Riccan.

Where did Riccan sleep last night? Glancing toward Amanda's bedroom, his gaze traveled over the couch. He spotted the pillow. At least Riccan was an honorable man.

He turned to his wife and said, "We should probably get going now so you can make arrangements with Elder Debbon. Amanda has to go to work anyway." He looked down fondly at Juila and said, "Have you been good for your mommy?"

Juila instantly nodded in her silly, exaggerated manner.

"That's my good girl. I've missed you, Juila. We'll see you again soon, maybe even tonight, okay?" Bryon moved to set her on the floor when he was interrupted by Riccan.

"I'll take her." He lifted her out of Bryon's arms and took her into the kitchen to get her breakfast.

"This seems like a cozy situation, doesn't it, Bryon?" Alena whispered to Bryon as they stood to leave.

Bryon smiled at his wife's assessment of the situation. Maybe the potential relationship would change Amanda's mind about leaving Tuala. With a grin still on his face, he yelled over toward the bedroom, "Amanda, we're leaving now."

Amanda rushed back to the living room and gave them both a hug. She had changed her outfit and was in the process of brushing her hair.

Alena still held onto Amanda's arms when she said, "I'll leave you a message when I get the meeting with Elder Debbon arranged. Okay?"

"Perfect! Thank you again, Alena. And you, too, Bryon."

They left the house with lighter hearts knowing Amanda would no longer have to live in a constant state of fear. They also knew she had a good friend and protector in Riccan. Her life was changing in a good way.

Rasa returned to her dorm room and turned on her patil. Huh, there's a message from Amanda. That's strange. She typically left the messages for Amanda, not the other way around. She touched the play button and sat in stunned silence as Amanda talked:

"Hi, Rasa. I have fantastic news! Petre was arrested last night here on Durseni. He even admitted to selling Jena to Elder Debbon! Alena and Bryon were here this morning to tell me the news.

"Alena's going to arrange for me to meet with Elder Debbon today. I might have Jena back soon! Wish me luck! Bye!"

Rasa reviewed what she knew of Elder Debbon. He was not one of the Elders who believed the people from Earth should be questioned or detained permanently. He and his wife had two children, their son Willian and their first-daughter—Jena!

It was true! Elder Debbon had Amanda's daughter.

However, where were their children since Elder Debbon and Chelesa were in the wise-woman training sessions? Had Elder Debbon used his Gate to send them both to Earth?

It didn't make sense, but then again, it made perfect sense considering the weakness of Jena's link. Maybe that was why Chelesa looked so sad on her first day of class. Realization struck as Rasa recalled Chelesa's arrival coincided with the day following Juila's nightmare of losing Jena's link.

It had to be true!

Rasa's break ended. She had a class to attend, cutting short her desire to dwell on the fascinating subject. Rasa believed she'd have difficulty concentrating with all of the questions she had for Elder Debbon and Chelesa competing for her attention.

Hopefully, Amanda would contact her later that evening to share how her meeting with the Elder went.

ALENA REMEMBERED how the daily schedule of training went. She timed her visit to the school just when they'd be getting out for lunch. She rushed forward when she saw her mentor and called out, "Elder Debbon."

Alarmed, he looked over to see someone rushing toward him. His expression instantly changed when he recognized his former student. "Alena, how have you been? What a pleasant surprise."

Alena didn't waste time with pleasantries. "I have an urgent matter to discuss with you. Do you have a few minutes?"

Debbon was baffled by Alena's sudden intensity and asked, "Is this about one of your patients? Do you need a consultation?"

Alena frowned. She glanced around them at all of the people nearby. She continued, "No, no, nothing like that. Is there somewhere private where we can talk?"

"Sure, we can go to my apartment. Will that do?"

Alena nodded. "Perfectly."

They went in silence as Alena considered how she'd approach this delicate subject. She was certain Debbon wondered what could be so important to bring his student to the island to speak with him.

He opened the door to his apartment and gestured for her to precede him into the room. She sat at the table and waited for Elder Debbon to do likewise.

Now that the moment was upon her, Alena couldn't get the words out. "This is such a complicated situation. I'm struggling to find the right words to broach the subject with you."

CHAPTER 51

Elder Debbon spoke softly to Alena, "Just start from the beginning, and we'll go from there, okay?"

Inhaling slowly, Alena said, "Okay, do you remember about two anons ago, I applied for the adoption of twin girls?"

Debbon nodded, tapping his fingers lightly on the tabletop. "Yes, I believe I do. I wondered how you'd have time with twins when you already had three small children. Have you reconsidered the adoption? Is that why you're here?"

Alena gasped. She'd never give up on those girls or her responsibility to them. Did Elder Debbon think so little of her? "No, it's nothing like that at all. One of the girls I adopted was kidnapped. We have reason to believe you know where she is."

Debbon's fingers stilled before he drew them together into a fist. "I'm not sure I follow, Alena. How would I know anything about your missing child?"

Alena rushed to finish before Debbon's anger erupted. "Petre MacVeen abducted her. He was taken into custody yesterday, where he admitted that he sold Jena to you."

Debbon couldn't have been more shocked than he was at that moment. He was having trouble breathing; his mouth opened and closed without making a sound. His fist flew up to cover his heart.

Alena's alarm rose as she watched Elder Debbon's face turn ashen, and he struggled to breathe. She stood and tapped into Elder Debbon's life-line to steady his heartbeat.

With her medical assessment confirming he was just in shock and not in need of medical attention, she removed her presence from his mind and waited for him to recover on his own. His reaction made it clear that he had some knowledge of Jena's whereabouts.

Finally, Debbon whispered, "I didn't know, Alena. I had a vision an anon before where Jena was presented to me in danger. I couldn't leave that precious little girl in the hands of the likes of Petre. She wasn't safe with him.

"His story about the child's mother being dead checked out. I had no idea Jena was taken from your family. I promise I didn't know."

Alena was satisfied the Elder spoke the truth. He had no reason to lie, nor was he the type to shirk blame. "Where's Jena, Elder Debbon?"

His face paled even more. "My family was being threatened. I sent the children to a safe house, and I brought Chelesa here."

Alena reached out and placed her hand over his fist, offering him her support. "Elder Debbon, you called her family. Did you adopt her?"

He shook his head and replied, "No, I negotiated a betrothal agreement with Petre. He lost his parental rights when he failed to show up before the three days expired. Jena's my first-daughter."

Alena was both elated and appalled at this newest revelation. If Elder Debbon had an agreement, it was binding; however, it also meant irrevocable. This wasn't good news for Amanda. She then told the Elder the final piece of her story, "Jena's mother has been found alive, Elder Debbon, and she wants her daughter back."

Debbon pulled his hand away, his surprise showing. "Jesa's alive? Where did you find her?"

Alena leaned back in her chair and sighed. Everything around Petre became so convoluted. "Petre lied about the mother's name. He called her Jesisca because he never knew her real name was Amanda. She's on the island and wants to meet with you. Can you see her tonight after class?"

Elder Debbon spent a moment absorbing all of these new facts before slowly nodding his head, "Certainly. Can you bring her to me around six tonight?"

"Yes. Thank you, Elder Debbon. I'll see you tonight." She stood and let herself out to return to the hostel. Alena sat at the patil in the room and sent a message to Amanda. She could hardly wait for the many hours to pass before picking up Amanda to finally get started on returning Jena to her mother.

Amanda rushed into Riccan's office. "Jena's been found, sort of. We definitively know Elder Debbon and his wife have been raising her. I'm meeting with him tonight. Can you believe it?"

Riccan stood from his desk and walked around it to give her a congratulatory hug. Just as his arms went around her, he looked beyond Amanda to see Ela Nena framed in his doorway. He immediately dropped his arms and said, "I'm glad it worked out so well. If you'll excuse me, Ela Nena has just arrived for our meeting."

"Oh, I'm sorry! Of course! Excuse me." Amanda was beyond flustered as she brushed past the small, frowning woman on her way back to her desk.

Ela Nena tapped her foot impatiently on the floor. "You know I don't approve of physical contact with the staff, Riccan."

"I'm sorry. Please have a seat. I have the drawings of the newest design for your review." He pulled out several large plasfilm sheets and rolled them out across his desk.

ALENA ARRIVED at Amanda's doorstep at five-thirty. Amanda was ready, with Juila resting on her hip, and she shut the door behind them. They strolled toward the school to have the most important meeting for Amanda's family.

Amanda was a bundle of nerves to get a resolution to this situation finally. How would Juila react to Elder Debbon? Was he going to be the same man whom Jena called Daddy?

The school was located on the island's far side from where Amanda lived. They took several flights of stairs until they reached Elder Debbon's apartment. Alena knocked on the door even though they were several minutes early.

Elder Debbon opened the door and stood in amazement. "You're the woman I treated so long ago for the broken wrist and beetlesnatch bite."

His gaze shifted to the child she held, identical to Jena. He looked at her birth crystal.

Amanda knew what he was doing. Where Jena's birth crystal had been dark black, Juila's stone was deep red; definitely not Jena.

He recovered from his initial shock and stammered, "Please come in. Come in."

The three entered the house to see a woman sitting at the table in the dining room. She had obviously been crying, and when she spotted Amanda carrying Juila, her sobbing renewed.

"They're the woman and child I told you about a couple of days ago, Debbon!" Chelesa spoke suddenly into the quiet room. Continuing her accusatory tirade, she added, "You told me it was my imagination. What do you say about it now?"

Debbon looked uncomfortable with his wife's question. "I'm sorry, Chelesa, I should've trusted your instinct. You were right."

Amanda recognized the woman, but now she realized why. The only one who didn't seem fazed was Juila. She smiled as though she already knew everyone, which naturally, she did through her link with Jena.

At Debbon's gesture, they sat, yet everybody remained in awkward silence.

Elder Debbon's strange admission when he first saw her made her question if he'd healed her when she first met Bryon. Finally, Amanda said, "I'm certain with the way you're looking at Juila that you don't need further proof of Jena's maternity. Where's Jena?"

Chelesa cried louder, causing Elder Debbon to raise his voice to be heard, "Our family has recently received threats, and we were forced to send our son and Jena away to a safe house. We don't have her with us."

His answer wasn't good enough. Amanda pressed, "Where is Jena, Elder Debbon? As her mother, I deserve to know."

Elder Debbon looked uncomfortable.

Amanda asked, "You healed me, didn't you, Elder Debbon?"

He nodded.

"Then you know who I am. Wherever you sent the children, I'll understand."

He exhaled and spoke bluntly, "We sent the children to Earth."

Amanda nodded. Finally, she had the truth. Then she asked, "Where on Earth is she? I want to get home to be reunited."

Chelesa stopped crying and gasped. "Debbon, did you know about this? Jena's mother is from Earth?"

Debbon winced at his wife's accusing stare and sighed, "Yes, I knew Jena was only half-Tualan. It doesn't matter to me, and it shouldn't matter to you, either. We're all Jehoban's creations."

"That's true, but you should've told me!" She sat back, glancing between Debbon and Amanda.

Would it have mattered to Chelesa before she fell in love with Jena? Amanda whispered her thanks to Jehoban for keeping that secret.

Debbon turned to face Amanda and admitted, "To answer your question, I don't know where Jena is or my son, either."

He raised his hand to forestall her next obvious question and continued to say, "I made arrangements with Elder Vargen to transport them to a safe house on Earth. Only he knows where they are. I suppose I should ask him since we know you're alive."

Amanda's heart sank with Elder Vargen's involvement. What if he figured out Jena's true heritage? As one of the Old Soul Engineering Facility founders, he was definitely not a sympathizer with Earth's people.

If anything, he was more ruthless toward them because of his son's mistake causing him such disgrace among the Elders. He deeply resented the interference the Earth people had made in his career.

"When will you talk with Elder Vargen?" Alena asked into the quiet that descended upon the room.

"I'll get him on the patil immediately." Debbon went to his patil and activated the emergency switch to contact another Elder.

Elder Vargen answered immediately, "Elder Debbon, how may I help?"

"Can you please tell me the location of my children on Earth?"

There was a pause before Elder Vargen answered, "There's been a problem, First. My contact hasn't returned to her post. I've been unable to ascertain where your children were placed. As soon as I hear from Shemalla, I'll contact you directly."

"Thank you, Elder. I look forward to hearing from you soon." He sighed as he disconnected the call and looked at the people in his dining room. Both Amanda and Alena wore unreadable expressions. Chelesa looked devastated. "I assume you could hear Elder Vargen."

Chelesa jumped up from her chair and screamed, "He said our children are lost on Earth. How can you be so calm about this? What are you going to do about it, Debbon?"

CHAPTER 52

Elder Debbon spoke calmly in the face of his wife's hysteria, "We aren't going to do anything right now. Let's wait until Elder Vargen's contact gets back to him.

"Once we know where the kids are, then we can make arrangements to get Amanda to where she can visit with her daughter."

Amanda didn't like the sound of Elder Debbon's disconcerted assessment of the situation. She wasn't planning on visiting with her child; she planned to take her home for good. A protest against the Elder's statement formed on her lips when she felt Alena's nudge against her knee.

She looked at her in time to see Alena shake her head swiftly. Amanda shut her mouth. Alena had some explaining to do once they left.

Alena cleared her throat to catch everyone's attention. "Well, it seems there's nothing we can do until you hear from Elder Vargen."

Alena pulled a piece of plasfilm from her purse and wrote down both her and Amanda's contact information. "Once you know something, please contact us right away. As you can imagine, we're quite anxious to have this matter resolved. Thank you for your time."

She plucked Amanda's sleeve to get her moving.

Amanda wanted to be well away from Elder Debbon before she started asking questions.

Alena opened the door for Amanda and Juila and then closed it behind them. She put her finger to her lips and set a brisk pace away from the school.

Amanda was bursting with questions. What had Alena figured out? What did she know? No sooner were they outside the school gates than she couldn't contain herself, "What's going on, Alena?"

"You heard Elder Vargen say his contact was Shemalla. You know who she is and where she's located. All you have to do is go back through the same Gate you used to get here and go ask. You don't need to involve Elder Debbon anymore. You can go home and reunite with your daughter on your own."

Amanda clutched Alena's arm in her excitement. "You're brilliant, Alena. I didn't particularly appreciate how Elder Debbon made it sound like he planned to keep Jena and allow me visitation. That's just wrong. She belongs to me, not him!"

Alena stopped walking and turned to face Amanda. "Actually, Amanda, Elder Debbon does have a claim to Jena whether you want him to or not. A betrothal agreement was signed, whether it was illegal or not, and the formal procedure was performed and then blessed by Jehoban. Your daughter is irrevocably linked to Elder Debbon's family, and her future is set with his son."

Amanda looked at Alena with growing horror as she imagined Jena's future. She didn't want someone to tell her daughter whom she'd marry. It was just not done that way on Earth. There had to be some sort of appeal to Jehoban or something!

Alena squeezed her arm to comfort her and said, "Let's concentrate first on finding her, and then you can worry about her future."

Amanda woodenly walked toward home with Alena, nodding her head in agreement. She reviewed her options for returning to Earth, not liking the idea of taking Juila through an unsanctioned Gate. The risk was too high, yet she couldn't leave Juila behind to search Earth for Jena.

Unbidden, an image of Riccan smiling at her came to mind. Where did that come from? Of course! That would be the perfect solution. Maybe Riccan could talk to his dad to send her and Juila to Earth. It was certainly an avenue to consider seriously.

They reached Amanda's house, where Alena took Juila from her so she could use the patil. First, she left a simple message for Rasa, letting her know the prediction of Jena being on Earth was correct. She told her she'd appreciate any ideas for getting home before signing off.

Her next call was to Riccan. She also expected to leave him a message but was pleasantly surprised when Riccan's image came onto the screen.

"Hi, Amanda. What happened with Elder Debbon?"

"He's been raising Jena, just as we suspected. He also told us he sent Jena and his son to Earth to keep them safe from threats to their family. The part which wasn't so good was when he called Elder Vargen—who transferred the kids—we found out nobody knows where the kids were sent." Amanda leaned into the edge of the table.

Riccan's eyebrows rose. "Hmm. So now, what are you going to do?"

Now came the tricky part. What would she do if Riccan refused? "I learned that Elder Vargen's contact was someone I already know at the museum in Roswell. I was hoping you could ask your father to send Juila and me through his Gate to Earth."

Riccan leaned forward, his grin growing wider by the second. "I can do one better; I can take you there myself!"

A thrill raced through her at Riccan's proposal, but she shook her head and said, "Riccan, it's kind of you to offer, but I can't take such a risk with Juila by using an unauthorized Gate."

He quirked his eyebrow, unfazed by Amanda's refusal. "Have you ever heard about the Elders having portable Gates?"

Hope surged once again. Could Riccan be saying what she thought? "Actually, yes, I have. Shemalla told me about them before I made my way back to Tuala. Does your father have one?"

"No, but I do. I built it into my telepod." His pride was evident in every nuance of his expression.

Amanda could hardly believe what he said was true. "You mean the telepod I saw at work has a portable Gate?"

"Exactly. When do you want to go?"

Amanda glanced away from the patil to where Alena played with Juila—if only they could go now, but that was too much to ask. "I'd say immediately, but we both have work in the morning."

"I'm honored at your commitment to your job, but work seems pretty irrelevant right now. Besides, I can time the travel just as easily. We can go over there, stay as long as you need, and still come back before work in the morning."

The final piece of the puzzle clicked together for Amanda. *Thank you, Jehoban, for the wonderfully supportive people you've brought into my life,* she said silently. Aloud, she said, "How soon can you be ready?"

"Meet me down at the office in ten minutes. I'll be ready!"

Amanda barely agreed before the screen went blank. From Riccan's reaction, he was thrilled to go on this adventure with her. She stood, turned toward the kitchen, and watched Alena serving Juila her dinner.

Alena looked up expectantly when Amanda entered the room. "Did you get some good news from either call?"

"The best news, actually. Riccan's taking Juila and me to Earth as soon as we get over to the office. This dinner is going to have to be on the run, Juila. We're going on a trip!"

Juila smiled at her mother as though she knew this would happen. Amanda looked at her daughter thoughtfully. Juila seemed to have a relatively accurate intuition about many things lately.

Alena, on the other hand, looked devastated by the news. "So soon? I'm not ready for either of you to leave. Please promise me you'll come back."

"I'm sorry, Alena, I honestly don't know what will happen. We've got to meet Riccan in ten minutes, which means I've got to get moving. Please tell Bryon I said goodbye.

"If it's possible, I'll do my best to come back to visit you both. Riccan did say we could be returning before tomorrow morning if we don't turn up anything. You two may as well spend the night here if you don't plan on going home tonight. Oh, and can you let Rasa know what I'm doing? I've got to run. Thank you for everything."

Alena grabbed Amanda's arm to get her full attention and spoke urgently, "At the girls' crystal ceremony, I saw images of your children's futures. I've had time to review what I saw, and you need to know they'll both be back on Earth as they get older. It will be okay."

Amanda froze, analyzing each word. "Thank you, Alena. I know how hard it must be for you to break your vows to reassure me that I'm doing the right thing. Now I know everything will turn out well. I really do have to go now."

Amanda grabbed up Juila and went to their room to gather the few things they'd need for an overnight trip. A minute or two passed since speaking with Riccan. Finally, she was able to do something productive.

Racing back to the living room, Amanda hugged Alena one last time before she whisked out the front door. Amanda practically ran to the office building. As she reached for the front door, Riccan opened it from inside.

She knew what he saw with her flushed cheeks and the twinkle of excitement in her eyes. His expression mirrored hers.

The elevator whisked them up to the roof. As soon as the doors parted, Riccan held out the remote to open the cargo door for them to enter the telepod. The door closed silently behind them, and Amanda placed Juila in the seat directly behind hers.

Juila's safety was paramount for this trip, so she opted not to carry her on her lap as she usually did for transport. She buckled Juila in before moving to the right front seat of the telepod. She fastened her seatbelt and saw Riccan buckled and waiting for her.

Now for the moment of truth: Amanda would finally get that ride in Riccan's amazing telepod with an epic journey landing them on Earth. With his hand poised over the plascreen console, Riccan said, "Tell me where we're headed so I can get the coordinates on the screen."

"I think Roswell should be our first stop. If we can't locate Shemalla in a reasonable amount of time, we'll head to my parents' house in Florida. They were supposed to be speaking with her regularly to get any updates on my status here in Tuala."

"Okay, Roswell, it is. We'll have to come in under cover of darkness so fewer people will have a chance of seeing the telepod. It wouldn't do to create a commotion, now would it?"

CHAPTER 53

Amanda grinned at Riccan's joke yet knew it was no laughing matter. Tualans valued secrecy to remain outside of Earth's inquisitive reach. What was Riccan waiting for? Did he change his mind after all?

Her worries disappeared as wholly as everything else around her when darkness overtook her senses. Her questions were answered; however, it did nothing to alleviate the nagging feeling something was terribly wrong.

In all the times she traveled this way with Bryon, it never took more than three heartbeats to arrive at their destination. Now, they were way past that marker. Still, the emptiness lingered.

A faint line of the landscape appeared outside the front window, and Amanda exhaled. They must have arrived in Roswell based on the stark desert countryside.

Riccan set the telepod down without a whisper of a jolt. "Whew, I greased that landing and preserved the paint on the bottom of the telepod."

Amanda doubted he ever had much trouble with his landings,

especially after watching him race. Telepods were like an extension of Riccan's body.

He scrolled through a series of screens on the flat panel with practiced ease as he deactivated the telepod. Riccan unbuckled his restraint and announced, "Okay, all systems are down, and we're ready to go."

Exiting the cockpit first, Riccan unbuckled Juila from the seat and carried her through the cargo door. Amanda followed immediately, turning to see the telepod door close silently after she stepped off the ramp.

What were they going to do about hiding the telepod? Before the thought even finished in her head, the telepod suddenly disappeared. Shocked, she turned to Riccan and asked, "Where did it go, Riccan?"

He laughed, held out his fist, and tapped his knuckles on the outside of the telepod as he answered, "It's still there. It's just using the colors of its surroundings to camouflage. I'd say the program works rather nicely!"

Whistling appreciatively, Amanda nodded. "You could say that again. How'll we find it when we get back?"

"I have a homing beacon programmed into the remote. Roswell is about a mile east of here. Let's get walking."

A strange, niggling awareness bothered Amanda, knowing it was something important. Suddenly the idea blazed through her mind: she had crossed the veil, yet she had retained her memories of Tuala! "Riccan! Something's wrong!"

"What?" Instantly on the alert, he scanned their surroundings to discover the trouble source.

His sudden tenseness made Amanda feel foolish for overreacting. She hastily touched his arm and explained, "Riccan, I still remember everything even though I'm back on Earth. The three other times I crossed over, I completely lost my memory. Don't you think that's strange?"

Riccan's shoulders relaxed, and his furrowed eyebrows rose. He considered her concern and asked, "What was different this time?"

"I can't think of any difference, really. Maybe I was more prepared? Well, no, that's not exactly true. I was as ready as possible when I went over there with Shemalla's help."

She strained to figure out anything else that could've changed. With a flash of inspiration, her mind centered on the pendant suspended from her neck. It prompted her to ask, "Do you think my birth crystal has something to do with it?"

Riccan pondered her question for a few moments. "I've received plenty of training from my father, and I'm well-versed in Jehoban's ability to change people."

He smiled and added, "More happened during your birth crystal ceremony than you'll ever know. Amanda, you're exactly right. When Jehoban decided to give you the crystal, he proclaimed you a child of Tuala.

"Even more than that, He bestowed all of the Tualan blessings upon you, including the birthstone, using the elemy, and the ability to pass through the Gates without any detriment to your memory."

Amanda simply stared at Riccan, hardly believing what he said was true, yet her full memory was a testament of truth to his proclamation. "Does this mean I can come and go from Earth with impunity?"

"I believe it does."

Her hand cradled the birth crystal, and she looked down at it with renewed respect. "Wow, that's so amazing!"

They resumed their walk to Roswell in silence. Thankfully, Riccan continued carrying Juila. Amanda would've been quite winded if she had offered to take her from him. Her musings were interrupted when Riccan suddenly began speaking.

"I'm happy I could finally help you with this situation," Riccan said. His words sounded clipped, as though he meant to say more.

"Me too." Amanda agreed wholeheartedly. She shivered at making this trek in the dark by herself.

"When we were at your house, I wanted to step in and arrange for you to meet with Elder Debbon. You do realize he's a friend of my family since my father's also an Elder, don't you?"

"I hadn't really thought about it. Why didn't you do it then?"

"Because I remembered you said how guilty Alena felt because Jena was abducted. It meant everything to her to make it right by arranging the meeting with Elder Debbon. I didn't want to take that from her; however, had she been unsuccessful, I would've stepped in at that point."

Amanda thoughtfully nodded. Riccan had paid closer attention to her than she realized when she had shared her whole story with him. He was probably the most thoughtful man she'd ever met, which only endeared him to her more.

She had no idea where they could possibly go, relationship-wise, that is, but she wished she'd have an opportunity to find out.

They arrived at Shemalla's house and knocked on the door. Was her friend asleep? The place was completely dark inside.

She knocked again before trying the doorknob and discovering it was unlocked. They cautiously walked inside as Amanda called out, "Shemalla? Are you home? It's me, Amanda."

They searched every room without finding any signs of Shemalla or a hasty retreat. Amanda worried something dire might have happened to her friend. They left the empty house without any other leads or options to travel back to the telepod.

The return trip seemed shorter, for which Amanda was thankful. She fantasized about resting in the comfortable co-pilot's seat. Her feet were killing her. She hadn't walked this much in one evening in as long as she could remember.

As soon as everyone was once again secured in the telepod, Riccan initiated the process to transfer them to Florida. Would her parents be able to shed some light on Shemalla's whereabouts, or at least pinpoint a time when they'd last spoken with her?

Obviously, her parents would have to get over the shock of seeing Amanda and Juila for the first time. She smiled in anticipation of the happy reunion. The emptiness of the transfer resumed, signaling that they were on their way.

There were more lights even on the outskirts of Amanda's hometown in Florida, making it a bit trickier for Riccan to navigate to a safe landing location. Amanda was confident at least some people would've spotted the telepod but hoped it wouldn't make the news.

Their landing ended up being in a brushy field west of her home. She recognized her surroundings and instantly felt optimistic that her two-year ordeal would soon be over.

Again, Riccan carried Juila, and Amanda didn't protest. She found her strides getting longer the closer they got to civilization. Eventually, they arrived at a major road where Riccan stepped forward to hail a cab.

At first, she was alarmed since she didn't have any money. Riccan leaned toward her as he opened the door and said, "I brought money. Don't worry!"

Naturally, Riccan would think of everything. Amanda should never have doubted his preparedness. *He'd been to Earth often enough to know how things worked.*

Relief washed over her that he'd offered to assist and accompany her on this investigative trip. She was sure this journey would've been quite dangerous if she'd made it on her own.

The cab driver called over his shoulder before they shut the door, "Where to?"

Amanda leaned forward, eagerly telling the address to the driver.

The cab sped through the streets toward her childhood home. Her heart thumped faster as she realized she was about to see her parents again. It felt like she'd lived several lifetimes since last being with them.

The car rolled to a stop in front of her house, and her fingers shook as she clumsily reached for the door latch. Riccan squeezed her knee knowingly as he handed a wad of cash to the driver.

They exited the cab and shut the door. The taxi sped away for his next fare as they stood looking toward her parents' home.

It was late, yet the lights were still on in the living room.

Amanda approached the front door and knocked three times in quick succession without waiting for another instant. She expected to see her mother or father's stunned reaction when they saw who came calling.

Amanda found herself in open-mouthed shock as her mother answered the door holding Jena in her arms.

BECAUSE THEIR SESSION lasted all afternoon and well into the night, Jasmine's shoulders slumped with exhaustion. She didn't dare take a break since her shortened time to discover Amanda's truths before Dr. Gascon drugged her again.

She wrote down Riccan's name. She'd check on whether or not he was a real person who lived in Florida. Amanda seemed convinced he was from both Earth and Tuala. He might just be the key to unraveling this whole tangled mystery.

She left Amanda sleeping on her office couch and stiffly rose from her chair. Her joints cracked loudly as they shifted back to their regular positions as she straightened up. Jasmine walked around her desk, opened her laptop computer, and turned it on. She sank wearily in her chair as she waited for the programs to boot up.

Finally, the internet search box showed on the screen where she typed in 'Riccan Stel, Florida.'

Within seconds, several articles popped up and a few photos of a man in his late twenties posing next to a Cessna 182S Skylane. She clicked on the first article to begin reading.

Riccan lived part-time in Florida as an engineer and a private pilot who volunteered for search and rescue missions. Oddly enough, no mention was made of where he lived when he wasn't in Florida.

Jasmine hit the back button and scrolled down through the search results to see if she could obtain any contact information for Riccan.

Nothing.

She pounded her fists on the desk beside the computer. How could she get in touch with him? He had to be the key.

~

WANT MORE?

IMPRISONED BY HER HAUNTING MEMORIES. The psychiatrist has crazy schemes. With no help in sight, will Amanda discover freedom and keep her sanity?

With her team of magical friends, who could stand against them?

THE TIME OF SHADOWS is the gripping first book in The Chosen portal fantasy series. If you like mysterious adventures, riveting self-preservation, and heart-pounding twists, then you'll love this supremely-crafted page-turner.

ABOUT THE AUTHOR

USA Today bestselling author, Amy Proebstel, writes epic dragon fantasy, magical realism fantasy, clean fated mate shifter romance, clean contemporary romance, and sweet young adult medical romance.

When she's not busy writing about young heroines and dragons saving the world, she spends her time binge-watching YouTube adventures, taking her husband and daughter flying, playing with her Pomeranian and Pomskies, or reading. If you like her books, she recommends you also check out Anne McCaffrey and Ava Richardson. They're the reason she started writing.

Subscribe to Amy's newsletter for a free book to get started on the journey today!

Feel free to email Amy at Amy@LevelsofAscension.com.

CHOSEN ORIGINS TRILOGY, A PORTAL FANTASY SERIES
    THE CHOSEN, A PORTAL FANTASY SERIES
    ROMANCES BEYOND TUALA, A FATED MATE SHIFTER SERIES
    BILLIONAIRE'S VENTURE ROMANCE SERIES
    DRAGON'S MAGIC: AN EPIC DRAGON FANTASY SERIES
    SWEET YOUNG ADULT MEDICAL ROMANCE SERIES

instagram.com/amyproebstel

PEOPLE

<u>Ahn</u> – / **ah** n / – Husband of Barla. Father of Gravin and Rasa. Harbor Master at the Port of Cresdon in Thulen. Former shipping captain.

<u>Alena</u> – / ah **leyn** a / – Born Ab 26, 3417. Maiden name: Bellen. Marriage Date: Tishri 16, 3436. Wife of Bryon. Mother of Justan and Kyelon. Adoptive mother to Jena and Juila. Trained as a wise-woman.

<u>Amanda</u> – / uh **man** duh / – means 'beloved.' Born September 28, 1972, in Florida. Maiden name: Covington. Daughter of Chris and Diane. Former fiancé of Nealand. Mother of Juila and Jena. First cousin of Gravin and Rasa.

<u>Andera</u> – / an **dair** uh / – Born Tishri 12, 3439. Daughter of Zeka. Betrothed to Justan. First-daughter of Bryon and Alena.

<u>Angie</u> – / **an** jee / – Nealand's new girlfriend.

<u>Barla</u> – / **bahr** luh / – Born January 21, 1945, in Wisconsin. Maiden name: Silnack. Formerly known as Barbara. Sister of Diane. Aunt of Amanda. Wife of Ahn. Mother of Gravin and Rasa.

<u>Bistea</u> – / bis **tee** uh / – Vendor at the marketplace in Kirma. Patient of Alena's.

Bryon – / **brahy** uh n / – Born Heshvan 2, 3416, in Kirma. Surname: Kesh. Marriage Date: Tishri 16, 3436. Husband of Alena. Father of Justan and Kyelon. Adoptive father to Jena and Juila. Manager of Kirma Shipping and Receiving.

Ceren – / **sair** in / – Born approximately 3412. Adopted son of Ahn and Barla. Works at the Port of Cresdon for Captain Ahn.

Chelesa – / **chuh** lay suh / – Wife of Elder Debbon. Mother of Willian.

Chris – / **kris** / – Surname: Covington. Husband of Diane. Father of Amanda and two other daughters.

Cleon – / **klee** on / – Transport operator at Kirma Shipping and Receiving.

Copa – / **kohp** uh / – Wise-woman for the district of Desio. Person who healed Ninan.

Corva – / **kor** vuh / – Foster child of Ahn and Barla. Her parents died in a house fire.

Crysta – / **kris** tuh / – Head maid at Elder Debbon's estate.

Daven – / **dav** uhn / – Surname: Stel. Husband of Nena. Father of Riccan. Student of Jehoban. Elder, whose base of power is on Pantano.

Debbon – / **deb** uhn / – Elder, whose base of power is on Elder Isle. Husband of Chelesa. Father of Willian.

Denana – / **day** naw nuh / – Employee in the Engineering Department at the Telepod Engineering Company.

Diane – / **dahy** an / – Born October 1, 1947. Maiden name: Silnack. Sister of Barbara and Saul. Wife of Chris. Mother of Amanda and two other daughters.

Dr. Flores – / **flohr** ez / – The doctor treating Amanda in the hospital in Cancun.

Ela Nena – / **eluh** nay nuh / – Married name: Dunless. Wife of Teden Dunless. Executive VP of Customer Operations at the Telepod Engineering Company. Riccan's boss.

Ellen – / **el** uh n / – Mother of Barla, Saul, and Diane. Maiden name: Hill. Married name: Silnack.

Fordin – / **ford** in / – Former seaman friend of Ninan. Confidant of Ninan's dealings with Petre.

Frasnia – / **fraz** nee uh / – Secretary at Kirma Shipping and Receiving.

Gatson – / **gat** suh n / – Personal bodyguard for Elder Debbon. Main home is on the Elder's Islet at the seat of power.

Gilora – / **gil** or uh / – Employee at the Telepod Engineering Company under Riccan. Interviewer of Amanda.

Gravin – / **gra** vin / – Born Elul 30, 3421, in Port of Cresdon. Son of Ahn and Barla. Brother of Rasa. First cousin of Amanda.

Gwenda – / **gwen** duh / – Employee at the Telepod Engineering Company under Riccan. Interviewer of Amanda.

Hashma – / **hash** muh / – A prostitute at the Lookout Tavern. Filed a sexual assault lawsuit against Petre. Mother of Petre's child.

Issyn – / **ih** sin / – Shipping captain who rescued Amanda from swimming. Friend of Captain Ahn. Main port of call is Port of Cresdon.

Jasmine Medin, MD – / **med** in / – Doctor at Cannon Memorial Asylum under Dr. Stephen Gascon.

Jehoban – / juh **ho** ban / – Means 'of all the people' who is the creator of everything. Earth equivalent: God.

Jena – / **jen** uh / – Born Iyar 22, 3443, in Kirma. Daughter of Amanda. Twin sister of Juila. First-daughter of Elder Debbon and Chelesa. Betrothed to Willian.

Jenny – / **jen** ee / – A dance team member from Amanda's high school.

Jern – / **jurn** / – A trusted friend of Bryon's.

Jesisca – / jes **is** kuh / – The name given to Amanda from Petre.

Jessa – / **jes** uh / – The name given to Elder Debbon from Petre for Jena's mother.

<u>Jessica Taivas</u> – / **jes** i kuh **tay** vuhs / – Wife of Nealand Taivas Sr. Mother of Nealand Taivas Jr.

<u>Jonan</u> – / **jawn** uhn / – Bullying neighbor of Ahn and Barla.

<u>Jose</u> – / hohz **ey** / – Mexican man who found Amanda on the beach in Cancun.

<u>Juila</u> – / **joo** ee luh / – Born Iyar 22, 3443, in Kirma. Daughter of Amanda. Twin sister of Jena.

<u>Justan</u> – / **juhs** tan / – Born Elul 21, 3439, in Kirma. Surname: Kesh. Son of Bryon and Alena. Betrothed to Andera. Brother of Kyelon.

<u>Kanekoa</u> – / kan eh **koh** uh / – Person who sells her house to Ninan in Kirma.

<u>Kendon</u> – / **ken** duhn / – Employee at the Telepod Engineering Company under Riccan. Interviewer of Amanda.

<u>Kenen</u> – / **ken** un / – Manager of the telepod crystal quarry in Beewa.

<u>Kiya</u> – / **kahy** uh / – A wise-woman in training with Alena.

<u>Kyelon</u> – / **kahyl** on / – Born Tishri 30, 3440, in Kirma. Surname: Kesh. Son of Bryon and Alena. Brother of Justan.

<u>Lana</u> – / **law** nuh / – Maiden name: Gurdin. Receptionist at the Telepod Engineering Company in Durseni.

<u>Lillia</u> – / **lil** ee uh / – A Tualan who gave the samara to Maria's family in Campeche, Mexico. Girlfriend of Lucinden.

<u>Lindon</u> – / **lin** duhn / – A friend of Bryon's who took him to Earth as a teenager.

<u>Lucinden</u> – / loo **sin** den / – One of the original angels of Jehoban. He confronted Jehoban for rule of the people, and Jehoban banned him and his followers to Tuala.

<u>Maria</u> – / mah **ree** ah / – The keeper of the crystal skull in Campeche, Mexico.

<u>Miorlen</u> – / mee **ohr** len / – Legal advisor for Elder Debbon.

<u>Nealand Taivas</u> – / **neel** uh nd **tay** vuhs / – Son of Nealand

Taivas Sr. and Jessica Taivas. Former fiancé of Amanda. Also known as Neal.

<u>Nealand Taivas Sr.</u> – / **neel** uh nd **tay** vuhs / – Husband of Jessica. Father of Nealand Jr.

<u>Nena</u> – / **nay** nuh / – Married name: Stel. Wife of Daven. Mother of Riccan. Occupation: Teacher. Lives in Pantano.

<u>Ninan</u> – / **nahyn** un / – Surname: Tigua. Unemployed seaman. Worked undercover for Petre to locate Jesisca. Traveled to Kirma to look for Jesisca. Works for Bryon at Kirma Shipping and Receiving. Address: Thursto Block 43-3, Kirma.

<u>Nurse Bota</u> – / **boht** uh / – The nurse who took care of Amanda in the hospital in Cancun.

<u>Petre</u> – / **pee** ter / – Surname: MacVeen. Formerly known as Petren, lost social status and forced to lose the honorific 'n' at the end of his name. Wears a black onyx ring showing his status as a Master Deceptor. First person on Tuala to encounter Amanda. Kidnapped Jena and sold her to Elder Debbon under the guise of a betrothal agreement.

<u>Rasa</u> – / **rah** sah / – Born Tishri 5, 3423, in Port of Cresdon. Daughter of Ahn and Barla. Sister of Gravin. First cousin of Amanda. Student of Jehoban.

<u>Riccan</u> – / **rik** an / – Surname: Stel. Son of Elder Daven and Nena. Chief Engineer at the Telepod Engineering Company. Popular racer of telepods.

<u>Rualin</u> – / roo **ahl** in / – A business associate of Petre.

<u>Saul</u> – / **sawl** / – Born in Wisconsin. Brother of Barla and Diane.

<u>Shemalla</u> – / shem **al** uh / – Maiden Name: Paramasivam. Born in Pantano. Employee at the UFO Museum and Research Center in Roswell, New Mexico. Apprentice to Elder Vargen.

<u>Sherry</u> – / **sher** ee / – Amanda's best friend from high school.

<u>Stavin</u> – / **stav** in / – A boyhood friend of Bryon's.

<u>Stephen Gascon, MD</u> – / **gas** cuhn / – Director at Cannon Memorial Asylum.

<u>Sydney</u> – / **sid** nee / – Father of Barla, Saul, and Diane. Surname: Silnack.

<u>Tana</u> – / **tan** uh / – Next-door-neighbor of Bryon and Alena in Kirma. Caretaker of Justan, Andera, and Kyelon.

<u>Teden</u> – / **ted** en / – Surname: Dunless. Husband of Ela Nena. Accounting Manager at the Telepod Engineering Company.

<u>Vargen</u> – / **vahr** guh n / – Elder. Co-founder of the Old Soul Engineering Facility.

<u>Willian</u> – / **wil** yan / – Son of Elder Debbon and Chelesa. Betrothed to Jena.

<u>Zeka</u> – / **zee** kah / – Daughter of Bryon's father's business partner. Mother of Andera.

PLACES

Acaim – / uh **kām** / – Island where Jehoban lives. Earth equivalent: Jamaica.

Ascension Gate – / ə **sen** SHən gāt / – A link between the levels of reality, most of the Gates are set between Earth and Tuala. Where the ley lines intersect, the elemental energy is the strongest, creating a vortex of plasma power where a person can control movement between Tuala and Earth.

Beewa – / **be** wuh / – Location where telepod crystals are mined. Earth equivalent: Merida, Mexico.

Cannon Memorial Asylum – Located in North Carolina. Built in 1962 and shut down in 1999.

Cerid – / **sair** id / – Location of creditors issuing a death and dismemberment order against Petre. Earth equivalent: Corpus Christi, Texas.

City of Thulen – Major city in the heart of Thulen. A place where Petre has many illegal business transactions. Earth equivalent: Mexico City, Mexico.

Desio – / **deh** zee oh / – Location where Ninan was dumped off by Petre. District where Copa is the wise-woman. Earth equivalent: Alvarado, Mexico.

Durseni – / **durs** en ee / – Earth equivalent: Cozumel, Mexico.

Elder Isle – Location of Elder Debbon's seat of power. Earth equivalent: Isla de la Juventud, south of Cuba.

Gulf of Thulen – / **thoo** lun / – Large body of water north and east of Thulen. Earth equivalent: Gulf of Mexico.

Ishal – / ish *uh* l / – Coastal town where Petre conducts illegal trade. Location where Petre dumped the freighter telepod. Earth equivalent: Tampico, Mexico.

Isla Mivua – / iz law mih **voo** *uh* / – Location where the storm transported Amanda to Tuala. Earth equivalent: Cook Island inside the Bermuda Triangle.

Kirma – / **kurm** a / – Hometown of Bryon and Alena Kesh. Location of Kirma Shipping and Receiving. Earth equivalent: Campeche, Mexico.

Lookout Tavern – Located in Ishal. Place where the prostitute, Hashma, works.

Matza – / **maht** za / – Small town where Bryon seeks healer assistance when Amanda breaks her wrist and is bitten by a beetlesnatch. Earth equivalent: La Isla, located south of Cancun, Mexico.

Mavuno – / mah **vun** oh / – Location where telepod crystals are mined. Earth equivalent: Villahermosa, Mexico.

Old Soul Engineering Facility – A place where they study objects from Earth and reverse engineer them for their own use in Tuala.

Pantano – / **pahn** tahn oh / – Home of Elder Daven and Nena. Location where Neal and Amanda started their journey. Earth equivalent: Boca Raton, Florida.

Porino's Café – A popular restaurant located at the southern port of Cresdon.

Port of Cerid – / **sair** id / – Location of the shipment bound for Beewa but quarantined for a beetlesnatch infestation. Meeting place for Ninan and Petre.

Port of Cresdon – / **krez** dun / – Main shipping port in Thulen. Home of Ahn and Barla. Earth equivalent: Cancun, Mexico.

Reesun – / **ree** suhn / – The large landmass north of the Elder Isle. Earth equivalent: Cuba.

Residence – Place of business for an Elder.

Southside Town Deli – Located in the Port of Cerid. Meeting place for Ninan and Petre.

Telepod Engineering Company – / tel *uh* pod / – Creator and manufacturing facility for telepods. Located in Durseni.

Thulen – / **thoo** lun / – Country where Port of Cresdon is located. Earth equivalent: Mexico.

Trilli Deli – A restaurant located at the main Port of Cresdon. A favorite place for Captain Ahn to frequent.

Tuala – / tōo a-lə / – Planet where Jehoban lives. Alternate realm of Earth.

UFO Museum and Research Center – Located in Roswell, New Mexico.

DEFINITIONS

<u>Aquaponics</u> – / **ah** kw*uh* pon iks / – A process for growing food floating on water containing nutrients supplied by live fish. The plants filter the water for the fish to survive. Since nutrients are readily available, the produce grows faster and in less space than traditional gardening.

<u>Beetlesnatch</u> – / **beet**-l snach / – Black beetle 3-4 inches long, migrates by flying, poisonous bite, lethal to humans and animals.

<u>Betrothal</u> – A formal union giving children even higher status in the community, approved and blessed by the Elders through a betrothal petition stating each family's different abilities and what color of crystal each child bears. Only approved if it is a superior union for the good of the society commemorated with a betrothal ceremony along with a pair of matching bracelets or rings with a precious stone. Once the age of majority is reached by both participants, they get married.

<u>Birth Crystal</u> – A circular pendant containing gemstones arranged like the leaves of a tree assigned to each citizen of Tuala within 24-hours of birth at a crystal ceremony, worn on an ornate chain around their neck. Once in place, the necklace cannot be

removed until they reach the age of eighteen. The stone's color can change with age, friends, or activities. Parents can both see and hear what their children are doing.

Bruskin – / **broos** kin / – An alcoholic beverage served cold similar to beer.

Chit – A small electronic disk assigned to respected members of the community. Each is unique to the owner and honored the same as money.

Clotted Cream – Sour cream.

Council of Elders – Elders who convene to arbitrate serious matters.

Deckhopper – Earth equivalent: pirate.

Elders – Individuals selected and trained by Jehoban in Acaim. Primary role to help/guide the people. Secondary role to protect the Ascension Gates.

Elemental Energy – The magnetic energy found in the earth used by the people of Tuala through their birth crystal to create. Slang: Elemy.

Elemy – / **el** eh mee / – Slang term for elemental energy.

Epeny – / **ep** eh nee / – Drug causing drowsiness and pain relief, an anti-inflammatory. Addictive when used too long.

Facultas – / fak **uh l** tus / – Meaning 'ability.' A book explaining the Tualan people's abilities used daily such as: teleportation, telekinesis, translation, deception, healing, amplification. Anything the mind can think of, the power can create without any limitations.

First-daughter – A girl who is betrothed to a son and brought into the son's family and raised as a daughter of the family.

Foxl – / **fox**-l / – Mammal with fur five inches long, straight when dry, curly when wet, head like a sheep, body size and shape like a cow, herbivore.

Gania – / **gah** nee uh / – A measure of distance equivalent to an Earth mile.

<u>Genero</u> – / gen **air** oh / – Meaning 'to create' or 'creation.' A book covering the creation of the worlds, Jehoban and his wayward student named Lucinden, and the beginning of the Elders.

<u>Glawlet</u> – / **glaw** let / – A common breakfast consisting of a fresh warm roll filled with a poached egg covered in a sausage gravy.

<u>Golden Jesisca</u> – 60-foot yacht owned by Nealand.

<u>Healer's Teaching Guide</u> – First book of instruction for wise-woman training.

<u>Inside Ascension</u> – Phrase to use at a Gate on Earth to get to Tuala.

<u>Invisibility Shield</u> – A plasma field around an object rendering it undetectable from viewing outside of the field.

<u>Java</u> – / jaw vah / – A stimulating beverage served hot or cold similar to coffee.

<u>Kittilee</u> – / **kit**-l ee / – A miniature feline similar to a common house cat.

<u>Krumpli</u> – / krump lee / – Edible tuber similar to a potato.

<u>Ley Lines</u> – / **lay** / – Concentrated lines of magnetic energy in the land. Ascension Gates are located where multiple lines inter-sect. Healers use the ley lines and crystals to assist with their talents to treat their patients.

<u>Life-line</u> – The non-physical core of every living thing which ties into the elemental energy of the earth. Wise-women access a person's life-line to accelerate healing.

<u>Lottery Pool</u> – The two lottery pools are called the short list and the long list. Draw from short list if the person declines post-study education. Short list retirement times range from nothing to one declan. Long list used for post-study graduates separated into two lists: one for general arts students where retirement times range from ten to fifteen anons; the other for declared major

students where retirement times range from fifteen to thirty anons.

Master Deceptor – A person who has mastered the skill of making people believe a lie augmented by the use of elemental energy.

Old Soul – A Tualan name for a person from Earth.

Outside Ascension – Phrase to use at a Gate on Tuala to get to Earth.

Patil – / pah **til** / – An electronic device used for storing/accessing information, making video calls, and scanning/printing documents similar to a computer.

Pika Juice – / **pahyk** ah / – A fruity beverage similar to orange juice.

Plascreen – / plah screen / – A large touch-screen plastic surface on a telepod that maintains all of the controls for telepod flight.

Plasfilm – / plas film / – An algae-based plastic used to make household items such as plates and cups, also used for making photographs and important documents such as schematics.

Plasprint – / plas print / – A large design schematic printed on plasfilm. Similar to a blueprint on Earth.

Post-Study – Advanced education similar to college.

Retirement – The amount of time immediately following formal education where the people are paid by the Elders to not work until their allotted time.

Samara – / suh mair uh / – Name of the crystal skulls.

Shill – Smaller denomination of money, a silver metal coin with ribbons of leaves curling around the edges. Ten shills equal one taj.

Sportsman Class – The middle racing class of telepods, with a mid-sized body and crystal drive, achieving decent speed and noise. Sometimes operated with sponsors.

Steena Tea – / **stee** na / – Sweet flavor with a minty finish, settles the stomach, refreshing.

Stock Class – The beginning level for racing telepods, with the smallest body, generally slower because of smaller crystal drives. Some of these racers use expensive technology to enhance the power causing contention among other stock racers. Almost exclusively privately funded by the drivers.

Supplemental Teaching Guide – Book of instruction inspired by Jehoban to help the Elders understand the way Jehoban wants the world to be maintained.

Swimmers – Anyone found swimming in need of rescue.

Taj – Highest denomination of money, a gold metal coin with a rose on the front. The average wage per anon is 350 taj.

Telepod – / tel *uh* pod / – A wingless aircraft providing a means of air transportation, powered by a large crystal drive where the crystal color and clarity determine the speed and reliability, operated by mind control, transfers from one location to another telekinetically.

Tocolas – / **tow** koh l*uhs* / – A red, corn-based chip colored and flavored by tomato juice, lime juice, and salt.

Top Sportsman Class – The highest racing class of telepods. The largest telepod body and crystal drive, achieving faster speed and noise. Almost always operated with sponsors.

Translate – The ability to move telekinetically from one location to another without the use of a telepod.

Tunic – / **too** nik / – An upper garment, either loose or close-fitting and extending over the pants or skirt to the hips or below.

Water craft – A smaller boat usually operated by one person.

Wise-Woman – A healer formally trained by an Elder. Giver of birth crystals and officiant of the crystal ceremony.